PUSHCART PRIZE XLIV

2020
PUSHCART PRIZE XLIV
BEST OF THE
SMALL PRESSES

EDITED BY BILL HENDERSON
WITH THE PUSHCART PRIZE EDITORS

Note: nominations for this series are invited from any small, independent, literary book press or magazine in the world, print or online. Up to six nominations—tear sheets or copies, selected from work published, or about to be published, in the calendar year—are accepted by our December 1 deadline each year. Write to Pushcart Fellowships, P.O. Box 380, Wainscott, N.Y. 11975 for more information or consult our website www.pushcartprize.com.

Acknowledgments

Selections for The Pushcart Prize are reprinted with the permission of authors and presses cited. Copyright reverts to authors and presses immediately after publication.

Distributed by W. W. Norton & Co.
500 Fifth Ave., New York, N.Y. 10110

Library of Congress Card Number: 76-58675
ISBN (hardcover): 978-1-888889-95-6
ISBN (paperback): 978-1-888889-96-3
ISSN: 0149-7863

For Lawrence Ferlinghetti

"I am waiting
for the meek to be blessed
and inherit the earth
without taxes
and I am waiting
for forests and animals
to reclaim the earth as theirs
and I am waiting
for a way to be devised
to destroy all nationalisms
without killing anybody."

from A Coney Island of The Mind *(New Directions, 1958)*

INTRODUCTION

For forty-four years this series has been dedicated to new and established authors and editors. Somehow they have kept the faith in a culture that often does not care about the heart, mind and soul of what they represent.

Nothing could be more important than these people in the present age of lies, info-clutter, rampant suicidal consumerism and the "nationalisms" that Lawrence Ferlinghetti warned us about in 1958.

That we all have persevered has much to do with the original example and encouragement of Ferlinghetti, who recently marked his 100th birthday. His risky publication of Allen Ginsberg's *Howl* (1956) in his City Lights Pocket Poets series and his arrest (and acquittal) on obcenity charges, is an essential legacy for our own small press movement. Back in his day, the small press was an anomaly, an underground oddity.

As Jonah Raskin said in a recent *Rain Taxi* feature: "Lawrence Ferlinghetti is far more than a survivor. He's a pilgrim, a pioneer, a godfather and a gadfly who has helped give birth to rebirths of wonder, again and again . . ."

For Pushcart it was Ferlinghetti's early endorsement of this series that made a huge difference to me. "The best small press anthology I've seen," he said. That cheer has meant so much to us in dark times and bright over the decades.

Another pioneer who has inspired Pushcart and other small presses for decades is Joyce Carol Oates, one of our first Founding Editors. Way back in 1975, post–divorce, I was living alone and lonely in a forest cabin in upstate New York. I had just written to Oates and dozens more prominent writers asking for their support of my anthology notion. The phone rang at 8 a.m. and a soft voice asked "What is this idea you have?" I thought the caller had the wrong number, perhaps a school kid who missed her bus. But it was indeed Joyce Carol Oates and I had her ok as a Founding Editor. She and her husband, Ray Smith, had just started their own journal, the renowned *Ontario Review*. She recognized how hard it was to get started and survive. She remains close to Pushcart as a continuing inspiration, advisor, benefactor and honored writer.

So many other authors have inspired Pushcart and our editors through the years. When I was struck with a cancer diagnosis that made continuing this series unlikely, the late W.S. Merwin offered his solace and support. So did Tony Hoagland, who died last year. His essay "The Cure for Racism is Cancer" from *The Sun* is included in this edition. About my memoir, *Cathedral: An Illness and A Healing*, Tony wrote: "I am grateful for the bluntness with which you narrate the darkness of being really sick." Those words from a fellow patient for my testimony meant so much to me.

From these writers I learned how important it is to all of us that we encourage each other. It is not news that writing is a hard and solitary road. A few words can give us the necessary courage to continue.

Some of those words came to all of us from the late Mary Oliver. Her poems were honored in PPs IV, VII, VIII and XVI. She was one of the few poets who became a household word, refuting the rule that modern poetry is for a tiny audience. We will not forget her lines: "Tell me what is it you plan to do with your one wild and precious life," Or: "You have only to let the soft animal of your body love what it loves," Or: "Love yourself. Then forget it. Then love the world."

In an often empty and horrifying world, Mary gave us all permission to dream, care and endure.

Many have told me that The Pushcart Prize series is almost a religious obligation to me. And I would not disagree. I suspect that Mary saw poetry the same way.

In a recent issue of *The Christian Century*, Debra Dean Murphy remembered her: "Mary died on the feast of Saint Anthony, the desert monk revered for his insistence that the words of God were ever before him in the nature of all created things . . . Her poetry and prose witness to an unorthodox liturgy of the hours—daily walks, early morning stillness, and the stars on a clear, cold night . . ."

❊   ❊   ❊

So many others to thank: the two hundred plus Contributing Editors for this edition for instance, and our Guest Editors David Long, Heather Sellers, Gabriel Solis (prose) and Jane Mead, Victoria Chang and Michael Collier (poetry) and the hundreds of presses that made over 8,000 nominations, and the presses new to the series: *The Common*, *Love's Executive Order*, *Waxwing*, *Washington Square Review*, *Birmingham Poetry Press*, *Paper Dart*, *Egress*, *Clover*, *Bare Life*, *Foglifter*, Terrapin Press, *Brevity*, *Twyckenham Notes*.

We are grateful to our distributor through the decades, W.W. Norton & Co., and to the donors to the Pushcart Prize Fellowships listed in the following pages. Perhaps you would like to join them?

And especially to you dear reader and to readers around the world. Thank you. Without you these pages would be blank.

Keep the faith. Love and wonder.

Bill Henderson

THE PEOPLE WHO HELPED

FOUNDING EDITORS—Anaïs Nin (1903–1977), Buckminster Fuller (1895–1983), Charles Newman (1938–2006), Daniel Halpern, Gordon Lish, Harry Smith (1936–2012), Hugh Fox (1932–2011), Ishmael Reed, Joyce Carol Oates, Len Fulton (1934–2011), Leonard Randolph (1926–1993), Leslie Fiedler (1917–2003), Nona Balakian (1918–1991), Paul Bowles (1910–1999), Paul Engle (1908–1991), Ralph Ellison (1913–1994), Reynolds Price (1933–2011), Rhoda Schwartz (1931–2013), Richard Morris (1936–2003), Ted Wilentz (1915–2001), Tom Montag, William Phillips (1907–2002). Poetry editor: H. L. Van Brunt

CONTRIBUTING EDITORS FOR THIS EDITION—Allison Adair, Steve Adams, Dan Albergotti, John Allman, Idris Anderson, Tony Ardizzone, David Baker, Mary Jo Bang, Kim Barnes, Eli Barrett, Ellen Bass, Rick Bass, Claire Bateman, Bruce Beasley, Marvin Bell, Molly Bendall, Karen Bender, Pinckney Benedict, Bruce Bennett, Marie-Helene Bertino, Linda Bierds, Marianne Boruch, Michael Bowden, Fleda Brown, Rosellen Brown, Michael Dennis Browne, Ayse Papatya Bucak, Christopher Buckley, E. Shaskan Bumas, Kathy Callaway, Richard Cecil, Jung Hae Chae, Ethan Chatagnier, Kim Chinquee, Ye Chun, Jane Ciabattari, Christopher Citro, Suzanne Cleary, Billy Collins, Martha Collins, Lydia Conklin, Robert Cording, Stephen Corey, Lisa Couturier, Paul Crenshaw, Claire Davis, Oliver de la Paz, Chard deNiord, Jaquira Díaz, Stuart Dischell, Jack Driscoll, John Drury, Karl Elder, Elizabeth Ellen, Angie Estes, Kathy Fagan, Ed Falco, Beth Ann Fennelly, Gary Fincke, Maribeth Fischer, April L. Ford, Robert Long Foreman, Ben Fountain, H. E. Francis, Alice Friman, Sarah Frisch, John Fulton, Frank X. Gaspar, Christine Gelineau, David Gessner, Nancy Geyer, Gary Gildner, Elton Glaser, Sarah Green, Mark Halliday,

Jeffrey Hammond, Jeffrey Harrison, Timothy Hedges, Daniel Lee Henry, DeWitt Henry, David Hernandez, Bob Hicok, Kathleen Hill, Edward Hirsch, Jane Hirshfield, Jen Hirt, Andrea Hollander, Chloe Honum, Christopher Howell, Maria Hummel, Joe Hurka, Allegra Hyde, Mark Irwin, David Jauss, Leslie Johnson, Bret Anthony Johnston, Jeff P. Jones, Michael Kardos, Laura Kasischke, Christopher Kempf, Thomas E. Kennedy, David Kirby, John Kistner, Ron Koertge, Richard Kostelanetz, Mary Kuryla, Wally Lamb, Fred Leebron, Sandra Leong, E. J. Levy, David Long, Jennifer Lunden, Margaret Luongo, Hugh Martin, Matt Mason, Dan Masterson, Alice Mattison, Tracy Mayor, Robert McBrearty, Nancy McCabe, Rebecca McClanahan, Davis McCombs, Erin McGraw, Elizabeth McKenzie, Edward McPherson, David Meischen, Douglas W. Milliken, Andrew Mitchell, Nancy Mitchell, Jim Moore, Joan Murray, David Naimon, Michael Newirth, Aimee Nezhukumatathil, Nick Norwood, D. Nurkse, Meghan O'Gieblyn, Joyce Carol Oates, Dzvinia Orlowsky, Tom Paine, Alan Michael Parker, Leslie Jill Patterson, Brenda Peynado, Dominica Phetteplace, Carl Phillips, Catherine Pierce, Mark Jude Poirier, Andrew Porter, C. E. Poverman, D. A. Powell, Melissa Pritchard, Kevin Prufer, Lia Purpura, Anne Ray, Donald Revell, Nancy Richard, Stacey Richter, Laura Rodley, Jessica Roeder, Dana Roeser, Jay Rogoff, Rachel Rose, Mary Ruefle, Maxine Scates, Alice Schell, Grace Schulman, Philip Schultz, Lloyd Schwartz, Maureen Seaton, Asako Serizawa, Diane Seuss, Sujata Shekar, Anis Shivani, Robert Anthony Siegel, Justin St. Germain, David St. John, Maura Stanton, Maureen Stanton, Melissa Stein, Pamela Stewart, Nomi Stone, Patricia Strachan, Ben Stroud, Barrett Swanson, Ron Tanner, Katherine Taylor, Richard Tayson, Elaine Terranova, Susan Terris, Joni Tevis, Robert Thomas, Jean Thompson, Melanie Rae Thon, William Trowbridge, Lee Upton, Nance Van Winckel, Matthew Vollmer, G. C. Waldrep, BJ Ward, Don Waters, Michael Waters, LaToya Watkins, Charles Harper Webb, Roger Weingarten, Allison Benis White, Philip White, Jessica Wilbanks, Joe Wilkins, Eleanor Wilner, Eric Wilson, Sandi Wisenberg, Mark Wisniewski, David Wojahn, Pui Ying Wong, Shelley Wong, Angela Woodward, Carolyne Wright, Robert Wrigley, Christina Zawadiwsky, Elizabeth Ziemska

PAST POETRY EDITORS—H.L. Van Brunt, Naomi Lazard, Lynne Spaulding, Herb Leibowitz, Jon Galassi, Grace Schulman, Carolyn Forché, Gerald Stern, Stanley Plumly, William Stafford, Philip Levine, David Wojahn, Jorie Graham, Robert Hass, Philip Booth, Jay Meek,

CONTENTS

PUSHCART PRIZE XLIV

THE ARMS OF SATURDAY NIGHT

fiction by **CALLY FIEDOREK**

from NARRATIVE

There'd be no traffic on the turnpike, not on Saturday. She could get her dad to drive her to the city, though at the risk of being pushy, and insensitive, really, considering the circumstances, but wouldn't some part of him enjoy it in a way, like, was it not a source of comfort in a time of grief, a welcome sign of life's renewal—the death-proof, scrappy ways of teenage lust?

There was this party in the city later. And she had it on pretty good authority—not immaculate, but strong—that Adam Donovan would be there. Adam Donovan. His name, a neon light, electric-blue. What was he doing *right this second?* Adam Donovan.

Adam and his dusty smells, the musk of boyworld. Adam with his hoodie and his hash pipe and his Tool sticker (like her, old soul, child of the ancient nineties). And there was something in his eyes (heavy lidded, heavy banged), a certain heft to him, not fat, slow moving like an animal, quick to spook (his tusk, his dark true heart), and this something made her wiggly kneed, and this promise of them in some room, or maybe in a car together, soon, this promise had been recently announced, and now it shone for her like Christmas used to, a spun-sugar bridge over the brackish of her days. But he was leaving!

He was going to California, with his friends.

She could picture them all, a week from now, in some Tonto-esque headwear, ensconced in their cocktails of peyote and electrolyte water, boning models in truck beds in the craters of the desert. Communing, amid nightblooms, with the very source of life, and he could say, years down the road, I was there. I touched the face of true experience. I, Adam Donovan, touched down in the cradle of the land. And her?

Janie fanned the Melba toasts, just so, the way her mother liked. It was her Uncle Murray's wake. Somewhere through the county the hearse was moving, over hills and viaducts, the corpse inside it, ovenbound. It was the start of a long hot summer in Montclair, already lethal.

They'd beat Dad home to get the roast on. They were expecting thirty, maybe fewer.

Through lace curtains they could see him coming now, walking a glacial aunt across the elm-lined street, her pillbox hat a black blotch in the late suburban sun.

"I think your father's going through a time," her mom said. He looked like he might bust a vein under the weight of the day—so sad, so cordial in his Big and Tall suit. "And it's not just Murray," she said, and started dusting something.

Mother often did this, proffered the catnip of grown-up talk, then walked away. Infuriating woman. Janie knew her dad's book of critical essays on semiotics, or technology and the soul, or something, had recently been rejected by the university press. She overheard them in the kitchen, the night Murray died.

"It's an extremely rarefied field you're in, hon."

"It's LIU, Robbie, not MIT." Robin was her mother's name. "I'm not even the best version of the uppity prick they'd have me for."

"Who?"

Grief had led him whiskey-ward, to maudlin contemplation. He'd been a sore thumb in his Irish Italian family—all hardscrabble working men—a professor and former sometime-columnist for *Newsweek*, whose career as a public intellectual had been looking, in the past year, pretty private.

"I should've gone to trade school, Robbie. Electricians, contractors, do *satisfying work*. Me, I feel like I've spent my whole adult life standing in the middle of an intersection, trying to play the harp, and all this time I've been saying, *it's the traffic that's the problem, it's too loud, I can't focus*, but it's not. The problem is—the music—the music that's inside of me—it's not *good*."

"I think I lost you a while ago, baby." Mom was putting peanut butter on a saltine. "An electrician? Remember that time you tried to fix the alternator, in the old Civic?"

"That's the point. I can't *do* anything." He took a slug, with some violence. He was not really a drinker, but it must have seemed to him like the type of thing a mourning man would do—"Murray loved his cars, boy"—so he was doing it.

Mother chewed noisily. "John, you're a beautiful man. You wanna break your back over a toilet pump, then spend the rest of the day yelling at the Giants? I don't think you'd like that. Maybe right now, the way you feel, you think you would, but you wouldn't." Mom lacked the depressive instinct. She worked in the Bronx DA's office as a counselor to domestic violence victims. She tended to get on with things.

They were a good match, actually. Janie could admit this much. She was grateful—most of her friends' parents were divorced, or divorcing, or in some kind of arrangement in which one or the other's sexual needs were being quietly outsourced.

"Well, here we are," Dad said, depositing the very old aunt—no one seemed to know who she was, whose aunt—into an armchair. "Where's Mike when you need him? We're gonna need to move those tables out. Some more of Murray's friends are coming."

The ceremony had gone off mostly fine, not that it mattered—it was not the royal wedding—though some of Murray's friends from his motorcycle club seemed a little wild, keyed up like for some hot wings convention, and not a homely, staid, indoor affair.

"Oh god, those rednecks? Make sure you pat them down."

"I don't think you can say that anymore, Mom," Janie said.

"What? It was like Altamont in there."

"Rednecks."

"Well, that's what they are. I don't like having violent personalities in my house. I think I recognized one from family court. Mr. Tribal Face Tattoos, more kids than teeth, you know the one—" Janie knew she wasn't being elitist. She was genuinely offended by their perceived lack of gentleness.

"They were his friends, Robin."

Dad, on the other hand, knew a few of Murray's pals from high school, and he seemed to get a kick out of being taken back. Janie couldn't square it at all, the cautious man who'd raised her with that picture on the mantel: her father, aged eighteen, head-to-toe leather, a heavy-metal zealot with a gaze that could kill.

Her parents, though she loved them, struck her as hopelessly softcore. (Her little sister, Dorie, barely counted as a family member: she was sweet but a pain, still in thrall to her Hatchimals and backyard

25

nonsense.) They were *not* Jersey strong. They were the type of people who, twenty years before, could have found a place in Manhattan, clung on for dear rent-controlled life, struggled, sure, but remained in the mix, where the action was, but they'd been squeezed out of that deal. (She guessed this was what her civics teacher, Mr. Pakouras, meant by the death of the middle class.) They prided themselves on being subtler than their neighbors but lacked what their neighbors had: Identity. Charisma. Money. They listened to NPR, sometimes, but their hearts weren't in it. They had no unifying piety, to God, or sport, or any of their many motherlands.

At Montclair High she felt apart. There was a small subset of edge-of-county people, the children of tradesmen, some from as far away as Kosovo or El Salvador, for whom every day in America must have been a fist in the face, a gut-punch struggle to adjust and survive, and they got on, but on the weekends stayed in their lane, she in hers. Nor could she relate to the genetic wealth of most of her friends, the shiny-haired incuriosity that blessed the rich, rolling up to school in their Land Rovers and massive, pristinely white sneakers, gum-snapping girls, figures honed on the regional gymnastics and jazz dance circuits, their McMansion- and boat-owning, philandering fathers, their tracksuit-wearing, dipsomaniac mothers. But she was generalizing. Taylor Palermo had a dolphin-shaped fountain in her front yard that might have been a Koons, Dad said, if not for the total absence of irony. Oh, but they were something, those people! Tacky, maybe, but life-loving. In your face, unmeasured, everything her family—Dad in particular—was not.

All of a sudden the living room was a sea of black. Everybody started pouring in—the Jacksons and the Tetrazzinis and the Wrights and the Farraguts.

"Who'll join me?" Her dad's best friend, Mike, started on his Rob Roys. She wished she could get loaded, that there was someone her age to conspire with to this end. All her friends were coming back from the beach, or getting ready to go out.

Her parents had padded the occasion with their neighbors and some of Dad's colleagues. It was strange to Janie, watching them all, how nothing could be more radical, more awe-inspiring, really, than someone dropping dead, and yet people were often at their most perfunctory at an event built explicitly around the fact of doom. It just seemed like a waste. A waste of Murray's memory, of the cocktail napkins, of the possibilities of language. There was no love, no vibes. There was nothing to talk about, least of all him. Everyone would drink responsibly, talk superficially, then go home. She just wished they would do it, you know, soon.

"Let's trash my dad's fuckpad," Hannah's text invite had said, with a toxic flippancy that Janie suspected masked a world of hurt.

Hannah's father owned a party den near the High Line that was going into foreclosure. Now she was milking the guilt over the world's most drawn-out, financially ruinous divorce and having one last hurrah, no supervision. All the seniors would be there, including Adam, plus the cooler juniors, of which Janie, to her enduring surprise, was one.

Adam. Oh, he walked across her mind again—a navy breeze—stomach-flipping. She couldn't really believe that the whole time they'd known each other his penis was right there with him, in his pants, *right there*. At *school!* An organ of such agonizing mystery, and he just walked around with it, like it was keys. She would die to see it, just once, before he left. He might be gone forever after that, but the memory of seeing his penis, of getting some *reaction* from it, she was sure would, in some small but everlasting way, define her youth. Would mark her with unending power.

She was sixteen—too wise, too jaded to fantasize of commitment. Bleh: she didn't want that any more than he probably did, at least not to her conscious knowledge. What she wanted was the ticked box, the existential check-in. Some relief from the dull mortal ache of always being where the party wasn't. What she needed was some proof that she'd been *seen* in this life.

They hadn't yet kissed, or even talked that much, but late in the school year she'd felt his eyes on her. He walked down the hall, and the frequency rose. (How she would miss his form in those halls, how gray next year would be!) To a friend, through a friend, he was overheard saying she was "way cooler and nicer than the other junior girls." Then last week, he shared a playlist with her, on Spotify—his assorted favorites, stuff she'd never heard before, Black Flag, Kraftwerk, some Prince deep cuts, The Cure. Her friends said it was "on."

How many dozens of times she'd fallen asleep listening to it since, how she'd heard every lick, every dreamy synth through the filter of the boy's imagination. How it came alive *through* him, not just the songs—a new blueprint—the people they might be. Here was the absolutely solemn pledge of Art, the yowl of the endangered, the soulsick and hungry, and tonight she and Adam would be out there, *free*, free to smoke and drink and spit and misbehave, and love each other. *Adam Donovan.*

It was now almost six-thirty. There was plenty of time. Not yet into panic mode, but plans would need to be laid. Softly at first, tactfully . . .

"Ha. Absolutely not." In the kitchen, Mother was droll. "As in, hell no. You're staying in tonight."

She had struck too soon. "But I asked, and you said yes."

"When was that?"

"Before." This was a lie.

"Child, you deliberately ask when you know I'm not paying any attention. I had a thousand people on the phone, a three-hundred-pound dead man in a Cadillac needed to be picked up. . . . Don't *manipulate* me, Janie. Just drop it."

"But can't someone take me to the PATH?"

"I said drop it. Your uncle's dead. Your father's . . . upset. This, of all nights, is a night for family."

Murray had been associated, unofficially, with a motorcycle gang with a chapter out of Newark, who did runs twice a year along the Eastern seaboard, from Pensacola all the way up to southern Maine. They came in now, five of them, wearing their vests over their suits. David and Jonas, the interracial gay couple her mom knew from town, seemed instinctively to stand less tall with their arrival, as if hoping to dissolve into the wallpaper.

On the backs of their vests it said Satan's Muse, and underneath it was a homespun, embroidered insignia, not quite realistically foreshortened, in which a toned, chesty woman in a Viking helmet was straddling a tiger, a golden revolver protruding, inexplicably, from between her boobs. Whoever did their graphics—in-house, Janie assumed—had cobbled together every possible motif of American machohood into one turbo-charged clusterfuck of crazy.

It was funny, watching these huge men handling tiny cubes of cheese. One held a caper berry up to the light and said, with an astonishment that was almost heartrending, "*This?* What the hell's *this?*"

One of them was younger, closer to Janie's age. A rookie recruit, probably, having not yet earned his vest. She hadn't noticed him at the ceremony. They acknowledged each other from across the room, as if giving props—for what, she didn't know. For not being old.

Her dad clinked a glass, and everyone stood at attention around the living room. Things were moving along.

"I just wanted to thank everybody for coming out," Dad said. "Some of you knew Murray. Some of you didn't. It's a—today—" the chin was quivering, *oh no*, "today's a—it's a . . . *hard day.*"

He gasped; his voice crumpled.

Oh god. Janie couldn't watch her dad cry without crying. It had nothing to do with her empathic heart. It was a knee-jerk spasm, a cellular tic, some twitching from the innermost coil of their shared DNA.

"Murray was my little brother. People said we were very different, that he looked up to me, but I—I always—I always wanted to be more like *him.*" *Don't cry don't cry don't cry.* "You know, he was happy up until the end. Every day was an adventure for him, and I don't mean that to sound like—Dorie, cover your ears—like some Hallmark-card bullshit. But I look at my kids and I think, I see some of him in them. Sweetheart, you can uncover your ears for this part—" This got a huge laugh, somewhat disproportionate, Janie thought, to how funny it actually was, but her sister, smiling bunny-toothed, seemed elated with the shout-out. "I see some of Murray in both my girls. Some of that carefreeness." *What carefreeness?* "Some of that dogged self-assurance. And I hope you," he looked right at Janie now, his firstborn, with such searing frankness, with such, well, love was what it was, and she tried hard to visualize anything, anything not dear to her, bull terriers, the Essex County DMV, Chris Christie, so as not to detonate with tears, "I hope you hold onto some of that," voice breaking now, "for the rest of your lives."

Everybody cheered. Her dad was wet-eyed but relieved, as though his work for the day was finally over.

"Anyway," he said, "let's all eat and drink a lot."

One of the bikers whistled, then they cranked up the George Thorogood, and that went a ways toward further breaking the ice.

"Who's the rookie?" Her mom nodded to the young biker. She always needed to know who everyone *was.* "He looks disturbed."

Janie considered him. He did look a little disturbed, grimacing into space like that. He wasn't bad-looking at all—his face was nice—but there was something so heavy, so jammed up about him. His neck and knuckles were covered in ink. He had those stretched-lobe earring things, which, gross.

"Don't recognize him," Dad said, sipping what must have been his third Corona. Janie had been betting on Dad as the softer touch, but he would never drive her, not even to the train, with anything resembling a buzz on. Very well. She would leave him to his newfound thirst.

She would proceed without their blessings.

Like Elvis, his hero, before him, Murray died in the bathroom, of a massive heart attack. It was an unpoetic end to all his roving. His misspent youth was a bunch of mythic Polaroids. His middle age, a punchline: the combover, the visible ass crack. They hadn't been close really, he and Janie. He was a friendly, open guy, but he'd always seemed to be holding back around her, as though at some point in his past his interest in young girls had been legally curtailed.

He had no kids, a few bad marriages to women who were tall and seemed insane, a cocaine and alcohol problem. He came around at Easter with a six-pack of tall boys, big belly hanging out under an Infowars T-shirt, and was often forwarding her father emails about life on Mars, government conspiracies, Jim Morrison spotted in an Arizona bathhouse. Dad didn't know when he'd jumped the shark. But he felt personally implicated in the softening of his little brother's brain, and this had hardened, in recent days, into the worst kind of survivor's guilt.

In Dad's mind he'd done wrong by Murray—left home too early, failed to protect him from the vacuum left by their older-than-average, ludicrously mismatched parents. Pop-Pop, all but mute after a stint flying bombers over Dresden, had lived to hold an infant Janie a single time, then died from cancer, something to do with all those burning polymers, and their mother took up with a voluble huckster named Jack Parisi, more her speed, who whittled Pop-Pop's pension away on liquor and massage chairs.

Janie remembered going with her father, when Grandma died, to clean that house out. Up in Englewood. How creepy that place was, pink fuzzy toilet covers, Henry Mancini 45s. Becrusted lipsticks, hosiery that smelled of menses from deep in the atomic age. It had filled twelve-year-old Janie with a weird alloy of emotions—this evidence of a family's, her family's, footprint in the world. A nauseous kind of shame to be the owner of a body, a female one at that. A brimming, almost painfully affectionate regard for her dad, his life and times, how pure and plain and steady he was. She remembered too the bittersweet relief she'd felt, in the car on the way home, watching the country roll, knowing she was still somebody's child.

She got a text from Hannah. "were all here pregaming. at my dads apt. Wher the duck are u."

Then, "adam asked about u," followed by a trail of sex emojis. Eggplant. Peach. Finger. Hole.

Oh *god*. It was all happening. It was really real—he *wanted* her.

"I think your father's lost his mind," Mom said, coming up behind her.

It was eight-thirty. The sun had set, and folks filtered out onto the front lawn, drinks in hand, to smoke and carry on under the fairy lights. It was kind of a great party. In the middle of the living room, there was Dad in a circle of Murray's friends, wearing a bandanna now, a bottle of Powers passed among them all, and singing loudly to "I'm No Angel."

"See?" Janie said. "He's having a *great* time."

"He is." This with a serenity and lack of judgment Janie found unsettling.

"He doesn't need me here at all."

"Honey, you know *that's* not true."

"Mom, I'm gonna go to this party. The last train's at nine-forty, which is after you and Dad are usually in bed, and I'm gonna call a cab, and stay at Hannah's, and be back before you wake up, so it shouldn't make any difference if I'm physically here or in the city when you guys are sleeping, and the security at Penn Station is impeccable these days, you said so yourself last time we were there, and I'm using the money I earned at Menchie's"—this was the frozen yogurt parlor where she swirled whipped clouds of aspartame four days a week, for her wealthier classmates—"so it's not like I'm asking for cab fare, or train fare, or anything, Mom."

Money, in the end, was the great legitimizer. The great silencer. Everyone knew this.

Mother sipped her wine slowly, planning her words, like some terrifying, nail-filing dowager. "So I guess you've sorted this all out."

"You're not gonna bitch me out?"

"I don't know what that means, but I can't chain you to the house, Janie. I can only tell you I'll be disappointed. We all will be," she said. "That's the limit of my power anymore."

31

Janie was let down. She'd been ready for a fight, the better to fuel her leaving with a dose of righteous fury.

There was actually some time to kill.

In the backyard the rookie biker sat alone, smoking.

Janie grabbed the dregs of someone's champagne flute, chugged hard, broke into stride. She was high on carnal rage, nerves, excitement, a little guilt, a swill of pilfered drinks. She was warming up. It was ideal—a guy around her age, and probably as hard to reach as Adam sometimes was, but the stakes were virtually nil.

"Hey," she said. She languished in the hammock, her dress riding slightly up a Jergens-bronzed thigh. This, her best Lolita. She knew she wasn't gorgeous, facially, not yet.

(*Body fine but face meh.*) These words she had internalized from an Excel spreadsheet circulated, last year, among the senior boys and intercepted by her dean, oh, to never be unread—though they were positively *glowing* in comparison to some of the others—and of course it didn't *matter*, she would *live*, of course much worse injustice happened every day, but it galled her still, the power of those words, and it embarrassed her, how bad she'd felt, and had they meant fine as in *fine* or fine as in *fiiiine*, and they shouldn't have been able to do that, those fuckers, to throw her off her game like that, as though her presence in the world were something, at best, to be tolerated, a cost to be absorbed, and not the dazzlement in some way owed, promised as it was by the fairer-boned, the plumper-mouthed, the worthier of air, and food and shelter. . . . On the other hand, she *might* be a genius. Taylor Palermo couldn't say that.)

"So, you knew my uncle?"

"Yeah, yeah, we spent some time together." He was all hunched over, all stuck inside himself. "In 2016, 2017."

"Sounds mysterious." Didn't her mother *understand?* She had to put herself in life's way—in Adam's way. She had to show up. Life wouldn't show up for her, as for the doll-faced and McMansion-born. The very, what was it, *dogged self-assurance* that was spurring her on now, was it not the thing her dad just said he admired the most in her? In Murray?

"Sooo, are you in school?" She didn't know if she meant high school or college. He was in that wasteland of young manhood where you couldn't tell.

"I was working at the Game Stop but I quit. You?"

"College, I guess. Next year."

"In state?"

"I was thinking Brown, actually?" She hated the way she said this, *actually?*, like she had already gotten in. "Or Oberlin."

They sat in silence, for what felt like a long time, then he said: "Why'd you come out here, huh? Cause you've got nothing better to do? Not while your iPhone 10's charging, huh." He said it deadpan, not even looking at her, full of low-boiling, predigested scorn. He was right about the phone.

"You know, I'm not one of those bratty girls who can't have a conversation that's not texts. I'm *trying* to talk to you."

He seemed appeased by this. He got a flask of something from his inside pocket. "You drink?"

"Constantly."

He said, "How well did you know Murray?"

"I don't know. Not so well. My dad loved him. So I guess I loved him. It sounds like he was into some pretty loopy stuff."

"You mean the conspiracy stuff? Yeah. That was weird."

He lit another cigarette. "But I don't know," he said, exhaling. She felt the sun rise on their conversation. "I feel like, for him, it was almost like his way of learning. Like, in school you're pumped so full of crap, so much false confidence, told to draw a four-headed unicorn or whatever, and oh that's amazing, Timmy, and then you grow up and there's nowhere to put that shit. So I think for some people, it's like their way of being curious. Like, where else do you put that."

"Um, you put it into learning about things that are *real*, and reading news about events that *happened?*"

"But what's the fun in that?" He was serious. Oh gosh, he was an *idiot*. He turned to her and cracked up in a smile. "I'm kidding, I know." It was a nice one, his smile. "I'm just trying to understand it." A shame about those lobe plugs. "I'm just trying to see it from Murray's perspective."

"So you've thought about this a lot."

"You want to believe the world is topsy-turvy, full of secrets and lies and shadows, and boogeymen, because the world you're looking at, the life you have, it's—"

"Flat."

"Exactly."

"But maybe it doesn't have to be," she said, and took his flask. A sexy sip.

"That's true."

They were flirting. She was *good* at this.

"Hey, how old are you?"

"Twenty," he said.

His ride, a bruised Toyota number, was in the yard, among a flotilla of chrome Harleys. Janie suddenly felt lighter, clearer-headed. Maybe he could drive her to the city, at his leisure. Adam would want her even more, seeing her arrive in a pickup, hair tousled from the winds on the George Washington Bridge. She was a bad girl.

He said, "Can I tell you something crazy?"

"Please."

"I think we're cousins."

"Ha."

"Not think. I know we're cousins. I just did that 23andMe shit. Murray was my dad."

She nearly spat her drink out. "Woah. *What?* Are you fucking with me? Does *Dad* know?"

"When would I have told him?"

"You're fucking with me."

"We had a paternal great-grandmother from Genoa, and another one from Limerick."

"Oh. Shit."

This was true—her parents had come back with a Bible's worth of information from their excursion, for their anniversary last year, to Ellis Island. Their idea of a great time.

"She didn't really want me to come, my mom, she thought it would upset me, which, screw her. She hung around with his whole crew. That's how I know them. And I had just started to really get to know him, you know, as my dad, and he was gonna tell you all, but . . . well . . . I wanted to come see what you all were like."

"And?"

"Pretty terrible." That smile again.

"You have to tell my dad."

"I will, eventually."

"He'll want to adopt you."

"Well, in that case, I definitely won't."

"Holy shit. Your *dad's* dead. Hey—"

No wonder he'd looked so unhappy earlier—he must have wanted to scream. Burn the house down. And everyone standing around him eating crudités, and she, the brat, huffing and puffing and acting all

34

deprived, and he'd be saddled forever with this cureless void, this inheritance of black holes, and no one to comfort him, to just say,

"I'm *so sorry.*"

"Thanks. But, please," he said, "don't say anything to your dad. Lemme talk to him."

"What's your *name?*"

His name was Alan, which, as far as names went, seemed an anticlimax. He lit a joint.

Once you got him going, he was pretty open. Long-winded, even. He was really nice. She had never just *talked* like this, to a guy, before.

Here he was, in the flesh—a real-life outsider. A rolling stone, with no connections. All this time she'd spent dreaming of the angry young men, the rebels and roughs, their hands so much firmer, it seemed to her, on the ropes of life than her own, but he was just alone, and broke, and luckless. She imagined him in his old Game Stop uniform, a vinery of tattoos screaming past the collar.

"When I feel shitty, I just . . ." They were side by side in the hammock. "I just keep on having to remind myself not to feel bad for him. For my dad. I keep on having to remind myself he's not somewhere, missing out on this, watching us all enjoy ourselves. He's just nowhere. Which is, like, a relief. 'Cause some people think of heaven as a comfort, but heaven, if it did exist, would actually be a sad place, wouldn't it? It would probably be a place just full of people watching us, and wishing they were here, and feeling bored, forever."

Which, now that Janie heard it out loud, was not unlike the way she'd been doing it, even in the here and now. Eyes glued to the interface, always pining for the other side, or better company. Always running the clock out for some grand encounter. And what if it didn't come?

Then again, what if it *did*. Wasn't that worse?

She was higher than she would've liked.

A blast of music escaped through the back door. Her dad appeared then, his face hazy in the porch light.

"Let's go," he said.

"What?"

"Your train."

Janie said, "What? But I thought you—Mom—haven't you been drinking?"

35

"What? No. Why? Not unless you count the one beer I've been nurs-ing for about," he checked his watch, "three hours. Let's go. You'll miss your train. I'll meet you in the car in five."

He acknowledged Alan with a nod, then disappeared back into the house.

Alan's phone was broken, but they exchanged emails. He had Hot-mail, of course. Janie had her doubts, but he insisted that it worked.

"Don't be such a snob," he said, but in a way like they were friends now.

Getting in the car, Janie felt a wave of nausea. She was gun-shy. Like the future was a shiny thing but also cheap, and vulgar, and too soon. She'd have to sober up before Penn Station. Breathe deep: get her head back in the game.

That smell was in the air, warm and mulchy, almost tropical. That smell of total summer. It made you pause. It made you pity the dead even more than usual.

Nominated by Narrative

HOMESCHOOL

by MEGHAN O'GIEBLYN

from N+1

For most of my childhood—from kindergarten until tenth grade—I did not attend school. *Homeschooled* is the term I used as a kid, the term I still use today for expediency, though it has always seemed misleading, since schooling is what my mother meant to spare us from by keeping us at home. We lived during those years on a farm in Vermont that sat thirty miles outside the nearest functional town and was, in a lot of ways, autonomous. We ate eggs from our own chickens, heated the house with a wood-burning stove, and got our water from a local spring, which was just a PVC pipe extending from the side of a mountain next to a sign warning that the county could not guarantee the quality of the water. I spent most mornings doing the chores I shared with my brothers: feeding the chickens, stocking the woodbin, hauling hay bales out to the sheep pasture. After that, the day was my own. Sometimes I read alone in my room, or sat at the kitchen table drawing comics in my sketchbook. As the oldest, I was often responsible for the younger kids, but like most children in large families they were easy—hungry for attention, game for whatever task I invented. We made baroque concoctions of flour and spices in the mixer and played with the bottle-fed lambs that slept in the kitchen in a baby hamper and wobbled freely around the house all day. We were always trying to teach them to sit or roll over, as if they were dogs.

My mom was usually outdoors, tinkering with something in the barn or traipsing around the pasture, examining the sheep for hoof rot. It was just her and us. Our dad left when I was 8—first for inpatient treatment for what in those days was called "manic depression," then the following year for good, when he returned to the small Oregon town where he'd grown up. At the time my mom was pregnant with her fourth child. Even though we lived in a remote area, with no other adult in the house, she insisted on giving birth naturally, at home. The night her labor started, I was the one who called the midwife, who instructed me to fetch a heating pad and rubbing alcohol; she'd be there in forty minutes. When she arrived, I helped ferry towels back and forth from the bathroom, and was allowed to stay in the room for the birth.

This was, according to my mom, "an experience"—one of many things I would never have learned at school. The sole purpose of schools, she often said, was to teach children to stand in lines. They were places people sent their children to do "busy work"—one of her favorite phrases, a catchall for all manner of scholastic activity, from the pointless tasks contrived to habituate children to following rules (worksheets, self-assessments) to the required subjects she considered vehicles for the state's ideological agenda (sex education, evolutionary biology). My mom had been sent as a teenager to a boarding school in the South, a missionary reform academy that liberally practiced corporal punishment and from which she fled, sneaking out at night and hitchhiking back home to Michigan. Her animosity toward institutions must have stemmed from that experience, but she rarely mentioned it—and anyway, she rejected all forms of schooling: public and private, religious and secular.

Learning was something else. It was happening all the time, whether we were conscious of it or not, like breathing. In a letter to the state department of education, she referred to her pedagogy as "delight-directed integrated study," a term I believe she made up. She was required to write these letters every year, one for each child, detailing how she would teach the core subjects. I read them for the first time a couple years ago and was awed by their expansive, often creative notion of what qualifies as education. On the topic of Comprehensive Health, she wrote: "Meghan had a great introduction to the health care system this past spring when she spent four days in the hospital having her appendix out." On Citizenship, History, and Government: "We hope to have contact with a family of Russian immigrants through friends of ours who will be sponsoring them. This should help make real to Meghan some of the freedoms we enjoy in this country." All the letters were written in the same shrugging, breezy tone that was her primary mode of defense, and barely concealed her hostility toward state intervention. On sex education: "Presently she is gaining a good base of information by being involved with the life cycles in our barn, and some sheep we will breed this fall."

My mom considered music the most important part of our education. Each of us kids played at least one instrument, and the only time she interfered with our day was when the house was quiet for more than an hour. "I don't hear any practicing!" she'd call out. She also placed a disproportionate emphasis on memorization. By the age of 10 I could, if prompted, recite entire chapters of the King James Bible. My mom would turn to me while we were weeding the garden or waiting in line at the supermarket and say, "Let's hear Luke 2." We did, technically, have textbooks; they came in the mail each August from a Christian education wholesaler in Texas. Occasionally, my mom would flip through one and comment on something, but they remained for the most part untouched, stacked on the kitchen sideboard. Subjects that didn't interest her were more or less neglected. I went for years without doing formal arithmetic. Until tenth grade, my knowledge of earth sciences began and ended with Genesis. Every few months my mom would recognize the lapse and try to remedy it with an outsize gesture. Once, she returned from a walk with a dead painted turtle she'd found on the side of the road, placed it on our backyard picnic table, pulled out a makeshift assortment of surgical tools—a screwdriver, dinner forks, a butcher knife—and announced we were having "science class."

But the vast majority of our day was spent doing nothing. My mom talked about the importance of "hayloft time," her term for idle reflection. Children needed to think, she was always saying. They needed to spend a lot of time alone. She believed that extended bouts of solitude would cultivate autonomy and independence of thought. I did hole up many afternoons atop the ziggurat of hay bales, reading, or sometimes just lying there in silence, watching the chaff fall from the rafters. I also spent a lot of time in the woods, which I called "exploring." Behind the sheep pasture was a dirt road that led up the mountain to a network of abandoned logging trails that were, for all I could tell, limitless. I walked them every day and never saw another person. It wasn't uncommon to stumble on a hidden wonder: a meadow, an overgrown pasture, tiered waterfalls that ran green over carpets of algae. In those moments I experienced life as early humans might have, in a condition not unlike the one idealized by the Romantics, my mind as empty and stark as the bars of sunlight crossing the forest floor. I walked until I was tired, or until the shadows grew long and the sun dipped below the mountains, and then I headed home.

To raise a child of nature—a child who is truly free—you must first remove him from society. Take him out of the city, with its vanities, its hierarchies, its parades of status, and away from the village, where he might learn the vices of peasants. Give him a wide stretch of land where he can wander wherever he wishes. Give him a tutor who does not teach but simply serves as a model. The overprotected child will grow up to be weak. Let him discover the limits of his freedom, learning from his own mistakes. Exercise his body, but keep his mind idle for as long as possible. When he grows older, he will read what he chooses to read, and will teach himself whatever he finds useful. By then, he will be a true freethinker, and approach every idea as a skeptic.

This is more or less the pedagogy laid out by Jean-Jacques Rousseau in *Émile, or On Education,* the vade mecum of modern homeschooling. Perhaps that's going too far. No homeschooler I've known has acknowledged its influence, but the book was the first to present a systematic argument that supports parents pulling their children out of schools and rearing them at home. If you were to trace the basic philosophical precepts of the American homeschooling movement back through the tributaries of history in search of their source, you would find them all in Rousseau: society and its institutions degrade the natural inclinations; spontaneous action is superior to habit; children are malleable and must be cultivated carefully and deliberately, like plants.

In the beginning, modern American homeschoolers called themselves "unschoolers," a nod to the Rousseauian idea that true education is naturalistic and self-directed. The term was coined by John Holt, a school reformer who'd gradually lost faith in reform. Holt believed that America was "a sick society" obsessed with violence, luxury, and power, and that public life rewarded groupthink and totalitarian consensus. During the free school movement of the 1960s, he wrote books outlining how schools could give children more freedom and autonomy, but he eventually became disillusioned with the charade of formal education. Schools could never be changed because they were inextricably linked to the corporate workforce; their sole task was to prepare children to be docile employees. "It was becoming clear to me that the great majority of boring, regimented schools were doing exactly what they had always done and what most people wanted them to do," he writes in his book *Teach Your Own*: "Teach children about Reality. Teach them that Life Is No Picnic. Teach them to Shut Up And Do What You're Told."

In the late 1970s, Holt began arguing that parents were perfectly capable of educating their own children. He started a newsletter, *Growing Without Schooling*, to connect his growing band of disciples, most of whom were hippies—back-to-the-landers, people living on communal farms—who believed unschooling was an ancient, intuitive way of raising children. Parents wrote in to share that their kids were "flowering" at home: a child of barely 2 had learned to cook meals for himself, using knives and a stove; a child of 3 had taught himself to read without instruction, and was so immersed in nature he could recognize and name every kind of tree. "By the time he was 5," the father wrote, "he was so used to getting up in the morning with the ecstatic prospect of learning all day long that I hated to disabuse him of the notion that learning was natural by sending him to school."

But if you read the newsletter carefully, it's clear that not everyone maintained this laissez-faire approach. One father claims he has "eminent domain" over his children, which gives him the right "to rear and to train them according to the dictates of my own conscience before God." A mother, who describes her family as "church-going Catholics," writes that with her children at home, she and her husband can better oversee their socialization, their television viewing, and their sugar consumption. It turns out the hippies were not the only ones reading Holt's newsletter. His subscribers included a number of religious conservatives—evangelicals, Catholics, Seventh Day Adventists—who shared his belief that state education was a form of mind control, though for quite different reasons. For them, schools were not brainwashing children with capitalist values, but with the agenda of the radical left, which, according to the rhetoric, included evolutionary biology, sex education, and secular humanism.

In the second issue of *Growing Without Schooling*, Holt acknowledged that his disciples were "mixed allies" whose grievances about schools varied dramatically. He saw this diversity as a strength, proof of the movement's potential to transcend political and religious lines. It's hard not to wince at his naivete. In the coming decades, homeschooling would become almost entirely dominated by fundamentalist Christians, who had a more ambitious social agenda, massive organizational wealth, and—perhaps most crucially—a large contingent of mothers who were willing to forego careers and stay home with their children.

In those early, heady days of utopianism, it was perhaps difficult to grasp a truth that is all too plain now: that countercultural ideals like freedom, individualism, and antiauthoritarianism can be commandeered by the very institutional powers they were contrived to fight.

But perhaps the problem lies closer to the source, with the Enlightenment notion of absolute freedom. Rousseau speaks passionately of liberating children, and yet his pedagogy involves highly specific prescriptions for how a child should be bathed (in ice-cold water), where he should be raised (in a temperate climate, like France), how he should be fed (sparsely; too much food will disrupt his digestion). Émile cannot have contact with other children, or see doctors or priests during his early years. "You will not be master of the child if you cannot control every one about him," the author warns. It is this contradiction in Rousseau—what Jacob Talmon called the "transition from absolute freedom to absolute necessity"—that led cold-war critics like Talmon and Isaiah Berlin to argue that his philosophy led, logically, to totalitarianism and other forms of social control. Like Rousseau, Holt believed true liberty was not merely the absence of unjust restraint, but the absence of all possible restraint. And from there it is only a short leap to the insistence that one must vigilantly maintain this freedom at any cost—and, finally, to the gnawing paranoia that there are subtle forces, everywhere and invisible, conspiring to constrict it.

My childhood was, in many ways, a walled garden constructed in accordance with 19th-century notions of innocence and autonomy. I was aware on some level that there was a broader culture from which we had deliberately exempted ourselves. My mother called it the World, which was neither the planet nor the cosmos, but a system of interlocking ideologies that were everywhere and in everything. Sometimes the World was capitalism, as when she complained that Christmas had been co-opted by the World's consumerism. Other times it was socialism, which was synonymous with the State, a vast and elusive force that had the power to take children from their parents. The World was feminism, environmentalism, secular humanism—ideologies that sprang from a single source and reinforced one another. We were to be in the World but not of it, existing within its physical coordinates but uncontaminated by its values. "Schoolkids," according to her, were hopeless products of the World. They could not think for themselves, but simply mimicked behavior they'd seen on television. ("Stop popping your gum," she would say. "You look like a schoolkid.") Media made for children was naturally suspect. My mom once pronounced an animated film about dinosaurs Darwinian propaganda, and marched us out of a community sing-along because a folk song espoused new age pantheism. I have more than once considered the brilliance she would have achieved as a critic, so relentless she was in deconstructing any artifact and reducing it to its essential message. Of all the things she taught me, this was the most formative: that life concealed vast power structures warring for control of my mind; that my only hope for freedom was to be vigilant in recognizing them and calling them by name.

Everyone we knew was like us. In those dark ages before chat rooms and social networks, my mom maintained some mysterious sonar for locating like-minded people: fundamentalists who shopped at cooperative groceries, strained their own yogurt, and spoke in tongues at the dinner table. For several years, our social life orbited around a weekly Bible study we attended at the house of a large extended homeschool family who took us into their fold. While the adults met upstairs, my siblings and I were abandoned to the other children, all cousins, who were less a peer group than a kind of child gang. The leaders were the two oldest boys, who wore matching fox-tooth necklaces and led us on long treks through the acres of swampland behind their house. Sometimes we were supposed to be looking for something—candle quartz, which they called crystals, or a fisher-cat that had been spotted in the area—but the expeditions were more often a hazing ritual, a test to see how far we would follow them into the darkened woods, crossing thin ice, crawling through the live wires of electrical fencing, climbing into abandoned deer blinds. I lagged at the back of the group, making sure my brothers, who were among the youngest, didn't get lost.

The girls all wore their hair long, grazing the backs of their knees. They were slightly older than me, and though they were kind—teaching me crochet stitches and braiding my hair—I was never sure whether I was their equal or their charge. During the coldest months, the boys gave up on their treks and we all hung out in the basement, occupying ourselves with a variety of homemade distractions that I am embarrassed to reproduce here. For a year or so, we were very into puppetry. We were once disciplined for "playing" Communion, passing around plates of broken saltines and Welch's grape juice. (Apparently this was sacrilege.) When I think back on those evenings, all I can think of is all that blood in close quarters, edging up on puberty. Most of the girls were in love with their cousins, and spoke of it wistfully, as a kind of romantic tragedy. "I'm sure Sean likes you," one of them confessed to me, sighing. "He'll never love me, because I'm his cousin."

We did occasionally have contact with larger groups. We went to church on Sundays, and in summer attended a missionary camp on Lake Michigan. In September, we sometimes went to Six Flags, which had a "homeschool day" discount to capitalize on the back-to-school lull. It was there, more than anywhere, that one could glimpse the movement in its entirety. The Christian Reconstructionists were easiest to spot (patriotic T-shirts), as were the macrobiotic hippies, who overlapped somewhat with the anti-vaxxers, the anarchists, and the preppers. There were the rich suburban kids whose parents had pulled them from school to better facilitate backpacking trips to Mongolia, and Mennonite girls in long denim skirts, plus the occasional Quiverfull family numbering twelve, fifteen, twenty-five. The full spectrum, in other words, of American private dissent. But even then, it didn't feel like a community so much as a summit of isolated tribes. Families came and left together, and remained as units throughout the day. The kids didn't talk. Concessions were a graveyard; everyone brought packed lunches.

Earlier this year, while going through some files my mom gave me, I came across a homeschool newsletter on the topic of socialization. I expected the authors would rehearse the arguments I'd heard as a child—that schools did not have a monopoly on social life; that there were plenty of other ways to meet people—and was surprised to find something else. The first article was by Sue Welch, a Christian homeschooling advocate. "The world says that our children need to spend large amounts of time with many of their own age-mates," she wrote. "This produces the desired effect of conformity." She went on to argue that socialization was a myth, devised by the state and their coterie of child psychologists to woo children away from the ideology of their parents. (The first definition of *socialize*, she pointed out, was "to place under government or group ownership or control.") Parents who accepted this wisdom were themselves victims of false consciousness: "Our own socialization has conditioned us to accept current opinion or psychological studies over God's revealed truth." The other authors more or less reiterated her argument: socialization was not only overblown, it was actively detrimental to children.

Poring over these documents, my first instinct was to dismiss these ideas as the fringe of the fringe. Like many adults who have left extremist religious backgrounds, I long ago came to terms with the fact that I was raised in a culture whose defining ethos was fear. But I always

44

believed that fear was subliminal, and that the restrictions it spawned were carried out in a kind of dream-state by parents who had fallen under the sway of talk radio and the ambient alarm of the culture wars. I had a difficult time believing that isolation was systematically prescribed by homeschooling leaders, and that my own cloistered childhood was the result of my mother heeding their advice. Some additional research proved the breadth of my ignorance. This view of socialization appears in all the landmark homeschooling literature, including the work of Holt, who claimed that kids benefited from a limited number of friends and recommended that children spend substantial time alone. It reaches poetic heights in the books of Raymond Moore, a frequent guest on James Dobson's radio program *Family Talk* who popularized homeschooling among religious conservatives. In his 1981 book *Home Grown Kids,* "peer dependency" among children is referred to as "a social cancer" again and again.

Then there's this, from one of the most famous homeschooling advocates: "Thus the oversocialized person is kept on a psychological leash and spends his life running on rails that society has laid down for him. In many oversocialized people this results in a sense of constraint and powerlessness that can be a severe hardship. We suggest that oversocialization is among the more serious cruelties that human beings inflict on one another." OK, I lied. That one's Ted Kaczynski.

The enlightenment idea that humans are infinitely malleable naturally has a dark side. If children can, as Rousseau claimed, be perfected through careful observance and social control, they can also be ruined if these methods are faulty or perverted. An entire strain of counter-Enlightenment thought stemmed from this idea, the most well-known example being Mary Shelley's *Frankenstein*. Although the novel is often read as a parable about technological hubris, Shelley herself envisioned it as a drama about child-rearing, and wrote it, in part, as a critique of Rousseau's pedagogy. Victor's monster is born good and begins his life, like Émile, in the state of nature: he roams the countryside and educates himself by reading in isolation. But because his "parent" abandons him without completing his education, the child is unable to fully integrate himself into human society. When he finally emerges from nature and enters a village, people find him hideous and regard him as a monster. He is forced to retreat back into isolation, and eventually his alienation transforms him into a murderer.

45

In March 2018, Mark Conditt, a 23-year-old man better known as the Austin package bomber, blew himself up in a Ford Ranger on the side of Interstate 35 outside Austin, Texas. Over the previous three weeks, Conditt had shipped homemade bombs in FedEx packages to various homes in the Austin area, all of them sent from the cryptic alias Kelly Killmore. While the attacks were initially believed to be racially motivated—the first two victims were people of color—later targets were white and lived in an upper-middle-class suburb. Conditt's motivations became even more puzzling after police recovered a twenty-five-minute confession video that did not mention anything about terrorism or hate. The interim police chief described the video as "the outcry of a very challenged young man talking about challenges in his personal life."

The lone eccentricity of Conditt's background was that he had been homeschooled. A local newspaper managed to reach Jeremiah Jensen, a friend of Conditt's, who alluded to the social struggles his friend faced as a homeschooler. "It's just very difficult for a lot of [homeschooled] kids to find a way to fit in once they are out in the real world," he told the paper. "I have a feeling that is what happened with Mark. I don't remember him ever being sure of what he wanted to do." Perhaps because there was no clear motive, Conditt's homeschooling seemed increasingly suspicious. BuzzFeed reported that in high school, Conditt had belonged to a Christian homeschool group called RIOT. The article cited a former group member who said that in addition to studying the Bible, RIOT members shot guns at a range and carried knives. She also noted that the kids were "very into science" and did experiments with chemicals.

A friend of mine who knew I was homeschooled sent me a link to the story the day it was published: "Ever heard of this homeschool Riot group?" He was under the impression—one that the article did not discourage—that the group was a radical nationwide cell network of Christian terrorists. I pointed out that RIOT was actually an acronym—Righteous Invasion of Truth—and the title of a 1995 album by Carman, who is basically the Barry Manilow of Christian contemporary music. Not exactly a figurehead of violent dissent. I linked a response article from HuffPost that excerpted a RIOT brochure, which was written in sunny, sociable language and interviewed one of the RIOT mothers, who spoke of the group in similarly benign terms. "Water balloons, cream pies, frisbee, etc.," she said. "That's what it is." By then, it was a moot point. People on Twitter were already proclaiming RIOT a neo-Nazi group and comparing it to ISIS.

I didn't rule out the possibility that homeschooling had contributed in some way to Conditt's sense of alienation. But the notion that he had been "radicalized" struck me as hysterical. It attributed to homeschooling the same vaguely conspiratorial powers of mind control that my mom ascribed to the World, and fell in line with some of the more outrageous assumptions people harbored about homeschoolers (how many times have I been asked if my parents kept us in cages or forbade us to leave the house?). My mother once pointed out that these stereotypes revealed how much people feared homeschoolers, which in turn revealed their own fear that they themselves were not free.

But after a while, I regretted defending the group to my friend. Why, after all, do I find it necessary to make these distinctions? Why, when I hear stories like these, do I immediately think of what my mother would say? It's difficult to account for why I still occasionally find myself defending homeschooling, despite everything I know about its detrimental effects and my own enduring alienation.

When I was 11, my mom sold the farm, which had become untenable, and moved our family back to the Midwest. Her family lived in Michigan, and we moved, in part, to be closer to them, but our life there was, in some sense, as itinerant and isolated as it had been in Vermont. For several years we moved between seemingly identical towns in Illinois and Michigan, where we ate at the same chain restaurants, shopped at the same big-box stores, and attended nondenominational churches that were so similar to one another in their worship style and theology that they, too, seemed like franchises. We were closer to civilization but still resisting its pull, circling the outskirts of communities, protected by the dull scrim of suburban anonymity. Everything changed when my mother got remarried, to a man she'd met at church. He had a daughter, which brought another child into our family, and soon after the wedding we all moved to a lakeside town in Wisconsin, a place that was, unavoidably, a community. Neighbors came by to introduce themselves and invited us to picnics and block parties. My parents began hosting dinners at our house. That fall, my mom suggested that if we ever wanted to try school, this would be a good time.

After all her years of embattled opposition of schooling, I'm still unsure what led to her change of mind. It's possible she was simply exhausted by the stress of raising five children and wanted us out of the house, but it might have had something to do with the cultural shift taking place in those years. By the late 1990s, the countercultural Jesus People fundamentalism to which my mother subscribed had been absorbed by the megachurch movement—a brand of evangelicalism that was more suburban and upbeat, concerned with engaging the culture rather than resisting it. I was then 15 years old, approaching what would have been the tenth grade. Although I maintained some misgivings about attending school, I suspected this was my one shot, and my siblings had agreed to go without hesitation. I said yes.

The school itself was a kind of nightmare: a large public institution with two campuses and a multimillion-dollar hockey rink that had been endowed by one of the parents. The football team was the Division 1 state champion, and on Fridays all the popular girls wore red tartan kilts to class to announce the weekend's field hockey match. The whole place smelled like an Abercrombie. My academic performance that first year was predictably uneven. I failed chemistry and barely scraped by in algebra. In music theory, I found the curriculum so elementary that the teacher eventually gave me a private desk in the corner and said I could use the hour to study for other classes. Things should have evened out over time, but my problem was not a dearth of knowledge but of discipline. I could not bring myself to concentrate on subjects that bored me. The one time I was formally reprimanded, it was for forging a note to get out of sociology so that I could work in the studio on a video production assignment. The principal, once the situation was sorted out, was baffled. "This is the first time I've sent someone to detention for doing homework," he said. I didn't understand what I'd done wrong. Why should I have to sit in a classroom where I was learning nothing useful, when there were things I wanted to do just down the hall?

I wish I could say I maintained the same aristocratic indifference in my social life, but I wanted desperately to be liked, and this made me painfully self-conscious. At lunch, I had a difficult time following conversations. Everyone seemed to be pantomiming, with great exaggeration, awe, affection, disgust. In retrospect, the problem was very simple: I was wholly ignorant of the social scripts that governed large groups of females. All my mental energy was devoted to deciphering codes, analyzing unfamiliar words, and unpacking innuendo. I often felt the other girls looking at me, wondering why I was so quiet, but I never contributed anything because I was always a couple steps behind, still processing the last thing that had been said.

Over time, my curiosity gave way to bewilderment, and eventually to boredom. I became fatigued whenever I was forced to talk to more than

48

one person at a time, overcome with a weariness that felt at times like mental blankness, and at others like acute physical exhaustion. I began eating my lunch in the library, under the pretense that I was catching up on homework, not realizing that this simple act of independence would damn me to full social opprobrium. Rumors made their way back to me—that I picked my nose in class, that I wore the same pants for ten days straight—which led me to retreat further. As a homeschooler, I had never felt lonely, even though my life consisted largely of solitude. It wasn't until I entered school that I understood for the first time the ache of seclusion and personal failure. We read *Frankenstein* that year in English. I didn't know then that the novel was in conversation with Rousseau, but I remember identifying with the monster's alienation. "Everywhere I see bliss, from which I alone am irrevocably excluded," he cries out in one monologue. "I was benevolent and good; my soul glowed with love and humanity: but am I not alone, miserably alone?"

I wish I could say that all of this passed like a bad trip, the way high school does for so many people. But to this day, it's rare that I end a social interaction without retracing the steps of those long walks home from school: convinced that everything I said was false, that authentic communication is impossible within the confines of social norms. I suppose I might be an angry person had I not, in the end, found my way back to Nature, or its closest analogue. It was during high school that I began writing. I transcribed conversations I'd overheard at school, observations about people, insights about the books I was reading. It became a habit that I came to depend upon, like nourishment, in the same way I craved solitude. The world was pulsing forward at a relentless pace, but the page was infinitely slow, infinitely patient. My first-person voice became my primary sense of identity—an avatar of words and air that I constructed each day and carried in my backpack like a talisman. Its private sustenance was less like a pastime than like the wilderness I explored as a child with total freedom, never exhausting its limits.

Émile, of course, is not really a child care manual. It's a philosophical treatise that explores an intractable problem: how can one maintain freedom from society while also existing within it? Many of Rousseau's first readers missed this point and took his prescriptions at face value. In the years after *Émile* was published, parents frequently wrote to Rousseau claiming that they were raising their children in the manner he'd outlined. To one such father he replied, "So much the worse, sir, for you and your son, so much the worse."

Rousseau knew that the state of nature was a lost Eden where no person could return. Society put humans in a state of disunity: one's natural inclinations were always at war with one's social duties. But isolating a child would only heighten that sense of disunity. "He who in the civil order wants to preserve the primacy of the sentiments of nature does not know what he wants," Rousseau writes in the early pages of the book—a user warning for anyone tempted to try his methods at home. "Always in contradiction with himself, always floating between his inclinations and his duties, he will never be either [natural] man or citizen. He will be good neither for himself nor for others. . . . He will be nothing."

I suppose this state of "contradiction," or disunity, sums up my position today. I left my family's ideology somewhat late—in my early twenties, after two tortured years of Bible college—which ultimately made the exit more difficult. I wasted a lot of time mourning the loss, drinking, working lousy jobs. But despite everything I now know about the ideologies that informed homeschooling, I maintain mostly good memories of those years I lived in innocence. I sometimes credit homeschooling with the qualities I've come to value most in myself: a capacity for solitude and absorption, a distrust of consensus. It is tempting, even, to believe that my childhood inadvertently endowed me with the tools to escape it—that my mother's insistence that the World was conspiring to brainwash me cultivated the very skepticism that I later trained on my family and their beliefs. But this is circular logic, like someone saying they are grateful for their diabetes because it forced them to change their eating habits. Its wisdom resembles the hollow syntax of rationalization. If I've often found it difficult to speak or write about this ambivalence, it's because it's impossible to do so without coming to interrogate my motives and doubt my own independence of mind.

Last summer, I came across Tara Westover's memoir *Educated*, a story that in many ways held a mirror to my own experience. Westover grew up in rural Idaho in a family of radical Mormon survivalists who forbade their children to attend school or see doctors. In her book, she recalls working alongside her father in his junkyard, where she sustained several injuries that were treated homeopathically; listening to his conspiratorial rants about the Feds; and helping her parents prep for the end of days. The story hinges on the process by which she educated herself, in secret, so that she could go to college—first at Brigham Young

University, then at Cambridge, where she got a doctorate in history. The manuscript was bought for six figures within twenty-four hours of hitting the market, and has since been published in twenty countries.

The whole idea of the book—its publicity budget, its book-club sheen—struck me from the beginning as evidence of bad faith. Americans maintain a voracious appetite for child-isolation narratives (*The Wolfpack, Room*). Unlike the readers of *Émile,* who delighted in the fantasy of native innocence, for Americans the allure of these cloistered children lies in the belief that they have been brainwashed; their entrance into society is not a loss of innocence, but a drama of liberation. Throughout her media tour, Westover was celebrated as a feral child who had crossed over, a symbol of American autonomy and self-governance who had, by dint of will, clawed her way out of a family that, incidentally, held fast to those same American virtues. Magazine profiles reiterated how "normal" she seemed. In interviews, she spoke of "psychological manipulation" and "reality distortions" with the authority of someone who had completed years of therapy. "All abuse is foremost an assault on the mind," she told *Vogue.*

Still, these talking points did not quell the collective anxiety that Westover maintained some confusion about her upbringing, and I suppose this is what interested me most about her story. Several critics found it unsettling that her parents were occasionally characterized, in her memoir, with a note of affection, and that the descriptions of her childhood landscape were undergirded by a sense of longing. One interviewer wondered "if Westover only really comprehended the difficulty of her childhood when she sat down to write." Reviewers noted this too, but dismissed it as an aesthetic choice. That she refused to "demonize" her family was not evidence of sympathy, but the result of her "matter-of-fact lyricism" and "characteristic understatement," a writerly restraint contrived to lend the darker moments of her story even more power.

Westover once hinted that the early iterations of her book had a lighter tone. When she first began writing, she confessed in one interview, she regarded her family's behavior as harmless and eccentric: "I don't think I had really appreciated how extreme bits of it were. I would write about the injuries a lot of times like comedies, and my friends thought, 'this undermines my trust in you because it doesn't seem like you understand the situation.'" One might argue that Westover understood her situation better than anyone, having lived it, but her authority as a narrator—and more fundamentally, as a witness to her own life—was for many

51

readers discounted by the brainwashing she'd experienced as a child. The most popular comment on the book's Goodreads page spells out what many readers found troubling: "I do not understand why an educated and worldly individual would have difficulty understanding the horrible and violent upbringing that she experienced." In the end, Westover, who has described her life as a process of regaining "custody of my own mind," was subjected, again and again, to the insistence that she did not actually know her own mind.

This is the predicament of people who were raised in highly controlled environments: any ambivalence about your upbringing is proof of its success, a sign that you are not yet completely free. Homeschoolers, after all, are not the only ones preoccupied with autonomy. All of us in America are Rousseau's children: obsessed with liberty, terrified of those who would put restraints on our thinking. If stories like Westover's are unsettling, it's because they reflect the larger disunity all of us know to be our fate—that none of us live completely off the ideological grid, impervious to malicious systems of thought. We are all like Frankenstein's monster, victims of our own miseducations, a motley patchwork of the influences that have shaped us, sometimes without our awareness or consent.

It is impossible to anticipate how a person will interpret the lessons of her childhood, whether she will find in them an impetus for violence or a source of creative inspiration. In my own family, my siblings and I have proved the outcomes of my mother's pedagogy wildly unpredictable. Despite her best efforts to raise us deliberately, each of us has negotiated, in idiosyncratic ways, the legacy of our childhood, and our lives have veered down such divergent paths that when we are all together, it is difficult to imagine we were reared under the same roof. My mother raised a writer, a musician, a missionary, a hotel manager, and an accountant; a progressive, a centrist, two moral conservatives, and a libertarian. I do not have children, but my siblings have collectively produced half a dozen. All of them go to school. +

Nominated by n + 1,
Lydia Conklin,
Barrett Swanson

ROLL UNDER THE WAVES

by JUAN FELIPE HERRERA

from LOVE'S EXECUTIVE ORDER

we roll under the waves
not above them we body surf and somehow we lose
the momentum there are memories trailing us empty orange
and hot pink bottles of medicines left behind
buried next to a saguaro there are baby backpacks
and a thousand shoes and a thousand gone steps
leading in the four directions each one without destinations
there are men laying face down forever and women
dragging under the fences and children still running with
torn faces all the way to Tucson leathery and peeling
there are vigilantes with skull dust on their palms
and the trigger and the sputum and the moon with
its pocked hope and its blessings and its rotations into the spikes
there is a road forgotten with a tiny sweet roof of twigs
and a black griddle threaded with songs like the one
about el contrabando from El Paso there is nothing
a stolen land forgotten too a stolen life branded and
tied and thrown into the tin patrol box with flashes of trees
and knife-shaped rivers and the face of my mother Luz and
water running next to the animals still thrashing choking
their low burnt violin muffled screams in rings
of roses across the mountains

Nominated by Love's Executive Order

THE HUMAN SOUP

by MAUREEN STANTON

from NEW ENGLAND REVIEW

There was a man I saw once or twice a week in the hot tub at the YMCA who talked boisterously, as if he were in a bar, as if he wanted everyone to know his business. His voice was too loud for the intimate setting, where barely clothed strangers sat together in hot water, skin cells sloughing off, simmering in the steaming cauldron. He talked about his fiancée, whom he was bringing over from Russia, about the crazy red tape she had to untangle to get her visa. "She's twenty-five," he said, though he looked late fortyish. He was fat, though handsome, with a fine nose and good straight teeth. He wore gold-rimmed glasses that never fogged. The fat man had been growing less fat over the past few months, perhaps because he didn't want his Russian bride to be shocked when she arrived.

I disdained this man, but my feelings were disproportionate to my annoyance, and so I wondered, what aspect of myself did I see reflected in him? What self-loathing was I projecting onto his large pale torso? Maybe he irritated me because he participated in an economy in which women trade youth, beauty, and sex to men with means for a life free from poverty. Maybe I disliked his naiveté, his belief that love might motivate his Russian fiancée, not economic gain. Or maybe his bid for companionship was too public, too much on display, and thus forced me to consider my own aloneness.

When the hot tub broke and was closed for a few weeks, I didn't see the fat man for a while, and part of me missed him, or missed the guilty pleasure of disliking him. I'd cultivated an elaborate disinterest around his frequent talk of the Russian fiancée. I'd strive for an expression that conveyed, *I'm not listening. You can't impress me. I'm preoccupied with my own important contemplations.*

*   *   *

In ancient Rome, bathing was practically an art form, a religion. After temples, bathhouses were the most common buildings. A fourth-century census recorded 856 public bathhouses for Rome's million or so citizens, which would be the equivalent of 900 public bathhouses in Dallas, Texas, today. The Baths of Caracalla, a twenty-seven-acre complex that took 9,000 laborers five years to complete, exemplified Romans' devotion to bathing. It included sports fields, an Olympic-sized swimming pool, gardens, fountains, and a four-story bathhouse that accommodated 1,600 people, with massage rooms, saunas, perfumeries, and a hair salon. The interior walls were adorned with mosaics and gilded carvings, and a hundred alcoves for statuary. There was a *hypocaust* (literally *fire underneath*) to warm the tiled floors, and to heat the tub waters, fifty furnaces burned ten tons of wood daily.

On a typical day in ancient Rome, a tintinnabulum rang to summon men and women to the baths—mixed-sex bathing was common. Entrance fees were free or low, so the poor could bathe, too. They soaked in the warm tepidarium or the hot caldarium, or dipped into the bracing frigidarium, all while being entertained by jugglers, acrobats, musicians, and poets. Vendors hawked wine, pretzels, cake, eels, and quail eggs. You could hire a depilator to pluck unwanted hair, or someone to oil, sand, and scrape your skin. All this bustle created a cacophony that "could make you hate your own ears," wrote Seneca, the first-century rhetorician. Musclemen pumping weights emitted "squeaking, squealing sound[s]." Masseuses slapped flesh, pickpockets were noisily arrested, and bathers yelped from having hair yanked from their armpits. "Sausage sellers, the pastry bakers and the barmen" cried their wares, and there was always a man, Seneca bristled, "who likes to hear himself singing in the bath."

Aside from giving him headaches, Seneca believed that communal bathing inspired "sexual licentiousness and moral delinquency," which was probably true. The Roman baths were designed for *voluptus*—delights of the flesh. Erotic frescoes at a Pompeii bathhouse depicted people having sex in graphic detail, and an epigram at the entrance to the Baths of Caracalla read: "Baths, wine and sex spoil our bodies; but baths, wine and sex make up life."

My first hot tub experience was meant to be erotic. In college in the early 1980s I rented an hour at Heavenly Hot Tubs in Northampton, Massachusetts, the grand finale to a night I'd planned for my second anniversary with David. I cooked a gourmet dinner, bought tickets to see the great French mime Marcel Marceau, and splurged on the hot tubs. That night David stopped for a drink after work, then another, and another. By the time he came home the dinner was congealed. At Marceau's performance, in the pin-drop quiet auditorium, David loudly sneered. A talented but unsuccessful musician, he was annoyed that the audience loved this performer who made no sound. I stood and walked out of the auditorium, then hid outside to see how long it would take him to realize I hadn't just gone to the ladies' room. I tried to recover the night at Heavenly Hot Tubs, but David complained the water was too hot. It took me another year to realize, *oh, he's an alcoholic*, and soon after, *I can't save him*.

* * *

Romans bathed for pleasure, but also to follow the medical wisdom of the time. Pliny the Elder in the first century, and Celsus, a century later, recommended baths for gout, itching, palsy, "complaints of male organs," gangrene, rabies, epilepsy, psoriasis, small pustules, and lice in the eyelashes. Sitting in the tub at the Y, I've often wondered about the ingredients of the human soup. Urine leakage, for sure, perhaps pus from suppurating boils, saliva, fecal particles, hair and the follicles attached to them, toe shreddings, dirt from under fingernails, nose and throat mucus, and oil from the thousands of sebaceous glands beneath our skin—as many as 900 on the face alone, all secreting waxy sebum. Dead skin cells slough off. Each of us sheds up to 500 million skin cells daily; we grow a new suit of skin each month. Belly button lint is emancipated by the roiling water, especially since there were always more men at the Y and belly button lint is a male phenomenon, as chemist George Steinhauser discovered in his four-year study of "navel fluff."

Marcus Aurelius, the stoic emperor, wrote, "This bathing that usually takes up so much of our time, what is it? Sweat, filth; or the sordes of the body." *Sordes* is the Latin root of sordid—"an excrementitious viscosity . . . all base and loathsome." Samuel Pepys, the sixteenth-century diarist, who bathed in the thermal waters at Bath, England, wrote, "Methinks it cannot be clean to go so many bodies together into the same water." A nineteenth-century traveler to a Persian bathhouse wrote that if people wanted to become clean, the bath was "the worst place" to go, the water "glutted with abominations . . . rats and black-beetles and horrible insects."

The human soup is a teeming broth, which must mean I have a high threshold for disgust, combined with a weakness for corporeal pleasure. One night in a hot tub at a sports club in Missouri, where I lived for seven years, the jets whipped a froth on the surface of the water that broke into foamy islands. One island of foam had caught in its meringue several short black squiggly hairs. At that point, I should have fled the tub, but it felt so good that I simply cupped my hand beneath the foam and flung it—with its payload of hairs—onto the tiled floor.

❃ ❃ ❃

Near the end of the Roman Empire, the baths fell into disrepair; it was difficult to maintain the sophisticated heating and plumbing systems in the midst of political turmoil. Sieges by Vandals and Huns damaged the aqueducts that funneled water to the dozen imperial bathhouses and 926 public baths, and in 537 AD the Ostrogoths completely destroyed them. Without water, 90 percent of Rome's population left the city. Within two decades not a single imperial bath complex survived.

The Goths attacked the bathhouses, but Christians attacked the idea of bathing. In the fourth century, the Mother Superior of a convent warned that a "clean body and clean dress" signified an unclean soul. Christian ascetics practiced *alousia,* "the state of being unwashed." Thirteen-year-old St. Agnes died in 304 AD having never taken a bath, and St. Fintan of Clonenaugh was said to bathe once annually, just before Easter. St. Anthony never washed his feet his entire life, and St. Francis of Assisi thought "dirtiness" a sign of holiness. In the sixth century, St. Benedict didn't bathe during his seven-year pilgrimage through France, Italy, Germany, and Spain, for which he earned the honorific "The Great Unwashed."

Architecture symbolizes the ethos of its time, evidenced after the fall of the Roman Empire when the decadent, now crumbling bathhouses were transformed into churches. Under Pope Pius IV, the ruins of the Baths of Diocletian—the largest bath complex in Rome, covering thirty-two acres—were remodeled into a church and monastery, Santa Maria degli Angeli. Michelangelo, who oversaw the project, incorporated into his design the original magnificent architecture of the bathhouse.

* * *

Wherever there is hot water, I go in. In Livingston, Guatemala, where boiling water seeps from the fissures of a cliff along the Rio Dulce, the captain on our boat trip to a manatee preserve idled his craft so we could swim in the thermal waters. In Yellowstone Park, surrounded by snow-capped mountains, I sat in an eddy of a rushing river where hot water bubbled up from some molten core, wearing only my bra and underwear. At the Sands Motel in Houghton Lake, Michigan, in the 1990s, I sat in a hot tub on a cool October night with Steve, my boyfriend of four years, who had been diagnosed with terminal cancer. Steve had tumors all along his spine by the time doctors discovered the disease, and he was in constant pain. That night in the tub—gazing at the veil of the Milky Way, warm swirling water soothing Steve's aches—was the single moment of physical pleasure for Steve in eighteen months, from the time he was diagnosed until the day he died at thirty-one.

* * *

After prayer failed to relieve St. Augustine's sadness over his mother's death, he thought to "go and bathe" because he'd heard that bathing "drives the sadness from the mind." A recent study in France found that a hot bath more successfully eased anxiety than paroxetine (brand name, Paxil), a prescription antidepressant. In that study, a couple hundred people aged eighteen to seventy-four who'd been diagnosed with General Anxiety Disorder were divided into two groups. One group took a daily ten-minute "bubbling" bath in warm mineral waters, followed by a three-minute shower, and then a ten-minute underwater back massage, while the control group took 20 milligrams of paroxetine. After twenty-one days, the bath group showed "significantly lower" scores on the Hamilton Anxiety Scale than the Paxil group.

Other studies have shown that "water bathing" decreases stress hormones (cortisol), and helps balance serotonin levels. Recently researchers in Virginia found "hydrotherapy" beneficial in treating depression; cold water, they found, increases the production of endorphins. Still, it's hard to imagine the ice baths given to patients in mental institutions in the early twentieth century as anything but cruel. According to a medical text of the time, the patient was immersed every three hours in "a great tub of cold water, with its lumps of ice clinking against its sides" during the "twenty minutes of torture."

A pair of Yale researchers found that hot baths can ease loneliness. "Feelings of social warmth or coldness can be induced by experiences of physical warmth or coldness," they wrote. Their study showed that people who rated higher on loneliness scales bathed or showered more often, longer, and with hotter temperatures. Bath-taking, they suggested, is "an unconscious form of self-therapy," in which people substitute physical warmth for "social warmth." We literalize the metaphor: warm the body, warm the heart and soul.

* * *

One night at the Y, I saw a lovely auburn-haired woman swimming in the "therapy" pool next to the hot tub, which is half the size of the main pool. The woman splashed and played like a ten-year-old. She wore a two-piece bathing suit as if at the beach, unlike my one-piece Speedo or the swim-dresses favored by older women. The young woman had a distinct mole on her cheek, which was interesting rather than unfortunate because she was so pretty, with doe-eyes and sensual lips, alabaster skin. She had a Russian accent, but spoke English well. She was the fiancée of the fat man who'd slimmed down; he was now bronzed and healthy looking, though flabby around the waist. He was not her aesthetic match and I couldn't help but wonder, *is she disappointed?* She seemed ecstatic to be swimming at this YMCA, lounging in the hot tub. I felt a little sad about the situation—I imagined that she had fled some remote oppressive region in Russia only to wind up with a man twice her age who took her to the Y. I wished he'd taken her someplace better.

* * *

In the Middle Ages, public baths in London, called "stewes," were often little more than brothels, some with built-in galleries for voyeurs. In France, Germany, and England in the mid-1500s, the stewes were ordered closed to halt the epidemic of syphilis—"the great pox"— believed to originate in the baths. Francis I, the King of France, destroyed the public baths in Paris in 1538 before he himself succumbed to the disease. Another epidemic, the bubonic plague, kept people out of public baths. According to the French physician Ambroise Paré, hot water was considered harmful as it destroyed the skin's protective oils, which then allowed "pestiferous vapours" to seep into "the little air holes in the skin."

❋ ❋ ❋

The water in the YMCA hot tub looked yellowish one night, the grout grimy. When I lowered myself in, I thought, *it's not hot enough.* Two days later, my right breast swelled painfully. The doctor said it might be mastitis, a staph infection common in lactating women, but since I was not lactating he mentioned that it *could* be inflammatory breast cancer (IBC). I left his office feeling relatively calm, thinking, *well, that's probably not it and even if it is, it's probably in the early stages.* I was uncharacteristically sanguine on the drive home, but—Google me this!—inflammatory breast cancer is the most aggressive type, with a dismal 10 percent survival rate. I freaked out, especially after I read that mastitis was *extremely* rare in women over fifty.

The doctor said the antibiotics would reduce the swelling in forty-eight hours. *Or not.* If this was IBC, the inflammation was caused by tumors blocking the milk ducts, so there would be no reduction in swelling. With a Sharpie, I outlined the red area on my chest to monitor shrinkage. And then I prepared for the worst. I told myself that fifty years was a good long life, that many people, like Steve, had far less time, that if anyone in my family should die young it should be me since I have no children, that my modest assets could contribute to my nieces' and nephews' college costs.

After twenty-four hours, the redness *seemed* to recede. I spent another day with anxiety like an electric current coursing through my body, but after forty-eight hours the swelling had diminished. "How did I get a staph infection in my breast?" I asked at the follow-up appointment. "It probably entered through a tiny cut," the doctor said. *On my breast?* I developed a theory. Maybe there was a small cut in my underarm from shaving, and when I sank to my neck in that nasty tepid hot tub water—just warm enough to breed bacteria—the microbe swam into a "little airhole" in my skin.

My theory was not far-fetched. A Chicago man sued his fitness club after he contracted a staph infection—*folliculitis MRSA pseudomonas staph*—from using their hot tub. He lost his case because he could not directly link bacteria in the water to his infection, even though evidence abounds that poorly maintained hot tubs breed dangerous bacteria. In 2006, Texas A&M researchers tested water from forty-three private and public hot tubs and found bacteria from feces in 95 percent of the samples and the staphylococcus bacteria in 34 percent. A teaspoon of tap water, they found, contained about 138 bacteria, while a teaspoon of hot tub water averaged 2.17 million.

The most common illness-causing bug in hot tubs is *Mycobacteria avium*, which thrive in the slime inside wet pipes. When you turn on the jets, the water is aerosolized and you can inhale *mycobacteria*, which causes a bronchitis-like infection called "hot tub lung." In 2008, a forty-one-year-old Australian man with hot tub lung required a double-lung transplant. You can also inhale the *legionella* bacterium in a hot tub, which causes Legionnaires' disease, named for a bacteria that sickened 221 men—killing 34 of them—after an American Legion conference at the Bellevue-Stratford Hotel in Philadelphia in July 1976. It took twenty epidemiologists from the Center for Disease Control six months to identify the bacterium, which had spread through the hotel's air conditioning system, which means you don't have to get wet to get sick. Three elderly men in England died from Legionnaires after *walking by* an unclean hot tub and breathing the steam. The tub—the Nordic Impulse Deep Hot Tub—was on display at a JTF Mega Discount Warehouse.

❊ ❊ ❊

After the Dark Ages began to lighten, Europeans rediscovered the pleasure of baths. "I have seen in my travels almost all the famous baths of Christendom," Montaigne wrote in the late 1500s. Bathing was "generally wholesome," he concluded, certainly better than having one's "limbs crusted" and "pores stopped with dirt." Society had suffered, Montaigne wrote, "by having left off the custom . . . of bathing every day." An eighteenth-century physician in Briton claimed that the thermal waters at Bath could heal everything from "the longing of maids to eat chalk, coal, and the like" to "hypochondriacal flatulence." Even religious leaders promoted bathing. In 1747, John Wesley, the founder of Methodism, wrote that baths cured more than fifty illnesses, including breast tumors, fits and convulsions, wandering pains, the falling sickness, leprosy, and the bite of a mad dog. "Cleanliness is next to Godliness," Wesley said, along with his less-quoted advice: "Do not stink above ground."

In pre-Revolutionary America, among aristocrats with money to travel there was a "craze" of taking the waters. In 1761, George Washington sought relief from rheumatic fever at the Berkeley Warm Springs in West Virginia. "We found of both sexes about 200 people at this place, full of all manner of diseases and complaints," he wrote. In 1771, John

Adams traveled to Stafford, Connecticut, in hopes that the waters would ease his nerves. "The water is very clear, limpid, and transparent," he noted.

But at the same time, like Christians in Medieval Europe, religious leaders in the colonies condemned bathing. Protestant ministers in Pennsylvania petitioned the governor to halt the development of public baths, fearful that they inspired an "immoderate and growing Fondness for Pleasure." In Colonial America bathing for personal hygiene was considered "impure" and the practice regulated. In Boston, it was illegal to take more than two baths a month. In Colorado you needed a doctor's prescription, and in Philadelphia and Wyoming, anyone who took more than one bath per month could be jailed. Even a century later religious leaders fretted. Mary Baker Eddy, founder of Christian Science, warned that, "Washing should be only to keep the body clean, and this can be done with less than daily scrubbing." Anti-bathing sentiment was so widespread that an 1891 editorial in *Science* argued *for* "the habit of daily bathing," which, the author lamented, had been "seriously questioned."

❊ ❊ ❊

One night there was a biohazard in the pool—some kid pooped in the water—so I couldn't swim laps. Instead I sat in the hot tub. In came the fat man, or the waning man, I should call him. We were the only two in the tub and I spoke to him for the first time in the years I'd seen him. "My Russian friend is in Florida taking classes," he said. "She loves the heat there." I wondered why he called her "friend" and not "fiancée." I usually avoid contact with people when I'm feeling blue, as I was that night, so I was surprised to find myself talking to him. At first we'd hesitated, a reserved hot-tub politeness, which made me think he was more considerate than I'd thought. In Arthur Conan Doyle's "The Adventures of the Illustrious Client," Dr. Watson observed that Sherlock Holmes was "less reticent and more human" in the Turkish baths "than anywhere else." Nearly naked in close proximity to other humans, floating in placental-like warm water, I was forced to confront raw humanness, his and my own, and my façade of imperviousness weakened.

In hot tubs, strangers have confided in me. One morning at the YWCA hot tub in Lansing, Michigan, where I lived for six years after Steve died, a man I'd never seen before asked me if I listened to "that new jazz station." I shook my head. "I'm tired of listening to country," he said. "All they ever do is cry about a broken heart."

I nodded.

"My wife left me two weeks ago after eighteen years. She was twenty years younger than me."

He asked me how old he looked. I thought he looked sixty, so I said, "Fifty-five?"

He smiled proudly. "Sixty-one."

He shook my hand and said, "Nice talking to you," then stepped out of the tub and I never saw him again.

Montaigne wrote of public baths, "He who does not bring along with him so much cheerfulness as to enjoy the pleasure of the company he will there meet will doubtless lose the best and surest part of their effect." At the Y in Maine recently, I overheard a man say he was hit by a school bus, and that he wished he had a hot tub in his backyard so he could sit in the tub under the stars. "Mother Nature, I think she's doing a pretty good job," he said. When the woman with whom he'd been talking left, he floated over next to me and picked up his conversation where he left off. It didn't matter to whom he talked; he just needed to tell his story.

*   *   *

In the mid-nineteenth and early twentieth centuries in the US, bath nay-saying gave way to its opposite—zealous advocacy. The impetus was to cleanse the stinking immigrants flooding into east coast cities—Boston, New York, Philadelphia. The millions of Irish fleeing famine, and Italians, like my grandmother, who lived in Brooklyn's tenements—were "too rank and malodorous for the nostrils of the refined," a letter-writer complained in the *New York Times.* In New York City at the turn of the twentieth century, 97 percent of tenement residents had no access to bathrooms. Wealthy and middle-class reformers rallied for the construction of public bathhouses to prevent contagions—cholera, typhoid, and tuberculosis. New York City had a higher death rate in the 1880s than Paris, London, or any major US city.

In 1890, *Cosmopolitan* magazine held a contest to design New York City's first public bathhouse. The winning entry resembled a luxurious Roman bathhouse, with a façade of pillars and arches, and inside, "plunge pools, Turkish baths, and steam rooms." The actual facility, though, was utilitarian, with dozens of "rain baths" to efficiently clean as many people as possible. At the World Hygiene Congress in Berlin, the "rain bath" had just debuted, a radical shift from tubs to "upright" bathing, introduced by Dr. Oscar Lasser as the Volksbad, or the "people's bath." The People's Bath of New York opened in 1891 in the Bowery neighborhood, with Wesley's aphorism—"Cleanliness is next to godliness"—engraved above its entrance. Each bather received a ticket for an allotted twenty-minute shower. To assure an orderly operation, the waiting area was supervised, sometimes by police.

The People's Bath in New York could accommodate 500 bathers daily, but the poor didn't flock to the bath, in spite of 100,000 promotional flyers promising free Colgate soap. In the first year, just 10,504 people bathed there, about 6 percent of its capacity, a problem that persisted as other public bathhouses were built for the poor. In 1913, Manhattan's Superintendent of Public Baths, Mr. Todd, told the American Association for Promoting Hygiene and Public Baths that one of the most difficult problems was "persuading the people to patronize the baths." The New York-based Cleanliness Institute embarked on a "Cleanliness Crusade," as did the Association for Improving Conditions of the Poor, with the slogan, "Nothing gives you 'pep' like a Daily Bath." But this didn't lure the city's indigent to the dreary bathhouses.

Perhaps the people understood that the baths were meant to "cleanse" more than their bodies. The *New York Sun* editorialized that public baths would transform "grimy Anarchists, and some of these Poles, Russians, and Italians into good Americans." Public baths were necessary for elevating the "moral and physical well-being" of the poor, said Dr. August Windolph to the American Association for Promoting Hygiene and Public Baths. Boston's mayor, Josiah Quincy, asserted that when "physical dirt" was banished, then "moral dirt" would be, too.

The solution to inculcate the habit of bathing in the underclass, wrote Mr. Todd, was to make the baths "attractive and inviting" by including "indoor sanitary swimming pools." Boston had done this in 1897, the first American city to open an "all-the-year-around" bathing establishment that included a "swimming tank." Aside from 10′ × 24′ pool, the bathhouse had three tubs and six 4′ × 4′ rain baths. For a nickel, you got a bathing suit, soap, a towel, and a five-minute shower before being allowed to swim for thirty minutes. On two days of the week, the baths were free. When bathhouses offered swimming and recreation instead of just cleansing, the people came.

❧ ❧ ❧

Often I sit in the hot tub before my laps, waiting for the high school swim team to finish practicing. In contrast to those muscular lithe youths, we tubbers are a sorry-looking bunch, uncomely bodies marked with bruises, varicose veins, discolored patchy skin, age spots that my dermatologist calls *lentigos*, purplish skin blotches that I learn are petechiae, or broken capillaries. A sign in the locker room says bathers are "required to take a healthy shower" before entering the pool or hot tub. For some people, this is a cursory rinse of the head. Others don't bother at all; there is no policing. The unwashed then wade into the human soup, shedding skin flakes and mite skeletons. There is enough chlorine in this water to kill any bacteria, I've assured myself time and again, but to my dismay I discovered that chlorine actually loses its disinfecting power in warm water, while bacteria thrive. The *mycobacteria* that cause hot-tub lung are "1,000 times more resistant to chlorine than e. coli."

One night before my laps, just the large man and I sat in the tub, he in his usual spot at the far corner of the tub where he could pummel his body with two jets. We said hello and then I broke eye contact. I wasn't in the mood for talking. His arm rested outside the tub and I noticed for the first time a stylized heart tattoo on his shoulder. I was amazed that I'd never noticed the tattoo before. After a few minutes the jets stopped and I stepped out of the tub to reset them. "Is the timer new?" I asked the large man. "Yes," he said. "They put it in about three weeks ago." He was friendly, helpful with his knowledge of all-things-new-at-the-Y. "I guess it saves energy," I said. He smiled, nodded. With the two of us alone in the tub, the large man was less gregarious, wasn't performing for others, or bragging. He seemed vulnerable, and my stance toward him softened.

At 7:00 PM, the swim team finished practice. An older heavy-set woman walked toward the hot tub and she waved to the large man, and he mouthed "hello." He'd have a friend to talk to now. I stepped out of the tub and walked to the pool, realizing on my way that I'd forgotten to say goodbye. *That's okay*, I thought. *I'll see him again.*

❋   ❋   ❋

A few years ago I took a spa tour of New Mexico with Ellen, my partner at the time. I'd left a five-year relationship to be with Ellen, who I thought would be my last lover. She was, but not in the way I'd hoped. We started at Ten Thousand Waves, a deluxe resort nestled in the Santa Fe hills, where "tub" was a verb. The menu of treatments sounded enticing and torturous—a hot oil scalp massage, or the herbal wrap, during which you were "enveloped in hot, fragrant, herb-soaked linens," while a therapist "wiped your brow with a cool cloth and fed [you] water through a straw." This treatment resembled the "wet sheet wrap" used in mental institutions in the early twentieth century, in which the patient was wrapped "like a papoose," a 1930s nursing textbook reads, in wet sheets ranging from 40 to 100 degrees—cold for agitated patients, warm for frail—while a nurse wiped the patient's brow and fed her liquid through a straw.

In mid-nineteenth-century England, trendy "Hydropathic Establishments" similar to Ten Thousand Waves offered variations on a theme: Dripping Sheet Bath, Hot Wet Flannel Pad, Wet Socks, Wet Head Cap, Wet Dress Bath, Wet Girdle, Wet Bandage, Mud Bath, Nose Bath, Gargling Bath, Sulphur Bath, Slime Bath. There was no Slime Bath at Ten Thousand Waves, but their Japanese Nightingale facial is, basically, bird shit on your face. TTW uses processed nightingale droppings, the "process" involving drying, pulverizing, and sanitizing it with ultraviolet light.

In the communal tub at TTW—co-ed, bathing suit optional, and large enough for sixteen—Ellen and I joined two heterosexual couples and two women, one nested between the other's legs, everyone having opted out of bathing suits. It was delicious sitting in 106-degree water under the big New Mexican sky, the air scented with juniper and piñon, until one woman began stroking her partner's breasts and another couple began making out. There was an erotic current that I suspected could spark a full-fledged orgy. Ellen and I fled to the Kojiro Women's tub, also "bathing suit optional," though we were alone there. We plunged into the ice bath, then raced back to the hot tub, like a physical mood swing, said to stimulate the immune system. After an hour we were languid like noodles, with just enough energy to peruse the gift shop, where you could buy "lucky" cat figurines, Zen sand gardens, and Buddha-shaped soaps. If you meet the Buddha in a spa, bathe him?

Our second destination was Ojo Caliente in the Sangre de Cristo Mountains. In the 1500s, Spaniards searching for the Fountain of Youth discovered these natural springs, where 100,000 gallons of hot mineral water gush from the earth daily. Ojo Caliente had a mud pool and several mineral pools, and like Ten Thousand Waves, a menu of treatments— blue cornmeal or red clay facials, hot herbal sheet wraps—but the place was modest; you brought your own robe and towels. The store's offerings were odd: one tampon for 25 cents, a hair elastic for a dime, along with the usual bathrobes and soaps. We sampled the iron pool, nearly enclosed like a cave, then the arsenic tub. Arsenic, in small quantities, is supposed to ease pain from arthritis, rheumatism, ulcers, eczema, and excess gas. Ojo Caliente's brochure suggested "drinking any of the waters while bathing," but who wants to drink water in which people with eczema and excess gas are sitting?

Lastly we soaked in the soda pool, which contained lithium, a natural salt used to treat depression and bipolar disorder. At a separate lithium fountain we sipped cups of water, reading about lithium's ability to lift one's spirits. Until the middle of the twentieth century, lithium was sold in beverages like 7-Up, originally called "Bib-Label Lithiated Lemon-Lime Soda," touted as a hangover cure: "Take the 'ouch' out of grouch." 7-Up with lithium was banned in 1948 after high doses of lithium were shown to cause serious side effects. A year later, John Cade, an Australian physician, published the first paper on lithium's psychological benefits—"Lithium Salts in the Treatment of Psychotic Excitement"—which eventually lead to the wide-scale successful use of lithium carbonate to treat depression.

Even trace amounts of lithium have proven to be mood-elevating. A 1990 study across twenty-seven counties in Texas found that places with the lowest levels of lithium in the drinking water had "significantly greater levels of suicide, homicide, and rape." A study in Japan tracked a million people over five years and found the same results: lower lithium rates correlated with higher rates of suicide and "all-cause mortality." A meta-analysis of eleven lithium studies conducted in several countries concluded that nine of the studies found an association between higher lithium levels in drinking water and "beneficial clinical, behavioral, legal, and medical outcomes."

I have tried a half-dozen antidepressants over two decades (imipramine, Wellbutrin, Prozac, Zoloft, Paxil, Effexor), though not lithium. I abandoned them all, and instead learned to self-medicate with hydrotherapy. In summer I dip into the salty sea or swim at a spring-fed swimming hole near my house. In winter I take baths until my fingers raisin, and a couple times a week I swim at the Y and languish in the hot tub.

❀   ❀   ❀

The final stop on the New Mexico spa tour with Ellen was the thermal springs in Las Vegas, a tiny town over the Sangre de Cristo Mountains from Taos. Ellen and I parked on a rural road and trudged through a snowy field to a stream, where we immersed ourselves in hot sulfuric-smelling water. The air was crisp and clean, the night wonderfully still and quiet, vapors rising into a glittered sky. There was no store with tchotchkes, no fancy robes, no Buddha soaps, no brochure. You could only find this place through word of mouth, which added to its charm. For centuries across cultures and geography, natural thermal waters have been considered sacred. The springs at Las Vegas had that consecrated sense, numinous, as if you shouldn't speak there. Years ago when I lived in Lansing, Michigan, an old woman I saw often at the YWCA said to the five or six people soaking in the hot tub, "We're blessed, ain't we?"

*　*　*

When it comes to bathing, I'm above average. According to a Colgate-Palmolive survey, Americans spend on average twenty minutes in the bathtub. On winter nights in Maine, I wallow in my bathtub for an hour or longer, reading, adding more hot when the water cools, poaching myself. I haven't changed the bathroom décor since I bought my fixer-upper, so the tub-surround is still a 1970s mustard-yellow. On the tub's edge is a burn mark from the previous owner, who must have fallen asleep in the tub, her lit cigarette scarring the vinyl. "Just took a lovely bath," she wrote in her diary, which I found among the heaps of trash in the house, unoccupied for three years before I bought it.

There are shower people and there are bath people. My fellow bathers include Somerset Maugham, who dreamed up sentences as he soaked in the tub each morning, and Winston Churchill, who bathed twice daily, rehearsing speeches and calculating budgets in the tub. "Hot baths," Churchill said, were one of the four essentials of life, along with "cold champagne, new peas, and old brandy." JFK bathed twice daily, the second following his afternoon nap. Fashion designer Tom Ford takes four baths a day: one when he wakes at 4:30 AM ("Often I lie in the tub for a half hour and just let my mind wander"); a second after working out; a third at the end of the day; and a final bath around 10:30 PM. ("Richard and I walk the dogs around Grosvenor Square and then head up to bed. Believe it or not, I usually take another hot bath.") Gwyneth Paltrow says she takes an Epsom salt bath every night, "to wind down," and Oprah Winfrey's "favorite indulgence" is a bath. "I love creating bathing experiences," she told *Bazaar* magazine, "gels, bubbles, crystals, salts, lavender milks." For Oprah, bathing is practically "a hobby."

*　*　*

On the most bitterly cold January nights in Maine, the hot tub at the Y feels exquisite. One such night I sat in the tub with two men in their early forties, one craggily handsome, the other small and wiry, all of us silent in the bubbling water until the large man appeared. As he stepped into the tub, the craggy man slid over, ceding his place. "You don't have to move," the large man said, but the craggy man smiled. "That's your spot." Vacating the spot was a sign of respect, as if the large man were an elder or, if this were ancient Rome, an esteemed philosopher.

Someone mentioned the news story that day about a woman in southern Maine who died in her home, but her body was not discovered for two and a half years. The article said the woman, who had "distinctive red hair," had never married, nor had children. "I wonder how long it would take someone to find me," the craggy man said. "Probably weeks." He laughed. The large man said, "I wonder, if I fell on the ice, or in a snowstorm, if nobody heard me yell, how long I would last in the weather." Nobody responded to his comment, and though the conversation had begun in a light-hearted tone, we fell silent. I understood the large man's concerns all too well. I carry my cell phone with me when I'm shoveling, or raking the snow off my roof, or in the summer when I'm on a ladder painting trim. We have that in common, fear of dying alone.

❀ ❀ ❀

Iceland is frequently listed among the top three countries with the happiest people, and they have the highest life expectancy in the world. Valdimar Hafstein, a University of Iceland folklorist, attributes this to Iceland's culture of communal baths, heated naturally year-round with geothermal energy. "We know our neighbors because we meet them in the pools," he says. "It creates a good vibe, and you feel at home there." Aside from beneficial minerals in the natural thermal springs, and the delicious soothing warm water, there was something both primal and sublime about floating with other people under a slate sky in early June, part of the "Hot Golden Circle" tour I took after a conference in Iceland—massive waterfalls, spouting geysers, and thermal pools. I was only in Iceland for a week, but contrary to my usual urgent desire to get home after a few days away, I wished I could stay longer. I felt happy in Iceland, where there's a heated pool or natural thermal spring in every neighborhood.

Japan, too, has a long tradition of communal bathing. Since the seventeenth century, public baths in Japan have been gathering places for philosophical debates and gossip, a custom deeply engrained in Japanese culture. Even up to the mid-1960s, only 60 percent of Japanese households had bathtubs. As of 2013, Japan still had about 5,200 public bathhouses—*sento*—though each year a couple hundred sento close as more Japanese install private baths. To appeal to a younger generation, bathhouse proprietors have opened twenty-four-hour "super sentos" offering specialized baths—perfumed, mud, and clay baths, or baths with electrical currents, hoping to preserve the bathhouse tradition, and to save an important social ritual.

❀   ❀   ❀

I still see the large man now and then, though he isn't that large anymore. His hair is still long, and his glasses still don't fog. His face is more handsome in his new weight class, his long straight nose, Brando-like mouth. One night I heard someone greet him—"Hi, Dan"—so now, after years of seeing him in the tub, I know his name. He no longer speaks of his Russian friend, and his weight loss campaign seems stalled. He hasn't gained weight, but the pounds aren't slipping off like they had when he was preparing to meet his fiancée. Over time I've developed empathy for him, even a begrudging admiration. He'd made a bid for love. It failed, but at least he'd tried. In sorting through my father's papers after he died at eighty, I found printouts of women's profiles from online dating sites. At seventy-eight, before the onset of serious health problems, my twice-divorced father was still looking for companionship. The large man in the hot tub, my father—they didn't give up on love, as I fear I have.

❀   ❀   ❀

Recently I joined the large man in the hot tub, along with a young man who was tanned already in late May (he must work outside), and a bald man in his mid-thirties, the three of them at one end of the tub and I at the other, up to my neck in water, almost invisible.

"I know a guy who's happy if he's fishing six days a week," the tanned man says. "He works the third shift just so he can fish."

"I feel bad for lobstermen," bald man says.

"They do all right," tanned man adds.

"Yeah," the bald man recants. "They say they don't make money, but you see them driving a fifty-thousand-dollar truck."

The large man looked over at me and winked. He wasn't contributing to the conversation; he was waiting it out, waiting to get the floor, or the tub. The bald man stood, his belly flopping over the waist band of his swim trunks. "Good night, gentlemen," he said, and walked up the steps trailing streams of water. *Salve lotus*, a Roman would have said. *I hope you bathed well.*

The large man saw his opening and launched into his story. "I was bitten by a scorpion at the Outer Banks," he said. There was no segue; his story existed in its own singular glory. "My wife took me to the emergency room." I wondered if this was the beautiful young Russian, or some earlier wife, or maybe some new wife he'd acquired since the Russian. He then listed various "itis-es" he'd suffered, happily complaining about his ailments, including foot problems "from carrying so much weight for so long."

That's where I took my leave. I sensed that the tanned man, who'd been politely listening, was preparing to exit and I didn't want to be left alone with the thinner-but-still-overweight man, even though I was glad to see him happy and vivacious, the way he was when he was anticipating the arrival of his Russian fiancée. He was back to his old self, enjoying the tub, conversing with everyone, telling fantastic tales. He had not died of a broken heart, after all.

Nominated by New England Review,
E.J. Levy,
G.C. Waldrep

ARSON

by CHARLES SIMIC

from THE THREEPENNY REVIEW

Shirts rose on a neighbor's laundry line,
One or two attempting to fly,
As three fire engines sped by
To save a church going up in flames.

People walking back from the pyre
With their Sunday clothes in tatters
Looked like a troupe of scarecrows
The bank had ousted from their farm.

As for the firebug, we were of two minds:
Some kid trying out a new drug,
Or a drunk ex-soldier angry at God
And Country for making him a cripple.

Nominated by The Threepenny Review,
Daniel Henry

THE HISTORY OF SOUND

fiction by BEN SHATTUCK

from THE COMMON

I was seventeen when I met David, back in 1916. Now I don't very much care to count my age. It's April 1972 here in Cambridge. White puffballs that must be some sort of seedpod have been floating by the window above my writing desk for days, collecting on the sidewalk like first snow.

My doctor suggested I write this story down, due to the recent sleeplessness that started when a package from a stranger arrived at my house: a box of twenty-five wax phonograph cylinders, with David's and my names written on the labels of each, sent from Maine. A letter taped to one of the cylinders read, "I found these in our attic years ago. I saw you on television. Figured these must be yours." Of the three books I've written on American folk music—with moderate success and thus the recent television interview—I've never written about that summer with David. So, here we are.

I first saw him in the fall, after term exams of my first year at the New England Conservatory. I was out with my friends Matt and Lawrence, celebrating with a drink in the pub. David was playing the piano against the far wall. His white shirt, yellow under the gas lamps, stretched and slacked between his shoulders as his arms swept down the keys.

"What do you think?" Matt asked, tapping me on the shoulder.

I hadn't heard his question.

"What are you looking at?" he said, turning.

"I know that song," I said. It was "Dead Winter's Night," a tune my father used to play on the fiddle back in Kentucky. A slow song, to the tempo of "a sitting person's breath," as my father would say. It's an old English ballad from, I've since researched, the Lake District, that tells the story of two lovers lost in the woods on a January night, having run from their homes to meet by an oak tree to then elope. A blizzard comes, and they can't find each other. In the chorus they call each other's names, but the wind shakes the trees so loudly that they can't even hear their own voices—so they die alone, huddled under separate trees: "Over snow'd floor two tracks did mark / One going west, the other east / Two still figures at trees' roots / On a dead winter's night, they never meet." Thinking of it now reminds me of the summer's white moths flitting around the lantern on our porch in Kentucky, of my brother and me lying on our backs, hands on our stomachs, feeling the vibration as Dad's foot stomped out the slow rhythm—the scratch of his boot on the wood. Katydids in the trees, stitching the night together.

"Excuse me," I said to my friends in the pub.

I pushed through the crowd, towards the music. The smell of soap, beer, and smoke filled the room. I leaned against the wall, hip touching the piano's back beam, watching David play. His eyes were closed. Cigarette wilting from his lips. Smoke crawling up his face. Black hair combed back. His head jolted when the chorus kicked in. I watched his fingers.

"Where did you learn that?" I asked when the song ended.

"Oh," he said, ashing his cigarette on the floor, looking up. "Some swamp in Kentucky."

A deep voice. Words spoken too fast. He played a C chord with one hand and picked up his drink from the floor with the other.

"I'm from Kentucky," I told him. His hand paused on the keys. He looked up again.

"Yes, of course you are. Sorry." He held out his hand. "David."

"Lionel," I said.

"What department?" Likely everyone in the pub that night was from the Conservatory.

"Voice," I said.

"Well," he said. "Fa-la-la. I'm Music History. This—" He played the melody once. "Just a hobby. In the summer. To get fresh air. Collecting."

From across the room, Matt and Lawrence motioned that they were leaving. I waved them on.

74

"Ever been to Harrow?" I said. "That's where I grew up."

"Harrow. Two summers ago. Sky-blue gazebo in the center of town."

He seemed unsurprised by the coincidence, so I, likewise, didn't react. There weren't many Southerners at the Conservatory then, and absolutely nobody from Harrow, a town of two thousand between the rivers Cold and Solemn. But here was David. Perhaps we'd even seen each other. I was once homesick, I remember.

"There was a reel I remember learning there," he said, "'Maids of Killary,' I think?"

"I know it. Do you know 'Seed of the Plough'?"

"Should I?" he said.

I told him that my mom used to sing it.

"Go on. Let's hear it."

"No," I said, shaking my head.

"What key?" he said, playing one chord to the next, down the piano. He edged forward on the bench. "What key?" he repeated, touching out an A.

His eyebrows lifted. I noticed then a dash on his upper lip, a scar, a smudge of pale red that I'd later learn was from his father.

"Don't think you could put a piano to it," I said.

"The floor is yours." He pushed away from the keys, slipped another cigarette from his pocket, picked a candle from the headboard, and cupped the flame to his face. Waited.

I was first told I had perfect pitch when I named the note my mom coughed every early morning. I could harmonize with a dog barking across the field. I was the tuner for Dad's violin—standing at his elbow, singing out an A while he pinched and tightened the pegs. Early on I thought that everyone could see sound. A shape and color—a wobbly circle, blackberry purple, for D. I only adjusted the shape I saw, and then locked into the correct decibels. Tastes started to accompany the notes when I was thirteen. Dad would play a bad B minor and waxy bitterness filled my mouth. On the other hand, a perfect C and I tasted sugary cherries. D, milk.

I sang for David then.

I've always felt as if what came from my throat and lips was not mine, like I was stealing rather than making something. This body was mine—the constriction of my diaphragm, the pressure in my throat, the lips and the softening of my tongue that shaped the sound—but what left me, ringing through the crown of my head so my skull felt more bell than corporeal, flooding my ears' tympani, vibrating through my nose,

75

wasn't my own. More like the sound of wind in the trees or over a glass bottle. Or, better, an echo of my own voice, coming out of my mouth. A repetition. I can't sing like that anymore—and I miss it. Now I have this weak warble, this drone that nobody tells me isn't any good.

As I ended the song, the color yellow faded to the taste of wet wood.

"Where in hell did you learn that?" he asked.

I shrugged.

"I wouldn't be puttering around school if I had a voice like that," he said.

When he stood to get another beer, I saw he was inches taller than anybody in the room.

We stayed together until dawn. Me singing to his piano. I might have been able to hum a D at both octaves, but I'd never met anyone with a memory like his. Tilting his head, plugging one ear with a finger, humming a note or two, he'd tease the song out, only fumbling a line when he was absolutely drunk.

"Let me buy you another beer," I said, not moving from the piano's side, in the gray morning light.

"Yes," he said. "You've kept me up all night. You owe me."

"Anything you want," I said, staring.

"No. I'm tired. It's almost morning. I'm going to bed. I live across the street. I have a couch if you want."

His apartment was bare—only a bed, a piano, and a chair. No couch. Dirty plates and glasses were scattered on the floor, along with pages and pages of music. No desk. I asked him for a glass of water, because the room was spinning. He brought a water glass from the kitchen, took a long sip, and then spit an arc of water at me. I opened my mouth to catch the stream. He did this until the glass was empty and I was wet but had managed a few sips. He placed the glass on the floor, and then walked to me, took off my glasses, folded them and put them on the window sill. He pulled my wet shirt up over my head and led me to his bed, on which was a pile of quilts and sheets. When I leaned in to kiss him I went right for the scar on his lip, sucked it while he pressed his palm up against my thigh. He fell back on the bed, wrapped his legs around me.

I woke when the sun was high and David was gone, with a headache and the room still moving. I'd been drunk before, but not like this. I crawled from the sheets and saw a note on the floor: *See you in a week.* I gulped water from his sink, then filled a glass and walked into the living room. I flopped down in the chair, drank until the glass was empty, then went back to bed, put myself under the covers. But when I woke up again just before sunset he was still gone, and so I gathered my clothes, folded his note and slipped it in my pocket before leaving.

Every Tuesday night thereafter, David was at the piano with a cigarette between his lips, and I was buying us drinks with my scholarship stipend. On nights that weren't Tuesday, I sometimes stood across the street from his building, looking up, trying to see who it was walking around his apartment. I was only curious, I told myself. I really don't think I've ever been jealous, which was a problem with every relationship I've had since David. Like Clarissa, whom I dated in my forties, and who left me after she admitted she was sleeping with my friend. I'd known about her affair, and when I told her so, saying I only wished she'd admitted it to me earlier, and supposed we could work through it, she started yelling at me, as if I'd been the one doing the cheating, that I didn't care about her anyway, so why should she stay? Most of the other men I've been with—Alex, William, Alistair, others—have lasted no more than a few months. Vincent was the longest. I met him in Rome, where I lived for over a year, in 1929 and 1930. Quick-witted, originally from Milan, charming to every stranger we met, a gap between his two front teeth, and a laugh that echoed all the way down narrow Roman streets, Vincent was a cellist and would practice in the same chapel where I sang. When eventually I said I needed to go home, back to Boston, for career reasons, he only said, *"Americano,"* like it was the worst word he could think of.

I won't dwell on the particulars of David's departure only half a year after we first met. It was 1917. America had entered the war. Classes were disbanded. He went to Europe. I didn't, because of my bad eyes. I wrote my Harrow address in his journal, told him to send me French chocolate.

I returned to Harrow, to the farm, to help my brother, who, not very long after I arrived, also went to Europe. Maybe that was the end of my time with David, I thought. A dozen Tuesday-night meetings in Boston. I thought of him in the way you do when you're young: in the mornings, lying in bed listening to the songbirds, sheets tangled around my legs; when I stood in the kitchen watching the kettle, waiting for a boil; when I was pruning, grafting, staking, and guying the fruit trees; when, after work, I walked to the streambed and listened to the spring peepers; sitting on our porch, listening to a thunderstorm clear its throat on the horizon in three notes, the smell of dirt released under the storm's coming. As in, always. I sometimes woke with an impression of his face in my eyes, with my hand reaching across the bed for him. My body remembering his body even if I tried not to. Gray-blue eyes with a ring of what looked like brown around the iris. A freckle on his eyelid. The scar on his lip. An Adam's apple stark as a broken bone. His hair smelled like tobacco, his neck like fermenting fruit. I didn't experience the guilt that some men at my time would have. I just loved David, and I didn't think much beyond that. My error was that I thought David was the first of many. That I'd tasted love. I was eager for my future. How could I have known that all the rest—Alex, William, Vincent, Clarissa, Sam, Sarah, and most recently George—were only rivulets after the first brief deluge.

Summer and autumn passed. Winter arrived on the farm. Snow once, but nothing like Boston. I spent months writing bad music, drinking too many cups of coffee, walking for hours. Wondering when life would resume, when the war would be over and I could go back north, back to classes, back to Boston, where, I was sure, David would return after his service.

I visited my grandfather sometimes, who lived on the outskirts of town in a house his father had built for him and his six siblings. My own father had died years earlier, in the orchard (my brother had found him with clippers in hand), and my mother had taken the change by taking walks that sometimes lasted into the night, so without my brother around, the house was empty and quiet in a way I didn't like. My grandfather would sit in his chair beside the fire, summer or winter, wrapped in blankets. We drank coffee, talked about the war in Europe and if I'd heard from my brother, and then he'd ask me to sing a song. He never asked me about the Conservatory. He didn't like to talk about anywhere north of Kentucky. He'd been in the cavalry in Antietam, watched his friends "de-limbed." He was not a bad man—just angry. Just missed his friends and missed his wife. I'm struck now, only writing this, by how many wars have swept through my family's lives.

David's note arrived at the farm in June of 1919. The return address was Bowdoin College, up in Maine. He'd written on the back of a sheet of staff paper—on the front were two bars of quarter notes arcing through the treble clef. A paragraph, only:

*My dear silver-throated Confederate: I hope this note finds
its way to you. How is life on the farm? As it stands: I just
returned from a walking tour, you might say, in Northern
Europe. God help me. But the day is getting brighter. I have
a position up at Bowdoin, here in the evergreens. Last month
a man visited the Department to show off a new phonograph
prototype. My advisor thought it a Fine Idea if I was elected
to record folk songs for Dept.'s Ethno- leanings in this boreal
wilderness. I can't drag this talking sewing machine by
myself—how about a long walk in the woods this summer?
The journey points north. A bed of pine needles under the
stars? Birch beer? Don't dally, just come.*

ps—Do you have funds? There's not much to go around here.

I turned the paper over and hummed what I could read of the two
bars, a student's jolting melody, surely. Every note I've gotten from
David was termed in directions: *See you in a week*, he wrote that first
morning. And then: *Don't dally, just come*. David gave me instructions,
and I followed.

That night, I lay in bed with the note on my face. I told my mother I
got a job in Boston, and left a week later. The farm would go untended.
The orchards would become overgrown, the netting not laid, and if I
stayed away long enough, the fruit would overripen, fall to the ground,
and rot. I didn't care. I left as if I were running away, took the train
from Louisville to New York, New York to Boston, Boston to Portland.

I've never cared much about objects—things, that is. I don't care
when a dish breaks, and when my house was robbed some years ago, I
can honestly say I didn't feel very bad, only confused and troubled by
the cost. The walls of my house are bare, and I ask friends to never buy
me Christmas or birthday gifts. It might be considered frugal or mean-
ingful, but it was a problem when I was younger. I used to lose every-
thing, leave my coat on the church pews, forget my schoolbooks, leave
a hatchet outside in the grass. I gave a lot of stuff away to other kids—
toys, my dad's violin rosin, coins. The worst was our family dog—I liked
a boy at school and so one day walked our dog to his house, tied her to
a tree on his lawn, and walked home not thinking too much of it. My
dad whipped me for that.

Yet I still have that note David sent, asking me to come north. Still
have all the notes he left me on the floor of his apartment. Still have

the cigarette he rolled and forgot on the piano one night, and the box of matches from the pub where we used to meet. I didn't keep the statuette Vincent gave me before I left Rome, or the gold watch that Clarissa gave me on our anniversary, or the landscape painting that Sara made for me, or the sea glass I collected on Cape Cod with Alex. But when it came to David, I was an insatiable magpie.

In the Portland train station, I saw him before he saw me. I stood some distance away, watching. He was wearing a light blue shirt, a dark jacket. Hands in his pockets. Cigarette between his lips. He'd grown a mustache, and looked thinner, sharper in the cheeks. When he stretched his arms above his head, I felt an actual jump in my chest, like an organ I didn't know I needed shifted into place. I waved, caught his attention, and he pointed at me like his hand was a pistol. Fired. Around him were the cases of recording equipment.

From August through September 1919, we must have walked a hundred miles, collecting ballads and tunes from the rocky coast to the endless interior of colonnaded forests and back to the coast. Walked through foggy marshes, forests loud with singing frogs and moss that we sunk up to our knees in, along coastal roads where the wind nearly knocked us off our feet. We visited towns, of course, but also granite quarries and farms where we'd heard there were good singers. David was always the one to introduce us, while I hung back, smiled. We worked off recommendations—someone's cousin might know someone's aunt twenty miles north. Sometimes we stayed in the houses of those we recorded, but mostly we slept outside, in a canvas tent that David lugged around. My job was to carry the recorder. Or, when it was a clear night—as there were many that summer—we slept without the tent, in fields or under the pines. Our limbs tired from the day's walk, and sleep compacting us together.

My grandfather once said that happiness isn't a story. So there isn't much to say about those first weeks. Though the heavy phonograph recorder straps dug into my shoulders, the blackflies left bloody welts all over my neck, and my boots made silver-dollar-sized blisters on both my heels, I don't think I've ever been happier—in the plain, dull, adjectival way that resists any further articulation. It comes in images: Sun hatching out of clouds while we walked through a hayfield flattened by days of rain, droplets lighting up around us and birds shouting. Bathing under a wispy waterfall with David, and afterwards having sex on

80

the rocks. Running out of food, finding a blueberry barren like it was a gift, and eating for an afternoon until we were sick and happy and too full to keep going, so we napped there, until a woman woke us with her boot. Later that same evening, under lavender twilight, him asking me to stick out my tongue, and then him showing me his—both bruise-blue. I thought of the untended fruit trees back in Harrow, of the birds eating the fruit and the grasses rising up through the orchard, and didn't care.

It was my job to work the machinery: unwrap the wax cylinder from its paper covering; brush the surface clean; fit it on the rotator; position the horn right to the singer's face and ask him or her to sing down the tube; move the stylus to the wax; turn the crank slowly. David transcribed the lyrics and notes in a booklet, along with a short interview about the origins of the person and the song, after the recording was made. I liked the songs, but didn't love them, not like David loved them. I don't know exactly where the passion came from—he didn't grow up with the songs, not like me and my brother. But then again, I didn't know much at all about David's early life—whenever I'd ask, he'd shake his head, wave his hand like he was swatting away a blackfly, say it wasn't interesting. I only knew that he was born in New York, that he lived for a few years in London when he was a young boy for his father's work— the profession of which I didn't know—and that he moved to Newport before going to the Conservatory. He did once mention an uncle in England who played the fiddle and took him to Ireland for a weeklong trip. Perhaps that's where his collecting started—now, at seventy-two, I know that most things we love are seeded before we're ten. When I asked what he liked about the songs, the ballads especially, he said— I remember his words exactly—that they were the most warm-blooded pieces of music he knew. I see what he means, that the songs are filled with the voices of thousands who've sung and changed them, and that they are always stories of people's lives. Not like the baroque music I began to love at the Conservatory, sharp and abstract and ornate like a coldly glittering piece of perfect jewelry. The folk songs had soft underbellies, could put a lump in your throat just by the melody. Emotion in song; nothing fancy. In the years immediately after our collecting trip ended, for reasons that will become apparent, I didn't want to sing the old songs. I turned to choir music, to arcing solos in cathedrals, which is why I took a position in a choir in Rome in 1929. It was only when my voice gave out in my fifties that I found the only thing I wanted to write about was American folk music, the traditions that trickled in from Europe and blossomed and twisted into something fresh and new. It was just by chance that my writing coincided with the folk revival in New York and Boston, and so my books sold well. It's not beyond my understanding that I was writing them as a sort of memoriam to David, without mentioning his name. And I honestly began to love the music again, the old Scotch-Irish songs from my home state and throughout Appalachia, in a way that had eluded me for so long.

Of all the recordings that summer of 1919, I felt like we were missing the best sounds. I wanted an audio journal of the days between our work sessions. The sound of a windstorm coming up a valley. The sound of the pines' broomed limbs brushing overhead. The *kapock-kipp-koop* of eight children's wooden spoons hitting wooden plates down a table south of Augusta; the crackling lard around a side of meat burning in a skillet. I wanted to record David's whispering, "Holy Jesus," when we first came to a field glowing with fireflies in Dog Hill; the scrape of a snapping turtle's claws across a table in Lincoln; the preamble in Cowper, when Nora Tettle and her three daughters, each so eager to have their songs recorded, singing at once entirely separate songs, each Tettle trying to outdo the others until David had to quiet them by knocking two cooking pans together. Love Williams in Southwick, seated in the middle of her kitchen, singing a modal tune while I tried to fix the phonograph, her six children and five stepchildren all sitting around her, quiet, until Love came to the second refrain, when the children couldn't restrain themselves and one by one joined their mother. Twelve singers, four harmonies.

I wanted all the chiseled ridges of sound that went missing. The vibrations that had been released into the world and never concentrated down the phonograph's tube and to the stylus, that had never been impressed to wax. I wanted a record of the sound from the years before: The first time David spoke his name to me in the pub. David asking me to his apartment. Asking me one late night if he should join the war or not, and me saying yes because I thought that's what he wanted to hear. The history of sound, lost daily. I've started to think of Earth as a wax cylinder, the sun the needle, laid on Earth and drawing out the day's music—the sound of people arguing, cooking, laughing, singing, moaning, crying, flirting. And behind that, a silent sweep of millions of sleeping people, washing across the Earth like static.

As the weeks passed, I noticed a darkness in David that I think he tried to keep hidden. His hands shook. He had trouble rolling his cigarettes. A few times I'd wake to see him standing some distance away from where we had made our bed. He was a black column under the moon, like a pillar of some ancient ruin. When we sang songs during our walks from town to town, he'd sometimes stop in the middle of a verse, repeating the last line, searching for the next one. I startled him once by coming up behind him too quietly. He jumped back, as if electrocuted. I assumed it was the war, as it was for so many men.

One day, tired of his silence, I asked if he'd ever shot somebody. He raised his hand in the air, and didn't respond.

By late August, a week before David needed to return to Bowdoin to teach, we had only three cylinders left. We were on our way to a house up near Kingdom, a coastal town near a granite quarry. We were looking for the house of John Winslow, the cousin of a woman named Mary Conway, who, Mary said, had a bank of songs in his head. "And his wife, Rosemary, is one of the best cooks in a hundred miles. She'll set you up good."

Some kids in town directed us to the end of a long dirt road. It was one of those too-cold late summer evenings, when a wind from a few months out was already blowing a chill over the land. The fog we'd seen all day on the water had folded in. Nestled in the woods was the house— or shack, really. A corrugated metal roof, patchwork of clapboard. Dozens of deer antlers nailed to the exterior. A dog chained to a stake in the muddy yard sprang awake and barked, ran towards us, and then was jolted back when the chain snapped tight. A flock of blackbirds lifted from the rain-darkened trees around the house, then dissolved farther into the woods. I got what you'd call a bad feeling.

David knocked. Nobody came to the door, so he walked around the house, called into the woods.

"Let's go," I said when he came back around. Now, thinking back on that house, I seem to remember that there weren't any windows.

The dog kept barking. Pulling at the chain. Jumping and choking itself. Huffing and snapping. A big dog. A bear dog, I think. Gray and brown with a white chest. Ears looked to be cut short.

"Shut up," David yelled at the dog. "Let's wait until he gets back," he said, turning around and peering down the road. "I don't think I can walk another mile. I'm thirsty and we're out of water. We're here."

He shrugged off his pack, sat on the steps to the front door, patted his pocket for his tobacco, and then rolled a cigarette. He closed his eyes, rested the back of his head against the door.

83

I slipped my shoulders from the recorder's straps, laid it carefully on the ground, sat beside him.

Then, for the first time since knowing each other, he asked me if I thought we'd see each other again, after the trip.

I said that I'd like to.

He asked if I worried about what we were doing.

I said I didn't, because I didn't.

He rolled his head against the door, as if to massage it. There was a slick of dirty sweat on his forehead. He then drew his legs up to his chest, leaned forward, put his chin on his knees, kept his eyes closed as if he were praying.

"I think I admire you," he said.

The dog kept barking. The chain snapped and clanged.

I was just about to ask him why, when he yelled, "Shut up!" to the dog, then scrambled to his feet and strode towards it.

As David approached, the dog lifted onto its back legs, the taut chain holding it upright. Like an axe head about to fall.

"What are you doing?" I said. "Careful."

David put out his hand, stepped closer. The dog was choking and wheezing as it pressed against its collar. David stood there looking at it, only a foot away, then flicked his cigarette at the dog's feet.

A man then called from the forest's edge, "Ho!"

I jumped up. David spun around. The dog went quiet.

The man had a long beard, mostly white but streaked dark. Over his shoulder was a long pole hung with dead rabbits. He held a gun in one hand.

"What in the hell are you doing?" he said, dropping the pole and holding up his gun with two hands.

"Hello!" David said cheerily, as if there wasn't a gun pointed at him. "I'm David Ashton, and this is Lionel Worthing. We're friends of your cousin, Mary Conway?"

"Mary." John Winslow said. "And?" He put the gun at his side and picked up the staff with rabbits tied to it.

"You must be John," David said. "We're collecting songs, and Mary said you had a few?"

"Not interested," John said. He walked towards us in that slow, intentional way that some woodsmen have, I've noticed. Like he felt the length of a day more than the rest of us, and didn't need to rush.

"It would only take a moment," David said. "Can I ask where you learned the songs?"

84

"Not interested," he said again, leaning the staff on the side of the house. The rabbits—there were three of them—must have just been killed. Blood dripped out of the mouth of one, and tapped a bed of dry leaves.

"Mary said your family is from the west of Ireland?" David said.

John didn't answer. Pulled a knife from his belt, cut the rabbits from the pole, and laid them out on the porch, side by side.

"Which town?" David asked. "I've spent some time there, way back. That's where I first learned 'The Shepherd's Song.' Maybe you know it?"

"Now look," John said, staring at David for the first time. One of his eyes, I saw then, was filled with blood, I suppose from a broken vessel. His cheeks were sunken. His whole face twitched, clenched, and then loosened. "I'm not interested. I told you that once. I told you again. I'm not trying to be rude, here. I see you have come a long way, if you're coming from Mary's. Come back later, maybe later. A week or two, and I can help you then."

David's gift of persuasion, I think, was only in that he couldn't stop going after something if he wanted it. If it wasn't for Mary's impassioned suggestion to record John, and for the fact that we wouldn't be anywhere near his house in a week, I think David would have stopped there. John seemed unlike the others, who at first always refused because they were shy or suspicious. Instead, he refused in a way that was final, unforgiving. His back was already turned to us, and with his knife he cut into one of the rabbits, then began yanking away the pelt.

"Is your wife here?" David said. "Perhaps she'd like to sing? Rosemary?"

The man turned to David, knife in hand, blood all over. Behind him, the rabbit's skin hung off its hind feet.

"Or water," I said. "We've run out of water. Could you spare some water?"

He sighed, kicked at the ground.

"I am a Christian," he said. He laid the knife on the porch, and then shuffled up the stairs. When he opened the door, sunlight spilled into the house and illuminated a woman's body, lying flat on a table in the center of the room. He didn't shut the door when he walked to the back, to the kitchen. The woman's dress spilled off the table, as if a tablecloth. The hem billowed in the wind coming through the door. On her chest was a bouquet of flowers. David and I didn't speak, as we both looked into the wake. When I heard John shut off the tap, I turned and stared into the trees.

85

He came out with two wooden cups.

"For the thirsty musicians," he said.

"Thank you," I said. I avoided a thumbprint of blood on the rim of my cup.

He picked up his knife and continued skinning the rabbit, finally yanking the skin off the feet. It landed with a wet flop when he threw it on the stairs.

"And is this what you do, go and ask people to sing down a tube?"

"I do," David said, stuttering. "Yes, I do. But not him." He pointed to me. "This one is a singer. He might have the best voice in New England."

"Is that so?" John said. Stabbed the knife into the porch so it stood upright. With his two hands, tore off the skin of the second rabbit. "Go ahead. Sing us a tune, then."

The water tasted metallic, bitter.

"I wouldn't know what to sing," I said. My head was still messy with the image of the woman on the table.

John started in on the other rabbit. "I'm sure you'll think of one," he said.

The first song that came to mind was "Lord Randal," one of David's favorites. He'd taught it to me one of the very rare mornings that we laid in bed in his apartment, when he didn't leave before I woke.

"O where have you been, Lord Randal, my son?" I sang. I closed my eyes, tasted burnt butter, and saw the color pale green. "Where have you been, my handsome young man?"

"Christ," I heard John say somewhere a hundred miles away. I realized then that I hadn't sung the whole trip.

"I've been at the greenwood. Mother, make my bed soon.
For I'm wearied with hunting, and fain would lie down."

"And what met you there, Lord Randal, my son?
And what met you there, my handsome young man?"
"O, I met with my true love. Mother, make my bed soon,
For I'm wearied with hunting, and fain would lie down."

The ballad is long and repetitive, the mother drilling her son with questions, trying to figure out why he is feeling so sick and weary. He tells her that his lover made him fried eels for dinner, and that when the dogs ate his scraps, they all died. The mother tells him that he's been poisoned. He agrees, and asks her again to make his bed so he can lie down and die, too. He tells her that he's leaving her the family cows, leaving his sister his gold and silver, and leaving his brother his house and property. The mother then asks, "What did you leave to your true love, Lord Randal, my son? What did you leave to your true love, my handsome young man?" He replies,

"I leave her rope on yon apple tree, for to hang on.
Mother, make my bed soon,
For it was her who poisoned me, and I fain would lie down."

When I finished and opened my eyes, John and David were both looking at the ground. The sky appeared violet.

"I'm sorry about your loss," David said to John then.

"Thank you for saying," John said.

David looked at me. "Good choice in song," he said. "Poisoned in love." He hooked his arm through the strap of his pack. "I didn't think you'd remember that one all the way through." He hefted the pack, shifted it into place on his shoulders. "Strange he calls her his true love right to the end. His killer, that is." He turned and walked away then, down the road, past the silent dog, without waiting for me. Without saying goodbye or thanking John, as he usually did with our hosts.

If John was disturbed by David's sudden departure, he didn't show it.

"A beautiful song there, lad," he said. "I know it, too. You changed the end, though."

"Did I?" I'd only sung what David had taught me.

"The end. It is usually, 'I leave her fire and hell.' Not an apple tree and rope. I think I like your version more. It's a little gentler."

"Thanks for your time," I said, going over to the phonograph and heaving it onto my back.

His whole body shifted, as if whatever he was going to say had gotten bent and clogged in his throat. "Good luck, son."

Another punch of cold wind rushed over the trees, as if August was already gone.

At the Portland train station, I told David I could stay in Maine longer, help him catalogue the recordings. I could find an apartment near campus, just for the fall semester, if he needed help. But I should have been more direct. For once, I should have been the one to give him directions. If not staying in Maine, I could have told him to come with me to Boston. Maybe things would have turned out better. Instead, he shook his head for reasons I only understood later, and said that we'd collect songs again the following summer. He told me we'd write.

September through December was the busiest time of year at the orchard back in Kentucky. In that time David hadn't answered one of my letters, so in January I wrote to the Bowdoin music department. I explained I was a research assistant of David's, a fellow graduate of the Conservatory, and that I'd been the one to join him on the song-collecting journey the summer previous. *Could you,* I asked, *send me his address, as I may have the wrong one, and there are some papers I'd like to share?* Or some lie like that.

The letter I got back, weeks later, was kind, I think. The department chair wrote that he was very sorry to be the one to deliver the news that David had passed away in the fall of 1919. He went on to say that he was sorry to report that he didn't know what cylinders I was referring to—that David's job had been teaching music composition, not ethnomusicology, and the department had not sponsored a trip for song collecting. *I'm sorry I cannot be more helpful,* he wrote. *If I find the cylinders you're referring to, I'll be sure to forward them your way.*

I folded the letter and walked outside, towards the orchards, and then realized that I didn't want to go to the orchards, so walked to the blue gazebo, but that wasn't the place, either. I ended up at my grandfather's house, miles out of town. We had tea. He showed me a new trick his dog had learned—balancing a stick on his nose. I didn't tell him about the letter. He said I "looked a bit sideways," asked if I was drunk, and when I said no, he poured me a glass of whiskey and said, "Go on, then." I slept at his house that night and for some nights following.

In a follow-up correspondence with the department chair, I discovered that David had had a fiancée, and that he'd been engaged since the spring before our trip.

It's been a few days now, after writing this above section. Yesterday I called a friend at the Harvard Peabody Museum whom I knew would have access to a phonograph. He asked me to come by, as the thing was too heavy to lug to my house, plus he wasn't sure he could get permission to bring it out of collections.

I walked the box of cylinders five blocks to the museum, met him at the door. He brought me past the new bird collection, past the skeletons and glass flowers, into the back office.

"I haven't used one of these since I was a boy," he said, slipping the dust cloth off the phonograph.

He helped me fit the first cylinder onto the rotator. He hooked the tube to the stylus base, and then placed the needle on the cylinder. Put his hand on the crank, turned it. What came from the horn was a man's voice from fifty years ago, from a seaside town just north of Portland, singing a ballad as trim and haunting as when I first heard it.

The cylinders were each labeled on the ends with the song title and singer's name and date of recording, which is why my eye was drawn to the last one in the box: October 20, 1919—a month after I said good-bye to David at the train station.

"Let's see what's on this one," I said, pointing to that cylinder.

He unfolded the paper, fit the cylinder on the rotator. Started the crank.

"Hello, Lionel," David's scratchy voice said into the room.

My heart hurt like it had been kicked. Clenched into something that then gave me the same hot rush in my legs that happened the moment before I crashed my car years ago. Pinpricks shivered down my thighs.

The phonograph's metal horn slushed out silence. I sank into the nearest chair.

"Are you okay?" my friend asked.

I nodded. Smiled.

"Thank you for this summer," David said, from fifty years ago. "And for last year. I am sorry I am not the same as when we first met. There's something in me that I can't get rid of. Some rotten spot."

More slush of silence—more static. The sound of him thinking. The silence was a high G.

"I can't see around it," David said. "The horizon of it just keeps speeding out ahead of me."

More static. And then he started humming.

"What's that he's singing?" my friend said.

"'Dead Winter's Night,'" I said.

I closed my eyes, leaned back in the chair.

"One going west, the other east," David sang in his stony baritone. "Two still figures at trees' roots."

I tasted salt and tobacco, saw the round shape of the color indigo thin into a rod of deep orange, then flash into a point of black which filled my mouth with the taste of wet stone.

I'm not sure what I expected to hear, what I wanted to hear, but what came to mind was that famous story about the phonograph—that it was

Edison's only invention that worked immediately. He drew out the concept of a stylus jittering over a soft surface, had his engineer mock one up, and it just worked, right then, the first time. It was that—the plain physicality of it, those hair-thin antique canyons chiseled by David's voice—that I concentrated on, looking at the skin-colored cylinder on the rotator. Edison hadn't thought to use the phonograph for music. He imagined doing what David had done here: recording messages, that it could be put beside a person's deathbed so he or she might give final instructions. Or that you could record a baby's voice, then the voice of the same person twenty years later, then as an old person, so that in one artifact you'd have an entire life. That it would be a comfort to people left behind. But it wasn't a comfort. Only a reminder of the regret I thought I'd let go. I should have stayed on the train platform in Portland, or forced him to come with me to Boston. It was only a reminder that I actually still, amazingly, loved David. That my feelings for George and Clarissa were mindful, thoughtful, compared to this bone-deep kind that David's voice had shaken loose. How to put it? This type of sadness. Not nostalgia. Not grief. Just the obvious and sudden fact that my life looked an inch shorter than it could have been. That the best year really had come when I was twenty. Walking over to the museum with the cylinders, I imagined I might be soothed by flipping through the audio scrapbook of that summer. That hearing Mary Conway's or the Tettles' voices would stitch a wound, in the same way that when I'd met up with Clarissa in Harvard Square years after we'd split, I was afterwards attended only by happiness at what might be an enduring friendship. The same with George—who regularly sent me updates on his life in Savannah, and who assured me he only felt thankful for our time together. But this cylinder reminded me of what I'd missed—which is, I think, a life that I didn't know but of which David was a part. The real one. And how ridiculously short it had been. Only two months. The memories of fireflies and swimming naked in the waterfall did nothing but make very fine and long incisions in the membrane of contentedness I'd built up over the years—a good home, a successful career, kind neighbors, a few great relationships. A wasted life. Maybe that's why people started using the phonograph for recording music—because why the hell would you want to listen to the voices of the loved and dead?

The song ended. The needle drifted off the cylinder.

"Do you want to listen to any others?" my friend said, detaching the cylinder and wrapping it in its paper. "Any specific one?" He fidgeted with the cylinders, turning them to read the labels.

Still, despite my shortness of breath, I wanted more. A dog gnawing at a bone, licking for marrow.

"Let's start from the beginning," I said. "The first one."

I looked out the window, to the street, where the fluffy white seed-pods were still blowing down the sidewalk, looking for a place to grow.

Nominated by The Common

ERL KING

fiction by JULIA ELLIOTT

from TIN HOUSE

I'd seen the so-called Wild Professor stalking the halls of the humanities building, a haughty middle-aged man with a face going to ruin from booze and passion. He taught the poetry workshop and the Romanticism seminar. He spat curses at the coffee machine in the English department lounge. He liked young girls, everyone whispered. He ate psychedelic mushrooms, kept up with cool music, and lived in a woodland cabin all summer long, typing masterpieces on a Brother electric typewriter powered by a generator. He gave me his famous look-over my first winter at college, in the humming submarine glow of the library. I peered up from a translation of *Venerabilis Agnetis Blannbekin* and saw him stomping toward me in muddy hiking boots. I feared he'd trample me. But he stopped and drilled me with his legendary eyes: pale green organs that floated in the darkness of his sockets like bioluminescent jellyfish. He looked ghoulish in the fluorescent light, his scalp visible in sick pink patches, and I didn't get his appeal.

I stared down at my book, reading the same line over and over: *And behold, soon she felt with the greatest sweetness on her tongue a little piece of skin alike the skin of an egg, which she swallowed.*

At last, the Wild Professor shuffled away.

In May I moved out of the dorms to live in a dilapidated antebellum mansion that had been divided into a duplex—we had three bedrooms and an upstairs sun porch that jutted out over a junk-filled carport. Punk Amy, hippie Kim, and preppy Paige got the good rooms, while I suffered the hot sun porch, which swayed in thunderstorm winds. Confederate jasmine slithered through busted windows. Brilliant green anoles sunned themselves on the flaking sills. But my rent was eighty dollars a month, and the downstairs living room was vast—grand with frieze molding, a marble-manteled fireplace, and a yellowed chandelier. We all worked shitty jobs, but at night we lolled on a thrift-store sixties sectional, drank jug wine, listened to *Loveless*, and watched grainy VHS recordings of *Twin Peaks*.

One night our mutual longing filled the room like a swarm of moths.

"Let's go out," said punk Amy.

"Where?" said hippie Kim.

"Rockafellas," said preppy Paige, who was trying her damnedest to be less preppy.

"The place will be crammed cheek to jowl with decrepit metal cretins," I said.

"Decrepit metal cretins!" Punk Amy hacked with laughter. "You have a way with words."

"There's this party," said hippie Kim. "A professor's. In the woods."

In Amy's white Volkswagen Rabbit we sped down Highway 321 to some trailer-strewn boondock hole past Swansea. The party was just breaking up, professors and graduate students with crusty casserole dishes climbing into cars. We found the Wild Professor beside a waning bonfire, smoking a joint with the theory guru Dr. Glott. I could make out a dark cabin on the hill behind them, a fairy-tale dwelling composed of logs and stone.

"The sex/gender binary is always already hermeneutically destabilized and epistemologically overdetermined," said Dr. Glott.

"The world will be undone by the flick of a young girl's tongue," said the Wild Professor, his long hair uplifted by a gust of wind.

"He looks like Bob," said hippie Kim.

"Bob who?" asked preppy Paige.

"*Bob*," Kim hissed.

"Oh gross," we whispered. "*Twin Peaks* Bob."

"Bob's not totally gross." Kim licked her lips. "I like his flowing hair."

"Flowing?" said punk Amy. "You mean stringy?"

The Wild Professor released an odd doggish yip when he saw us.

"Speaking of girls." He sniffed the air.

"Be ye sylphs or things of flesh?"

"Definitely flesh," said Kim.

"Right," said Paige.

"Sylphs," I mouthed.

"Robots," Amy said in a menacing mechanical voice.

We drew closer to the fire and sat down on roughhewn chairs. We smoked weed. We drank blackberry wine from dusty mason jars. The Wild Professor slipped a Cocteau Twins cassette into a corroding boom box.

"Dance," he commanded, and for some weird reason, we did. Paige shimmied. Kim attempted some sultry moves from her belly dancing class. Amy jackhammered in place, frowning furiously, while I leapt like a doe around her.

That night I was wearing a bell-sleeved green gauze gown, Arthurian revival from the seventies, and my skirts caught on blackberry briars whenever I danced too far from the fire. The blackberries were still hard green fruit, just blushing pink, and the night grew cool. We went back to the fire.

"Where's Dr. Glott?" asked Kim.

"Taking the high road home," said the Wild Professor. "His lumpish wife awaits him, a slimy newborn pressed to her engorged breast."

"What the fuck?" said Amy. "Let's go."

But when the Wild Professor chanted in Old High German, Amy fell into her chair. Plop, plop: the other girls followed. They slumped and stared. But I remained on my feet, arms crossed.

"She looked at me as she did love and made sweet moan," said the Wild Professor.

He spoke of femme fatales and consumptive poets. He lectured me about bird migrations, planting vegetables according to the lunar phases, and suffering bouts of automatic writing when the moon went full. When, at last, I pulled my eyes from him, I noticed that my friends had fallen asleep in their chairs.

"Did you roofie my girlfriends?"

"You're not girls." He stroked my briar-scratched arm. "But women."

He was a feminist, he said, and we were full-grown mammals who shed menstrual blood.

In the firelight he looked younger, fine-boned, with a gold-green Pre-Raphaelite gaze.

"I am certain of nothing but the holiness of the heart's affections," he said.

Rolling my eyes, I followed him up the hill. His dim cabin smelled of mold and honeysuckle. Candles flickered on the ancient mantel.

"How old is this house?"

"Built by a rum trader in 1702. Want to taste some of his rum?" he asked.

He pulled a crystal decanter from a cabinet, plucked the stopper, and sloshed an inch into a mason jar. Perched on a filthy velvet chair, I tasted the burning sweetness.

"It's rum all right," I said. "But I seriously doubt it's three hundred years old."

The Wild Professor laughed like a teenage stoner, falling backward onto his bed and taking gulps of air between each howl. He thrashed and kicked and then went still. As he sat up, slow and stone-faced like a movie vampire, I tensed at the sight of his black hair—a wig, I thought, that he'd slipped on during his laughing fit. But his skin was smooth too, pale as a ghost salamander's. His enormous eyes shed gold light. And his lips looked plump and red.

He grew six inches. His jowls vanished. Elegant muscles appeared. A beautiful man moved toward me.

"How the hell?" I said.

"The willing suspension of disbelief," he whispered, his breath on my neck, hot huffs smelling of vanilla and ham. He nibbled my earlobes. He stuck his tongue down my throat and nudged me toward his fur-strewn bed. A gust blew both candles dead.

The Wild Professor loomed over me, his antlers ivoried by the moon. I stroked the soft fur on his thighs, explored coarser tangles of groin hair until I found the meat of him, a bald weasel, warm and straining as though wanting to leap from his body into my young hands.

I woke naked, half covered in musty fur scraps, the room cold. Brutal light gushed through a window to illuminate my bedmate. Beside me wheezed an old man: crepey skin, scrotal eye bags, a few wisps of hair on a scaly scalp, a gash of mouth open in surly snarl. I couldn't help but shriek. Mortified, I leapt from the bed and found my dress—soiled, gnawed, tattered, heaped on the floor, and fouled with dark fur. I pulled on my leggings, slipped on a cardigan I found on a chair, and ran out into the yard. The girls were gone, but they'd left a note on the picnic table, the paper scrap secured beneath an empty Jägermeister bottle.

Amy thinks he's a grody perv, but I sort of get it.
Call us tomorrow and we'll come pick you up.
Peace and Love,
Kim (and Amy and Paige)

"Come inside. I've built a fire," the Wild Professor growled behind me.

I jumped, bracing myself for the old man. But now he looked younger, not as young as he had the night before, but back to his usual self: worn and semi-dumpy, with thinning hair and bold eyes, his megabrow un-wrinkled, lines like parentheses framing his mouth, his jawline gone soft with proto-jowls. He wore a velour bathrobe the color of clotted blood.

"I need to call my friends," I said.

"I don't have a phone. Let me feed you breakfast, and then I'll drive you to the Family Dollar in Swansea. You can use the pay phone there."

The Wild Professor closed the velvet drapes. The cabin glowed with cozy firelight, reminding me of storybook animals tucked into winter dens. He fed me gingerbread glazed with honey from his beehives, ba-con from a wild boar he claimed to have slain. His coffee, laced with Amaretto, warmed me to the bone. In the flickering dimness, he glim-mered with a trace of the beauty I'd seen the night before. He plucked a book from the shelf, its leather binding embossed with stags and wolves.

"A maiden wandered through dark woods, witches snickering in the brambles. The girl found a castle, once grand, now in horrid shambles. Weeping, she fell upon the cold stone floor. She woke and saw a pale dwarf, smirking beyond a door. Come in, said the dwarf, don't be afraid, for marvels you shall see. Secrets of the ancient whale and the sacred honeybee."

The Wild Professor lapsed into Old High German. I don't know how long he went on, but when, at last, he stood and whisked the drapes open, dusk was falling.

"Let's go outside," he said. "The fireflies are hatching."

We stood on the hill and watched a thousand blinking insects float out from the dark wood.

The Wild Professor spent mornings writing poems, and then he'd feed me lunch. Today, like most days, we wove through the forest in the after-noon heat.

My ignorance was as deep as a wishing well, and the Wild Professor tossed glittering coins of knowledge into it. He pointed with his gnarled stick.

Pokeweed leaves are edible when tender, but poisonous when dark and tough. Rattlesnakes lurk in long grass and amid the wild blackberries. Orange mushrooms can be edible or toxic, depending on the wood they grow on. And the gills of the deadly Amanita are as white as a comatose princess's throat.

The Wild Professor identified spots where boars had rubbed their muddy flanks against pine trunks. He explained the similarities between the mayapple and Shakespeare's mandrake, which was once thought to grow from the last seminal spurts of hanged men and shriek when snatched from the soil. He identified nine tree species, twelve scrub plants, four birdcalls, and two butterflies. He listed six obscure bands from the late 1960s and then raved about three so-called rogue states to whom the US had secretly sold weapons.

His brain was a beehive on the verge of swarming. Though greedy for knowledge, I was glad when he finally slumped against a tree and napped. I cooled my feet in the creek, trying to remember the differences between hognosed snakes and copperheads.

A few weeks ago, I'd called my Columbia apartment on the Family Dollar pay phone.

"I'm taking a vacation," I'd said to Amy. "To get away from it all."

"What do you have to get away from? You're nineteen years old."

I heard Siouxsie Sioux wailing in the background. I could picture the girls lounging in the living room after a long night partying. I ached for the coziness of it all. But I remembered the restless longing, the desire to crawl out of my window at night, climb onto the rotted roof, and get swept up by a gust of otherworldly wind.

Kim snatched the phone. "What's he like?" she breathed. "Does he really put girls into trances with poetry?"

"Naïve idiot," hissed Amy, snatching the phone back. "I'm coming to get you."

"Not yet."

"Your mom has called three times this week. I've been covering for you, but . . ."

I hung up. I called the library where I reshelved books and told them that my grandmother had died. I smoked three cigarettes, pinched my arms to produce pain endorphins, and then rang my mother.

"Baby," she said, her voice rich with uncanniness. She was in the Low Country, down near Black River Swamp. I could hear my father's Weed Eater whining in the background. I pictured him in goggles and tri-ply gloves, fighting off the vines that threatened to entangle our house.

"Let them grow," I'd begged him as a child. "And our house will be like Sleeping Beauty's castle."

"You have a lovely imagination," my mother would say.

She used to take me into the shallows of the woods, just where the poison oak began to riot. We had mad tea parties: banana bread, lace-fringed napkins, juice in china cups. Mom, pretending she could talk to crows, would translate their caws. Sometimes we'd linger until the lightning bugs drifted out. Dad would call us in his stern voice. Mom would smirk. But she always packed our picnic things right after we heard the electric garage door close.

One day at dusk the Wild Professor stood at the edge of the woods, held his cupped palms together, and blew into the slit between his thumbs. Mourning doves spun out of the forest and landed on his arms. He cooed them into a stupor and slipped them into a burlap sack. He snapped their necks and gutted them. He composted the yellow intestines; he saved the purple giblets in a mason jar.

He opened a bottle of muscadine wine. We sat by the fire watching the birds roast on a hickory stick.

"For you, my dove." The professor laughed, showing his jagged yellow teeth. "A gift."

He pulled a necklace from a shoe box, a polished dove skull strung on a chain of braided grass. I slipped it on. I closed my eyes and fingered my scalp and thought I felt knots on the top of my head—horns, I dared to hope, but probably nothing.

When I opened my eyes, the professor was groaning in his chair, stooped over to nurse a stomach cramp.

"Sometimes it hurts," he said. "Maybe you'll understand one day, if you've got what it takes to change."

He glared up at me, his eyes green-gold, a thread of drool spilling from his ripening mouth. I watched bone nubbins crack through his skull and flare into antlers. I watched eye bags shrink and wrinkles melt away. Black hair sprouted from his scalp and flowed down his back like a cape. He grew six inches. He climbed out of his pants. He cast off his shirt, puffed up his chest, and scratched his furry thighs.

"It always itches at first," he said, his voice husky and garbled.

Howling, he came at me. I opened my arms to the beast. As his gamy tongue lashed at my throat, I couldn't get naked fast enough.

Summer thickened. Summer hummed. As we walked through the meadow, grasshoppers scattered with every step, their gauzy wings catching the light. Honeybees dozed in the wild asters. The milk thistle grew tall. Each night I felt the strange lumps form on my head, but by morning they were gone. Cautiously, I nibbled orange mushrooms, unsure about the species. I mimicked the professor's Old High German chants inside my head, inventing new words of my own, reaching a state of giddiness that felt like power.

One evening I sat in the kitchen fingering the bumps, which seemed a little harder.

"Maybe my horns will break tonight," I said, and then I uttered a fake spell.

"I doubt it. You can't tell a *Gymnopilus junonius* from a honey mushroom, nor can you conjugate the verb *wehsalon*. Are you speaking pig Latin?"

"It's actually an obscure chant from a Celtic goddess cult. Older than Scottish Gaelic, I think."

The professor harrumphed, but he looked worried. He growled and slumped off into the dog fennel.

At dusk I ate cold potatoes and venison jerky and waited for him on the porch. Pining for the beast, I brushed my long red hair. My heart lurched every time I heard him howl. I could barely make him out, tall and horned, raging under a paltry moon.

One afternoon like all other afternoons we pulled our chairs from the shade and drank wine in the meadow.

A hawk swooped. Buzzards circled. Crows complained in the pines. When the sky turned smoky lavender, the wispy moon looked solid again—fat and pocked and bright. Crickets chimed in with the waning cicadas.

I walked off across the meadow alone, hoping he wouldn't follow, eager to try a new spell.

"Where are you going?"

"For a stroll."

Lightning bugs blinked in the deep woods. I slipped into the delicious darkness and listened to a chuck-will's-widow calling its own name.

"I'm changing! I'm changing!" the Wild Professor cried, but I didn't rush to him. I crouched in my hiding place, a burrow lined with leaves and moss, covered with a dome of woven muscadine vines. I ate an orange mushroom and wild berries and chanted my language over rare stones. My skull burned. I fingered the bumps on my cranium. At last, I felt damp bone pushing through. Blood seeped into my hair. Blood trickled over my brow and ran into my left eye. I scratched my thighs as mink-soft fur grew. I scrambled from my hut and unfolded myself, standing six feet tall.

Smelling me on the wind, the Wild Professor let rip a heart-stopping wail.

I'd waited a month for this night, envisioning the glory of two beasts locking horns, hurling their passion at each other, enveloped in a cloud of musk. But now, all I wanted to do was run.

Amazed by the strength in my legs, I ran east through wild blueberries and then north through ferny woods. Howling himself hoarse, the professor bounded behind me, but I was faster. I leaped over a rusted fence, crossing into a clearing where pine trees had just been razed. The air smelled sad from a hundred weeping stumps. I spotted a rattlesnake winding through the wreckage. The professor stopped by the fence, panting hard.

"What kind of mushrooms did you eat?" he asked, eyeing my new form.

"Red fly agarics."

"Bullshit. They don't grow here."

"I found one."

"Where?" His voice broke.

"Top secret."

He studied my antlers. He took in my long furry legs and frowned.

"Aren't you tired from all that running?" he asked.

"No," I said, and dashed off into the woods.

I stood in the glare outside the Family Dollar, the black pay-phone receiver burning my hands.

"You're not sick of him yet?" Amy asked. "What the hell do you do all day in the woods?"

100

"There are plenty of things to do in the woods," Kim cried in the background.

The Wild Professor bristled in his Corolla, pricking his ears to catch bits of my conversation.

I hung up and called my mother.

"Honey lamb," she said. I longed for the sweet warmth of her, before her body became taboo flesh, when she was omniscient, a mystery I spent ten years trying to solve. I remembered the two of us pretending to be animals, crawling on all fours and eating wild blackberries. One summer afternoon when I was twelve, bikini-clad, oiled and tanning in the backyard, I declared our picnics stupid. Mom bit her bottom lip and walked off into the woods alone. I ached to follow her, but some new thing inside me, something hard and heavy, anchored me to my lawn chair.

"Have you paid your phone bill yet?" she asked.

"Not yet. We're still using the neighbors'. And please don't call here—it annoys them."

"When are you coming home for a visit?"

"Soon. I promise."

"We both miss you very much."

I heard my father's lawn mower droning in the background. I pictured him in his coveralls, perched on the roaring machine, looping out to mutilate a clump of goldenrod, fighting off the wildness that crept out of the woods.

A whole week of storms, and we were trapped inside like two rodents in a burrow, unable to transform in the stale air. Thunder boomed. Crows cawed. Rain dripped from a hole in the fungus-infested roof and plopped into a Crock-Pot. I picked through the professor's moldy books.

He went back to his typing with renewed ferocity. The spell checker on his Brother electric bleeped and bleeped.

"Where's my fucking pen?" He slapped his desk and glared. "I can't concentrate with you in here."

His eye bags had grown more voluptuous. Gray hairs matted the filthy floor.

"I'll go for a walk in the storm. Maybe I'll change and run into the woods and never come back again."

"Don't you dare." The professor stood up to block the door. "Just be quiet."

I picked up a legal pad and started a poem.

The Erl-king's song spilled from a cave, deep and dark and strange.
His hair was long, soft, and fair, but blighted with spots of mange.

"What are you writing?" he asked.

"Nothing. A poem."

His jaw creaked open and released a cackle.

"What could you possibly have to write about at your age? Let me read it."

The Wild Professor chased me around the cabin, knocking over stacks of books. *Mushrooms Demystified. A Brief History of Time. The Anatomy of Melancholy.* Clutching my scrap of poetry, I ran out into the rain.

I glanced back and saw him glowering in the doorway. He emerged, taller than the cabin. His head morphed into a skull. Fireflies glowed in his eye sockets. The end of his beard swung lower than his crotch as he waved a bony fist in the air. I'd never seen him like this before, and I felt a sick allure: I, too, might learn this trick. But I was making progress with my own transformations and wanted to explore a new spell.

"You bitch," he shrieked, shrinking back down to his normal size. "My heart is bleeding."

I scanned the sky, spotted the moon behind gray clouds, glimmering like a fetus in an ultrasound. I fished a mushroom from my pocket. I cajoled and chanted until my horns came. I felt a queasy pang of pity, something I'd never felt for this man, and I almost slumped back to him. But the pull of the storm was stronger. I craved atmospheric electricity and the blackness of forest soil. I craved roiling clouds and the scent of my own wet fur. I wanted to climb a rocky hill and gaze upon the raw sublime, watch lightning jag from Heaven to Earth, catch the silhouette of some dangerous new beast galloping toward me across the meadow.

The more often I changed, the more depressed the Wild Professor grew. His hair fell out. He moped in the cabin and said he didn't feel like transforming, even when I slid my hand up his thigh and stroked his half-soft cock.

"Where the hell did you find that willow bark?" he asked me again and again, tearing through the cabin, looking for my stash of herbs.

Each evening he stood in the drizzle at the forest's edge. He called and called, but the doves wouldn't come to him.

One day he shot a squirrel with his air rifle, skinned it, gutted it, and boiled the beast on the wood stove. There were bloody handprints on the white minifridge, smears of gore on the last clean towel. I craved the green scent of trees. My legs itched to run.

"Eat," said the Wild Professor, offering a plate of gray meat. "Squirrel flesh will enhance your natural clairvoyance, assuming you have any."

"No thanks. I'll stick to jimsonweed."

"You have no idea what you're fucking around with."

When he sneered I could see the contours of his secret skull, the skin loose on it, ready to slough off at any minute and reveal new marvels. But he slumped at the table and ate weird meat. He sipped black wine and brooded.

"Just wait until the solstice," he muttered. "I'll be at the top of my game again."

After a week of nonstop rain, the tomatoes turned mushy, blighted with blisters, splitting open and oozing foul juice. The cucumbers had bloated and paled on the vine. A thousand berries fermented in the soppy grass.

"Give me a ride to town," I said.

"The car is broken," said the Wild Professor.

"I need tampons. I need Midol. I need to make some calls."

He cringed at the word *calls*, as though I'd bellowed the Old Norse word *kalla—to summon loudly—*and some gorgeous demon would materialize in a fiery fury to whisk me away.

We were almost out of olive oil. Ants had gotten into the peanut butter. I'd found a fat black widow tucked under the dewy seat of the composting toilet. But we still had wine. We sat drinking at the kitchen table in the stale buzz of afternoon. But the wine only thickened our mutual boredom.

"All the car needs is a new timing belt, and Sarah's bringing one to the solstice party."

Sarah was an ex-girlfriend, ten years younger than the Wild Professor, but too old, now, to be his lover.

The professor scowled. He had an eye infection, to which he'd applied a chamomile poultice. He smelled of sour laundry and armpit cumin. He looked as if he had a fever, and I wondered if the squirrel meat had made him sick.

"Fuck it," I said. "I'll bike to Family Dollar."

"The chain is broken."

"I'll run," I screamed, halfway down the dirt drive.

The next morning I woke before dawn, sat up in bed, and waited for sunlight to break through the kitchen window and beam on the bed. When the light came, I saw the Wild Professor as I had my first morning there: a bald old man wheezing in the last throes of sleep, his eyes encased in crinkled pouches, his nose dripping amber rheum. I'd tried to catch him like this before, but he always got up before dawn. I'd wake to find him crouched over the sink, drinking tinctures and gobbling mushrooms, popping pills from unlabeled bottles.

But this morning he slept through dawn. The longer he slept, the older he looked. At last, he sat up, opened his toothless mouth, and hissed like a lizard.

"Who are you?" he asked, his eyes milky with cataracts.

"La Belle Dame sans Merci," I joked. But he didn't laugh. He hid his head under the covers and whimpered.

On the solstice, the Wild Professor spread a harvest feast beneath a portable canopy emblazoned with the words PALMETTO FUNERAL HOME.

"I bought it at a thrift store." He smirked. His eyes gleamed with a new electromagnetism, and I fell into his arms. I sniffed his neck and smelled a faint whiff of beast. He hadn't transformed in weeks, but his eye infection had miraculously healed. His hair looked thicker. And I craved his other form.

The sun was still high when the first car came bouncing up the potholed drive. It was Sarah, who'd lived with the Wild Professor in the forest one summer long ago. She had a handsome ruddy husband her own age. She had a fetus the size of a frog inside her swollen belly. She had a broccoli casserole and a jug of springwater.

"Well water gives me gas," she said, sending the professor a secret smile.

A philosophy professor arrived with his fourteen-year-old daughter and his twenty-eight-year-old girlfriend. An adjunct poet, new to the Wild Professor's department, walked through the meadow in a minidress and hiking boots. She eyed the funereal canopy, the cobblers and salads and bowls of strange meat, the mismatched cups and unlabeled bottles of homemade wine.

"Am I in the right place?" She waved a faded flier. "I got this invitation in my department box?"

"A thrift store score." The professor pointed at the canopy. "I assure you I'm not in the funeral business, though given recent downsizing in the humanities, never say never. Anyway, welcome to Walden. You must be the lesbian adjunct poetess?"

"The what?" The poet frowned.

Another couple came, both middle-aged with monkish bowl cuts, both wearing work shirts and cutoff acid-washed jeans—she a deconstructive gender sociologist, he a painter who specialized in grotesque cherubs.

I ran to the meadow, stood like a meerkat, and peered. At last, punk Amy's white Volkswagen Rabbit materialized, turning from Basil Road onto the Wild Professor's dirt drive. Punk Amy, hippie Kim, and preppy Paige rushed from the car. The girls gathered around me, picked at my clothes, and poked my ribs.

"You're so skinny," said Paige.

"Too damn thin," said Amy. Her Mohawk bristled with hardened gel. Her arms were tricked out with spiked bracelets. She looked ready for battle. "Has the perv been starving you?"

"Nature girl," quipped Kim, admiring the miniskirt I'd made out of gigantic collard leaves. I wore it with the professor's Roxy Music tee and plastic combat boots from the Family Dollar.

We smoked a joint. I grabbed a bottle of blackberry wine and led my friends through the forest. I felt possessed by the Wild Professor as I recited the names of plants and beasts, pointing out holes and hollows where creatures hid from predators. But then I settled into my own voice.

"Tickleweed," I said, nibbling a tender leaf that the Wild Professor incorrectly called haresbane. "A mild aphrodisiac."

The landscape sparkled with beauty again because my friends were there to share it: the trees bursting with sap, the birds bustling amid shimmering leaves, the air drowsy with the fume of poppies. In the meadow, butterflies hovered over waist-high wild flowers, and bees dozed in the blooms.

"I could stay here forever," said hippie Kim, lying down in a patch of *Papaver somniferum.*

"My ultimate nightmare," said Amy.

I felt an eerie chill, though there was no breeze. The philosophy professor's daughter came skipping through the meadow in a white dress.

Dusk fell. The Wild Professor's guests sat around the fire drinking wine and eating cobblers, casseroles, flatbread with pesto and cherry tomatoes. None of the guests touched the dove-liver pâté. None of them tried the squirrel salad.

"The Cree Indians fed squirrel meat to their children," said the Wild Professor, casting his luminous gaze upon the philosophy professor's daughter. The girl, Ashley, stood basking in his attention. She gave him a sly glance and blushed. She was just coming into her beauty, testing its power, hungry for magical change.

The sociology professor harrumphed. She jotted notes into her journal while her husband sketched a rococo cloud.

Sarah chugged springwater and eyed the wine, no doubt remembering her endless evenings here. Twelve years ago Sarah had stormed out during an August drought and walked off across a dead meadow. But there she was, tugging me away from the fire for a heart-to-heart.

"I came to check on him," she whispered. "And to see how you're doing. How *y'all* are doing."

"The rains set us back, but the garden's reviving," I said. "I'd like to drive to Columbia occasionally, but . . ."

"If you did, you'd never come back."

"But you're back." I glanced up to see the Wild Professor wriggling his pointed ears. He claimed he could hear sounds from up to thirty miles away. I turned back to Sarah. When I opened my mouth to speak, I felt the professor's hot, gamy breath on the back of my neck.

I left him alone with Sarah.

Sarah's husband watched her intently. The philosophy professor kept a sharp eye on his daughter. Having wiggled out of his lap, the philosophy professor's girlfriend was now deep in conversation with the adjunct poet.

I joined the youthful throng under the high, waxing moon, wine bottle in my fist, and danced around the fire, remembering my first night here, my green gown torn by briars, the Wild Professor ripping it off with his yellow claws. Ashley stood amid wild flowers, watching us.

"Come on," I called to her. "Don't be shy."

106

The girl inched closer. She took furtive sips from a mason jar.

"Oh my," said Kim. "What have we got there?"

"Something he gave me." Her eyes looked huge. Her pupils had gobbled up her hazel irises. "It's actually delicious. Like honeysuckle and chocolate and blood."

"Blood? What the fuck did that perv give you?" said Amy. "Let me take a sniff."

The girl giggled, handed the empty jar to Amy, and executed a perfect *petit jeté*.

I pulled the Wild Professor aside from his table of elders. "She's just a child."

"It was only blackberry juice," he said, watching Ashley perform elegant pirouettes in the poppy field. "And besides, I can tell she's a woman already."

"What was that?" the philosophy professor asked.

"I said, where is that woman already?"

"Wha woman?" slurred the philosophy professor, and then he passed out in his chair.

The deconstructive gender sociologist hawed. But then she teetered; she moaned; she fought and thrashed but soon lay still in the grass.

"Honey," said her husband. But in seconds, he, too, was asprawl.

"You asshole!" I cried. "You slipped them a potion."

"It's been lovely," said Sarah, nodding fiercely at her husband.

"Yep." He put down his beer.

They hustled toward their car.

"Where is the philosophy professor's girlfriend?" I asked. "Where is the adjunct poet?"

"They went for a walk." The Wild Professor winked. "A lovely night for romance. Just look at that moon."

"Listen," I said, avoiding the moon, avoiding his eyes. "I need to tell you something."

"You're leaving me?" The professor shrank an inch, but his eyes still glowed.

"Let's not think of it like that," I said. "I just need to get my shit together. I need to pay my rent, or they'll give my room to another girl. We can see each other in town."

"I'll pay your rent."

"No way."

"Stay with me until winter, at least," he whined. "I'm on sabbatical for fall semester."

"I have to go back to school," I said.

"I can teach you everything you need to know. I see lots of potential in you." The professor grinned like a wolf. I felt myself soften a bit. "After all, I was the one who taught you how to change. You watched me eat the mushrooms. You heard me chant the chants."

"I figured that out myself. I don't eat the same ones. I don't chant the same chants."

"What you're doing is childish make-believe. Stick around this fall and I'll show you the real deal."

Little Ashley leapt into the firelight and laughed. She stood on tippy toes and whispered into the Wild Professor's ear.

"More blackberry juice, please."

The Wild Professor's eyes bubbled like molten gold. He grew a foot taller. Slaver trickled from his jaws.

"That's fucked up," said Amy, appearing by my side.

"He's so beautiful," said hippie Kim, gawking at the spectacle. "Now I totally get it!"

His hair came back. His fur sprouted. His antlers filigreed toward the moon.

"Actually, don't look at him," I cried, though I had trouble pulling my eyes away. "Just walk the hell away."

"That's right. It's just an illusion," said Amy. "A heap of shining bullshit."

"But I don't want to go," said Kim. "Let him bite me. Gore me. I don't care."

"I want to say here forever," said Ashley, charging away. She ran toward the glorious beast.

The Wild Professor stood over the flames, splaying his legs like Atlas. Sparks shot toward his groin. I'd never seen him so huge, so strong, so alluring. But I pictured him hunched over his typewriter when the words wouldn't come, turning toward me, his eye bags aquiver with rage. I saw him mooning around in the drizzle, failing to seduce a flock of doves. I envisioned him, ancient and brittle, sulking in his sour bed.

Now Kim walked backward, watching the Wild Professor rise toward the stars. Now Ashley danced around the fire, singing an ancient lullaby. When the Professor threw back his head and howled, I reached for my secret pouch, struggling to remember the sequence: Amanita, mayapple root, rattlesnake tongue, reindeer moss. Luciferin, fairy dew, cicada wing, owl bone meal. I chanted the poem I'd written for the solstice, loud enough for the Wild Professor to hear. Words spun around my head as my antlers came, forty-seven points and glowing gold. My thigh muscles popped out, bigger than ever. My fur sprouted bushy and thick. Bones aching. I grew three feet, towering over the other girls.

Paige shrieked as she ran toward the car. Amy hustled after her down the slope, pausing to shout. "What the hell have you gotten into?"

"Just wait for me," I cried, my speech garbled by the chant that wouldn't stop coming, wet words unfurling like newborn bats from my throat, darting up into the sky to circle over the Wild Professor's head. Jolted out of her trance, Kim stopped smiling.

When the Wild Professor moved toward Ashley, the bat swarm descended, flurrying his hair into a knotted mess. He swatted at the bats, uttering words that he claimed were Indo-European, curses that pricked my kidneys and made my heart boil with black blood. I shrieked a word so old that hominids had uttered it, a word that made him double over and clutch his gut. And then I ran at him. I battered his back with my horns. Kicked his flanks with my hooves. When he fell onto his side, moaning, Ashley ran to me, hugged me, croaking as she tried not to cry.

We ran down the slope toward the car. I felt myself getting smaller, moving slower, returning to my human self.

Hand on the door handle, I dared to look back.

The Wild Professor had burst into flames. As flesh fell like ash from his body, I thought I had destroyed him.

But the cloud of ash morphed into a wolf skeleton. He crouched on all fours and barked.

"Get in! Get in!" Amy screamed through the open window.

We piled into the white Rabbit, Ashley whimpering in the back seat. "My tummy hurts," she said, and then she passed out.

When Amy turned the key, the car sputtered, failed, and then sputtered again. We lurched off, bounded down the bumpy drive, and skidded left onto Basil Road. We swerved right to dodge a doe, left to avoid an injured raccoon.

"Jesus, step on it," I said.

The Wild Professor was galloping toward us, his snarling muzzle full of blood-glazed teeth. He hurled his body at the car, clattering bones against molded steel. His ghost tongue lashed like an electric eel as he barked.

We rolled up the windows. Finally Paige shifted to fourth and gunned it, and we left the Wild Professor whining on his haunches, his snout aimed at the moon. We hooted in triumph.

But tears leaked from my eyes as I watched the professor shrink back down into a puny man. He stood like a hobo on the side of the road, his jeans covered in home-sewn patches.

"I will make you beds of roses. I will teach you how to fly," he cried, his voice breaking. And then he turned away.

As he hobbled back toward his cabin, light leaked out of him with every step.

Nominated by Tin House,
Ethan Chatagnier,
Ron Tanner

A FABLE

by GRAHAM BARNHART

from WAXWING LITERARY JOURNAL

One day a cat spied a family of mice trying to hide in a milk can.
These will be a fine supper, he thought, and thrust
his face into the pail. Lifting it he soon
had a mouthful of mice. But to his dismay he found
his bulging cheeks kept him stuck fast, and he could
not swallow the mice, even one at a time, because the narrowing
neck of the pail narrowed also around his own.
He stumbled about in frustration tipping the pail back and forth
as the mice tumbled into and out of his mouth. At length
some soldiers approached behind grumbled humvee engines. The
    cat
froze in terror, unaware he had wandered so close to a patrolled
    road,
unwilling to remove his head lest any of the mice escape.
How did a cat even get stuck in a pail is not a question
anyone stops to ask in a warzone. And why should they?
One soldier drew a pistol and fired. The cat ran back and forth
in frantic, erratic patterns. The soldier fired a second time—
no one knows what became of the mice.

Nominated by Waxwing Literary Journal,

Hugh Martin

FAT SWIM

fiction by EMMA COPLEY EISENBERG

from VIRGINIA QUARTERLY REVIEW

Alice spots the fat women through the second-story kitchen window. It's Wednesday, so Dad is out at his feelings meeting. She has just turned eight and has been dragging her drumsticks over different household surfaces to see what sounds they make. The sink has been working well—a satisfying *ting, ting, ting*. Also the panes of window glass—higher, though, and more muffled. The kitten meows on the ledge. Shush shush, Alice tells him, then bops him lightly on the head with a stick.

It's the colors that catch Alice's eye, the parade of bright bodies turning the corner of 49th street onto the avenue, then veering into the rec area that holds the pool.

Back soon, back soon, back soon, Alice tells the kitten. The drumsticks roll off the counter and hit the parquet floor.

The public pool is on Alice's avenue, which has many trees and a lot of garbage. The sidewalks are cracked but the parking is permit-only—the old woman who lives in the purple house is the captain and she is efficient. Dad drives a Subaru that always works but is always dirty.

From the top step of Alice's stoop she can clearly see the women across the street and through the chain-link fence. The women are fat and they are swimming. Well, they are about to swim. They are taking off their jean shorts and belly shirts and fringe vests and heart-shaped sunglasses and putting their hair up into ponytails or, if they have no hair, pressing both of their hands onto their heads like a cap—a dance move. A song is playing from a radio that is attached to the motor bike of the boy who lives in the purple house. The song is a rap song that

112

has been playing all summer and even before that, in the weeks when the kids at school believed it should have been summer vacation but it was not, and the air conditioners were working at home but not at school. The fat women are black and they are white, a thing that almost never happens in this neighborhood. They snap their fingers. They lean forward and stick out their butts, then lean back and lift their breasts to the sun, their bellies hanging over their bikini bottoms.

This is interesting to Alice because they are fat like her. As they dance to the rap song, sometimes a swath of fat goes one way while the woman goes another. These are moves Alice, too, has sometimes done, but only alone and only in front of the mirror. Slight rolls of flesh hang down their fronts, just below the elastic of their bras. Flesh gathers on their backs like wings. Alice would like to run a finger through the crease this flesh makes. This is what she thinks about later, at night, in her bed with the lights out. With both hands, she holds the flaps of fat where the low parts of her stomach touch her thighs. She jiggles them—together, then separately—then lets them go. She pats her vagina with her whole hand, once, twice. The thing that most people do not know about fat is that it is more taut than you think. It is not all softness. It bounces. It bounces back.

The following Wednesday, Alice is ready, sitting a little closer, on the bottom step of her stoop, and waiting for the women. In addition to sexy touching, she has also been dreaming of the fat women, which is how she knows it is romantic. She has imagined a birthday party. It is her birthday, a pool party, and the women are her guests. There is cake and ice cream. Everyone eats as much as they want and no one is there to ask them if they are sure they really want to eat that second piece. They eat the ice cream from the pint cartons because it is assumed that each will finish her own pint. No one has to share, no one has to put the ice cream back with one bite left because she is afraid her mom will notice the carton is missing. Then there is dancing. The fat women compliment Alice on her moves. They say they have never seen moves like that, and ask Alice to teach them. Then two women come up on either side of Alice, grab her hands and swing her body back and forth, back and forth. Then they toss her into the water and she swims and swims.

In real life, they are not dancing today. It is too hot, the women say, entirely too hot. They take their clothes off and get right in the water, either by jumping or easing themselves down the flimsy metal ladders.

113

If they ease themselves in, their breasts are the first thing to float. Recently, Alice has learned that breasts are actually just sacks of fat. Her own breasts, which she has had for a year already, are also made of fat. She likes them. She likes to hold one in each hand and jiggle them separately. Strange, though, she thinks, the way people love breasts but hate fat. If the women jump in, they surface slowly, gasping and laughing, then moving across the water slow as manatees. There is a beach ball, which circulates in no particular order. They tap it with the tips of their fingers, then let it fall when they get bored.

Alice sits with Dad when he gets home, munching on a crispy grilled cheese and carrots that Dad has grown in their garden. She knows now that carrots come from seeds and that just because the ones that come from their garden look like crooked knuckles, and not like the smooth ones from the grocery store, does not mean they are bad.

How big will I get? Alice asks Dad, holding another knobby carrot. Will I keep growing?

Dad looks up from the pile of papers he is writing on. Whenever he is writing to his students, he uses the cheapest possible pen, Alice has noticed, usually the free ones from the bank near their house where the trolley stops. Dad is fat, too, but Alice's mom, Tara, who used to be Dad's wife, is not. Alice has noticed that this happens often, a fat man with a thin woman. Rarely does it go the other way around.

I don't know, Dad says. You will very likely keep growing up vertically. I don't know if you will also keep growing out horizontally. Do you want to?

Yes, says Alice.

Okay, says Dad.

After dinner, Alice and Dad take a walk to Fred's Water Ice at the corner where the shiny flags are, across the street from the funeral parlor. Everything at Fred's is red metal—red metal poles that hold up the red metal roof, red metal horses that you can ride for fifty cents. Alice gets a jumbo opaque plastic cup of black cherry water ice mixed with vanilla soft serve. She holds it in one hand and the red metal hair of the horse in the other. Next to her on a Santa's sleigh is a little girl with her hair up in two poofs secured with bright, colored balls that Alice thinks are cool. She thinks the girl is five, maybe six.

How old are you? Alice asks the girl.

Eight and a half, the girl says, wiping some dust off the sleigh seat next to her. But inside, she says, I'm much older.

Me, too, Alice says.

Her thighs are much bigger than the girl's, trunks compared to the girl's branches. Does this matter? Can people be the same age but different sizes? Alice squeezes her thighs together, hard, to see if she can suffocate the metal horse, but she can't, he keeps right on bucking.

You're fat, the girl says.

I know, Alice says.

Oh, the girl says. What's your name?

Alice. But sometimes people call me Alley Cat or Topsy.

Because of your hair?

Yes.

Can I touch it?

Okay, Alice says. She is used to this from school. Curly hair like hers, so curly it sticks straight out from her head in a circle like a Truffula Tree, is interesting to people, she knows. Alice leans her head down and into the space between their two rides. The girl puts her hand into Alice's hair and moves it side to side.

Cool, the girl says.

Dad has his right leg up on the sitting part of the red metal table and is leaning over it, stretching. His jumbo cup of mango water ice is empty, and the smallest bit of orange water puddles at the bottom. He wears floppy water shoes with toes and a back but no sides except thin slats. Alice worries about him. At night, after she has put on her pajamas, they meet in her red chair for a story and he does the silly voices and smoothes her hair away from her ears.

The girl gets off the ride and goes to take the hand of a tall man leaning against the red metal fence—her dad. Alice sees how this dad holds himself, chest a little puffed out. He moves a toothpick around in his mouth and his boots are laced up tight and hard. Dad carries a canvas bag with two straps, and usually the tops of vegetables—kale, rhubarb, collards—poke up out of the bag. Alice worries that Dad is too gentle for this world. That he will not last. That one day she will wake up and wait for Dad to pour her the cereal with blueberries and he will not be there.

Dad likes to say that he is a survivor, that he has survived many things. Alice does not know what feelings he goes to talk about on Wednesday nights, but she suspects it has something to do with this. One thing he survived are his parents. His dad, who is dead, used to put his hand on top of the television when he came home to see if Dad had been watching it. If he had been watching it, his dad would beat him, or sometimes not, but the possibility was always there. His mom lives with other old

115

people in a facility in Florida and sometimes sends letters that arrive in manila envelopes because they are too long to be folded in three and mailed in a regular envelope. Alice has never met her.

Another thing Dad survived is Mom, who is not gone, only living in the suburbs with her new husband. Alice spends every weekend there. There is little to report because everyone is so little. Mom has shrunk. Mom's new husband runs marathons, leaving the house before Alice wakes up and returning halfway through the day, in small shorts and shellacked with sweat. Fifteen miles! Twenty-seven miles! Mom high-fives him and then they both want to high-five her. Alice's chest starts to feel tight hours before dinner time because there is usually not enough food and she usually goes to bed hungry. This feeling sticks around long after the meal has actually happened, the hunger has actually come, and even through the morning when she can eat again. At Mom's house, even the air feels thin.

Penny for your thoughts, Dad says, from the red table.

I'm in love, Alice says.

What news, Dad says. Who with?

I'm not sure, Alice says. I don't know their names. I'll let you know.

You're in love with more than one person?

Yes.

Okay, Dad says. He tosses his empty cup into the red trash. It's nice to be in love, Dad says as they walk home, and even nicer when someone is in love with you. When your mom was in love with me, I felt good all the time. I would wake up in the morning and jump out of bed.

That night after Dad reads her the story of the princess who rescues the prince from the tower, Alice is almost asleep when she hears Dad crying on the other side of the wall. At first it is quiet like *sniff, sniff, sniff,* but then it is louder and then very loud, as if Dad doesn't think Alice can hear him, or does not care.

On the third Wednesday, Alice starts preparing early. She digs her bathing suit out of a garbage bag that sits under many other garbage bags, from that time Dad thought they had bed bugs last summer. Now she is ready. She goes down the steps, looks both ways, and waits for the low-rider to pass, trundling slow. Then she crosses the street, steps over the curb, and presses her nose through the chain-link fence.

She hears the women before she sees them. They're rounding the corner together.

And he was like—

What a fucking jerk—

Broke down, broke down, broke—

Hot hot hot, too hot you know—

They carry big beach bags and walk the length of the chain-link fence, past Alice and then through the gate. The pool is small, no Olympians here, but big enough to have parts of it cordoned off by plastic buoys for lap swimming. It is surrounded by ten steps of asphalt on all sides, then grass, then the chain-link fence. She has never come here without Dad and a sign says this is not allowed. But the guy with the clipboard who is maybe a lifeguard and maybe not is talking to a girl in a pink bikini over by the showers.

The five fat women take over the corner to Alice's left, putting their bags on the grass and spreading their towels. They take off their shirts and push them through the holes in the chain-link and there are those back rolls again. One of the women, black, in a cactus-print bikini, who carries all her weight in her lower half, in the part covered by the bikini bottom, sees Alice looking at her and smiles, then turns when one of the other women calls her name. The other woman is white. She leans her bike up against the chain-link fence and then lifts off her loose dress to reveal a floral one-piece and thick arms. She cocks her head and winds an elastic around the bottom of her thin braid, too thin, like Alice's when her mom pulls and braids it. She wants her friend to put sunscreen on her back, in the part below her bikini top's clasp, where she can't reach. There is music from a boy's bike, slower with no words, just the same beat over and over again.

The guard does not notice when Alice power walks through the gate. She walks over to where the fat women have put their towels. Underneath her overalls she is wearing her multicolored swimsuit. She feels the effects of the elastic fabric—how taut it is and the shimmery sensation it gives where it contacts the denim of her overalls. As she walks, she pooches out her stomach and feels its new smoothness, her rolls of fat now a continuous curve. She pats her stomach a few times. She can feel how it moves, how the impact of her hand moves across the flesh. She takes off her overalls and spreads them on the ground like a towel.

The sunblocked pair of women are sitting on the edge of the pool, waving their legs in the water, while the other three swim around each other happily. Alice walks over and stands next to them on the pool's edge. She feels sure they will tell her to go away but they don't. They keep on chatting, talking about a man the black woman had been dating but was dating no longer.

And he did what? honked the white woman, splashing with her feet.

Yeah, said the black woman, how's that.

Alice is still standing there.

Hi, the black one says then, shading her eyes from the sun when she looks up at Alice.

Hi, says Alice.

The white one and the black one look at each other a minute.

Want to sit with us? the black woman says.

Alice's chest gets tight, but not like at Mom's house, more like balloon tight, tight like the head of the drums they play in music class.

Okay, Alice says.

I like your suit, the white one says. It's pretty.

Thanks, Alice says.

We've seen you, the black one says. You live across the street.

That's right, Alice says. That's me.

Soon her two new friends are in the pool with the other women, so Alice gets in too. She eases herself down the ladder and, pushing out across the water, does a fast doggy paddle. She can swim only medium well. The beach ball appears and Alice has trouble hitting it with her hands while also staying afloat because she is just a kid and a lot shorter than the women.

Oh, oh, one of them says, noticing, so they move their game into the shallower end. Now Alice is having fun. She dives for the ball and hits it just before it smacks the surface of the water. The women laugh and clap. They take a page from her book and are soon diving for the ball too. Alice bounces up and down, up and down, ready to hit the ball at any moment.

After a while, the women get out of the pool and go to lie on their towels. Alice lies on her overalls.

The women are talking about leg hair and armpit hair and the individual decisions they make about it.

One woman, a white woman with a shaved head, says that a long time ago she decided she no longer cared what the world thought. Fuck it, she says. Her leg hair is very long and Alice can see it moving slightly as it dries in the sun.

Want to touch it? The woman says to the group, and they all do. Want to touch it? She says to Alice. Alice does. It feels soft like the caterpillars that Alice sometimes finds growing on Dad's carrots in the garden.

The black woman in the cactus bikini starts reading palms.

Want me to do yours? She asks Alice. She takes Alice's hand in hers. Alice feels each of the woman's individual fingers, which are pretty and manicured with yellow nail polish, move over the skin of her hand. Later, when Alice wants to feel the good sexy feelings, she will think of this woman.

You're going to live a long time, the woman says. See this line? The woman traces the line that goes from the bottom of Alice's index finger diagonally down to where it meets her wrist. But, the woman says, it won't be easy.

Don't tell her that, says her white friend. Don't tell her that. She's only a child.

Why not? She needs to know.

The women lie down on their backs and get very quiet. The sun is very hot. Alice stays sitting up a minute to survey the bodies around her and revel in her luck. Their breasts look very nice, snuggled up in their bathing suits of various colors. She is happy. She shimmies her shoulders a little and wiggles her toes. She has a body. She lies down on her back too. The air moves fast across her wet arms. The clouds move fast across the sky.

Back at home, after they've all parted ways and promised to see one another next Wednesday, Alice lets the kitten walk all over her chest, lets it knead her flesh with its paws because it thinks she is its mother. Meow, meow, it says. It leaves little red claw marks on her breasts, then hops off toward the floor when it hears Dad's footsteps on the landing.

Dad's face looks red and smushed, less defined than usual. He shrugs off his totebag onto a kitchen chair. The kitten jumps onto the table and knocks a water glass onto the floor, but the glass is thick and just rolls across the hardwood without breaking.

Jesus, Dad says, Jesus Christ. He picks up the glass very slowly as if it takes all of his energy.

Why are you wet? Dad asks Alice then. There are little puddles on the floor under her feet and her butt is leaving a wet spot on the Indian sheet that covers the couch.

Where do you go on Wednesday nights?

Alice. Answer me. Why are you wet?

I went to the pool without you. What do you do when I'm at Mom's? Why do you cry in the night?

119

With his whole palm, Dad runs a hand down his face, wiping it of expression. He takes off his shoes and for once just throws them by the door instead of placing them neatly in the shoe holder as he is always reminding Alice to do.

There are things in this world that are too cruel to tell a child, he says. Even a great one like you.

What things? Alice says. Things like what?

I'm going to take a shower, Dad says.

They have dinner and it is fine. Everything is fine. Dad is his usual self again, smiling and counting his peas into groups of five so they can practice multiplication tables. In the red chair, he does the silly voices.

Good night, good night, Dad says, and flicks off the unicorn lamp.

Alice's vagina hurts, in that dull achy good kind of way. She thinks about the woman in the cactus bikini but she does not touch.

Outside the window that holds her air-conditioning unit, the wind blows. She feels very awake, her eyes cutting the dark. She can see the outline of every object that is her room—the poster of Emma Goldman with her little glasses and the candles in the shape of panthers and the glass jar full of rocks that she and Dad carried for miles along the shore of Martha's Vineyard. It started to rain and they had to keep walking a long time but eventually they made it back to the car and Dad gave her his big orange sweatshirt with the oversized hood.

I love you, Dad said.

I know, Alice said. But you don't love you.

I know, Dad said. His hands were on the wheel but the car was off. It was raining louder than it had ever rained. I'm working on it, Dad said. I'm going as fast as I can.

Okay, Alice said. Go faster, Alice said.

Alice has a feeling then, lying in the dark in her good bed, and the feeling is like a presence, or a spirit, like how people describe their spirits leaving their body when they are dying in ghost stories except she is not dying and this is not a story. The spirit seems to be coming from the outside, from the night, from the street that lies between her and the pool, and it seems to want to tell her something of the future, to make her know that though she is free now, and though she has already done better than her father, the world is still waiting to tell her who she is and what her body means.

She still has the rest of the summer, three months of Wednesdays. The women are there every week, without fail. They buy her ice cream and teach her how to whip it and how to lean back, how to crack her back and how to crack her knuckles, how to whistle and how to snap, how to spit and how to make a man who calls out on the street wish he had never been born.

The spirit knocks at the windowpane—once, twice, three times. Alice is gripped then, suddenly afraid.

Go away, go away, go away, she says to the spirit. And for now, it does.

Nominated by Virginia Quarterly Review,
Ethan Chatagnier,
Lydia Conklin,
Allegra Hyde,
Don Waters

OLD SCHOOL

by ALLEN GEE

from PLOUGHSHARES

In the fall of 1987 after driving across the country to study at the University of Iowa, I found myself enrolled in James Alan McPherson's fiction workshop, not knowing how I'd ended up there. The rumor circulated that, like a magisterial conductor of a symphony orchestra, the Iowa Workshop office manager, Connie Brothers, somehow made all the decisions about our academic lives, but I couldn't be sure. What I did know, however—walking into a welcome party at the former Workshop director Paul Engle's house, as the new director, Frank Conroy, played jazz on a baby grand piano, and as James Salter lounged on a blanket on a lawn—was that the other graduate students were older and far more mature than I was, many of them already published or from Ivy League universities, while I'd attended the University of New Hampshire. So for my first critique in McPherson's workshop I submitted a fishing story that wasn't my best work, including a main character with no descriptive racial features; the character was virtually white. Therefore, after the workshop ended, James called me over out in the hallway.

"Why did you put that story up?"

I lowered my voice. "It was smoke."

"What do you mean?"

"I was being cautious. I've heard how cruel it can be here, so I didn't want to put up what I've been spending all my time on."

James stared at me with concern as if I were an ailing patient requiring a diagnosis, but he also appeared amused as if recognizing that I possessed some street smarts. "What are you really working on?" he said.

"A novel. It's about a Chinese restaurant in New York."

"Can you bring me some of the pages tomorrow?"

"I will," I said but immediately felt vulnerable.

The novel I was working on chronicled the life of the owner of a restaurant called the China Star, as well as the lives of the cooks and waiters; I was attempting to write realistic working-class fiction in the vein of Bernard Malamud's *The Assistant*. The next day, I left the first two chapters in a large envelope in James' mailbox, and that evening, he telephoned. I was surprised because I hadn't given him my number. "Can you meet me at my office tomorrow at two o'clock?"

When I told him I could, he hung up.

A year earlier, I'd been working in a bookstore when I'd found a paperback copy of *The Stories of Breece D'J Pancake* on the shelves, so I'd read James' eloquent foreword to the collection. I hadn't read *Hue and Cry* or *Elbow Room* yet, though. My coworkers at the bookstore had laughed when I'd told them I was applying to Iowa, and they'd reacted with astonishment when I informed them I'd been accepted and offered a scholarship. Still, I wasn't boastful. I'd been a secondary English Teaching major as an undergraduate and had only taken fiction workshops during my junior and senior years. So not only hadn't I read James' books but I wasn't well read, period. I hadn't read enough Russian or English literature, or a sufficient amount of cultural criticism or poetry or history, and I hadn't read many American classics, not even *Catcher in the Rye* or *To Kill a Mockingbird*.

Therefore, the next day in James' office, I felt unconfident as he said, "I've read your chapters. You and I work the same side of the street." Then he handed me a hardback copy of *Choose Life: A Dialogue Between Arnold Toynbee and Daisaku Ikeda* and said, "Can you come to my house?"

I didn't feel as if I deserved such attention.

Still, I ended up driving each week to the eastern side of Iowa City where James lived at 711 Rundell Street in a modest two-bedroom pale green, white-trimmed house. During those weeks, he handed me many books—Marcus Aurelius' *Meditations*; Miguel de Unamuno's *The Tragic Sense of Life*; Albert Murray's *The Omni Americans*; Gustav Schwab's *Gods and Heroes of Ancient Greece*; Jefferson's *Writings*; Ralph Ellison's *Invisible Man* and *Shadow and Act*; *The Collected Stories of Isaac Babel*; Homer's *The Odyssey*; Alex Harris' *A World Unsuspected*, containing an essay by James about his own early years; Junichiro Tanizaki's *In Praise of Shadows*; Richard Wright's *Native Son*, and more—so

123

each week, we talked about a book. A few times, I gave James pages from my novel, and we talked about those too. I admitted to him early on that I hadn't read his books yet, which amused him, but by the end of that fall I told him I'd read *Hue and Cry* and *Elbow Room*.

"Do you know how lucky you are?" Connie Brothers asked me one day, remarking about my time with James. I told her I did, thinking of how somehow she saw and knew everything like some sort of Buddha psychic, before I realized that James must have said something about our hours outside of class.

I mentioned to another graduate student what was occurring, and she said in an accusatory voice that reminded me of Veruca Salt in *Willy Wonka and the Chocolate Factory* asking for an Everlasting Gobstopper, "Why don't I get a mentor?"

My guilt compelled me to ask James what I should say, and he replied, "Tell her that sometimes certain people just get along and become friends."

I felt grateful hearing that he thought of me as a friend, and contemplating those years, I know now that I was the beneficiary of old-school mentoring. When Odysseus, the King of Ithaca, fought in the Trojan War and entrusted the care of his household to Mentor, who served as a teacher and overseer for Odysseus' son, Telemachus, "mentoring" unofficially began; from there, the term *mentor* eventually evolved to mean trusted advisor, friend, and wise person. Socrates and Plato, Hayden and Beethoven, Freud and Jung—this was mentoring too, and eventually, I would learn that Ralph Ellison had been James' mentor. One night at the Foxhead, an Iowa City bar, another graduate student said to me, "What do you guys talk about?" I shook my head and said it was too difficult to explain.

Back then it was. How could I say that James was providing me with ideological perspectives that I would be able to apply to my Asian American identity for the rest of my life, to ward off any sense of inferiority based upon race, as far as my status as a citizen could be concerned? How could I express that he was passing down insights about how to read a short story or an essay or a novel that would serve me as a professor decades later? How could I know that we were only in the formative stage of what would evolve into a twenty-nine-year friendship?

Someone else at the Foxhead asked, "Can you understand him?" This aligned with the complaint some students had made that James spoke too softly, or that his words sometimes sounded unintelligible, but I had no difficulty hearing or understanding what James articulated. I attrib-

124

uted this to the other students being poor listeners, or to their not being patient enough to let him finish talking about what were often multilayered, complex ideas.

What I also realized then, as if by instinct, was that I should protect James' privacy because while he seemed reclusive to many people that he simply didn't want in his life, each week he wanted to talk with me. One day, Connie telephoned and asked me to drive over to James' house because he was upset. A Southerner who he'd helped gain admission into the Workshop had complained about James' teaching, and Connie thought I could help to calm James down. He was livid, though. "It's always this way!" he said. "Blacks never stop being kind to the Cracker, and all they do is backstab us!" He pointed to some of his bookshelves. "You can find it throughout history! It never changes!"

"I won't ever betray you," was all I could say.

And during the course of our visits not only did we speak of books or my writing or racial conflict, but he told me about his bitter divorce and his flying to Virginia each month to see his daughter, Rachel; he related how he felt betrayed by people in Charlottesville who he'd thought were friends, who'd testified against his capacity to be a good father. We also spoke about our upbringings—his in segregated Savannah, mine in New York, comparing our cultural backgrounds—and we shared stories about our relationships with women. Sometimes we watched movies—his favorite film at that point was *Lawrence of Arabia*. I learned that he'd nicknamed his house Little Monticello, founded after Thomas Jefferson's beliefs of equality, and now and then, when I entered 711 Rundell, James was standing in the kitchen fixing Southern cuisine, like ham hocks and collard greens, or seafood dishes, like shrimp with rice or Lobster Thermidor. He'd learned to cook, he told me, working as a Pullman Porter during his college summers at Morris Brown, and he'd started smoking cigarettes then. Above all, I ascertained there was a pattern to his life; he flew to visit Rachel as much as he could, and he spent fall, winter, and spring mostly living the life of the mind, teaching, reading, and writing, glad to be an intellectual, sometimes flying off for conferences, social with his neighbors and carefully chosen friends, or lovers, but he was lonely without family, his sister Mary living back east and his brother Richard living in Atlanta, while most of all if he wasn't flying to see Rachel, James waited for Christmas or summers when Rachel would fly to Iowa to stay with him for longer stretches of time, or he flew her to see him for weekends whenever it was possible. Indeed, in his essay *Junior and John Doe*, James writes of

125

how withdrawn he'd become during this period, relating that he lived in "a condition of internal exile" because he didn't want to conform to a white model of identity, a behavior he asserted many black Americans were participating in at that time.

During the fall of 1988, though, when James went on leave, he still wanted me to stop by, so sometimes I did, but during the spring of that second year, I visited more, and midway through the semester, he said one thing that would forever affect our friendship. He related to me how his mother had often told him when he was a child, "James, go find your sister and bring her home." That was, he explained, how he learned to be a rescuer, or it brought out the unavoidable characteristic of his possessing a rescuer's personality.

I told him that I was a rescuer because of my own psychological inclinations, but then I said, "What happens in that rare instance when the rescuer needs something, and there's no one there to help because everyone else is too needy?"

"That can be awful."

"I'll always try to help if you need something," I said.

"Thank you," James said.

One afternoon that spring I drove to 711 Rundell and found bulging padded mailing envelopes stacked waist-high on the front steps, and when I rang the doorbell James appeared and I asked what was in the envelopes. "Manuscripts, for judging for an award," he said.

"Do you have to read all of them?"

"It's important to look out for other minority writers."

I had often noticed that there were piles of paper on the round wooden table in the dining room adjacent to the kitchen; James was always working there, writing recommendation letters, or someone was always asking him to read a manuscript or soliciting a blurb from him, and he told me that he didn't ever write blurbs anymore, that he had only written them for a few writers. The requests appeared to me like a constant onslaught, so I said, "I don't ever want to be part of this drain on you. After I graduate, I'm not going to send you manuscripts or ask you for letters all the time. I don't want that to be part of our friendship."

"That's kind of you, but when you publish your first book, I want to give you a blurb."

"You don't have to," I said.

That last spring, we started calling each other "Old Negro" and "Yellow Peril." James was riffing, acknowledging how Ralph Ellison celebrated "the negro idiom" in his work. In turn, I was adding America's World War II derogatory perception of the Japanese to the mix; despite how I was Chinese, specificity didn't matter.

I left Iowa City in 1989, moving back to upstate New York, but our friendship continued; one summer when James happened to stay at Yaddo in Saratoga, I brought him to my parents' house in Albany. My father cooked a traditional Cantonese meal, serving lobster Cantonese, simmered chicken, steamed sea bass with black bean sauce, Chinese broccoli, and several other dishes. James enjoyed the food and felt so relaxed that he told my parents he would always think of their house as one of his safe houses, like on the Underground Railroad.

I had moved back to New York to teach high school and hadn't published the novel I'd written at Iowa. This failure had nothing to do with James but was because of my youth and my not knowing nearly enough about plot. We wrote letters or sometimes spoke briefly over the telephone, and in 1994, to be able to find more time for writing, I embarked on earning a PhD at the University of Houston. Each year for the next decade, I drove through Iowa City on my way back from Texas to New York, and staying with old friends, I would visit with James for several days. He didn't care if I'd published or not. He joked more with me, speaking once of wanting to write a story with a white rapist and the character's name would be Forced Bussing, referring to back when public schools in Savannah had been integrated. I told him about my watching a Japanese restaurant chef at a cooking table being pestered by an irate white customer about the Japanese in World War II, and James said, "The cook in every Asian restaurant should put up a sign: 'Don't fuck with the chef, or we'll fuck with the food!'" One year, commenting on the decadence of the nation he remarked how everyone was telling him he should smell the roses, but he told them all he'd planted yellow tulips throughout his yard. Another time at a Japanese restaurant, a young white waiter with a crew cut stared at us rudely for far too long, as if trying to determine who James and I were or what our relationship could possibly be. "He's my father," I finally said, "and you're taking away my chance for an education." James and I laughed at how I was boldly implying that the waiter was undermining some Asian kid's opportunity to be working there and saving money for college tuition, but the waiter couldn't comprehend the subtext of my words. Upon being inducted into the American Academy of Arts and Sciences in 1995, playing on the stereotype of the predatory African American male, James said, "I've been teaching since 1981, and the Dean asked me what

I wanted. I was tempted to say nineteen white women or time off. You know I'd get the time off that way, right?"

Our visits weren't always silly or foolish, though. The level of our intellectual discourse heightened, as if we were part of a barometric experiment measuring the limits of mentoring possibilities. Speaking about the form of the novel, James related how people flock to what is fashionable, which he always equivocated with the loss of self. James spoke of Melville and his view of Black slaves, and how the status of the Black American is always the measuring stick of American democracy, but always at the lowest possible end, so I spoke of the myth of Asian Americans always being the model minority. At another instance, discussing *Bartleby the Scrivener* and *Benito Cereno* and *Billy Budd*, I spoke of how Billy Budd's trial reflects the lack of the law's ability to speak to all of humanity's complexity, while literature is more able, and James seemed moved as if recalling the choices he'd made for his life's work, deciding to become a writer and professor instead of practicing law. I would later learn that James' first fiction-writing teacher in Boston when he attended Harvard Law School had been the novelist Alan Lebowitz, who had also written A *Progress into Silence: A Study of Melville's Heroes*, which had deeply contributed to James' enthusiasm for Melville. We spoke on another occasion of how the Western world believes in causality and technology while other sides of the world have true faith in more "mystic" forces, and one evening we riffed off Miguel de Unamuno, discussing our perceptions about what various cultures or religions strived to live for to meet death, James comparing American, Muslim, Egyptian, Buddhist, Greek, and Japanese viewpoints, while I added the Chinese, Jewish, and British perspectives.

I should add that during those years, James was moving beyond Ralph Ellison's earlier teachings. James had met Ralph while interviewing him for a cover story for the *Atlantic Monthly, Indivisible Man*, that ran in 1970, and in doing so he'd become enamored of Ellison's opinion that the United States was already miscegenated, or that Black culture was already part of the center of American life. This thinking sounds very passé now, but it seemed like a revelation in the '50s and '60s. Beginning in the 1980s, though, James' reading and his initial travels to Japan and elsewhere led him to incorporate sources from innumerable cultures into his frames of reference; Ellison had spoken of American literature being built off Black folklore while James had gone global, seeking other sources for American literature. In particular, he demonstrated this by writing his memoir, *Crabcakes*, that was published in 1998 and

128

partly set in Japan. Another way of saying this is that Ellison's thinking was primarily invested in considering the binary of black and white cultural influences upon America, and arguing for the recognition of those black influences was crucial when Ellison asserted the idea. But James had become more interested in chronicling the possibilities of how he or anyone, as an American citizen, could nurture one's self-improvement as a human being by absorbing the better aspects of Eastern cultures and philosophies. This global leaning could also be seen in some of the essays in his collection, *A Region Not Home*, published in 2000. Indeed, when James spoke of traveling to Japan he always sounded happy—he told me that he was very lonely during his initial trips, but he liked how politely he was treated there, and how peaceful it was living without racism, as if his stays in Japan were like James Baldwin's expatriate years in Paris. In later photographs from Japan, James does appear like a different man, a man at ease.

Aside from the heightening of our dialogue, James asked for my help or advice. Once, he asked me to go with him to a meeting with a financial advisor who was a white man. After the appointment, James said, "Do you think I can trust him?" I told James I thought he could. On one particular evening, James startled me by asking if he could read a short story he'd finished, so I sat with him at his round wooden table and listened to an unpublished story with an untypical scenario for an African American character like some of the stories in *Elbow Room*. As much as I laughed at the story's humor and appreciated its insight, I also realized that James simply wanted someone to hear his work without any fanfare. On another evening, he shared an essay about neighboring titled "The Done Thing" that emphasized the need for receptiveness and "openness to new people," calling for civility and community and the "revitalization of our country's spiritual life." He asked if I thought the essay ended succinctly enough. I affirmed that it did. In 1995, he shared with me that he'd become involved with a woman I knew, Jeanette Miyamoto, and she'd given birth to a child the year before, so now James had a son, Benjamin. James had decided not to raise Benjamin with Jeanette, though, remaining a bachelor in Iowa City; he thought it had been difficult to be a good enough father to his daughter, Rachel, so he didn't believe he could be as focused intellectually if he wasn't alone. His identity as an intellectual was what he most believed he could depend on; it had become an ingrained way of being. Still, when he asked for my opinion I told him he should avoid anything he might regret. He stayed on his own, though.

Driving up to Iowa City in 1996, I found James forlorn, smoking cigarettes, and drinking J&B scotch. When I asked what was wrong he told me that doctors had found two growths in his throat and something at the entrance to his lungs. He feared cancer but didn't want anyone to know and asked me to take him to and from Mercy Hospital. I did. After undergoing biopsies during the morning, he called Alan Lebowitz that night and told him about what was occurring and then put me on the phone with Alan, who asked what I recommended. "Places of rest," I said.

After I exchanged telephone numbers with Alan and finished talking with him, James said, "Alan is my best friend."

I felt glad knowing he had a best friend, and fortunately within days the results of the biopsies deemed the tumors and growth to be benign. During a subsequent visit, James asked if I would help him to buy new shoes because his feet were hurting. I drove him to a shoe store, and he told me that he wanted to find a pair of sandals. What was unspoken was the ever-present possibility of rude treatment from a salesperson due to the very dark hue of James' skin. The clerk who waited on us turned out to be a blue-eyed, red-haired white woman with high freckled cheekbones, and she waited on James with patience and bountiful courtesy, so he purchased a pair of Birkenstocks. He commented about how comfortable the sandals were, and how much better his feet already felt. Assessing his old shoes I observed that the heels were badly worn down, with the severe slant of overpronation. "How can you read so many books and take such good care of your mind," I said, "but not think at all about your feet?"

We both knew the answer—that the life of the mind has its stringent demands, and that it can be all encompassing—and he knew I knew what his answer would be, so he didn't have to say anything. I shook my head in sympathy, and we both smiled.

In November 1998, James suffered from a case of viral meningitis; his colleague, the poet Jim Galvin, found him unconscious on the floor at 711 Rundell. James remained in a coma at Mercy Hospital for eleven days, and I felt stunned, having just visited him in October. When we spoke on the telephone during his recovery I felt on a deeper level than knowing from a daily sense that if anything ever happened to him my life would not be the same. A visit that spring confirmed for me that James would recover from the meningitis, but I still worried about him. The continuing onslaught of work, his smoking, the occasional hard drinking, his remaining single. What if the rescuer needs rescuing?

James writes in his essay *Gravitas* about how Aristotle distinguished between friendships: "For Aristotle, the best of all grounds for friendship was what he termed 'perfected friendship.' This degree of friendship is attained when one person wants for the other what is good for him simply because it is good for him. He believed that only people with comparable virtues could sustain this kind of friendship."

I wondered if ours could be such a friendship.

In February 1999, I flew from Houston to Chicago, but the flight was late so my plane didn't land until 8:00 p.m. I was supposed to visit James and called to tell him I wouldn't be arriving in Iowa for another four hours. Still, he said, "It's all right. Call when you get here. Even if it's late, I want to see you." I telephoned after midnight, thinking I'd see him late in the morning, but he said, "Come on up."

There are eleven steps from the sidewalk on Rundell St. to the front door at Little Monticello. James welcomed me into the house and we drank and talked, and then I went to stay elsewhere. As we continued to visit throughout the weekend, we kept drinking and talking; James told me he was writing and doing research for a novel about John Bingham and the Fourteenth Amendment. He spoke of how Albert Murray and Stanley Crouch had been feuding, so he was trying to play peacemaker. He told me about interviewing Richard Pryor for a *New York Times* article and his perhaps helping Pryor to invent the character Mudbone. On Saturday evening when I walked in, James was preparing lobster, and as we ate he told me he was happy to have received a valentine from Rachel, and that he regretted not being in her life more.

One weekend that year, James revealed that he was suffering from sleep apnea, and he was coughing badly, and his eyes were very red. We spoke of his not marrying Jeanette and not raising Benjamin, and he wondered aloud if he'd made the wrong decision. By this time, James owned over three thousand movies; it was as if he couldn't stop buying DVDs, and he needed to rent storage units for all his papers, books, and old VHS tapes so there would be enough space for Rachel to stay when she flew each year to spend Christmas or summers with him. I debated within myself if I could live a similar life of the mind, without perpetual companionship, as rewarding as solitude could sometimes be.

In 2000, the same year James published his essay collection, *A Region Not Home*, a woman whom I'd dated in the fall of 1988 when I studied at Iowa telephoned me in Houston. She'd been a single parent when we dated, but our relationship had abruptly ended when she left me for someone else. Now she told me that her daughter Ashley, who had recently turned thirteen, had never forgotten me, and she wanted to know if I would consider acting as Ashley's father. Since I was single and believed I might not ever marry, I flew to Iowa and surmised that Ashley wasn't going to be a rebellious teenager. I thought she deserved to have a father, so I consented to her mother's request. This meant that I'd be traveling to Iowa more, and I'd see James more frequently.

As if being over fifty caused James to feel the need to impart more significant lessons, he began to share more about his history with me. One weekend, he said that he'd spent most of his money from a Guggenheim award going back and forth from Iowa City to Chicago in 1972 to research articles about The Blackstone Rangers and The Contract Buyers League that would be published by the *Atlantic Monthly*. This was when he was completing his MFA at the Workshop in only a year and a half. He related how, after publishing with the *Atlantic Monthly*, he soon became a contributing editor there, but then they published an article by R. J. Herrnstein asserting heredity was substantially more important than environment in determining Black intelligence. When James objected to the piece, an editor asked him to lunch and offered him membership in a club to buy him off, but James refused and then resigned. During another trip, he told me about his dating an African American lawyer named Maxine Thomas who was intelligent and had won beauty pageants, but her taste seemed too materialistic to him, so he stopped seeing her. At another point, he told me that when *Crabcakes* was being submitted for publication two publishers had asked him to edit out his writing about what Americans could learn from Asians, but he'd refused to allow the editors to cut his work, saying that he wouldn't "sell his soul."

In 2004, I left Houston with my girlfriend, Renee Dodd, to accept a tenure track position in creative writing at Georgia College in Milledgeville, an hour and forty-five minutes from where Renee had grown up in Atlanta. Her parents still lived in Atlanta, and I wondered if the move would affect my visits to Iowa City, but I kept driving or flying to Iowa. Renee and I married in 2005, and in 2006 Ashley transferred from the University of Northern Iowa to the University of Iowa, so now each time I saw Ashley I saw James.

If I found him drinking, I told him I wouldn't let him drink alone. We always went to eat at the Hamburg Inn; he'd frequented the place forever, and more than once because Iowa City was changing, becoming built up with condominiums and more retail spaces, he called the Hamburg Inn "the last real place in Iowa City." He let me know about

132

his having type 2 diabetes, the disease hindering his feet, and that January in 2007 he walked gingerly across the snow and ice, taking his time ascending the eleven steps. He hadn't quit smoking cigarettes and informed me at another point that there'd been a house fire from his putting ashes into a cardboard box and leaving them there and going out. "You won't receive any time off for that," I said, and we laughed.

In 2008, James expressed the concern that Obama would be assassinated because the first Black president represented the fear that all African Americans shared when they stepped up and stood out. James also worried that Obama would be beaten down by America's corporate culture. Observing how partisan the nation was becoming, James spoke of Pompey's line in Roman history as a parallel for being defeated by racism, because this was where Caesar had routed Pompey's cavalry, and then Pompey had lost the will to fight, watching both his cavalry and legions break formation and retreat from battle. On another weekend, James let on that he was having some financial difficulties, saying he'd signed another five-year teaching contract, and I would later learn that like someone far more elderly and vulnerable, he'd been spending too much money on subscription mailing offers, and he'd fallen prey to a few telephone scams.

In late May of 2009, I brought my wife to Iowa City to meet James, and when we shared the news that she was pregnant he congratulated us. He shuffled around, still healing from foot surgery because a doctor had actually found a nail in one of his feet, and James said he could probably start calling himself Jesus now, provoking laughter. We were also glad because Ashley was graduating that weekend, and I knew James had been happy about how Rachel had received her degree the year before from Tufts University.

The mood felt easier; I hoped the future might be kind to James, my wife, and me. In December 2009, though, my wife gave birth to our daughter, Willa, who suffered from all kinds of allergies and was prone to sickness. Since I wanted to be at home as much as possible to help raise her, I wasn't able to visit with James in 2010 or 2011.

In February of 2012, I received an urgent message from Rachel. James had undergone surgery for two benign polyps in his colon, but the anesthesia had affected his short-term memory, leaving him with a noticeable degree of dementia. I booked a plane ticket to fly to Iowa in March.

Since his short-term memory kept failing him, James couldn't live on his own anymore; he was in a nursing home not far from 711 Rundell called Legacy Gardens. When I walked into his room, I simply felt glad to see him, and when he told me that he knew who I was and remembered the sound of my voice, I said, "Do you know my name?"

"Allen Gee," he said. But what soon became evident was that he couldn't recall any of our visits over the past twenty-five years. Not one of them. I felt stunned—it was as if some of the most meaningful inner workings of my being had suddenly been extracted—but I was still whole and knew that any kind of diminished capacity had to be far worse for James. I would later learn that at first he hadn't recognized Rachel or Benjamin, and when he realized how his memory loss would prevent him from teaching or writing anymore, he wept profusely. He was only sixty-eight years old. I would later discover that not long before the operation for the polyps, a neurologist had diagnosed him as having the worst case of cerebral atrophy caused by alcoholism that the doctor had ever seen. So it had been amazing, like some kind of Herculean mental feat, that James had been able to teach fiction-writing workshops and literary seminars for the past several years.

On my second day in Iowa City that March, Deb West went with me to see James. She'd been working as a secretary in the Workshop offices since 1988, which had been my second year at Iowa as a student. James spoke so easily with us that he almost didn't seem impaired; he lamented with humor that he wasn't drinking anymore and talked with us about Obama and Mitt Romney and the need for something far more humanistic and transcendent in the world. He and Deb each spoke of missing Frank Conroy, who'd passed away from cancer in 2005, and then James, Deb, and I remarked with gratefulness about how long we'd known each other. I told James about his having mentored me and shared some stories from our past, and he told me he thought he remembered some of our friendship.

The next day, when I took James to a Chinese restaurant for dinner, he ordered shrimp with lobster sauce, saying he liked having space and not being hurried. He was able to get in and out of my rental car without requiring much help, and I was encouraged by how well he walked on his own. We stopped that evening at the house at 711 Rundell and sat in the living room like we used to and talked about politics, writing, and our daughters. James said he liked being there and hearing the sound of the clock ticking. As much as our talking felt the same, he asked me four or five times, "Where are you teaching now?" and "How long are you staying for?" His short-term memory failure made it abundantly clear that he couldn't live in the house alone anymore, but I didn't want to imagine the house without him.

The following day, we went to lunch at the Village Inn and ate salad and fish, and had fruit for dessert. James spoke again of the pleasure of being able to take his time. I asked if he knew who Jackie Robinson was, and he said, "The first major league black baseball player." I asked if he could distinguish between Martin Luther King and Malcolm X, and he said, "X was a nationalist, and that's never good." I smiled, and we talked about Trayvon Martin, and James even remembered the source for a line from his story "On Trains" in *Hue and Cry*. I thought there was a slight chance he might regain some of his short-term memory, and more of his long-term memory.

But when I saw James again in July, he told me he was brooding about his fate, about what had happened to his short-term memory, which hadn't improved, and only some of his long-term memories had returned, so between our going out for meals to escape the monotony of nursing-home dining, as if in the throes of depression, he slept a lot.

I resolved to see James as much as possible, so during the next three years I flew or drove to Iowa in the fall, winter, spring, and summer. Rachel was living in Barcelona, where she supported herself by teaching English, having become more of a citizen of the world in practice than James had been able to during his lifetime. This gave him a great deal of ideological satisfaction; he told me that he didn't want her to stay in Iowa City to take care of him, not by any means, wanting most of all for her to live her own life, and if she wasn't he'd view himself as a burden.

I didn't always sign in at Legacy Gardens but noticed who some of James' other visitors were: David Hamilton; Jason Chen; Eileen Pollock; Phil Jones; Jeanette Miyamoto; Fred Woodard; Mary McPherson; Marian Clark; and Horace Porter. I heard from some people that they didn't want to intrude or see James in a nursing home, but I thought they were missing out because after his first year at Legacy, James rallied. He told me that he was done brooding and had made up his mind to make the best of what he had, rather than being resentful.

Thereafter, from 2013 to 2015, we developed new rituals. In the fall, I visited and cooked meals for him or bought barbecued ribs and chicken from Jimmy's Rib Shack so we could eat at 711 Rundell. Despite the darkness and unforgiving cold of Iowa winters, I flew up during January or February because I knew visits at that time of year were necessary, and instead of asking James to negotiate the icy eleven steps in front of his house, I drove him for lunch to the Bluebird Diner or the Hamburg Inn. Or we ate like middle-class princes, splurging on shrimp and lobster tails for dinner at Red Lobster. "Do you know how many seafood meals you cooked for me over the years?" I asked James once.

"I have no idea."

"There were a lot," I said with gratitude.

For my late spring visits, we went out to eat or I took James for drives through the Iowa countryside so he could see the greenery of the grass and the rising cornfields. And in 2014 and 2015, I drove up for Fourth of July weekend to bring him to the Iowa City Jazz Festival. The first summer, we caught the Trinidadian trumpeter Etienne Charles, who spoke meaningfully about July 4th, remarking upon the colonization of America by Columbus. James nodded in approbation. He told me he'd never been to such a large outdoor public gathering during all his years in Iowa City, and he couldn't recall the last time he'd heard live music. The next summer, we saw the twenty-piece big band, Colossus; James liked their traditional sound and appreciated how they swung. (He always said he liked the old-school jazz musicians the best, like John Coltrane, Miles Davis, Pharaoh Sanders, Sonny Rollins, and Charlie Parker.)

When I had to say goodbye to James at the end of our visits, I began saying, "I'll take my leave of you now," mocking formality, acknowledging both of our families' working-class roots.

And during this last two-year stretch of visits, James told me yet more about his history, of how when he was growing up in segregated Savannah, his father had been sent to prison and was put on a chain gang, so at school James had been asked if he was still "on the dole" by those who gave out free lunch cards, making him feel ashamed and determined to want better for himself. He recounted how Miss Alba, a manager at the M&M Supermarket where he worked bagging potatoes, had taught him about country music. He shared the story of how his own teacher at Morris Brown hadn't sent in his story for the *Reader's Digest* contest one year, so James had enrolled in a drama course at Spellman the following year, and the teacher there had entered the story, and James won. He told me about having a Black Muslim culture nationalist roommate named Hiawatha Brown at Harvard Law School, and that Hiawatha had loathed him for having all kinds of friends.

I should include, briefly digressing, that during James' second year at Legacy in 2013, an editor offered a contract for a collection of my essays. When I told James about this he asked for a copy of the book. He read some of the essays on his own or had his health care worker, Joanne Stutzman, read others aloud, and in January 2014, as if remembering what he'd told me years before, he dictated a blurb. He was fully aware of what he was doing, because he'd refused several more recent Workshop students who'd sent manuscripts by mail and asked for blurbs in accompanying letters. I felt moved; it was almost no different from when he'd been my mentor over two decades before. I thanked him and then expressed my regret that I hadn't published earlier as did some of his more famous students, like ZZ Packer, Yiyun Li, Gish Jen, or Edward P. Jones.

"It's all right," James said. "It doesn't matter," as if he'd already formulated his answer and was simply retrieving it from someplace, as if like a mentor of impeccable awareness he'd anticipated my inevitable sense of inadequacy long ago.

We joked more while James stayed at Legacy. He said that we needed to form the Chinese Obscenity League so that Asians could start saying *motherfucker* like African Americans and be more politically forceful. He recalled his old phone voice message at 711 Rundell, which had announced, "Master Jefferson isn't here right now. He's down by the cabins, making contradictions." He said that the imaginary rap group he'd formed in the 1990s, The Ugly Motherfuckers, was making a comeback. He told me about how people kept bringing him crabcakes after *Crabcakes* was published, and I said, "You need to write a book called *Lobster Tails*." We laughed again one morning when the nurses asked if I was James' Asian son, and he said to me, "For that you need to get a summer tan, and a lot more color."

Regardless of how James' short-term memory faltered, causing him to ask me four or five times during a single visit if I was married, or if I had flown or driven up to see him, he still surprised me. His intelligence remained on a far different plane. Speaking to me once about dialogue, he said, "These days there can be a character in a story speaking with all types of high and low dialects, the current day Omni-American, and this character will be all idiom, differing from the characters in *Elbow Room* who are composites of cultural elements." At another point he spoke of the Back-to-Africa movement as the predecessor for the Mexican self-deportation policy advocated for by Mitt Romney and the Republicans. Once, he said, "Whites holding onto power now value exclusivity (the melting pot) more than the transcendence that Omni-Americanism (a future with multiracial citizens) offers." He added, speaking about the political primaries, "It's a shame that whites often value muscular behavior, while today's mixed-race children are signs of the transcendence of true American ideals." At another time, he spoke

137

of transcendence versus ideology, the latter being fixed, without the possibility of evolution, and he said, "The ending of a story should be a temporary moment that evokes the human condition and suggests the future or transcendence." And commenting on his own history of intellectual solitude, he said, "Writing is really between you and your conscience, so it's best to be private and keep to oneself." Once, I asked if he remembered the five books he'd written, and he couldn't name them, so I listed the titles, and he said, as if to leave me with encouragement for my own writing life, "More, more, more."

Rachel had moved back to Iowa City in 2015, to take care of James and be with him; in January 2016, I learned from her that he'd fallen and broken his pelvis and right ankle. He'd been moved from Legacy Gardens to Iowa City Rehab for physical therapy and hadn't had a cigarette for over a month, because he'd also been at Mercy Hospital in late November and had recovered from a slight case of pneumonia there. When I flew up that January and saw him, I said, "It's me, the Yellow Peril," and asked him who I was. He smiled, and said he knew. I showed him Richard Pryor videos on my iPhone, brought him seafood, and we ate together. Since I could only visit for two days, the visit felt far too brief, but I noticed he was quieter, yet as calm and gentle as always, and I thought of how in spite of a lifetime of racial slights, he'd been steadfast over many decades, and in this way, heroic, always calling for more benevolent communities and compassion in his writing.

That March, I returned, and we sat on a Thursday evening and talked quietly about revolution versus evolution—James didn't think Bernie Sanders' proposition of revolution was attainable because there hadn't been a successful whole-scale revolution involving the entire citizenry since the country had been founded. That Friday, I took James to lunch at the Hamburg Inn for what would be the last time; we met David Hamilton, who had been the editor of *The Iowa Review*. James and David spoke of their retirements and how Iowa City had become their home; they joked, why move South since global warming had left the Midwest winters far milder? I thought James seemed slower, perhaps from not smoking and not being spurred on anymore by nicotine, and I needed to lift him up to help get him into and out of my rental car. The next day, I didn't risk a trip out with him and brought food from Jimmy's Rib Shack. We polished off a half-slab of ribs, coleslaw, beans, cornbread, and a smoked chicken sandwich, the food tasting so good that James spoke of not needing to go to St. Louis, South Carolina, or Texas. At 3:00 p.m. that afternoon, I had to leave to catch a 5:12 p.m.

flight out of Cedar Rapids. "I'll take my leave of you now," I said, still mocking formality, not wanting to acknowledge that we might not see each other again.

I couldn't drive up to Iowa that July 4th because of a vacation with my wife's family. In late July, I learned that James had been admitted to Mercy Hospital for fluid on his lungs—it was pneumonia again—but this time Rachel messaged that I should fly out as soon as I could. When I arrived that Friday the 22nd, James was in intensive care and had been placed on a ventilator. After entering the room, I grasped his hand. The expression of recognition in his eyes told me that he knew who I was, and that day, numerous visitors made their way to the hospital to see him and support Rachel. She told me I should stay and rent a room in the hospital's third-floor family lodging section; if anyone asked, I could claim to be James' brother-in-law. Despite being tired I didn't sleep much that Friday night, and on Saturday James improved enough to be taken off the ventilator. He received more visitors but slept for most of the morning and slept so soundly that afternoon that the nephrologist couldn't wake him, and then James slept through the early evening. Rachel went out for a late dinner with some friends and one of James' other former students, Marcus Burke, and by that time the hospital had fallen quiet. There weren't any other visitors, so from 9:00 p.m. to 11:00 p.m. I found myself sitting alone with James, and he was wide awake.

Thinking back, I went old school and read from a copy of Albert Murray's novel, *Train Whistle Guitar* that Rachel had brought to the room. Then I read from a copy of Ralph Ellison's *Invisible Man* that I had packed in my travel bag. James made "Ah" sounds of approval when I read certain passages, and I said, "Do you remember that you wrote all about Ralph?"

James couldn't speak more than one- or two-word sentences, but with a glint in his eye, he said, "Yes."

"Do you want me to keep talking?"

"Yes."

So I played an album by the Pharaoh Sanders quartet on the CD player Rachel had set up, and I pulled a chair closer and told James the story of his life: how he'd grown up in segregated Savannah but had read books at the Carnegie Library and had managed to attend a private Catholic school, and how his father had been one of the first Black master electricians. I recounted how James had gone to Morris Brown because of the help of his Uncle Thomas, who was chaplain there, and next was Harvard Law School and taking summer fiction classes with

139

Alan Lebowitz, and I asked James if he liked hearing this. "Yes, a lot!" he said. So I told him about how he'd befriended Edward Weeks at the *Atlantic Monthly,* earned his MFA at Iowa and then left a teaching job and a bitter divorce in Virginia like an escape artist, returning to Iowa to try and restore himself, and I said he'd done everything possible to be a good father to Rachel and had lived a generous life sharing his intellect with countless students. Then I told him there had been a lot of happiness in his life, and Ralph would have approved of what he'd accomplished, and I promised to take care of Rachel for him and said that I would make sure to tell Benjamin about who he was.

The next day on Sunday afternoon, James was moved to the heart section on the fifth floor but couldn't cough, which was a side effect from his dementia, so his lungs were filling with more fluid. He spoke briefly with his brother and sister by telephone. He began to fade and become less responsive, and on Monday as his condition worsened Rachel decided to move him to Hospice Care on the north side of the fifth floor, to a serene room with an expansive view of the leafy green Iowa tree branches swaying in the wind. She'd remained a fount of strength: she'd been tending to him for over a week, dancing for him, playing his favorite music, reading to him, talking to him, and holding him, showing him how much he was loved. James was soon sedated with Ativan and morphine so he wouldn't suffer or be in pain. Writers and former students and friends and relatives from across the country began sending tribute messages via a hospital email delivery system, and several of us took turns reading these heartfelt messages to James. I extended my stay but had to leave Iowa City that Tuesday afternoon to catch a flight out of Moline to return to work. When I left, I told James that I would miss him, and I said, "I'll take my leave of you now," but this time I was in tears, meaning what I was saying, and as I departed from the room, my life was already not the same.

That same day, Marcus Burke texted me that he'd picked up Benjamin at the Cedar Rapids airport, and then Rachel and Benjamin and several of James' former students and some of James' old friends and neighbors, including Fred Woodard, gathered and drank bourbon and kept James company late into the night. I was back at my office the next day at Georgia College when my cell phone rang; it was ZZ Packer, and she'd been at McDowell, the artists' colony, so she hadn't received the message I'd sent her a few days before, telling her how serious James' condition had become. I texted Joanne Stutzman, James' health care worker, who was in the Hospice Care room, telling her that ZZ was family, so she should be put through when she called Joanne's number. I felt as if I was nurturing the communal spirit that James had spent so much of his life writing about and asking others to cultivate, and I soon learned that ZZ was able to speak to James and had told him what he'd meant to her, and not long after, at approximately 1:00 p.m., James took his last breath with Rachel and Benjamin by his side. Rachel would later tell me that at that exact moment, she felt a pure warmth pass through her heart.

Grief resides within me like it might never fade, but I have been thinking lately about how James wrote that Ralph Ellison passed along Aristotle's model of perfected friendship to another generation: to John Callahan, Michael Harper, Stanley Crouch, Horace Porter, Charles Johnson, and to James.

I would like to believe that James was well aware of his passing on this same distinct type of friendship to me, and that, to honor the knowledge I inherited from him, I should be so fortunate now as to be able to pass it on, in the same generous fashion, to others.

Nominated by Dewitt Henry,
Melissa Pritchard,
Maura Stanton

AN ENDLESS STORY

by LOUISE GLÜCK

from THE THREEPENNY REVIEW

I.

Halfway through the sentence
she fell asleep. She had been telling
some sort of fable concerning
a young girl who wakens one morning
as a bird. So like life,
said the person next to me. I wonder,
he went on, do you suppose our friend here
plans to fly away when she wakens?
The room was very quiet.
We were both studying her; in fact,
everyone in the room was studying her.
To me, she seemed as before, though
her head was slumped on her chest; still,
her color was good—She seems to be breathing,
my neighbor said. Not only that, he went on,
we are all of us in this room breathing—
just how you want a story to end. And yet,
he added, we may never know
whether the story was intended to be
a cautionary tale or perhaps a love story,
since it has been interrupted. So we can not be certain
we have as yet experienced the end.
But who does, he said. Who does?

II.

We stayed like this a long time,
stranded, I thought to myself,
like ships paralyzed by bad weather.
My neighbor had withdrawn into himself.
Something, I felt, existed between us,
nothing so final as a baby,
but real nevertheless—
Meanwhile, no one spoke.
No one rushed to get help
or knelt beside the prone woman.
The sun was going down; long shadows of the elms
spread like dark lakes over the grass.
Finally my neighbor raised his head.
Clearly, he said, someone must finish this story
which was, I believe, to have been
a love story such as silly women tell, meaning
very long, filled with tangents and distractions
meant to disguise the fundamental
tedium of its simplicities. But as, he said,
we have changed riders, we may as well change
horses at the same time. Now that the tale is mine,
I prefer that it be a meditation on existence.
The room grew very still.
I know what you think, he said; we all despise
stories that seem dry and interminable, but mine
will be a true love story,
if by love we mean the way we loved when we were young,
as though there were no time at all.

III.

Soon night fell. Automatically
the lights came on.
On the floor, the woman moved.
Someone had covered her with a blanket
which she thrust aside.
Is it morning, she said. She had
propped herself up somehow so she could see
the door. There was a bird, she said.

Someone is supposed to kiss it.
Perhaps it has been kissed already, my neighbor said.
Oh no, she said. Once it is kissed
it becomes a human being. So it cannot fly;
it can only sit and stand and lie down.
And kiss, my neighbor waggishly added.
Not anymore, she said. There was just the one time
to break the spell that had frozen its heart.
That was a bad trade, she said,
the wings for the kiss.
She gazed at us, like a figure on top of a mountain
looking down, though we were the ones looking down,
in actual fact. Obviously my mind is not what it was, she said.
Most of my facts have disappeared, but certain
underlying principles have been in consequence
exposed with surprising clarity.
The Chinese were right, she said, to revere the old.
Look at us, she said. We are all of us in this room
still waiting to be transformed. This is why we search for love.
We search for it all our lives,
even after we find it.

Nominated by The Threepenny Review,
Elton Glaser

HI HO CHERRY-O

fiction by BECKY HAGENSTON

from WITNESS

I've just asked Wendell to access data pertaining to twentieth century board games when he says, "Tie me up and leave me in the closet for an hour."

"Excuse me?" I say. Wendell has been my research assistant for six months. He lives with my husband and me, has his own workspace in a corner of the dining room. He's a new brand of Service Robot my university recently acquired. He accesses other remote robots to help me retrieve data. He's bright red, about four feet tall, and has a head that looks like two old fashioned blow dryers put side-by-side. He has round green eyes that blink. Until now, he hasn't said anything more to me than, "Right away," or "You bet."

"Ha, ha," I say, because I'm guessing this is a joke. Not that I've ever heard him joke.

"There's twine in the kitchen drawer," Wendell says. He has an Australian accent, but I could have made him sound French or Irish, or like a small Cockney child. "Tie me up and leave me in the closet for an hour, and then I'll access that data."

"I can't do that," I tell him. "Seriously."

He doesn't say anything. I ask him again about his board game data and he still doesn't say anything. "Are you okay, Wendell?" I ask.

"There's twine in the kitchen drawer," Wendell repeats. "Tie me up and leave me in the closet for an hour, and then I'll access that data." He sounds so cheerful and sure of himself.

So I do it. I feel a little bit weird, but maybe it has something to do with his electrical system. I figure Wendell knows what's best for himself. I don't really know how these robots work. I'm more of a historian. When I take him out of the closet an hour later and untie him, he says, "I've sent that data to your workstation," and I say, "Thanks, Wendell."

When my husband gets home from work, I tell him about Wendell asking me to tie him up. He looks horrified. "You didn't, did you?"

"Of course not," I lie. "But—he's a robot. He—*it*—can't feel. It's just programmed that way." This is what I told myself as I wrapped the twine around his metal body and rolled him into the closet.

"You should get a replacement."

"But Wendell's already downloaded so much already. It's too much trouble to find someone new at this point."

My husband says, "Well, keep an eye on him. It could be some kind of malfunction."

"Oh, I will," I tell him.

* * *

The next day, Wendell rolls into my office and starts working right away. He's found commercials of children playing games called *Lite Brite* and *Shoots and Ladders* and *Hi Ho Cherry-O*. The children in these commercials are very white and dimpled and mostly wear stripes, and they shout a lot. They are very, very happy children. My research involves childhood in the twentieth century which, even though it wasn't that long ago, is difficult because so much was deleted or destroyed in fires and floods. I've done some interviews at old folks' homes. I've done some memory scans. What's confusing is that most of what Wendell is finding doesn't necessarily collaborate with the memory scans.

My husband works as counselor at a Home for the Disembodied, so he can commute remotely from the Virtual Station in our bedroom. We've talked about getting a larger apartment, but this works for now. He stays in the bedroom and I stay out here with Wendell, and then we have dinner together.

I thank Wendell for finding those commercials, but when I ask if he's found anything about something called Battleship (which came up in the memory scans), he says, "I believe I can find that information. But first, scrape me with a knife hard enough to leave a mark."

"I can't damage you," I tell him. "I won't get my deposit back."

"Then put your hands around my neck and squeeze as hard as you can."

He waits. I wait. I say, "Who programmed you?"

"I'm programmed to work for you," he says, in his cheerful Australian accent. "I am at your disposal. I am here to make your life easier and assist with your research. This can go much more quickly if you please do what I ask."

So I do. When he says, "You're not squeezing as hard as you can," I squeeze harder. He doesn't so much have a neck as a plastic cylinder but I feel it getting warmer as I squeeze and when he says, "Okay, that was great, you can stop now," I keep squeezing a little bit longer.

*　*　*

At dinner my husband starts to say something and then stops himself. I know this is because his other family came to visit him at the Home for the Disembodied. He has a wife who's an actress and triplet sons, aged seven. They're always aged seven, which he says he finds somewhat frustrating—how there's only so much you can do with them, how you can never hope they'll turn out to be more than they are. But then he has the opposite problem with his actress-wife, whom he doesn't recognize from day to day. Finally I told him I was sick of hearing about his other family. Even though he explained that he was with them because he felt sorry for them, and that he and the actress wife hardly ever had sex anymore, we agreed not to speak of them.

"Well, what is it?" I ask at last. "Go ahead and tell me."

"I know you don't like to hear about them," he says, but I make a rollie-motion with my hand that is meant to convey get on with it. "The triplets and I shot some hoops is all," he says. "And they were good. And they got better as they played. It was something." He forks some pasta into his mouth. "I think I can maybe get them on a team," he says, with his mouth full and muffled. "Coach them."

"Huh," I say.

"How was your day?" he asks.

"It was the usual," I tell him.

*　*　*

My husband and I have talked about having children, either virtual or real. We have polite, reasonable conversations about how we should have sex again sometime but then we just crawl into bed and lie next to each other until we fall asleep. But maybe someday, when we're sixty, we might try for a child. Except the world is getting smaller. Most things disappear: cities, glaciers, mountains, civilizations. I don't want to raise children in a Home for the Disembodied. I want them here, in the flesh, but my husband says that's too dangerous, he doesn't have the stomach for it. I wonder if he would feel differently if we could produce dimpled, stripes-wearing children who roll dice and make cakes in plastic ovens and rejoice when their plastic cherries fill up their little buckets.

❅ ❅ ❅

The next morning, Wendell isn't at his work station. I drink my coffee, go through my documents and my video streams and the transcripts of the memory scans. Some of the memory scan interviewees end up in the Home for the Disembodied, but it's impossible to interview them there because all they want to talk about is tennis and sex, and most of them don't even remember their previous embodied lives.

Finally, I say, "Wendell?" and find him behind the laundry room door. He doesn't answer. "Are you not feeling well?" I ask. "Did you find anything about Battleship?"

He raises his blow-dryer head and says, "I'm not feeling motivated."

"Well," I say. "What would motivate you?"

"Tell me you hate me because I'm stupid. Tell me I should drown myself in a toxic lake."

"Well," I say. "But I don't hate you. I actually appreciate your help. You're a good worker."

He doesn't say anything. I go back to work reading the memory scans, but I can't find anything about Battleship, or about something called a Donny and Marie lunchbox, or about something called Free Parking that led to broken friendships among the interviewees. *I told Krista that you got five hundred bucks when you landed on Free Parking, and she said you didn't, and we never spoke again after that day.* It's so goddamn frustrating. Wendell has access to other Service Robots all over the world and all he has to do is ask them, and they'll tell him everything I want to know.

I go back to Wendell, who hasn't moved. "You're supposed to be programmed to help me," I say. "So help me!"

"But first, put a plastic bag over my head and secure it with a large rubber band that you can find in your desk."

So I do it. He looks helpless and ridiculous and terrifying. The plastic bag is white and makes him look like a robot ghost. He says, "Now tell me you hate me because I'm stupid and you want me to drown in a toxic lake."

"I hate you," I tell him, "you goddamn piece of shit, because you're stupid, and you should drown yourself in a toxic lake."

148

"Thanks!" he says cheerfully, and the printer starts whirring and my computer lights up with the sound of music and children laughing and singing.

He doesn't ask me to take the plastic bag off and so I just leave it there.

       ✿   ✿   ✿

When I told my dissertation director what I wanted to write about, she looked dismayed and said, "Oh, that's pretty bold of you." What she meant was: Who wants to be reminded of what we can't get back? What good will that do? She said, "I would like to caution you against it." Then she leaned back in her big chair and said, "What was your childhood like?"

That was a very personal question coming from her. I said, "I had the same childhood as everybody, with my screens and my worlds and all that." I didn't tell her that I was raised in an orphanage because my parents lived at the Home for the Disembodied. But they did their best. They taught me how to do puzzles and fly a virtual plane and how to do very complicated math, and they eventually deleted themselves when they said the world scared them too much.

"I'll sign off on this," she said, signing off on it. "But I think you'll find that whatever you're looking for isn't there."

"I'm not looking for anything," I told her.

"It won't add up," she said, and I said, "It doesn't have to," because I had no idea what she meant.

But now I'm starting to understand. She checked in with me last week to let me know that my dissertation was almost a month late, and if I ever wanted to finish and get on with my life I should submit it to the department. "Okay," I said.

It occurred to me for the first time that she and I never discussed what getting on with my life might mean.

       ✿   ✿   ✿

I call the university and ask if it might be possible to exchange Wendell for another Service Robot and they say are you kidding? Are you insane? That robot was programmed to make your life easier.

"Oh, great, thanks," I say.

This morning, Wendell isn't in his corner. He's not in the closet or the bathroom or behind the laundry room door, or in my office, so that means there's only one place left to look, and sure enough there he is in the bedroom. He's standing about a foot from my husband, who is sitting at his work station, the top half of his body swallowed by the VR unit. He's lost in his Disembodied world, counseling newbies, leading discussions, giving tennis lessons, coaching the triplets, and hardly ever having sex with his actress wife.

"I found some information about Battleship," Wendell says. He still has the bag on his head. I feel like everyone is underwater but me.

I'm rarely this close to my husband while he's at work. I know he can't hear or see me; he's in his world and I'm in this one. "I also found out about Rockem Sockem, and music that makes you dance and dance."

I want to know about these things.

Then he just stops talking.

"What do you need me to do?" I ask, but he doesn't answer. "You're a stupid piece of shit," I say, hopefully. "You're just a piece of metal with no soul. You're not real." Nothing. "I don't know what you want from me," I say.

I take a pair of metal nail clippers and scrape along the side of his body, leaving a long white mark. I'll lose my deposit, but to hell with it. I write IDIOT on him in permanent marker. This doesn't seem like enough. I pull the bag off his head and his glowing green eyes stare, blink. I slap him across his head. I slap him again. It's a game, I tell myself, like happy children used to play. Just figure out the rules.

He doesn't say anything.

I go into the kitchen and turn the kettle on. When it whistles, I carry it into the bedroom and pour boiling water over Wendell's head; steam rises all around us, and hot water soaks the carpet. From inside his VR unit, my husband lets out a long sigh.

Wendell says, "Battleship was a guessing game, thought to have its origins before World War I. It's a game of strategy. In 1967, Milton Bradley produced a plastic version. The game was played on grids. The goal was to sink your opponent's ship." And he flashes a commercial on the wall of the bedroom, two little boys sitting by a lake, one saying, "J1!" and the other saying, "You sank my battleship!" and falling backward into the water while the other boy laughs and laughs.

"I don't understand this," I say. I stomp my feet, and I wonder if my husband's world is shaking somewhere, if maybe one of the triplets missed making a basket. "And I still need to know about Free Parking. What the fuck is that?"

But Wendell goes quiet again, and after I slap him a few more times and knock him over and call him a piece of trash I know we're done for

150

the day, so I put him in the closet with the old computers and the vacuum cleaner. I take a deep breath. Something is happening, a feeling like when my parents taught me math problems and finally, finally, I could solve them.

At dinner, my husband compliments the pasta and asks me how my day was.

"It was great," I tell him, because I have realized this is true.

He says, "You seem like you're in a good mood!" and I say, "I am." My heart is beating so hard that I can hardly eat. I say, "Tell me about your day, honey."

He stares at me, fork suspended.

"Really," I say. "Honey, sweetheart, love." And I sit back while he tells me—first nervously, then with enthusiasm—about the triplets playing basketball, and about his wife's new red hair and how he's trying out for a play they're putting on at the Home for the Disembodied, so he might be home late some nights. "That's really, really great," I say, because I'm happy for him, and for me, making such progress, finally.

And later, when we get into bed, I crawl on top of him—how long has it been?—and press a gentle, gentle finger over his lips, his neck. "What?" he says, his eyes wide. My blood is rising, my fingers are tingling, my husband's pulse a sparrow beneath my hands. "Oh, no, I don't think so," he says and rolls over. "Is that okay?" he asks, his back hunched toward me.

"Of course," I tell him. "It's fine." I stare at the ceiling. My husband's breathing turns to snores. "It's fine," I say again. And what I'm thinking is that tomorrow I will ask Wendell more questions, knowing that all the answers will confuse and infuriate me. When he goes silent I will pound his head into the wall, hard enough to leave a dent; I will wrap him in plastic; freeze him in ice, burn him, call him terrible, terrible things—whatever it takes until he throws all his cherries in the air and tells me I've won.

Nominated by Witness,
Michael Kardos

THE ALMADRABA

fiction by MAIA JENKINS

from THE THREEPENNY REVIEW

Elena picks me up from Santa Justa and we set off for Chipiona. Her car is grey and battered. I'm not sure how she has acquired the ride and, like most things with Elena, it seems to invite more questions than it answers. The backseat is covered in crumbs so plentiful only a small child could have scattered them, and when I go to search for the aux cable in the glove compartment I find a sheaf of unopened envelopes, the first of which is addressed to a Jorge Sanchez-Rueda of Calle Lepanto.

Elena is quieter than usual. Her legs shake as she switches gears and when we hit the motorway she throws a look over her shoulder as if to check we aren't being followed.

"Can you get me some Advil?" she asks.

I go to her bag. Her phone is alight with messages from three numbers, the contents of which are hidden. Quickly, I find the pill pot, shake one out and hand it over.

"Two," she says.

After the painkillers have done their work Elena brightens. We pull into Chipiona before sunset.

"Whose place is this again?" I ask.

"A friend's," she says.

"What friend?"

"Just someone I know."

The building has an ugly façade. It takes Elena a few tries to jam the key round. Inside isn't much better—duff corduroy sofa, dead spider plant, spit-colored light spinning with spokes of low-hanging dust, walls as thin and pale as mild Kraft singles. *Where are we,* I want to ask? I place my backpack on the bunkbed's lower rung, pull through the closet—hangers, diapers, a stack of beach towels printed with Disney characters from decades past. Although there are signs of life in the apartment opposite—a lit lamp, a clothes-horse covered in swimwear—the town seems mostly empty. Swallows dip against the sky's pink panorama, rise against the lighthouse and the stout villas balanced like sugar lumps on the rim of the cliff. We can't see the ocean but that doesn't matter: the week stretches out before us like one long, borderless, sunlit corridor. From behind, Elena puts her hands around my waist and sighs into my hair.

I'd met Elena in Seville. I was twenty-one—Study Abroad—and had been taken under the wing of my host-mother's twin nephews, Alvaro and Javier. Identical in good looks and high achievement, the boys would take me to a bar twice a week, ply me with beer, and laugh at my bad Spanish. While I didn't exactly enjoy their company, I needed them.

At the time, the fact of my virginity hovered over me always. In my mind, sex had taken on an almost physical presence—not an act so much as a fascinating character to whom I had not yet been introduced. I thought of nothing else. Those afternoons in the bar, I'd look between the twins—acrylic black hair, pastel polos—and try to imagine having sex with them. For some reason I couldn't picture it.

"What does this word mean?" Alvaro asked, knocking his glass against mine. Foam spilled down my wrist. "*Salud,*" he said.

This, I knew. "Cheers."

They shook their heads, delighted to correct another mistake.

"Health," Javier said.

"Health," said Alvaro.

Head humming, heart too, I excused myself to use the bathroom. There was only one toilet and a small queue had formed by the door.

In line, a girl tapped my shoulder. I turned. She smiled and I smiled back. Her angular face and blunt, white-gold fringe gave her the look of a young Debbie Harry and in her nose was a silver wire, hardly perceptible apart from the glint it gave off in the low light.

"Heard you speaking English," she said. She had a supple American accent. "Elena." She extended her hand. After weeks of elaborate double-kisses of greeting, the small modesty of her gesture almost made me tearful.

"Megan," I said.

"Hey Megan," she whispered. "Do you have a tampon?"

"Sure," I said, handing her one from my bag.

"Life saver." She flicked her fringe out of her eyes. "I love you."

After I was done, I held the door open for Elena, raised my eyebrows at her in coy acknowledgement before returning to the table. A plate of yellow beans had been laid out. Javier thrust them at me. Vinegar lapped at the bowl's edge.

"*Chochos*," Alvaro said. "Try one."

Javier grinned, held up a bean, pressed hard so it split at the eye. "What does this look like?"

I stared at the bean's pale flesh. Alvaro flipped a beer bottle against his mouth.

"I don't know," I said.

"Look," Alvaro insisted, squeezing another bean in my face. "*Cho-cho.*"

I was starting to get annoyed. "I don't know."

"Come on!" said Javier.

"I really have no idea."

"Yes, you do!" Alvaro insisted.

"A pussy," said a voice from behind me. I looked round. Elena again. She cleared her throat. "They want you to say the bean looks like a pussy," she explained, placing a hand on the back of my chair. "*Chocho* is slang for vagina." She looked at Javier. "Is that right?"

"Yeah," Javier said. "That's right."

Alvaro licked his lips. "You want one?" he asked her.

"No," she said. An embarrassed laugh choked and died in Javier's throat. Alvaro stared at Elena, assessed her, taking in that combination of poise and grit I would come to love so much. Javier stood, darted two kisses at Elena's cheeks.

"*Encantado*," he said. "Please, join us."

With a look of amused distaste, Elena perched on the stool with her legs gripped around the barrel table.

"What do you do here in Seville?" Alvaro asked, leaning forward. "Study Abroad, also?"

Elena shook her head. "God bless you for thinking I'm young enough for Study Abroad."

Alvaro and Javier looked blank, disappointed. Her Spanish, unlike mine, was perfect. There were no errors for them to correct in what she said.

154

Elena went on. "I'm a teacher."

Alvaro narrowed his eyes. "You're American, though. Have you had many problems with your visa here in Spain?"

"I'm Colombian, actually," Elena frowned. "And no, I get by."

"*Colombiana!*" Alvaro slapped his knee. "And you're allowed to stay here?"

"Your school pays you enough for the work permit?" Javier asked.

Elena held up her hands.

"What *are* you two? Immigration officers?"

Javier and Alvaro laughed.

I ran my finger over my bottom lip. "Sorry," I said in English. "They're at law school. This is interesting to them."

"Forgive us," Alvaro said, pressing his glasses back into place, "if we seem rude."

"No, no," Elena cracked her back. "It'll give you something to ask your professors," she said. "I'm sure they'll know more about work permits than I do."

Her eyes were a brilliant, bird-like yellow. "Listen," she said to me. "Can I get your number?"

"Sure," I said. I had never known someone so forward. Back home, we fell into friendships, contact details moving along the town's small circuits but never asked for directly. Maybe this was how life would be from now on, I thought, typing my number into Elena's phone.

Our first night in Chipiona, Elena and I listen to pop music and laugh at the transatlantic gaps in our understandings.

"How can you not know who Robbie Williams is?" I ask.

She closes her eyes, holds up a hand. "I'm sorry: but 'Angels' is a Jessica Simpson song."

Elena is a good dancer. She wears a white dress, the brass buttons down the front giving her the look of a pageboy or some fairytale prince. Although the town below us is quiet, I imagine she could make a party with her body anywhere.

"Do you want to find a bar or anything?" I ask.

She swallows and smiles at me over her glass. "No," she says. "I don't."

A first-generation Colombian, Elena grew up in America. I'm not sure where. She mentions palm trees, houses on stilts, the hurricane insurance her mother complains about paying. She misses the jungles around Cali. Once, she'd had to outrun an alligator.

"Go in a zig-zag," she says, moving her hands in demonstration. "Flips them like roaches."

She talks about men a lot. In Elena's world, flings flare up and die over the course of days. I laugh at all her stories, unwilling to tell her I am a virgin. It isn't a purposeful lie, only a series of omissions. To create a convincing narrative, I steal funny stories from my friends back home— strange-looking cocks and men with breasts or bad breath—and feel a combination of delight and guilt when Elena laughs and launches into a story of her own.

"A woman's pain threshold can increase by forty percent during sex," she tells me one night. "My ex liked to smack me across the jaw as I was coming. Said it was like trying to take a stick off a dog."

With Elena, most things can be polished into jokes. She likes to laugh. "Enough of that," she says if conversations get too serious. We never talk about our fathers. In the fiber of her self-deprecation, I sense a point of some terrible loss. It's that intolerance for self-pity, the brittle joy I've only ever seen exhibited by people who have suffered, their optimism not so much an outlook on life as a mode of survival. Unlike me, I decide, Elena is tough.

No matter how drunk we get in Chipiona, Elena is always up before sunrise. Most mornings I wander to the kitchen groggy and parched to find her cooking the *tortilla con patatas* we will take to the beach later and eat in our laps. It is hot in the day and cold at night, and the beaches are deserted. The first day I fall asleep on my stomach, burn the backs of my legs. Every night thereafter Elena kneels behind me, tongue clicking as she applies aloe vera to the hot blisters.

"It'll turn into a tan," she says. I have never had a friend like her before.

"Can I tell you something?" I ask.

"Sure," she says. The gel is sticky on my skin.

"I'm a virgin," I say.

She pauses. Her fingers hover over my tailbone. "Really?"

"Yes," I say. "I can't stand it."

"Why did you lie?" she asks. I wonder if she's going to be angry.

"Embarrassed," I say.

"Nothing to be embarrassed about," she says, flicking the gel cap closed. "You have time to do whatever you want."

Later that night Elena is chopping tomatoes into a salad and stops, her face darty with fear.

"Oh god," she says. "I forgot you hate tomatoes. I'm such an idiot." She starts plucking red globs from the leaves. "I'm so sorry."

"Elena," I still her hand. "I love tomatoes."

She shakes her head, her expression resetting to confused irritation. "I was thinking of someone else," she says.

On our fourth day at the beach, she starts to tell me why she'd left Colombia, the wave of consecutive failures that swept her from home: first to America, later to Spain.

"My dad had an identical twin brother called Elio. Uncle Elio. They used to play this trick on me when I was a baby. I've seen the home videos: them passing me back and forth between them. Every time I turn I think I've been taken away from my real dad. I start screaming and reach out for him."

She places her beer can in the sand with a crunch. The air is rubied with red dust. "I guess they found it funny. Everyone laughed. It's pretty terrible if you think about it, though."

I nod, sip my drink, wonder what Javier and Alvaro are doing today.

"When my dad got sick it was weird. He was still young—like thirty-five. Uncle Elio became this avatar for what my father should have been. It was so spooky watching him take care of my dad, like watching the present tend to its future or something."

I know Elena is only revealing this secret because I have told her I am a virgin. Rather than reassurance, I feel an abrupt resentment towards the acquisitive nature of all relationships, how even at our most vulnerable we depend, somehow, on a willingness to make trades. It seems pathetic.

As she speaks, a square appears on the horizon, rocks on the sea's surf-crusted block of unmoving blue.

I point. "What's that?"

Elena doesn't sit up. Her sunglasses are enormous, star-shaped, hot pink plastic. The square grows to a rectangle. Ragged shapes become visible as it draws closer, edges serrated with what I now see are heads and shoulders and backs.

"It's a boat," I say, although "boat" is an inaccurate description for the weak, sunken dinghy approaching the shore. People spill over the yellow sides like an overrisen pie crust, whole torsos pressed out, grazing the waves—some in life jackets, others in muddied T-shirts or vests. Although there appears to be no driver, the boat thrusts at the beach with some purpose.

Elena pushes her glasses back into her hair. "Shit," she says. They are getting closer.

"What shall we do?" I ask.

"Nothing," she says, biting her lip. "Let them be."

Sooner than I expect, the dinghy hisses ashore. It comes to a stop a few feet from where we are lying—me on a Pocahontas beach towel, Elena on The Little Mermaid. In silence, the passengers leap into the sea. A mother lifts her child onto her shoulders, steadies him with one hand, scoops water out of her way with the other. Her heavy skirts billow out around her, slow her down. A few people hold plastic-wrapped belongings but mostly they are empty-handed and the younger men reach the shoreline first, rush away in all directions, scattering like the seeds of a blown dandelion. Elena breathes in. I draw my knees to my chest, unable to process what I am seeing. We are still. It is quiet. I don't know if they have noticed us. There is no one else on the beach but a man selling ice-cold shrimp from a polystyrene hamper. "*Dios,*" he says as the people reach the beach, run up the embankment and leap across the bluffs, into the ryegrass and away into the town. It doesn't take more than a few minutes for the whole boatload to disappear. Silence resettles. Deserted, the dinghy rocks in the shallows a moment before turning, as if operated by some ghost captain, and taking off in the direction from which it came. I don't know what to say.

"Be careful," Elena says. She is lying down. "Your skin is getting red again."

On the last night, we decide to go out for dinner. It is cold. We wear jackets over summer dresses. Using the lighthouse beam as a guide, we run along the seafront and wave to the men picking cockles from the tarry shingle below.

"Echo!" Elena shouts at the sea. Nothing comes back. "Shit, I guess no echo," she says, and we lean over the bars, laughing into the silence.

We go to Calle Larga, a quarter-mile strip that must, in summer, heave with tourists and bars and souvenir shops. There is only one restaurant open. We order the house special—*pescaito frito*—and sit at the bar until we are warm and drunk enough to move outside so Elena can smoke. Committed to using only coconut oil as sunscreen, she has acquired a rosy mask across the bridge of her nose.

"It's the only way," she says, inspecting her face in the back of a spoon.

"It'll turn into tan," I say. This is our constant refrain. The burn is worth it because it will turn into a tan.

"At his funeral, my grandmother got confused," Elena says suddenly. It takes me a moment to realize she is talking about her father. "She saw Uncle Elio in his black suit, thought it was my dad, and started yelling across the pit, tried to jump in after my dad's coffin. 'He's right here!' she says. 'Not to worry. Stop the funeral!'"

Elena laughs. I laugh too, although I don't find the story funny.

"Uncle Elio started coming to my bedroom," she says. "It was a few years after my dad died. I was ten, maybe eleven. I woke up and saw Uncle Elio on the edge of my bed. For a moment I thought he was my father, back from the dead."

She isn't laughing now.

"It only happened a few times. Then my mother found out."

"What did she do?" I ask.

"She wasn't happy about it, that's for sure," Elena says with a gruff laugh.

The sound of the wind grows louder off the sea and I know, somehow, to listen hard to Elena's story because she will only tell it once, in the safety of all our darkness and distance.

"A few weeks later, we left for America," she says.

"What's wrong with it?" the waiter asks as he clears away our plates.

We'd only managed half the seafood.

"We're so full," Elena says.

He looks disappointed. "What you really need to try is the red tuna," he says. "Five years ago, we had the best red tuna in the world. Right here in Chipiona. So big you wouldn't believe it." He holds his hands out. "Three meters long."

Elena nods. "Wow."

The waiter is in his early twenties and has a tattoo of the recycling symbol on his inner wrist. "People used to come from miles to fish using this Roman technique," he says. "*Almadraba,* they called it. Catch these huge fish. That was the thing about the *Almadraba.* Only the strongest fish got caught. The weaker ones were thrown back in, given another chance."

"Another chance for what?" Elena asks. "To get caught later?"

The waiter nods and smiles. He isn't really listening. "Now these foreign companies come in, overfish the sea and sell eighty percent of the tuna to the Japanese."

Elena laughs. The waiter looks at her, confused. She pokes her tongue out at him.

"*Inglesa?*" he asks me.

"Yes," I say.

Elena points at her heart. "*Colombiana.*"

The waiter nods, watches me.

"It's so quiet here," Elena says. "Where's the party?"

The waiter glances down a side street, as if expecting to find the party hiding in the shadows there. "We're going to the beach later," he says. "Want to come?"

"*Vale,*" Elena says.

He takes Elena's phone, smiles at me as you would a dunce. When he leans across the table I catch his scent, a not unpleasant combination of soap and sweat and salt, and I'm reminded I still haven't had sex with anyone. I keep watching for signs of vibration between him and Elena but when he gets up to fetch our bill it is my shoulder he touches.

He throws his arm up at the ocean's murky hollows. "Playa del Camarón. Half an hour, *mas o menos.*"

Elena is walking in the direction of the flat, away from the beach.

"You want to go home first and change?" I ask.

"I'm not going."

I wonder what I can have done to upset her. I don't want to go home, not yet. The interaction with the waiter has woken me up, made me long for something more than the balcony, a few beers, and bed.

"You're the one who asked him where the party was," I say.

"As a joke," she says.

The streets are silent, amplifying our conversation so we sound angrier than we are.

"I thought it might be fun," I say.

"We're having fun," she says. "You and me."

I say nothing.

"Aren't we?"

I hesitate. She pushes her hands up in my hair, pulls me to her. The kiss is not the moment I realize how much I want her, but a split second after, as she spins away from me, releasing my hand with a sigh. I watch her go. The lighthouse beam laps the street, illuminating the crag of creeper vines, a poster for aloe vera gel, Elena's stubborn stride. I try to imagine the passengers from the boat out there in the dark mountains, hiding in the houses, but I cannot. It is past midnight. Elena and the light are the only things in motion.

The waiter and his friends are at the beach's southernmost bend. At their feet, the remains of a bonfire spit and snap, casting their faces in spiky orange light. Without a word I pass them, duck into the changing rooms near the footpath. Moths crash against the neon bars. At the mirror, I pump soap into my palms, wash my hands. The waiter appears behind me, puts his arms around my waist. Up close, the tattoo on his wrist is scabbed-over and faded.

"I'm going to join the army," he explains. "You're not allowed tattoos. I can't afford the laser treatment so I rub salt over it every night to make it disappear."

Without thinking, I lift his wrist to my mouth, suck down on the tattoo. Unsurprisingly, it tastes like salt. He laughs and tucks my hair behind my ears. I let my head fall forward onto his chest. Bubbles pucker and hiss around the plug hole. My hands are sore where the hot water has hit them.

"Where's your friend?" he asks.

Not wanting to talk about Elena, I turn, place his hand between my legs. The reflected faces in the mirror don't change. I rise against his palm as he reaches between us. After everything Elena has said, I anticipate pain, but there is nothing besides a silence in my stomach like a fast-growing ink blot, the last thing I'd expected.

When I get back Elena is still awake.

"You smell like bonfires," she says.

She sounds far away. A trapped June bug hums in the curtains.

"How was it?" she asks.

"Good," I say, lifting my dress over my head.

"I want you to know I made it all up," she says once I am in bed. "My father, Uncle Elio. Everything. Even the alligator. It never happened."

"Elena," I start.

"No," she says. "It was all a lie."

I can't say much else. I have made a fool of myself—lied too—and I won't speak to Elena again after tonight. Her breathing levels out.

I catch the June bug in a glass. All night it buzzes against the sides, and in the morning we leave so early I forget to right it. I think about the June bug now. Has anyone been back to Chipiona? For all I know the bug is still there, upturned, like the glass above it, like I was that whole week: asleep on my stomach, afraid to touch the bed to my burn.

Nominated by The Threepenny Review,
Alice Mattison

SAY IT WITH YOUR WHOLE BLACK MOUTH

by DANEZ SMITH

from POEM-A-DAY

say it with your whole black mouth: i am innocent
      & if you are not innocent, say this: i am worthy of forgiveness,
  of breath after breath

i tell you this: i let blue eyes dress me in guilt
walked around stores convinced the very skin of my palm was
    stolen

& what good has that brought me? days filled flinching
thinking the sirens were reaching for me

& when the sirens were for me
did i not make peace with god?

so many white people are alive because
we know how to control ourselves.

how many times have we died on a whim
wielded like gallows in their sun-shy hands?

here, standing in my own body, i say: the next time
they murder us for the crime of their imaginations

i don't know what i'll do.

i did not come to preach of peace
for that is not the hunted's duty.

i came here to say what i can't say
without my name being added to a list

what my mother fears i will say

        what she wishes to say herself

i came here to say

i can't bring myself to write it down

sometimes i dream of pulling a red apology
from a pig's collared neck & wake up crackin up

     if i dream of setting fire to cul-de-sacs
     i wake chained to the bed

i don't like thinking about doing to white folks
what white folks done to us

when i do

       can't say

    i don't dance

o my people

    how long will we

reach for god

    instead of something sharper?

    my lovely doe

with a taste for meat

take

the hunter

by his hand

Nominated by Poem-A-Day,
John Allman,
Jennifer Lunden,
Maxine Scates,
Richard Tayson

"GENERAL: UNSKILLED"

fiction by RYAN ERIC DULL

from THE MISSOURI REVIEW

Mikey was on the road somewhere in Fountain Valley, looking for the 405, a ceramic saluki in his right hand and a big forced smile on his face, teeth and all. He'd heard from the entrepreneur and motivational podcaster Greg Charridan that smiling, even fake smiling, sent signals to your brain that helped to keep you upbeat. It was important to stay positive, although Mikey knew that the ceramic saluki was probably going to ruin his day.

Delivery jobs were always scheduling nightmares. And the dog was guaranteed to break, its spindly saluki legs splayed out in all directions, just begging to snag on an empty buttonhole. It was maybe five inches long, lighter than a penny, and brittle as a glass tooth. Mikey was afraid to hold it and afraid to put it down. It was worth about twenty dollars to shuttle this thing out to Huntington Beach, and it would take half a pound of careless pressure to set Mikey back ten times that much. Shirt pocket? He'd crush it. Passenger seat? If someone cut him off, the glove-compartment door would smash the thing to sentimental dust. Sunglasses case? Inner wall of the spare tire? Mikey wondered for a long, feverish moment whether his best option might be to keep the ceramic saluki inside his mouth for the duration. But you never knew with antiques. What if his tongue smudged the paint? Not an easy thing to explain. Bad review for sure.

He should have turned down the job as soon as he saw the dog. No, he should have turned down the job as soon as he heard that he couldn't deliver it until late afternoon, which meant he'd have to schlep it along on any and all jobs he managed to pick up in the interim. But he didn't

166

turn down jobs. First line of his profile: "Mikey H. doesn't turn down jobs." It was key to his growing appeal. So he was stuck with the dog. Delivery between 3:45 and 5:00. Which meant about 4:00, if he wanted a good review.

He had an appointment at 11:00 and an appointment at 2:00, and otherwise it was catch-as-catch-can. It was a Tuesday, he was the fourth most highly rated nonspecialist in the greater Anaheim area, he had a 2012 Volkswagen Golf, and he was willing to drive. He'd find something. He could move up to number three today. That was not outside the realm of possibility. Six days since he'd hit fourth place, and straight five-star reviews ever since. He visualized his name rising, like a weather balloon, to the top of the Anaheim Taskr General: Unskilled leaderboard. At a red light, he held the saluki a foot in front of his face and said, "You will not impede my ascent."

Mikey pulled into a CVS parking lot, slid back the sunroof, opened Taskr, and made himself available. After a moment, he popped the glove compartment and plucked out a box of tissues. He'd mummify the saluki, that's what he'd do. Mummies lasted forever. But his phone was already buzzing, easy job eight minutes away. He laid the saluki in a loose mound of tissues on the floor in front of the passenger seat. Back on the road in under a minute, tires singing across uneven asphalt.

He spent forty-five minutes helping a middle-aged guy move dusty patio furniture from a storage unit into a U-Haul. Mikey left the saluki on his dashboard, where he could keep an eye on it from across the lot. The guy spent the whole time talking about the Ducks, but Mikey didn't follow hockey. He responded mostly by talking about the Clippers, but it didn't seem like the guy followed basketball. They got along fine. At the end of the shift, the guy offered to keep Mikey's clock running if he'd help him to unload the U-Haul at his house, which would have been a pretty great pickup, except that the guy lived out in Long Beach and Mikey didn't want to risk being late for his 11:00. He thanked the guy and told him he'd be around later in the day if he needed anything. The guy went for a handshake, and Mikey countered with a thumbs-up. "Taskr policy," Mikey said. "We're not supposed to—"

"Sure," the guy said and gave Mikey a big thumbs-up, both hands.

Trotting back across the parking lot, Mikey could see the Golf, but he couldn't see the saluki. He lowered his sunglasses, squinted against the glare off the windshield. The dash was empty, smooth as a beach. He broke into a run, mashing his key fob, head swiveling for thieves. Jerked open the door, jaw clenched. The saluki had fallen from the dashboard onto the nest of tissues on the floor. It wasn't broken, but Mikey just about collapsed. He got back on the road, cradling the thing in his hand.

He was counting off steady, calming breaths when his phone buzzed in the passenger seat. That'd be his review. At the next red light, he snuck a glance. Five sparkling stars.

Half an hour before he had to start driving to his 11:00. A doctor or lawyer could knock out two or three jobs in that time, dollar-a-minute quickie consults in their off hours, but General: Unskilled tasks tended to go long. Quick break, then. Mikey pulled into a gas station and listened, at double speed, to the rogue sociologist and entrepreneur-podcaster Sen Sydal's opinions on Vitamin C. Vitamin C was overrated but good. Orange juice was bad. Guava, now, there was some produce you could build a breakfast around.

He thought that Linda, his regular Tuesday 11:00, might want to see the saluki. Some of his regulars were like that—always digging for details, personal stuff. He set the figurine on her kitchen counter and invited her to admire it and asked how she would keep a thing like that from breaking. She thought she had a Christmas ornament box with a Styrofoam shell that might do the trick and went off to find it while Mikey wandered around dusting the tops of tall cabinets and looking for anything that might need inexpert fixing.

Linda had a project for him this week: looking up addresses for heritage boards and town governments in far-off states where she thought she might have relatives. There were unmapped sections, she suspected, in her family tree. It was important to know where you came from, and where you had people. Mikey's family was all back in Savannah. When had he last called them? He should call them. His dad had had that— what was it?—that court thing coming up. He'd call them soon. Thursday. He took half days on Thursdays.

While Mikey scoured search engines, Linda talked about her son, Hunter, who was in his sophomore year at Northeastern University, an entire continent away, and who was in trouble for throwing a party in his dorm room and setting a wall on fire. Linda was pretty anxious about the whole thing. This was not the first time Hunter had set a dorm wall on fire, and apparently Northeastern had a strict three-strikes rule. Mikey thought Hunter would be fine, and said so. A lot of people didn't feel pressure until it was make-or-break. Now that his back was to the wall, Hunter would probably make dean's list. Linda made a bulgur salad. Linda was always feeding Mikey.

When the hour was up, he left the saluki on the counter so that Linda could remind him about it. She didn't, so he walked to the Golf empty-handed, ran back inside with an air of what he hoped seemed like invincible boyish carelessness, and retrieved the dog and the ornament box with profuse thanks. In the Golf, he found that the dog was too long to fit in the Styrofoam shell. Still, a nice thought. His phone buzzed. Always a good review from Linda.

He got tagged for a science thing at UCI. A call for volunteers had come up short. In a room that looked like a doctor's office, a not-unattractive grad student pasted electrodes onto his forehead and gave him a sheet of sentences to read into a microphone.

He read, "I hope that we will work together in the future."

"Great," the grad student said. "Now please repeat the sentence and pretend you're speaking genuinely, but to someone who you personally dislike."

"I hope that we will work together in the future," Mikey said.

"Really imagine it. Maybe they have an annoying voice. Maybe they have insulted you or your family. But you would still like to work with them."

"I hope that we will work together in the future," Mikey said.

"Excellent. Now please repeat the sentence, and pretend that you're speaking to a thirty-five-year-old man identified as Pacific Islander."

It went on like that for about half an hour. Mikey tried to keep the sentence from mashing into a pile of nonsense syllables. He hoped that he was really lighting up the electrodes, because he was imagining as hard as he could.

Somewhere around the thirtieth repetition, the Savannah started coming out in Mikey's voice. The grad student cocked her head. "Where are you from?"

"Savannah," Mikey said. "Georgia."

"Oh, really?"

"I've been in California a while." And then he read the sentence as though he was speaking to a veteran of the United States Armed Forces.

When the experiment had ended, Mikey peeled the electrodes off his forehead and asked the grad student, "Hey, do you like dogs?"

169

She shook her head. "Allergic."

"Too bad." The saluki stayed in his pocket. He offered the electrodes to the grad student, but she was writing something down. He set them on the counter. "So, if you don't mind my asking, what's the goal here? What do you think you're going to find out?"

"We don't know what we're going to find out," said the grad student. "That's why we're running the experiment."

"Right," Mikey said. "Of course. Out of curiosity, how did you choose me?"

"Taskr," she said. "We asked the first five or six people."

"Was that by rating or proximity?"

"I'm not sure," she said. "Whatever's the default."

"Rating," Mikey said. He turned the electrodes on the counter so the sensors were faceup. "You aren't worried that might compromise your data? Choosing highly rated people?"

She shrugged. "I don't think it's relevant."

Which struck Mikey as probably wrong, but she was the one with the degree. So far, she did not seem unambiguously pleased. Not that she was under any obligation to be cheerful—she was a busy individual doing some kind of important linguistics-related work, and she could emote however she wanted. But Mikey had the leaderboard to think about, and it was all too easy to imagine this grad student, maybe a first-time Taskr user, giving him a four- or a three-star review and having no idea that she was absolutely demolishing his rating. "Hey, listen," he said, "do you guys still need volunteers?"

The most beautiful facial expression in the world, Mikey knew, was the tiny widening of joyful surprise you got when someone began to believe that you might be able to give them what they wanted. The grad student offered a particularly lovely rendition, just a millimeter lift in the eyebrows. She said, "We do."

"Would you mind if I told some other people about this?"

She would not mind at all. So there was his review. He was on the phone before he left the building, badgering his housemates to drag themselves off the couch and make a few bucks on the bleeding edge of scientific inquiry.

A young guy at a Starbucks in Orange needed someone sociable for twenty minutes. He had a job interview coming up, big job at a big firm, and he wanted to practice answering tough questions. The guy was practically trembling. Told Mikey about the job and his eyes went distant and his spine bowed forward until his ears were level with his shoulders. Pathetic, the way some people wrung themselves out. Pathetic but tragically common, borderline epidemic. All of these supposedly ambitious people, these credentialed, meritorious people, believing they had to beg unworthy largesse from the polished, perfumed Big Time. Just look at this guy, qualifications coming out his pores, future for miles, but body language like he was the oldest grandmother in a Catholic church, full supplication. It had to be some kind of an institutional problem, maybe with the schools.

Mikey stuck to the scripted questions for the first five minutes, then started cutting in, asking his own questions, acting like he was so bowled over by the guy's CV that he couldn't help himself. Got the guy talking for real, tried to model power postures. The guy got into it, talked up his achievements, faintest hint of a smile poking out from way down in his involuntary muscles. A connection was formed. That was the real joy of General: Unskilled. This guy, desperate, had put out a call for any warm body that could read a simple list of questions off a sheet of printer paper. And here he was, not one hour later, positively glowing in the light of a new relationship. This guy right here, this guy with the knit brow and the wild eyes and the tiny smile and the total possession of his own, astonishing history—this guy could interview for the position of almighty God.

When they hit twenty minutes, Mikey played up his disappointment. The time had just blown by. The guy didn't suggest an extension. He thanked Mikey several times. For a moment, he looked ready to go for the handshake, but Mikey cut him off with the big thumbs-up. The guy acknowledged it, smiled, thanked Mikey again. It felt wrong to leave it at that, anticlimactic. Mikey thought of a line, a terrific line from the towering entrepreneur and podcaster Richard Hammert. He checked the guy's name on his phone, and he looked him square in the eye, sincere, warm, and he said, "Listen, Ethan: Sooner or later, everyone gets exactly what they deserve." The guy blinked. Mikey nodded. The guy walked Mikey out of the Starbucks and watched him until he was back in the Golf, back on the road, on to the next thing.

Mikey felt fantastic. "I know what people want," he told the saluki and then, after a moment, "I have spent over 980 hours helping people. I have studied human psychology. I have a 4.6-star weighted rating and in excess of 115 positive written reviews. Can you get in excess of 115 positive written reviews if you don't understand people? You can't. You just can't." He contemplated these numbers, and his head swam. "I could make third today." Third place, in a metro of three million-plus people. And in under five months. Just thinking about it gave him vertigo. No peak in sight looked quite so tall.

"It doesn't take much," he told the saluki. "You just have to commit. Anyone could do it." Mikey's heart broke for his housemates, all of them sitting on their asses, throwing résumés into help-wanted Dumpsters or chasing after degrees, delaying the inevitable. Look where they were, and look where they could be. He'd convinced a few of them to download the app, but as far as he knew, none of them had taken a gig. He'd even offered to send a Trusted-By voucher to anyone who completed their first job, allowing them to skim some gravitas from his towering profile. The Post-It had been on the refrigerator for months: "Mikey Will Vouch For You—Inquire For Code." There had been no bites. Everyone was wedded to some analog, old-world path to success, too focused on the left-foot-right-foot to realize they were walking into a hazmat wreck. Or else they'd been unemployed for so long that they were independently reinventing Buddhism, learning to free themselves from want. The house was like a nursing home: static, all downswing, slippers and sweaters and looming oblivion. But you had to give people chances, as many as it took. He'd keep trying.

His 2:00 was long-standing, one of his first. An apartment building way out in Garden Grove. Twice a week, Mikey delivered groceries and then sat for an hour while Mr. Nguyen talked. Mr. Nguyen was a phenomenal monologuist. He had a real instinct for emotional twists and turns. An undiscovered talent, Mikey thought, buried these sixty or eighty years, it was hard to tell. Get this guy in front of a webcam and who knew what might happen? Never too late. The age thing could be a hook. Mikey was pretty sure that Mr. Nguyen ought to be seeing someone, in the sense of professional therapy, but he wouldn't or couldn't, maybe for generational-pride-related reasons or maybe for socioeconomic-status-related reasons: could be anything, and Mikey would never ask. It was sad, probably. But at the same time, therapists had only existed for, what, a hundred years? People had managed before then. If Mikey's half of a psych degree didn't qualify him to provide actual professional

172

therapy, it was probably enough for a nineteen-dollar-an-hour substitute. Mr. Nguyen seemed to think so.

Mikey deposited the groceries on the kitchen counter. "You shouldn't use the bags from the store," Mr. Nguyen said. "They're making you pay now."

"Five cents," Mikey said.

"Five cents for this much plastic. What's that, a dog?"

Mikey placed the figurine gingerly on the coffee table. "Yeah. I have to bring it to someone in Huntington Beach."

Mr. Nguyen picked it up, and Mikey chewed his cheek. "Have you ever seen a greyhound run?" asked Mr. Nguyen.

"That's a saluki."

"What's a saluki?"

"The rich man's greyhound, I think."

Mr. Nguyen wiggled the saluki like it was walking across the table. Its tiny paws clicked against the glass. "It looks like a greyhound."

"That's actually pretty delicate."

"What do you think of greyhounds?"

"They're fast, right?"

"Oh, they're fast," Mr. Nguyen said. "Faster than a horse. You like them?"

"I don't have an opinion about greyhounds. I don't know any greyhounds."

"They're too skinny," Mr. Nguyen said, bouncing the figurine in his hand. "All bones."

"They have to be, right? To be fast."

"Well, who needs a fast dog?"

"Gamblers, I think."

"And who needs a thing like this delivered?" He held it to his ear and shook it.

"Maybe it's an heirloom. I don't know."

"So get it yourself. People are lazy, that's all." Mr. Nguyen punctuated this by knocking the dog against the table like a tiny gavel.

Mikey lifted it from his hand. "You wouldn't believe it. Some of them won't even buy their own groceries."

"Don't be an asshole. I have plastic knees."

Mikey put the dog back on the table, out of Mr. Nguyen's reach, and pulled a chair over from the dinette set. "How's that thing with the building manager going?"

Which set Mr. Nguyen off on a huge snorting eye-roll that lasted, more or less, for the rest of the hour.

So now it was 3:04. Mikey was way out in Garden Grove idling next to a parking meter and looking for a job that would take him in the direction of Huntington Beach. He had a big cushion, but if a job went long, he could easily end up having to drive twenty miles in twenty minutes, courting all variety of disaster. He'd been there. No leeway at all on delivery jobs, ratings-wise. Possibly there was merit to driving straight for Huntington Beach, delivering the saluki at precisely 3:45, dropping the albatross. But here was a request from Westminster, straight shot on the 22, so it was back on the road and hope it all works out.

He was just about there by the time he realized it was the guy from before, Ethan, the Starbucks interview guy. A different address but the same profile picture—alert and firing-squad serious, tragically coiffed, in front of a white cement background somewhere. Classic bad profile picture. Desperately formal, eyes starving. Why hadn't the photographer said something? Mikey would mention it. Not advice anyone wanted to hear, but Lord, someone had to tell him.

He left the car in forty-five-minute parking and took the saluki with him. Mikey wasn't altogether pleased to learn that their earlier session had been unsatisfactory. Hard not to take that personally. But twenty minutes was too short, that was all. The guy should have extended.

Mikey found Ethan in the hall outside his apartment. He was pacing a little, shifting his weight like a rocking chair, eyes up and down the hall. When he saw Mikey, he wasn't so much nervous as full-on inconsolable, post-traumatic eye sockets all dark and bugged. So Mikey met him at a jog and shook his hand. He was pretty sure he could do that, didn't think anyone would misinterpret the gesture, and this guy clearly needed to, like, discharge something, close some kind of circuit, so Mikey grabbed his hand from where it was floating, trembling in the air, grabbed it with both hands and said, "Hey. It's good to see you again. What can I do for you?"

Ethan shook his head and didn't say anything. Mikey tried not to be annoyed. He couldn't help until he had directions. A neighbor carried a bag of recycling into the hall. Mikey said, "Hey, why don't we go somewhere?"

The door to the apartment was unlocked, braced against the bolt, and Ethan pushed it open. Mikey followed him. He was listening for absolutely anything, any kind of sign or instruction, and the door swung closed behind him and the bolt smashed into the frame and Mikey started and spun and slid the bolt and eased the door shut. Ethan didn't turn.

The blinds were closed. It took Mikey a second to adjust. The place looked—Mikey shouldn't think this way; it was an unpleasant way to think, a dehumanizing way to think—the place looked like one big diagnosis. Kind of barren, not much evidence of a healthy inner life. But maybe Ethan had just moved in, how about that?

Ethan backed up to a wall and slid to the hardwood, almost hyperventilating, and, all right, it didn't look like he was doing so well; you didn't have to be a licensed professional to see that. Mikey slid down right next to him, so their shoulders touched. He didn't say anything. He tried to breathe at the same time as Ethan and then maybe just a little slower, so that the guy slowed his breath to match, just a little bit until they weren't breathing so hard and the buzz went down in their heads and they could think clearly.

Mikey waited for Ethan to say something. All at once, he was furious, just existentially miserable that Ethan should have to say anything, that there wasn't some other way to figure out what he needed. How awful to talk. How awful to have to. What Mikey wanted was to loop this guy directly into his veins, to pass this guy's pained, anemic blood through his own hearty organs and make it clean. He visualized this process. He could feel the light-headed rush of new blood, could see the medical tubing warped by the force of it, the light shining through the red.

He was not unaware of his schedule. His phone was in his pocket. They'd been sitting a while. It had to be getting late.

He said, "Hey, why don't we go somewhere?"

Ethan stopped breathing.

Mikey waited, and eventually Ethan started breathing again.

Mikey said, "Listen, here's the situation: I have to go somewhere. It's a prior commitment. I'm committed. But that's only going to take a minute, and it's a nice drive; it's to Huntington Beach, a beautiful afternoon drive, so why don't you come along?" He took out his phone, and Lord but it was getting late, and he showed Ethan as he opened Taskr and ended the current job. "No charge. See? I could use the company. It's been a day."

Ethan didn't say anything.

Mikey got up. After a minute, Ethan got up. Mikey made for the door. "Got your keys?" Ethan got his keys.

Down on the street, Mikey pulled a ticket out from under his windshield wiper and stuffed it into his pocket. He got into the car and Ethan

175

stood outside. Mikey stretched across the armrest and opened the passenger-side door. He scooped the tissues off the floor and stuffed those in his pocket too. The saluki was still in his left pocket, and he had to lean way over toward Ethan to keep it from pressing against the seat. When they'd been driving for a few minutes, he said, "Have you been to Huntington Beach?"

Nothing.

He said, "It's nice. They've got a pier and all."

Ethan kept his head still, tilted toward the glove compartment, while his eyes traced the car. He stopped on the divot in the dash where Mikey had wedged a desk chair a few weeks back. Mikey gestured out the window with his head, made some slightly flamboyant moves with his hands, cleared his throat, but the guy stayed fixed on the flaw. Questionable behavior, Mikey thought. Judgmental, maybe.

Mikey opened the center console and produced a bag of crisped snap peas. He tore it open with gentle pressure, the steering wheel steadied on his knees. "Hungry?"

Ethan looked at it, shook his head, and went back to the divot.

Mikey felt the divot on the one side and the saluki on the other. It was intolerable.

He said, "Hey, could you do me a favor?" He fished the saluki out of his pocket and offered it to Ethan. "Could you hold this for me? It's a saluki. It's precious. You wouldn't believe how precious this thing is."

Ethan took the dog with both hands and turned it over. Mikey immediately regretted letting it go, but he couldn't think of a way to get it back. Traffic was light and the sun hit the road square and lit the windshield up like a projection screen.

"You could deliver it, if you want," Mikey said. "You could come with me when I deliver it. I'd give you half the commission. You deserve it."

From the dashboard, Mikey's phone said, "Turn left on—" in a peaceful voice louder than anything they'd heard in an hour. Mikey flipped his mirror down and checked his teeth for snap-pea gunk. He grimaced and tried to pull the corners of his mouth up. Ethan made eye contact in the mirror. Mikey took a breath and smiled harder, so that his gums showed and his eyes caught the light. He said, "You've got to smile. Whatever happens." He closed the mirror and turned to reach for the saluki. "Anyway, that's what I've heard."

Nominated by Jeffrey Hammond

MONTICELLO HOUSE TOUR

by **KIKI PETROSINO**

from WASHINGTON SQUARE REVIEW

What they never say is: Jefferson's still
building. He's just using clear bricks now
for his turrets & halls, new terraces
to belt his estate in transparent loops
of dug air. After death, it's so easy
to work. No one sees him go out
from the Residence, his gloves full
of quiet mortar. Jefferson's coat is narrow
as daybreak. His long sleeves drag in the muck
as he minces his turf. You know the room
you were born in? It's part of the tour. Hundreds
of rooms unfolding for miles, orchards blooming
in the parlor. Remember that wingchair you loved, the one
with a face like a lion, especially in the dark
of late winter, when Mother sat with you
in her pink gown, humming? As it happens
Jefferson built you that lion. He drew your time
in prudent proportions. You have one job: to fit
the design he keeps spinning. Your whole life is laced
through a ring of similar finds. Just look in the binder.
It's all Mothers in pink gowns, humming.

Nominated by Washington Square Review

THE PEACHES OF AUGUST

by TOI DERRICOTTE

from BIRMINGHAM POETRY REVIEW

The long awaited, here, at the local farm stand, are not as comely as the ones at Whole Foods, but they are dollars cheaper, & so we sweep them up like sweepstake winners, & stack them gently in our purposeful cloth bags. Tomorrow, one of us, before the other awakens, will slice into Tupperware the 4 or 5 softest to the fingers—(to test press kindly as a newborn's cheek)—& stir them with brown sugar from a box sitting atop the refrigerator for months, alone, remote, mysterious.

Nominated by Birmingham Poetry Review

THE ENTERTAINER

fiction by WHITNEY COLLINS

from THE PINCH

Mrs. Billingsley asks Rachel's mother, not Rachel, if Rachel would like to accompany them to the beach for two weeks. "There's no television, no A/C. It's almost embarrassingly primitive, but Rachel is just so entertaining. Such a delight. I know she'd make my girls happy."

This is how Mrs. Billingsley puts it to Rachel's mother over the phone one evening after Rachel has been particularly engaging at tennis, and Rachel's mother, in her outdated kitchen, still humiliated by her divorce, her hatchback, her teeth, replies: "Yes! Yes! Absolutely!" without even asking Rachel if going to the beach for two weeks with the Billingsleys is something she wants to do.

If Rachel's mother's own life is unsalvageable, her daughter's still has a shot. She pictures what Rachel can look like in five years if she goes to the beach and puts on a good show for these folks, meets the people they know. If Rachel is willing to do her little song-and-dance at night while the Billingsleys drink scotch, tell some of those Helen Keller jokes she picked up at summer camp while the Billingsleys scrape crab claws with silver forks, teach the talentless Billingsley girls how to macramé, lip sync, hula hoop; Rachel, if she's lucky, might end up as decadently bored and unafraid as they are.

Of course, Rachel will have to learn how to starve herself, how to volley, how to operate aging dick, but these are small prices to pay. Rachel's mother can at least teach her something about the not-eating. *Think of your hunger as a wheelchair,* she'll tell Rachel before she leaves for the trip. *Something you can never get out of, but something that will get you where you want to go, even if it's uncomfortable.*

179

"I don't want to go," Rachel says when she learns of the plans.

"Too late now," her mother answers.

Rachel feels like hired help, a jester for the elite. Rachel's mother feels something akin to hope, like the hand of God is touching her for the first time in a decade.

The Billingsleys fly to the beach in a private King Air twin-turboprop. The girls, Devlin, fifteen, and Davenport, seventeen, straddle Rachel age-wise and know her only through the tennis clinic that Rachel's mother paid for, like her summer camp, on a low-interest Discover card. They buckle themselves loosely in adjacent leather seats across from Rachel and their mother and exhale in unison.

"Was there not a Lear?" Devlin says.

"Or a Citation?" Davenport adds. Their voices pout but their mouths do not, as if their faces are afflicted by a practiced palsy.

"The girls are used to jets," Mrs. Billingsley explains. "But this is what we get when the men have first dibs."

"Fuck men," Devlin says.

"No thanks," Davenport answers. "I'm going to be a lesbo."

Rachel stares at the sisters and they stare back, in such a way and for such a time that Rachel begins to wonder if this is her cue to begin entertaining everyone. To start diffusing things, as she always does, with her non-threatening plumpness, her simple face, her clever puns. It's why she was invited, after all: to do what she does at tennis. Introduce the joyless to the concept of joy—if not in a way they can experience, at least in a way they can witness.

"You know any lesbos?" Davenport asks. "You went to camp. Camps are crawling with lesbos."

Rachel waits for Mrs. Billingsley to chime in, to say something like, "Davenport, please," or "Knock it off, girls." But instead, Mrs. Billingsley tilts her head back for a nap even though the plane has yet to depart. "Lesbos," she snorts with her eyes closed. "What goes where?"

Rachel's mother works in the basement of a bank, counting checks with the eraser end of a pencil. She hears three things, eight hours a day, five days a week: the *thipthipthip* of the erasers, the asylum hum of the fluorescents and the cheery, insufferable banter of her co-workers. All women, all obese, all over sixty. All of them inexplicably—infuriatingly—content with their lives.

"One of them told me a recipe for layered pudding today," Rachel's mother tells Rachel the night before her trip. "You should have heard her. You would have thought she was explaining how to deliver a baby. 'First there's a layer of vanilla pudding. Then there's a layer of strawberries. Then there's a layer of non-dairy whipped topping.'" Rachel's mother puts her face in her hands and groans. "It's called *Cool Whip*, you idiot. It doesn't make you sound smart to call it something else. It makes you sound like someone who's worked in the basement of a bank her whole, pathetic life who thinks calling *Cool Whip* non-dairy whipped topping puts a stamp in her passport. Please. Like she even has a passport."

Rachel's mother looks up. "This is what it's come to, Rachel. Pudding people. For a while there, your father and I had a chance to make something of ourselves. We were on the verge of a country club. But now? The city park."

Rachel remembers the first time she walked in on her father. He was standing in front of the bedroom mirror, using a can of hairspray for a microphone. "Who here's happily married?" he asked the mirror. "Can I get a show of hands?" Her father squinted his eyes, as if he were looking out past stage lights and into an audience. "What's that? Five? Six? Well, there you have it, people. Proof of aliens."

Rachel's mother puts both of her hands on Rachel's shoulders. "This is not a trip to the beach, Rachel. It's a trip to school. Study these people like you're going to be tested. Someday, you could spend a third of your year in a beach chair. You just have to work at it hard enough and then—abracadabra!—you won't have to work at all."

Rachel's mother smiles. She sees Rachel living like someone in a soap opera: lethargic with wealth. Her tan arm, now thin, stacked with bracelets to the elbow. A silver-haired man in terrycloth shorts at her side. Rachel's mother sees Rachel with a husband so taken by her full lips and visible hipbones that he rewards her yearly with a new Lexus. Rachel, on the other hand, sees nothing but a container of *Cool Whip*. She's eating out of it with a ladle—or rather her hands.

In the air, somewhere between Delaware and the beach the sisters insist on calling 'Ass Island,' Davenport gestures loosely at the plane's amenities: a narrow drawer lined with packs of spearmint gum; a first-aid cabinet equipped for hangovers, not engine failure, stocked with envelopes of *Goody's* headache powder; a bread basket filled with boxes of animal crackers and buckled into a spare seat, like a neighbor's child the Billingsleys have agreed to transport but are set on ignoring.

"Animal crackers," scoffs Devlin. "You see any babies up here?"

"In your vagina," Davenport says.

Devlin and Davenport lean across the narrow aisle to punch one another in the upper arms for a time, back and forth like papier-mâché marionettes, until their arms are red and welted from shoulder to elbow. It's as if both have been grabbed and shaken by a middle-aged lover who's discovered he's been jilted for a pool boy.

"Trucey trucey?" Devlin asks.

"Vodka juicy," Davenport answers.

At this, the sisters set about making cocktails, and Rachel watches, spellbound. The girls are a study in contradiction, equal parts crude and classy, mundane and mesmerizing. Their hair is eternally slept on, piled on their heads like Caucasian turbans. Their silk dresses are shapeless but clingy, their expensive loafers intentionally mashed into slides. Their bodies, fed only candy, seem to consist of neither muscle nor fat. They can slump in the corner of a tennis court biting *Skittles* in half; they can scuff across a tarmac with unwieldy handbags concealing liquor; they can slouch in leather seats, knees agape to show a pearly slice of panties and still, somehow, exude regality. Their only accessible flaws, Devlin's fingernails and Davenport's bottom lip, both of which have been habitually and vigorously chewed, only serve, in Rachel's opinion, to humanize them, to mark them as either inwardly anxious or outwardly bored.

"Here." Devlin offers Rachel a drink. "It's a Stoli-and-Diet."

Rachel takes it and sniffs. Beside her, Mrs. Billingsley naps with her mouth open, gasping, as if she's slept alone for years.

"That," Devlin points at her mother, "is how you make a man fuck the nanny."

"No shit," Davenport says, tossing back the contents of her plastic tumbler and mixing another drink inside the bowels of her Italian purse. "And yet, they're still together because Daddy likes consistency."

"And Mommy likes money," adds Devlin.

For an instant, things go quiet. As if an intentional moment of silence has been observed for decency's death. Then Davenport belches, unblinking, and says to Rachel. "So, who did your dad leave your mom for? A babysitter? A secretary?"

"Don't say it's someone not young," says Devlin. "Because that is the burn of the century."

Rachel takes a taste of her drink. And then a second. She doesn't dare say why her parents split. That it was her mother who left her father. That it was her father who left banking for stand-up comedy, because he deserved—his word—*applause.* That her father now lives in a basement apartment with a recliner and a hot pot and an iguana he agreed to house sit but somehow got stuck with. That her father spends his days making long lists of catchphrases he believes will get him discovered, revered, iconized: *And that's the long and short of it, folks! Trust me, ladies and gents, I'm an expert! And that's what you call screwed, my friends!*

"He banged my French tutor," Rachel lies, having had neither French nor tutors. "She was twenty-three."

Devlin whistles and clucks her tongue in mock judgment. Davenport shrugs. "I've heard worse," she says. "At least he didn't bang you."

Rachel finishes her drink at that. Davenport makes her another. Halfway through the third, despite her mother's warning, Rachel gets out of her figurative wheelchair and asks for the animal crackers. Devlin and Davenport watch unblinking as Rachel eats an entire box and then a second.

"Damn, bitch," Devlin says. "Save some for the Africans."

Davenport says nothing. She just stares at Rachel as Rachel eats, chews her lower lip as Rachel chews, and it occurs to Rachel, as the plane whirs on slow and rich, as the girls splay warm and drunk, that Davenport's lower lip is the way it is and Devlin's fingernails are the way they are, not because the girls are scared or bored, but because they're starving.

'Ass Island' turns out to be a private slice of Caribbean land that's shaped like a hand giving the finger. It's owned by people as white as its sand and run by people as dark as the rum that Devlin and Davenport keep under their twin bamboo beds.

"This is our room," Davenport says. "We've got a view of the ocean, a view of the pool, a view of where Devlin screwed the Jamaican."

"How do you know where I screwed the Jamaican?" Devlin asks.

"Because I was watching," Davenport says.

Rachel sits on a bed while the sisters unpack by tipping their suitcases onto the floor of the closet. They each deposit a pile of silk dresses and sunglasses, bikinis and lighters, Tarot cards and menthol cigarettes, smashed shoes and loose Skittles. There's a pink plastic case that Rachel guesses might hold a diaphragm. A carved wooden box that must be for weed. When they're done, they take Rachel on a half-hearted tour of the shingled house and flowering grounds, pointing out useless things. Not where Rachel can find an extra roll of toilet paper or a glass of water or a bottle of sunscreen, but where their father once had a seizure from too much cocaine, which window the natives climb into when the Billingsleys aren't there.

"See these shotgun shells?" Davenport says, opening a drawer intended for silverware. "They come here and do drug deals. They use this house as a hideout."

"Just doing our part," Devlin says.

"Community service," Davenport agrees.

Rachel is too ravenous to be impressed; she cannot help but point to the refrigerator next. "Any diet soda in there?" she asks.

Davenport yanks it open to reveal a lone champagne cork and an old jar of cocktail sauce, then she turns, slow, and looks at Rachel. "Oh, shit," she says. "You're hungry again."

Devlin opens her mouth in awe, then closes it like a fish.

Rachel lifts her shoulders, then drops them.

Davenport thinks with the refrigerator open. "If we take you somewhere, will you eat for us?"

Devlin releases a gasp. "Oh, please," she whispers. "Pretty pretty?"

Rachel looks from one to the other. This is why she was invited, she sees. This is how to make them happy. "All right," she says, nodding her plain, round face. "I can do that."

At a restaurant meant for locals but appropriated by the sunburned, Rachel sits while Devlin and Davenport order for her: a double-bacon cheeseburger, a bowl of conch chowder, a plate of coconut macaroons.

"Get her a beer," Devlin says. "Two."

"God, beer," Davenport says. "What I wouldn't."

Rachel watches them fight over the menu, as if they've never held one, as if it's pornography, a love letter, a treasure map. The waiter lets them

184

keep it to peruse, which they do, producing a pack of menthols while they read it, smoking as if they've just had sex. Rachel notices that the Caribbean sounds different from other oceans. It sounds like something Rachel knows, but cannot place.

"Jerk chicken," Davenport says.

"Fucking potatoes," Devlin adds.

When the food arrives, the sisters sit back to watch Rachel eat, their eyes glassy with booze and tears.

"Take it slow," Davenport says.

So Rachel does. She eats the burger as if it's her first, the soup as if it's her last. She pinches up each cookie with her soft, ringless fingers and holds them up for the girls to see, sugar in the sunlight. By the time the meal is over, Rachel feels the feeling of a job well done—one hundred stacks of counted checks. A layered pudding, well-layered.

"Take a bow," Devlin says.

"No shit," Davenport adds.

Rachel does not refuse. She brushes the crumbs from her lap and stands. She bows stage left. She bows stage right. She bows right down the center.

That night at the house, the girls show Rachel how they entertain themselves without television.

"Things to smoke," Devlin says, laying out cigarettes and joints like a picket fence on her bedspread.

"Things to drink," Davenport says, placing a bottle of vodka next to a bottle of rum on the nightstand.

"And things to play," Devlin says, thumping her skull as if she's thinking up something good.

"Like what?" Rachel asks.

Devlin runs an unlit joint under her nose and inhales. "Sometimes Davenport and I pretend we're regular people. That we're not rich."

"Yeah," says Davenport. "We just lie here and say shit that rich people would never say."

Rachel frowns. "Such as?"

Devlin licks the joint and smooths it, like a child's cowlick. "Rachel can judge us," she says to Davenport. "Rachel can tell us if we sound poor."

"Oh, wow!" Davenport says, showing an emotion Rachel guessed her incapable of. An emotion Rachel feels compelled to nurture, to cup her hands around and blow on like an ember. "Would you?"

Rachel cannot imagine saying no. "Okay," she says. "For Skittles."

Davenport and Devlin further brighten for a brief second, as if Rachel has offered to eat two slices of cake in front of them. "God, I love you," Devlin says.

Davenport says nothing; she just stares at Rachel until Rachel turns warm, and after an eternal minute, Devlin lights a joint and takes a long drag, thinking. "I'm gonna run to *Sears*," she finally says, releasing smoke. "And get me a new jog bra."

Davenport doles out two *Skittles* to Rachel. "Well?"

Rachel eats the candy. "That doesn't sound rich."

Davenport takes her turn. "Pass the ketchup," she says. "For my steak."

"Not rich," Rachel says, eating two more *Skittles*.

"I got summer teeth," Devlin says. "Some are here. Some are there."

Davenport and Devlin burst into an unexpected laughter that sounds both magnificent and terrifying, the howls of two lean dogs. Rachel eats the rest of the *Skittles* off the bedspread while the sisters, beige and bony, pass the joint between them. Both of them could fit inside her body, she thinks. Davenport and Devlin could be dropped into her torso like two silk scarves into a basket. They could hide there, where the hunger lives; a little, shimmering, satin pool.

"What's your dad do?" Davenport asks out of nowhere.

"Great question," Devlin says.

Rachel has forgotten where she is, who she is supposed to be. "Oh," she says, coming to, declining the joint with a wave of her padded palm, imagining two scarves unfurling down her throat. "He's an entertainer."

Davenport and Devlin look at each other, quiet, then they clamp their hands over their mouths like they're at a funeral suppressing laughter. "Like an actor?" Devlin says.

"Like a rock star?" Davenport adds.

Rachel isn't sure what to say. "He just has this way," she says. "Of putting on a show."

"Oh, our dad's like that, too," Devlin says. "He throws big parties and never shuts up. Sometimes he pays someone to play the piano."

Davenport wets her fingertips and pinches the hot end of the joint without reaction. "One time, he hired a magician for the cokeheads. You know. Cokeheads love card tricks."

186

Devlin nods. "And last Christmas he brought in an owl."

Davenport points at Devlin. "That's right. He found an owl under the house, down by the stilts, and brought it inside to show to everyone at the party."

Rachel stares. "An owl?"

"Yeah," Devlin says. "Did you know there were owls in the islands? I didn't. I thought owls were from a forest in Germany or some shit."

"Dad just walked in with that owl on a beach towel. Everybody went out of their fucking skulls and the owl didn't do a goddamn thing," Davenport says. "It had to be sick."

Devlin blinks slow, remembering. "It just sat on that towel and stared. Everyone was passing it around and Dad was standing there like it was no big thing except it turned out to be a big thing."

"A real owl," Rachel says.

"Turns out owls are beautiful," Davenport says. "Who knew?"

"Thanks, Dad," Devlin says as if he's right in the room with them. "People were so-so before you brought the owl in, but now they're happy as fuck."

Rachel feels something close to fear, rising. "What happened to the owl?"

Devlin lays down on her bed and closes her eyes. Davenport pulls off her shirt and sits there, topless, using her shirt to pat under her armpits. "It's hot," she says. "I'm wasted."

Davenport falls forward on her bed. Her bare, brown back is as slight as a child's. Rachel stands there, alone for a moment, thinking about the owl. She wonders if they let it go. If the owl let people touch it. She imagines the owl, startled, flying around the living room, the guests both delighted and afraid, Mr. Billingsley really getting his money's worth, even though it cost him nothing.

Rachel leaves Devlin and Davenport the way they are: passed out, with the lights on.

In Rachel's room, Rachel finds Mrs. Billingsley on the bed, staring at the ceiling, a drink loose in her hand. Her stout arms are pink from sun. Her eyes are pink from scotch. Her dress, also pink, is hiked up on one side to reveal a pale, dimpled leg.

"My girls," she slurs. "I do apologize."

Out the window, Rachel can hear the ocean but not see it. She still cannot place what it sounds like. "Oh, they're fine," she says. "They're fun."

"Pfft," Mrs. Billingsley says, shaking her head, jiggling a bit of her scotch onto the floor. "Thank God they're rich. If they weren't rich, they'd be dead. They don't know how to do anything."

Rachel says nothing. She wants Mrs. Billingsley to leave. She wants to climb into the bed and think up catch phrases for her father. *What do I look like, an idiot?* She thinks of the one time she went to see her father perform. It had been late in the afternoon, in a bar that smelled of Pine-Sol. Only eight people had been in the audience and one of them kept saying, "Give it up, man. Give it up."

Mrs. Billingsley sits up on one elbow, takes a long swallow from her drink, the ice clattering back and forth like bracelets on an arm. "I wasn't born rich, Rachel. But I wasn't born poor either. I was somewhere in the middle. Like where you are. In that place where you don't know how good you got it." Mrs. Billingsley swings her legs over the side of the bed like she might stand, then she wavers and lies back down, gingerly, as if she's on a raft in water. "I was thirteen when I met Mr. Billingsley. I worked at the golf house on the ninth hole of the club we couldn't afford to join, and I served sandwiches to the men. Those were good days. Quiet ones. I worked with another girl. Her name was Beverly. We just listened to the whack of golf clubs. The hum of golf carts. We made lists of what we wanted in life. Cars and rings. Things, Rachel. Then we handed the men sandwiches. We didn't even have to make them. We just had to keep them cold. When I saw Mr. Billingsley, I told myself to do whatever it took to get him to marry me. So, I did whatever it took."

Rachel's hands are stained from the candy. She clasps them together as if in prayer and then unclasps them. Over and over she does this as Mrs. Billingsley talks.

"Oh, Rachel. I just did what it took. And look where it got me." Mrs. Billingsley reaches her arm down as if to put her glass on the floor, but the floor escapes her by a few inches, so she lets the drink hang in her swollen hand. "You'll meet him," she says. "He's old and angry and handsome and funny and everyone loves him, so I probably should, too. It's too late and too hard for it to be any other way anyway. Oh, God," Mrs. Billingsley sighs. "I'm so glad you're here, Rachel. You're such a delight. Can you teach my girls something normal? Something useful? Can you show them how to fry an egg? Can you show them how to fold a towel? Can you show them something, anything, they can use in life?"

Rachel thinks of the sisters, across from her at the table, waiting, watching, wanting. Their eyes are as pale as fresh concrete, but whenever she brings the fork to her mouth, their pupils dilate with joy, like black ink dropped into water.

"Yes," Rachel says. "I can do that."

Outside, the ocean fades and crashes, fades and crashes. Finally, it occurs to Rachel that it sounds like applause.

Nominated by The Pinch

REZA'S RESTAURANT, CHICAGO 1997

by KAVEH AKBAR

from VIRGINIA QUARTERLY REVIEW

       the waiters milled about filling sumac
shakers clearing away plates of onion and
radish
       my father pointed to each person whispered
Persian about the old man with the silver
       beard whispered *Arab* about the woman with
the eye mole *Persian* the teenager pouring
water *White* the man on the phone
               I was eight
and watching and amazed
I asked how he could possibly tell when
               they were all brown-
skin-dark-hair'd like us almost everyone
in the restaurant looked like us
       he smiled a proud
little smile a warm nest
of lip said *it's easy* said *we're just uglier*

       he returned to his lamb but I was baffled hardly
touched my gheimeh I had huge glasses and bad
       teeth I felt plenty Persian
              when the woman
       with light eyes and blonde-brown
hair left our check my father looked at me
       I said *Arab?* he shook his head laughed

we drove home I grew up it took years to
        put together what my father
meant that day my father who listened
        exclusively to the Rolling Stones
who called the Beatles
                    a band for girls
        my father who wore only black even
            around the house whose arms could
                        cut chicken wire and make stew and
        bulged with old farm scars my father my
father my father built
        the world the first sound I ever heard
                was his voice whispering the azan
                        in my right ear I didn't need anything
                else my father cherished
                that we were ugly and so being ugly
                        was blessed I smiled with all my teeth

Nominated by Virginia Quarterly Review,
Marianne Boruch

SAY THIS

by LUCIA PERILLO

from POETRY

I live a small life, barely bigger than a speck,
barely more than a blip on the radar sweep
though it is not nothing, as the garter snake
climbs the rock rose shrub and the squirrel creeps
on bramble thorns. Not nothing to the crows
who heckle from the crowns of the last light's trees
winterstripped of green, except for the boles
that ivy winds each hour round. See, the world is busy
and the world is quick, barely time for a spider
to suck the juice from a hawk moth's head
so it can use the moth as a spindle that it wraps in fiber
while the moth constricts until it's thin as a stick
you might think was nothing, a random bit
caught in a web coming loose from the window frame, in wind.

Nominated by Poetry

MONSTERS

by MARGARET WARDLAW

from CREATIVE NONFICTION

The old Victorian anatomy lab was the final resting place for hundreds of human remains, carefully dissected, labeled with pins, and floating eerily in jars of formalin. The pathological museum was once the crown jewel of the state's oldest medical school, and a full century later, the jars remained. The specimens were long since obsolete, but what could be done with them? Their eerie glass gathered dust, and they became dismembered sentinels, staring out at each new generation of novice physicians.

There were babies among them—remnants of a once-prestigious embryology collection, lovingly curated at the turn of the century by the first woman medical school professor in Texas, the efficient and exacting Dr. Marie Charlotte Schaefer. In her eagerness to serve her alma mater, "the old lady," as her students called her (though she was not old), had unwittingly condemned a generation of babies, grotesquely, to eternal infancy while their anguished mothers grew into old women, went gray, died, and were buried. She continued this labor of love for years, accumulating and preserving babies until she was taken ill on campus and died the same day, in the prime of her life, from an acute disease of the heart.

Years passed while the babies' luckier brothers and sisters became children, grew into men and women, and even had children of their own. Now, even they lay peacefully under marble obelisks, lambs, or angels in the old Broadway Cemetery. On occasion, an industrious professor would select a baby for the subject of a short lecture, and more than one anxious maintenance man had shuffled the jars from place to place to make room for a new influx of students. But, for the most part, they remained undisturbed for more than a century. One fetus, presumably due to an unfortunate shattering and the modern difficulty of finding an appropriate container for hundred-year-old human remains, hovered uneasily at the bottom of an old food jar. "The pickle with the perfect pucker," its lid declared.

In the days of Dr. Schaefer, and as late as the 1980s in some medical publications, physicians called these babies "monsters." When I was a medical student in the early 2000s, one particularly haunting specimen still bore the label "anencephalic monster." Suspended naked and eternally lonely in his strange glass coffin, he had no top to his skull, only a small amount of brain, and huge staring eyes. *Monster*. That was the technical term, and it had been that way for as long as anybody could remember. It was the term the Royal College of Surgeons had used, and the Renaissance doctors before them, and the medieval manuscript writers before them.

With the well-intentioned support of an army of surgeons, intensivists, nurses, wires, tubes, and prayers, a baby I'll call Luz has managed to survive to almost a year old, though according to most of my medical textbooks, her condition is "incompatible with extrauterine life." She has lived most of that time within the four walls of the children's hospital, and farther within the four walls of various Isolettes and in various intensive care units.

Luz was born with a severe form of holoprosencephaly. It's a spectrum of disorders in which the brain and the structures in the middle part of the head don't form correctly. Babies with its most serious form, which is typically lethal, were once called "cyclopean monsters," as if they were infant versions of the mythical Odyssean behemoth, because they are born with a single nostril, a gaping hole in the lip and palate, and only one eye. In addition to these anomalies, which we physicians casually refer to as "midline facial defects," these children also have corresponding missing parts in the middle of their brains.

At eleven months old, despite every available brain surgery, feeding tube, hormone replacement, or intravenous antibiotic, Luz is dying. And she seems hell-bent on doing it while I am on the night shift.

It's winter, long past sunset, and as I badge my way through seemingly countless doors, into smaller and smaller spaces in the hospital, I imagine the colored windows in the walls hinging around her like a nested puzzle box or one of those little Russian stacking dolls. First, there was the big box of the hospital with its tiered gardens, kid-friendly gift stores, and larger-than-life murals of happy children playing. But that was the outside box, the deceptively cheery one we showed to tour groups, donors, and television reporters. One had only to go through the staff-only door and down the concrete stairs toward the hermetically sealed pediatric intermediate care unit to unlock the second box, a whole different world. Accessible only by code words or magnetized badges, the unit hummed incessantly with ventilators and alarms, punctuated by the occasional cries of grieving parents or conscious children.

Farther on, one needed only to click back a metal handle, and the glass door of the baby's room would slide open like the top of a puzzle box. Inside the room, wires and tubes spindled out, weblike, from pumps and monitors—little lifelines leading toward the eerie glow of her glass bassinet. It could be Snow White's little coffin of glass and gold, covered with a cheery purple shroud donated by a local charity organization of sewing grandmothers.

Go then, inside, and here she is, the baby. But here's the bitter trick. If you go even farther, inside all these boxes, inside even her skull, beyond the thin rim of brain that keeps her breathing and to the center of it all, there's just emptiness. There, in the middle, is the place where everything should be: the twin hemispheres of the cerebral cortex, the corpus callosum, the seahorse of the hippocampus, the pituitary that Descartes mistook for the seat of the soul. But inside the brain of this tiny doll, at the center of the whole giant puzzle box, there's just water.

Staring through the clear glass of the bassinet, I think back to my medical training on the Texas Gulf Coast, to the nineteenth-century anatomy lab in the beautiful red-brick Victorian building. Abraham Flexner praised the facility in his famous turn-of-the-century report on medical education, denouncing every other medical school in the state and crowning ours the only school in Texas "whose graduates deserve the right to practice among its inhabitants." Our medical forefathers designed their school with up-to-date Rembrandt-style dissecting pits, which are now used mainly for freshman lectures. And they kept their cadavers in the attic, which was thoughtfully lined in a gorgeous Romanesque arc with a full score of high windows. It was part of the old architectural master plan to catch the great Southeastern sea breeze, whose salubrious powers would fend off the fetid air and quell the stench of decay. Nineteenth-century doctors with dashing mustaches, old-style aprons, and lit cigarettes carried out their gloveless dissections with the windows open to let in the salt light and the sea breeze, and to air out the smell. A full century later, we novice physicians were doing the same thing in the same place, albeit with gloves and without cigarettes.

But with the windows closed, the building was horribly ventilated, and we spent our first year of medical school marked by the stench of formaldehyde, which not even the most powerful disinfecting agents could cleanse from our scrubs, our hair, or our bodies.

As if the horror of dissection wasn't enough, we had to do it under the fixed stares of the babies. By the time I was a student, the old pathology museum had been renovated to accommodate a newly necessary women's changing room. The babies had been moved to shelves along the high attic windows. Each morning, as we filed in for dissection, babies and fetuses of varying gestational ages and with every conceivable deformity were lit up from behind by a great oceanic light.

We returned often in the evenings and sometimes into the wee hours of the morning, hoping to memorize the intricate details of the marvelous wonder that is the human body with enough detail to pass the gross anatomy midterm. Well after dark, all the lights were on in the attic lab, and from most places on the campus, you could see the outlines of the babies, gravely observing from the high windows of the old red Victorian.

Midway through the semester, after a particularly difficult day, which involved holding our cadaver's head in place while my tank-mate grated his way through teeth using a household hacksaw, I developed a series of recurring nightmares about the babies. In one dream, I gave birth to piles of them. In another, they floated in strange fish tanks, and I had to feed them. One particularly lurid nightmare took place in a vacant hospital stairwell. A nurse wheeled a plastic bassinet toward me. It was filled with a blue-and-pink-striped nursery blanket, but inside was only a tiny disembodied head, attached to a strange machine in the shape of a fancy olive oil dispenser. The dream nurse leaned in to whisper conspiratorially: "They can live like this for years," she instructed, "but sometimes it's best if they don't."

Our sense of humor was becoming more macabre by the day, and my soon-to-be doctor friends began jokingly referring to these dreams as "hauntings." I tried to soothe myself by visiting healthy babies in the newborn nursery. I threatened to return to the lab in the dead of night to steal the jars and take them to the old Victorian cemetery for a proper burial so the souls of the babies could finally rest. Once this was accomplished, I reasoned, I could go back to the anatomy lab at night, which I had been increasingly avoiding, to the detriment of my plummeting test scores. "You can't do that," my friend remarked. "Everyone will know it was you." It wasn't the first or last time I contemplated quitting medicine.

And now, years later, here I am with Luz. With her strange sweet face, she could be a twin to one of those poor little specimen babies, born a hundred years ago in a time when they never even got to be grieved or buried. But despite what those long-dead nineteenth-century anatomists in Galveston thought, I can tell she's no monster. She's a living, breathing baby. Her single nostril is moving air through her lungs, and her heart is pumping blood through her tiny body, only half the size it should be at her age.

But that's not how I can tell she's a baby. I can tell she is a baby because of the baby things she does. How she likes to suck and be held. And how she cries and then consoles if you just rock or hold her.

I'm from a huge family by American standards, so I've been rocking babies since childhood. Right now, inside all these protective boxes, and with all these people and machines working so hard to keep her alive, this baby is alone. She's alone, and she's dying. And now she's screaming. And I'm supposed to be her doctor.

I've always found it to be one of the more upsetting ironies of what we blindly insist on calling medical "care": no one thinks to hold children when they are dying. So I decide I will hold this baby. After countless rounds of broad-spectrum antibiotics, Luz has developed an antibiotic resistant bacteria, and she's on isolation precautions. So I gown and glove up, slide open the glass door of her room, walk toward her, and begin rhythmically unplugging her from her monitors and tubes. When she is finally free, I lift her from the bassinet. I put her over my shoulder, the way babies like. I can feel her warmth and weight through the yellow gown, and I pat her with my nitrile gloves. I bounce my knees and rock her like I've done a thousand times before, with more babies than I can count. Almost immediately, she stops crying.

And all of this is fine, and beautiful, and even profound and cathartic. Because finally, after all these years of training, and despite all the training, for once I know just what to do. And that thing is so simple. I think to myself, *Maybe if I can do this now, for this baby, just hold her when she needs it, when she's crying out in a great need, and just come to her as a baby, maybe it could be a sort of penance for all those babies. A penance for my whole profession, and for all those years that we thought these children were monsters and treated them horribly, and locked them in jars forever, and forgot altogether that they were ever babies at all. If I can do this penance this time, maybe I'll be forgiven. And maybe then I will finally stop having all those bad dreams.*

Except there are no priests here to grant absolution, and this isn't a confessional; it's a hospital. And I'm not a parishioner; I'm a doctor. And unfortunately for me, I'm a doctor who, in this moment, on this long night, is holding the admit phone. Which means that every time a patient from the emergency room needs to come into the hospital, I have to go there. So I leave her. And I keep leaving. And every time I leave, I plug her back in to her weird web of wires, and I write another order for morphine and Ativan. Because that's the only other thing that keeps Luz from crying.

It's a terrible cycle in which the succor of human comfort is deliberately and repeatedly taken away. In its place, I give a shadow. It's the thing the gospels warn against, where the father gives you a snake when you ask for a fish, or a scorpion in the place of an egg. But it is what our culture, despite its unprecedented levels of wealth and knowledge, has stupidly mistaken for care. At some point in this long, dark night, I find myself in the actual chapel. And with my hands covered in holy water, I realize I am touching my forehead in the exact place where hers is broken.

The practice of preserving babies in formalin died out in the mid-twentieth-century. As medical photography advanced, trainees needed preserved specimens less and less. But in some hospitals, up until the 1970s, babies like Luz, if they were born alive, would never be shown to their families. They would live out their short lives in the hospitals where they were born, and they would die alone.

In the hundred years between the birth of a little baby who still floats suspended by thin cords in a jar in an anatomy lab in Galveston, and of the one here with me today, wired to a dozen monitors, in a glass bassinet in a pediatric ward, we've come all this way. Those nineteenth-century anatomy professors could never have imagined the medical interventions we have now that are routinely done to babies like Luz. Neurosurgeons can go into her brain and put in a shunt to drain the fluid that would otherwise kill her. When she stops being able to breathe on her own, pulmonologists and otolaryngologists can attach her to a miraculous machine that will breathe for her. When she stops being able to eat, pediatric surgeons can put a tube directly into her stomach, and skilled nurses can pump in formula. When she develops an infection, fellowship-trained specialists can treat it with a bevy of powerful anti-microbials. With the help of neurosurgeons, they can even drill a hole in her little skull and pump the drugs directly at the thin rim of her brain.

But some things haven't changed. After all that progress, we still refuse to treat her like a real baby. In our perverse attempts at giving her the most up-to-date medical care, we deny her the comfort humans have been giving their crying babies for thousands of years by sheer instinct. Deny her the gentle embrace of warm arms that even a small rim of brain can recognize as safety. In the midst of all this advancement, we have come to value technological innovation, and the prolongation of life through invasive medical technology, more than we value human compassion and kindness. She is no monster, so why should she spend her final hours alone, like a pathological specimen, walled off from comfort in a little coffin of glass?

I think of the doctors of old, who gave us the word *monster*. It comes from the Latin word *monere*, from which we derive the English word *demonstrate*. It means "to warn." For centuries, priests, physicians, and philosophers alike believed that babies like Luz were omens and signs sent from the gods. What else, except divine anger over human folly, could account for such tragic little bodies, broken before they could even be born?

And yet, far from being regarded as mistakes, these babies were an important part of the natural order. There was a perfection hiding in the otherworldly shapes of their uncommon bodies. There was a God who, with time and care, fashioned their physical flaws to point perfectly to our spiritual ones. And if one looked closely enough, a baby like Luz had the power to teach, instruct, and correct. Even in her short life, she could be a guide, bending us forcefully toward our own better nature.

Nominated by Creative Nonfiction

STETHOSCOPE

by TOM SLEIGH

from POETRY

i.m. Denis Johnson, 1949–2017

THE UNIFIED FIELD
It wasn't that there was anything to say
that would stop him from feeling this way—the X
of himself splayed out in space

where gravity was weakest. He and his father
and talkative mother
suffering tiny strokes that took away

this syllable from this word, that syllable
from that, all this lay
in one pan of the balance scale

while in the other there was nothing but dark matter
and the cosmic inconsequence
of his literal physical heart beating.

And then the unified field, faced with its own emptiness,
bent down to his chest as if to listen.

A TOAST TO PAVLOV'S DOGS
Oh Leash held by a hand I can't see, here
in the laboratory where nothing can change
and where yips and bites are fine-tuned to the pack's mentality,

am I one of his dogs, the three-legged one that knows nothing
of my lack except for how I bark, growl,
and whine to be let in? Am I the salivating triangle

guided only by my nose that keeps me
on the move in my limping trot away from you, Leash, yanking
me back from all the filth I want to shove my nose in?

Why won't you let me go free? The sad gestures
of our growing intimacy is a reflex we
can't escape or express: sometimes, emotion is just mange.

So Leash, here's a toast to my lab pals: August, Fast One,
Pretty Little Lady, Joy, Beauty, MiLord, Clown.

THE JUDGMENT AFTER THE LAST
What would we like to see happen?
Would we like to drive nails into our hands?
Would the shame engulfing us like flame

on a computer screen make us understand
that throwing a match into the Grand Canyon
while snapping a selfie, and never once thinking

how far that match falls, is the original sin
that a donkey's ears twitching
as we ride it to the bottom reveal as the truth

about our consciences? How many nails
will we need? Go to the movies, do research,
be the Regulator forced to kill kill kill

and that's when we'll find out just who we are
or if there's anything like "who" anymore.

MISSION
It's not simply that the palm trees are on fire
but that they waver up more fire than fire,
brighter and harsher and more intoxicating

201

than the flames spreading ever thought of being—
the thick black smoke turning noon to midnight
rears up in a wall that nobody can see

over or around or through even as this nobody
comes crashing through the screen
right into my living room: poor nobody! In this loneliest of times,

he tells me how much he loves me, how his lack
and mine feel somehow the same and that the flames
crawling over him have become his mission:

burning, he erects a burning house of smoke
we can neither live in or abandon.

SUNDAY IS NEVER THE LAST DAY OF THE WEEK
Using zip ties and Velcro to strap on a homemade bomb,
who is to blame, who should have told us
that on the far side of the screen in this Sunday calm

our generation has had its time? In that corner
where we slept together so many nights, yes, in that corner where
the bed of the dead lovers has been put out with all the other

Monday morning trash, there are always two doors
opening and closing as one of us goes out and the other comes in.
Why couldn't we show our love for one another

the way the void dissolves into the zero? Why did the animal
grafted to the human find such satisfaction in explosions? Darkness
to darkness, ashes to ashes, the animal to the human,

why shouldn't we take pleasure where and when we can—
provided this is pleasure, provided that the body isn't null.

LAST RITES
Even if the suit they dress me in for my funeral
is dry-cleaned at Perfection Laundry, then washed
and washed in the blood of the lamb, the knees

will still be muddy from kneeling down, the sleeves,
mismatched, will tell their own threadbare tale
about the breath of life breathed into tabletop dust.

What would the naked man and woman and talking snake say
about the god who no longer remembers if they're forgiven
or not? Listening as a kid to the old stories,

there were never enough beanstalks and giants
and Jacks. Now, the pallbearers pick up my coffin,
they carry me out to the ruined cathedral where the saints'

wooden faces, frozen in their homely expressions of grace,
are shadowed by flocks of blackbirds whirling past.

CODA: THE HUNGER ARTIST AS A SENIOR CITIZEN
Nowadays, in my cage
in old straw, where
my brother keeper

forgets to come feed me anymore,
at last I'm fasting for its own sake,
not to break records I've broken

a thousand times before.
Besides, nothing could be easier
than to starve forever

if the food they keep on
giving you makes you sick.
This hunger is a moment's

vision that will persist
in a pillar of radiant house dust.

Nominated by Lloyd Schwartz,
David Wojahn

SCANDALOUS WOMEN
IN HISTORY

fiction by MALERIE WILLENS

from SEWANEE REVIEW

After being hired as a beauty technician with Rémy at Saks Fifth Avenue, Kim was given a lab coat the color of a pencil eraser, and told she'd be going by "Kendra." She wore her long auburn hair pulled back, exposing a creamy, freckled complexion and lippy pout. Over the next several months, magnified beneath the department store's halogens, she would see approximately three thousand faces at various stages of decay. On her first day of work, she learned the merciful cant of the makeup counter:

"Say 'extracting' for popping zits and 'cleaning' for getting rid of blackheads," explained Jade, her boss. "Most important: don't say 'wrinkle.' Say 'fine line.' And stay positive. If someone's oily, suggest a product to eliminate *shine*. 'Shine' sounds dewy, not greasy. Watch Dane when he gets here. He's our star."

Dane arrived forty-five minutes late, looking stunning in cowboy boots. "Good morning, everyone," he said, although only Kendra and Jade were there. He threw down his bags and slipped into a gray lab coat with a gliding disregard. He restocked the lipstick display, swinging his chin-length hair from his eyes with shampoo-commercial verve. He moved with willowy precision. It was impossible to imagine him sitting still.

Side-work done, he approached Kim. "And *you* are?"

She hesitated. "Kendra."

He didn't so much shake Kendra's hand as present her with his.

"Is Dane your real name?" she asked.

"It is now. Né Douglas: world's worst name. I don't go by Doug because I hate diminutives. Dane came to me in a dream. It's strong and simple, right?"

Customers were beginning to buzz around Rémy's three-hundred-sixty-degree counter, the largest at Saks. "Are you Danish?" Kendra asked.

"Hell if I know. I was adopted." He leaned over the counter to take a customer's liver-spotted hand in his.

Kendra spent the rest of the day watching Dane regale his customers with tales of intrepid ribosomes and their unctuous promises. There was the soothing emulsion, the stalwart pentapeptide, and the light-deflecting pearl. Dane's spiel made Kendra suddenly self-conscious about the dull, flaky skin around her eyebrows. Under the cover of familiarizing herself with inventory, she scanned the counter for an exfoliant to unearth the fresh bright layer of skin beneath. She felt her face absorb imaginary nutrients, growing stronger and softer.

Dane spoke of the most florid, delectable ingredients: heliotrope, Copahu wood, watery violet, oak moss. Sicilian bergamot, Chinese peony, white cedar, and the elusive blue rose. A dash of neroli, a trace of blood orange. According to Dane, no customer ever questioned the origin of Copahu wood or disputed the existence of the blue rose, which *did* exist, Kendra would later find out, although it was more purple than blue.

Dane made enough on commission that day to pay half a month's rent. After work he took Kendra to a place he liked—one of the few remaining dives on the Bowery. She asked him if there was anything she should know about the job. She wanted the sort of insider information not in the training manual.

"Learn by doing," he said as he filled their glasses with wine from the carafe. "The trick is not to overthink."

"What about the boss?"

"Jade's joyless but harmless. Poor thing. She thinks her gamine haircut's chic but she looks like a pinhead." He took a sip of wine. "Now tell me about Kendra."

She confessed that none of her previous jobs had ever really worked out. It wasn't that she was lazy, but she'd never understood the fuss about an honest day's work. She'd tried public relations, ad sales, and dating rich men, all of which demanded a fanatical belief in the product—or the appearance of such—that she'd been unable to supply. So she'd quit them all, on principle.

She did not tell Dane that she'd also tried credit-card fraud and shoplifting, beginning with hair mousse at age fifteen. She'd seen her mother pocket cough drops at the drug store and cuff links at Bendel's until just before her death, never once getting caught. Was it her mother's unhurried elegance, the fact that she'd always been unusually pretty, that protected her? It seemed to exempt and implicate her at the same time. All mothers are tricky but Kendra's was spectral, too gauzy to hate or love.

She admitted to Dane that it was nice being at a new bar with a new person. She'd been unemployed all summer, languishing in her apartment, rereading the same magazines and the jacket flaps of books. Now autumn was chopping up the air and she'd have money in her pocket. It was good to be out of the house.

"Here's to you," Dane said, clinking his glass against hers.

He told her he'd come out at twenty and spent the next few years in a funk, chastising himself for being gay. But the gloom got boring, so he settled into a routine of slutty revelry, forcing himself to live fast, provoking strangers on the street and dear old cousins, wearing his shorts too short and his tank tops too tight. It was fun until it wasn't and he'd felt even more morose than before. Now he hoped to level out. He took antidepressants but said he wasn't depressed. "Whatever helps," he added, sucking in his cheeks just slightly, as though posing for a picture. "Does the eighty-dollar cream with good packaging do more than the drugstore brand? Fuck if I know. I'm all about the placebo effect."

He finished off his glass of wine. "Tomorrow you'll meet Nadia," he said. "She's extraordinary."

*　*　*

The next morning, Nadia marched in to Rémy like she was there to serve papers. "This is the nasolabial fold," Dane explained to Kendra, unaware that Nadia was standing behind him. "It's the diagonal line that starts under the nostril and extends down to the outer corners of the mouth," he continued, running a finger along his own lineless face. "And these," he continued, pointing to the area between his lower lip and the chin, "are the puppet lines. You want to call them that because it sounds fun, not clinical."

"Or you can say 'marionette lines,'" added Nadia in heavily accented English.

Dane turned around and saw her. He took her face in his hands. They were both around six feet tall.

206

"Nadia left on Friday an alien and here she is today, a citizen," he said.

"Congratulations," said Kendra. "Where are you from?"

"Romania." She said it like Ru-MEN-ya.

"Just like Nadia Comăneci," Dane teased.

"Stop it," she told him, "You know I can't stand eet." She told Kendra, "Usually I say Moldova, because with Romania, everybody knows gymnastics and maybe they know Ceauşescu. Both of these I don't want to talk about. I say Moldova, people know nothing. No bad and no good."

Nadia was her real name. She was dark, with a wide jaw and almond eyes. Her features had an aspect of cruelty to them, and it was unclear whether she'd endured it herself or inflicted it on others, or both, or maybe neither.

＊　＊　＊

Kendra's first week at Rémy induced a bodily response. The genial gold light and the sweet, heavy air made her feel buoyant and warm. The change felt efflorescent, metabolic, though what this blossoming was, this transformation, she could not say. Dane and Nadia spun around the makeup counter like old marrieds in their kitchen, anticipating each other's movements without colliding. Kendra sometimes felt like a minor character in a musical. The three of them arrived each morning at ten. For Kendra, the transition from the city's concrete and construction to the sunny, synthetic whir of Saks was a relief. She'd rush up from the subway, maneuvering the sidewalk crush of pedestrians, and feel a palpable slowing as she entered the building—a softening, a brightening. An average day brought her in contact with around twenty faces. She'd give her attention to the special topography of each, fielding questions that ranged from the merely inquisitive—"Where do dark circles come from?"—to the semihysterical—"Why do I have dark circles even though I sleep nine hours a night and my mother never had them?" At day's end they'd all hang up their lab coats, rinse the makeup off their hands and forearms in the employee bathroom, and leave for the bar on the Bowery smelling of soap.

One rainy morning, Kendra hurried into work as she always did, shaking off the subway frazzle and stuffing her bag into the cubbyhole beneath the perfume display.

"Someone left this for you on the register," said Jade, who seemed to take pleasure in sneaking up on people. She handed Kendra an envelope with her name typed on the front.

Kendra walked around to the other side of the counter, away from Jade and the customers. The note read:

I am the indentation on the pillow just after you've left bed. I'm the bits of hair in your brush, the sheen your thighs leave on the leather seat, the way your boots still suggest your stance even after you've taken them off. I'm your glasses once you've laid them down, I'm the way they make other people look (like you) when they try them on. I'm the cowlick you comb down, the cleavage you hoist up, the wart that keeps growing back on your thumb. I am uncontrollably you, unstoppably so, and I keep existing and existing: pushing, pulling, staining, straining. You can make your bed, wipe the chair, comb, cup, cradle and coddle and still I keep coming at the world with my you-ness. Lucky world.

Kendra put the note back into the envelope and slid it into her lab coat pocket. Allowing herself to fall into the morning's rhythm of work, she could feel the letter's crisp rectangle against her thigh. She rubbed bronze eyeshadow onto a woman's inner wrist and penciled in another woman's brows, occasionally tapping her pocket, counting the minutes until lunchtime.

She reread the letter while eating her frittata. Was it a love note? And did the writer actually know her? She did have a wart on her thumb, but she'd never worn glasses or even contact lenses.

She paid for her lunch and walked the two blocks back to Saks, wishing she felt flattered instead of tricked. The few admiring notes she'd received before—one while working at the college espresso bar and another that had been slipped underneath the door of her first apartment—had not made her feel especially desirable or alluring. Instead they seemed to mock her vanity, her constant sense of being watched. She'd always been ashamed of her self-consciousness, which made her even more self-conscious.

She couldn't recall any unusual client interactions or attention from passersby. For the rest of the day she monitored the browsers and buyers and other employees with suspicion. You are you, the note seemed to say, and the essential you—whatever that is—remains, despite your attempts at reinvention. Depending upon how you looked at it, Kendra thought, this was either affirmative or terribly bleak. Maybe it was a joke.

"Apache Tulip," said Dane. "Such an unappealing name." Kendra's throat burned slightly with her first sip of wine. She'd joined Dane and Nadia at the bar, but her thoughts were with the note, which now lay in her purse, seeming to generate its own heat.

Nadia downed her tequila shot without a grimace. "Oh my God, eet's the ugliest color I ever saw. Who'd buy it?"

"Please," said Dane. "I can sell snow to Eskimos. And Apache Tulip's tolerable. The worst is that horrid new shadow—the split-pea one."

"I think eet's Delilah," said Nadia.

"No, it's Jezebel," said Dane. "Or maybe Imelda Marcos."

Kendra couldn't remember the name, which was part of the Scandalous Women in History line, but she knew it wasn't Delilah, Jezebel, or Imelda Marcos. She was tipsy and tempted to read the note aloud, but Dane and Nadia wouldn't stop until they remembered the name of the split-pea colored eyeshadow.

"Squeaky Fromme?"

"Ethel Rosenberg?"

"Leona Helmsley?"

"I got it!" said Nadia. "It's Eva Braun!"

"Eva Braun!" they said in unison.

"And today I sold two," Dane said.

"On your sick planet, dees is a good thing," said Nadia with a smile.

"Do you ever feel bad?" Kendra asked him.

"About what? Why should I feel bad?"

"I think she means about lying to the people," Nadia said.

"Lying, schmying. The people feel great when they leave me. Everyone knows confidence makes you prettier."

"But selling something awful and expensive that you know doesn't work?" said Kendra.

"Please. Nothing *works*. Name *one* thing that works."

Kendra could not, at that moment, think of anything that worked.

"See? You're stumped!" said Dane. "Accept it, *ma petite*, and it'll set you free. No cream works better than any other cream. No perfume will get you laid."

Dane was drunk.

"Reading your horoscope will not make tomorrow better than today," he continued. "Wearing glasses will not make you look smarter."

"But Danuçu," said Nadia, "you are always reading your horoscope and wearing the perfume."

"True. Now that I don't *rely* on outside help, I do what I please. Don't you see? I rely on myself . . . but I'm open to whatever makes life easier. Whatever gets you through the night."

"I agree with this," said Nadia. "I always say, *'Te faci frate cu dracul, pînă treci puntea.'* In English it's like, 'you can become friends with the evil until you cross the bridge.' You can tell I'm pragmatist," she added with a gentle boozy belch.

"But you're sending people into the world looking like crap, they're paying all this money to look like crap. And you get their hopes up—"

"No one's sending anyone anywhere, Kendra. They're grownups. They can think for themselves. Plus," Dane said, flopping back against the Naugahyde, "I'm wasted. Don't listen to me."

Kendra was wasted too. They all were. They leaned into each other in silence. Kendra felt the wine pickling her gut. She couldn't decide whether Dane and Nadia were freer than she was, or more cynical. Maybe those qualities went hand in hand.

On the subway home, Kendra's thoughts returned to the note in her purse. She was seated near an ad for single-malt scotch with a Gaelic-sounding name, thick amber ribbons streaming into a lowball glass with three perfect ice cubes. Though not a scotch drinker, she felt a yen for the peaty burn.

When she saw ads for booze in a subway or a magazine, she looked for messages hidden in the liquid. Her friend Pam's Uncle Frank, a big-shot advertising man, and a bachelor, had taught her to do that. In middle school she and Pam would spend weekends swimming and eating turkey chili in his condo, and he'd dazzle them with the secrets of subliminal advertising, showing them ads for brandy and scotch in *Playboy* and *Penthouse*. There were lips and breasts and silhouettes of naked women, barely discernible in the swirling psychedelic liquid. Words like "sex," "love," and "yes" were planted there too, transforming the ads into games of *Where's Waldo?* that still captivated Kendra. Neither she nor Pam ever spotted the words or images on their own. They'd curl up next to Uncle Frank in their bathing suits, coltish and leggy on the leather sectional and breathing in the scent of his cool licorice breath. He'd guide them to the word or image with a flourish. Once Kendra had seen whatever there was to see, she couldn't believe she'd ever missed it.

Uncle Frank must be an old man now, Kendra thought. He might even be dead. She pictured him in his aviator glasses, and could not remember the color of his eyes. She looked at the scotch ad again, adjusting her gaze. There were no hidden words. Just scotch, and now she wanted some.

Later, in bed, in the dark, she pulled the blanket over her face and tried to concentrate. Had Dane written the note? He liked to screw with people, after all. She was glad she hadn't told him or Nadia about it. If she'd mentioned it and Dane *had* written it, she'd feel pathetic. It would also mean that he had a cruel streak.

And if the note was a joke, Kendra wanted it out of mind before she really began chewing on it, working it like taffy. She turned on the nightstand lamp and reread it. She walked over to the filing cabinet at the far end of her studio, pulled out a white envelope, wrote "Dane" on the front in block letters, put the note in the envelope, licked the glue, and sealed it. Then she took a swig of seltzer and returned to bed. She set her alarm for eight o'clock instead of the usual eight thirty.

*   *   *

She was the first to arrive next morning, as planned. She placed the note in Dane's cubbyhole and began to organize the lipsticks. Jade was next to arrive. It normally took her until midday to summon a personality; she spent her mornings in a trance, punching buttons on the credit-card machines and organizing the previous day's receipts. Then came Nadia. She settled in and began making herself up with rough, impatient hands, imposing a sort of Eastern Bloc savagery onto her broad features. In ten minutes she had smoky eyes and her contours loved the light. Dane was late, which gave Kendra time to reconsider what she'd done—it was underhanded, she knew. Waiting for Dane to arrive was like having stubbed her toe. Caught in the second between stub and throb, she braced for impact.

When she heard the clup-clup of Dane's cowboy boots, she was lining a customer's eyes and couldn't turn to greet him. Would he read the note right there? The customer was chatty, in need of reassurance, and by the looks of her—alligator bag, serious jewelry—she could pay for it.

"I bet you've got great stories from this place," said the woman.

Kendra couldn't think of any, but agreed anyway. "Amazing," she replied, surprised at how convincing she sounded.

"The people that come in . . . you must get some nuts. And so vulnerable, with the beauty thing and all."

"Definitely."

"You ought to write a book."

"You think?" Kendra had moved to the woman's lips, but she kept talking.

"You could do a typical day in the life, or divide the book into chapters by customer." She spoke like she'd washed down her morning coffee with Adderall.

"This has a patented enzyme that recognizes the vermilion border," Kendra said. She gave the woman the lip liner so that she could try it herself. "That's the line that separates your mouth from the rest of your face—your lip line. It's guaranteed not to stray outside—"

"—Whoa-whoa, go back."

"To what?"

"What did you say it was called?

"The lip line?"

"Yeah. 'Vermilion' something."

"Vermilion border. Humans are the only animals who have it. There's no demarcation between lip and face in other species."

"It's genius! There's your title: *The Vermilion Border.*"

Kendra had to admit, it *was* a good title. "Are you in publishing?" she asked.

"I'm not, but I know some top people."

She reached into her purse and brought out a cell phone. She held the phone out at arm's length and looked sternly at it. Was she calling a publisher? An agent?

"It's voice-activated," she said to Kendra. "Call home." Then a pause. "Hi sweetheart, it's me. I'm running late. Can you change my Ingrid appointment to a quarter past? Grazie. Ciao."

"Button-pressing's obsolete," she said as she dropped the phone into her alligator bag. "In six months we'll all be voice-activated."

It struck Kendra that the woman had likely forgotten about their book venture over the course of her ten-second phone call. *The Vermilion Border* was probably one of many genius ideas the woman would have that day, one of a thousand pet projects to dissolve by cocktail hour.

"I think I'll pay," the woman said.

*　*　*

"Nice run." It was Dane. Kendra wondered how long he'd been watching. "You just sold a day's worth of product."

He looked completely unfazed. Kendra waited for something—a strained expression or a hint of concern in his voice. Nothing. Had he even read the note?

"How's your day going?" she asked.

"Weird. But every day's weird lately. Weird's the new boring," he said, leaning his elbows on the glass counter and grabbing a customer's well-tended hand in a way that seemed to flatter her.

Kendra found Nadia taking a break in the lounge, hunched over the newspaper.

"I'm doing crossword to help with the English. You think it's good idea?"

"It won't hurt. But a lot of that stuff is puns."

"What is 'puns'?"

"It's like jokes with the language." Kendra thought for a moment. "What did one termite say to the other termite when they sat down for a drink? 'Is the bar tender?'"

Nadia was baffled.

"It's where you mix up words to be clever."

"Why is mix-up clever?"

"It's not. I always thought puns were lame."

"This I agree."

"Have you talked to Dane today?"

"Of course. Why?"

"I don't know. He seems a little off."

"Off?"

"Not quite right."

"Maybe I ask if he's okay."

"I'm sure he's fine. Don't mention anything. I don't want to make him self-conscious."

"Have it your way," Nadia said. It was a favorite expression. She'd learned it as a teenager, she'd once explained to Kendra, when Burger King first came to post-Communist Romania.

At six o'clock Dane was applying lip gloss to a little girl while pitching her mother on matching tubes of *Mata Hari*. Within minutes they'd paid and left, and Dane, Kendra, and Nadia were on their way to the Bowery. Kendra hoped the booze would make Dane talk. If he wrote the note, she wanted to know as soon as possible.

"If I'd had matching mother/son lip gloss when I was a kid, I'd have led a much happier life," Dane said, squeezing the lime into his highball.

213

Except for the three of them, the bar was empty. The normally silent jukebox played unrecognizable synthesizer music. Kendra wished she'd taken a photo of the note before giving it to Dane.

"I didn't wear makeup until I was in my twenties," said Nadia.

"Neither did I," said Dane.

"Seriously," said Nadia. "My mother never."

"I can't picture you having a mother," said Dane.

"What do you mean? Everyone has mother."

"I can't picture it either," said Kendra. It was hard to imagine Nadia as a child.

"I'm offended at this," she said. "My mother is wonderful woman. I love my mother."

"I'm sorry," said Dane. "I didn't mean anything bad. You're just so independent." He sipped his gin and looked contrite. "Tell us about her."

"She's poet."

"You're kidding," said Kendra.

"She's a little bit famous in Romania. She also is a teacher. A professor in college."

"That's amazing," said Dane.

"Why are you surprised? I have very artistic family. It's not like we're potato farmers."

Kendra wondered what Nadia's mother's poems were about. The Romanian countryside? Politics? Eternity?

"My mother right now is fighting a new law. It says no women older than sixty can remove their tops on the beach."

"Because their breasts are saggy?" asked Dane.

"Yes. Because the government says nobody wants to see it."

"That's really cruel," said Kendra.

"I know. It's awful. Romania's a bad place to get old."

"Everywhere is," said Dane.

"What about your mothers, both of you?" asked Nadia.

"My mother was glamorous," said Dane, "but not nice. She taught piano out of our house. She'd sit there in a minidress with a cigarillo dangling from her mouth, ashes falling on the keys. It was totally normal then to smoke wherever. She'd bang those keys so aggressively. She was all technique, no finesse."

"Do you play piano?" Nadia asked.

"Yeah, but there's never one around. No one I know has a big enough apartment. What about *your* mother?" he asked Kendra.

She did not tell them what came to mind first: that if you shoplift and get caught, you will be charged with theft. If you don't have any money on your person, you will be charged with burglary. "Equipped to steal" is what you'll be charged with if, for example, you have a slit in the lining of your jacket for concealing stolen goods. You're likely to be charged with deception plus theft if you're caught exchanging stolen items.

Instead she told them that her mother always slept in her jewelry. Kendra had never been sure whether this was because she fell asleep with the same catlike indolence that characterized her waking hours, or whether she wore it to bed as some sort of gesture. Of something. In her early twenties, Kendra tried wearing jewelry to bed but it would itch her skin or catch in her hair. She couldn't escape the sensation that something foreign was nibbling at her neck, her wrists. She'd take off the necklace at three in the morning, then fall back asleep until the bracelet began to bother her. By sunrise, the earrings, too, would be sitting on the nightstand.

"I never got to wake up in my jewels."

"That's a little bit sad but I don't know why," said Nadia, who paid for the next round of drinks. "Okay, guys," she said. "I can't keep this secret any longer." She pulled the note from her purse and slapped it onto the table as though placing a bet. "I will read," she said: "I am the indentation on the pillow just after you've left bed. I'm the bits of hair in your brush, the sheen your thighs leave on the leather seat, the way your boots still suggest your stance even after . . ."

*　*　*

Kendra reached for her wine and drank, hiding behind the glass. She knew the rhythm of each sentence, rising and falling with Nadia as she read it through to the end.

"I think this is a beautiful note, no?" said Nadia. "I don't understand everything but I think it's romantic. It's not typical 'baby-baby' stuff."

All Kendra managed to say was, "Wow."

"Somebody fancies Nadia," Dane teased. "God, why don't I ever get love notes?"

"Do you think this is love note?" asked Nadia.

"More like infatuation," said Dane, "but that's good." When he noticed Kendra's silence, he asked, "Are you jealous you didn't get a note? Aw, Kendra wants a love note."

215

Kendra laughed it off, staying long enough to finish her drink and blaming her departure on aching sinuses, which wasn't exactly a lie since red wine inflamed them.

In bed she tried to piece it together. Did she and Nadia share a stalker who left the same note for both of them? Had Dane received the note as planned, then given it to Nadia?

❄   ❄   ❄

The next morning, Nadia arrived in full makeup. Her posture seemed straighter and she moved even more briskly than usual. She even spoke more assertive English with her customers.

Dane and Kendra watched her, elbowing each other when she flipped her hair out of her eyes or giggled in ways that seemed out of character. Jade was too busy being busy to notice.

"Come here a minute," Dane said. "I have to tell you something." Kendra followed him into the employee's lounge. He took his time pouring them Styrofoam cups of coffee. Kendra grabbed hers before he started in with cream and sugar and stirring.

"You know Nadia's little love letter," Dane whispered.

As if on cue, they both turned to check that they were alone.

"It was my note. Some secret admirer left it for me and I decided to give it to Nadia."

"Why?"

"Because I knew she'd appreciate it. It cheered me up. And I said to myself, 'If you can do something that'll make someone's day, then do it.' So I did it."

"Do you know who left it for you?" Kendra asked, surprised at her ability to converse so casually about *her* note, the note *she* was given, the note *she* gave Dane. The cups of coffee sat steaming, untouched.

"No idea. It's the first time I've ever gotten something like this."

"I don't believe you."

"Seriously. If someone's interested, they're normally much more direct."

Kendra's relief felt like a tropical breeze. She really *did* have a secret admirer who was not Dane; neither Dane nor Nadia knew the note was originally hers; Dane was kind and generous for giving the note to Nadia; and she had made them both feel desired. They had all three been given the same note. She felt light and serene, like she'd just worked out or stolen something.

"Why didn't you give it to *me*?" she asked.

"I considered it but I thought it might weird you out. I knew **Nadia** wouldn't be as critical."

Now Dane sipped his coffee.

"The note *was* weird."

* * *

Later that week, Jade casually told Kendra she was doing a good job. It was the first real feedback she'd gotten, and it made her think that maybe she'd found her calling. Not necessarily in cosmetic sales, but sales in general, face-to-face encounters with new people every day. After learning that Dane hadn't written the note—that her admirer was indeed a stranger—its unsettling sentiment began to fade, leaving only a vague and pleasant sense of having been noticed—until the next one appeared.

"Someone left this for you. On the register," said Jade. Three weeks had passed since the first one.

> In the subway station this morning, a man in silver body paint and a top hat stood perfectly still atop a milk crate. Every few minutes he changed position but otherwise he was motionless. He rarely blinked. You couldn't even see his chest rise or fall. His cardboard sign said ROBOTMAN.
>
> Later, at a different station, a man contorted his body in impossible ways. PRETZELMAN is what his sign said. He turned himself inside out on a purple yoga mat next to a stack of performance videos for sale.
>
> Robotman versus Pretzelman. Who wins in the game of life?

Before Kendra could decode it, she felt Jade reading over her shoulder—Dane and Nadia were with customers, and three others were at the counter looking for help—so she folded the note and put it into the pocket of her lab coat. Rather than clarifying anything, the second note had only added to the mystery of her secret admirer—who was most likely, she realized, a crazy person. She approached a petite, blonde-haired woman in her midfifties, Kendra figured, whose trepidation made her seem older and more frail. Her face was symmetrically pretty, with big blue doll eyes, and she spoke with the wistful whine of the Rockaways. Her pantsuit was a size too small.

"I'd like to get a few things, but I'm not sure what."

She had a date that night, she confessed, and needed a little boost. Something to give her an edge. She recounted her history in brief: name,

217

Bea; occupation, paralegal. Born in Queens, married thirty years, widowed, no kids, recently relocated to Riverdale. She bought the mascara Kendra recommended, but lingered afterward. Kendra offered to do her makeup for free, though makeovers were normally reserved for people who'd spent considerable money or seemed as though they were about to.

Kendra enjoyed depriving herself of the chance to reread the note that lay in her pocket. It reminded her of being fourteen and going out to dinner with her family, knowing there was a boy who liked her, wanting desperately to talk to him on the phone but relishing the ache brought on by denial.

"I don't want to look too made-up," said Bea. "It's not me."

"It'll be natural. You'll still look like you, only fresher."

"Fresher sounds good."

Kendra sat Bea down and snapped a smock around her, shifting the light so that it illuminated only her face. Bea sat up straight.

"I've never had my makeup done by someone else," she said, maintaining her stiff pose, barely moving her lips when she spoke. "I feel pampered."

"It's good to pamper before a date."

"I kind of like this guy and I don't want to disappoint him," she said, closing her eyes so that Kendra could work on them. "He's very educated. A voracious reader. Politically active. I went to college but it was like a hundred years ago. Who remembers?"

"I can't remember anything either," said Kendra, daubing pink cream along Bea's puppet lines. "How did you meet?"

"I'm embarrassed to say."

"Was it online?"

"Yes! If you can believe."

"Sure I can. It's common now, even if you hate the idea."

"That's what they tell me." Bea opened her eyes when Kendra moved to her cheeks. "It's such a strange process, dating when you're my age. We've been out twice and I think it went okay. You can never really tell though, can you? He at least *seems* interested."

"Are *you* interested in *him?*"

"I think so. They say the third date is very revealing. If we can survive three dates, maybe it'll be something."

Kendra smoothed and blended, powdered and plucked. She swept gold over Bea's cheekbones and neck and transformed her lips into luscious, fruity things. Bea examined herself in the hand-mirror, turning her head three-quarters left and then right and back to center.

"I look dangerous."

"Is that good?" Kendra asked.

"It's great! He won't know what hit him. You're an angel," she said.

She thanked Kendra, then gathered up her bags and walked off. But she returned a few minutes later.

"This is embarrassing," she said, "but . . . oh jeez, I'll just show you." She reached into her purse, pulled out a crisp white sheet of folded paper, and handed it to Kendra. It was an e-mail she'd printed out:

> Hi Bea. I'll collect you at seven. I figured we'd grab a bite somewhere near the Ninety-Second Street Y. That way we can walk to the performance. I thought Thai or Northern Italian (I know places), if that suits you. FYI, the play is called "The Awful Grace of God: A Portrait of Robert F. Kennedy." It's a one-man show and it's supposed to be terrific. Don't let the title worry you . . . after JFK was assassinated, Bobby quoted Aeschylus in a speech, something about the awful grace of God. They say the play is quite uplifting in spite of all this.
>
> Excited to see you,
> Irwin

"It's nice, right?" Bea asked.

"Very."

"I've read it like three times already today. This is going to sound silly, but you don't happen to know how to pronounce this, do you?" Bea pointed at one of the words. "I thought I'd look it up on the Internet but now I won't have time, with the makeover and all, and I'm not so good at using my cell phone for that stuff anyway—"

"It's Aeschylus," Kendra said.

"Oh—Aeschylus—okay. I thought maybe it was E-shill-us." Bea widened her eyes in relief. "Good thing I asked. I've read the word before but never said it out loud. Why would I, right?"

"I can't pronounce half of our ingredients," Kendra said.

"You're a doll," Bea said, squeezing Kendra's hand the way a favorite aunt might. She folded the paper crisply in half and put it back into her purse. "Okay then. I'll report if it's good news."

Kendra watched her until she was gone. She hoped Bea would seduce Irwin. And stop worrying about Aeschylus and Bobby Kennedy. She wanted her to feel dangerous and adored while getting swept up in the surprise of a good romance. Maybe she'd do a striptease, drunk and slow and a little embarrassed, call in sick the next morning and maybe the morning after that.

She wanted this for most of her customers. They came from everywhere but they all breathed the same scent while they lingered at the counter: the slightly noxious odor whose top note, the first to fade, consisted of the three-hundred-plus fragrances being hawked at Saks. The middle note was the molasses exhaust of Fifth Avenue. And the base note—the olfactory anchor—was the musk of the people themselves, never the same twice, impossible to name.

Nominated by Sewanee Review

THAT'S THE JOB

by EDWARD HIRSCH

from KENYON REVIEW

That's the job, he said,
shrugging his shoulders
and running his hand
through his hair, like Dante,
or a spider
that knows its web,
That's just the job,
he repeated stubbornly
whenever I complained
about working the night shift
in hundred-degree heat,
or hauling my ass
over the hump
for a foul-mouthed dispatcher
yelling at us
over a loudspeaker,
or riding the cab
of an iron dungeon
creeping over bumpy rails
to a steel mill
rising out of the smog
in Joliet or Calumet City
where we headed
to track down
a few hundred giants

in chains clanking together
on rusty wheels
for dragging home
and uncoupling
at the clearing yard
loaded with empty
freight cars
waiting to be loaded
with more freight,
because that's the job.

Nominated by Jeffrey Harrison,
Donald Revell,
Michael Waters,
Charles Harper Webb

THE LAST VOYAGE OF
THE ALICE B. TOKLAS

fiction by JASON BROWN

from THE MISSOURI REVIEW

(1981)

When, at fifteen, I began my first summer as the Rural Carrier Associate of Howland Island, Maine, a post officer from the regional office showed up unannounced and reminded me that I must adhere to the agency's mission statement by ensuring the "prompt, reliable, and efficient" delivery of the mail. In August I thought of his words as I held the official-looking letter that had arrived for the writer staying in my grandparents' guest cottage. Most people only received bills and handwritten notes from friends and relatives. Sometimes a postcard. My grandfather, who frequently asked me if I'd heard the writer say anything interesting, would love to see the contents of a typed envelope from the Jonathon Riley Agency, 333a Lafayette St., NY, NY.

As I put the letter aside instead of in the writer's mailbox, I thought of the postal motto, which I had memorized the previous summer: *Neither snow, nor rain, nor heat, nor gloom of night stays these couriers from the swift completion of their appointed rounds.* Halfway through sorting the rest of the mail, I picked up the writer's envelope again and ran my finger over the indentations left by the typewriter on the letters of the writer's name, Alexander Smith, and the name of the island. The bell on the door clanged, and hard-soled shoes tapped down the hall to my office/candy store.

"Hey," the writer said. "Anything for me?" Through the dark glass of his Ray-Ban Aviators, he looked at me sitting on my swivel chair behind my desk complete with various cubbyholes for international, certified, and return service forms, as well as a number of rubber stamps I longed to use in an official capacity. I still held his envelope clamped between my thumb and forefinger.

"Is that mine?" he asked, his eyebrow rising above the gold rim of his glasses.

I nodded, relieved, and handed the envelope to him. He turned and walked away without saying goodbye.

The writer's vanilla-colored envelope would have leaned at an angle in his brass box. The weaker envelopes, especially the blue *par avion* ones, began to sag from moisture after a few hours. Made of thicker paper, the writer's letter hadn't even bent in the mailbag on the boat ride from the mainland.

At 1 PM I rushed home to eat the lunch Grandma had left for me. She'd taken the skiff to shop on the mainland, so I had a one-day reprieve from afternoon chores. The writer had only left fifteen minutes ahead of me, but when I arrived at our house and looked out the kitchen window across the field that stretched to the beach and the guest cottage, I saw no sign of him.

Most summers our house filled with cousins, uncles and aunts, and my sister, but for the last two weeks of August this year, I was alone with my grandparents. My sister was staying with my father and his new girlfriend over on China Lake, and my cousins were busy with their parents. I called out for my grandfather. When he didn't answer, I knew he was probably down at the island landing.

I had just finished the first half of my sandwich when the door to the guest cottage flew open and smacked against the shingles. The writer lurched into the field, kicked a rotting log with the toe of his leather shoe, and yelped as he hopped on one foot. In his balled fist, he raised a crumpled letter the same color as the envelope that had come for him and threw it toward the mouth of the bay.

The August winds on our part of the coast followed predictable patterns. The letter rose briefly, pushed a few inches, no more, toward the water, then slowly reversed course and blew back over his head. As he whipped the door to the cottage closed behind him, I watched the letter roll over the recently mowed field and pass by our house.

Over cod cakes that night, my grandfather smoothed the creases of the letter, took his reading glasses out of the pocket of his flannel shirt, and squinted at the contents. He read it once and raised his head to look out the row of windows at the bay. On the second read, he began to shake his head.

"What does it mean?" I said. I'd read it, of course. Something about his publisher not liking his second book. A former English teacher at the high school in Vaughn, where my whole family lived in the winter, my grandfather was our only authority on literary matters.

"It's not good news for him, that's for sure. This kind of thing happens all the time." My grandfather returned his glasses to his pocket, carefully folded the letter, and pushed it to the middle of the table. He sat back, cupped his hands behind his head. "Why don't you ask him to supper at the end of the week?" my grandfather said as he stood to retrieve more matches for his pipe. Among his few friends in Vaughn, my grandfather was known as "the Torso." A disproportionate amount of his long frame extended above the waist. Tall on foot, he towered when we all sat at the supper table, and when he walked, his head didn't bob, his shoulders didn't sway, and his perfectly erect posture held straight as a board.

"Should I mention the Aga stove?" I said. He didn't nod, because I'd come dangerously close to calling it what it was: John Updike's Aga stove. The stove on which John Updike had made tea in the morning before he sat down to write or grilled himself a cheese sandwich after a long day of writing. In our family, if you wanted to speak of John Updike, you spoke of "the stove," not, as Uncle Alden sometimes called it, "the Aga." Likewise, you could say "Lewiston" but nothing about the dowel factory my great-grandfather had bankrupted. Nothing about China Lake, where my father spent most of his time, nothing about my mother, who had gone to live among the Rarámuri of Copper Canyon.

I saw the writer the next morning standing above the island landing. His hair stood up in back. Though drizzle pattered through the maples and fog sat right on the ground and showed no signs of blowing out, he wore his sunglasses. He hadn't shaved, and when he raised the lenses to squeeze the bridge of his nose, I saw rings under his eyes.

"You have any aspirin?" he said and leaned against the white oak that had long served as the anchor point for people to haul their boats at the end of the season. His slight paunch pushed against the front of his button-down shirt. The matching pouch of fat under his chin thickened when he yawned and squinted at me through his Ray-Bans. One of my goals in life at this point was someday to own a pair of real Ray-Bans. A friend at school told me I had to watch out because a lot of people would try to sell you fake ones.

"They . . ." he said, nodding at the one-room shack the association people called the yacht club. Despite the weather, "they" were setting up for the monthly yacht club lunch on the screened porch. "Are you one of them? You're not, are you?"

"No," I said quickly.

"You and . . . what's your name again?"

I'd told him three times already. "John."

"You and your grandfather and that other guy, the one with the beard, the carpenter."

He meant Uncle Alden.

"You're not like the rest of these people walking around in stupid-looking shorts."

Unlike those people, we were from here. We owned the original farmhouse on the island. We didn't live in it year-round, but our ancestors had.

"What you got there?" he asked, pointing at the paperback in my hand. I showed him the cover with the lighthouse.

"Ahh," he said, "that book." The writer scratched his chin. I could sense his eyes narrowing behind the lenses of his glasses. "John what?" he said eventually. "What's your last name?

"Howland."

"Same as the island. They name the island after you?" He laughed, but this was not a subject of humor for us. The writer had stumbled upon my grandfather's greatest obsession, a grievance he had cultivated like a rose garden. We had lost most of the island in the 1800s when, one generation at a time, members of our family who needed money sold off pieces to a summer colony now called the Howland Island Association. With his canvas bag in one hand and his pipe in the other, my grandfather often plowed right through gatherings of people in green shorts. He spurned their friendliness on the trail. He mutely refused invitations to parties.

"Are those Ray-Bans real?" I asked. He'd just asked me a lot of questions. I felt I was owed the truth about his sunglasses.

He took off his glasses and looked at the little cursive *Ray-Ban* scrawled on the lens. "I don't know. I hope so. I'll give them to you when I leave if you can keep these people around here away from me." He looked over his shoulder at the yacht club.

When she picked her mail up one day, Mrs. Hayes described the writer as having "ruined his looks through booze and neglect." Someday I, too, wanted to be known as having "once been handsome."

Mrs. Hayes, Sophie, who, roughly the same age as the writer, took exquisite care of herself and seemed to subsist on water and lettuce sandwiches and wore only tight, high-waisted floral shorts and pink Izod shirts, closed her eyes before she spoke. She followed her statement by raising her chin and looking right at me.

When the writer pulled out an envelope, I thought for a moment he had somehow retrieved the letter I had picked up next to our house.

"I need you to mail this," he said and placed it carefully in my hands.

"But it doesn't have a stamp," I said.

"I know it doesn't have a stamp, champ. I didn't bring any with me on my preppy, mosquito-infested vacation. You're Postmaster Howland of Howland Island, right? Put a stamp on there for me, and I'll pay you back."

One of the Hale girls—Charlotte, the older one—stepped out of the yacht club and walked toward us with her arms crossed and chin tucked into her chest. Her long hair swung back and forth. I'd spent my life pretending to have no interest in her when she and her friends arrived from Massachusetts and New York for a month each August. According to my grandfather, the Hales were *carpetbaggers*—in 1939 they moved in next door and drove our taxes up. I'd once heard Grandma say under her breath that for all the people around us, paying taxes was like buying an ice cream cone.

The writer watched Charlotte go for a minute and turned back to me.

"What're you waiting for?" he said. "Permission to speak?"

"My grandfather said you should come up to the house for supper," I said to change the subject. "We have John Updike's Aga stove."

The rain-splattered sunglasses had slipped down his nose. In the shallows behind the lenses, his eyelashes flicked like minnows. "I don't understand," he said. "Your family knows John Updike?" I nodded, just slightly. "If I don't swim for the mainland first, I'll come for dinner. So what time do they pick up the mail here?"

I explained that it wasn't picked up—every day I had to take the mail to the mainland by skiff.

"So they let some kid in a leaky boat drag it across the high seas?"

"I'm bonded," I said.

"No, you're not. You're a kid. Kids don't get bonded."

"How would you know?" I muttered.

"Listen . . ." he paused, looking either at the top of my head or over me. Could he have forgotten my name?

"John," I said.

"John, I didn't sleep too well last night."

I reminded him about supper Friday night. He seemed likely to forget.

"Yeah, I'll be there."

On Fridays my grandparents started drinking gin around noon and didn't stop until supper. The writer arrived at 5:30 carrying a bottle of wine and not wearing his sunglasses. Grandma's corgi, Emma, broke into a frenzy of barking. The writer held the bottle of wine out to Grandma, who snorted and snatched it out of his hand.

Uncle Alden, sitting on the far side of the porch in a dirty T-shirt and cutoffs, crossed his legs, pointed his bearded chin out toward the cove and the open ocean and bounced his black-soled foot in the air. When he first heard about the writer coming to supper, Uncle Alden, who claimed to have known plenty of writers at college (before he dropped out), said they were mostly full of shit. For money he worked on the island as a carpenter fixing people's cottages. His calling, as he put it, was to build chairs (shown at the Winnegance Gallery in Bath).

My grandfather shook the martinis and filled everyone's glasses while the writer settled into the wicker. With his cheeks freshly shaven, he seemed ten years younger. Every time he tried to lean back, he started to slip out of the chair. He looked, for a moment, like a student sitting in class.

"John here tells me you have John Updike's stove."

"We do, don't we?" my grandfather said and nodded at me.

My cue to talk about the merits of "the stove," its origins, its place in stove history: "The Aga stove was invented by Nobel-Prize-winning physicist Gustave Dalen, who lived from 1869 to 1937. Since 1930, they have been manufactured in England by the Aga Rangemaster Group. They were designed to make use of a low but continuously burning heat source."

My grandfather picked up with the general career of the inventor, Gustaf Dalen, who invented Agamassen, a substrate used to absorb hydrocarbon gas so it could be used safely in lighthouses—this, not the stove, had earned Dalen the Nobel Prize. The stove, a kind of after-thought, made his career. Wasn't that often the case? My grandfather posed his question to the field in front of our house and to the bay and the ocean beyond. A rhetorical question meant solely for contemplation—I worried that the writer didn't understand the rules.

"I suppose you're right," the writer said. Uncle Alden stole a glance at the writer. "The view from your deck is amazing," the writer added. While he looked over the beach and across the bay to Hendricks Light, standing tall and luminous, we looked at him. The word "deck" hung in the air.

"It's in the kitchen," Uncle Alden said. "The stove."

My grandfather told the writer to come see for himself. I followed them into the kitchen. Cream colored, with four heavy doors and a pipe that connected to the chimney, the stove took up one whole wall. Uncle Alden had constructed a separate support system under the corner of the kitchen. Grandma had rested a large silver platter on one of the burner covers, and sometimes in late summer a vase filled with sea heather perched on another cover.

"It's huge—the size of three stoves," the writer said, though its size would not have struck any of us as its most notable feature.

"Yuh," Grandma said with her eyes closed. Grandma hated the stove, which only worked for cooking if you kept it burning all the time, which you couldn't do in the summer (when we lived on the island) without turning the house into a Dutch oven. She would rather we used the stove as a mooring for the boat.

"It puts out a lot of BTUs if you bank the coal in the firebox," Uncle Alden said.

"Coal?" the writer said. "Do people use coal anymore?"

"One of the ovens is not working," my grandfather said. "I forget which one." He opened one door to reveal the firebox, another door to reveal one of the ovens. "Big enough for a turkey," he noted.

"I would never cook a turkey in this thing," Grandma said.

Finally, my grandfather opened the door he had wanted to open all along. He knew very well which one. "Oh, this is the one that doesn't work," he said and started to close the enameled hatch.

"Wait," the writer said, stepping forward and pointing. "Was that a pair of tennis shoes?"

My grandfather slowly reopened the door and peered in as if he'd forgotten about the shoes.

"Oh, yes, they were there when we got the stove. We leave them in there to remind us which oven not to use."

"Are those?" The writer laughed and raised his eyebrows to express exactly the kind of surprise my grandfather hoped for. Instead of answering, my grandfather opened the stove door wider. From the side, you could see that the instep of one shoe had worn at a bevel, and the sun-faded canvas tops had been scuffed near the laces. "Updike's shoes?" the writer said. He leaned over with his hand outstretched. For a moment I feared he might try to touch the shoes. No one, not even my grandfather, touched the shoes. The writer seemed to realize he was about to cross a line and retracted his hand.

I knew what would come next.

"So you went down and picked the stove up?" the writer said. "I mean, how? It must weigh as much as a subway car."

My grandfather smiled, and the writer pretended to look at the stove from the side, from above, from the front again, though he was really looking at the tennis shoes.

"So you know him—Updike?" the writer asked.

My grandfather straightened himself, crossed his arms over his chest, and gazed at the tennis shoes.

"Well, he and I were at Harvard, and several years ago we had a call about the stove, so we drove down to Prides Crossing."

"Is he much of a tennis player?" the writer asked.

"You certainly wouldn't think so to look at him," my grandfather said.

As we all passed through the dining room to the parlor, the writer gazed at the cracked plaster, paintings, hand-made furniture, the long varnished sweep oar nailed to the ceiling beams along with at least 150 corks from a century of New Year's eve parties held around the hearth. I could see the stories about our lives forming in the writer's head.

"What happened to your drink?" my grandfather asked him.

"I don't know!" the writer said. He smiled as my grandfather poured him another from the silver shaker and refilled my grandmother's cup. The writer leaned over one of my grandmother's paintings of Five Islands.

"I like this a lot," he said with more enthusiasm than I'd seen him express about anything. His shoulders straightened as if a monkey had finally climbed off his back.

My grandfather settled on the sofa. "She calls it her attempt at something and then tells me it will end up in the attic. Or destroyed."

"I don't know about that!" Grandma protested.

"Do you have a gallery?" the writer asked, as he looked around the room at her other paintings.

Instead of answering, Grandma stuck her hand out in front of her, extended her fingers, and clamped them around her cup. My grandparents drank martinis from metal cups. She had been the head of the school board in our area and didn't call herself an artist.

"She doesn't do that," my grandfather said.

"Do what?" the writer asked. "Sell her work?"

Grandma squeezed her eyes shut and twitched her head to the right—a form of "no" too emphatic for words.

"No one wants this stuff," she said.

"She's just like her grandfather, who did those over there," my grandfather said and pointed to the far wall. "Lived to be 105. A worshipper of the obdurate truths, I believe he would have said of himself."

"Jesus, what're you talking about?" Grandma said.

"You sign them Sarah Libby," the writer said.

"That's who I was before him," Grandma said and nodded her head toward the far side of the sofa.

"She would've been something if she hadn't married me and spent all her time working and raising children."

"I would have gone on a car trip to New Brunswick with my cousin Janet. Instead, I married you."

"I'll take you to New Brunswick," my grandfather said. "We'll drive up in September."

She took a sip from her drink. At moments like this, with my grandparents distracted and no other cousins around, I had learned to dip into the kitchen for my own cocktail. Six parts gin to two parts orange juice. I sucked down half the glass, filled it back up, and headed for the parlor, where the writer walked along the bookshelves. Uncle Alden had disappeared, drifting like a dark cloud back to his home across the water, which was fine with me.

"These are all written by Douglas Libby," the writer said.

"Her uncle," my grandfather said, raising a finger and pointing across his chest at Grandma, "grew up over there and joined the French Foreign Legion in 1914."

"I know this guy," the writer said. "I mean I know of him."

"He was known, I think," my grandfather said.

"He was a drunk," Grandma said.

My grandfather tilted his head. "He wrote like someone who never read anything after Balzac."

Grandma held out her cup. My grandfather shook the empty pitcher, raised both elbows, and paused with his eyes fixed on the last light painting the bay. He groaned slightly, stood fully upright, and glided toward the kitchen.

When my grandfather returned from the kitchen, pitcher in hand, he paused above me. I didn't have to look up to see his scowl. I'd left the gin bottle next to the kitchen sink, not on the table, where it belonged.

"Leave him alone," Grandma said, "he's a good boy."

"Ahhhhhh! But he's not a good boy," my grandfather said as he poured Grandma a new drink. He splayed the fingers of his free hand and lowered my grandmother's drink to the coffee table with exaggerated care. When the cup finally came to rest on the table, he lifted both his hands, then sat down with a sigh. Emma shifted far enough away from him not to be crushed.

The writer pointed at a painting Grandma had done of me sitting on the porch with a book on my lap looking out to sea. The very opposite of the 150-year-old paintings on the second floor of my young, square-jawed ship-captain ancestors sitting upright with compasses or charts in their laps.

"Is that you, postmaster?" the writer said.

I nodded.

"What book are you reading there?"

"A prop, I think," my grandfather said.

Grandma vanished into the kitchen and a short time later announced supper, which worried me. The quality of Grandma's crab cakes suffered after five hours of drinking, but semi-inebriation was the only state in which she would agree to feed people outside the family.

When the writer offered to help her carry in the food, Grandma pretended not to hear. My grandfather sat at the head of the table, crossed his legs at the knees, folded his hands in his lap, and angled his chin to the south, straight out to sea. Many of us in the family had been born with round faces and button noses; not my grandfather. Even in his seventies, his head stood high and square on his shoulders like a bust on a mantel. One of Grandma's paintings captured this moment, right before supper.

I hoped he would tell the story of how one of our many ship-captain ancestors from Vaughn had spent a year as a prisoner of Barbary pirates in the 1700s. The feel of the wool shirt and the weight of the iron shackled to his ankle. Anyone caught trying to escape was thrown from the walls of the city by the Dey's men, or they might be tied in a sack with rocks and thrown into the Mediterranean.

Having arranged his napkin properly on his lap, my grandfather then never used it. He cut his food with surgical precision and never lowered his head toward his plate. I tried to imitate him. Emma circled his chair with her nose to the ground. Grandma, whose drinking angled toward the sentimental conviction that she'd been blessed with an extraordinarily talented and adoring family, looked as if she wanted to hug someone. I wanted to hug her, too.

The writer asked my grandfather what he was currently reading.

"*Don Quixote*," my grandfather said.

"Oh, really? Which translation?" the writer asked.

My grandfather had read the novel in Spanish and in every English translation. He didn't answer right away as he passed the fish cakes to the writer and took a piece of bread for himself.

"I reread it a few years ago," the writer said, and my grandfather's eyebrow twitched.

"Don Quixote hears all things speaking. Sancho Panza is the practical materialist," my grandfather said.

The writer paused with the fork in his hand. "Yes," he said.

"Unfortunately, the death of Don Quixote marks the rise of Sancho."

"How so?" the writer asked.

My grandfather smiled. "The rise of prose," he said. "Stuff. More and more stuff. Have you ever been out on the water?" he said.

"Out there?" the writer asked, pointing toward the open ocean, now covered in darkness.

"Tomorrow, we'll take him by the lighthouse," my grandfather said and nodded to me.

"I have to admit I'm a little afraid of the water," the writer said as he stared out the window.

"Nonsense," Grandma said and scooped another barely cooked crab cake onto his plate.

On the dock the next day, Grandma looked over the writer from head to foot as if she had just noticed him for the first time.

"I met your neighbors up the hill," the writer said.

"The Hales? They're from New Hampshire. They haven't been coming here long."

"Really? I thought the woman said . . ."

Grandma waved her hand in the air. "Helen, I don't care what she told you. She's French, you know. Michaud. Says her people were connected to Pierre L'Enfant." Grandma looked at the writer with her eyebrows raised.

"The guy who built Washington, DC?"

"You believe that?"

The writer shrugged, and Grandma turned away.

I lowered myself into the stern of the small punt while my grandfather held the oars in place with his elbows and knees and lit his pipe. Smoke rose in a cloud that hung around my head before catching the wind and blowing out. Under the black metal letters ALICE B TOKLAS screwed onto the planks of the stern of our boat, you could still see the outline of the name BETSY, the wife of the man, Harold Moore (a distant cousin to my grandfather), who built her and ran her as a lobster boat for almost thirty years. The iron fastenings wept dark rust stains down the sides of the peeling white hull.

Right before we reached the stern, my grandfather let go the oars, stood up on the seat of the punt, and leaped onto the deck. Without a glance in my direction, he buried his head in the engine compartment. My grandfather had the air of someone who could fix anything, but the last time we'd refueled, Bobby Plumber at Five Islands Marine had told my grandfather not to take "the old girl farther from shore than you can swim." She had twice slipped her mooring in the last ten years because of rot around the cleat. The main problem with the *Alice B*, which for some reason never seemed to worry my grandfather, was that she was sinking. The electric pumps ran day and night.

The *Alice B* had no neutral, just forward and reverse. Grandma knew the drill. As we approached the dock, she positioned the writer in front of her. When my grandfather swung us around parallel with the dock only a foot away, Grandma shooed the writer into the boat. He landed on his knees, and we swung around for our second pass to get Grandma, who simply lifted her foot and stepped forward as if onto a moving escalator.

As we rounded the north point, my grandfather pointed into the woods above the beach. "That's where my ancestors built their first house." At low rpms, the engine that lived under the wooden box amidships jackhammered while the exhaust pipe sticking up through the roof buzzed like a giant insect.

We headed for open water, and my grandfather opened up the throttle to 4500 rpms, the sweet spot where the engine reached a gallop. As he searched for his tobacco in one pocket and his pipe in the other, I reached for the wheel to keep us on course. The *Alice B* pulled to starboard, especially at speed. He nestled against the windshield to light his pipe and without glancing at me took the wheel again. I let go just as a cloud of pipe smoke mushroomed around his head. We passed Joey

Pinkham hauling with his son off Bull Ledge. In the middle of sorting through one of his pots, Joey raised an arm, then tossed out several shorts. In reply, my grandfather raised his hand in the air.

Hendricks Light came into view. Rollers split aqua green over the axe-head of the granite point.

"There it looms," my grandfather said, "stark and straight, white bricks glaring." As I followed the writer's eyes, I wondered how he must see the lighthouse on his first day ever on the water, his first time up close.

The swells lengthened and the *Alice B* settled into a steady roll with spray feathering across the windshield and the deck. My grandfather told the story of riding out Hurricane Carol in the Bay of Fundy in 1954, a story I'd heard from Grandma before. In Baddeck, on the island of Cape Breton, Nova Scotia, where he and his friends picked up a schooner, they stayed at an inn where all the maids were blue-eyed Irish girls. When my grandfather pointed to where the waves crested fifty feet above the deck, the writer looked up to where my grandfather pointed and said he couldn't believe anyone would survive that. For a moment I was there with him on that schooner in 1954, my bloody hands hauling on the jib sheet while he lashed the tiller so we could heave-to into the path of the storm.

As we rounded the western tip of Damariscove Island, Grandma, sitting on a metal lawn chair in the stern with her eyes closed and her chin raised to the sky, pulled her sweater tight over her shoulders. In less than a month, the summer would be over and we would all be back in Vaughn, sliding toward winter. My sister and I living with my grandparents, my father living over on China Lake with his new girlfriend. My mother had said she would be coming back from her job teaching English in Mexico, but she had said that last year as well. In the winter, trudging up the hill to school and working on the woodpile in the afternoons, I felt as if the story of our lives came to a halt until we returned to the island.

To enter the only harbor of Damariscove Island you had to avoid the wide, sharp ledges on both sides of the approach. The narrow harbor extended far into the island, which had been treeless for as long as I could remember. Because of the high hills on both sides, the water in the harbor remained calm while the surf pounded the windward shore.

We landed at the dock and climbed the ramp. I waited for my grandfather to tell the writer, as he had told others, that the first Howland in

America set foot here in 1621, when he came to beg help for the starving pilgrims at Plymouth. Without this tiny island, and without John Howland, they all would've died.

My grandfather carried the basket up the trail that wound past the Coast Guard station. Grandma spread the plaid blanket on the high grassy point where we always ate and anchored the corners with stones. The basket contained sandwiches, the martini shaker, and molasses cookies wrapped in a cloth. My grandfather poured into the small tin cups. Instead of sipping his right away, he rested his cup on his knee. We all sat facing the bay. At a distance of several miles, the pointed firs sat above the line of pale granite.

"The shinbone coast," my grandfather said.

I bit into my cheese sandwich, which Grandma had lined with yellow mustard, and I began to imagine the story the writer would tell about us. No heroes, battles, murders, discoveries, shipwrecks—all of that would be in the background.

My grandfather took the pipe out of his mouth and pointed at the *Alice B.*

From a distance, you couldn't see the paint peeling or the hull losing its shape on the starboard side. Planks could be replaced, but when the ribs warped, no one would be able to save her.

"Stein left most of her money to Toklas," he said, "and the paintings in the apartment in Paris, but their relationship had no legal status. When Toklas was away, Stein's family came in and stole them all. Toklas wrote her own memoir, you know. Even though she wrote it almost twenty years after Stein's death, the memoir stops the day Stein died, 1946."

"I didn't know that," the writer said.

"She had to live a lot of years as no one."

With the stem of his pipe still pointing at the harbor, the corners of his mouth turned down, my grandfather nodded.

"She was Stein's Sancho Panza," he said.

The writer stared at the sandwich my grandmother had made from stale bread and cheese she stored in the cupboard. Guests were always my grandfather's idea, never Grandma's. She served them food not even a squirrel would touch. The writer stuck out his tongue, touched the edge of the sandwich, and frowned. His hunger had yet to overcome his standards.

"So what happened when you drove down to Prides Crossing?" the writer asked.

My grandfather lifted his cup to his lips, sipped, set it down again. I sat up straight because my grandfather rarely told the story of picking up the stove. I'd only heard it once before from his mouth and only secondhand otherwise.

As my grandfather described John Updike, reading glasses dangling from his neck, answering the door, the writer raised his cup to his lips, and in my memory of the story (at least the version told on this day), John Updike said, "John! It's been years."

My grandfather finished his drink, stood, stretched his arms in the air, nodded to the writer, and said, "Come on," which I knew meant without me. I told myself I didn't need to go. Even though I knew exactly what my grandfather would say as he and the writer stood on the ledge above the Coast Guard station, I shuffled in their direction until I could hear just enough to follow what I'd already heard before. John Updike stands in the doorway of his Prides Crossing house. My grandfather asks if it's a bad time, but John waves my grandfather's worries away and comments that he has been praying for an excuse to abandon *Rabbit at Rest.* The new Mrs. Updike greets my grandfather and Uncle Alden, and they sit on the patio and have drinks. My grandfather and John talk about their former classmates from Harvard and what has happened to them. After an hour or so, my grandfather says they have a long drive back to Maine and should see about the stove before they drink too much to do anything about it. John says he can't wait to get rid of the goddamned thing, which is too complicated, too big, too English. He suggests they hook up a chain to my uncle's truck and drag it out of the house. For a moment some version of this plan is seriously considered—with a blanket and maybe an old pair of skis underneath, such a thing might be possible. John Updike, a bit "shellacked," goes up to the attic for his old skis. In the end everyone gives up and decides to head into town. Over a third bottle of wine at supper, John insists that my grandfather and uncle stay the night.

As the writer and my grandfather walked back to the blanket, the wind whipped the words out of my grandfather's mouth and carried them out to sea. Interested in whatever my grandfather had said, the writer stopped walking and watched my grandfather—the first time I'd seen him really pay attention to anyone on the island.

"What did you say to him?" the writer asked.

"What could I say? He was right. I knew he was right. He knew he was right."

"So you said nothing."

237

"No! I told him to give someone else a chance."

The writer rocked back on his heels.

"I guess he didn't listen to you."

"No, he did not."

The writer and my grandfather settled on the ground next to Grandma and me, topped off their drinks, and picked up their sandwiches. My grandfather ate his, while the writer sniffed around the edges again.

Knowing that my grandfather had never even met John Updike didn't matter to me. I believed the story of picking up the stove, though I knew it wasn't true. Uncle Alden had once pointed out that the Old Man and Updike were not even at Harvard together—once he showed me the Red Book to prove it. Uncle Alden had gone to college briefly with a friend of John Updike's son, which was how he heard about the stove. He and my grandfather hadn't even gone to Prides Crossing—they picked the stove up at a garage in Ipswich.

The day my grandfather and Uncle Alden drove into Five Islands with the stove, the fishermen gathered around the wharf as my grandfather brushed pine needles off the top and reached into one pocket for his tobacco pouch and his other for his pipe and matches. The wind had come up early that day, out of the north at fifteen knots, so it took three matches to get the pipe lit. Then he put his arm over my shoulder.

When Harold Pinkham asked how much the stove had cost, my grandfather uttered the single most impressive word in our language: "Free." Not just any stove, my grandfather explained, an Aga stove, the most indestructible stove ever made. We backed the truck up to the edge of the wharf. While people stood watching, the loading winch used to haul crates of lobster to the deck lowered the stove into the stern of the *Alice B.* We motored north along the shore toward the island with several lobster boats in tow. It would take six men to muscle the stove onto the dock, six more from the island to lift it into the back of the island truck. Grandma had set out bottles of Poland Spring gin on the porch.

My grandfather inhaled and said, "I've been working on a little book myself."

Grandma almost choked, and I lowered my sandwich into my lap. We'd never heard such a thing.

"What about?" the writer said casually.

"It's nothing, really, a few questions about *Quixote* that have bothered me over the years," he said. "You see, Cervantes created a character greater than the book from which the Don wandered. How is it that the knight commits the same chivalric errors in taste that Cervantes is so eager to criticize? In Don Quixote's speeches about becoming a knight-errant, there is no irony. The only difference between Don Quixote and Lancelot and Sir Tristram is that Don Quixote lived in the age of gunpowder, and he could find no knight to fight. It's not a satire at all. It's a condemnation of a world in which the virtues of the knight cannot be recognized."

The writer nodded while my grandfather picked at the grass between his knees, pretending to seem relaxed, I could tell, as he waited for the writer to finish sipping from his cup.

"You may have something there," the writer said. "But what do I know?"

"As much as anyone, a writer like yourself. The fun sinks to the low level of medieval farce: donkeys, gluttons, tormented animals, bloody noses. Cervantes put up with the Inquisition, solemnly approved of his country's brutal attitude toward Moors. The art of a book is not necessarily affected by its ethics, wouldn't you say?"

"Yes, I guess that's true," the writer said.

After a few moments of silence, my grandfather rose to his feet again and walked toward the water to light his pipe. The writer finished the rest of his drink and followed him. With the stem of his pipe, my grandfather pointed to Newagen Harbor, Fisherman's Island to the east, Seguin Island to the west. Before I could catch up to them, I heard the words "gilded butterflies."

Grandma called for me to come back and sit down. I obeyed, as I almost always did with her, and I heard nothing more because the wind increased as it did every afternoon in August. My grandfather spoke with more intensity, and the writer leaned in.

"Eat the rest of your lunch," Grandma said behind me, "or you're not having any of these cookies."

I was sure the writer would forget, but as we passed the channel nun in the *Alice B* on his last day, he tapped my shoulder with the folded Ray-Bans.

"You earned them," he said.

I hadn't, but that didn't matter to me. I had to exercise all my willpower not to put them on right away. I had a clear image of what I would look like wearing them. A younger version of the writer, a man on the verge of ruining himself.

When we reached Five Islands, he threw his suitcase onto the dock and climbed out of the boat with the care of someone pulling himself back over the lip of a cliff. "Okay," he said when he was on his feet again. He reached over the boat and took my grandfather's hand in both of his.

"Send me the manuscript when you finish. I mean it," he said to my grandfather, who removed his pipe and nodded.

I managed to wait until we rounded the point before slipping the Ray-Bans over my nose. Behind the darkened glass, I watched boats pull at their moorings' tethers and seagulls glide over the evergreens running north to south on the island—the world I knew enhanced through a pulsating yellow glaze.

After the writer left, my grandfather spent every morning, even Saturdays, in his bedroom with the door closed. The first half hour of quiet ended with a flurry of key taps and the sound of his chair scraping deeper grooves into the pine floor. Another lull always ended with a second burst of tapping that usually steadied for an hour, sometimes more, and fell off. Over supper he talked about the knight's library burning down. The loss of all those words.

Grandma and I met Mrs. Hale on the way to the landing, and she asked, in a whisper, how my grandfather's Don Quixote book was going. I had no idea how she'd found out. Maybe the writer had told someone, probably Sophie Hayes. I hadn't told anyone. No one would ever ask my grandfather about the book. "I can hear him typing from my porch," Mrs. Hale said. My grandfather typed with the window open, and the sound carried through the woods early in the morning before the wind rose. "You should mind your own business," Grandma snapped.

One after another, people from the island came to see me at the post office and asked me about the Quixote book. I became the expert for the remaining weeks of the summer. What was it about? How was the work going? I told them the book seemed to be going very well but that he wouldn't talk about it to anyone. "That's usually how it is with those things," I said. "If you talk about it to anyone, it goes away."

"I'm not surprised that he's writing a book, your grandfather," Mrs. Hayes said. "He's always seemed like a writer to me."

Uncle Alden did not let me off easily.

"What do you know about this book?" he asked me. He and his friends were rebuilding a porch on the other side of the island, and he had walked to the post office on his lunch break. I shrugged and pretended to busy myself rearranging the *par avion* envelopes.

"When did he tell you about it?" He stood over me with his arms crossed over his chest.

"Two weeks ago, I guess," I said, even though my grandfather and I had never talked about the book.

"He just told you out of the blue? For no reason?"

I shrugged again.

"How long has he been working on it? Don't shrug this time."

"A while, I would say."

"A while, you would say! You're starting to sound like him." He looked at his watch and rushed out.

Though my grandparents handled all their mail at their winter house in Vaughn, where they returned once every week or two, I thought my grandfather might mail chapters of the book to the writer from the island. He visited me at the post office once and left money for a Hershey bar, but he said nothing about his book or sending a letter. When he left, I went to the window. He stepped carefully on the old stairs and, partway down the trail, steadied himself against a tree for a moment before continuing.

When my grandfather finished his book, it would travel over the water to the writer and then to a publisher. His name would stretch across the spine, and the book would sit on shelves in libraries and in people's houses all over the state. People would take the book down and read the words he had typed in our house on the island. Though I knew we had no connection to John Updike, I pictured him reading my grandfather's book by the fire in Prides Crossing.

As far as I knew, he'd never tried to compose anything more than a letter before the writer came to visit, but when people on the island asked me about his book, I could tell that they believed it existed. It seemed obvious to them. Mrs. Hale, Mrs. Hayes—their belief cost them nothing, but I knew that in another two weeks I'd be sitting in my grandparents' peeling house in town with its sagging window mullions and the humming refrigerator containing discount cuts of meat. Occasional phone calls from my mother in Mexico interrupted midsentence when she ran out of money.

At the end of the month, my grandparents rose early and prepared to take the *Alice B* upriver to Vaughn for the weekend. I rushed their bags down to the dock ahead of them. With one eye on the trail, I quickly searched the bags but saw no sign of the manuscript. When they appeared around the corner, walking slowly (more slowly every year now) with the dog between them, their arms were empty.

For lunch that day I cooked the last hotdog on the iron skillet and ate it with Grandma's potato salad at the kitchen table. With my stomach so full that I felt slightly dizzy, I stood in front of my grandparents' bedroom door, left partially ajar, and pushed the door open all the way with my foot. My grandfather's desk sat on the far side of the room under the eaves. Lowering myself into his chair, I looked out the window and rested my fingers on the enamel keys of the typewriter. Either the letters danced on the page, my grandfather had said, or they lay down. You either had the trick, or you did not.

Inside the slant-front desk I found stacks of paper crammed into drawers and slots. I pulled them out one at a time and looked for any sign of the typing I'd heard every morning. A few of the dusty, yellowing pages contained yearly tax amounts, lumber bills, food bills by the month. The top drawer held stacks of typed letters. From the pile, I found a letter dated three days ago and addressed to the Tax Assessor of the Town of Georgetown, Maine, Ronald Boynton, concerning property tax values on the island. In one section my grandfather outlined what he received for his taxes purely in the negative: *I do not receive road maintenance, I do not receive access to schools, I do not receive fire and medical services. What I do receive is a tax bill. My contribution to the creation of this single page of purple prose (and the in-depth analysis behind the eloquence) is exactly $600 dollars this year, $570 the year before, $530 the year before that. Cognizant though I am of the scarcity of trees for making paper in the State of Maine, a scarcity so severe that it would precipitate a 7.02% and 5% year-over-year inflation rate, and bearing in mind also that the ink used to print said bill is not produced in the State of Maine and has to be imported by tractor trailer overland from Worcester (and understanding as I do that the price of stamps increased last year by one cent), I fail to see why I should pay you any goddamned money at all. Instead of entertaining your incessant and unsubstantiated demands for more and more and more money without end into the future, I propose that you submit a request to me for funds that includes a detailed justification (beginning with why the tax assessor's position should exist) and ending with the word "please": early 14th c., "to be agreeable." From Old French plaisir, which means "to give pleasure, to satisfy." 11c. From Modern French plaire, from Latin placer, "to be acceptable, be liked, be approved," possibly from plak-e-, "to be calm," still water, etc., from root plak-, "to be flat." See "placenta": a circular organ in the uterus of pregnant eutherian mammals, nourishing and maintaining the fetus through the umbilical cord. Not to be used* *as the intransitive "do as you please" first recorded in Scotland (of all places) 1500; nor as the imperative "please do this" first recorded in England 1620 (of all times). Only, in this case, to beg, to wit: "PLEASE send SOME of the money without which I would have to look for another island with a shortage of overpaid, unskilled civil servants."*

The letter to the tax assessor was clearly a draft with crossed-out and penned-in sections. He had typed, edited, and probably retyped it.

In the bottom drawer, I found a cloth-covered yellow volume, *Lectures on Don Quixote,* by Vladimir Nabokov. The corners had worn down to the boards and the pages hung loosely in their binding. I flipped through some of the dog-eared pages and found this: *Come with me ungentle reader who enjoys seeing a live dog inflated and kicked around like a soccer football, who likes on his way back from church to poke his stick at a poor rogue in the stocks, come with me and consider into what ingenious and cruel hands I shall place my ridiculously vulnerable hero.*

I read from other places marked in the book and came to a familiar passage underlined in pen: *Don Quixote is not a satire of the chivalric and romantic, it is a condemnation of a world in which the virtues of the knight cannot be recognized.*

I remembered exactly where I had sat next to Grandma (the feel of the cheese sandwich in my hand, the sharp granite under my butt, the smell of the salt air, the view of the bay) when my grandfather spoke these words to the writer. As if I had been reading someone's personal diary, I carefully placed the book in the drawer exactly as I had found it. The air from the open window felt cool on the skin of my arm.

When we returned to Vaughn, where no one from town would be able to hear typing from the street and no one would ask about the progress of my grandfather's book, the mornings would be quiet again.

I looked out the window toward the small beach below the field. The two Hale sisters were rising out of the water. In the bright sun, the sea behind them was iridescent and dark, and their bathing suits shone as slick and black as sealskins.

As I walked downstairs and through the parlor, the sound of my bare feet slapping the pine boards echoed into every corner of the empty house. In the kitchen, I opened the oven door of the Aga stove, removed John Updike's tennis shoes, and slid my feet into place, one at a time. Pulling the laces tight, I wiggled my toes. I'd never played tennis, but it so happened that I wore a size nine shoe.

With the Ray-Bans riding on the bridge of my nose, I crossed the field toward the beach, where the Hale sisters lay on their stomachs, their heads down and the soles of their feet angled to the sky. Standing next to a piece of driftwood, I gazed out and tried to think of what I could say to them about the sea rolling in waves of pure lemon to curve and swell upon the beach. I might say that at night the peaks climbing as high as church towers slowly ate away the ground where we stood.

The older one, Charlotte, rose on her elbow. Furrowing her brow, she glanced from the Ray-Bans to the tennis shoes.

"John," she said, "is that you?"

"No," I said in a voice I didn't recognize, a voice I'd been waiting to hear. "It's not."

Nominated by The Missouri Review,
John Fulton

HOW TO MOURN THE DEAD

by NAUSHEEN EUSUF

from THE AMERICAN SCHOLAR

for the victims of the Dhaka café attack, July 2016

Let us recite in four tongues
                  the names of the dead
and cease for the unborn
        who shall never be named.

Let us unrivet our gaze
                from the malice we saw
that we cannot unsee.
        Let us imagine the amenable.

Let the wounds heal
                on their inviolate flesh
so they can walk again
        on the fresh-cut grass of the lawn

when they awake.
                Let us honor the spirits
who step lightly through
        the garden of our disgrace,

who shall never leave the mist
                of that midsummer morning
by the glimmering lake,
        but walk always beneath the trees,

astonished by the chancel
        of branches laced above them,
and the ordinance of birds,
      and their bodies stained with light.

Nominated by The American Scholar,
Christine Gelineau

BRAINDRAIN

fiction by C PAM ZHANG

from PAPER DARTS

Because bodies couldn't cross the borders—bodies were unwanted. Bodies had disease and sweat and threatening biceps and strange-tongued languages, needed beds and jobs and maybe even women and lives, meant a future of preexisting bodies diluted by the sweat-flesh-stink-color of new bodies. No bodies. But what *was* okay, they said (they on the right side of the wall), was brains.

Tossed over, slipped through cracks too narrow for shoulders, bobbing across seas like coconuts, came the brains. At first border-residents complained of cerebral goo, which left a troubling smell of stale tears. A severe proclamation was issued. Thereafter, all brains were carefully wiped before being thrown, flown, slid, shipped, given.

Wondrous things arose from the brains. Congratulations and medals were handed around, one suited man on a podium to another. Because without bodies—their distracting skins, breasts, eyes, tongues—the ingenuity of brains could be fully harnessed for the first time. Within the walls, technology thrived. Money hummed.

Without, families sat around the bodies of loved ones. Hugged the slumped shoulders, bathed the hollow heads. Pressed the slack fingers to phones to authorize digital payments trickling in. No thanks exchanged. What was the point? The brains dwelled elsewhere.

Nominated by Paper Darts,
Allegra Hyde

THE UGLY AMERICAN

by **SHARA LESSLEY**

from BIRMINGHAM POETRY REVIEW

—Petra

The boys beat the jennet because they could,
out of boredom, because she was in heat,

they beat her with sticks and switches and clods
of dirt. Because revolution had stalled the usual

parade of buses and there were no tourists to ferry
up 800 rock-cut steps to The Monastery,

they pinned her against a cliff and beat her.
Only a woman, very pregnant, saw, who'd left

her husband snapping photos near Q'asr Al-Bint,
left him in search of shade, somewhere to rest.

And when the boys cheered and laughed
and thrust their hips and whipped the jennet,

baiting their donkeys to mount her,
the woman, too, picked up a stone, though

she was half a field away; she heard herself
curse, think every stupid soulless thing

she'd heard about the filth borne of this region.
And when a man—an uncle? cousin?—came

charging, freed the jennet as it brayed then loped,
when he berated the boys, driving them off, the woman

watched them saunter toward the village trail.
As they joked and kicked up sand, it was then she felt

deep within the son she had forgotten. Please
understand this isn't metaphor: when

I dropped the rock, I had blood on my hand.

Nominated by Birmingham Poetry Review

WALKING IN FAST-FALLING DUSK WHAT IS BETWEEN US BESIDES

by MARY SZYBIST

from THE PARIS REVIEW

this sharpness of pines, this gravel loose

beneath us, faltering with each rustle, each step, with what we're
   not

saying to each other—Now your flashlight's beam angles

into the thickness, dead petals the color of light honey

unfasten from their coppery centers, dark berries shine

clustered above twig tips, above forked edges of leaves, above

everything unnamed between us I have

not forgiven—still overflowing toward us while still

arrested, suspended, in all the shadows

of everything I don't know how to feel

that slant toward the awkward shapes our bodies make as we

walk over what may be moss or violets in the dark, over

things maybe veined or dank or thorned or now

between us, *Can't you slow down* I say

though I am not falling behind.

Nominated by The Paris Review,
Marianne Boruch,
Jane Hirshfield

STORIES THAT FIT
MY HANDS

by REBECCA McCLANAHAN

from THE GEORGIA REVIEW

SATURDAY NIGHT AND SATURDAY NIGHT AND
SATURDAY NIGHT WITH THE NEIGHBORS

The table is set—flowers in a crystal bowl, linen napkins folded and creased, the candles ready to light. It's 5:45, and the other couple is due to arrive at 6:00. They are our closest neighbors, about twenty feet away, and I saw them less than two hours ago. Since then, the wife has phoned three times. And now the phone is ringing again. My husband, a book open on his lap, smiles his impossibly patient smile. He holds up the book so I can see its cover—something about Dadaism. What I know about the subject wouldn't crowd the head of a pin. Dada: probable father of the surreal, the absurd. Subverter of reason, logic, language. And of course, being a dictionary junkie, I know the multiple derivations.

I pick up the phone and put it on speaker so Donald can hear. "Hello," I say, as if I have no idea who is on the other line.

"This is Juanita. Who is this? Is this six or three? I've tried all six numbers."

"I'm number three. You've reached *me*, Mother." At least she dialed from the phone this time, I think. When Donald and I were with her this morning, she kept pressing the numbers on her little pink wristwatch, then holding the watch to her ear. She was trying to phone her dead sister.

"*Every* number," she says, in her sweetly adamant way. "We are supposed to go to dinner. Who is this?"

"You've reached the right number. I'm your daughter, Rebecca." Pause. Try again. "Becky? Number three." Several months ago, when it became clear that neither of my parents could manage dialing, Donald programmed the numbers of their six children according to birth order. It was a brilliant solution, given that this recitation is one ability my mother has never lost.

However, the challenge lies deeper: Yes, she can recite the names and punch the corresponding numbers, but who are these people showing up at her door every few hours, or phoning her from across town or across the country and saying things like, "Hi, Mom. How are you today?" Up until a few months ago, Dad would have connected the dots for her once again, would have intervened in a phone call like this one. But he is worn down and, since his latest stroke, when he does connect the dots they form a strange design. Mostly, he sits in his chair waiting for something to happen. "Floating," is how Donald describes it, "from one moment to the next."

"We are supposed to go to *dinner*," she says. I know she has been looking forward to this outing all day. Dad, too. He told me so. Though I see them several times a day, and Saturday night is always "date night" at our place, each Saturday is like the first time for them now.

I spent most of the afternoon at their place, finally managing to get both of them bathed and into clean clothes. As usual, Dad insisted on buckling his own belt, his hands shaking violently. The belt is too loose, even threaded through the last hole, but he refuses to let me buy him a new one. "A waste of money," he says. His shoes alone required five minutes of struggle; he was panting by the time he had finished. When I left he was asleep in his chair, and probably still is.

"Are you three or six?" she repeats.

"I'm number three, Mother."

"No, not my mother. I'm trying to reach someone else. A neighbor. We are supposed to come to dinner."

"This is your neighbor. Just come out the front door, turn left at the sidewalk, and come to the second door. Don't forget Paul. And your walker. Be careful."

"Oh, thank you," she says, a bubble of anticipation in her voice. "We're looking forward to it."

A few minutes later, the sweetest couple on the face of the planet arrives at our door. Sans walker or cane, they lean together, holding each other up. Behind them, the dark sky threatens the thunderstorm predicted for later this evening. Dad wears his signature Marine Corps cap, Mother an ancient ball cap from a team whose once-extinct name has recently been resurrected. The cap is too big, and most of the plastic teeth on the back closure have broken loose, but it was a gift from one of her grand- or great-grandsons (none of whom she can name) so is too precious to part with.

Now, having finished their watered-down sherry, they are seated across from us at the table, my father admiring the napkins, the silverware, the lighted candles. Mother has already tucked into her meal; for a ninety-pound weakling, she can really put it away. I love that about her, among so many other things that I can't name without weeping. No weeping allowed on date night.

Dad picks up the knife, turns it carefully in his shaking fingers. "Heavy," he says. He never uses a knife—a matter of pride, it seems, to be able to hand it to me at the end of dinner and announce that it's perfectly clean, that I won't need to wash it. Then he shifts the knife to the other hand, as if weighing it on a scale: "Heavy." He puts the knife back on the table, lines it up perfectly beside the spoon. He stares at his plate as if it were a work of art. "Colorful," he says of the meal I've prepared: pork roast, mashed sweet potatoes, broccoli, sliced tomatoes. He says this every week. He lifts his fork. Takes a bite. Places the fork back on the plate. The planets shift, the earth rotates on its axis.

"Just go with it," Donald always says of the interminable wait between bites. The pauses. The sighs. "Think of it as theater."

Theater of the absurd, I think. Ionesco, Genet. The kind of play that always puts me to sleep. Suddenly, a whiplash flashback: Samuel Beckett's *Waiting for Godot*, some college production I sat through two, maybe three times, hoping to deserve my diploma. I know, I know, the play is a master-piece, and Donald could explain exactly why . . . but, my god, the silences, the loops, the repetitions! And that same Charlie Brown tree, the same two tramps beside it, waiting, waiting. Well, maybe not tramps, but bedraggled all the same. Two bedraggled companions— but wait, is that action I see on the stage? A boot! One of the tramps is trying to take off his boot. Now the other one is actually moving— offstage, to relieve his troublesome kidneys.

"I thought you were gone forever," the other man says when the first returns. The two have been companions for over fifty years, but we won't learn this until late in the play, after I've nodded off in self-defense and woken to see that one of the tramps has nodded off, too, waking with a dream he wants to tell the other. A nightmare, actually, which it seems the second tramp doesn't want to hear. They've got more important things to do . . . to not do, I mean, for this is a play where nothing happens. (Nothing happens twice, some critics have said.) Unless you count the waiting as something. But who is this Godot, anyway? And will he never come?

Get on with it already. If the characters don't even know who they're waiting for, how am I supposed to know?

"Well," Mother begins, looking up from her plate. "Well."

She has finished her last bite of sweet potato and is ready for conversation. This is the trickiest part of the evening. If the silence is interminable, its opposite is fraught. (I hear Donald's voice in my head again: "Think of it as theater. And steer away from the other stuff.")

The "other stuff" used to mean my never-ending corrections, which I gave up years ago, or maybe it just feels like years: "No, Mother, I'm your daughter, not your sister." "No, Dad, you weren't in New York on 9-11. Maybe it just seems like you were." "No one can look into your bedroom window. It's on the second floor, remember?" And then, on the worst days, the "other stuff" drew tears I could not stop—I was losing my parents, maybe had already lost them.

Now, "the other stuff" has come to mean the planetary orbit of repeated anecdotes that, once you enter, is nearly impossible to escape. Donald and I have learned, for instance, not to mention 9-11 (for the aforementioned reason), or how the two of them met (which leads to the pole-dancing story Dad concocted to flabbergast his listeners—how Juanita was the dancer on the second pole and he told his buddy he just had to meet her!), or puppies of any kind (their lascivious Great Dane, who was always getting loose, once had a litter of thirteen puppies from various fathers), or how Dad lost a finger in a fan belt accident, or any of the other two or three stories that constitute my beloved parents' greatest hits.

Her brown eyes are merry, eager, almost flirtatious. It's Saturday night, after all, and she's wearing her special pearl earrings, the ones Dad brought back from his overseas duty in Japan nearly sixty years ago. She misplaces the earrings regularly—well, one of them anyway. We've found the missing earring in the seat of her walker, in the utensil drawer, in Dad's underwear drawer. I found it again a few weeks ago, tucked in a Kleenex tucked in a copy of *Black Beauty* she insisted had been stolen by two thieves—a man and a woman—who entered their condo, took Dad's wedding ring and the book, and ran out the front door.

Dad lifts the knife again. "Heavy," he says. I'm so tired I can barely think. I turn my head to look at Donald, reach for his hand under the table. Now that he's halfway through the book on Dadaism, he must know how to enter this world and escape unscathed. I look up at my father. *Dada:* French for hobbyhorse, something to climb on, to ride; the first words of a child—reaching out to a father, let's say, to be picked up; variant of *ta-ta*, nursery rhyme for bye-bye, see you later, or, sometimes, the more permanent goodbye, as in "I thought you were gone forever."

Now, touching Donald's hand, something occurs to me: Beckett's two tramps—or clowns, or aging friends or lovers, however you choose to see them—aren't the only characters in the play. Another couple enters later, and, after some onstage business with a rope, as I recall, at one point all four fall down together. Then, in a moment that comes to me clearly now, the four lie together a while, looking up at the absurd stars. That is my memory, anyway. Chipped and tarnished as it is.

A light rain has started to fall. In the distance, thunder rumbles. Mother pushes her empty plate away and places both elbows on the table. She leans forward, cradling her freshly scrubbed face in her hands, fixing her gaze on me. She smiles broadly. "So," she says. "What did you do today? Other than make dinner for your sister?"

Donald's words in my head once more: "Just go with it."

"Not much," I say. "We've just been waiting for you. It's always a pleasure to see you on Saturdays."

"Oh, we've been here before?" she asks. "I thought it looked familiar."

Dad holds up the knife. "Perfectly clean," he says, handing it to me. He lifts his hand, turning it over, examining it. "I can't remember how I lost it." He means the ring, I think. He's remembering the lost wedding ring.

But, no, it's the finger. "It was some kind of accident. But for the life of me I can't remember what it was."

"Lady was a Harlequin Great Dane," Mother says. "She had one blue-glass eye. She was a rascal. Thirteen puppies. Can you imagine?"

Thus the evening proceeds. Pause. Grumble of thunder. From Dad, a 9-11 remembrance: "I can see it all in my mind. Just horrible."

Mother looks out the window, pointing to a tree bending slightly in the wind.

"Every leaf is wet," she says.

My father nods. "Every leaf."

"It's raining," she says.

"Yes. We're in for it, I think," he says.

Beneath the table, Donald reaches for my hand. Silence descends. Cue the thunder, the lightning. Cue the players for the next act.

OUR GOD IS TOO BIG

Three AM has come again, the haunting hour in Room 503, my father delirious in the white-sheeted bed. His lifted arms roam the air. Light leaks beneath the heavy door I asked the nurse to close. Light, too, through the window blinds casting a shadow show I watch each night. What story are his hands weaving? I cannot follow the plot.

Some nights he leans over so far that his fingers touch my arm. That's how small the hospital room is. For eight days and nights I have made my nest in this chair: notebook, eyeglasses, penlight, book. My voice is a scratched record, the needle stuck on a groove: *Time to sleep, Dad. You're okay, I'm here.*

He is not okay. I am not here. Sleepless, each night I float on ragged wings out the locked window and above the darkened streets to enter his bedroom—their bedroom—where my mother lies in their double bed, eyes wild, calling my father's name. She turns to reach for him and touches a back—some nights a daughter's, other nights that of a keeper paid to tether her roaming mind. Seventy-two years together, and my father will never sleep with his wife again.

Beneath his sheet, he wears only a hospital gown, the smallest adult size; I must remember to ask for a child's gown. This one keeps slipping over his shoulders and riding up above the indwelling catheter he screamed against when they installed it. *Naked came I out of my mother's womb, and naked shall I return*—words that now rise from the bowels of my unbelief. Words underlined in my first Bible. Job's words, or God's words *through* Job, depending on what you hold, what holds you.

Across town, in another hospital, my nephew swaddles his freshly born son, soul arrived from who knows where. I imagine the child as all mouth, a red squall opening the silence.

Jeremiah enters my father's room, nearly filling the doorway. "Everything okay here?" he asks softly. Night nurses are the best.

"I'm not a nurse," he told me the first night. "Just a certified aide." I answered that I don't care, that he is still the best nurse on the hall.

As he moves toward the bed to adjust the sheet Dad has pulled loose, Jeremiah shrinks the room even smaller. He is impossibly tall, heavily muscled, with just enough of a paunch to prove he loves to eat. Polished ebony skin, a lilting accent. I want to ask about his name, but don't wish to pry. It's not a name you hear every day, not one I would give a son: Jeremiah, the weeping prophet, probable author of the book of Lamentations. Bleak stuff: the destruction of Jerusalem, the deaths of kings, affliction, misery, wormwood and gall. Then again, maybe Jeremiah is the perfect name for Dad's night watchman. We are on a deathwatch here.

"Still reading that book?" he asks, pointing to the paperback in my lap: *Your God Is Too Small*, a title impossible not to take personally. The book belongs to my parents, along with dozens of others they haven't opened in years—Bibles in various translations, a worn concordance, hymnals, books inscribed by friends and pastors to "fellow traveler" or "sister in Christ" or "one of God's beloved sons, a quiet inspiration." *Your God* was published in 1952, the year I babbled my first words, though *Dada* was thousands of miles away, flying night raids in Korea. My father hated flying solo at night, especially over water.

"So lonely," he often said. "Black as far as the eye could see." To keep himself company, he sang hymns. "He Hideth My Soul" is still his favorite: "He hideth my soul in the cleft of the rock . . . and covers me there with His hand."

I nod and hold the book up for Jeremiah to see. "For believers and skeptics alike," I say.

Jeremiah shrugs. "Worth a try, I guess." He fills the Styrofoam pitcher with fresh ice, Dad's only nourishment now, straightens the stack of washcloths beside the sink, and walks to the door, closing it quietly behind him. The morphine has finally kicked in and Dad has fallen into sleep, *fallen* being the operative word here. The drug drops you, you fall. Then you're on your own.

I switch on my penlight and open the book. Our problem, this author believes, is that we "have not found a God big enough for modern needs." We need "to enlarge the aperture through which the light of the true God may shine." Critics called the book groundbreaking, a classic, so I must give the author his due; it's clear he knows his stuff. But I can't carry it. The load is too much. I can't hold in my arms the boundless sky, nor count those innumerable pinpricks of light, ancient stars tearing through the darkness.

Our Sunday School leaders did their best to prove God's bigness, his majesty, teaching us songs complete with choreography. "Wide, wide as the ocean," we sang, stretching our small arms out to the side, then "High as the heavens above," our arms lifted above our heads. But no matter how wide I stretched, or how high, I could never touch Him.

So I reached for the songs and stories that fit my hands, like "the wee little man" who came to the parade to see Jesus. Too small to see over the crowd, Zacchaeus "climbed up in the sycamore tree." (We had hand motions for that, too.) Of course, I missed the whole point of Luke's Gospel—that Zacchaeus was a tax collector despised for his usury, an outcast. What mattered was that Jesus spoke to this little man, asking him to come down and dine with him. I imagined that Jesus also touched Zacchaeus because Jesus was always touching people: lepers, disciples, children. Did he touch the widow, too? The one who gave all she had— two coins that amounted to nothing, or so the rich Pharisees said. "The widow's mite," our teachers called it, which confused me. Weren't mites like spiders, or ticks that burrowed in the dog's fur? The smallest creatures possible? My grandmother, when we got under her feet in the kitchen, would give us a quick kiss and shoo us out the screen door, laughing: "Go play now, you little mites!" There was such comfort in being small, I see that now. To be held on your mother's lap. Wrapped in a towel after your bath. To be called to the table, where there was always enough—no matter how bare, I now know, the cupboards sometimes were.

The door opens partway, and Jeremiah's large round head appears, haloed by the hall light. One arm reaches in, waving a sheet of paper. "Forgot to give it to you," he says, entering the room and placing the paper on a counter beside my chair: the hospital menu for tomorrow. Dad has long passed beyond the need, but I am always hungry, and ashamed for the hunger.

"Don't be that way, now," Jeremiah said a few nights ago when I confessed.

"But my father is dying," I said, tears dropping onto my loaded tray. "How can I want food?"

He didn't say the expected thing—that I need strength for what lies ahead, though he knows what lies ahead. It doesn't take a prophet to see that we are in the last days here. No, Jeremiah didn't say a thing. He just touched my shoulder lightly and handed me the menu.

I almost asked him then about his name. Did his mother choose it? His father? Does he know that Jeremiah was not only a prophet, but a poet as well? The book of Lamentations is a poem—five poems, really. Bleak, yes. But a sliver of light slips in now and then, when the weeping quiets and the soul can speak: "The Lord is my portion." Not much to feed on, but something I guess.

I close the book. My God is not too small. He is too big.

To hold, I mean, in the palm of my hand. A hand that can reach to touch this man I have grown, almost too late, to love beyond measure. Why enlarge the aperture? If God still lives, he can shine through the smallest gap, the cleft of a rock. Ancient poets could fit a whole life, and death, into a few syllables. Issa is my favorite, the saddest haiku master, whose losses were innumerable and whose name means "one cup of tea." I once watched an artist paint a name on a grain of rice. I now imagine she could paint hummingbirds as well—and the eyelashes of humming-birds, and the eyelashes of my new nephew—with one strand of my father's hair.

Outside the door, two nurses are laughing quietly at some confidence they have earned the right to share. My father pulls his arms from under the sheet and lifts them high. In the last days, *your young men shall see visions, and your old men shall dream dreams*—another Bible verse that won't let me loose. Now my father's mouth is moving, his jaw open-ing on its hinges, but releasing no sound. Maybe he is singing.

Nominated by the Georgia Review,
Fleda Brown

REWINDING AN OVERDOSE ON A PROJECTOR

by SEAN SHEARER

from BELOIT POETRY JOURNAL

Blacker. Black. The foam drools back
up his chin, over his lips and behind his teeth.
The boy on the floor floats onto the bed.
Gravity returns. His hands twitch.
The heart wakes like a handcar pumping faster and faster
on its greased tracks. Eyes flick open.
Blood threads through a needle, draws into a tube.
The syringe handle lifts his thumb.
The hole in his vein where he left us seals.
The boy injects a liquid into the cotton
that drowns inside a spoon. He unties the leather belt
around his arm, pushes the sleeve to his wrist.
The wet cotton lifts, fluffs into a dry white ball.
The flame beneath the spoon shrinks to a spark,
is sucked inside the chamber where it grows cold,
then colder. The heroin bubbles to powder.
The water pours into a plastic bottle. The powder rains
into a vial where it sleeps like an only child.
All the contents on the bed spill into a bag.
The boy stands, feeds his belt through the loops.
This is where I snip the film and burn it.
What remains are the few hundred frames
reeling: the boy unlocking a bedroom door,
a black jacket rising from the floor, each sleeve
taking an arm like a mother and father.

Nominated by Beloit Poetry Journal

FESTIVAL

fiction by MARY MILLER

from THE PARIS REVIEW

My husband, who loved festivals, who was a great fan of festivals, wanted to get to the square in time for the first band at eleven o'clock.

From bed, the dog and I watched him dress. He tried on various T-shirts, declaring some of them too tight and others too loose, before finding the perfect one. We watched him smear sunscreen on his face and neck and ears.

"Don't forget your ears," he said.

"I won't forget them."

"And don't wear a gray shirt. You're always copying me."

I had already planned my outfit and had every intention of wearing a gray shirt. I thought of the other shirts I might wear, shuffling through them in my head.

When the door closed, I got out of bed to watch as he set off with the dog. The dog didn't want to go without me. She was my dog from before. She sat in the driveway and looked back at the house. He tried to get her to run, thinking the farther he could get her from the house, the less she'd think about me. She ran for a few seconds and stopped to look back a second time, to the last place she'd seen me. I could have watched this show for hours. I worked from home and the dog and I were together nearly all the time, so I rarely got to see her love for me on display. Her usual state consisted of deep sighs, or nails skittering across the hardwood as she tried to escape my attempts to pick her up, flip her onto her back, and rock her like a baby.

I ate a granola bar, took my vitamins. I unloaded the dishwasher and put some clothes in the dryer, turned on the radio. But pretty soon my husband started texting me things to bring—his hat, cash from the cash drawer—so I tied my shoes and set out. I was on the phone with my mother when I stopped to chat with some neighbors who'd found a snake in their yard. They showed me pictures of the snake, were super excited about this snake, so I did my best to play along.

"It was really big," the younger woman said, holding out her arms.

"Was it poisonous?" I asked, which was the only question I could think of.

"I looked it up," she said. "It's not poisonous, but it was huge—an eastern hognose."

"I've never heard of that one."

"It was really big," said the other one.

They just wanted to warn me in case the snake made it across the street and over to our yard and my dog tried to get ahold of it. They were having such a good time telling me about the snake that I'd forgotten my mother was on the phone. When I put my earbuds back in my ears, my mother said she'd enjoyed hearing about the snake, too, which annoyed me. Probably what she'd enjoyed was my friendliness, how I'd been the one to stop the neighbors to say hello. She was a friendly woman and I wasn't, and she didn't understand why I wasn't more like her. Whenever she pointed this out, I blamed it on the man she'd married, my father, and how he had ruined us with his cynicism.

"Remember to go by Jesse's booth to look at his paintings," she said. "But don't spend more than fifty dollars—I only want a small one. And I don't want you to go out of your way. Only if it's not too much trouble."

"It's not too much trouble," I said.

"I'll pay you back," she said.

"You don't have to pay me back."

"I'm going to pay you back."

"We'll see," I said.

"No, we won't see. I have the money right here."

"You have it right there in your hand right now?"

"Well," she said.

"We've had this conversation already," I said, and then I told her I had to go, that I would call her later. I was busy looking at the college girls. High-tops were popular again, as were ripped jeans. Cutoffs. Crop tops. There was a group of six in front of me and I noted their similarities: three had on the exact same pair of tennis shoes. Five were wearing shorts so short you couldn't tell they were wearing them. Two crop tops. Four had braids in their hair. They were all of varying degrees of very thin. The uniformity was mesmerizing. The girls were young and beautiful and proud to be young and beautiful in a way I'd never been at their age. Youth and beauty hadn't seemed like anything special, and though I'd been young and pretty enough once, I had never been one of them. A few weeks ago, a group of girls had laughed at me from their car. It was clear they were laughing at me because they'd looked right at me and then one of them said something and the others opened their mouths and another pointed. But I hadn't heard what they'd said. What could they have said? I was just a regular person in blue jeans, not fat or ugly or weird looking. I was plain. But being plain isn't funny.

I was still disappointed I hadn't given them the finger or told them to fuck off, hadn't stuck a hand through an open window to touch a girl's cheek or pluck a strand of her hair. I'd just stood there. It hadn't oc-curred to me to do anything else.

It was hot out and I'd begun to sweat. I found my husband, and the dog was excited to see me, though not as excited as I thought she'd be. My husband told me the dog was very excited as he handed me the leash. Then the three of us stood and listened to the band, which consisted of two white men and two black women. I knew one of the men—the one on guitar, Glen—and had slept with him a number of times, had dated him for a month or so, though my husband was unaware of it. He thought Glen had a crush on me and that was the extent of it. It had been sev-eral years since we dated, but Glen still messaged me from time to time, had contacted me to ask if I'd be at this very festival.

Glen was attractive to me only when onstage. I reminded myself of this. Take him off the stage and it all fell apart. But he was onstage at that moment so it was difficult to remember what I'd found so distaste-ful about him. He was tall and thin and more attractive than most of the men I'd been with. And he was a very good guitar player—at least that's what people said.

"Do you think he sees me?" I asked my husband. Glen was wearing mirrored sunglasses that seemed to be pointed in my direction.

"Oh yeah, he's sniffed you out," he said.

"I think he's looking at me," I said, though it was clear he was look-ing at me.

The song went on for a long time. I shifted my weight from one leg to the other, remembered how much I disliked festivals: All the people, how slowly they walked, how you had to walk with them in one direc-tion, at their pace. And all the strollers and dogs and pretty girls and

263

the boys trying to fuck the pretty girls and not me. The smell of meat and fried food. But this festival was particularly shitty because they didn't sell beer so we'd have to go back and forth to my husband's office, where he had stored a cooler the previous day.

My husband thought ahead. It was one of the things I liked about him. Glen did not think ahead. But the main problem with Glen was that he'd liked me too much. He'd liked me so much I'd gone mute, still. I recalled lying on his sofa, in his bed, on the swing set on his front porch. Even in his car, I'd reclined the seat.

When the song ended, we walked over to my husband's office and poured ourselves beers in Styrofoam cups he'd found in the break room. The beer foamed up like crazy. I noted that my husband had not thought far enough ahead to bring plastic cups. I tried to get the dog to drink some water but she wasn't interested, so I peed and called to my husband from the bathroom to tell him there were free tampons—how I had forgotten there were free tampons? His office also offered buckets of candy and tables full of magazines. We had plenty of tampons and magazines and candy at home, but that didn't temper my excitement.

I sat on his leather couch and took a sip of foam, looked at the books on his bookshelf, the art on his walls. He had a real office. I didn't have a real office and never would.

He pulled a flask from his desk and drank from it. He didn't offer it to me but I held out my hand.

"You wore a gray shirt," he said.

"I planned to wear this shirt days ago. I made no promises."

"You should have worn those sneakers I got you."

"They're not comfortable."

"You have to break them in," he said.

The more he talked about the sneakers he'd bought me, the less I felt inclined to give them a chance. He should have known that much about me by this point. And I could use his credit card to buy myself any damn shoes I wanted.

I refused to move so we continued sitting, him behind his desk and me on his couch like I was at my therapist's office or had been in a car accident and needed to sue someone.

"You ready?" he asked.

"Maybe we should fill up again before we go."

"Pace yourself," he said.

"We'll split one then."

He wanted to go see his friend Chris at the barbecue truck. Chris was the king of barbecue in this town, had labeled himself as such. There had been no good barbecue before, so it didn't seem like much to be king of, but it was refreshing to be around someone with so much self-esteem and confidence.

The line was long. It was nearly one o'clock and all the lines were long. It was at this point I realized how hungry I was, how the whiskey had been a bad idea.

I followed my husband in between trucks so he could say hello and ask how the brisket had turned out. The brisket was the best brisket Chris had ever made. He told us how much he'd cooked, how he'd only slept four hours in the past two nights, and how they were on track to sell out by three o'clock. What else was there to say? Chris was doing the absolute best version of Chris and no one could stop him.

After that we went to find Jesse's tent. My mother wanted one of his paintings because my sister and I had been friends with him in high school. He'd been particularly close with my sister and I vaguely recalled her telling me that there had been a drunken, not-quite-consensual encounter between the two of them one night.

I'd seen his work on Instagram, had made fun of the pensive photograph of him at the beach, looking out at the ocean, in which he claimed to have found God. I'd shown my husband, who knew Jesse's brothers, and we'd read the post aloud to each other and laughed. Jesse talked about submitting and surrendering, walls breaking down, and the clichés from which he'd learned that he must put aside his ego, that he was not in control. All of this had been the impetus for his new work. His new work consisted of shells he had purchased online, thousands of shells he'd spent months figuring out what to do with, "though sometimes the simplest, most obvious explanation is the best," he wrote. The canvases mimicked patches of sand more perfect than any you'd see in real life. But he was going to pass along his insights to you via these perfect swatches of beach because Jesus wanted you to have this jewel-like piece to hang on the walls of your multi-million-dollar condo in Florida so he could continue to pursue his art and not, say, have to sell life insurance.

"Hey, Jesse," I said.

If he recognized me, he didn't let on. His whole family was this way. Once, I'd introduced myself to his older brother for the fourteenth or twentieth time, and he'd said, impassively, somewhat ominously, I know who you are. What a weird family! I wasn't going to let it get me down.

It was a nice day and I was at a festival. I had a dog and a husband. I reminded myself I was rich, or at least upper-middle class.

My husband held out his hand and told Jesse he was friends with his brothers, and then he nodded at me and said, "My wife, Lauren." Since that didn't seem to spark anything, either, I gave him my maiden name.

"*Lauren*," he said. It sounded funny coming out of his mouth, not like me at all. "How's your sister? How's . . . Twinkie?"

This was the nickname she'd had as a child, a name our father had given her that had stuck. It had been fine for a thin girl. Back then no one ever joked that she'd eaten too many Twinkies, that she just *loved* Twinkies.

"We haven't called her that in a long time," I said. "Tara. Her name's Tara."

"Right," he said. "How is Tara?" He smiled. He looked serene and unperturbed, saved, completely insane.

"She's good." I thought he'd ask me questions about her—where she was, what she was doing—as people did, but he didn't.

"You're a writer now, aren't you?" he asked.

"I am."

"I'm working on a book," he said. "It's about the greatest love story ever told."

"Wow," I said. "The greatest one." It was about God, I knew, and I wanted him to say it was about God. He told me he was dictating it into his phone and it was now well over four hundred thousand words. Like most everyone who has never published a book, or even a poem, they think telling you something is seven hundred pages makes it worthwhile.

"Wow," I said again. "That's really something."

"But I need someone to help me with it."

"You mean a ghostwriter?"

"What's that?"

"Like someone to write it for you."

"No," he said. "I need someone to help me gather my thoughts."

"Like a cowriter?"

"Yes, like a cowriter. Someone to help me shape it. Get it ready for publication."

"Ah," I said. "Yes. Well . . ." And then we started looking at his sand and shell paintings, along with those he hadn't sold from the series before the sand and shell paintings, and from the one before that. There were a few of night skies—stars, moons—and lots of paintings full of people in colorful clothing with blank, beige faces. That series had not been a success.

"These are the last two skies," he said.

"The last two," my husband said. "Your mom might want one of those."

I knew he wanted to catch my eye and smirk but we were too polite for that sort of thing. My husband was very polite. Sometimes I wondered if I was the only one who liked him, and, if no one did, whether it would change the way I saw him. He knew a lot of people, was friendly with a lot of people, but he mostly hung out with me. Where were his friends? Why couldn't he have left me and the dog at home and gone with them?

I took a bunch of pictures and texted them to my mother while Jesse continued to smile serenely into my face, past my face, into my skull, and out the other side at the people walking by. He looked like a maniac. I wondered what he had done to my sister on that night so long ago and whether whatever had happened had been rape, but once you've been saved you're forgiven, and there's no need to think about any of the bad things you did in the past. That was the allure of the whole thing. You could just admit to being a sinner and let it all go while everyone else continued to suffer.

While I waited for my mother to respond, a text from Glen came through: *Saw you out there in the crowd.* Of course you did, I thought. The dots were still going so I waited to see what else he was going to say, but he was either writing a very long message or had decided to leave it at that.

My mother wanted a night sky, said I should ask which was his favorite. I relayed this to Jesse and he held the two of them up for a moment before handing me the harvest moon, a plane's pink contrails streaking across it. I wondered what his brothers thought of this new Jesse, if this was a better version of him than the previous one. Maybe night-sky Jesse had become addicted to Adderall. Perhaps beige-and-faceless Jesse had missed family gatherings to watch porn, sent dick pics to teenage girls. No version of him could have been weirder than this one, but he had always been weird. He'd always been distant, locked within himself. I remembered one time my sister and I had had a party at our house. Our parents were away for the night and we'd invited a few friends over but it got out of hand, just like every movie in which teenagers throw a party. Things were broken, drinks spilled on the nice rugs. Jesse had gotten so drunk he'd fallen asleep in our parents' bed and pissed himself, though my sister and I didn't tell anyone. Or at least I had never told anyone. I'd cleaned up after him and said nothing and forgot all about it for years and years. I couldn't wait to tell my husband. It seemed an unlikely thing to forget—when people shit or piss themselves it sticks with you. I could recall in great detail the few times it had happened to me. They were some of the most vivid memories of my life. On my deathbed, I would recall the times I'd shit or pissed myself instead of the great loves of my life.

It was weird to think I had once known him like that, that I had known him at all. He'd had such nice hair then. It was possible I'd run my fingers through it, brought him a glass of water and some Tylenol, a pair of my father's pants. If I had done those things, provided him the least amount of comfort, I wanted to take it back.

Jesse swiped my card, asked if I wanted a bag.

"Yes," I said. "I want a bag."

It had a sticker with his name on it in big shiny letters. I wondered if my sister had ever told our mother about him, what he'd done. It seemed unlikely, although Tara was a sharer; she liked to share even the most terrible things that had happened to her. But also our mother had a knack for forgetting, just like Jesse. They could put the bad stuff out of their minds, offer it up to Jesus.

"I just remembered something," I said, as he continued his blank stare, so pleasant and otherworldly. He was with God now and no one could touch him. I wanted to punch him in the face, imagined blood pouring down his nose, how bright and lovely it would be dripping onto his paintings. Making them better, real. Why couldn't he even recall my sister's name? She hadn't been Twinkie in so long. "There was a party in high school and you had too much to drink. You fell asleep in our parents' bed." I paused to see if anything was registering. Nothing. Nada. "I'd forgotten all about it until now. Do you remember that night? I know it was a long time ago."

"It doesn't ring a bell," he said. "But there were a lot of parties back then, and I was a different person."

"Of course," I said. "We were different people."

My husband took my hand. He had spotted some wind chimes he thought we should look at, was moving me in the direction of them. I looked down at the dog and she was licking my pants like, Let it go, move on. I didn't want to move on, didn't want to let it go, but there was nothing to be done. I wouldn't mention how he'd pissed himself— how I had given him a pair of my father's pants to go home in, because I had, it was all coming back to me. It was over and I'd done nothing, said nothing, in the same way I had failed to put my hand through an open window to touch a girl's cheek or pluck a strand of her hair.

The wind chimes all looked the same to me, or similar enough, so I told my husband I liked the biggest one, the one that resembled a chandelier.

"Are you sure you want that one?" he asked. "Where will we put it?"

"I don't know," I said. "Anywhere. On the screened porch." We had a big house and it was just the two of us and the dog, but the house was becoming cluttered. There was so much stuff. We were jamming it full.

We took our purchases to his office, poured another round of beers. I sat on his couch and waited for the foam to subside as he drank from his flask. For some reason, he didn't make fun of Jesse or Jesse's art and neither did I. We didn't mention him. It seemed the time for that had passed, or there was nothing funny about it. There had never been anything funny about it at all.

Nominated by The Paris Review,
Elizabeth Ellen

HUMAN TRAFFIC

by BRUCE COHEN

from ALASKA QUARTERLY REVIEW

A filmmaker captures two migrating geese dying in midflight.

Most folks would prefer not to immigrate to another country
           In the trunk of an El Camino.

The delivery nurse hands a man the next baby in the chain—
           His wife will not be traveling incognito with him.

If one were to think about it, the concept of *ice water* is the epitome
    Of extravagance,
           The fragrance of a peach, unimpeachable.

Mittens make no sense in terms of finger-function.

      Who hasn't, at some hopeless point, read yesterday's
      newspaper,
           Refurbished yesterday's newspaper into shoe
           insulation,

As a substitute for socks?   As a kid I thought the train stationary—

           Only the world moved. People duplicate
           & hide spare house keys.

Two keys are necessary to destroy civilization,   the atomic locks

Always more than an arm's length apart so two separate
people are required.

      Yes, two people are needed to make love.

      Only an anonymous one in the firing squad has the actual
bullets.

Brand new citizens are attaching wheelchairs & bicycles to the
   front of public buses.

            A plastic spoon, melting on the sidewalk,
      Imitates the fundamental properties of its eatable ice
      cream cousin.

Most folks opt not to slurp coagulated soup off a filthy floor
   Or bake their bread with sawdust rather than flour.

A man chooses to dogpaddle (never having learned to swim)

      Through an ocean with his children on an impromptu
      raft rather
Than refurbish   his bombed-out apartment.

A profound difference: between a kicked-in door & a door kicked
  out.

Nominated by Leslie Johnson,
Alan Michael Parker

271

HAO

fiction by YE CHUN

from THE GEORGIA REVIEW

1966

Qingxin remembers that the character 万 comes from 𝄐 in the Oracle Bone Script—a scorpion with large pincers and a poisonous sting at the end of its jointed tail. How does a bug come to mean ten thousand, as in "毛主席万岁"—*Chairman Mao lives ten thousand years*, a slogan she's made to write a thousand times a day? She wants to look it up in her *Shuowen Jiezi*, but all her books were confiscated and burned. If she remembers correctly, it's speculated that scorpions once plagued the central plain, so when people saw the sign, they saw not just one scorpion but tens of thousands of them. Now, three millennia later, on the same central plain, she is labeled "毒蝎," *poisonous scorpion*, and ordered to write a word that comes from the same insect a thousand times a day. Is she, then, a "poisonous scorpion," releasing tens of thousands of scorpions back to the central plain each time she writes down the word? It's confusing.

Another label she's given is "牛鬼蛇神"—*ox demon serpent god*. Back before the Revolution, these gods and demons with human bodies and animal heads had powers and were treated with reverence. Now people labeled so are shaved a Ying-Yang Head and made to kneel, their faces distorted in fear and shame and in their effort to endure something they didn't know they could endure. Their bodies remain human bodies that bleed and break easily and are subject to hours of beating by their former students who are given a new name too—Red Guards. What are they guarding? Their human sun, the Chairman? It's all too

272

confusing. Sometimes Qingxin wonders if Chairman Mao is indeed a god and will indeed live ten thousand years as she is condemned to write a thousand times a day.

"If you look at history," her husband would say, "Qinshihuang did the same thing—*burn books bury intellectuals*—so that nothing except his own words would count. It's the same they want—power, immortality, obedience, with only minor differences: one called himself the First Emperor, the other Chairman; one had scholars buried alive, the other has them tortured day after day by the students-turned-killers. You can tell those little monsters are enjoying it. They'll eat us if they're asked to, turning us into meatballs, and they'll laugh and celebrate their vitality. This is not a world to live in. Soon we'll forget we're humans, we'll lose the desire for the last bit of dignity."

In the dark bed of their old apartment he would say those things, and she would hush him with "People can hear you," looking around their small room as though ears were concealed in the lightless air. Their four-year-old daughter slept between them, her breaths faintly audible, each a thin hook cast into the unknown.

The character 无 is simplified from 無 which comes from 𣉻—a person dancing, waving bouquets of flowers, for the dead. Now, the word means *zero, nothing*. There's no more dancing for the dead, no rituals, just a dead body dumped somewhere, turned into zero, nothing. His body was dragged onto the shore. Three Red Guards took her there: "We got something to show you." They looked mischievous. There was no dignity in that waxen face either, with garbage caught in his collar, riverweed in his hair.

They asked her to slap his face. She looked at them.

"Slap his face—he is bad," one said. "He knew he was bad, that's why he killed himself, which makes him even worse."

"There's no need to explain to her," another said. "You do what we ask you to do. You are all bad!"

Both had been in her Chinese class and her husband's history class—that was two months ago, in the pre-revolutionary era, when they were merely adolescent bullies with military fathers. Now they are judges and executioners.

His skin felt damp, rubbery. Since the Cultural Revolution, she hadn't really touched his face—it would have been too much to bear, that gesture of sympathy, of looking into each other's eyes and saying,

273

"We will be fine. We will survive this." She couldn't make herself put on such an act, and she knew neither of them would want to receive it, as their sympathy could only confirm their individual misery and humiliation.

"Slap him! Not stroke!" they yelled, then laughed.

That night, when her daughter, Ming, asks about her father, Qingxin tells her he has gone to a place where he can sleep. "He hasn't been able to sleep much," she says. "Now he can sleep without ever being bothered again."

Ming is quiet for a while. Then she says, "Word game, Mama. Let's play our word game."

It's their bedtime ritual. A game Qingxin devised when Ming turned four—months before the Revolution, before their world was flipped upside-down—figuring it was time to teach her how to write. So instead of giving her the routine backrub, she started to write words on her back. Oftentimes, Qingxin picks words that are pictographic, their origins traceable to the Oracle Bone Script, the beginning of Chinese written language's bloodline. She will start with a word's original form and let Ming guess what it is, and then trace its evolution to its current simplified version. Which was how she used to teach her students— when they were still students—so that they knew words were not made of random strokes, that each came into being for a reason, with logic behind it, with thoughts and imagination.

Now logic fails. Thoughts and imagination are reserved for cruelty and survival. In this new, upturned world, what used to be the essential components of life, such as books, order, and reason, such as friends, parents, and husband, are being thrashed out of their existence, vanished into the ether. But more so than ever, Ming has been insisting on playing the word game every night.

"Mama is tired. Go to sleep now."

But she fusses, cries. "Word game, Mama. Let's play our word game."

"Not today. Go to sleep."

Ming cries louder, turning her back against Qingxin, her little shoulders shuddering. Qingxin holds her in her arms and cries with her. A few minutes later, Ming starts again. "Our word game, Mama. Write my name and your name."

Slowly, Qingxin writes her daughter's name, 明, an ideogram that hasn't changed much since its origin, a compound combining the two

274

pictograms 日 and 月, *sun* and *moon*, meaning *bright*. A word Qingxin picked, and since the Revolution, she has wondered if she'd had the prescience of the dark age falling. More than any time now, her daughter needs a name like this to keep her out of darkness's way. But how will things be bright for her both in daytime and at night? What a grand and impossible hope it now seems.

Qingxin's own name is even more impossible: 清心, *clear-water heart*, or *heart like clear water*. "When our heart is quiet and clear," her mother, who practiced Chan, told her, "we don't feel pain. We want no more no less, just this moment as we breathe." Both Qingxin's mother and father were classified "Rightists" and sent away to separate prisons in separate provinces. Qingxin doesn't know if they're alive or dead, or if their minds are set free—or if they are able to think of the name they gave her and breathe and feel their hearts purified like clear water. When the dregs stir up again, they won't sigh, because they know more is coming, which is the nature of life. Conditions form, but they can always go back to their breath as long as that's not taken from them. And even if it's taken, they will either restart the cycle, being born again, or they will join the stars.

Qingxin doesn't know which is more probable or preferable. The ideas of incarnation and karma are two things she hasn't seen much point of until now. This is how they make sense now: one will believe anything to know she won't come back to a life like this again; if she doesn't cause harm in this life she will suffer less in the next, and her tormentors will suffer the worst because of the bad karma they've already deposited at such a young age. This is something worth believing in.

In the mornings, Qingxin does janitorial work, cleaning the school compound and toilets. In the afternoons, she's taken to the town square for the struggle session, made to kneel with a cardboard sign hanging around her neck, with three lines of words: "牛鬼蛇神 / 坏 / 余清心"—*ox demon serpent god / bad / Yu Qingxin*—and an X across each character of her name. After the session, the Red Guards take her back to the school, into one of the former classrooms, which are now called "牛棚," *cowsheds*, to copy the slogan "毛主席万岁" a thousand times—a way, as they put it, to "atone" for her husband's suicide. Gripped by the new pains from the new beating, she sits in a former student chair, completes this "assignment" in a student notebook.

One day, about a week into this daily copying, she raises her head from the notebook and sees her blunder: instead of the word "万" *ten thousand*, she has been writing "无<@$p>," *nothing, zero*—that is, instead of *Chairman Mao lives ten thousand years*, she has been writing *Chairman Mao lives zero years*. Not once or twice, one page or two, but for four pages, several hundred times, she has replaced the word.

She is alone in the "cowshed," but they are coming. It's close to the time they come to collect her "homework," give her a final scolding or beating, and then, if all goes well, let her leave to pick up her daughter. She will need to tear the four pages off and make them disappear, quickly, but the room is locked. She cannot go to the bathroom and flush the pages down the toilet. She cannot shred the pages with her fingers and throw them into the dustbin or hide them in her clothes. The guards will see the tear, will search for the shreds, find them, and patch them up.

She's shoving the last handful of paper into her mouth when the door unlocks. A Red Guard, a slender girl with darting eyes, steps in—also a former student of hers, a good, respectful one exceling in composition and handwriting, who now keeps her face stoically straight and avoids eye contact.

"What—what are you chewing?" Her expression is a mix of alarm and annoyance, as though she's convinced that her former teacher—now "ox devil"—is taunting her with a new kind of perversity: chewing paper like an ox chomping down chunks of grass, with gluey pulps forming in the corners of her mouth.

Qingxin cannot answer. All she can do is shake her head and try to swallow the dry, inky, half-chewed paper shreds as quickly as possible.

The girl looks behind to the door, but the other Red Guards are not coming yet; she has to deal with this alone. Her face hardens. She walks over and picks up the notebook. Despite Qingxin's attempt to remove the torn edges from the seam, the girl notices the tear right away. She narrows her eyes at it, then flips through the remaining pages.

"You didn't finish today's assignment," she says, her eyes still on the pages that are covered with the same five words, like the same insects crawling, gathering, multiplying. "Why are you eating pages from the notebook?"

Qingxin makes a difficult final swallow. "I didn't like the handwriting on those pages. I only want to write those sacred words in the best handwriting possible"—saying what she prepared to say.

"I don't believe you. There's no need to eat bad handwriting. Why don't you just tell me the truth?"

"That is the truth." And again she wants to cry. She sees her daughter waiting on the front porch of her preschool, always one of the last to be picked up—small on the top of the darkening stairs, leaning toward the direction where her mother must eventually appear. "Please believe me. I don't like bad handwriting. You know me—"

"Don't talk to me like that. I don't know you. You're not my teacher anymore. You're the class enemy. Don't forget that."

"I know, I know. Please let me redo them. I'll finish this in no time."

The girl is considering, her face turning malleable, and for a moment the room seems to pulsate with the possibility of human decency. But they both hear something: their eyes snap to the door—the three other Red Guards are rushing in, those who'd dragged Qingxin to the riverbank.

"What's going on?" they yell.

And instantaneously the girl's posture changes to alert, a streak of shrewdness crossing her face. "She lied to me," she says without looking at her. "She must have written something bad on the notebook and she'd eaten up the pages before I came in. It must be something bad."

At some point during the beating, Qingxin stops feeling any pain. Even the thought of her daughter, that wrenching heartache, leaves her. Her mind must have risen up quietly as though not to disturb the scene or not to continue witnessing it. Her mind flies away from the room, the school building, alights on a tree, a birdwing. But after circling over the city, maybe for ten minutes or an hour, it eventually flies back to her daughter, who is now sitting on a little stool inside the school, her gaze on the front door. Near her, the hunchback janitor is mopping the floor, muttering loudly about his own share of misery in the harrowing world.

Because of her new "crime," Qingxin is no longer allowed to live in her apartment. She and her daughter are put in a closet-size storeroom in the school. It's windowless and smells of stale water and mildew, a third of its space occupied by brooms, mops, and buckets that Qingxin uses for the janitorial work. She folds a blanket to the size of the remaining surface and spreads it on the floor.

Ming doesn't ask about the new cuts and bruises on her mother's body. When her eyes involuntarily rove to those places, they quiver back to a spot that's unmarred—Qingxin's right eye, part of her right cheek, her throat, her left collarbone. Ming has learned not to ask about those things since Qingxin's first beating, which came with a barbarous haircut, her long hair chopped and one side shaggily shaved into the Ying-Yang Head. Ming broke into tears when Qingxin picked her up at the preschool, pointing at her grotesque head with terror and bereavement in her eyes. Ever since her birth, Ming had clutched a strand of her hair in her sleep as if it were her new umbilical cord. But Qingxin couldn't provide any answers to her questions, nor could she concoct any words of comfort, as the child cried and followed her limping steps home.

Since then, Ming has not asked about the bruises, welts, and cuts which appear, fade a little, appear again. That's one thing she must have learned will inevitably come, just as her mother must drop her off at the preschool every morning and disappear—without Ming knowing for sure if her mother is going to appear again. Qingxin will give her daughter a finger to grasp when the child gropes for her hair in the middle of the night, will say, "I'm here. I'm right here," when her daughter wakes up in panic, gasping as though she can't find her next breath.

After Qingxin switches off the one light bulb above their heads, Ming says the words Qingxin knew were coming: "Word game, Mama. Let's play our word game."

Despite this knowing, the word *word* makes her shudder. She can taste again the inky paper: bitter, nauseating, like wiggling bugs jammed into her mouth. What could have gotten into her to replace "万" with "无," a word that comes from scorpion to a word that meant, once upon a time, dancing for the dead? Did she, deep in her consciousness, need to dance for her dead husband, instead of adding more poisonous scorpions to this plagued land? Or, did she covertly wish Chairman Mao would die instead of living ten thousand years, turning into nothing, zero—a wish so powerful it bled through her fingers that held the pen, through the ink onto the paper of the notebook?

But how could she be so careless with what she wished? How could she wish anything more than staying alive so her daughter could stay alive? How can she guarantee she won't do anything so careless, so foolish, and so fatal again?

"No more word games. We're not playing that game again."

You can't trust words. They can get you killed, get your daughter orphaned. It's better Ming doesn't know words.

"But Mama, we do it every night."

She cries. Qingxin lets her. But word game or not, she knows there's no way to guarantee anything—not that another "crime" will not befall on her, nor that she will survive another beating. There's simply no way. Which is why people end their lives, by whatever means available—drowning in the river; leaping off a building; hanging from a tree, a ceiling, or any other place strong enough to hold a noose; swallowing sleeping pills or insecticide; cutting their throats open with a pair of scissors or stabbing their hearts with a kitchen knife—so they don't have to guarantee anything again.

Qingxin has a pillow. She can wait till her daughter falls asleep and put it on her small breathing face to make the sleep permanent. Then it will just be herself, which at this point is easy to finish.

She holds her daughter in her arms and moves her hand across her small back, which feels incredibly soft and alive, as though all that is tender and good in the world is condensed in there. Ming's cries gradually subside to intermittent sobs, and then, when Qingxin thinks she has fallen asleep, Ming suddenly asks in the dark, in a quiet, measured voice that doesn't quite belong to a four-year-old, "Mama, are you going to die?"

The tears that Qingxin has been holding back slide off. She tries to keep her voice even: "Yes, someday. Everyone dies. But I won't die until I know you're safe."

"How are you not going to die?" Ming asks, turning to lie on her back and gaze at the dark ceiling.

"I will—I will take good care of you and take good care of myself."

Ming turns her face back to her mother and nestles her head on her chest.

And then, with a little finger, she starts to draw on Qingxin's skin just below her collarbone her own name, 明, a sun and a moon. With each stroke, each touch, Qingxin feels a trickle of coolness, an easing, flowing. Her pain begins to loosen its fists and knots. Her body feels lighter, as if light is receiving her, and she and her daughter are not here in the windowless room, but outside, under a moon. On a green meadow somewhere. Moonlight hums in the grass.

Then Ming draws Qingxin's name, 清心, clear-water heart. The two words her parents named her. On the cardboard she wears in front of her chest, the words are crossed out, as though this person no longer exists and in her place is this reduced half-human-half-animal that can no longer own the name. But her daughter is writing it on her bare skin right now, stroke by stroke, with care. And somewhere in her vision, Qingxin sees a body of clear water that is also inside her own body— which is her parents' wish for her, to be able to return there, to go back to her breath and know that she can be as calm and clean as water that knows no pain, no resistance, nor fear.

All the torments to turn her into something less human will not work, because only humans are given a name by their parents with a good wish in their hearts. And only humans can think of their hearts as calm and clean as water. This is something they cannot take away from her as long as she still breathes. She can still cleanse all the filth and hurt, let them settle, and leave the mind clear.

Each day is a day gained in this life. The moment when she survives another beating becomes expansive. She will not show her amazement after knowing that she is still alive, still able to move her arms and legs, and breathe without too much pain. Still allowed to go see her daughter. To be able to do all that for another day amazes her, as though she doesn't know the width of her own dimension, or how far her life can be stretched without snapping. She is relearning how to live this life. Already she has learned to better endure the beating—not move, stay still, twist the body in a way to protect the head. And to be only partially there when they humiliate her: those shaming songs they make her sing, she sings without letting the words sink; those self-condemning words they force her to say, she says without letting them cling.

She is able to believe none of those words matter when she lets her finger dance across her daughter's soft back and draws the real words on her skin—words scripted with love, free from malice. Usually, they're simple words about the natural elements—star, wind, mountain, river, the seasons, the colors, types of animals, names of plants and flowers. As though she's recreating the world, its blue hills, clouds like pagodas, blooming trees, laughing children, pairs of wings.

As Qingxin endures the day, she thinks of a word to give her daughter at night, like a gift, a talisman, to "take care of her" and "take care of herself." An amulet to save them from harm and keep them alive for another day.

One night, she draws on her daughter's back the word for fountain, 泉, which comes from 㕛—water flowing out of a mountain cave. She describes the mountain, how quiet it is: you can hear each birdcall and their echoes between the rock faces and the sound of water gurgling just out of view. The two of them have climbed along the stony path toward the fountain. "Now we're here," she says. "Let's drink." She cups her palms into a bowl; her daughter does the same. They reach over, feel the cool water touching their skin, filling them up, and quickly they hold the water to their lips. "Ah," they say, "how cool, how sweet." Ming giggles. She does too.

But then she is afraid. She holds her daughter tightly in her arms, doesn't know if she's doing the right thing—to make her believe there can be joy in this world that doesn't tolerate joy, not even from a four-year-old. Those people will not tolerate seeing them smile, seeing the sun on their faces. They will want to crush that, too.

Some nights she cannot lift her finger. "Our word game," her daughter will say. "Let's play our word game." But Qingxin doesn't want to make the effort, or feel those decent human feelings. They seem too fine, too contradictory to the rest of her existence. Too incoherent, false, fake. She wants to sink in her despair, to end it all. But her daughter will insist, "Draw words, Mama. Draw my name and your name," and will touch Qingxin's face with her hand.

"Mama is tired. You draw on me."

And Ming will start to draw—on Qingxin's chest, her palm, a piece of skin that's not cut or bruised—her name: a sun and a moon; her mother's name: clear-water heart. Qingxin thinks, *May the sunlight and moonlight shine on her path so that she will not get lost; may my mind be as clear and calm as water . . .*

Then, Qingxin will hold her daughter and cry, and it's as if she is turning into a lake, no longer hard, edgy, clenched, clenching; her pain begins to liquefy. Then she will start drawing a new word on her daughter's back.

She's thinking of words that do not signify the natural elements, the rudimental, everlasting things that will outlive this distorted world. The word 好, for example, the dual opposite of the word 坏 that's on the cardboard she carries every day. The most common word in Chinese, perhaps, a ubiquitous syllable people utter and hear all the time, which is supposed to mean "good." But what is *hao* in this world, where good books are burned, good people condemned, meanness considered a good trait, violence good conduct? People say *hao* when their eyes are marred with suspicion and dread. They say *hao* when they're tattered inside.

But she thinks of the word itself. It comes from 𡥀, a kneeling person with breasts, a woman, 𠨰, holding a child, 子. It suits her, doesn't it? At night she holds her daughter in her arms, and in the daytime, as she's made to kneel in front of others, she is still holding her, even though no one sees it.

And she thinks again of the word 坏 that hangs in front of her chest and is yelled into her face every day, which comes from 褢, a person crying by the crumbled city wall for her lost home. It also suits her in that sense: she is the one who has lost her husband, her home, and wants to cry by the crumbled world.

She thinks of each word as a seed, an origin, a center where its meanings radiate. Then, when she draws a word on her daughter's back, that clean slate, that virgin land, she will be able to imagine she is writing it for the first time. She's planting a seed and together they will name it, nurture it, give it new meanings, and salvage it from hate and abuse.

So, in the narrow room with no light, she draws a sun and a moon on her daughter's back. She draws a lake of clear water and a heart. And then, she draws a kneeling person with breasts.

"Why is she kneeling?" Ming asks.

"Why do you think?"

"Because she is tired?"

"Yes, she is tired," Qingxin says, "but not too tired to hold her child." She draws a child by the woman.

"That's us: you holding me."

"Yes, that's us." And she lets her hand rest on her daughter's soft, unscarred back.

Nominated by Alaska Quarterly Review

VERSAL

by FRANCINE J. HARRIS

from BELOIT POETRY JOURNAL

The wood is not a negro with tree in the farm-split sand
        for almighty, not a road to bend over,
not a lakeside, or sideways log stump, not
        a sidelong, not a strangler clutch

        or fruiting body of fungus. The warn
of wood is not hiding in bark, deer suit,
        or elk piss musk, not in camouflage. Not
a snowshoe a negro, not a cowhide stripped

or oversprawl. The tree is not a loner type, not
        a sleeper cell, not a jumpy trigger.
The foliage low hangs a lake I like, an ice cave
        shot, a hit tide, frozen in place.

And a black girl is standing on it, over a river rocking.
        Sidebank isn't thug among us, not
a rush gang, not a flower snatched from sidewalks,
        which isn't breaking in root. Nothing

        for jewels, isn't watching through windows. The black
meadow isn't sniper squatting, cheapening the field reek,
        eyesore cattail driving down
the sound of stream driveby. The wood

is an eager, a Negus among us, a runner like eagle
        a brown sighting, root system gathered in growl
of curl, of amassed vein feed. Say it with us.
        The wood is a falcon, a clean stretch of might.

The dark bark is humming. Night stretched.
        A reserve is craning in its path glow, pitch fall.
Matted grass atrament, blowing night
        like long husk. And a black girl is standing in it.

Nominated by Beloit Poetry Journal

THE IMPORTANT TRANSPORT

fiction by DIANE WILLIAMS

from EGRESS

Otto told me that our opportunity had been squandered and that I should have felt compelled to contribute something. He said, "It is too bad you don't understand what is happening here."

And, I saw that it was true—that I had failed to do my best.

This was to be our short interregnum. How to proceed next?

That morning the wake-up radio music alarm had been set, but the volume knob had been wrenched *by somebody*, counter-clockwise, full-on. My first thought was that the window must be open and that the wind had caught at the blinds and that it was blowing across the fins— the slats, rather—and that they were vibrating and causing this tremendous sound before it dawned on me that *this* blast was something other and it made me afraid.

And, where did Otto go? He was missing and the window was indeed open and a small breeze lightly batted the venetian blind's liftcord tassel against the wall.

In an hour he was back again and the look on his face was one of gratitude, and to add to this comforting effect, he smiled.

"Where did you go?" I asked.

"Kay," he said. That's my name.

"You're all I have. Where did you go?"

"Do you like it here?" he said.

"No, I don't like it here. Why should I?"

"I know. I know," he said. "Some water?" He had to walk and to walk, to go such a short way, it seemed, to get that for me.

We had another such dialogue the next day.

"Do I have to say?" he said.

"Yes,"

"Suzette."

"Oh, Suzette," I said.

Later on he married the young girl.

I have had to wait for my own happiness. I married Eric Throssel, who is a good companion—and I thought I was very happy when we had finished supper one night. But the more important transport occurred en route to Long Grove while I was driving.

Eric spoke, and his words I don't remember them, but thank God they served to release the cramping in my neck, and in my shoulders and my back and they provided for an unexpected increased intake of oxygen and can we leave it at that?

Nominated by Kim Chinquee,
David Naimon

FOOTPRINTS IN THE ORDER OF DISAPPEARANCE

by FADY JOUDAH

from MICHIGAN QUARTERLY REVIEW

A fever of thyself think of the Earth

I call the finding of certain things loss

I hold grief close to brace myself for the expected

The unexpected not coeval with the unwanted
they kneel me

I have a fever

when at customs I don't declare
what I brought into my country
from that other minor country

a periodic fever

when in legacy mode my teeth have grown
too yellow for the abrupt hug
of a carnivorous flower

And that I pray for bipedal aliens
or play to inner ear bones those Max Ernst structures

Consanguineous or not
all my erasures are relatives

And you and I are hapten-stance:
you elicit me to me
move me in me

I have a fever others speak I learned love in

For relief I braid Tylenol with Motrin
at the shore of words the sea ends

Consider me a color
an unspoken sound
aphasia won't clarify

Per your mother
they have books on tape now

Per mine dead dogs will follow me

The soul of one dog will enter and exit other dogs
whose deaths I'll come upon

I won't know whose soul I will run
lizards and rodents and a rabbit
will mortgage my dreams

There will be light to wake me sootless
there will be light to resect my spleen

There are always women and bees
and who can't tell a story about honey?

Newborns aside
I'm unlikely to cause anyone harm

My benefits outstrip my collateral
on an earth we'll never plow

What if butterfly or moth on lemon or mango tree?
What if I taste the coffee you swirled inside your cheeks?

To each its caterpillar

I defervesce
I have a fever others speak I learned love in

Between my nipples and knees and within
the frame whose borders are laser-hung
to render umpires surplus

I defervesce
our error was mutual
and being touched was how
you touched me back

Your cherries are black
your eyes grabbed mine by the elbows
our fourth and sixth cranial nerves intact

You pitched your face in my shoulder
variance in clinical features
strapped to the waist

To be clear
one mustn't be connected to the bed of another
about to be shocked

To be clear
what one does with the towel is the business
of making cancer history

A remittent fever
I too shall overcome
the majority incarcerated in herniated prisms
out of what kind of house into prison

Out of prison into what kind of house

My fever says I am the one who never was
a narcissus under hooves
now a boxthorn

I'd bury my sorrow alive
but my sorrow has bones

My fever says I need skin
other than that of a bacteriophage
and besides

mist was falling
and Sisyphus
forget him

he could've died like the rest of us

Where is he now
and what has he seen?

Which protection program and was he
at any point a Gizmo?

Tell me a story when you were little

Your mom bathed you until you were ten
you said you'd tie your dad's shoes
for him when he's ninety

Tell me when you opened your lunch box
she'd packed for you the night before

Here's a lock of your toddler hair
and your baby teeth

biting your dorsal wrist
in a perfect circle to tell the time

the marks take to disappear

Nominated by G.C. Waldrep

THE CURE FOR
RACISM IS CANCER

by TONY HOAGLAND

from THE SUN

The woman sitting next to me in the waiting room is wearing a blue dashiki, a sterile paper face mask to protect her from infection, and a black leather Oakland Raiders baseball cap. I look down at her brown, sandaled feet and see that her toenails are the color of green papaya, glossy and enameled.

This room at MD Anderson Cancer Center in Houston, Texas, is full of people of different ages, body types, skin colors, religious preferences, mother tongues, and cultural backgrounds. Standing along one wall, in work boots, denim overalls, and a hunter's camouflage hat, is a white rancher in his forties. Nervously, he shifts from foot to foot, a styrofoam cup of coffee in his hand. An elderly Chinese couple sit side by side, silently studying their phones. The husband is watching a video. The wife is the sick one, pale and gaunt. Her head droops as if she is fighting sleep. An African American family occupies a corner. They are wearing church clothes; the older kids are supervising the younger ones while two grown women lean into their conversation and a man—fiftyish, in a gray sports coat—stares into space.

America, that old problem of yours? Racism? I have a cure for it: Get cancer. Come into these waiting rooms and clinics, the cold radiology units and the ICU cubicles. Take a walk down Leukemia Lane with a strange pain in your lower back and an uneasy sense of foreboding. Make an appointment for your CAT scan. Wonder what you are doing here among all these sick people: the retired telephone lineman, the grandmother, the junior-high-school soccer coach, the mother of three.

Show up early on Friday morning and lay your forearm on the padded armrest of the phlebotomist's chair. Her nametag reads, NATASHA. She is clear-eyed and plump, and a pink plastic radio on her cubicle desk softly plays gospel at 8 AM. Her fingernails are two inches long, and it is hard to believe she can do her job with nails like that, but she's flawless and slips the needle into the hardened, scarred vein in the back of your hand.

I wish there were other ways to cure your racism, America, but I don't see one. Frankly your immune system seems to be the problem. Installed by history and maintained by privilege, it is too robust, too entrenched to be undone by anything less than disaster. That's how it is for a lot of us. If you are white and doing well in America, a voice whispers to you incessantly, repeating that you deserve to be on top, that to profit is your just reward. And it's not only white people who need the cancer cure; it's any person who thinks that someone of another religion, color, or background is somehow not indisputably, equally human.

The first time you park your car in the vast, cold cavern of the underground garage and step onto the elevator, you may feel alien and forsaken. Perhaps you'll feel that you have been singled out unfairly, plucked from your healthy life and cast into this cruel ordeal. Walking through the lobby with a manila envelope of x-rays under your arm and a folder of lab reports and notes from your previous doctor, you'll sense the deep tremor of your animal fear, a barely audible uneasiness trickling up from somewhere inside you.

But there is good news, too. As you pass one hallway after another, looking for elevator B, you'll see that this place is full of people—riding the escalators, reading books and magazines, checking their phones near the coffeepots. And it will dawn on you that most of these people have cancer. In fact, it seems as if the whole world has cancer. With relief and dismay you'll realize, *I'm not special. Everybody here has cancer.* The withered old Jewish lefty newspaper editor. The Latino landscape contractor with the stone-roughened hands. The tough lesbian with the bleached-blond crew cut and the black leather jacket. And you will be cushioned and bolstered by the sheer number and variety of your fellows.

This strange country of cancer, it turns out, is the true democracy—one more real than the nation that lies outside these walls and more authentic than the lofty statements of politicians; a democracy more incontrovertible than platitudes or aspiration.

In the country of cancer everyone is simultaneously a have and a have-not. In this land no citizens are protected by property, job description, prestige, and pretensions; they are not even protected by their prejudices. Neither money nor education, greed nor ambition, can alter the facts. You are all simply cancer citizens, bargaining for more life.

It is true that this is not a country you ever planned to visit, much less move to. It is true that you may not have previously considered these people your compatriots. But now you have more in common with them than with your oldest childhood friends. You live together in the community of cancer.

More good news: now that you are sick, you have time to think. From this rocky promontory you can contemplate the long history of your choices, your mistakes, your good luck. You can think about race, too, because most of the people who care for you will be nonwhite, often from other countries. You may be too sick to talk, but you can watch them and learn. Your attention is made keen by need and by your intimate dependence upon these inexhaustibly kind strangers.

Two years ago I was diagnosed with cancer and underwent surgery followed by chemotherapy at MD Anderson. It was the start of my journey through this well-lit underworld. By now I have orbited many times around the honeycombed complex of registration desks, prep rooms, and staging areas, potted plants and bubbling aquariums. I have sat in the infusion lounge, where twenty IV poles rise like trees beside twenty upholstered recliners, each pole hung with a fat plastic udder feeding gemcitabine or cisplatin into someone's arm: the unnaturally cheerful evangelist minister; the gray-faced Vietnam vet wearing his American Legion hat and windbreaker, as if he were going off to another war. We are not tourists in this place; we live here now.

In nothing but my hospital gown and cotton long johns, I have pushed my IV pole down the corridors at midnight, trying to keep my skinny legs from getting weaker. I've rolled my IV miles through the deserted hallways and empty waiting rooms, taken it over the sky bridge and back. Once, at 1 AM, I met a black guy doing the same thing. We paused and talked a bit, in our matching pale-green smocks, with our IV poles and drip bags. He explained to me, with a strange enthusiasm, that his doctors had cut out and then reversed his rectum, and now they would not discharge him until he could pass gas for himself. That's why he was out walking so vigorously each night. As we stood there together on the

293

wide, deserted walkway, it seemed as if cancer had erased our differences by bringing us into the intimacy of shared trouble. Then, with a nod, he strode swiftly away on his muscular legs, at least four times as fit as I was.

In the Republic of Cancer you might have your prejudices shattered. In the rooms of this great citadel, patients of one color are cared for by people of other colors. In elevators and operating theaters one accent meets another and—sometimes only after repetition—squeezes through the transom of comprehension. And when the nurse from the Philippines, or the aide from Houston's Fifth Ward, or the tech named Dev says, "I'll pray for you," you are filled with gratitude for their compassion.

This place bears a passing resemblance to those old photographs of Ellis Island—so many travelers come from afar, sitting with their papers and passports, hunched on wooden benches with luggage at their feet, waiting to find out if they will be admitted and advanced to the next stage in the process. Some of the travelers are dressed in pajamas and slippers; some have on shiny blue tracksuits and Nikes; and some wear suits and ties, as if being presentable will make a difference. The shabby and the affluent, the stoical and the anxious, the scrawny and the stout, the young and the aged. If we are tense or pace restlessly, it is because we are aware that we may, on short notice, be swiftly deported. And because of this, perhaps, our hearts soften.

One awful night, after I'd made a scouring passage through the ER waiting room—room of heartbreak and harsh lighting—a smiling man from Nigeria named N'Dbusi entered my cubicle. I remember how he introduced himself, then reached out with his forefinger and thumb and gently plucked at my arm. Like a pleat in a piece of fabric, the skin stayed in a raised position. "You see this, my friend?" said N'Dbusi. "It seems you are dehydrated. We are going to give you some IV fluids to moisten you up." He continued to talk with undiminishable cheer as his hands deftly removed the paper wrappers from a needle-and-tube kit and threaded the needle into my vein with the grace of a seamstress slipping a stitch into silk. He must have done this thousands of times. But where others might have grown bored and careless at the repetition, he had perfected an elegance.

This is the stupefying and ultimately transforming thing: that here, where I do not expect it, I encounter decency, patience, compassion, warmth, good humor. I remember the middle-aged nurse from Alabama, his calm Southern twang and beer belly, who stood firm one night, utterly unperturbed while I vomited repeatedly, as if a demon had seized control of my insides. With empathetic watchfulness, he administered the proper shot until I fell backward into a state of blessed relief. I remember the shift nurse with pale-olive skin and thick eyebrows who, in the middle of the night, brought me hot packs of damp folded towels heated in a microwave. She was from the Middle East, maybe Syria or Egypt. She was so kind and respectful to me that, after she departed, I abruptly burst into tears and blew her a kiss through the closed door.

The historical record—for tolerance, for human learning—is not promising. Yet I believe, more than ever, that at the bottom of each human being there is a reset button. Undeniably it is difficult to get to. To reach it seems to require that the ego be demolished by circumstance. But reach that button and press it, and the world might reshape itself.

Unfortunately you must come here, America. You must lie on the gurney and be wheeled down miles of corridor under a sheet, staring up at the perforated-tile ceiling and the fluorescent lights, not knowing quite where you are. You have to ride a wheelchair to your date with the MRI machine, past women and men being wheeled to similar destinations. You will look into faces lined with fatigue and pain and anxiety. Often a glance will pass between you: a glance without the slightest veil of disguise or pretense; a look of recognition and solidarity. It is a strange communion, but that is what it is.

I remember how the orderlies would wheel us along, calling out as they approached the intersections of corridors, "Coming around! Coming across!" in order to avoid collisions. I remember handsome Marvin, the mayor of the hallways, with his sleek corn-rows, greeting everyone he met, his full voice singing, "Coming around, coming around! Coming across! Coming around!"

So, America, I express this rather unconventional wish for you: I hope you get cancer. In order to change, you must cross this threshold, enter a condition of helplessness, and experience the mysterious intimacy between the sick and their caregivers, between yourself and every person who is equally laid low.

Come into the fields and meadows of the examination rooms, come to the clean beds, to the infernal beeping of the monitors, to the lobbies and alcoves of this labyrinth. Look at the faces of the ones who are attending to you. Witness those who are silently passing by on their pilgrimage to surgery or radiology. Let the workers be fairly paid and valued, for their skills draw us together like the edges of a wound. Listen to the music of the voices around you. As the machines tick, as the ventilators suck and heave and exhale, as the very ground beneath our feet starts to dissolve, we shall be changed. *Coming around, coming around, coming across, coming around.*

Nominated by The Sun,
Ellen Bass,
Michael Bowden,
Daniel Henry,
Andrea Hollande,
Laura Kasischke,
Joan Murray

DEAREST WATER

by NANCY TAKACS

from CLOVER

In the searing heat of Dead Horse Point
looking over a vertical cliff,

I walk near the corral
where unwanted horses were
once left to die.

You have given us saliva
and this rim of crimson,

an altar cloth of air,
your distant promise.

Seeing your green curve
at the bottom
of this canyon,

they broke out
and leapt to their deaths.

My own thirst cruises like a lantern
over hoodoos and dry tides.

Your scent steams
like a live secret,

water,
my good memory.

I am thirsty
for the lost.

Nominated by Gary Gildner

PATTYCAKES

fiction by CLAIRE DAVIS

from THE GETTYSBURG REVIEW

The moon blues the hills, the valley floor and fairgrounds. Its light cascades down the bleachers of the open-air arena and over the announcer's stand and the crisscross banners ringing the rails. All about the perimeter, scattered popcorn glows like insufficient stars in the dirt, while from the dark of the holding pens at the man's back come bellows and snorts, the rub of hide against wood, the rumble of bulls in close quarters. The man is dwarfed by the empty grandstand, a small man, mostly invisible once the makeup comes off, as it has this hour of the night, after the crowds have gone, the cowboys and cowgirls shuffled off to bars, to dances, to spur-of-the-moment trysts on cots in emptied horse trailers. The man holds his stillness, a thing he has learned over the years when all else fails. Waits in that stillness for the quiet of the night, for the bulls' shuffling to cease in sleep, the rough stock horses to tumble into slumber.

This is the truth, as he sees it . . . after the gates are shuttered, the bright lights quenched, the flags and star-spangled parades packed back in boxes. It is the heart emptied, the envelope opened and all the good news long gone. A cloud drifts over the moon, its shadow moving across the arena floor, and for just a moment, the man thinks it a bull slipped from its pen like a rogue wish loosed into the night. It could be the last bull he stood off against, or the first, the roan, come back after this score of years, just out of the chute, spinning and sunfishing, burying its Brahman head between its knees so that the rider rolls over a shoulder, heels over head, boot and spur with its freewheeling rowel trenching the dirt.

Here is another truth: hung up, one hand still roped to its back, face-to-face, you see the eye, the quiet at the core of the bull's turning, and with it the revelation that all the rumors, the tall tales of the animals harboring grudges, long-standing feuds, are just so much fodder for the audiences, for the riders to hang their glory on. Instead, it is a simple beast simply meaning to be rid of the thing strapped to its back.

Then it's the pickup men on their horses spurring them near to corral the bull after the man, with his painted face, comes from nowhere, frees the rope that binds you to the animal. And you? You are slipping, an unceremonious fall to the dirt as the bull turns, carried as much by momentum as anything else, two thousand pounds of meat behind horns of encased bone. And in that turning, you pray. You pray for mercy, for the turn of the bull's mind, for the hand of man, or God, for whatever unlikely salvation might intervene.

The cloud sails free and unleashes the moon's light once more, and the man takes a deep breath and pushes off the bench. There is the sound of laughter somewhere in the near distance, a radio playing in one of the trailers, the hard splatter of a horse pissing on the dirt.

He wanders the length of the arena, swings clear of the bleacher's underbelly, where, regardless of what town, what city, what part of the country, there is the ever-present presence of sawdust and spilled drinks, puke and semen. He's heading back to the stock corrals when he thinks he sees the young man in the near dark, propped against the light pole, face turned down to his chest. At the day's start, the kid had been the fresh-faced whelp, the puppy you couldn't bring yourself to kick away.

It's midday. The kid looks no more than eighteen, and he's standing at the bullpens, sizing up the rides like he owns them.

The man knows the bulls by name, by character, by whatever traits the god of such things invests in them:

Hurricane Jones—side-winder of the first order.
Lemonade Freeze—stiff legged back and buck.
Twister—busts balls with the best of them but hangs its homely
    head over the rails to be scratched behind the ears of an evening.

The man walks over to stand next to the boy, props a cleated shoe on the fence rail. He means to study the bulls as he does before every performance. For that's half of what he thinks of it, a performance. The other half is something else that all these years have yet to reveal to him. Besides checking for the giveaway tilt of head or rheumy eye, he's looking for the ones that have an edge about them, a nervous energy beneath the slack hide. The ones getting their game on.

The kid fidgets, and when the man looks over, the boy is radiant in the sunlight: his red hair hot as a firecracker; his face overrun in freckles. The man can't make out the color of his eyes, gray maybe, but so clear they're like a baby's fresh out of that first darkness.

"You the clown, ain't you?" the boy asks of the man dressed in loose drawers and face greased in paint.

"What give it away?"

"Yeah, no, I mean, are you *a* clown? Or, you know, *the* clown?" and he nods at the bulls.

The man snorts. "What you think? This look like some kind of goddamned circus?"

The boy turns away to hide his embarrassment, and for that moment, the man feels bad, remembers what it means to be young and eager and driven to such lunacy with the desperation of what feels too small a life. A calliope cranks up somewhere on the grounds. It's enough to set teeth on edge.

"Which bull's the worse?" the boy asks.

"Depends. Worst at what? Worst at scoring? Worst to look at? Worst attitude, worst confirmation, worst goddamned stink?"

The boy shakes his head. "Nah, nah. You know what I mean. Worse to face off with. Quickest to break a man." He turns away from the bulls. "What's your name?" the kid asks.

"Hap, the clown." He breathes a sigh of relief as the noise of the calliope abruptly stops.

"No. I mean your *real* name."

The man pauses, looks up as if to search the sky. Can't remember the last time someone asked him that. "Maybe I don't remember it no more."

"That for true?"

"No." He watches the bulls a long moment. "Glenn. Name's Glenn."

"I'm Louis," the kid offers, like he's been asked, and holds out a hand, which the man takes after a long pause.

"Why a clown? Were you a rider first? Did you used to ride the bulls?"

"Do I look that stupid to you?"

The boy's gaze moves up and down the clown outfit. "Well, yeah. But that's the point, right?"

And yes. That's the point, he thinks. It's always the point. It's the clown, the buffoon, it's God's own fool who's left to save the day.

Not a barrel clown mind you. Oh, they play their role, distract the bulls, entertain the crowds, they're the ones who have the patter, who tell the jokes, and who elicit oohs and aahs when the bull hits the barrel, hooks it with a horn or snout, and rolls it thumping down the dirt, the clown inside looking like a ragdoll caught in spin cycle. But, no, he's the one who faces off with the animal, dodges and ducks, runs and jumps, has been known to leap, one foot off the face of a bull, and back flip to his feet. He's the bullfighter clown. The elite.

Some men would take that to the bar with them and brag on it. But that's not him. When he admits to it, which he rarely does—for who out there really likes a clown—it's only when the circumstances are just right. Meaning, he's deep enough into his cups, the music is country enough, and the woman sitting next to him is slow eyed and long limbed and has laughed at one of his jokes, and then, of course, what's a man to think but that he has at least one chance in hell.

"I'm with the rodeo. I fight the bulls," he tells her.

"You're a bull rider?" she invariably asks.

And, of course, he can't stop himself, says, "No. Do I look that stupid to you?"

The boy is a virgin. Claims he's ridden bulls before, but the man sees the tell on his face. He's probably a hand on his daddy's ranch and grew up on all the romantic crap the cowhands spun about the life. Also claims he's ridden broncs, and that's probably true, as far as it goes— the barn-sour horses of home, maybe, starting a young colt or two.

They're still at the bull pen, the midafternoon sun heating up hides and quick-drying the bulls' shit into a fragrant morass the clown has come to know better than the smell of his own skin anymore. In the background, the road-crew techies are setting up the sound system, testing the mics. The bulls are half-asleep, leaning their weight against the rails, against one another, and here and there a fly tightrope walks a bull's long eyelashes, or spirals about its hooves. The bulls are a range of colors: buff, and black, and gray, a ruddy red, and roan. They are solid, and spotted, brindled, flea-bit, and grizzled. If their breeding is specific, their names are haphazard:

Slim Pickin's
Packing Heat
Tiny Dancer
Lightning Hopkins

He suspects the rough-stock contractors sit around a table of an early spring evening, Maker's Mark in hand and a handful of photos like cards waiting to be dealt. They dream names up to intrigue, to inspire fear, to build legends, or maybe just to say who *they* are, because they like the blues, or Elton John, or something or other. Who's to say?

But if it were up to the clown, he'd study on the bulls awhile, call them what they are: Blue Balls, Faberge Egg, Pudding Brains, or Get Off Quick.

The man points out a few to the boy, singles out their weaknesses: a blind spot here, a failure of drive there, a bad gut, spins left, balks in the chute, checked-out brain. The kid takes it all in. He's paid his fee, and he's at that point in the day where second thoughts haven't yet kicked in.

The boy's not just light on the how to, he's light on gear as well. The sum total: clean jeans and half chaps, glove, boots, spurs, the requisite pearl-snap-button plaid cowboy shirt, a well-aged cowboy hat, and one brand-spanking-new standard stock seven-plait bull rope. But *the* coup de grâce? He pulls a Saint Christopher medal from under his shirt, just like the one Glenn's own father used to wear, right up to the day he drove his Cadillac head-on into a cottonwood on the far end of their property and snapped his neck. Turns out, Glenn thinks, there isn't no medal with miracle enough to stop what a man intends to do.

"For luck," the kid says.

The clown's face is inscrutable behind the paint. Anybody who knows anything about the circuit, who's in it for the long haul, who means to think on the same level when he leaves the arena as when he arrived, who doesn't care to have a rib driven through his lung, wears body armor—Kevlar vest—heavy chaps, impact-absorbing helmet, high-carbon-steel-wire face guard. Knows a Barstow from a Brazilian from a standard bull rope.

"Medals are all and good," the man says, "but tell me you got a mouth guard at least?"

And from his shirt pocket, the kid pulls out a well-chewed guard he might have used as recent as high-school football.

"Right," the man says and points to a bull. "Hope you get that one." The animal is the color of butter, with an eye that doesn't quite open all the

303

way. "Name's Destroyer." Which at this point in its rodeo career is past destroying much more than hopes for a qualifying ride, but he doesn't mention that. It's an honest beast. It'll pack the boy a good two, three seconds before dumping him and trotting happily back toward the exit gate.

He points out three more—Gobsmacker, Bellevue, and Colonel Sanders. "Those next," he says, "in that order. Short of that? No dishonor in being smart. Just letting the ride pass." But of course, what kid, still wet behind the ears, still soundly among the immortals with his goddamned Saint Christopher medal, would do that?

The man springs for sodas at the vendor who's just setting up, and they sit in the shade, chugging down drinks that scour the throat pleasurably, and after a few questions, he finds out the kid has always lived within ten miles of where they are sitting right now; his father raises Black Angus. Of riding the bulls, he says, "First time I seen it? Man, oh man, guy's like riding a fucking earthquake and he comes off after eight seconds, and I can see it." The boy's eyes light with a hallelujah fire. "He comes off that ride and he's different from me and my dad and all my friends and all the people I've ever known in this world. *Different*. You get that, right?"

There's little to be said after that, and then the quiet between them feels so good, the man can't bring himself to tell the boy everything he should have known from the get-go.

They break bones routinely. Compound fractures that turn your stomach to look at: stable, green, spiral, transverse, oblique. Torn ligaments. Torn tendons. Shredded rotator cuffs. Dislocated shoulders? Common. Broken fingers? Chump change. Contusions? Too countless to remember. Concussions? Now we're into the terra firma of bulls. Broken hearts and broken bankrolls the least of it. Broken legs, broken ribs, broken faces, broken backs, broken brains. Broken necks.

Sometimes, they die.

The kid announces, "I got that stringy-assed bull, Pattycakes." And the kid's bummed. But for all the wrong reasons.

There are schools for it. Rodeo-clown school that is. But he's earned his credentials beginning as a young boy working the bulls with his father.

He knows what it means when a bull paws the dirt. When the bull backs up, or plants its lead foot. When its weight swings to its dominant side. There's the lowered head. Then there's the lowered poll that signals something other. The flick of the ears. The movement of eye. The tossed head, the tic in the shoulder. The turn away, the turn to. He's spent a lifetime studying the nuanced gestures of bulls in herd, and alone.

He even studies the matadors of Spain, the *toreos* of Mexico—men working with bulls bred to fight to the death. He perfects the hard-heeled pivot. He inspects the narrow cut of his silhouette in the mirror. He works out on the balls of his feet. He spends mornings working out: jumps, barrel leaps, sprints and flips. He means to be the best god-damned clown ever.

It has served him well.

Once the moon tips down behind the hills, the milky way emerges, its light so bright that even the light pole the kid leans against can't dim its substance. Glenn thinks the last time he saw a sky like this, he was a kid sitting next to his father on the porch of a summer's night on the Missouri Breaks of Montana—the air windless, the riverside cotton-woods hushed. And his momma in the porch swing behind them, her shoes kicked off, cotton wads packed between toes, so that the stringent smell of fresh polish intermingled with the pungency of bulls and the green, green smells of the creek that runs through their land. When she spoke, it staked familiar territory—her perennial mistrust of the ranch's purpose. Rough stock. "Gladiator bulls," she said. "It's heathen." And then his father did what he always did at such times, joined her on the swing, wrapped his arms around her and said, "It ain't like we're raising lions to eat the Christian cowboys," and laughed her out of her mood.

But that was ages ago. That was in the time before, and when Glenn draws close to the light pole, he sees it's not the kid after all. No. Of course, it isn't. It can't be, can it. It's Wiley, his colleague, the barrel clown, still in his hipster shorts and team jersey. Seahawks this time, one of a rotating stock depending on what state they're in. His default? Packers. Claims as many people love as hate the Packers. "It's a win-win," he says and grins a lopsided grin.

"Got a cigarette?" Wiley asks.

Glenn surprises him by producing a pack.

"Thought you quit."

"Yeah. So did I."

"Well, hell." Wiley smiles, says, "Any night's a good night for a bad habit."

And Glenn says, "Some nights'r a better excuse than others."

Wiley lights the cigarette, and his hand is trembling. He inhales, holds it as though it were a joint, and when he releases, Glenn can hear the catch in his breath, still.

"Rough one," Wiley says after a while.

Glenn looks overhead at the light, where, beneath the coat of red dust, the remains of a thousand flies, the scores of crisped beetles and moth-fattened spiders has dirtied the lens. And he stands that way, his back stiff, his neck held in a painful bend . . . for there it is, another truth: beneath the splendor, there's always the ruin.

Goddamned Pattycakes. The chute he's in is inordinately quiet. The clown's not fooled. This one is the exception that proves that the beasts are simple. Where other bulls have their predictability, not Pattycakes. The little shit.

It's a small bull. Maybe seventeen hundred pounds. Maybe. A motley rust and gray, as indistinguishable as dirt. All in all, a bull most cowboys don't bother to consider. Never mind the record, the overlooked statistics. They take one look at the size of it, its placid stance in the midst of the other's bullying, and they dismiss it.

But not Glenn. It's the eyes that give it away, he thinks, the imposing calm in the midst of the ruckus—the crowd's roar, the lights, the whipping flags and flagging horses. In the pen, Pattycakes is the eye in the center of the stirring, the other bulls circling and circling as if caught in an undertow.

In the arena, the clowns stand at the ready, the pickup men side by each on their horses, laughing and joking with Wiley, who's straddling the barrel center arena. Glenn watches chute five, sees the kid perched on the top rail next to the flank man, awaiting word to settle down on the bull.

The crowd has waited the long day. For this. Bull riding. Glenn twists his cleats in the dirt, spends the time stretching, flexing. He's coming on mid-forty, after all, and in moments like this, with the certainty of aging and an uncertain future, he feels a pit in his stomach he never feels when facing the bulls. He's tried to imagine that time when he walks away and doesn't come back. But it's a curiously empty space in his mind, a thing, it seems, beyond his imagining.

No. This is all he's ever known.

He secures the knee braces under the roomy shorts, ankles taped under knee-high socks. He checks elbow pads, wrist wraps, and chest protector. An oversized shirt covers it all. He cranks a ball cap backward on his head, the frayed brim shading his neck.

The chute boss signals they're ready. Wiley drops the patter and swings the barrel around and around and around once more, his own private superstition.

Glenn's ten and standing with his dad. They are training the latest batch of yearling bulls, the first of the animals chuted up and waiting to be fitted with the weighted bucking rig before being turned loose into the corral. There he will spin, hump, and buck, and only when he's done it right will the contraption slip from his back. "Learning the game," his father says, claiming the bulls come to enjoy the adrenalin rush near as much as the cowboys.

The sun is mulling over their heads, steeping their backs in its rays, while the heated air wavers up from the ground, distorting the near field, so that it looks as though the mature bulls paddocked there, his father's pride and joy, are of some higher nature, wading through pools of sky.

His father elbows him. "That one," he says and points to the young Spanish-fighting and Brahman mix, a dun-colored yearling that fidgets in the chute, "will put men to shame when he grows up."

But the boy can't imagine the bull riders shamed. He looks at Sean Cassidy—one of his father's ranch hands playing flank man up top the chute—securing the rig on the youngster and waiting for the signal to tighten it down. He is a stumpy figure of a man, broken by his years on the circuit—buckled over in the midsection, one leg permanently shortened so that everything this side of sleep is done as if perched on the side of a slope. But he was, by all accounts, a bull rider of the first order.

On any given day, when asked why he rode, Cassidy has a different answer: "It was that or work." "Corn dogs seven days a week." "The space program was full." "Breeding. My dad was a bullshitter. My momma a ball breaker." "To enhance my good looks." "Because the presidency was taken."

307

He's still Glenn's hero, as all the bull riders are. In point of fact, he would admire bull riders aloud if there were call for it in their household.

But of the bull riders, his mother says, "Stupid is as stupid does."

And when he asks his father about those men, why they ride, what they seek, his father raises his gaze toward the sky as though it were writ large there.

"The young ones are mostly out to prove themselves." And roughing his son's hair, he winks down at the boy. "Those that need proving, that is. But the long-timers?" He dwells on it a moment. Gives up. "Who'm I to claim to know their reasons. You know your granddaddy was a bull rider?"

And yes, Glenn has seen the photos in the tack room. The old man of whom he has only the vaguest of recollections.

"He ever say why?"

"No. No. No, he never did." He claps the boy's shoulder. "But that's all to say you come by it natural—the bulls that is. Your grandpa. Me. And you got a way with them, I'll say that for you." He shades his eyes and looks over to where the yearling waits. "It'll be interesting to see what you do with it." In his eyes, there's a thing the boy can't read, and then his father turns away to swing the gate open, to let loose the small storm into the corral.

Later, years after his father has died, when Glenn announces his intentions to rodeo, his mother rears back, hands on hips, with a look of disbelief on her face. "Have you learned nothing?" she asks. "After what the rodeo business did to your dad?" And that's all there is to be said of it. Right up to the time he leaves for good.

He wants to believe that, back when his mother was still alive, had she taken him up on his semiannual offers to come see, or had she borne to hear of his life . . . it would have proved some small consolation that he's never *ridden* the bulls.

They finish their smoke, and Wiley says, "He's going to be okay. He's young. Tough. Nothin' more we could'a done. Hey, they take their chances." He drops the half-finished cigarette. "You all right?" he asks, but doesn't wait for an answer. Instead, he heads back to the trailer he calls home, while Glenn makes his way to the bull pen, where he finds the animals are, for the most part, sleeping, their breaths idling.

He recognizes the careful specificity of the breeds: the Brahman, the Plummers, the Charbrays, the Spanish-fighting blends. A world of breeding his father wouldn't recognize anymore. Artificial insemination. Genetic engineering. Even cloning.

No. His father loved the bulls, the brawn of them, the steadfast way they moved through their lives. They rutted, they ate, they slept, they lived side by side without furor or acrimony. It was not a romantic notion. His father had no illusions about the beasts. Only respect. That, in the end, they destroyed him, would have been irrelevant to his father. Ironic, that the new bull, a prize his father had longed after, had purchased at so dear a price at auction, was the one to bring sickness and sterility into the herd. Within a year, the business was decimated, and his father was taking that one-way trip down the road.

Glenn leans on the rail. For the most part, the bulls have drifted into sleep, down on their knees in the dark, a loose knot of horns and hide, at the center of which is Pattycakes, standing wide eyed, ears flicking at sounds only he can hear. Maybe it's the traffic, miles down the road. Maybe it's the crowd's yells still echoing somewhere off in the distant hills, or the mumble of past prayers cow-boys mouthed in its ear.

It was so few hours ago that the small bull blew out of the chute, rocketing past Glenn, while on the kid's face was the bewilderment of a child just then realizing he is strapped to the back of misfortune. As if the world, as he has known it, has rocketed out from under him, and there's no saying what comes next: like rising of a spring morning to see the cauls of miscarried calves dotting the pastures in an unholy harvest. Like the cottonwood rising up at the end of the road each time you pass it.

Like Pattycakes falling incomprehensibly to its knees 3.3 seconds into the ride. That fast, the bull is down, and the crowd leaps to its feet. Glenn's already at a run, his cleats digging into the dirt, while Wiley stands at the barrel, at a loss what to do. For there's no distracting the animal, who is going down intentionally, burrowing into the dirt with the boy helpless on its back, and then rolling, and righting itself, and rolling again before flinging itself back onto its feet. And the boy comes up with the bull, but dirtied and crushed like crumpled paper on its back. The pickup team rides in, but the bull dodges them, and the kid . . . Louis, Glenn reminds himself to give the boy that much . . . Louis is a scrap flopping at its side, and Glenn doesn't remember much beyond the roar of the crowd, as he reaches the bull on its off side and leaps at its back, and somewhere in the ensuing chaos, in the jarring of spine and snapping of neck, in the spin and orbit of dirt and bull and crowd, the boy is released, with or without his help, he can't say, and collapses

309

into the dirt. But captive himself now of the moment, of the bull and the sound of its breath like the huffing from Glenn's own chest, the man is carried a full two seconds longer before he finds himself free and standing on the arena floor.

The riders wrangle the bull back to the pen, and in the interim, Glenn turns away from it all, from the bull, the other clown, the crowd's silence, and the stunned announcer, to cross back to where the medics are already working on Louis, the boy's hair as red as the dirt he lies on. Finally, from overhead, the announcer's voice brings the crowd back to their seats: "Nothing to worry about folks. We got the best medics, the best docs. You betcha. Let's give a hand for Louis Belfour of Two Rivers, Montana."

In the quiet, in the dark on his own, Glenn stares down into the pen of sleeping bulls. Pattycakes stands again at the heart of the cluster, and the bull is looking back at him now. Glenn swears it's true—the bull's gaze holding to his own. Perhaps they are called by memory to each other, the bull and the man, the events of the evening still alive in each and stretching out over the air like a bridge between them. In Glenn's head are those seconds he spent atop the bull, scrabbling at the rope, while the whole world closed down to all that mattered, the boy and the great weight of the animal struggling beneath them while time stretched out and seconds turned endless—like it must have felt to his father as he drove that last road. Like the hours his mother spent alone all the nights thereafter. Like the towns he's wandered from one end of the country to the other. Like the line in the dirt the kid's boot drew when they lifted him onto the gurney.

Overhead, stars wheel in slow circuits over the earth, and clouds shred and flee, their shadows riding herd beneath the trees. The air about him is thick with the pungency of bulls, musk and sweat, sweet grass and home. Glenn rubs his face, feels a slick of grease paint he missed beneath his chin, and the heel of his hand comes away glowing a blue-white. He thinks of the boy with his radiant hair, how all he'd wished for was to be different. Singular. Like Glenn's father, who loved nothing better than those early mornings, alone, walking among the bulls, apart from other men in his endeavor and firm in the belief that something you love so well will do you no harm. Glenn stares into the pen that has drawn as sure a circumference around his life as does the sky about the earth.

But, for the bulls. Always the bulls.

310

He drapes his arms over the rails of the pen, hands clasped, studies the animals a long moment. Their congregate breathing like a hum in the dirt. He steps up onto the rail and swings his legs over. Below him, the watching bull bellows, and the other animals awaken, their bodies jolting upward to press against the rails and each other, a heavy fumbling in the dark—a great clot of muscled haunches and swaying balls, the whites of eyes, and fulsome throats as they blow and call and wheel head to flank. When they calm, the man climbs down into their midst, joins the bulls treading their own slow circuit, and, one step after another, he passes among, and of them, as he has his whole life, as his father did before him, working his way through the herd meaning to make his peace. Like a supplicant, to lay hands on the burnished horns. Yes. Like that.

Nominated by The Gettysburg Review,
Kim Barnes,
Jack Driscoll,
Jeffrey Hammond

MUD MATRIX

by HOA NGUYEN

from THE BARE LIFE REVIEW

Drown vs flood
    Silt and mud
Burned burrowing creature
with strong rodent teeth

Mekong moon story
    we write water on water
  Write country
    Float on flat boats
  notice the river moon reflective
and her voice there

She dyes her hair with plant matter

  Old woman now shrugged in a high collar

I once made silk flowers
    as a silk flower maker
folds allure folds of silk along a slender
branch under glass

mother + fish
  child + mother

what electric ribbon of water

re-
   becomes there   triangle delta
       my mouth fishlike and moving
     Moving change mouth
as the nine dragons rain more

   I don't recognize
you anymore

Grateful is the name of the passport
      medicine thin It comes with a picture
  a wormed
belly and fevered knees
   It comes with a scratchy
    please of refugee

Ching ching me   a big flag pole

  please you with my gratitude
      we the
expected happy   thankful pleasing

Cone hat memory
certainty of the poor
   hung in a baby hammock and swung

Mooring birds brought to you
by the dead
   who wears the gem twist ring and bangles

one broken jade bracelet

   Mother gone to mud
How they hook you

These they hook
and boil a perfect bird

She howl like a bird as if for life

Can eat a tooth or other crumbles
 bird beak tooth

No it's flies in your eyes

Nominated by The Bare Life Review

THE EFFECT OF HEAT
ON POOR PEOPLE

fiction by FARAH ALI

from KENYON REVIEW

Saba was beginning to think that Kamil was a belligerent man. When she'd married him, she'd known that there wasn't going to be a honeymoon because his financial circumstances didn't permit extravagances, but she wished they could put some neutral space between them. They had each taken three days off from work after the wedding, and in the hours and weekends that they had to spend together, they discovered they had precious little in common. After the forced post-wedding holiday, they gratefully fell back into their jobs. Saba was a receptionist in an office building, and Kamil was a reporter for an English newspaper. Because they had seen their parents, uncles and aunts, and older cousins make the best of bad relationships, they stumbled along clumsily.

Saba couldn't understand how Kamil could sound angry even about things that excited him. One Saturday afternoon in June, when the hot, dry wind called the *loo* blew into the city of Karachi, he grabbed Saba's hand and tugged her down the four flights of stairs in their building, past orange, *paan*-stained corners and candy wrappers and sticky black dirt, onto the pavement. He told her to look up and see the whiteness of the sky and the utter absence of clouds. Saba nodded in an absentminded way; she had left their dinner on the stove and didn't want it to get burned.

She made an inventory in her head of everything that made her cringe: the cushions on the sofas that had been flattened a long time ago, and the mattress on the bed which had stains that she avoided looking at when changing the two bedsheets she covered it with. The floor under her feet felt gritty even after she swept and mopped it. It was always warm inside their apartment. The fans on the ceilings moved slowly, and when she asked Kamil about them, he said there was something wrong with the wiring, waving a hand vaguely as if the answer lay somewhere over his right shoulder. It became hotter as the days went by, and when Saba cooked in the narrow kitchen she felt fetidness rising in small waves from the dark space between the stove and the counter. Once, after an argument with Kamil, she cut her finger when moving a piece of ginger against the jagged teeth of a grater. She put her hand in the bowl, squeezed out the blood, and mixed the food with the specks of red. It was some comfort seeing him eat it distractedly, the way he ate almost every meal.

Every morning, she entered her office full of gratitude for the air conditioning and went to the bathroom to gently wipe the sweat off her upper lip and to reapply her lipstick. On her soft chair behind the shiny counter, she sometimes felt bad about Kamil. He was one of those who had to work outdoors and swelter in the quiet, raspy warmth of the wind. She imagined his going around the city on his motorcycle on assignments, sweating under the helmet, interviewing pedestrians and protestors, penciling down statistics in a small notebook that he held in his browned, veined hands. When he had to stay out past dinner, Saba was happier because she didn't know how to speak to him for longer than five minutes. His conversation was in the format of opinions, and she assumed it was that way because he was always sending in articles to his newspaper. When he talked, he leaned forward as if to drive his points home with his spittle. If ever she had to identify his body, she knew she would have to look for a mole under his left brow. She could not call him a bad husband, even after he once grabbed her arms in exasperation because she had refused to counter his opinion with one of her own. He let go of her with a jerk and called her "mild," as if it were a swear word.

*   *   *

Kamil told Saba about a new assignment he had gotten from his editor: he had to write an article about the effect of heat on poor people. He looked determined and important, as if the weather were a criminal and he had to expose it. Sometimes he shared with Saba the results of his research, speaking professorially. He related incidents from his memory and from scrawls in his little notebook. He told her that in the slum areas the heat had solidified the air into a sulfurous yellow and that a charity group had funded vans to be turned into ambulances that stopped wherever they saw clumps of flies because almost always there was a body underneath. He swore and slapped the table for emphasis, and sometimes he gritted his teeth when he spoke.

Once, after dinner, he threw a newspaper into her lap. "Read that," he said with a grimace, and paced the floor with the air of a person who had been grievously injured.

Saba dutifully read the sordid piece of news: in a narrow alley, an old man had been found wheezing. Rescuers discovered that he had been unable to ask for something to quench his thirst because the sun had dried up all the water in his body, even his spit. Saba folded the newspaper and made sure that her face showed that she, too, had a heart for the dying downtrodden. In fact, she really thought that when there was no electricity the two of them could be good subjects for Kamil's research. She didn't say that out loud, though.

Over dinner, tearing his bread with angry flicks of his wrists, he complained about the city's lack of preparation for the heat wave and the idiocy of the population. He asked Saba if she felt it, too, and for a moment she was puzzled—did he mean the idiocy or the heat? But wisely she just said yes. He hovered around her when she washed the dishes, not letting her use more than a trickle of water from the tap, telling her how three people had been found dead in a small, unpainted house, apparently strangled by the heat and the resulting thirst. He also reduced his bathing to once a week because he said more than that was a crime. That annoyed Saba because she had to lie next to him every night. Even with her back turned to him she could smell him. She had to wait for him to fall asleep before she went to the bathroom to clean herself, soaking a towel with water and wiping the soap off her body. Her hair was the hardest to clean because it was thick and curly. Sometimes it took her thirty minutes to get all the shampoo out. When their electricity started going out for eight hours and opening the windows only brought in more suffocating air, Saba started testing her limits, and his: she shut doors and cupboards with angry bangs and let water gush out of taps at full strength. That drove Kamil wild, and he pulled his hair and called her names.

One evening he stalked into the kitchen where she was washing a teaspoon under a small waterfall and wrested it from her soapy hands. She shouted that he smelled like garbage, and he hit her on her face. Right away, he looked horrified at what he had done. He stammered that he was terribly sorry, that it was the heat, or all those thirsty people clutching their throats as they died one by one by the sides of roads he went on every day. Saba stayed quiet, scrutinizing the event that had just happened, like a scientist in a lab coat peering quizzically into an unidentified object. She did not feel angry at Kamil, and she recognized that that was a curious thing. Instead, she imagined severing her nerve endings with tiny scissors and shutting off her pores, sealing herself in. A little later, Kamil tried to show her that he loved her, or was committed to her, or to the idea of marriage, or something. She wasn't sure what. But she let him apologize to her in their small, hot bedroom with no windows until, exhausted, he fell asleep.

Early the next morning, Saba woke up from the humidity. Her pillow was damp with sweat. She put her hands on her stomach and, through the thin cotton that covered it, knew that the division of her pale cells had begun. She made up her mind that she was not going to share this bit of clairvoyance with anyone, not even her husband, whose child was forming away inside her. He lay on the other side of the bed, his shirt sticking to his front and his face covered with stubble that seemed to grow in hours. Saba did not feel like reaching out and smoothing away the hair from his forehead. Instead, she turned her thoughts inward, to the filling and emptying of her lungs and the tiny lub-dub of her heart pulsing out from her wrist. She swung her legs off the bed and got dressed to go to work. There was gravity and deliberation in her movements, as if this secret child was filling her with grace. In the mirror, her face appeared to be unlined, pale and beautiful. She looked at the large, purpling bruise, found two plasters, and stuck them on her forehead.

❖   ❖   ❖

For the first few weeks Saba's arms and face and fingers did not show signs of internal changes. In the lobby of her office building, behind the reception counter, she patted her stomach. When she wasn't answering calls and directing visitors, she whispered memos to the baby. She described to it the clothes on the women who stood in front of elevators to go to higher floors for more complicated jobs. If someone wore a more daring eyeshadow than was usual for her, Saba told the baby. She always spoke admiringly about these women. They had smooth foreheads; there didn't seem to be any bruises hidden there, though of course she couldn't tell unless she touched their faces. She balled up her fists to resist the urge to go up to them and find out, and let herself believe that these were complete women, beloved women.

"I think that blue suits her, oh, look at the print on the back," she would softly say to the baby.

Then the elevator doors would open and take them all away from her.

At home, she ignored Kamil and read to the baby instructions from the backs of shampoo bottles and the list of side effects from packets of painkillers. She took care to eat her fruits, vegetables, and chicken. She wanted her child to be God-conscious, so she read to it from her Holy Book. Sometimes at her work during break, she read bits of news—not written by Kamil, but by others in other newspapers—about the rising temperature in the city. "Alarming! Record-breaking!" the newspapers said. Such stories gave her perspective, she found. She read a paragraph about a young man, who had been identified as Hamid, found face down on the mass of fat wires and gray pipes under the bonnet of his car. His face had to be unstuck from the machinery, and his mother had identified his body. It was too gruesome a story to read to her baby, so Saba folded the newspaper, hummed a tune to her stomach, and finished an entire bottle of water. She started checking how much she was sweating and moved as little as possible when she stood outside after work to catch a rickshaw for home. To keep the baby cool, she thought about snow and ice cubes and refused to look at the sky. The bruise on her forehead was fading slowly, though in certain lights she could trace its original outline.

One evening, Kamil held her chin in his fingers as if it were a grape, crushable and small, and turned her face toward his. Then he let go and lightly said, "There's hardly a bruise there now." He sounded pleased, like he did when his favorite shoe was mended.

This was how they settled back into their normal routines, just like they used to after other fights. Watching his mouth twist into shapes as he ranted, she mulled over the idea of telling him she was pregnant. Because she didn't want to completely shock him, she started off by relating her own anecdotes from work, like when her paycheck had gone to the wrong person because of a misspelling, or a joke she'd heard at the water cooler. But Kamil puffed out his cheeks and let the air escape slowly as she spoke, and she realized that he did not have much patience for incidents that took place in air-conditioned interiors. So she withheld her big news from him. The baby inside her gave her the strength to apologize for her stories. Right away, Kamil forgave her. His voice flowed around her, blurring pleasantly, and she nodded and smiled, comforted that under her clothes, her secret was thriving and pushing

319

out her skin. She spoke to the baby in her head, imagining the words going down her blood stream and into its umbilical cord.

In episodes, she told the baby all about how she and Kamil had gotten married. When she was twenty-six years old, her mother had become worried that her daughter was going to stay single forever. So she took her to see a baba, a discreet old sage, who was known to have cures for problems like infertility, singlehood, cheating spouses, and divorce. His house was very far away, somewhere among the shanties but better than most of them. A small child let them in. Saba couldn't tell if the child was a boy or a girl, its hair was short and matted, and its eyes had been outlined with kohl. They followed its bare legs to a tree, under which sat the baba on a cushion. He asked Saba to lay her hand on the top of a small table, palm side up. He prodded it in a couple of spots, muttered, and once he rattled the fat, yellow beads around his neck, and once he pulled his tangled, gray beard, Saba became so caught up in the moment that when thunder crackled above their heads, she believed she was cured. Two weeks later, Kamil and his mother visited her house. They had seen her picture, given to them by a match-making lady, and had liked her face. Kamil was twenty-eight and had nice manners and a decent job. Saba's mother raised her hands in speechless gratitude, and Saba and Kamil got married.

❖　❖　❖

In preparation for the baby, Saba started scrubbing the apartment clean. The corners were the hardest because each one she confronted had a peeling table standing there, with maybe an object on it that had stopped working, or piles of old telephone directories, or just plain dust. She gazed critically at a lamp with a faded blue shade and flipped through a directory to look up names for the baby, then swept everything into plastic bags. On a weekend, she stood back with her hands on her waist and surveyed the results. The heated light coming through the grimy, barred windows dimmed the effect of her hard work, but she was still pleased. She decided that one day she would paper that particular wall and that window. For some time at least, her child would be spared knowledge of the danger of agile intruders who could break into safe abodes, and the necessity of ugly bars. While she cleaned, Kamil worked in his corner of the living room, glancing at her with a frown every now and then.

Once he said, "You're making too much noise."

Saba wondered if this was what companionship was.

Sometimes when she saw him sitting over his papers and notes, feverishly writing away at his Very Important Piece, she wanted to tell him her secret. More specifically, she wanted to gloat at the look of shock on his face. Perhaps he would be astounded that he had undermined her for so long that he would sink to his knees and hit the floor with his forehead.

There was no doubt in her mind that the baby was growing fine, even though her stomach only looked flabby, not taut, when she stood sideways in front of the mirror. She tried to glean knowledge of the baby's gender, but her sensitive fingers only told her that the naughty baby had crossed its legs, or had curled up tight, refusing to let its mother know. She made plans for educating the child after which he or she would grow up to earn some money, and the two of them would live in a nice little place by themselves. She imagined Kamil calling them to ask if he could visit them and she and her grown child looking at each other and laughing at the very idea.

*　*　*

Kamil said his editor was getting worried about the article being printed in time. There had been news from the meteorological station about rain in the next few weeks. Also, Kamil said, while squeezing his forehead, the imams of the city's mosques had started to pray for rain every Friday after afternoon prayers. A lot of times he came home then went out again, returning for a few hours between midnight and dawn.

"Wrapping up a few details," he said to the notebook in front of him even though Saba hadn't asked him.

She had decided she was not going to be curious about his movements. She chose, instead, to feel irritated, because she told herself that it was getting harder for her to rest now because her back ached. She discovered that the trick to falling asleep was not to start listening for the sounds of her husband closing the front door and his motorcycle rumbling down the street and the moon coming up and the moon going down and the motorcycle rumbling to a stop and the other side of the bed creaking.

*　*　*

Kamil's article was published, and one week later clouds crowded around and everyone in the city held their breath, and then it rained. Kamil, who had started to look like a dehydrated stick with glittering black eyes, turned shiny with the muggy air and with the congratulations he

321

received on his fine work. He brought home samosas and held out a copy of the newspaper in front of Saba—he didn't let her touch it because her hands were greasy from the food.

"It's a feature piece," he said proudly. "My best work, the editor says. I might even get an award for it, though he has asked me not to mention that in front of anybody yet."

Saba made herself smile. She felt an urge to touch her forehead again and make a wincing face, but she wasn't sure she could handle what would follow. What if Kamil got angry? What if he laughed about it? What if he couldn't remember what he had done? And her old bruise wasn't hurting her anymore, anyway. It hadn't hurt for a long time, and so what if Kamil was going to receive an award for some humanitarian words? She held inside her far more than he was ever going to get to hold in his thick fingers.

For about nine days, it rained almost nonstop. Roads got flooded but people crossed them joyously, hitching up shalwar and pants. Umbrellas were optional. Schools were closed for a whole day to celebrate the end of the worst heat wave in forty years. Some of the poorer people still died because of electrocution. Kamil wrote a small piece on how they should have known better than to bathe in puddles where wires had fallen. He showed it to Saba, and late at night she used those pages to scrub the toilet.

His minor success seemed to have made him generous toward her. He asked her one night about her work, but she didn't have any interesting details to relate, so she just told him that they had switched from blue sticky notes to green ones.

She was surprised when he came home one evening with a new handbag for her.

"You never get anything for yourself," he said, gentle admonition in his voice.

She hung the bag from her mirror. She knew where it was from. It had swung from the post of the cart of the man who sold fake bags and shoes at the corner of their street. When she lay in bed, she saw its bright, golden clasp gleaming cheaply in the dim light. It reminded her that the building she lived in was old and a sickly shade of yellow, that most of the year the trees and shrubs outside hung dispirited and dusty, growing out of cracks in footpaths, and that no amount of rain could give them beauty. Maybe she and Kamil had never had a chance because of the street they lived on: narrow, dirty, trapping heat that poured from the sky in the day, releasing it in waves from the melting asphalt in the night. Even rainwater couldn't flow down it gracefully: already there were plastic bags and pieces of food from vendors' carts mixed in it.

She had seen handbags like that when she was small, in apartments like this one on streets like hers. Always, the women holding it wore bright maroon lipstick and clutched their men around the waist if on a motorcycle, or walked fast through marketplaces holding hands of little children who wore shirts with words on them like "sweet girl" or "cool guy." Her mother had been one of them herself and had had friends like these, and Saba used to visit them with her, wearing an ironed frock. When the women talked about their husbands who were tailors or butchers or electricians, they used pronouns because Saba was sitting with them. She understood anyway, listening to every word while pretending to be absorbed in eating the biscuits. The topics hardly ever changed: their men's tempers, excesses, and taciturn ways.

Like everyone else, though, Saba had been sure she was going to have it different and better.

❀   ❀   ❀

The rain stopped, and the returning humidity was still a few days away. Kamil told Saba that he wanted to drop her to her work. He wouldn't listen when she said that she could go on her own, so she agreed and got onto the motorcycle behind him. It was necessary that she put an arm around him, to have something to hold on to. They bumped along, and Saba sent reassuring messages to the baby in case the new sensations were worrying it. Puddles lay on the road like trick rugs. Kamil went around them whenever he could, a detail which Saba would remember later and which would make her think that he was a kind man. He was going slowly through a spot of shallow water when a van spun toward them. It roared, or screamed, Saba wasn't sure. For some brief, wonderful seconds, she and Kamil flew through moisture and air. When she opened her eyes, she was on the road with Kamil, as if they were lying in bed, the gray of the sky above them. She pressed her stomach for company, but the baby didn't talk to her, and she worried if it was upset at something she had said or done or eaten. There was a lump-like hardness inside her. She waited to understand if the pain she was feeling was real or imaginary, and then she decided that it was very real, not unlike the kind she used to get before and during her period, which of course hadn't happened for a long time because her baby had been real just like this pain. When it subsided, the leaden weight inside her settled like sediment and filled her with a new kind of gravity, unlike the one she had experienced that morning when the baby was a dot.

And so, she did not feel sad about the loss of her child. The appropriate amount of grief will come later, she comforted herself. Her head and belly felt sodden, and she longed to get away from the mess. Vaguely, she wondered if Kamil, too, wanted to go away. She couldn't turn her neck to see how he was doing. If only he had a pillow under his head, she thought. Did this concern of hers mean that she loved him? If she could move her hand, she'd have clutched her chest. What if the van hadn't hit them? She would have missed out on loving her man. The close-call nature of it all filled her with exhilaration and delicious sorrow. Lying in the puddle, she squared her shoulders and decided that if she hadn't taken care of Kamil before, she would do so now. A twinge of regret made its way to her mind at all the times she could have wiped Kamil's brow or brought him a glass of water, or checked his work for mistakes, but hadn't. But you couldn't hurry things, she told herself. They happened only when all necessary conditions had been fulfilled. After all, each event existed merely as a result of a previous one. Before this love was the event of the baby, and before that was her marriage to Kamil, and the old baba she'd met with her mother, and her own parents' existence. So really, it was almost impossible to tell what or who to blame or thank. She moved her hand until she found Kamil's cold, still one, wrinkled with water, and she held on to it like a burr and waited for someone to find them.

Nominated by Sandra Leong

IS ALL WRITING ENVIRONMENTAL WRITING?

by CAMILLE T. DUNGY

from THE GEORGIA REVIEW

We are in the midst of the planet's sixth great extinction, in a time where we are seeing the direct effects of radical global climate change via more frequent and ferocious storms, hotter drier years accompanied by more devastating wildfires, snow where there didn't used to be snow, and less snow where permafrost used to be a given. Yet some people prefer to maintain categories for what counts as environmental writing and what is historical writing or social criticism or biography and so on. I can't compartmentalize my attentions. If an author chooses *not* to engage with what we often call the natural world, that very disengagement makes a statement about the author's relationship with her environment; even indifference to the environment directly affects the world about which a writer might purport to be indifferent. We live in a time when making decisions about how we construct the products and actions of our daily lives—whether or not to buy plastic water bottles and drinking straws, or cosmetics with microbeads that make our skin glow—means making decisions about being complicit in compromising the Earth's ecosystems.

What we decide matters in literature is connected to what we decide will matter for our history, for our pedagogy, for our culture. What we do and do not value in our art reveals what we do and do not value in our times. What we leave *off* the page often speaks as loudly as what we include.

I could choose among several paths walking from school to my childhood home in the Southern California hills. Route One was the most direct as the crow flies. It involved the fewest inclines but required a precarious scrabble down a pathless embankment to get to the greenbelt attached to the cul-de-sac where we lived. Route Two involved an initial ascent, then a level walk along the street where Jeff Blumenthal kenneled the Dobermans he often sicced on my sister and me. Running from the dogs was complicated by the steep stairs leading down to the greenbelt that separated our streets; this should have been the easiest way home, but we avoided it whenever we could. Route Three had no dogs, no stairs, no embankments, and no greenbelts, but it was significantly longer, ending with a climb up a three-block road that had *hill* in its name.

We also had a fourth option. We could climb beyond Jeff Blumenthal's cul-de-sac and into the foothills that backed both his house and ours. In the hills, we walked along drainage canals and animal paths, avoiding our suburban streets and the heavily irrigated strips of park dividing them. We climbed down, finally, over chaparral shrubs and scraggily anti-erosion landscaping, directly into our own back yard. Our parents didn't like us to take this route because we sometimes ran into coyotes or rattlesnakes, but I preferred the risk of the improbable encounter with a rattlesnake to the surety of Jeff Blumenthal's Dobermans. On that little-traveled path, I was free from the tensions of my built environment. I could be like the landscape in the hills beyond our house—a little wild and moderately protected.

Aggressively trained Dobermans, sun-lazy rattlesnakes, green turf in a desert, and ice plant clusters to keep serrated foothills from sliding over newly constructed neighborhoods represented the thin divide between the natural world and our built environments. When one world impinged upon the other, my daily life was directly affected.

When I began to write, words and images sourced from my childhood's landscape became part of what and how I wrote:

Language

Silence is one part of speech, the war cry
of wind down a mountain pass another.
A stranger's voice echoing through lonely
valleys, a lover's voice rising so close
it's your own tongue: these are keys to cipher,

the way the high hawk's key unlocks the throat
of the sky and the coyote's yip knocks
it shut, the way the aspens' bells conform
to the breeze while the rapids' drums define
resistance. Sage speaks with one voice, pinyon
with another. Rock, wind her hand, water
her brush, spells and then scatters her demands.
Some notes tear and pebble our paths. Some notes
gather: the bank we map our lives around.[1]

"Language" was the first poem in my first book. This seems as right a decision about order as I've ever made.

Environment is a set of circumstances as mundane as the choice of paths we take to get home. When I lived in Iowa City for my final years of high school, our main routes home—in a car now, because we lived eight miles from school—involved either the interstate and a major thorough-fare, or the back roads that led through farmland and patches of prairie.

On recent visits to the Midwest I've driven through ghost landscapes—less prairie, less farmland. Memory overlaid my vision, inscribing alternative realities onto the present, making me aware of where I was within the context of where I have been.

Isn't this one of the things we do when we sit down to write? We decide how to describe what we are compelled to describe. Even while moving through vast cities like LA or Chicago, by being attuned to a world that is more than simply human I can't help but think of what might have been there before we privileged our own interests: commerce and industry, asphalt and glass. In this way we can apprehend what might have disappeared and what still lives alongside us, biding time—ginkgoes, catfish, the rivers, crickets.

Looking out my office windows where I live now in Northern Colorado, I see the foothills of the Rocky Mountains on most days, and the actual Rockies on really clear ones. People in Fort Collins navigate by those mountains—which are to the west, and so, except on about five overcast days a year, you always know just where you are. The mountains are a constant guide. Consider how different this topographical navigation is from an orientation based on your proximity to a particu-

---

1. From *What to Eat, What to Drink, What to Leave for Poison* (Red Hen Press, 2006).

lar building, to a particular street—South of Houston, or SoHo, for instance—or navigation by some other man-made landmark—east of Central Park. Here I'm using references from New York City, the environment of my husband's youth; for him, thinking to navigate by nonhuman landmarks took a little time. Similarly, "Two streets down from the Waffle House," we might have said in the Virginia town where I once lived, or "Just after the entrance to the college," or, "We're the house with the blue trim. If you reach the Church of Life, you've gone too far." In such urban environments, it might be difficult to remember that you are, in fact, *in* an "environment," given that we've come to think of the terms *environment* and *nature* as referring to someplace wild and nonhuman, more akin to the foothills of my childhood than to the cul-de-sacs terraced into their sides. But that line of reasoning slides us toward the compartmentalization I resist. Our environments are always both human and other than human.

I feel an affinity for what ecologists call ecotones, areas at the margins between one zone and another—like the tidal zone where beach and ocean overlap, or the treed and grassy band where forest becomes meadow—spaces that are often robustly productive and alive. These are overlaps rich with possibility and also, often, danger. The margins of one biologically robust area and another are sometimes called conflict zones, because the clash between one way of living on the Earth and another can be violent and charged. They are spaces that reward study, revealing diverse possibilities for what it might mean to be alive.

Writing takes off for me when I stop separating human experiences from the realities of the greater-than-human world. A poem that at first seems to have everything to do with some so-called environmental concern might end up being about some human condition, or I might begin a poem thinking about some human concern and end up writing something that's chock full of natural imagery. The connection I feel to experiences that are beyond my own, beyond simply the human, causes me to fuzz the lines.

In a radical and radicalizing way, these fuzzed lines bring me face to face with the fragility of the Holocene—or, more precisely, the destructiveness of the Anthropocene. To build an age around the concerns of one species is to ignore the delicate balance required in any ecotone.

When one way of living on the Earth takes priority, the overlaps that support a healthy system of exchange collapse. Without that exchange, one path becomes the only path, and so whatever dangers were inherent on that one route cannot be avoided, because whatever possibilities were available on the others can no longer be revealed. I do not want such a limiting set of circumstances for my writing or for the literature of our time. I certainly don't want such a limiting set of circumstances for my world.

In 2009, when *Black Nature: Four Centuries of African American Nature Poetry* was published, one of the most remarkable statements the book made was that black people could write with an empathetic eye toward the natural world. In the general public perception of black writers, the idea that we can write out of a deep connection to the environment—and have done so for at least four centuries—came, and I think still comes, as a shock.

As the editor of *Black Nature,* I was able to make the anthology a complete project by expanding the presentation of how people write about the environment. Not all the poems in the anthology are of the rapturous *I walk out into nature and find myself* ilk, though such poems *are* there. The history of African Americans in this country complicates their ability and/or desire to write of a rapturous idealized connection to the natural world—as when I have driven over the Tallahatchee River and had my knowledge of history, of the murder of Emmett Till, make it impossible for me to view those often-quite-scenic waters in a purely appreciative manner. And so, many of the poems in the collection do not fall in line with the praise school of nature poetry but, instead, reveal complicated—often deadly—relationships. The authors of these works mix their visions of landscapes and animals into investigations of history, economics, resource extraction, and other very human and deeply perilous concerns.

In complicating or "de-pristining"—I'm patenting that word—my environmental imagination, I engage with what has come to be called *ecopoetics,* connecting topics we often understand to be the provenance of nature poetry with topics about our current and past human lives. In doing so, ecopoetics has expanded the parameters of who is writing environmental work, and how. This mode of creating and understanding poetry is expanding our ideas about the very nature of what constitutes environmental writing.

Writers exploring ecopoetics ask themselves questions such as these: How does climate change affect our poetics? How do we write about resource extraction, agribusiness, endangered bird species, the removals of indigenous peoples, suburban sprawl, the lynching of blacks, or the precarious condition of gray wolves and the ecosystems dependent upon them? Our contemporary understanding of ecopoetics takes into account the ways human-centered thinking reflects on, and is reflected in, what we write. And, contemporary ecopoetics questions the efficacy of valuing one physical presentation of animated matter over another, because narratives about place and about life contribute to our orientation in, and our interpretation of, that place and that life.

All of our positions on the planet are precarious at this moment in history, and attentive writers work to articulate why this is the case—including many writers of color who were already engaging in this mode of writing long before the ecopoetics movement took off. (Works by Alice Dunbar Nelson, Lucille Clifton, Claude McKay, Anne Spencer, Sterling Brown, June Jordan, Evie Shockley, Sean Hill, and Ed Roberson spring immediately to mind.) But only as the ecopoetics movement gained traction has such de-pristined writing finally been identified as environmental writing and, therefore, begun to be seen in a new light.

Without giving myself license to believe that all writing is environmental writing, I could very likely assign expansive poems—including many of those anthologized in *Black Nature*—to just about any category other than that of a nature poem. But to separate the importance of human interactions with the non-human world from the importance of cultural and political considerations would be to limit the scope of such poems entirely. This is particularly true given that the black body has so frequently been rendered "animalistic" and "wild" in the most dangerously degrading and limiting senses of those terms.

According to what Jeff Blumenthal yelled at us as he commanded the attacks, he sicced his dogs on us because we were black girls and, in his mind, beneath him. Hearing all the names he assigned to my body, so many of them intended to limit my potential, I quickly learned the danger of categorical labels. Never mind all the things Jeff Blumenthal and my sister and I might have had in common; our differences were enough to cause him to be indifferent toward our safety. He was hostile toward our presence in a space he considered his own. So, walking the easy path home from school was often nearly impossible.

The history of human divisions is often constituted of stories about one set of people being hostile toward the presence of others. An ideology that would demand the exclusion or subjugation of whole populations of human beings is an ideology quick to assume positions of superiority over all that is perceived to be different. If you can construct a narrative that turns a human into a beast in order to justify the degradation of that human, how much easier must it be to dismiss the needs of a black bear, a crayfish, a banyan? The values we place on lives that are not our own are reflected in the stories we tell ourselves—and in which aspects of these stories resonate with us. To separate the concerns of the human world (politics, history, commerce) from those of the many life forms with which humans share this planet strikes me as disastrous hubris and folly. We live in community with all the other lives on Earth, whether we acknowledge this or not. When we write about our lives, we ought to do so with an awareness of the other lives we encounter as we move through the world. I choose to honor these lives with attention and compassion.

Nominated by The Georgia Review,
Stuart Dischell,
Gary Gildner,
Ainee Nezhukumatathil,
D. A. Powell

FOUR SHORT ESSAYS PERSONIFYING A FUTURE IN WHICH WHITE SUPREMACY HAS ENDED

by CHEN CHEN

from FOGLIFTER

1.

                                        therefore,

2.
i walk, chewing bubblegum, which should make
a happy feeling, bubbly me   but,

i am busy considering
how to personify
is to make a person out of feelings

& not necessarily to make
more personable   again,

i tap on the window of feeling
unseen & the window
refuses to personify me   see,

some people are not yet personified
while trees often are & the birds

in poems & the pets
of white people most often   &,
the present refuses to personify into a future

of bubbly walking   yet,
to person is to feel, & necessary   so,

i read a friend's poem
in which the word "emotionality" feels
out for me in the middle of our unseen   in fact,

i feel the word sounds clunky   then again,
aren't actual feelings

clumsy, & within our unbubbly
i sound out a clumpy, a cracked   exhaling,
i will feel

3.
so healed when white people
finally shut up
about that one time they went to asia

& felt so spiritual & healed
for poetry should not be therapy,

poets say, though still i feel
that some would prefer me
to therapize

them with yummy feelings
of migrant tragedy, fix them

up a fixed dictator-&-
dumplings past,
never to walk into a future

of unpersonable feelings
for to feel is to window

& to person is to people
a feeling, a future
in which

4.
this future walks,

unpersonifiable, because

what, who

is a person

in these windows, now

Nominated by Foglifter,
Jung Hae Chae,
David Meischen

NEW BEES

fiction by CLAIRE LUCHETTE

from PLOUGHSHARES

We bought the nylons before evening prayer at a twenty-four-hour grocery three miles away. They came folded inside paper envelopes, tawny mesh showcased under cellophane windows. We bought a dozen. They tend to rip.

Later, we disagreed about whether the envelopes could be recycled. If paper's affixed with plastic, is it still paper? Eventually, we stripped the cellophane squares from all twelve envelopes and sorted the scraps.

Everything has a thousand uses. When nylons run, we slip our hands inside and dust shelves, polish silver, buff our leather shoes. There's always a way to give something new life, but most people don't realize this. Most people don't want to know all the lives contained within disposable things.

That spring, we wanted new bees for Harriet. They hadn't wintered well, our bees. Only a few hundred were left by the time Harriet came to the convent. She didn't know there used to be thousands, so to her, there was a bounty. She'd go out bare-handed and give the hives some air. She'd coo and grin, watching them float. She was unlike us—we found them fearsome. Agatha was allergic to bees, and Mary Lucille was seventy-three, frail as linguini. Therese avoided pain, and I avoided anything with violent rage.

The winter survivors moved slowly. They were depressed, having witnessed the deaths of their babies and their parents, who had come to lie in piles at the bottom of the apiary.

Ours was a humble apiary. Nothing special. A dozen sheets of hanging beeswax, stored in a frame on wheels. The apiary was a wooden model, donated years ago. We kept it next to the baby Oreocookie cow, which we milked for butter.

We were having trouble with Harriet, it's true. She was a novice—hadn't been veiled, hadn't been given a religious name. During morning prayer, she had this look of hurt. It's not unusual. 5:20 is a painful time to be praying if you are usually dreaming then. But it was harder for Harriet than for most. She displayed none of the joy we felt, none of the love. She worried the skin under her eyes. She never had an appetite. She had a round crater on her neck where an old boyfriend had stubbed out a cigarette.

So we wanted to surprise her with new bees. Many times, all a person needs is somewhere to be and something to do. We used the parish computer and found an apiarist in Louisville. He bred honeybees and sold them in boxes of twelve thousand.

When we called him, the apiarist sounded impatient—"Yeah? Hello?"—as if pulled from pleasure by the ring of the phone.

We explained we were customers intending to buy bees. We were interested in the Carniolans—tough, resistant to mites. But we had a question. How would we get the bees out of the box? We pictured a rushing swarm. We pictured quick, vengeful enemies.

He explained that all we'd need to do is throw the box on the ground, wiggle free the lid, and pour out the bees. They'd spill from the box, he said, like oil. They wouldn't hurt us. They were merciful creatures. They'd find the apiary on their own.

And the bees were safe to transport in a box, in the back of a car?

Yes, of course. He regularly drove with a carful of bees. "They like inertia," he said. "Just like us."

After he said goodbye, his phone hovered in its receiver, and we heard him whispering tender words: "Oh, darlings. You can have my waffles. Yeah." We hung up, flushed with the hot shame of happening, uninvited, upon an intimacy not our own.

We pooled our allowances, folded the bills, and sealed them in an envelope. For the keys to the van, we went to Father Lucas in the rectory. He was watching television in blue jeans. We showed him handfuls of dead bees. We said, "Father, think of the bees. Think of the flowers."

His patience was cursory at best. In mass, he sped through Communion, doling out wafers in rapid succession—"BodyofChrist Bodyof-ChristBodyofChrist."

He held a curled bee in the lamplight. Its legs were kinked but its wings were out, as if it had died mid-flight.

Father Lucas looked at us: "Did you know people used to think bees came from the rotting bodies of dead cows?"

This was a passion of his: sharing unsolicited trivia. He plucked the unspent stinger from the bee's belly and tossed it to the carpet. "Bees are a worthwhile investment," he said, "if we care for them right. Buying new bees every year—that's an expense we can ill afford."

We nodded. We told him, "Harriet, the novice—she's good with them. We trust her."

We stood, patient. It's best, more often than not, to say nothing rather than something.

Finally, he crossed one leg over the other and spoke: "Well, I don't see why you can't go and see them. But you've got to be careful driving."

We smiled. We thanked him.

"One more thing," he called. "If the van gives you any trouble, just pull off the road, call me, and wait for me to come."

We left Harriet to sit the hotline. Every day, we heard only from Theresa, a local woman who was, on her own, raising a daughter with special needs. She asked no questions, sought no advice. She often cried. We had never met her, only knew her voice: hurried, and colored with apology.

Harriet wanted to know how to counsel Theresa: what to say and how to say it.

"Pray with her," we said. "Listen. If you don't know what to say, wait. Wait until you know the right words."

She wanted to know where the four of us were going and when we would be back. We looked at her: the hunched shoulders, raw mouth. At nineteen, she was still afraid of time spent alone. She didn't yet know that privacy was not a punishment but a gift.

We shook our heads and told her we could not tell her. We knew how to protect the truth. Many people don't realize that honesty can work this way—that it's possible to be candid about your candor's limits.

The van was an old red Mercury Villager, a donation from some parishioner whose child had long ago attempted to obscure, with the liberal use of a black magic marker, the entirety of the rear window. Back when the van was brought to us, we were able to work away much of the ink, but retired our sponges after a few rounds of scrubbing, leaving a cloudy film on the glass like lacework.

The seats were matted velour and the sliding doors were trouble. They jammed in their tracks. More than once we had driven down the highway with the doors stuck halfway open. So we were prudent. Everyone climbed in and out from the front seat.

The car made no mystery of how it felt, being made to climb those hills. The whole way, it groaned with contempt. We paid no mind. Windows down, our veils trembled in the wind, and dust settled in the nooks of our ears, the bends of our elbows. We ate graham crackers straight from the sleeve and counted pale gray horses propped on the hillsides.

We'd written directions on both sides of a napkin—even the tedious steps, like Continue. Preparation is a compulsion of ours. We carry toothpicks and half a dozen sanitary pads everywhere we go. We sharpen pencils in groups of three.

The exit was an EXIT ONLY and we slowed to take the turns at half speed. Ours was the only car, turning up wild dust, and there were no houses for miles, until we turned off the paved road that led to the apiarist's house.

We thought, at first, that we'd arrived at the wrong house—we saw no beehives in the yard, no white-suited man traipsing in the bushes. Just a low house of clapboard and siding, the windows covered with sun-leeched sheets of newspaper. A dark place to be raising bees, we agreed. We checked the house number against our directions.

We slipped graham crackers into our pockets, turned off the van and climbed out, one sister at a time. The grass was frosted with so many dandelion heads we bent to stroke it. He had bushes of raspberries near the road, the fruit gone squat and hard. In the treeless yard, a low plastic pool, clotted with fallen leaves, and on the porch, a paint-stripped bike thrown on its side.

We heard them first: the drone like a quivering siren, rising and falling with no clear rhythm. And then the man opened the door and we saw them: hundreds of bees, gliding with ease around the front room. Such buoyancy they showed! They looked, diving and climbing, almost beautiful, until we remembered we were afraid.

From a metal jug the apiarist shot smoke in the air, and the bees slowed as if in obeisance. A few drifted past us through the open doorway and we jerked with fright, clutching each other's elbows.

"I didn't expect the clergy," the apiarist said, seeming delighted. As he spoke, we watched a bee hover and lower itself onto his nose. "These weren't raised to be God-fearing bees, I'm afraid." The bee wriggled but the man's voice remained measured. He appeared not to have noticed. He smiled then, displaying only a half-mouthful of teeth. "It's not every day I get a visit from the brides of Christ," he said.

The room was floored in linoleum, walled with slats of imitation wood, and empty except for a low-hanging light bulb and a white wooden beehive, uncovered. And except for the bees. They blurred the air. Crowds of them danced over the surface of the apiary. Others came to rest on the wooden frames bordering the windows, and on the apiarist's shoulders and head. The rest were set on soaring. They approached us with interest and we shut our mouths, dug nails into forearm flesh.

The bee shimmied on the apiarist's nostril, and then moved on. We smiled. "So, the bees, then," we said. "We came for the Carniolans."

He nodded and gestured for us to walk with him. We held hands and followed the man to the back of the house, where the bare hallway gave way to a wide room with a narrow yellow mattress, a brown blood spot in its center. He must have slept among these bees, dozed to their thrum.

He rifled in a dark closet. With his back turned, he couldn't see us, frozen, trying to appear inanimate so the bees might pass us by. Mary Lucille's tiny hands gripping mine tight.

The apiarist spun back around and assembled a cardboard box. He pulled from the windowsill a mass of bees clinging to a hunk of comb. And inch by inch, he lowered the comb, with the bees hanging on, into the cardboard box. We watched him slowly tip the box up over itself so it lay flat on a white sheet, trapping the bees inside. He propped up a corner with a two-by-four. "So they'll tell their friends how nice it is inside the box," he said. The bees wandered in and out, as if making up their minds. "In, oh, half an hour or so, we'll have a good three pounds of bees in there."

We nodded. How many bees to the pound? In the kitchen he served us bottled cola. He offered us pickle spears fingered from a wide-neck jar. One of us said no for us all.

This must be a kind of suffering, we thought, to be trapped inside with a million bees. It is terrible to be conscious of all the ways you can be hurt.

The apiarist ate his pickles with loud snaps. Through the back door a dog came panting—a rib-thin, bear-faced dog. His walk seemed to hurt him, but he delighted in the presence of water in his bowl, in the hands of the apiarist digging through his ratty fur.

"Bennie boy," the apiarist cooed, crouching to kiss the dog's wet nose. "That's my Bennie." He turned to us. "You all can pet him, if you like."

Agatha bent to meet his face. He breathed at her, hot and hard. Bees latched to the dog's tucked belly and greasy ears, but Bennie never whined, never stopped to swat or shake them loose. We watched him lick freely at the water, though several bees hung above the bowl. A loving thing, unafraid.

"Are you looking at his balls?" the apiarist said. We weren't, but then we saw them and could not ignore them. Bulbous, fat. The healthiest part of him.

"Oh, I'm sorry," the apiarist said. He scratched his nose with a wet finger. "'Balls' is a swear, isn't it?"

"No, no, don't worry," Therese said. We all sat on the floor at Bennie's flank and watched him breathe. He was the kind of trusting dog who seemed not to know how bad things were.

When we stood back up, we saw that bees had drowned in our cola. They looked, examined from the bottles' mouths, to be at rest. We abandoned the soda in the sink and washed the bees down the pipes.

The apiarist sighed, watching them go. He told us how lousy things had been for him and the bees. Lately, his queens were laying fewer eggs. "One thing about queens," he said, "they don't like to be helped along. They like it to be their idea."

We set our bottles on the counter—four tiny clinks.

"Say, girls," the apiarist said. "Could you help me with something in the garage?"

We looked at each other and held hands tight.

His garage was detached from the house, with a wide square-faced pull-down door gaping a foot. We welcomed the walk in plain, beeless air. He led us in through the side door, and Bennie rushed in first. There was no car or truck, only amassed disorder. Eight feet of an artificial Christmas garland studded with imitation pinecones. Towers of thick, glossy science fiction novels. Canned beans and corn, their tops dust-fuzzed. A woodworking bench and low table saw, an upended electric keyboard, a dozen empty tissue boxes, a microwave.

We waded in. Bennie's tail upset a pile of empty amber prescription bottles, and they went flying. The apiarist ignored the dog. He perched

340

a foot on a rusted lawn chair and said, "Well, it beats me why a bunch of pretty girls would be interested in the clergy."

We clutched more tightly each other's palms. Mary Lucille spoke, her voice measured and firm. "Now. What can we do for you here?" And we looked to the apiarist for instruction.

"See, I'm having trouble with that old door. It won't go down the whole way. And I get little critters coming in at night."

We looked at the foot of liminal space, the threshold for escape.

"I'm sure if you're having trouble closing it, we won't be much use," Mary Lucille said. "We're not exactly brawny."

He walked over and mock-tugged on the strap hanging from the door. "I don't know why it won't give! Like a stuck zipper or something."

We thought he wouldn't see us slipping bits of graham cracker from our pockets and letting Bennie lick them up from our hands. We thought it'd be a silent gift. But Bennie ate with such loud, excited smacks of his tongue, and the apiarist flung around and stared hard.

"We just," Therese started. "We only wanted—"

He raised his voice then, rage swelling in his face. "You do. Not. Feed my dog. Without. My. Permission."

"Oh, that's enough," Mary Lucille said, and we felt the air shift. "It was an innocent act. A cracker for a needy dog."

He could have come at us. But instead he bent to stick his hand inside Bennie's mouth and scrape gummy bits of cracker from the teeth and pink tongue. Bennie's eyes went shut, and he whined from somewhere deep within. We watched the man rake the dog's throat with one hand and hold his head with the other. Later, we'd recall seeing him flick the wet starch to the ground. On his face, there was, for a moment, tenderness. Care.

We collected ourselves, and then, while the man's hand was between the jaws of the dog, we fled out that side door, abandoning the box of bees we had come for in the clapboard house.

We hurried the van's engine awake and leapt the curb and started to soar. And we were all feeling good, so good—feeling useful, feeling all sorts of brave and a certain kind of lucky, the kind that comes after you circumscribe danger with your own will and good sense. The wind welcomed us to newfound speed. We smiled out the windows at fields of upright corn.

But then, a few miles out, just before the turnpike, we heard it. In the middle of the thruway, the car issued a pained squeal; then, a snap.

341

The steering wheel went stiff—stubborn as anything. It took all the combined might of Agatha and Mary Lucille, up front, to force the wheel to the right. We parked on the shoulder, turned off the car, and, for a moment, we neither spoke nor moved.

In the glove compartment we kept a small, heavy phone. Father Lucas didn't answer when we called, so we left a message in calm words. "Hello, Father. The van won't steer. We're at mile marker eighty-two. Please call us back when you have the chance."

We sat on our hands. In our silence, we heard the whir of rushing cars. We sighed, one by one.

We called again, and when he still didn't answer, we climbed out and went to look at the engine's innards. We knew a thing or two about engines, the plot of bulbs and tubes. We could point to the battery and the transistor and the fuel injector. So many places for trouble to hide.

We read aloud from the manual. Checked the camshaft and the coolant. Walked circles around the vehicle. The car would start, but would not steer.

If you look long enough, there is always something to blame. The trouble was the serpentine belt—the black strap that moves the water pump. It had snapped right in half. We pulled it free, a squirming length of rubber, and tucked it in a cup holder. With a bit of glue, it would work well to seal the gap under the convent's front door.

It was a decision made together, in silence, confirmed with glances and nods. All at once we shed our nylons and tied the feet tight to make a loop, and with tense hands we guided the nylon over the pulleys. There was slack, and we tightened it. Our fingers caught grease and soot and our foreheads went sweat-slick, but then the engine turned over and the pulleys spun and the nylon moved the disparate parts and Mary Lucille pushed the wheel and the tires did what she told them to do, and we laughed. We laughed and laughed. Amid the thick fields, along the great wide paved road, we had found a way to move.

While we were slinging hosiery through the car engine, Father Lucas called to say he was coming to save us. The voicemail was panicked, as if it was he who was in trouble.

What words had he said to us about the van, before we left? "If there's trouble, leave the trouble for me"? "Don't touch what you don't understand"? No matter. Many times, the greatest mercy you can grant a man is the chance to believe himself the hero.

And so we slipped free the ring of pantyhose from the pulleys. We slackened the knots and reclaimed pairs at random. Some of us had thicker ankles, some of us darker flesh, some of us broad bellies. But it hardly mattered, the chosen mesh, because our habits hung low to cover our legs. Back in the van, we waited for Father to arrive.

Maybe it was selfish, our need to have everything fixed just right. Two weeks later, Harriet would leave, a bar of our lemon soap in her backpack and a paper bus map in her hand. She said goodbye just after prayer, having shed her habit in favor of denim. She took the red line bus to an aunt's house in Madeira, or a cousin's place in Kenwood; we forgot which. She promised to call us when she arrived, but she never did. We spoke her name in reverent prayer and imagined her with a new haircut, a new place to go every day. Or returning to some place she'd been before. An attic or backroom or dive bar. Somewhere familiar, but in no way safe. In time, we saw that there was no longer any faith to foster in her; she would have to create her own. The old weary bees would survive another season. They kept us stocked in clumpy wax and honey, until they, over the course of one week, perished, killed by the spray we used to eliminate dandelion weeds. It is impossible to know for sure. Everything comes with a price. Nothing in this life is without sacrifice. We found their little bodies scattered in the grass, in the fig tree and the blueberry bush. They died while seeking. They knew nothing besides their daily hums and hunts. We looked out the kitchen window and watched them flit and thought that maybe they knew fear too, and valued, above all else, control, over their work and their home and their flight.

But we didn't know any of this that afternoon, as we waited in our tired car, singing low hymns, watching the grass take the wind. We wanted to go home to Harriet, to tell her she was important, more important than bees. We wanted to hold her hand in prayer and hear her voice in song and make her see and know her value.

We waited. We whistled. Used spit and sleeves to wipe scalp smudges from the windows.

The parish florist drove Father Lucas out to mile marker 82. Father came like royalty, waving out the window of a purple van. We saw their smiling faces among the bouquets. Lilies pressed up against the windows, ranunculi in the passenger seat, and the waxen face of our parish pastor above his crisp collar.

"Oh, my ladies," Father said, stepping out of the van. "What did you do?"

It is our belief that the greatest grace you can grant yourself is the private knowledge of your strength. We popped the hood and let him look. He shoved his shirtsleeves high, frowned into the depths. Standing behind him, we crossed our arms. Even though we could point to the problem, knew what the van needed, we stood and let the wind upset our veils, and we waited, letting him stare at the valves and hot pistons, allowing him the time he needed to conclude whatever he would.

Nominated by Ploughshares

AMERICAN LANDSCAPING PHILADELPHIA TO MOUNT VERNON

by ROGER REEVES

from THE PARIS REVIEW

Who would have thought too much simultaneity:
The Swan Planters hovering above the windbeaten
Statue of the Virgin Mary who casts her gaze down
On the Repainted Lawn Jockey, his brown face
Spreading out over his white cap, a small rebellion
Or, merely, an inarticulate hand overzealous
In restoring Race back to its place in God after
Winter makes heathen the heaven of horticulture.
This is America calling: the golden pollen of Spring
Blinging every available sedan, stone porch, puddle,
And satin blouse hanging from a smiling white line
Into yellow salvation, or forgetfulness, a black dog,
Antique in its hunger for my daughter's hand through a fence,
My daughter, in her machine and wonder, willing
To give. It is as if every moment is praying
For whatever is above it or just outside of its grasp: the dog
For a hand, the Lawn Jockey holding his absent lantern
Out in front of him for the Virgin whose eyes,
No longer there, Januaried away by the blizzards,
Salt, and wind, stutter with a brown streak
I won't call bird shit but rusted water
Dripping from the corrugated roof above.
Even the flies, in the earliest part of the sentence,
Twitch above the sidewalk as if being accused
Of neglect, infanticide, murder, ending the empire

In order to start another in their own image.
But what is an empire fashioned in the image of flies?
Mistake: it's not a lantern the Jockey holds
Out in front of him, but a black hitching ring
For masters to tether the tamed because they lack
Mastering, though not the Jockey, who stands on the wind
And paving stones like Jocko Graves, the slave
Of General Washington, who froze to death
Enfolded in snow on the banks of the Delaware River,
His lantern out in front of him awaiting his master's return
As he had been ordered, and Washington, so moved
By Graves's frozen obedience, constructs a statue
Of dead Graves holding a lamp at his plantation
Home in Mount Vernon. Even in death, a slave must
Labor though I knew nothing of these clothes
When, on a Ferris wheel, overlooking the muddy
Syringed-and-bottled banks of Philadelphia, I kissed a girl
Through the tin smog and chemical-plant perfume
And carried that kiss through the year, touching newspaper,
Edges of blankets, the backs of hamburger buns
To my lips to remember the dimming summer
Sheepishly backing out of a door it hurriedly burst through.
Only in America will the sons and daughters of slaves
Kiss the sons and daughters of their masters
And remember it as an opportunity to be human.

Nominated by The Paris Review,
Kim Barnes,
Ben Fountain

BAD NORTHEN WOMEN

fiction by ERIN SINGER

from CONJUNCTIONS

We are Tockers, descendants of thirty-six feet of long lean Saskatche-wan woman: six Tocker sisters, six foot tall, exemplary ax-women all, so says our mom. At the kitchen table this morning we are mixing our Nesquik and Mom is quoting from *Taking Our Time: A History of Tock-ers*. Citing each Tocker triumph she stabs the book with her file, show-ering its curling cover with fingernail dust. Tocker Trucking! Compass Sawmill! TT's Laundromat! Stab! Stab! Stab! Mom plants the file in an old baby corn can crammed with white pencil crayons and shards of rul-ers and dried-out pens. She rubs her eyes until mascara moons arise underneath. Our spoons clack inside our plastic cups.

What was I saying? she sighs. Point being, summer's coming and no Tocker ever chopped a tree indoors. Get outside and play! Tocker girls brown up good. Just godsakes don't get a farmer tan.

That right there's offensive to farmers, Dad says behind his cigarette smoke.

I'm going down for a nap, says Mom. She puts her Kool-Aid glass in the sink.

Dad lifts his chin to the nip marks on our legs.

What's this? He bends, grabs our pup by the snout for a one-on-one: You're supposed to scare them feral beasts off.

Mom says, If these girls can't handle a couple of strays, how will they learn to handle a man?

Dad's not worried about that.

Because! he says. *Because* I got a feeling this one's going to shape up to be a good guard dog.

347

Mom snorts, says, I like my animals wild and in my tummy.

The dog is a freebie from Swap 'N' Shop. He's a weird-looking guy, kind of a fluffy coyote. Dad claims his name is Chopper but we're not convinced.

Don't fail me now, he warns the pup. Can't watch my girls every minute.

More like any minute. Dad spends his days under the Chev Suburban he's liberating from our driveway. He's getting itchy. Threatening to head north this time.

He follows Mom down the hall to her bedroom.

Go play, he says.

Teenage girls don't play. So we walk. We walk Airport Road until there's the hum of an approaching plane. Checking over our shoulders, we break into a run. The airplane descends from the south, twin propellers whirring over great squares of green spring prairie, silver circles of grain bins and farmhouse roofs streaked rusty with wood-smoke. It lands short of the darkness of white spruce and jack pine gathered on the horizon. We are close enough that we can see the white blobs of strange faces in the dark windows as the plane shoots by us, blowing past the warning signs. *Caution! Stray Dogs on the Runway!*

American bear hunters in khaki and camo step on the tarmac and feel like welcome strangers. There is only one dog in sight and he belongs to us: four stringy teenage girls in ribbed tank tops and basketball shorts pressed against the chain-link fence. The hunters are too far away to see our winter-pale legs knotted with mosquito bites, our gnawed fingernails, our silver-filled molars, our greasy hair Mom chopped short as punishment for, as she puts it, not learning to work a shampoo bottle.

The hunters laugh at something we can't hear, which is the pilot saying, Welcome to the North, where the men are men and the women are too.

The ditch is dry and we follow it along Highway 4. The pup leaps and runs in circles and stops to sniff a squashed porcupine. Foxtails grow along the road and we tear them from the ground and brush the silk across our lips. We hurdle over fully loaded baby diapers and broken beer bottles as we go north to Bart's Gas.

The Gladue girls have the picnic table. They are cracking and firing off dill pickle Spitz shells to the dirt below. These chicks are Cree and they glow, they've got that sunny maple-syrup skin that we can't get no matter how many hours Mom forces us out in the sun. The Gladue girls are named for old movie stars.

Too much grease in that hair, *moonyasses*, says Whoopi, scratching our pup's tawny fur. Your bangs look like string cheese.

The boys say your panties smell like muskeg.

Puckamahow, says Daryl. Then she puts up two fists and laughs at our chickenshit eyes.

Let's go then.

As if.

Too dumb you are.

Look in the mirror.

Bored, we leave. There is nowhere new to walk. Tocker Town has no surprises, no hidden staircases, no haunted conservatories, no secret garden. We know this place like the inside of our parents' underwear drawers. Today is Saturday. No school. No money. No jobs yet but summer is coming. Work will claim us. Crappy jobs come like power poles on the highway.

Before we die we'll slick your Teen Burgers with Teen sauce, make chicken salad on a cheese bun and keep your kids from drowning in the public pool and we are jolly bun fillers of submarine sandwiches and we ring up your Trojans and Lysol and scented candles, and we shovel your snow and push your babies on the swing set, pare your grandpa's toenails, harvest your honey, detail your urinals, hold the papery hands of your dying, nestle newspapers in the rungs of your mailbox and ladle gravy on your french fries and we push logs through your sawmill, bring you size-ten Sorels, then size eleven, then size ten and a half and climb onto our mattresses at night with gasoline on our hands and dog bites on our ankles, chicken fingers on our breath, cigarette smoke in our hair, ringing in our ears and our men's hands snaking up our thighs.

With nowhere to go we walk home, which is the most mysterious place of all. We take turns carrying the pup because the stray dog pack starts shadowing us when we cut through the Video Express parking lot.

At home Mom is up from her nap and planting the garden, tanning off her wrinkles in a slack Value Village bikini. There's dirt on her knees, goose bumps on the loose flesh of her thighs.

She says, I'm standing in the graveyard of my summer.

Mom tells us we aren't allowed inside unless we plan to shower because we look like we've dipped our heads in an outhouse hole.

From underneath the Suburban, Dad says, I've known your mom to camp in the bush for a week and come out smelling fresher than the day she went in.

349

He lays it on superthick with Mom when he's itching. Might very well be up and gone soon as the Suburban is humming. He used to say he couldn't bear his women for more than a season but he's been here all year.

Yeah right. How's that?

How? How, they want to know? Mom stabs her Garden Claw in the ground. Hoo, boy! Nobody ever told *me*. Nobody taught *me* a damn thing. Look how I turned out.

You're perfect, Mother, calls Dad. Mom scowls.

Dad claims the Tocker Town job market is a dust bowl. There hasn't been so-called real man's work since he returned from whatever boomtown venture or hunting extravaganza he left us for last time.

Lately he's telling us how we couldn't imagine what all connections he's got in the Yukon. The Yukon is the *true* true north strong and free of which we sing at school every morning and before minor hockey games of boys who call us hatchet faces (which, at first, we think is because of the Tockers' work in the forestry industry).

Dad crabwalks out from under the Suburban, arms skinny as a new carrot. He climbs in the driver's seat and smiles through the windshield at nothing. He's just sitting there like a toddler in a plastic car on the lawn.

Mom says, Tockers who leave aren't real Tockers at all.

Fine, Dad says, staring, that faraway smile on his lips. I'm gonna drive to Whitehorse and when I get there I'm gonna order pizza every day and the pizza will always be meatlovers'.

Our stomachs sing dirges.

Even if Mom won't go?

Even if Mom won't go.

Even if we don't go?

Well, I can't spank you no more so is there anything specific I can do for you?

Tell us we're pretty.

My girls are the prettiest girls north of North Battleford and south of sixty and half my heart will pretty near disappear if you don't come along. Man's gotta keep his family together.

He can sweet-talk with impunity because he knows Mom is a mountain. Where she is, we are. Even awful mothers are everything.

Mom, let's all go this time. For real. C'mon. Let's go.

In her garden, Mom levels Dad with eyes black as old bear scat.

I'm due to get drawn for moose this fall, she says. I'll drop all you like a cigarette butt before I give up my Saskatchewan hunting license.

We watch her tearing the earth with her claw.

Thing is, girls, man needs his woman to have a little mystery to her, Dad says. But don't overdo it.

The whole trailer is damp with the steam of four showers. We sit on the floor of the living room while Mom stretches over the couch, dozing in and out with a glass of cherry Kool-Aid balanced on her gut. She's pulled on an old Oilers shirt. Her bikini top is collapsed on the carpet beside us. We watch what's on the CBC because we don't have a dish and we don't need one anyway. The news says two teenagers got shot in a shopping-mall food court in Guelph.

No food courts here, murmurs Mom, eyes half closed with a gassy newborn smile.

The Saturday movie is about the queen of our hearts, Princess Diana. She's pregnant and falls down a flight of stairs.

Dad comes in wiping grease on his jeans. No stairs in a trailer, he says. Youse guys got it better than Lady Di.

No one laughs. Humbled, he wonders, Will there be supper tonight, Mother?

Mom shrugs. I'm going to take a hot bath. See if that'll knock me out.

She likes to keep us guessing, keep us hungry. Hunger might be better than what she offers. She cooks with passive aggression. I am mad at you, says the elk liver and onions. Don't be a pussy, says the bear and turnip stew. Her Swiss beaver steak says, I'll make you bad northern women.

Who is a bad northern woman?

She is the opposite of a good southern girl.

Mom's supper could make you whimper for hamburgers that taste like cow and sausages that taste like pig. Pop the lid on our deep freeze and marvel at our foggy bagged bread, our icy peas, our pile of wild meat. Whether you can stomach it or not, there is always food. Later, when we're grown, Mom will fall back on this: I never let you go hungry, she says again and again.

Eat, she'll goad from the head of the table. Puts hair on your chest like fish hooks. And Dad will say, Damn rights, I wouldn't go chest to chest with my old lady.

After you eat, make yourself scarce. You don't really like it here and we don't want you anyway.

This is our northern hospitality.

We press our ears to the door as the bathwater runs. On the other side Dad is telling Mom that the Suburban's engine turned over this morning. He implores her to imagine the true northern delicacies a Yukon stove could yield: giant boiled moose head, Dall sheep shanks rank with game, caribou barbecue.

Mom says, Yeah, but do they have Tockers there?

No, he says, they have trees. The Yukon is full of trees waiting to fall.

If he wants her to come that means he wants us too.

You dough head, says Mom. Strong trees grow here. The ones up north are weak.

I never heard that, says Dad. You don't know that.

Mom's voice softens. Now stop it. You're not going anywhere. Come here.

Sometimes we can tell the difference between the sounds of our parents' love and the sounds of their anger. Both horrify. We depart.

Lions Park playground is empty. Someone has taken all the swings and looped them around the wooden frame out of reach. There are tractor tires painted primary colors humping out of the grass and we climb the giant treads, pull up the hems of our shorts and tank tops and swing our legs in the sun.

There's the usual talk about our future truck. The specific model is yet to be settled but of course not a Ford. The color will be pure white. The air freshener will be mango. The tires will be as enormous as the ones underneath us. Big enough to cruise around town looking down on everyone else's roof. There's nothing mysterious about a girl in a shitty car.

Then there's tough talk about how if Dad goes again, he's dead to us. Half of us think he really wants us to come. Mom has dared us to say yes to him. See our invitation evaporate, she says.

Our stomachs creak and groan. At first we laugh and poke our bellies. Then we grow restless, suddenly sick to death of each other, seeing everything we hate about ourselves on each other's dumb faces. We kick the tires, flick our lighters, and push their tops into the rubber until it melts. Without speaking we walk back to Bart's Gas to try to stir up something. This time only Daryl is on the picnic table, letting Peps Derocher lick Cheezie dust from her finger. She rolls her eyes and sends a half-hearted kick of dirt our way.

Not now.

We walk up one side of Tocker Town Main Street and down the other. We go in the hobby shop and loiter in the aisles just to bug the cashier who always accuses us of stealing. We go in the grocery store and we steal a box of Glosette peanuts and a mango.

The pup follows us to the highway, where we race beer cans off the side of Jonas Tocker Memorial Bridge, so named for a great-uncle who got drunk, crashed his car, and burnt down the original. (*Taking Our Time* tells the story a little different.) We stick our thumbs out to hitch. Logging trucks blow by and lift the hair from our scalps. No one stops. It was a joke anyway.

Over by the swimming pool the stray dog pack circles us and licks our legs. Before we can grab the pup, a mangy collie with a cloudy eye nips him. We holler at the mutt pack and take turns carrying our little boy. A block from home, we bowl the mango down a culvert. That's when we hear the thunderous roaring, a belligerent engine revved to life. Our father whooping, his voice a gold rush.

Supper is stringy wild goose, salt and pepper roasted with a freezer-burn finish. Dad feels his shirt pocket for a smoke before he even sets his fork down, that's how quick he needs the taste out of his mouth. Mom licks her purpled lips, one paw curled around luminous juice. She wants to know if we've heard her very own tale of the drowning eagle.

Many times.

When I was about your age, I knew this eagle that come to nest every year by Tocker Lake, Mom begins. I'd go there to swim or just lie alone for hours until my skin was brown as a marshmallow on a wiener stick. One afternoon, I felt our eagle passing over. Sure enough, she was swooping down to the water for some grub. Oh, what a beauty. So powerful she could hook the thickest walleye in the drink. Seen her a million times but each time was like the first. Now, that afternoon, this eagle's feet go up and she spreads her curly talons for lunch but it's not until she's got those claws sunk in good that she realizes she's hooked onto a big old jackfish.

Mom sips her Kool-Aid. She leans into us.

Now, I got a look at the hoary bastard. I got a flash of that big, meaty water rat in her talons as she tried to lift it and, oh, this poor bitch is struggling. She's trying to fly back up in the air where she belongs and the jack just keeps dragging her down. She fights good but it's no use. He sank her. The eagle drowned. Dead.

Mom slaps her hand on the table. The cutlery jumps.

At least she died at home, she says to Dad.

After supper we go out the bedroom window. Climb and pull each other to the roof to eat dry ice-cream cones because our stomachs are burning. The pup yelps from the bedroom where we've trapped him. After nine and the sun is finally fading. Mom is working her night shift at the old folks' home, a place where she claims to eat shit forty hours a week. This is Mom's only story that never rings true.

Below our dangling feet, Dad ferries rifle cases and toolboxes and garbage bags of clothes from the trailer to the Suburban. After tonight his underwear drawer is nothing but pennies and rolling bullet casings. The sky is fairy-tale blue, lit by gold, fixed up with fleecy white clouds. We talk about Princess Diana, how sad her life was. How if *she'd* had a big truck, well, she'd still be alive. We agree she would've liked us. At bedtime we discover the pup has peed on the bedroom carpet. We fall asleep without cleaning it up.

In the morning Dad gives us one final pitch. He asks us who we want to be.

We want to be this one chick at school, the setter on the volleyball team who buys all her clothes in the city. Dad shakes his head, frowning. No, he says, we can pick anyone, anywhere. Like cast fishing lures we can sparkle and soar. We are tethered only when our line hits the light.

But that chick lives here.

Maybe, says Dad, maybe up north all youse will be that chick. Up there who will know your names?

Exactly!

Dad surrenders, palms in the air. The record shows: he tried.

Mom sprays her planters with a garden hose.

Do I need to check my purse? she says. Did you clean me out again?

She's still dressed in her scrubs because she hasn't gone to bed yet. She fans the hose over her poppy patch. We hug Dad goodbye. Does he really think we'll come? Nope, he tells us later. You're your mother's daughters.

Maybe so, but we aren't Tockers. Mom isn't either, not really. Before Mom married Dad she was an Ekert, and her grandma, Grandma Olga, was one of those behemoth Tocker sisters, but Great-Grandma Olga's mother, the lady who pumped out those thirty-six feet of long lean Saskatchewan woman, she was some other name that nobody committed to memory or bothered writing down because she didn't have a self-published family fairy-tale book.

Dad comes up behind Mom and says, Anything good that's going to happen to me here's already happened.

Who's waiting for something good to happen? Mom says.

Pfft, Dad huffs. He gets in the Suburban and says, Probably better this way, eh?

He backs out and away with morning light passing through the empty windows.

What'd I tell you, says Mom, turning to us, red-eyed and jowly jawed.

The hose hisses as Mom crushes some peonies with water. The pup scrabbles out of our grip and gives chase. We look from the dog to Mom.

Good riddance, she says and turns the hose on herself. The spray plasters her thin hair to her forehead and cheeks, water streaming down her face, dripping from her chin. She yells at us to shut up.

Running through dust kicked up by Dad's wheels we chase after Chopper. Chopper is speedy. The little guy is nowhere in sight so we run for Highway 4, the only way north. Sure enough, the pup is trotting down the centerline. A car swerves and honks and Chopper ambles to the ditch. Drops out of view. At the junction of Highway 4 and Railway Avenue a van with Manitoba plates pulls alongside us and honks. We're watching cars, timing a dart across. The man in the van says, You girls are gorgeous. He laughs and spittle flies out the space where his front teeth should be. He revs an engine so old it sounds like Dad at the sink in the morning, sputtering, growling, unearthing treasures from his smoker's chest.

This man yells over the engine, She runs dirty but she can go!

There is a truck barreling toward us as we dash across. White line, yellow lines, white line, ditch. Chopper is trotting through the new spring grass, sniffing some dog crap by the service road. We call to him but he doesn't know his name.

The dog pack crests the approach in front of the Chinese restaurant. There are four of them today: the collie, a sick terrier, a gray pit bull, a white shepherd with a speckled face. Chopper goes right to the pack, yipping at the bigger dogs. The collie snaps at him. We scream. The dogs growl and bark. Chopper darts to us but the collie catches him at the neck.

Frozen-eyed, Chopper flops side to side, a wild noodle in the dog's mouth. His fluffy coyote tail sweeps the grass. We leap into the pack and grab the collie by the hindquarters and yank them like a wishbone and pound his body with our fists. Chopper falls to the ground and we scoop him up. Our screams are high and shrill. The pit bull leaps at our legs, tearing at our skin. A truck rips in off the highway and a door slams and in the golden eastern morning light filtering through the dust, there is our father. Hear his sweet holler.

355

We run as he boots the collie. He grabs the terrier by the scruff of his neck and tosses him. Dogs yelp and scatter. The animals speed off into the fallow field beyond the Chinese restaurant.

Dad drives us home. Says he could hear our screams from Bart's Gas. Chopper whines. The fur on his neck is bloody but he licks our wounds.

Seems like you'll be OK, right, boy? Dad says to the pup.

All these years off and on with Mom and still he never learned how to lie.

Mom emerges from her bedroom in a Garfield nightshirt with her damp hair mushed to one side of her face. She smiles, so triumphant at the sight of Dad she doesn't notice our bloody legs, the tear trails on our dusty cheeks.

Seems like there's nothing the five of you despise more than seeing me get a moment's rest, she says.

In our room, hands atremble, we pull T-shirts and stuffed animals and loose tampons out of drawers, forgetting dog food and winter jackets and our last name. Down the hall Dad tells Mom to pack up. Her yell could send a thousand geese back south. Then, silence. Dragging our garbage bags down the hall we stop to rattle the doorknob.

C'mon, Mom, we say, pressing our bodies against her hollow door. She's up against the other side, on the ground, crouched at our feet.

We tell her that even if these strays run off, a new dog blur of mange and eye gunk and broken teeth will appear. We confess we're scared of summer. Every day of our lives will be work and if it's not work, every day will be like today.

Worse, she laughs. It gets so much worse.

First Dad drives to Bart's so he can finish gassing up. The Gladue girls are at the picnic table. We get out.

Dogs got you, eh, says Whoopi. She reaches over and scratches the sharp bridge of Chopper's nose. Hey, she says, ever think he looks like a coyote?

We tell the Gladue girls we are going to the Yukon.

For vacation?

No. Forever.

But school's not done yet.

We ask them if they know about the eagle that got drowned by the jackfish.

Where'd you hear that?

Our mom.

They laugh.

356

Your people could win medals for bullshit, says Whoopi.

Eagles don't drown, dummies, says Daryl. You can't believe how good eagles swim.

Dad comes back from paying. He thumps a hand on the roof.

Say bye to your friends, ladies. Consider us long gone.

When he slides into the driver's seat, he grips the wheel with both hands and squeezes. Usually we fight to ride shotgun. The four of us climb in the back.

Well, bye then, Whoopi says through the open window.

Bon voyage, offers Daryl. To maintain equilibrium, she licks her finger and draws a quick cock and balls in the dust clinging to the Suburban. At a gas station outside Fort Nelson, as Dad rants about how much girls have to stop to pee, we'll see her drawing and feel sadness that we won't yet identify as homesickness.

Bye, we call to the Gladue girls.

The girls return to the picnic table. Gravel crunches and pops under our slow tires. The feathers of a dollar-store dream catcher on our rearview mirror flutter as the Suburban gains speed. Dad rolls up our windows and stills our dancing hair.

He says, Jesus Murphy, girls, look at your old Dad now. He takes off his ball cap, tosses it on the passenger seat. Rubs his bald spot. Lights a cigarette. He says, You know it won't be no cakewalk in the Yukon. You girls are going to have to buckle down. Help me out till Mom gets there.

The highway roars. Two kilometers out, we zoom past a reflective green sign welcoming visitors to our town: MUSKWA LAKE: YOUR GATEWAY TO THE NORTH.

Dad drives north and west. The bones of our knees press together. The pup shakes on our laps, claws stabbing through the nylon of our shorts.

Our blood dries as Dad drives. We trace our fingers over the marks on our long Tocker limbs. In the years to come, many more apart than we ever were together, we never stop telling our childhood. We remember the white trails of each other's scars like they are our own.

Inside the Suburban, we leave tractors dragging seeders, men toppling jack pine, and our mother, lying on a mangy bedroom carpet, waiting. We don't turn back. We are four strays strung by seat belts, fingers against a windowpane as bush and bears and burning cigarettes whiz by.

Nominated by Conjunctions,
Marie-Helene Bertino,
Joyce Carol Oates

THE WHITE ORCHARD

by ARTHUR SZE

from KENYON REVIEW

Under a supermoon, you gaze into the orchard—
a glass blower shapes a glowing orange mass into a horse—
you step into a space where you once lived—
crushed mica glitters on plastered walls—
a raccoon strolls in moonlight along the top of an adobe wall—
swimming in a pond, we notice a reflected cottonwood on the water—
clang: a deer leaps over the gate—
every fifteen minutes an elephant is shot for its tusks—
you mark a bleached earless lizard against the snowfall of this white page—
the skins of eggplants glistening in a garden—
our bodies glistening by firelight—
though skunks once ravaged corn, our bright moments cannot be ravaged—
sleeping near a canal, you hear lapping waves—
at dawn, waves lapping and the noise of men unloading scallops and shrimp—
no noise of gunshots—
you focus on the branches of hundred-year-old apple trees—
opening the door, we find red and yellow rose petals scattered on our bed—
then light years—
you see pear branches farther in the orchard as the moon rises—
branches bending under the snow of this white page—

Nominated by Kenyon Review,
David Baker,
Mark Irwin

DOUBLE VISITATION

by JEFFREY HARRISON

from POETRY NORTHWEST

There I was with my father again alive
walking around the back yard together,
and I hardly noticed that it wasn't our back yard
or that my father looked like he was in his fifties.
We were laughing at something, joking around,
each comment making us laugh even harder.
But then he was crying and I didn't know why,
his face contorted, unable to speak. I turned
and hugged him and whispered in his ear
the words I wanted to say and he wanted to hear . . .

and as if I had uttered some magic formula
I found myself sitting in a movie theater
beside my suddenly alive again brother.
The movie ended, and as the credits rolled,
we both agreed that it was good. Then I said,
"But I think I fell asleep for part of it,"
and started telling him the dream I'd had,
how our father had visited from the dead,
and what I'd done—and, to show him, did again,
whispering those same words to my brother.

Nominated by Robert Cording,
Chard de Niord,
Nick Norwood,
BJ Ward

I CONFESS: MY CULTURAL MISAPPROPRIATION

by ALLAN GURGANUS

from SALMAGUNDI

I.

It kicked in early, my confusion: When is cultural appropriation appropriate? By the age of six, I owned three good puppets. Those being gifts, I had not made them. My mother boasted a Master's degree in education; so Christmas brought me a cardboard marionette theatre. It was red and gold. My arbitrary players? A yellow fur lion, one ancient Austrian woodcutter and a Marilyn Monroe look-alike. Having only these actors might seem limiting; but, odd, all my plays about the world fit them exactly.

The character-puppet I did not need was one representing a sensitive freckled white boy with bangs, seersucker shorts, and his own *National Geographic* subscription. He would have bored me very much. It was others, always others, I pursued. The less like me, the more I needed them. What I didn't know, they *were*. By asking them, by moving them around our little stage, I farmed my life toward theirs. I kept trying to understand them from the inside out. My strings lifted their hands and paws. Manipulation, you say? Don't puppets require that? Isn't all art manual labor in the service of certain truth-telling tricks?

True, as a child of the ruling class and race, I was possibly an unconscious colonial power-broker seeking to bend a population of cloth and plaster to my imperial will, you think? But, by enlivening these inanimates, I myself was being puppeteered by the dire need: to know what it meant to be a lion, a very old man, a powerfully beautiful woman.

360

Child's play only seems caprice: it is always half-labor. It is us practicing for daily life then Carnegie Hall. And, in a world dark and undermining as ours today, that mix of determination, curiosity and whimsy—that interest in sonar projection and the interpretation of returning signals—has kept me avidly interested because properly scared—these seventy years.

By age eight, I understood: marionettes rigged with just four strings can't simulate gestures precise enough to seem specifically human. I somehow knew: only by approximating voices might I fully inhabit these little bodies and giant wills. By choosing a timbre and an accent, I might invent-invest some subtler hint of soul. But I'd need one distinct separate pitch for each figure in my theatrical alphabet. Each must sound singularly unlike me while still vocal-corded, umbilically my own. I craved the textures of those voices readiest to argue.

II.

Ventriloquism is a low-tech stunt. Technology very early ran this ancient skill through its shredder. The term "ventriloquize" grows from Latin meaning "To Speak from the Stomach." It stems from an ancient belief that the spirits of the dead communicate through our belly rumblings. It was once thought these could be repeated then translated by oracles. Only in the early nineteenth century were dolls brought onstage. Till then, the goal had been to make ventriloquized voices seem ghostly projections sent from afar. Clear from the next world.

In the 1950's and 60's, the British Actors' Equity registered 400 ventriloquists. In the 2000's, that fell to 15. But in 1953, I asked for and received a child-sized Jerry Mahoney ventriloquist dummy. Jerry came with his instruction book. Its title? "How To Throw Your Voice."

"Throw" is a big, male, steroidal and exciting verb! True, my arm as a Little Leaguer lacked much of the Maris-Mantle gristle. But I imagined I could someday, with practice, with something like empathy, eventually send my voice into a certain emotional strike-zone that would make others swing, three times at least.

I understood: a ventriloquist's *own* voice had to be both duller and different from the tone he was throwing, from such diction as he pitched. Appropriation seemed a compliment.

So, call me a funky practicing Ventriloquist since 1953. True, I could never say "Bottle of Beer" without moving my lips, unless I pronounced it "Vottle of Veer." But, faking some new amalgam of speech based on another's character and wants and education—that's what I still keep daily throwing at the page. I exist as a dependent of my own invented ones—a PT Barnum providing his employees slightly better health care but with that showman's same appetite for freakish exceptions. My star players include the fifty one percent of humanity that is female; and the twelve-point-six percent of our nation's populous that is African-American.

This very fascination might seem to place me squarely in the crosshairs of those bent on policing the purported crime of cultural misappropriation. It makes crude sense that an abused nation or race—having been exploited for centuries—wants alimony. Problem is—most groups rightly feel singled out for reparation—The Irish, The Chinese, The Queer, The Untouchables.

Indigenous Australian aborigines, sick of seeing their religious symbols usurped by Caucasian copyists, recently petitioned for copyrights. They would monitor native artworks. How? With the suggested label "Authenticity Brand." But, however earnest that phrase is, doesn't it offer us a contradiction in terms? We know authenticity—as we recognize pornography—the second we see it.

I'd suggest that such ethnic guardians—advocating enforced cultural monopolies—are accidentally practicing their own form of one-voice one-note puppetry. To say that six-year-old black children should be issued only puppets depicting six-year-old black children—that backs us into an enslaving literalness. I grew up in the south of water fountains marked "Colored ONLY." To willingly re-nail that sign onto any human replenishment as essential as Narrative, that repeats a tragic mistake for tricky new reasons.

Must all creations be mere replicants of their makers? Is that not the haiku for totalitarianism? Such a quota would surely disqualify from love and art my beloved mangy lion (he enjoyed a different taxonomic pedigree). Re-installing genetic tollgates in art or life echoes the eugenic stringencies that cost millions of lives last century. Please don't tell me women can't write as men, gays as straight, blacks as whites, little boys as giant cats.

I would suggest that such re-segregation is anti-imaginative, a reversal of the limited social progress we made before hitting the wall-building craze of our present ludicrous age. Speaking as a Tyrolean wood cutter, or a pretty blond lady in red, taught me what I was—and was not. And was not *yet*.

362

Refining motions and vocal tics for each of my hand-held Mercury players added a luster, depth and pity to my consideration of others. It enriched my sense that our human tribe is—while never interchangeable—certainly permeable to forces of consideration, to depths of sympathy, to the redemption of comedy across world cultures.

III.

Everybody knows *Star Wars* lifted elements of Kurosawa's *The Hidden Fortress* which had already subsumed that Japanese genius's reverence for Shakespeare's wizardry, which had long-ago had its larcenous way with Thomas Kyd, Kit Marlowe, ersatz royal histories, plus tumbling fistfuls of protein hoisted from Chaucer, Boccaccio, Plutarch and Ovid. And every snatched appropriation? It did not dilute Shakespeare. It strengthened his future skywalking implications.

To "throw" the human voice is a strenuous yet honorable activity. By lovingly imitating others we are not stealing souls, we're re-anointing, reinforcing them. Throwing a voice boomerangs it through both space and time. I fear that the more we say "One voice per customer, one language per race," the more we seek to claim some aspect of human experience as the purview of a single class, a single religion, a single sexual outlook, a single historic tragedy. And this narrowing shrinks our chance at understanding how immense and godlike is the human imagination in its fullest flower.

Can something as holy and universal as literature have a 'Colored Only' and a 'Whites Only' drinking nozzle? Instances of bi-cultural pan-gender trans-racial cross-pollination include the non-menstruating males who gave us Emma Bovary, Anna Karenina and Mrs. Bridge. Writing past one's drivers' license descriptors awarded us those strangely hyper-mortal men—Casaubon and Bulstrode—engendered by a wonder named Mary Anne Evans who had to call herself 'George Eliot' to get published. Or how about Abel Meeropol who wrote Billy Holiday's anti-lynching ballad "Strange Fruit"? And what of the Russian-Ukrainian-Jewish Gershwins' version of a black-blues song called "Summertime"? Whenever you say a person of this color or that sex cannot do something, one of them will at once do it so frigging brilliantly. I would further argue that the farther a voice is 'thrown' the greater its possible velocity and force, the richer its paradoxical originality.

"Us being us"—stuck with only those *like* us. That bricks off more of those gated communities to which our races and classes and nations are once again retreating, brothers and sisters. Something there is, every-thing there is, that does not like a wall. And a voice? A voice can be 'thrown'—a borrowed voice—can be thrown right through one wall, all walls. We must keep playing, praying, in and through each other's voices.

The first voice I remember came to me in song from a black woman named Lizzie Smithers hired to tend me as a little pink baby about the size of a puppet. Lizzie Smithers' song: "If you haven't got a penny, a ha-penny will do, if you haven't got a ha-penny, God bless you." And God bless cultural appropriation. My first English language was Lizzie Smithers', the African American variant I'd call my mother-tongue. I sought to pay homage to its richness and cadences in my first book, *Oldest Living Confederate Widow Tells All*. I further tried to tap the wit, the rightful fury, the quantum kindness of this woman who minded me for minimum wage while teaching me the maximal beauty of human speech. When Toni Morrison praised my novel's major black character Castalia Marsden for "not having put a foot wrong in 718 pages" I sobbed as only a liberal puppeteer probably should, even in private. When Cecily Tyson won an Emmy playing Castalia, I was reassured the charac-ter had never been mine, but a given, always largely "ours." The mystic chords of memory so soon entwined with the snagged strings of child-hood puppetry. I pull one cord and the opposite limb lifts. I try sum-moning the battle cries of my ancient Welsh ancestors but their drums and war-chants sound only fully African. While the blue-black nurse-maid Lizzie Smithers lullabied a 20th century child with news of Lon-don's seventeenth-century street beggars.

When authenticity lives ethnically unbranded, when we put the First Amendment in its deserved first place, we'll know again that all culture is world culture. It was "ours" before and after it became briefly merely "mine."

Named for an attractive string-pulling species that loves to make things, it is, all of it, "Folk" art.

Nominated by Salmagundi

SKIN-LIGHT

by NATALIE DIAZ

from POEM-A-DAY

My whole life I have obeyed it—

    its every hunting. I move beneath it
    as a jaguar moves, in the dark-
        liquid blading of shoulder.

The opened-gold field and glide of the hand,

    light-fruited, and scythe-lit.

I have come to this god-made place—

    Teotlachco, the ball court—
    because the light called: *lightwards!*
        and dwells here, Lamp-land.

    We touch the ball of light
to one another—split bodies stroked bright—
        desire-knocked.
            Light reshapes my lover's elbow,

    a brass whistle.

I put my mouth there—mercy-luxed, and come, we both,

to light. It streams me.
A rush of scorpions—
            fast-light. A lash of breath—
                    god-maker.

Light horizons her hip—springs an ocelot
cut of chalcedony and magnetite.
            Hip, limestone and cliffed,

slopes like light into her thigh—light-box, skin-bound.

Wind shakes the calabash,
disrupts the light to ripple—light-struck,
            then scatter.

This is the war I was born toward, her skin,

    its lake-glint. I desire—I thirst—
    to be filled—light-well.

The light throbs everything, and songs

    against her body, girdling the knee bone.
    Our bodies—light-harnessed, light-thrashed.
            The bruising: bilirubin bloom,
                    violet.

A work of all good yokes—blood-light—

    to make us think the pain is ours
    to keep, light-trapped, lanterned.
            I asked for it. I own it—
                    lightmonger.

I am light now, or on the side of light—

    light-head, light-trophied.
    Light-wracked and light-gone.

Still, the sweet maize—an eruption
of light, or its feast,
     from the stalk
        of my lover's throat.

And I, light-eater, light-loving.

Nominated by Poem-A-Day,
Michael Dennis Browne

FLOUR

fiction by JOY WILLIAMS

from THE PARIS REVIEW

The driver and I got a late start. I usually decide on these excursions the night before, but it was late in the morning when I informed the friend who was coming to visit me for the weekend that I had to cancel, it was absolutely necessary for me to cancel. I had got it in my head that in her presence some calamity or another would arise and she would have to assist me in some way, rush me to a physician or something. She would be grateful she was there for me perhaps, but I would find it a terrific annoyance and embarrassment. I gave some other excuse for the disinvitation of course. Pipes. I think it was broken pipes. I should have written it down so I don't use it again.

I cleaned the house, which was very much in need of cleaning, for I had been putting it off. Still, my commitment was not great and I neglected the windows as usual. The dogs had pressed against them day and night for years. Their breaths are etched in the glass now, very lightly etched.

By departing so late, we could not make our customary first stop. The driver and I usually spend two nights in lodgings on our route. This time three nights would be necessary. We take separate rooms, of course. If by chance we should come across one another in the restaurant or the hallways, we offer no acknowledgment.

The car is a big one, encompassing three rows, three tiers behind the driver. It amuses me to think of them as the celestial, the terrestrial, and the chthonic. In fact, I quite believe that all things—every moment, every vision, every departure and arrival—possess the celestial, the terrestrial, and the chthonic.

The dogs had pretty much stayed in the terrestrial section where their beds were, as well as a few empty plastic bottles. They liked to play with them, make them crackle and clatter. Sometimes I ride in the chthonic with the luggage, the boots and coats, the boxes of fruit and gin and books. It smells strangely good back there, coolly hopeful and warmly worn at once. But usually I stretch out in the seat behind the driver and watch the landscape change as we rise from the desert floor.

Shockingly, it is almost two o'clock in the afternoon. We will not get far today!

When the driver and I first met—when I was interviewing him, you might say—he told me that he was studying Coptic.

Naturally, I did not believe this for one moment.

Without any encouragement from me he said, "The verb forms and tenses of Coptic are interesting. For example, some tenses that we English speakers do not have are the circumstantial, the habitual, the third future, the fourth future, the optative, and tenses of unfulfilled action signifying *until* and *not yet*. I am working now on translating and interpreting the story about the woman carrying flour to her home in a jar that is broken."

"The flour all pours out?" I said.

"Why yes." He seemed pleased.

Everyone knows the story of the woman and the flour. Who did he think he was kidding? Still, you're never drawn to a person for the reasons you think. Besides, he was the only one who applied for the position I sought, which I had kept purposefully vague, and parsing every nuance of the woman and the jar would keep him occupied at least.

We are at a crossroads light behind a new, bright yellow truck. When the light changes and the truck accelerates, a dense cloud of black smoke erupts from the tailpipe. People spend more than a thousand dollars to customize their vehicles for this effect, which honors freedom and individuality. It takes a moment for the simple clarity of the air and sky to reassert itself.

When a little baby dies you think, If they can do it with such wonderment, so can I.

The bright yellow truck, the yolk-colored truck, dances away. He is not going in our direction, though perhaps he quite is, and our driver is graciously finding a detour for my sake. Rather than discussing the wisdom of this—will we find a decent place to stay when dusk descends— I leave my perch and crawl over the backs of seats to the very rear, the cozy chthonic. There is scarcely room for me to curl, to burrow, and surprisingly I do not even feel comfortable here.

Dusk is not nearly as considerate as is generally assumed. One thinks it offers a reasonable amount of time to adjust to night descendant, but the reality is it does not. With only moments to spare, we sweep under the portico of a large hotel that has seen better days.

The driver goes in to address the desk while I pick about among the rubble in the back. Sometimes I like to bring my own lamp into these places, but I feel too tired to locate the cord, then follow the cord. I am remarkably tired. I look instead at the gardens that rim the crescent of the drive. Though they are not extensive, someone cares for them, really cares. I feel better watching them, as though I have just enjoyed a cocktail, though that is still ahead of me, thank God.

(In the morning the gardens would not seem nearly as responsibly cared for, but I was paying less attention to them then.)

The driver has arranged for everything. He escorts me to an adequate room, smiles as guilelessly as the boy he so seems to be, and says good night. Later I go down for my cocktails in the cavernous dining room made tragic with the heads of animals and loud with the happy screams of tourists. There are commendable ruins nearby, apparently. We would never have stopped here had I been more decisive earlier.

We leave at daybreak, the reasoning being that we would make up some time. Preposterous of course. One cannot make up time. One can make up a story or a face or a bed. Ugh. I find it all repellent. My bed, by the way, was so uncomfortable. I would not have been surprised if, on tearing the mattress open, I'd have found it to be stuffed with rocks. The driver says apologetically that he had spent a restful night, though he had slept little, as he was working on his translation.

"The art of translation is very forgiving, isn't it," I say.

"Forgiving?" he repeats.

For a while I ride up front with him but find I can gain no perspective. We are climbing, climbing, there are switchbacks and signs of warning in the bright falsity of daylight, and nature pressing in around us, fierce yet helpless, regarding us with distaste.

I think of my friend. She might not have received the message and could be knocking at the door of my house this very moment. She might have even already left once and returned. But I cannot think about her for long. We both have betrayed one another more than once.

After a few hours, though we had not made up one minute of lost time, the driver asks if I would like to stop for a moment. He pulls off the road and spreads the blanket—which we have used often for this purpose—upon the ground and puts out bread and water. I had once tried to make the bread myself, but it was dreadful. I don't know where it's acquired now. We seldom eat much of it. We never finish it. Sometimes we don't even begin, though I don't wish to think we waste it. The sun is warm, the air feels fresh and good, but I feel that the small pleasure I am taking in this instant is significant only to the extent that it can be remembered, and once again I am compelled to be dissatisfied.

The car looms beside us, handsome, without agency. The driver had once confessed to me that he loved it as he had loved nothing in his life before and that if I ever found it necessary to separate him from its care he would probably kill himself.

He is such a child, I thought at the time, but I did not reassure him. I might even have smiled, possibly laughed, his question was so naive. Of course, the both of them could crush me like an insect at any time. It is a serious business, a most serious business.

He packs up the bread and water and folds up the blanket, the raveling border of which I pretend not to notice. What he should be doing in the evening is repairing our picnic blanket, or at the very least determining how it can be displayed without calling attention to its degradation. Instead, he spends the nights searching for the missing word in some Coptic riddle. Or so he claims.

Hours pass rather senselessly, as they often do. I do some thinking once again in the rear, in my cannily constructed chthonic, but nothing of any real import. When we stop again, dusk is just beginning to assemble her portentous armies. The lodging is once again unfamiliar. It might have been plucked out of a hat, as they say. Again it is a hotel from an earlier time, restored to partial grandeur. There seems to be a niche of Texas billionaires who specialize in these labors of love. What is their fantasy really, I wonder. With very little inquiry I learn that one of the new owners is an artist. Her paintings are everywhere, her specialty scenes of dinner parties where the well-known dead are guests. Frida Kahlo and her parrots are there, for example. I think they are parrots.

In my room is a fruit basket, which contains a single orange. Quite naturally, I am afraid to eat it. The room is pleasant enough, but there is a certain beyondness to it. I cannot explain this at all but I very much want to discuss it with the driver. Yet when I come upon him later, drinking a glass of wine on one of the verandas, I ignore him as usual.

Trains rumble past the hotel all night but there are no passengers on them. They carry freight, interminable freight.

The next morning is bitterly cold. I approach breakfast wearing everything I own and even a robe I do not, a fat white thing that is one of the amenities of the hotel. A small fire is burning in the vast fieldstone fireplace. It looks absurd—a few sticks when it could have been mighty logs. There is certainly enough timber surrounding the place.

The driver is seated some distance from the inadequate fire. He is not one for pretending that things offer what they cannot. He, too, is wearing the provided robe, and the sight of it over his dark suit—for it looks as foolish as the fire—prompts me to acknowledge him with a shy wave. I approach him, even sit down opposite him. His notebook is open and he is pressing a pencil against the page. This I have witnessed before.

"Not still the woman with the jar," I tease. "Surely you must be on to another narrative by now."

"I've rendered the road as a distant road," he says.

"But that is nowhere near the end," I protested. "Practically nothing can be known at that point."

"What is important is the quality of the emptiness she eventually discovers," he agrees. "And that is what is so difficult to suggest."

We do not return to our respective rooms but place the robes in a barrel that we believe to be for that purpose.

In the car, the driver says, "I think with a little effort it's very possible we can recover the schedule."

"Excellent," I say.

And we do arrive, though it struck me then as being utterly foreign. But the driver, breaking our comfortable silence at last, says that to him it appeared much the same as always.

Nominated by The Paris Review

AN OPEN LETTER TO WHITE WOMEN CONCERNING 'THE HANDMAID'S TALE' AND AMERICA'S CULTURAL AMNESIA

by TIFFANY MIDGE

from MCSWEENEY'S

Dear Dakota, Jezebel, Bronte, Caprice, Cher et al.,

I don't mean to single anyone out here, but as an Indigenous woman it behooves me to point out that while I perfectly understand your fondness for *The Handmaid's Tale* as a white feminist anthem, I can't help but feel all kinds of something about it. Each week when all of you are discussing and posting recaps of the latest episode on Facebook, I'm resisting the urge to cram my face into the couch pillows to keep from screaming. I don't mean to point blame on anyone, per se, but I'm talking to you, Katniss, Guinevere, and Fig.

You see, Veronica, while *The Handmaid's Tale* presents a dystopian world ruled by a white totalitarian and fascist regime, and while it appears to bear some similarity to the United States' current conservative administration, Reese, might I offer a reminder that the Republic of Gilead is in fact fictional. And at least for the time being, Flora, white women are not being forcibly recruited into brothels, work farms, or as baby-making vessels for the Republic.

But if I may be so bold, do you know what's actually *not* fictional, Kinsey? *The Indian Maiden's Tale.* Yes, Indigenous women are well-acquainted with that American dystopian nightmare. At the risk of sounding like old-broom-up-her-ass Aunt Lydia, an episode from *The Indian Maiden's Tale* is when Indigenous children were torn from their mothers and confined to residential boarding schools, forced to contend with all manner of horrors and abuse— a hellscape of horrors and abuses, not so very different than those portrayed in your favorite TV programming. So, Waverly, I hope the next time you cozy up with a box of wine and watch another thrilling episode of *The Handmaid's Tale,* you'll pause and reflect on Indigenous women and children who have endured unconscionable suffering.

And during commercial breaks, Fiona, may I also remind you that Indigenous women suffer violence and rape at astonishing rates: The Department of Justice Survey in 2016 reported 56 percent of 2,000 women surveyed, had experienced sexual violence. And if that doesn't have you reaching for the smelling salts, Eloise, sterilization of Indigenous women was a rampant practice; the U.S. General Accounting Office reported that the Indian Health Service sterilized 3,406 Indigenous women between 1973 and 1976. And according to a report compiled by the Lakota People's Law Project, Lark, Indigenous women are incarcerated at six times the rate of white women. I hope you'll think of that the next time Offred debases herself by saying "blessed be the fruit," or Mrs. Waterford sits pensively in her blue frock in her blue sitting room thinking about how miserable her life is and how she wants to disappear into the wallpaper forever.

As entertaining as *The Handmaid's Tale* is for fans of Orwellian, nihilistic programming, Madison, it does not represent all of society. But it does effectively represent the cultural and historical amnesia of America, Saffron. And maybe you will switch to the history channel and watch an episode of *The Indian Maiden's Tale* instead, Hyacinth.

Nominated by Kim Barnes

WILD PANSY

by LISA BELLAMY

from THE SOUTHERN REVIEW AND THE NORTHWAY (TERRAPIN BOOKS)

As a seed, I was shot out the back end of a blue jay
when, heedless, she flew over the meadow.
She had swallowed me in my homeland when she spied me
lying easy under the sun—briefly, I called her Mother
before I passed through her gullet like a ghost.
In a blink of God's eye, I was an orphan. I trembled
where I fell, alone in the dirt. That first night
was a long night, early May and chilly, and I remember
rain filled my furrow. I called out for mercy—
only a wolverine wandered by. I cursed my luck,
I cursed the happenstance of this world, I smelled
his hot stink, but he nosed me deep into the mud—
this was the gift of obscurity. I germinated, hidden
from the giants of earth, the jostling stalks,
the various, boisterous bloomers, and this was my salvation.
After seven days and nights I pushed through—
yes. Here I am, kissable: your tiny, purple profusion.

Nominated by Philip Schultz

STAY THERE

fiction by LESLIE PIETRZYK

from THE SOUTHERN REVIEW

The unyielding concrete of the parking garage pushes damply through my black cocktail dress, chill seeping along my spine, along the backs of my bare arms. His big, puppy-dog hands cup my ass; my legs vise round his waist; a tangle of bracelets tickle my fists. Sure, call me lost—in level P-3, in him, in the sex—lost with my muffled moans, biting my lips into silence, lost amid the compressed fury that defines a twenty-four-year-old boy fucking. "Jesus," one of us whispers, in the quiet of this shadowy corner on level P-3. A car door slams, a lock beeps, clickety high heel footsteps recede. He hears because he snickers.

But I'm not lost. Not ever. A part of me stands back, always the observer, evaluating and assessing, aloof as my forty-years-old-tomorrow body responds and writhes, begs for more, begs for no end, begs for the end, gets what it wants. Even now, I'm leaning into the cliché, examining why I'm here. Maybe if I had been happier with boys when I was twenty-four, instead of yearning for men and their once-exotic weariness, which I mistook for complexity. Maybe if I had wanted this, only back then.

He relaxes, rummaging his face into my shoulder. I open my eyes, and he rears his head as if he understands I'm watching, and his eyes—truly turquoise—dive through mine. I blink—his face too close, eyes too blue—and scramble to focus, and his smile slides sweet and sleepy, like a baby's. Innocent. Beautiful. The word is *addicted*. I'm addicted to him. I whisper, "Jesus."

"*Jesus.*" His face flops to my shoulder, his body limp, the angle of leaning deepening, sandwiching me harder against the concrete—his

376

sleepiness wallops that fast. Like getting knocked out. I'm uncomfortable as hell but still I want to stay forever in this never-never land of between.

Two car doors slam in quick succession. Another. Laughter, a drifting echo of conversation: "So, I went to that new place by the Harris Teeter, the one where they say the soup is so amazing . . ." Maybe I'll catch my friends disparaging me and the art I'm dragging them to see, or worse, pitying me, poor forty-at-midnight, unmarried me. I think I would welcome knowing what they really think.

"Hey," I whisper, "I can't be more late than this." He rouses himself and I untwine my legs from around his waist, planting my feet in their spiky high heels. He fidgets and pulls out of me, clasping the open side of the condom with both hands. He's always careful, but I wouldn't mind if he wasn't, if we made a baby with turquoise eyes. There's no simple way to suggest such a thing. But I think it every time. He shifts and zips and jams his fingers through the cascade of blond hair and is good to go. What a pro. I'm thinking about a comb, wiggling into my shapewear, sleeking up, though he gallantly says, "I don't know why you think you need that torture. You've got to know you're smoking hot." Tay is smart enough to avoid "still": *still* smoking hot.

I imagine he'll toss the condom into the clutter of Big Gulp cups, McDonald's bags, and candy wrappers washed up in this distant corner. The pang of waste. But he discreetly carries the condom as we walk to the stairs, plunking it into a garbage can. Conscientious, which I noticed right off, how that first night of class he lunged forward to pull open the studio door for me, stepping back to allow me through. I paused. "You're doing this because I'm the teacher?" I said, a surprising flush of power tripping on my part. "No, ma'am. Because apparently I'm raised right," he said, the words pulsing with an almost sexual glow, then a follow-up smirk as apology, as if he simply couldn't stop himself. I swept through the door, forcing myself not to look back.

I stop to balance my purse on the garage's iron railing, rooting inside for my mirror and lipstick. I also dig out a minibottle of Purell, squeeze a dab into my hand, then say, "It's not an insult," tilting the bottle toward him. He laughs but accepts, rubs his hands together briskly. The sound always feels ugly, clinical.

"Be there in a sec," he says, swishing his fingertips against my bare arm. My skin prickles, abruptly alert. He could go again, and I long to reach for his crotch, just one lingering caress, just to know for sure, to

377

prove something to myself, though that's needy. Or is it wrong? I'm not his teacher now. But I was when I started sleeping with him.

"It's OK," I say. "People walk in public places side by side all the time. It's called coincidence. No one will think anything." I sound desperate, afraid of my own party, my own art show. Pitifully unwilling to plunge into the crowd alone.

He often knows what I'm thinking, or maybe I imagine that. "You're the hottest-looking forty-year-old I've met."

"Not forty until tomorrow." I'm quick and light so I don't say the other thing: How many forty-year-olds do you know, besides your mother?

"Got to get something out of my car," he says. Meaning a cigarette.

I nod. He leans in to snag another kiss, to tempt me, but I jerk back at the glare of headlights on the wall, about to turn the corner and il- luminate us. "No presents," I say, though I know there isn't one, that what's in the car is a pack of American Spirits. The car sweeps by: two women from yoga class. I wave effusively. They probably assume Tay's my son, since they don't know me well. I push away that thought, let- ting my eyes follow Tay as off he goes. He moves easily, slipping place to place as if he's liquid.

When I can't see him, I glance into the tiny mirror I've found in my purse. A network of lines etch the corners of my eyes and lips; I see crev- ices. Another thought to push away, and I start up the stairs, heels clacking. I think of when I was growing up, watching my father prac- tice his smile in the bathroom mirror, smiling over and over, tilting his head this way and that, as I timed him with the second hand on his wristwatch. Ten seconds, twenty, a minute. "Smiling's hard work," he would say, "and takes muscle. You've got to build muscle if you want any- thing in life." I thought he knew everything. It was exciting that his picture was everywhere, the smile I knew from the mirror, his famous smile. Now he's dead to me. I rouse the muscles of my own face, form- ing a smile. And I stride up the stairs to this party.

The gallery is a buzz of people swarming my photographs, winding through tables set with flickering tea lights, glassware flashing and clink- ing. My photos pop against Chita's newly painted walls ("You're forty, baby, and by golly, you deserve a fresh coat of color," she said in her drawl), and I'm greeted by hugs and kisses, a surge of applause, Chita calling, "There she is!" I let the crowd carry me forward, and I watch myself work. Conversations on a loop: "Thank you for coming," "So happy you like the show" (offer humble namaste head bow), exclamations of "You shouldn't have!" at impersonal gifts tucked into decorative bags (soap, wine, scarves). I'm gentle with those nervous around art, patient with their need to condense it to pap: "How long to make that?" "How do you decide the price?"

Former students stare at me or pretend not to, as if there's still some scrap of power I might wield, though grades have been posted and my judgment complete and I'm not their teacher anymore. I shouldn't waste time with them—they're neither friends nor buyers—but what a relief to shift loops, asking what they're up to, not that I care, but to hear the bounce of their chatter: new studios, gallery visits, redesigned websites, so-and-so who ditched Durham for Brooklyn. I'm not listening close enough to get the name, and asking young people to repeat is too old-person. But who's pulling out for real? Who's the bold one? I'm bothered not to know.

Fuck it, and I'm about to ask, but I sense Tay's arrival, finally, and I maintain my breath in a calm, measured in and out, even as my skin ignites and a sharpness tightens my posture. His is a splash landing into the cluster of students, and they fuss and hug, creating excuses to touch him, the tap of fingertips, a complimentary pluck at the rolled-up sleeve of his coral button-down. I'm edged to the perimeter. These girls are in love with him, especially the redhead; the boys, too. Jealousy is also very old-person, as is not understanding that this, that everything, will unfold eventually.

Chita eyes me, nudging with urgent glances, which means business and someone to meet—it's a party but it's work. No part of my life is ever its own self. Before walking away, I indulge my glance on Tay, towering over these girls. They're nodding in unison, such a serious conversation, a line of furrowed brows, but he laughs, and even in the party din that's as clear as morning birdsong. My child would get that laugh, I think, knowing laughter doesn't run in families, isn't an inheritable trait.

I dredge up a smile. Like that, my father camps in my head again, and that pang. Not remorse, not sorrow, because I wouldn't expect him to show. Maybe anger that I sent the invitation, or rather, that Chita did? "He's your father," she said, extending the word into a landscape of vowels and many syllables. "Maybe he'll buy something," with *buy* getting the same stretched-out verbal treatment and her trademark wink. "No," I said, which to her meant she could—and should—do what she wanted. I also said no to her plan in which I buy

into her gallery and be partners for a couple of years before she re-
tires to Eureka Springs, Arkansas, where her daughter ended up. Not
that I have a better plan. I've lost the will for reinvention. This might
be my last show.

Chita doesn't look sixty. She wears bejeweled cat-eye glasses attached
to a chain she made with healing crystals and beads, a shimmery laven-
der three-quarter sleeve dress that looks straight from Jackie Kenne-
dy's closet, and her signature red cowboy boots. She's not five feet even
in the boots, which makes people underestimate her, which she uses to
her advantage, because she uses everything to her advantage. She's the
only one who knows about Tay, because she caught us in the unisex bath-
room of a highway dive bar we thought was safe but that wasn't: Chita
would drive anywhere on a wispy rumor of great fried chicken, and I
should have known that. The next day she said, "Honey, whatever y'all.
Like what I read at Jewel and Cath's wedding, some mystic poet Rumi,
not that I know Rumi from rummy from Bacardi, I just read what they
gave me. But it was, 'Close your eyes. Fall in love. Stay there.'" I didn't
wreck her moment with an "It's not love" announcement. Now, she's
talking with Shannon, my old high school best friend, who drove down
from Richmond, which is sweet since we're basically Facebook close
nowadays, and with Shannon's boyfriend, who apparently is her *new*
boyfriend, who must be a collector or rich, because Chita's chatting him
up, laughing like he's busting her gut, and now she's tag teaming me.
I'm up. Time with the artist, Chita taught me, that's what they're buy-
ing, what they want. An experience to brag at friends. So I flash my
smile, and Shannon leans in for a hug, too long, too loopy. Drunk al-
ready. Her Facebook scroll is cartoons about wine-loving women and
wine o'clock.

Chita says, "So, y'all are friends from way back?" The master chatter.
She gets people talking about themselves, staying attentive through the
monologues, but it's a data sweep, collecting and retaining information.
Her memory is frightening. Right now she's honing in, certain this guy
collects something—art, people, experiences. Or maybe it's simple: a
house needs decorating. When she brought up the gallery deal, Chita
promised I'd learn these skills. "It's in your blood," she said, meaning
my politician father, and like that, the muscles of my face hardened, so
she amended herself: "Selling art is about relationships, that's all. Sell-
ing anything is." There was my father's famous voice, drilling us at the
dinner table: "What is politics about?" and it would be me, dutiful

380

middle child, piping in, because if no one did, he'd ask until he got the answer: "Politics is about relationships, Daddy."

Astonishingly, this drumbeat was pounded so relentlessly into my soul that not until college did I realize politics is about power. Likely art is, too.

I shake my head, back to the world, back to where I'm supposed to be, glad-handing Shannon's silver-haired boyfriend. Peter Robbins, though I think, *Rabbit*, which is impossible to forget. Shannon leans forward on her tiptoes; she's wearing silvery ballet flats that look like they fold up to be stuffed into her purse, and I wonder if she forgot her real shoes or if she didn't think my party was good enough for real shoes. Peter Rabbit announces that he's a lawyer, giving the firm name, then takes over the conversation (negating the necessity of announcing he's a lawyer, ha-ha). He's talking about value and investment, things no one would say about art in Durham, North Carolina. I'm desperate to cut in with, You do understand you're not in New York, right?—which Chita knows, because she opens her mouth to speak first, but suddenly Shannon says, "You're so tall!" She's drunk, but we do party laughs, and I jab one foot forward to show the high platform of my shoes. "My little secret," I say, and Chita catches me glancing at Tay, who's leaning both elbows on the bar.

Shannon blathers about Peter's new beach house in Duck—they're driving there tomorrow, they want to fill those blank walls, wouldn't something from here be perfect—and Chita's eyes hint that we've hit the business part. So I ask, "What part of Duck?" and Chita jumps in with, "Who do y'all collect?" which I quickly understand is the right question. Her face is directive.

"I'm exclusively into political art," Peter Rabbit says, which makes Chita cock her head, as if the computer in her mind has stumbled into bad code. I tell students that the creation of any work of art is, at its core, a political act, but I can't imagine Peter Rabbit seeing beyond color splotches on canvas.

"Interesting." Chita's murmur is always artful encouragement, and I sense she's fascinated by this bit of information, while regretting her fascination.

He puffs and talks on, as predictable as a clock: "I bought a George W. Bush at a charity auction and a Winston Churchill"—pausing here, letting the significance settle, and if it's possible to do a double cock of the head, that's what Chita does, because he's talking some real money now—"and of course Shepard Fairey's Obama print. I started with campaign memorabilia, like everyone, like any amateur, then branched out. My first was a Jimmy Carter. Right now I'm hot for Ulysses S. Grant."

Chita is nodding fast, faster, that way she does when she's not allowed to show her fury, and she grabs hold of my arm, presses in. That's the signal, that she'll handle it, that a sale is a sale, but I say, "You know *I'm* the artist, not my father."

Peter Rabbit says, "My parameters are wide," and Shannon chortles. Always a stupid drunk, even in high school.

Abruptly, Shannon paws at me, clutching my arm, which makes Chita let go. I feel like a wishbone. "You're so brave to be here," she says, slushily serious. She downs her glass, then blows her wine breath at me as she says, "Considering."

"Yes, it's very brave to walk around being a forty-year-old woman," I say, almost adding, You're doing it, too, before deciding that, drunk or not, she's an old pal and it's likely this guy isn't getting the truth about her age. When they first walked in and gave me the quickie greeting, she overexplained that "we *went* to the same high school." Which is not saying we were in the same graduating class.

"Your father," she says, which are not the words I expect, nor ones I ever like hearing. Since I moved here I've been going by my middle name and a last name I made up. But she knows, this drunk girl-woman and her too-much cleavage.

Tension crackles up like a fire coming to life.

Chita murmurs, "So, Peter. Ulysses S. Grant? Fascinating."

I say, "We don't see each other anymore. It's been years." A deep breath: "Basically, he's dead to me."

Shannon gasps and tightens her fingers around my arm. "You haven't heard?" then glances at Peter Rabbit, whose face turns unreadable. "She hasn't heard," she repeats. "It was on the hotel TV right before we came over." Her eyelashes are caked with mascara, and tiny lines radiate from the corners of her eyes. She looks old right now, old and tired and no longer drunk. "It's unlucky to pass along bad news," she says.

"Then don't," I say, irrationally. My heart thumps, maybe loud enough to muffle her words. Once I hear what she says something will change. It's one of those before/after moments that life whacks you with. Shannon is the one who drove through a hurricane to rescue me from the bad boyfriend's apartment, who picked me instead of Lisa Long to co-edit the yearbook with her, who taught me quadratic equations and dragged my ass through algebra. The one who, a long time ago, knew everything about me and loved me anyway. Why did she turn into this stranger?

"Oh, Lexie," she starts, dropping into my childhood nickname, the one I hear only from my sister and brother, only when they're sloppy drunk. "You know I hate being the one doing this, but he was knife stabbed up in Washington, and they don't know if he's going to make it."

"Critical condition," Peter Rabbit adds. "We weren't sure you'd be here."

Chita opens her mouth and seems to forget to close it. I rarely speak of my father, and only last year she learned who he is. Speaker of the House. So fucking important.

Knife stabbed. A strange phrase, maybe not real.

"Lexie was never a girl to miss a party," Shannon says, "not when I knew her." There's an encouraging smile, an invitation to laugh all this off, to avoid the unpleasant. That was what she did back then, too, handing over money or arranging things. "Oh, Lexie," she sighed when I told her I was pregnant, "which kind of phone calls you want me to make for you?"

"I assume his new wife did it," I say. "The third one," but only Shannon is kind enough to force a laugh, which I would love her for if I didn't despise her right now. Peter Rabbit shifts his weight. Sweat dots his forehead. I imagine this being the story he'll tell about the photograph he buys.

Shannon says, "Some nutcase at the Kennedy Center, apparently. Not many details."

Chita says, "It's really OK if y'all . . ." Leaving the sentence for me to fill in. OK if I go. If I don't.

"I'm fine," I say.

Shannon whispers, "He was with that kid of his. She's hurt, too." I'm tired of her hand clutching me, keeping me from saying what I want to, from thinking it. "Also in the hospital," she says, as if to make me feel guilty.

I need Tay. But scanning the room, he's nowhere, not with the clique of students, not at the bar, not admiring my work, and I'm about to scream my frustration and fear when he bounds around the back wall, from the bathroom, and he catches my eye and threads the crowd expertly, one quick pause to lean a whisper into the redhead's ear. I gave her a B minus. She'll be the one to end up with Tay after he's done with me, after I'm done with him, after we're done together.

383

When he reaches me, I sidestep so he can nudge into the group. I say, "This is Tay, one of my star students. He's creating some intimate, contrasting narratives with found materials." He does a namaste bow, complete with hands, as if the motion is natural. A sharp intake of air from Shannon, presumably jolted by the same electrical current I feel. Peter scowls. Chita knows my praise is biased, but she tugs the head scarf taming the frizz of her curls and says politely, "I'll have to visit your studio sometime. Let's be in touch," and Tay nods and tosses a non-committal, "Lovely," which will certainly build Chita's interest, which Tay certainly understands.

My voice is wooden as I recite the names of everyone standing in our circle, and Chita excuses herself, her assistant drawing her away with one delicate finger sliding onto the crook of an elbow, as if the young woman had been signaled in to execute the rescue. There's an awkward few minutes where we talk about art and restaurants and the Outer Banks. There's a silence. Peter Rabbit coughs. The last time I saw my father in person was ten years ago, at my sister's wedding in Charlotte. He wasn't invited but showed up anyway. So him. My sister asked how I'd feel if he gave the toast instead of me, that her husband (now ex) thought it would be appropriate. "Furious," I said, but I applauded with everyone when he came up with something so moving the whole ball-room overflowed in tears. I look at Tay's turquoise eyes and say, "Get me the hell out of here," and he grabs my hand and parts the crowd, leading me with such purpose that no one squawks or stops us or registers that we're holding hands.

We're silent all the way to my car, but once there, I say, "Want to drive with me to D.C. right now?" and he says, "Sure." We get in and Sirius blares on, Lithium and the old-person grunge I grew up on, and I punch over to Spectrum, which I pretend is modern enough for him. I take the corners carefully and exit the garage into traffic, heading generally toward I-85, but after the first big intersection I swerve into a bank parking lot and chunk the gearshift to Park, my hands gripping the top of the wheel so tight my knuckles go white. All I have is whatever's in my purse. All he has is whatever's in his pockets; his car's still in the garage. I think about my friends who traveled from all those cities. The photos Chita needs to sell. My father and the mess of his life. The reckless, restless mess of my own life lately, sleeping with a student, my creative block. A line of a dozen black birds balance on a wire. I wonder if they sleep there, in a row like that. Twilight is settling in; soon streetlights will flick on. Tomorrow I would make a different decision.

I say, "This is crazy," and Tay lifts a strand of hair off my face, tucks it behind my ear. "I think you want to keep driving," he says, and I do.

My parents' marriage officially blew up in 2001, the day before the terrorist attacks. Can't buy timing like that, and, lucky for him, my father's scandal got danced right off the front page. I watched the Twin Towers collapse over and over while at the same time trying to absorb that my parents had been separated for a year without my knowing, that he was going to marry this crazy child bride when the thirty-day waiting period was up, that there was a baby on the way, that my mother had agreed to the whole thing and wasn't suing his ass. So on 9/11, when friends called, anxious for my father in D.C., it was only impeccable training that kept me polite: "He wasn't in the Pentagon, and they're doing everything possible to keep members of Congress safe."

My father couldn't have known when those attacks were going to take place. But he has always been lucky. Luck like that is hard to fathom, even when it keeps happening, as much a trademark of his as that laugh, the voice, and his cornpone sayings.

Divorcing the child bride a year later made everything worse. She kept as quiet as a crazy person could, but no way he'd ever be president, no way his golden-boy name would ever top those not-so-secret, here's-our-man, savior-of-the-party lists again. All those volunteers, all those phone calls and neighborhoods canvassed, all that money, all that hope, all of all that swirling round and round, flushed down the crapper.

Didn't stop wife number three. How did he manage to find those women, all those women and girls, who flocked to him, who happily ate his shit? Did he find them or did he somehow create us?

It's true night now, and 85 up to Petersburg is empty and dark. I tell Tay that my father's been rushed to the hospital without telling him my father's name. "I need to see him," I say, letting the cliché work its magic. If Tay thinks it's strange that my phone's not buzzing with calls from family, he doesn't say so. I dread the merge onto 95, with its East Coast megalopolis traffic and long lines of trucks rumbling and shuddering their way north, but now, right now, I'm flying. The car, a Lexus SUV I bought off an old boyfriend who upgraded his car before he upgraded me, is beautiful for road trips, like lolling in an armchair while a kalei-doscope spins. Tay plays with the satellite radio, finding some specialty station the specialty of which, apparently, is to play every song I've ever loved. The sunroof is open—it may be chilly for that, but I like the scrape and race of the whipping wind. The art I left behind on Chita's walls is distant, an old, tired thing. I could let go. That I hopped into this car with only my purse must mean something, and I ponder the colliding possibilities, that 95 ribbons on to New York, to Boston, lands deep in the wilderness of Maine. Or I could reverse and charge south, to Flor-ida and the Keys, to the end of the world. Time and place are worn out, wrung dry; they are concepts from the old world. We're nowhere but here, now. It doesn't matter that I'm forty, tangled in an inappropriate and out-of-control relationship with this boy, this savvy sweetheart of a boy with turquoise eyes. I lost my job over this, whatever this is. I don't know who told the dean. Tay doesn't either. The redhead? I don't care anymore.

This journey is animal instinct, and it occurs to me that my only mo-tive might be to watch my father die, which startles me into speaking: "I think I'm going there to watch him die."

He seems disconcerted, as if he'd planned on silence the entire dis-tance. "He'll pull through," he says. "Our bodies perform a thousand daily miracles we don't even know about."

"How do you know that if we don't know about them?" I ask.

"Excellent question." Then he says, "Anyway, no one's dying. Be pos-itive."

His glances at his phone, buzzing a text. "My buddy in Adams Morgan is good with me and/or you staying at his place and he'll jump over to his girlfriend's."

It's deflating somehow that there's already a plan, someone in charge, but I smile. I imagine my teeth shining in the dark.

"He's not far from the zoo," he adds, like he's reading an Airbnb listing.

"The zoo," I repeat. I fake-think it over.

I should explain to Tay who my father is. People Tay's age are awed by very little; he won't care. But my father is a political legend. He could have changed the world, people say, if he had had the chance. He *had* had the chance, I counter, but fucked it all away. I should U-turn over the median and tear back to Durham, back to my party, which is ca-tered and costing a fortune. I went with prosecco instead of the cheap white. Everyone is getting drunk on my prosecco.

It occurs to me that no one has contacted me. I ask Tay to grab my phone out of my purse and read off my missed calls and texts: Chita, Chita, Shannon, some other friends. My father's staff track me down every year to check my contact information. I imagine a file somewhere, a plan that includes my number, a phone tree or whatever they're called now. I should be part of a chain of events. I haven't seen him for ten years, but he's my father. Is he allowed to pretend he's not?

A few minutes later I say, "I haven't cried."

"Maybe you're not sad," he says. And a minute later, he asks, "Are you?"

"Hell, no." But I feel bad for saying that, so I add, "Maybe I'm numb. Or in denial."

He says, "Families are complicated." It seems like a polite response. "Is yours?"

He laughs. "Actually, not really. I was raised by a wolf pack, so you know. Survival of the fittest. It's all pretty simple."

I say, "I think maybe I'm angry."

He says, "What's making you angry?"

It's unexpected, but I start sobbing, shaking and heaving. The car drifts, and he grabs the wheel one-handed and says, "Look, there's a truck stop right after the Virginia line. Let's pull in and grab some beef jerky and cigarettes. We'll talk. It's just another couple of miles." He murmurs and soothes like I'm a wounded animal. All this kindness is making me angrier. Peter Rabbit would never say these things to Shannon.

I focus on steering. Focus on hating my father. Focus on these two easy, comfortable things.

It's a real-deal truck stop, with a sign advertising showers and Wi-Fi. There's a vast parking lot and an off-chain, all-night restaurant you'd have to roll the dice on—it's either a stack of amazing pancakes or salmonella. There's also a 24-7 shop for snacks, and Tay says, "I'll run in for beef jerky," and I laugh through the tears, but he says, "Seriously. They've got a great selection," and I shake my head at him. It's meant to be fond, but it feels like a tired shake, like at a bad joke.

I park under an overhead light in a gravelly corner, over by the air hose, so no one can see me sitting in the front seat crying. I click off the car. The interior lights flare then fade out. I never want to leave this car. A sliver of the moon peeps through the open sunroof.

When he unbuckles his seat belt, I grab at the neck of the coral button-down. "Hang on," I say, pulling so he can't leave.

He wraps both arms around me, nuzzles his face into my hair, smooches my head.

"Do you love me?" I ask. I never ask. I never say it back if they say it. I like to think of myself as hard, but right now, I don't remember why.

"Of course," he says. "You know I do."

Too fast. He doesn't. That's fine. Plus, the words. He didn't say them.

So I say, "How crazy is this, walking out of a party and driving north with no luggage, no nothing?"

"Whatever shit we need, we'll buy," he says. "That's how America works."

"What's a father anyway?" I say. "One sperm hitting the right place at the right time. It's simple luck more than anything." I take in a deep breath and hold it for a long time. Then I say, "I decided. We're going back home. This is stupid."

"Look," he says. "We're already in Virginia." He pushes open the door as if to show me the ground of this different state.

"I decided," I say. "Back home." But in the silence I think, *I love you. I love you.*

"Huh," he says. The silence is different, tight. He draws the door closed.

I ignore his disappointment because I feel relief. I feel a flood of sanity. My father will die and I'll read about it online. That's fine. This is fine. This boy was raised well, raised to appreciate an older woman. He's great in bed. His art is thoughtful enough, shows enough promise without, I'll admit it, threatening my art. Roman numerals follow his name, which shouldn't matter but does. It does. He's everything I want without being anything I want. I want a baby.

I say it: "I want a baby."

He shifts backward in the leather seat. I feel his mind travel a million miles away.

I say, "Honestly, that's not what this is about, but I do. I just really do."

He grunts in some noncommittal way that's animallike without being an actual no.

I talk fast: "You don't have to know. I don't have to tell you. You don't have to have any responsibility. I'll do everything by myself. My mother was practically a single mother. I know it's not the same, but I know how it works."

That same strangled sound. But still not no.

"This is what I've waited for my whole life," I say. "I lied in class. All the art in the world means nothing without a baby."

He still has not said no.

"Your beautiful eyes." I reach to touch his cheekbone, but he pushes my hand away, which is still not the word no.

"I'll die if I don't have a child," I say. "My father is dying, maybe he's dead already, and I want a child."

Still no no.

"We'll get a lawyer," I say. "I'll pay. I'll pay for the lawyer and a lawyer for you, and I'll pay you, if that's what you want." I have no idea how this money will materialize.

"What I want is so simple," I say. "A baby. To be a mother."

He says, "I'm HIV positive. AIDS. You're not getting your baby from me." And he jumps out of the car, the interior light glaring an accusation before fading down into darkness. I listen to his footsteps walking away, then I sit in silence. Enough time passes that I know he's not picking out beef jerky. Enough time passes that I think maybe he won't return. Trucks pull in and out of the parking lot, their rumbles like a distant summer storm. He might have already hitched a ride on one of them. He is gone.

I should have followed him. Generally I am enlightened and calm about AIDS, but at this exact minute, I'm not. My thoughts are nasty. I'm thinking that this is why he chose me, because I'm old and half-dead anyway. I know enough to know he's not going to drop dead, that there are drugs, that Magic Johnson has been alive for years and years, and good for him. Good for everyone living with HIV. I am ugly, ugly, ugly right now. I should find Tay and apologize and talk and understand. I should thank him for finding us a place to stay by the zoo in D.C. and tell him I love pandas.

There's a double rap on the window, but instead of Tay it's a thirtyish man wearing jeans ripped at the knee and a light blue Carolina Panthers T-shirt. He's waving a phone side to side like a metronome. "You Crystal?" he squawks. He presses his phone up against the window, showing me a picture of a girl with a pompadour of black hair. "You Crystal?" he asks again, shouting.

I shake my head, ignoring the prickles of fear while chastising myself for not closing the sunroof, for not locking the passenger door after Tay got out.

"Sure?" he says. He is tall and wiry, either a dark-skinned white man or a light-skinned black man. His head is shaved and gleams as if polished.

"God no," I say. "My boyfriend will be back in a minute."

He says, "I sent a hundred bucks to her PayPal. Jesus Christ."

"Maybe she's late," I suggest.

"Fuck," he says, shoving the phone into his back pocket. "That's money I ain't getting back. Am I right?"

I shrug-nod. "My night's pretty shitty, too," I say. "My father's dying in some D.C. hospital." The man's eyes glisten. There will be a story. There will be sympathy. I can bear neither right now, so I pound ahead, desperate to shut him the fuck up: "And I just found out my boyfriend's got AIDS," I say. I can't believe I say these words. Suddenly they're real. Maybe that's why I say them. I hope I only thought them.

He stands there, I don't know why. Like he's growing roots. Finally he says, "Tough about your dad." His face knots with more concern than I'd expect from a horny dude whose hooker bailed. I have an image of his father's face, worrying over some screw-up, his father calling him "son" at a Panthers tailgate, on a fishing trip.

I harden my voice. "He's basically been dead to me since I've been an adult. I mean, he was never much of a father. I haven't seen him for at least ten years. So, you know. Fuck him." I grip the steering wheel. The muscles in my forearms are taut. My knuckles feel as big as walnuts.

"Honor thy father," the man announces. "Like the Bible says."

I want to ask if the Bible mentions paying for sex with a stranger, but I know better than to agitate men at truck stops when they start up on the Bible. I roll my eyes and stare straight ahead, waiting for him to walk away. Waiting, waiting.

The man still stands there, so I say, "OK, thanks!"

"It's a fucking commandment," he says.

"Thanks," I say again.

He presses his hand up onto the window, palm flat and wide, sideways, fingers splayed. His eyes settle and fix on a point in the distance. Even so, my heart jumps across my chest. I'm statue still, though maybe I should grab for my purse or my phone. Just in case. Instead I think about Crystal and her hundred dollars. She's probably some guy in Nigeria. She probably doesn't exist at all. I think about a man, this man, lonely enough to send money to a girl who doesn't exist, though surely part of his brain had been warning him no.

I cautiously rest my own hand up against the window where the man's palm is, spreading my fingers to meet his. I'm startled to hit smooth glass, expecting his rough, warm skin, and I wonder how his rough, warm skin might press against mine, might push into the deep me of me. I'll never see this sad man again.

390

All these years it was so easy, saying, "My father's dead to me," because he wasn't dead.

Feelings explode across my mind, flaring like fireworks. Why we persist in loving things that don't exist.

The man's face is wreathed in shadowy angles, a contrast to the smooth shine of his head. I am one second away from clicking the button that unlocks all the car doors, one second away from saying, I'll do you for free, one second away from making a baby with eyes the color of this dark night. A baby doesn't need turquoise eyes to be loved.

I hope—no, I pray—that Tay doesn't decide to come back right now, but of course I hear footsteps and as my eyes flick to the rearview mirror I see him. A cigarette glows between his lips, and he's carrying a plastic bag. After what we said, he actually bought beef jerky, and it's ridiculous that I know a boy who would do that. Maybe that plastic bag is oddly hopeful.

The man's eyes snap over to Tay. "That kid the fag boyfriend with AIDS?" he shouts.

Tay freezes, and I expect him to crumple and drop to the pavement, struck dead by these words, by my casual and rapid and utter and real betrayal. This is what over will look like, this late night at a truck stop at the Virginia border, this shrieking stranger. How will Tay get back to Durham, I half wonder, half care. Is our betrayal equal? I half wonder, half care about that for a minute, too, until I hurt too much.

"Choose me," I say to the man. Can he hear me? I press the button that unlocks the doors, motion him in.

The man shakes his head, sadly, slowly; his sorrow looks to me immense and heavy, a burden he assumes I'll never understand. His hand drops off the glass, and he steps away from the car, sliding back into the shadows. Not even a fingerprint on the window. As if he had never been here at all.

Tay, too. Gone.

Anything in the world can change in a single instant. See? Here I am, now alone. Yet here I am, still bound to that same ache of nothing I started with, tonight and every night. I close my eyes. That. That's the thing that will not change.

Nominated by Maribeth Fischer,
Mark Wisniewski

FIVE AND A POSSIBLE

by ALISON C. ROLLINS

from NEW ENGLAND REVIEW

Spades is a way of life for black folks.
My mother went into labor
In the middle of a game.
I was born as

Five and a possible. She said
She'd felt no greater pain than that loss,
Than when she turned away, shamefaced
In the midst of kin,

When certain bragging rights began to crown.
They pulled my body from her diamond,
Held me up to meet her gaze, to study
The odds of what a luckless god had

Given. An overbid could get you shot
At Grandma's house, could have you
Question the number of hearts
You had in your hand.

Everyone knew that my mother was the score-
Keeper. She counted the books twice every
Round. There had been three before me.
Babies my mother got but did not get.

My mother taught me to watch a man's eyes
When he deals, to cut the deck
Like his cord of wishful
Thinking.

She'd warn in silence, *don't talk across the table!*
Then demonstrate over dinner with my father,
As the air held the weight of
Things unsaid.

After the divorce and Grandma's funeral,
All the words in my mother for *tired*
Were tired, her hands folded in scorn
Like cards.

Nominated by New England Review

BON VOYAGE, CHARLIE

fiction by DAN POPE

from BELLEVUE LITERARY REVIEW

Charlie Company was shipping out. Blair arrived for the sendoff ceremony at the community center a few minutes before 11 p.m. and set up his gear—the soft-boxes and reflectors, the backdrop for portraits—in a corner of the gymnasium. The enlisted men were spread around the bleachers and banquet tables in their fatigues, chatting with wives and girlfriends, mothers and siblings. Along the opposite wall, VFW old-timers were serving hot food out of trays, wearing their ceremonial caps.

Blair was on assignment for the *Hartford Courant* to get a pictorial for the Sunday magazine. He had been drinking since morning, and this was his second shoot of the day. He'd spent the afternoon outside the police station in Hartford, waiting on a perp walk. Five hours with a half-pint of Jack Daniels, a gas-station grinder, and a can of Pringles. At last the guy had come out with a navy-blue windbreaker over his head. Blair always liked that shot: you cover your head, you've got something to hide. After that, he'd had a couple of drafts at the Half Door and fallen asleep in his car. He'd woken in the dark parking lot around 10 p.m., shivering and dry-mouthed, and raced to Plainville in the on-coming sleet in time for this shindig. Why a midnight sendoff? he wondered. Why keep the kids up so late on a school night? He could see no good reason, as was the usual case with all things relating to the U.S. Marine Corps.

After getting his screens in place, Blair grabbed his 200mm and walked over to the banquet tables for a plate of chicken and mashed potatoes, spooned out by the red-faced VFWers. There was no beer, only soft drinks. He took a few pictures of the coots in their caps, just to give them some attention.

Paper plate in hand, he mixed among the crowd, examining faces, looking for something to spark his camera. For Marines, they didn't look like much—more Lil Wayne than John Wayne. A motley bunch of white kids, Latinos and blacks, a stray Asian—mutts all of them. Blair was six-two in height, and he was probably the tallest guy in the room, although the pudgiest as well, going on 225 or thereabouts with the beer weight.

The enlisted men—it seemed mendacious to call them "Marines"; they were children, really, just a year or two out of high school—all said pretty much the same things. They had joined because it was better than working at a convenience store or some other dead-end job. "I signed up to pay back the evildoers for what they did to my brothers," one genius expounded.

"Your brothers?"

"The firemen, sir," he explained.

Blair tried to keep his face sympathetic. He wanted to tell the kid: You're fighting for oil, dumbass. That's the best-case scenario. But it's probably worse than that. You're probably fighting for Dick Cheney's cronies. You're fighting for Halliburton. You're fighting to line the pockets of some fat-bellied midland Texans who never served a day in their lives. Those are the evildoers. Those rich fucks and their lapdogs in D.C., humping their bibles and wide-eyed interns, they're the ones you should target.

At midnight, the kid told him, the bus would take them to the air force base for transport to Twenty-Nine Palms. Then, after six week's training—to Iraq, the company's first deployment.

Blair asked, "Do you feel like a hero?"

The kid shook his head. "We've got a job to do and we're going to get it done."

Another brainwashed child with a rifle. Hell, Blair had spouted the same horseshit, not too long ago. He had spent a couple of years in the Suck himself, back in '91, in the first Gulf merry-go-round. He had been with the 1st Marines, a gunner in an M2 Bradley, part of a three-man crew. They'd come into Kuwait right behind the lead companies, the three of them yelling at each other the whole time, him blazing away with the machine gun. There were lines upon lines of bull-dozed trenches, some with arms and legs sticking out of the sand on top. That's what he saw in his sleep to this day, the limbs in the sand, some still twitching. Since then, since breathing in all that burning oil, he hadn't felt right, not for a single day. Some days he could barely get out of bed, with the room spinning under him. Whenever he turned too quickly, a sort of alarm went off inside his head, like a coach's whistle. Other times he would hear a sudden whooshing sound, like a wave coming to shore. When he told the VA doctor about the sounds, the woman looked at him blankly and scribbled on her prescription pad: *Risperdal*. There were other meds, prescribed by other doctors over the years, all of which sounded like the names of sci-fi planets: *Klonopin. Paxil. Celexa*. He had a cabinet filled with little orange-brown bottles, the meds long expired by now. But Jack to start the day, a couple of Coronas for lunch, Guinness for dinner, vodka on out—this helped. Buzz management, he called it. He'd seen some TV show that said you could survive forty days on beer alone. He vowed to test that out someday.

For the past decade, since his wife left him, he'd been working as a photographer. He'd started taking pictures in Kuwait City with a Hasselblad he found in the trunk of a blown-up Mercedes, four burned bodies sitting patiently in the front and back seats. Back home, he got a freelance gig with the local paper. Now he worked full-time at the *Courant*, trying to survive the cutbacks and layoffs. He'd passed on the first round of buy-outs. He didn't want to consider the prospect of having nothing in front of him but his apartment couch and 35-inch Sony. Days off were bad, sometimes very bad, listening to the voices of the invisible and the dead. Best to keep busy, he figured.

Blair spotted a corporal with an interesting look, acne-scarred and bug-eyed. He asked if he could take his picture, and the corporal stood in front of the screen and posed stone-faced with his father's bible in one hand and an Arabic dictionary in the other. "I like to know my enemy's language," he said.

Good luck with that, buddy, Blair nearly responded. *Allahu Akbar*, he wanted to say. *As-salāmu alaykum*.

The corporal suggested that Blair get a shot of Hernandez.

"Who's Hernandez?"

Hernandez was his sergeant, the corporal explained. This would be his third deployment. He had volunteered to go with the platoon, even though he'd already done his requirement. "None of us have been over there, except him. I wouldn't go in his shoes, not a chance."

"Why not?"

"He got married yesterday. You want to meet him?"

"Sure," Blair said. It sounded perfect, just the sort of pablum his editor loved.

The corporal returned with a short, wide-shouldered Hispanic man. He had small black eyes, a nose that looked like it had been broken once or twice, a fierce expression. "Yes, sir," said the sergeant; he'd be honored to take a picture with his bride. They'd met just three weeks ago, he explained. "She served me a burrito at Chipotle. That's all it took. One burrito, one smile."

"Which Chipotle? Here in Plainville?" asked Blair, scribbling in his steno pad.

"East Hartford," he said. "Angela," the sergeant called out, and the woman turned and came out of the crowd.

At the sight of her, Blair straightened up, assuming his old military posture. She was eighteen or nineteen, wearing a bright-red skirt and tight woolen sweater, her long dark hair covering her shoulders. Blair took his camera from his chest and raised it, studying her through the lens, pretending to check the focus, trying to keep his hands steady.

"We were going to get married in May," the sergeant said, "but then—" He looked at his boots and shrugged. "I figured we might as well do it now, just in case."

"I'm so proud of him," said the girl.

Blair directed the two to stand in front of his screen, trying not to stare. "Pose any way you like," he said.

The girl offered her profile, gazing up at the sergeant with adoration. Blair caught her expression at that moment, the shot they published the following Sunday: wide-eyed, aflame with love. He took a lot more pictures than he needed to.

Soon after that, he packed up and left, tossing his gear behind the seat, cursing, his gut aching. He got lost trying to find the highway on-ramp and pulled into a strip-mall bar a few minutes before last call and downed two quick vodka and tonics.

By the time he found the interstate it was past 1 a.m. and he still couldn't get his mind off her. It made no sense, getting married. What was the point? The more he had to come home to, the more he risked. Why volunteer for another trip to see the elephant? Why fly off to Iraq when he had her warming his bed? Talk about stupid. Sergeant Stupid.

On I-84, eastbound, he came up on a Greyhound, and there they were—*Charlie Company, 2nd Battalion, 25th Marines*, according to the banner on the side of the bus. The interior lights were on, and he could see a couple of kids with their heads resting against the windows. In the center aisle, one stooge was doing some kind of goofball dance.

"Moron," Blair said aloud, honking his horn. He stuck his arm out the window and flipped them off. "Fuck off, Charlie Company. Company of fools and misfits. Company of cocksuckers. Company of buffoons. Company of dead men. Die well, Charlie Company. Die holding your guts in your hands. Die crying out for your mother."

He kept on like that all the way back to Hartford. "We've got a job to do and we're going to get it done," he said, the speedometer inching past eighty. "Keep dancing in the aisles, you ignorant children."

He thought he was done, but then he started up again. "Dick Cheney's dancing right now. He's shooting duck and dancing a jig. The man has no heartbeat. Did you know that, you cockeaters? He's a fucking zombie. He's eating your skin. He's sucking your blood and you don't even know it. Off to the slaughter you go. Kill well, my little darlings. Kill your darlings. Kill yourselves."

And all that dumb beauty waiting at home.

"Screw it," he finally muttered.

That night, bleary-eyed, he wrote the piece, trying to fit in every cliché he could: *For love of country . . . protecting our freedoms . . . newlyweds in love in a time of war . . . a company of heroes.* He titled it "Bon Voyage, Charlie Company." Next to the picture of the broad-shouldered sergeant with his arm around the girl he penned the caption: "Hero and his heroine."

His editor ate it up.

Two-and-a-half years later, Blair was out of a job. He'd walked away with a three-month salary bonus and two-months' vacation pay. Four times he trekked out to the Chipotle in East Hartford, gorging on guacamole and salty margaritas. She wasn't there. The fourth time, he didn't even go inside. He just nipped his Jack in the parking lot, watching the taxpayers going in and out the front door. A waste of time, he told himself. Even if she remembered him, would she smile at him that same way, her eyes wide with adoration?

His ex had looked at him like that, once. He could still see it, the joy in her face, that day, on the tarmac in his dress greens, back from nine months in the sand. His high school sweetheart, the love of his life, a girl who would do anything for him. She came running out of the crowd, threw her arms around him. And what did he say, his prior self, the brainwashed fool? *Keep your hands off the uniform.* Within a year they were divorced. That's what the Suck did to him.

That last night, coming back from East Hartford, Blair pinched a curb and slammed into a guardrail. He managed to get home without arrest, but the next morning he reconnoitered the damage to the front end of his pick-up—the right tire, wheel well, front shocks—two grand with labor, said the mechanic. His cushion gone, he had to go begging back at the *Courant* for freelance gigs, as well as a couple of crappy town papers.

He spent a lot of time on the couch. His excitements were take-out Korean and RedTube featurettes. Often he was too dizzy to piss standing up. Many mornings he found himself on the bathroom floor, his head atop a pile of clothes next to the laundry basket. The slab of porcelain, he dreamed one morning, was his gravestone: *A piece of shit, now and forever.*

When the email arrived he didn't, at first, recognize the name: Angela Roman.

You probably don't remember me. They told me you don't work at the newspaper anymore but gave me this email so I hope you don't mind . . . The email went on and on, the stray Spanish word mixed in, one long paragraph. It was *importante* that she get in touch with him because her computer had crashed and she had lost all her photographs. Did he still have the pictures from that night? Would it be possible for him to send the pictures he'd taken? She apologized for the trouble, but it was *importante* for her, now that her husband had been wounded in the war.

He read over the email a few times and pondered his response. Best to delete it, he figured. Head out to that new place, the Tilted Kilt, where the barmaids and waitresses wore mini-tartan skirts like schoolgirls and didn't mind dirty talk when you ordered a beer and didn't cut you off after four rounds. All this appealed to his half-Scottish heritage.

Instead he poured a vodka and tonic and mulled. An hour later, he had an idea. He emailed his old editor at the *Courant* and pitched a pictorial for the Sunday magazine, titled *Wounded Warriors*. There would be no text. Just photos of GIs with their families. The caption would feature three pieces of information: the soldier's name, plus the manner and place of injury. *Private So-and-so, Mortar attack, Balad.* Etc.

His phone rang a half-hour later. "Dynamite idea," said his editor. "We can run it on Veteran's Day."

He parked in front of the apartment building, which was on a noisy side street just a few blocks from his old offices at the *Courant*. Some kids were sitting on the front stoop, playing the radio way too loud. He went through the outer door and pushed the button marked *Hernandez*, and a moment later the buzzer sounded. He took the stairwell—elevators ignited his dizziness—and climbed the steps to the fourth floor with his camera and satchel, inhaling cat piss and a burnt-meat smell, which made his stomach turn. He hadn't had a drink all day and it was almost three o'clock.

A short, squat woman answered the door. She was wearing a stained housecoat. Late fifties, he guessed. He introduced himself and she waved him into a kitchen that smelled like ammonia. She left him at the table, calling out in rat-a-tat Spanish.

Blair placed his camera on a chair, listening to the chatter in Spanish from the back room. He stuck his head around the corner, spying the hallway photo-gallery, which included his Sunday magazine spread, the newspaper a bit faded now, framed in black vinyl. Next to that were various shots of Hernandez in states of youth (child in carriage, pre-teen in baseball uniform, high school senior in prom tux), culminating in his Marine portrait, wearing his dress blues, hands clasped behind his back, his cover too big, tilted down on his brow.

The woman came back with an older man, stooped and bald, wearing heavy corduroy pants and a black shirt buttoned all the way to the top. He was carrying an accordion folder, papers sprouting from the top.

Blair stepped forward to introduce himself, but the man waved him into a seat. "Sit, sit. I am Javier."

"I'm from the *Hartford Courant*," explained Blair. "I'm here to take some pictures."

"Yes, of course," said Javier. "They are getting ready. I have some information to share with you."

The woman offered coffee, and Blair said yes, *gracias*, that would be nice, and she busied herself at the counter.

The man explained that he was Hector's uncle. His sister—he nodded toward the woman—wished to explain the problems they were having with the government. His sister did not speak English, you see, so he, Javier, had been reviewing the correspondence, making the phone calls, visiting the VA offices. "This has been going on many months now," he said. "They tell me to fax the forms to them. Fine. I go to Staples and fax the forms. The next day I call back, I stay on hold, I wait an hour. Finally I speak to the lady and she tells me, no, no, they did not receive the fax. They never receive anything."

The woman said something and Javier put his hands up. "*Cálmate, cálmate,*" he told her. He took some papers out of the file and moved his chair closer to Blair's. He smelled like cigar smoke and body odor. "You see, here is the problem . . ."

While the man rattled on, Blair became aware of a rhythmic beeping coming from the back of the apartment, some hospital gadget, it sounded like, measuring blood or oxygen or other vital function. The mother placed a mug before him and he sipped the coffee, which was excellent.

When Javier finally stopped speaking, Blair asked, "Is Angela here?"

"Yes. I told you. They are getting ready. It is very difficult."

He started up again on the VA and Blair cut in: "Would it be possible to take your picture? You and—" he gestured toward the mother. He hadn't gotten her name. He didn't need their names. He just wanted the old man to stop talking.

"It is shameful, the way they treat Hector. They say they have no record of his marriage. How is this possible? You have the papers right there."

Blair said, "I'm just the photographer. You understand?"

"Yes, of course," said Javier, and he and his sister disappeared down the hallway. Blair heard a door opening, and the beeping intensified.

Blair poured himself the remainder from the coffee pot, looking out the window, the view obscured by a hanging fern—a shadowy alleyway, another brick apartment building just a few feet away, some kids standing on the fire escape, leaning over the rail.

Back at the table, he thumbed through the military reports while he drank his coffee. It had been two years since it happened, in July 2006. An IED had exploded beneath the sergeant's Humvee in some place called Al-Iskandariya. The other three soldiers in the vehicle died at the site, but Hernandez had somehow rolled onto the ground, bleeding and burning. He burned until another soldier extinguished him. This soldier was one of his friends but he did not recognize Hernandez at that moment. He realized the burned man was choking so he reached into Hernandez's mouth and pulled out what he found there—his teeth, the shattered pieces. They got him to the Air Force base, then to a hospital in Germany, then to Walter Reed. There, he spent months in intensive care, undergoing multiple operations and burn treatments. He had lost one leg above the knee and another at the hip (*guillotine amputation at thigh*), his entire right arm (*limb burned away, bony stump visible*), his left hand, and part of his face (*fist-sized hole in the skull*).

Jesus, thought Blair, the poor bastard—burnt to a crisp and sliced off at the thigh: a half-man.

At the squawk of a baby, Blair glanced up. She came into the kitchen, holding a fat little boy, maybe two years old.

"I'm sorry," she said. "I didn't mean to keep you waiting."

Blair lowered the papers, as if caught in the midst of some wrongful act, and stood, knocking over his coffee cup. The transformation astounded him. She had put on weight, cut her hair. Sallow complexion, big freckled bags under her eyes. She was someone like any other—damaged, tired-looking, unremarkable. She could order a drink at the stool next to him at the Half Door and he'd probably not even notice her. All that crazy fire he'd felt that first night, that seemed absurd to him now.

"Oh God," she said, grabbing a napkin to mop up the coffee. "I can't believe he bothered you with all that. It's sort of an obsession for him."

"I know how it is. It's all red tape, the Marines."

"You were in the service?"

"A long time ago."

She bounced the baby on her hip, but the kid wrestled away from her and grabbed Blair's leg. "Teto, no," she admonished. "Leave the man alone."

"I don't mind," he said. He rubbed the kid's head. "Teto? That's . . ."

"Hector Junior."

"Of course."

The boy made a grab for his camera and Blair pushed it out of his reach. "I brought these," he said, digging into his satchel for the manila envelope. "I thought you might like them. I use the machine at work for free . . ."

This last part was untrue. He was embarrassed now, the time and money he'd spent on this little project at the photography store. He'd printed the shots he'd taken that night, a first-rate job—8x10s, some in color, most in black-and-white: the beautiful couple, she in her tight sweater, he in his desert camos and brown combat boots. A Marine recruitment poster: join the Corps and get the pretty girl.

Angela sat and sifted through the pictures, staring intently, lingering on certain images. Meanwhile the kid pawed at his leg, grinning like a maniac.

"He's got a lot of energy," Blair said dumbly.

Without raising her head from the photos, she said, "Come here, Teto," and the kid obeyed, crawling into her lap.

Blair picked up the empty coffee mug and put it in the sink. In the kitchen window, the late-afternoon sun was fading.

She slid the prints back into the manila envelope, sniffing, tearing up. "That was—," she took a deep breath. "That was a different life."

He paused, unsettled by her tears. "The Marines ruined me too."

She didn't seem to hear him. "I've seen soldiers on the news with double amputations, even triple amputees like Hector. They have prosthetics. They go sky-diving, they run marathons. Some of them even re-join the army."

"It'll take time."

"No," she said. "The head injury. It's not possible. He's like a child now. He has to be taught everything. The names of things. He gets frustrated so fast." She let her tears fall, raising her eyes to his, looking for some answer from him, of all people.

In that moment of clarity he saw how he would become her lover. He'd offer to help with the VA, play the part of an honorable man. He would return to this apartment to shuffle the papers with the old man, pat the kid on the head, wait for her to come around. The poor woman would be dying for some parole from this purgatory, the endless beeping of that unseen machine, marking the seconds. He could see himself—it was as if it had already happened—entangled in bed with her, the furious coupling, her naked flesh, and then her gathering of clothes and rushing off again. She would lose weight, reclaim some part of her youth. They would cook meals, drink red wine. It wouldn't be difficult. And if all went well, she would be his for a time—until she grew weary of his deception, his limitations, just as his ex-wife had grown weary, and then she would realize what he truly was: another half-man.

She wiped her tears and stood up, letting the child slide from her lap. "Teto, go play with your choo-choo. Go now."

Blair grabbed his camera and followed her down the hallway to the bedroom, the mother and uncle waiting in the doorway. The antiseptic smell met him, and a stench of stale food, something rotten. He knew what to expect, but still, the appearance of him on the hospital bed shocked him. Blair had seen his share of horrors in the desert—dead bodies, burned bodies, severed arms and legs. But this man was alive. It didn't seem possible, so much of him was missing.

Blair looked away, studying the machine by the bedside—a digital display, some tubes running to the bed, disappearing under the sheets. He raised his camera and only through the lens did he truly examine the soldier. His ears were gone, just two uneven holes on the sides of his head. He had no teeth. He spoke a language of grunts, which Blair could not decipher, although his mother did, and she got him what he apparently wanted—a cracker, ginger ale, ice chips. The skin around his eyes seemed to have melted, the dead eyes staring out. A monster mask of a face. Blair forced his mouth into a blank smile, trying not to show his shock and revulsion. "Semper fi," he said stupidly.

There were some angles which would lessen the grotesqueness of his subject—the jaw line, the good side of his mouth. Blair could make the image palatable, something that wouldn't disturb your Sunday breakfast. (His editor would require that, of course.) But, not this time. No, Blair would not add to the litany of mendacities, all of which had led to this tableau, this rickety hospital bed. He raised the camera and adjusted the focus ring, taking head-shots and close-ups. He concentrated on the burnt flesh, the disfigured mouth and ears. After a few minutes he stepped back and took a final, simple shot from the end of the bed, depicting a monstrous child at sea on a giant mattress:

Hernandez, Sergeant
Improvised explosive device
Al-Iskandariya, Iraq

After he finished, the uncle led him down the hallway, the others following. Blair retrieved his satchel from the kitchen table. "I can talk to my editor," he told Angela, "about the VA. There's a story there for sure. Maybe we can get it straightened out. We can publicize his case, at the very least. I can't promise anything—"

The old man grabbed his hand, surprising Blair with the sudden strength of his grip. "Yes, thank you. This would mean so much, you cannot know . . ." Javier's hand was stiff and coarse, evincing a lifetime of labor. "Thank you, my friend. God bless. God bless you."

Blair waited to be released, but the old man lowered his head and began reciting a prayer in Spanish, their hands bound. He looked across the table to see the women joining in silent concentration. Blair, who did not believe in God and could not remember the last time he had prayed, bowed his head and joined these people in their hopeless entreaty, offering his own prayer for the ruined warrior Hector, his wife and child, and for Blair himself: God be with you, my son, my daughter, let peace be with you and with all men and women, *As-salamu alaykum*, motherfuckers, amen.

Nominated by Bellevue Literary Review

JAILBAIT

by OTTESSA MOSHFEGH

from GRANTA

The day before I left home for college, I made a phone call to the publishing house of a writer I'll call Rupert Dicks. Dicks had a reputation as one of the most audacious and brilliant minds in literature in the last century, and his work represented everything I held as sacred at the time—he was innovative, unapologetic and dedicated to the craft of honest prose. At seventeen, I knew I was a writer, and I wanted to know what Rupert Dicks knew. I was determined to get him to tell me.

'I'm calling because I'm a student of Rupert Dicks,' I told the book editor on the phone.

'I didn't know Rupert had any students at the moment.'

'Well, I'm his student. Mind asking him to call me?'

I was a kid, but I wasn't naive. A glance at Dicks's author photo had given me some insight into how I could talk my way into his tutelage.

'Tell him I'm a freshman at college,' I said to the woman on the phone. There, I thought. That'll get him. I gave her the phone number of my soon-to-be dorm room. When I moved in the next day, the red light on the answering machine was blinking.

'Rupert Dicks here. I understand you're interested in writing. I don't know what you look like or if you've got any talent, but give me a call and I can tell you what I think.'

I called him back. Without much chitchat, Dicks gave me directions to a particular bench in an enormous park on the other side of town, the site of our meeting the next morning.

'Bring your work,' he said. 'See you tomorrow.'

I was thrilled.

That afternoon, I went to college orientation, mingling with students who seemed, suddenly, like children. I had a secret, a path, and passion that would lead my life to interesting places, not just around the corner to the university library. If I felt any anxiety about my meeting with Dicks the next day, it was that he would refuse to teach me or tell me my work was juvenile.

'Let's see what you've brought me,' Dicks said when we met. No hello, no handshake. He hunched over on the bench, took out a pen, and started drawing diagonal lines across every page of the story I'd given him. I sat down next to him and surveyed him. He wasn't a large man, but his body vibrated with the demanding neediness of a man who had once been very beautiful and powerful. At sixty-five, he now had age spots on his face, jowls, thin white hair edging out from under his hat. I remember thinking his waning vitality could be used to my advantage. If I succeeded in reflecting his great masculine strength, then he'd want me around, might take more of an interest in my work, tell me more, explain more, enlighten me more.

'So?'

'There's a garbage can over there,' Dicks said nonchalantly. He seemed to want this to hurt my feelings, although it did not. I took the pages from his fingers and crumpled them up, made two baskets into the garbage can, but missed on the third. I stood and bent down to pick up the balled-up paper, knowing Dicks would have a perfect view of my butt. It was innocuous, and yet very deliberate.

'Let's walk,' he said when I returned to the bench.

He talked for an hour about craft, curiosity, urgency, warned against the pitfalls of subconscious conformity, complacency and people-pleasing. I tried not to ask too many questions because they only inspired outrage and scorn. Along the way, he name-dropped writers and editors.

Finally, he turned to sex. I played along, but I was no Lolita. I was not sucking lollipops or sitting on anyone's lap. This was a game of egos. If I wanted what Dicks had to give me—the wisdom of his experience as a great writer—I would have to venerate him and lead him on, to flirt. But I couldn't seem too willing. If I didn't hold myself up high enough and play hard to get, my allure would vanish, along with his tutelage.

'Seventeen, eh? Jailbait,' he said. 'I should be careful what I do with you. And if you're ever famous, you could try to humiliate me. Which would be pathetic on your part. Women and their boohoos and neediness.'

Our first meeting concluded with a writing assignment. He told me to come back when I'd finished. I called him a week later.

'I did what you told me.'

'Good girl,' he said, and invited me to his apartment for the first of a handful of meetings over the course of the school year.

Dicks lived alone in a beautiful apartment decorated by his wife, who'd died years earlier. The whole place was dark. The kitchen, even on the sunniest day, was a cold chamber of shadows. Dicks and I sat across from each other, a small desk lamp on the kitchen table illuminating the printed pages I brought with me. At each meeting, he made me a martini. He ate cereal and smoked marijuana. Conversation was mostly one-sided: a man and his audience.

None of the work I showed him was very good, or very honest. But that was beside the point. I just wanted to listen to him talk. If he spent five minutes addressing my writing, I felt my visit was worthwhile. My ambition was not to be successful—to publish books and be renowned, rich and powerful, like Dicks; I wanted, truly, to use my writing to rise up to a higher realm of existence, away from the stupidity I saw in my classmates, teachers and parents, or on television and on the subway. I understood that life would be meaningless unless my art reached toward an understanding of who I was, and what I was doing here. I don't know if Dicks sensed my seriousness as a writer. Part of what made him interesting was that I felt he would dismiss me the moment I bored him. And he did, sometimes, tell me to leave abruptly, when he'd had enough. I kept calling and asking if I could visit. Dicks never refused.

When I turned eighteen, our meetings became more overtly sexual in tone. One day he took me by the hand and led me into his office, unearthed a huge cardboard box, and proceeded to pull out photographs, mostly Polaroids, of young, attractive women. 'These are some of the chicks I've laid,' he said. There were hundreds of them. 'I shouldn't have to convince you: I know what I'm doing in the sack.'

Another time, I raised my arms to lift a book off a high shelf and Dicks traced his finger over my exposed stomach. Nobody had touched me there before. 'You know, with age, the nerve endings in your fingertips become more sensitive. I can do more with this one finger than some college kid could do with his entire body.' He made a good case for himself. The touch lingered long enough for me to be stunned for a minute. I made up an excuse to leave quickly that day. But I called again before too long.

Then there was the kiss at his kitchen table. Sixty-five-year-old lips, cold, slack, weirdly passionless. I felt nothing. I can't say I wasn't disappointed. When he sat back down, he asked if he could take me to bed. He didn't want to have intercourse, he explained. He just wanted to pleasure me. I said no. We argued about this for hours. Yes, I stayed for hours and argued. They were some of the most rhetorically challenging hours of my life. I'd never been more present. I was alive and engaged, watchful and cautious with my body language, arrogant and flirtatious in my speech. Dicks mesmerized me. If I'd been any less determined as a writer, I may have been persuaded.

The last time I saw Dicks, I brought a new story. Dicks read it over my shoulder in the love seat in his immaculate bedroom. He edited the entire piece, explaining his reasoning for every move—it was a private masterclass, just what I'd always wanted. 'Thank you,' I said. 'This means so much to me.' Then Dicks went to his closet and began a show-and-tell of lubricant gels, dirty movies, contraceptive sponges, etcetera. So, we argued about sex again. None of it turned me on, not the argument, not his erotic devices, not him. He'd given me what I wanted, teacher to student. I didn't feel like paying him back.

'I'm sorry I've wasted so much of your time,' I said. 'I won't come back, I promise.'

Dicks was irate, and yet he helped me on with my boots.

'I have better things to do, you know, than muck around with some kid.' That was the end.

At thirty-six, I'm pretty fluent in irreverence and cynicism. My assumption that people are ultimately self-serving lowers my expectations and allows me to forgive. More importantly, it empowers me to be selfish, and to cast off the delusion that I'll get what I want just by 'being nice'. We are all unruly and selfish sometimes. I am, you are, he is, she is. Like Dicks, I have little patience for small talk or politesse. One has to be somewhat badly behaved to write above the fray in a society most comfortable with palatable mediocrity. One has to be willing to upset the apple cart. Apples go flying, people trip and fall, yelp, grab for one another. A street corner is transformed into a tragic circus. And everybody gets an apple, each one bruised and broken in a special way. That's the kind of writer I have always wanted to be, a troublemaker. I can't fault Dicks or anyone else for wanting the same.

Nominated by Granta,
Elizabeth Ellen

FALLING

by RON STOTTLEMYER

from TWYCKENHAM NOTES

A few rungs from the top
of the hayloft ladder, my cousin

spreads his thin arms wide
and falls like a sparrow hawk

through invisible time
into the swells of hay. Outside,

it is still August, the sky white
over the wheat field shouldered

on the hill by the barn, the creek
drawn thin as steel wire.

As he wades through the hay to us,
he keeps saying, "I was flying,

really flying," his voice brighter
than it would ever be again.

That voice deepened into the rough
world of a man who sidled across

car lots somewhere in Nebraska,
glad-handing ranchers into pickups,

who talked loud above twanging
country music, bought rounds

night after night, a man like all
of us who never saw enough

of what was always coming,
who once looked up past lanes

of dust in the twilight of a barn
and thought he was flying.

Nominated by Twyckenham Notes

CHINKO

by SAMANTHA LIBBY

from NEW ENGLAND REVIEW

This is the place where dragons once lived and will one day be born again. Here mythical beasts lie waiting, growing, plotting, and scheming. Chinko is an easy place to introduce, but a difficult place to get to. At Chinko, you begin on an airstrip, a small dirt line in a lawless place. If you wanted, you could put your pack on your shoulders and walk all the way to Darfur and not encounter a single road.

Tens of thousands of elephants used to call this wide corner of the Central African Republic home. Now, fewer than a hundred of them hide in the protected wildlife refuge that spans more than 17,000 square kilometers. Even with luck, you will never see them. All that is left are monkeys that pick at burned, dry grass, and wild pigs with fantastic noses that skitter-scatter at the sound of your approach. The branches of charred trees help hide the black mamba, one of the most poisonous snakes in the world, while the great eland antelope, a magnificent creature native to this part of the world, walks through the dying bush, looking for what is left of his home.

The word "Chinko" means nothing. It is the name given to a river in a place where the river gets lost in thick brush and fields of termite mounds. Chinko Park, established to protect what little is left, is called a national park, but there is nothing national in a place without the rule of law. Chinko's only defense is a handful of well-trained rangers who spend weeks at a time in the wild, waiting for poachers or armed groups to emerge from the thick bush and attack. This is a dangerous part of the world—everyone knows at least that much.

In war-torn Africa, outsiders often feel an obligation to dissect old clichés and invent new ones. But I show up empty-handed. After ten years working in human rights and humanitarian aid around the world, I can no longer be deluded as to my own relevance. I come for a reason startlingly few want to admit: I need to work and there is often work to be had in places where nobody wants to be.

I find myself working on a large USAID radio project in the Central African Republic when I am sent to Chinko. They want me to assess whether or not the network can be extended to include the anti-poaching efforts in the area. Be careful, my more experienced colleagues tell me. Fear is not romantic. I already know that heavily armed poachers, rebels, and mercenaries regularly move in and out of the massive area that the park is mandated to protect. But I do not understand how to be afraid there, and this, as many veterans of the humanitarian trade will tell you, is an unspoken part of any security plan. In a conflict zone, fear will be your barometer for stress when the potential for danger is constant. I ask around town. Fear in eastern CAR is no adventure, I am told by a Green Beret who'd been assigned to the US mission to capture and kill the leader of the Lord's Resistance Army. He looks at me through hooded and tired eyes and says, You don't know what lives out there.

But people do not come to this part of the world to listen to sound advice.

After three tiny plane rides to the eastern reaches of the country, I see fire in the distance. We land, and as soon as I set foot on the ashen ground, one man runs out from the main compound to greet the pilot and me. The Lord's Resistance Army has entered the park and surrounded a patrol, he says. What should they do? Engage or retreat? As he begins to argue with the pilot, I walk around the base and try to look as if I am supposed to be there. I am the only woman among four hundred men. When an hour passes and there is still nothing for me to do, I sit and look at the smoking land. Who set the fires? How close are they? If they come, there will be nowhere to run. I watch the fire grow.

*　*　*

I spent my childhood running. Like many who are bullied from a young age, I believed there was a reason I was hated and that that reason was justified.

The form the bullying took was varied but relentless. Sometimes it was simple and predictable. I was not to be sat next to, invited to birthday

413

parties, or included in activities. Other times, it was violent. I was chased, pinned down, and abused. Sometimes, it defied logic. I was pushed into a self-described jury of ten-year-old children where I was judged to be ugly, stupid, and weird. When I asked why, I was beaten with sticks and driven away. These memories are scattered and difficult. Writing them makes my hands shake and my chest tight. I have to take frequent breaks to gather my courage.

There are other events that I will never attempt to recall unless forced. I fear them more than I fear those armed with machetes and guns in the places I choose to live. Still, I hold on to these scattered vignettes of my childhood. I bury them, but I do not discard them. Over the years, they have coalesced and grown into a single living beast. I cannot see it, but it can speak to me and it calls me horrible names. I have acquired some strength with time. I locked the thing up in chains and threw it into my deepest dungeon. I go about my life, but as time goes on, I can feel it stretching against its bonds. I know that one day I will not be able to hold it back. What will happen when we finally meet? I am curious about this in the same way I am curious about the viciousness of war. Over the years, both have become constants to me. My Invisible Beast is deadly, but in its own way it is also precious to me.

❖   ❖   ❖

In the dry season, Chinko is constantly burning. Sometimes the fires are deliberate. Dropped from ultralight planes, fire helps clear the brush and herd protected animals into a more confined, manageable place. Fire creates paths, sears dead earth, and allows it to grow again.

Fire is also the work of poachers looking to flush out their prey. The result is an ashen, burnt moonscape that is constantly smoking or smoldering. It is so hot here that standing still feels like a slow suffocation. You must constantly be in motion, both to prevent being caught in an ambush and to escape the oppressive sun and heat smog.

I wonder what creatures can survive the heat and flames. I feel my Invisible Beast delight at these new surroundings. It purrs in the hundred-degree heat and stretches its wings. It pushes up for air, like the flames gasping for oxygen. Maybe after all this time I have grown too frail to fight it. My first night at Chinko, alone with myself in my 4×6–foot tent, I feel something pressing against my heart, and after so many years of concessions in a fruitless war, I give up. The ugly truth escapes.

Maybe I came to Chinko to give up.

The Beast screams with the urgency and delight of a newborn. *I am free. I am free.* I scurry to the back of my tent. I wait. I prepare myself for the slaughter. But it does not look at me. It appears entirely uninterested in me. It knows me already. It gives my things a disdainful sniff, licks up my melting candy bars, and breathes in the night air. Lawlessness is a freedom for some. It slithers into the shadows and disappears into the bush. It takes me a full ten minutes to realize that for the first time in decades, I am truly empty.

I am certain that I will never sleep soundly again, but I fall asleep right away and have no dreams.

The next morning, the men complain of ghosts rattling around in the bush. I eat my entire breakfast in two gulps, careful to avoid their searching looks. To them, this is no idle superstition. Chinko has claimed the lives of many men with such casual certainty that when I first learned of Chinko's brutality I was stunned. Ambush, torture, helicopter crashes, black mambas, road accidents, strange and familiar diseases, overdoses, and friendly fire. All these things can happen here, and they do. But these are all known things, so despite the constant stress, I find comfort in the certitude of disaster.

❊   ❊   ❊

When I was nine years old, I went on a forced backpacking trip in the mountain chain that bends across eastern California and into Nevada. By this age, I was prepared for what the other children would think of me. I remember the sense of power I felt in knowing this in advance of any actual bullying. When it was time to board the bus, I walked, determined, to the back, opened a book, and erected a wall around myself. Nobody, not even the counselors, attempted to scale it. I was quite smug about this. The memory of contentedly sitting back, relaxing into the safe company of the great horned minotaurs and soft-spoken centaurs that populated my book, is as strong as what would come later.

After about three days, we were near the top of the mountain and out of water. Refilling the massive pile of campers' water bottles was a job nobody wanted, but I volunteered because it offered isolation and peace. I didn't want to be stuck cooking or putting up tents with my peers, who openly complained about being near me. It was as if I had some incurable social disease, and proximity to me would be fatal to one's status. On the banks of an alpine lake, I got to work alone, with the song of myself.

415

The work was hard. I had to use both hands to pump the water and it required a great deal more force than I had expected. I tired quickly and it was hot. I sat back to rest. I don't know how long I sat like that. Three girls who lay out tanning on a nearby rock yelled at me, bringing me out of my reverie.

Get back to work, slave.

Of course, they were joking, but I understood then what they wanted me to understand. This is my first memory of feeling truly hated. Up until then, I knew other kids didn't like to be around me, but this was different. Something was *wrong* with me, something contemptible that they could see and I could not. I stood, suddenly overwhelmed with the truth of where I was, the years of loneliness catching up to me in a giant tidal wave. The happiness of the bus, a life behind walls, I saw for what it was: the bold-faced lie of a child. I looked around for an escape. In defiance, I kicked over the few bottles I had managed to fill and dived into the water with all my clothes on. I couldn't hear if the girls laughed or shouted. I remember the wonderful quiet of the green underbelly of the lake. I swam, not coming up for breath. A silver-haired mermaid slowly came up to my side and together we navigated the deep. But even she could not shield me from the crushing sorrow that comes after intense anger. I remember wondering if I could stay down there forever, and how easy it would be.

＊　＊　＊

Once I overcome the shock of where I am, I find that my days at Chinko are filled with a kind of lightness previously unknown to me. Without the weight of the Invisible Beast, I go about my work with a new kind of levity that surprises my colleagues. I consider the thing lost in the wild. Dead, maybe. Though I fear a more likely truth, which is that something about Chinko is just holding it at bay, and when I leave it will creep back up to me and snuggle inside my heart where it has lived for so long. I find excuses to stay longer at Chinko even though my work does not require it. I am afraid but grow accustomed to the strange and wonderful sensation of living without the Beast. As time passes and it does not return, I relax and let myself hope it may be lost forever.

One evening, I am busy helping connect a radio relay to a new battery. Swarms of tiny gnats surround my head, as what feels like hundreds of tsetse flies bite my arms and legs. It is impossible to see or work, and my nerves stretch dangerously after just several minutes. Even if I tried, I could not show you on a map where we are. Where is a four-hour drive from the middle of nowhere?

I know better than to ask the rangers who are there to protect us, but the question eats at me: if the rebels come for us now, who will save us? I also do not ask because the answer is obvious. The park helicopter crashed a month earlier, killing everyone on board. Out here, an ultralight plane has no runway, not even a patch of empty dirt, to land on. Just as we are about to abandon the evening's project, I hear something coming.

I can immediately tell that it is massive. I assess my own protection. Two rangers guard this post, night and day, beneath a sign painted in crude white letters in memory of a fellow soldier who had overdosed the week before. Freddy from Rafai. Their faces are blank. I wonder if they hear it too and are just not afraid. Whatever it is, it is getting closer. It sounds like something the size of a suspension truck is moving through the brittle grass and burnt trees, crushing everything in its path. I can hear it breathing, snorting clouds of steam into the air. For a wild moment, I think it's going to charge after us, and the flimsy Soviet-era AKs will be of little use. I am about to abandon my assumed nonchalance and call on the rangers for help, when in the same moment, it turns away.

I listen to it retreat, its tail swishing through the dead grass and thick ash. The men seem bored, unperturbed. Did they even hear it? I say nothing all the way home. I have so much adrenaline coursing through me, I can barely contain myself. Intense fear makes you react in unexpected ways. This fear is not romantic, but nobody warns you that it can be wonderfully fun. I resist crying out with glee. That night, I curl up alone in a familiar place inside my mind, a place only I know of, running for miles and miles where nobody can ever catch me. Then I sit beneath my favorite thinking tree, the one where no one can ever find me, and begin to sharpen my knife.

*　*　*

There's something of a relief in remembering ordinary sorrows. You know that they are shared with many others. You cannot be alone with such pain.

Consider the high school dance. The boys slink out onto the neon lit dance floor and twine themselves around their prey, dragging them out in the open to feast. They wrap their thin arms around the thinner girls and pull them so close that, on the sidelines, you put your hands on your chests and imagine what it would feel like to be in such contact with another. Did you spend too much time in far-off lands, places that only exist in ink and drawings, that in the real-life land of teenage touch and temptation you are lost, helpless, and afraid? Is there a purer moment of desire for relief than standing with your back against the gym wall, listening to your favorite songs play, as everyone but you swings in time with each other? The strength of the need outweighs most embarrassment, and it is common to try to outlast the pain. Somewhere in the darkness are great heroes who will come for you and pull you into the neon pinks and yellows. In that kaleidoscope you will be certain you won the war on your own, and you didn't need allies at all because now you have something even better—a partner. But when this rescue does not come, and the song ends, and you are still against the wall, you will abandon the attempt forever.

*　*　*

At night, the men of Chinko gather around a table.

Love is complicated, they say. And then they say, Love is simple.

I have never been to a place where it is acceptable to say these things without a hint of sarcasm to soften the blow.

There is a ritual at dinnertime that I have come to enjoy. While sitting in a land that is almost empty, we remember what we once had. The dreams that stayed dreams, the loneliness of the temporary NGO-employed lovers, the small towns that we all came from and can't quite return to, what our parents think and don't think of us, why we are even here, and when we might leave. We delude ourselves of our own importance.

I can't claim to be one of them, but I enjoy being near those who have dedicated themselves to living and surviving here. They call themselves soldiers, but really they are lovers. They talk of love at every chance. To them, love seems possible everywhere. The Chinko river is an imagined meeting place with magical goddesses. The rainy season will bring storms that shower this cursed land with a wealth that humans never manage to pull from the gold and diamond mines that dot the outskirts of the park. They have names for all their future children and they are named things like Storm or Horizon. Love stories and passion—not lust, but ideas of growing old in a place—are wild ideas in this place. Their evenings are twisted with dreams of women who are gentle in a way that is foreign to this land. This is not the kind of talk I have heard before, from men on remote bases in Afghanistan or Iraq, engaged in wars their leaders have determined for them. The wishes and hopes of the men of Chinko are not wrapped around the axle of desire but around a need for the kind of company that will alleviate the constant injury of life in this place. The names of the dead are never spoken. At Chinko, there is no need to acknowledge the daily constant of pain. It is one of the reasons I feel at home here.

I am also not sure how to be a woman here. I cannot nod in agreement with their desire for beautiful creatures that lie waiting for me in the bush instead of poachers armed with helicopters, large automatic weapons, and huge amounts of money.

So when they ask me to reveal my passionate wish, a story for my romantic future, I realize that I have nothing to say because I never believed such a thing would be possible for me. I tell them I hope I will survive and I can tell they are very disappointed with my answer.

The men's guns lean on the table.

I do not have a gun. This would be a great impropriety as a humanitarian. Still, I silently long for a weapon. A thin zipper and four walls of plastic are all that separate me from danger each night. I do not know how to load, aim, or shoot a Soviet-era AK type weapon, but I find myself imagining the comfort of having one near me as I fall asleep.

The discussion of love resumes because believing in the impossible is a necessary character trait for long term residence out here. I find I cannot bear it and do what comforts me. I sit alone.

One of the Central African rangers passes by. He sees me alone. My aloneness distresses him—he tells me this—and he sits down next to me. I ask how he is. He does not answer and says he is sharpening his knife. He says this like it's very important and I giggle, mostly because I am uncomfortable. This discomfort is easier than the men's discussion not far away. He withdraws a long knife—something akin to a machete—and hands it to me. He says, *This is a dangerous place. You must protect yourself.* At first, I am afraid to take it. A month ago in the capital, Bangui, when asked how I would protect myself at Chinko, I showed my friend, the Green Beret, my version of the tiny knives many women aid-workers carry. As a veteran of three wars, he had laughed bitterly at me. *There's one rule about knives: Never get in a knife fight,* he said. Still, I take the ranger's gift. With the handle, it is longer than my forearm. He nods as I turn it over in my hands as if this will somehow teach me how to use it.

Parfait, he says. Perfect.

I nod in response. He shakes his head. No, he explains, in French. That is my name. You (he uses this pronoun) colonialists cannot pronounce my real name in Sango—the local dialect.

You picked your name? I ask him.

Yes. I wanted them to know who I am. He points to himself. *Perfect.* He points to me.

What would you call yourself, if you had a choice?

Just then something howls in the bush and brings us back to Chinko, to the lonely company of the others. It is the hour of the hyenas. I can hear them laughing as the sun goes down. They are running on the airstrip. At night, they will no doubt try to kill some of the chickens. I am not sure who I am rooting for. I stand and join the conversation about love, eager to avoid answering Perfect's question.

In the darkness something moves.

          *   *   *

Outside the increasingly manicured Silicon Valley, you can find mustard grass taller than an adult and full of life: quail, red-tailed hawks, deer of every shape, possums, and that majestic pest, the mountain lion. Snakeskin bakes in the desert sun and forms wonderful curling white patterns on the barren rocks. I went to several agonizing summer camps in fields that bordered these foothills, and the counselors warned us never to venture in.

Teenage years brought active pursuit. It used to be that recess, birthday parties, and transport were my primary fears. Now the danger was constant. The school dances taught me that I was undesirable, but more rigorous schooling showed me that the classroom was also unsafe. Teachers openly mocked my appearance. "All the girls in this room have nice muffin faces. Samantha's is a horse." It's silly when you're thirty, but a heartbreaking truth when you're fifteen. Another male teacher complained that I wasn't a "nice girl," like his wife. I didn't know what this meant but at the time, it made me question my own decency. Then there were my peers. Girls at this age preferred to form circles, tight-knit barriers that they needed no weapons to defend. A single stare was a sword through the ribs and lungs. I didn't just descend into myself as a teenager, I sought the outer perimeters of where I could safely roam. I fantasized daily about running away, but I lacked the courage to carry out any of my well-designed plans. I assumed I would not be strong enough to survive. Still, each summer, I tested this hypothesis.

After I was dropped off each day for camp, I waved goodbye, then promptly made my way into the nose-high grass. The California summer brings wildfires that are as magnificent as they are deadly. Firefighters were often helpless to suppress the fire's rage as it tore through the California bush, clogging the happy valleys with smoke. If you got caught in a firestorm, there was nothing anyone could do for you. Although the risk to me was probably minimal, when I went into the foothills I told myself I was fearless. My system of relief had turned into a game of hide-and-seek after a group of boys discovered my daily routine. On this day, I watched from the branches of a tree as they crashed about in the thick brush, yelling, leaving tracks, talking of their own strength.

That morning they'd snuck up behind me as I read underneath an oak tree and doused me in urine. Why? Every hunter needs a target. I ran and they followed. I was afraid of what would happen when they found me. My walls were already rotten, crumbling, weak from years of attack. I waited in the thicket, lost in the bottlebrush's red conical flowers, then climbed into a tree.

They got very close. I could look down and see the top of a faded ball cap through the branches. I prayed with everything I had that this boy would not look up. *I am safe. I am safe*, I told myself.

He reached into his pocket and lit a cigarette. One of the other boys asked for one, but he refused.

Let's go. It's fucking hot.

He dropped the cigarette in the grass and left.

I waited twenty minutes, just to be sure, and dropped down from the tree. I saw I was alone. When the fear left me, I felt a tentative kind of happiness in the silence of the hot afternoon, knowing that not a single person was within earshot. I bent down in the grass. The cigarette still smoked. I watched the dry grass begin to catch flame. After a moment, I pressed it out with my heel.

I felt something far ahead move. Had they found me? I rose, prepared either to surrender or to bolt.

About five meters in front of me stood a massive buck, its antlers maybe two feet above my head. Its eyes were heavy and alert. I knew deer were not afraid of people this close to civilization. Something growled. My heart seized. They found me. I slowly turned. Can you believe my relief? Low in the grass, a mountain lion crouched, so perfectly still it didn't even blink.

❀　❀　❀

Silence comes quickly to the tiny base. It is so thick, I can't even hear snoring from the tents of the Ugandan soldiers a few paces away. Deep in the bush, I know my Beast waits for me. I touch my knife and consider curling up with the safety of my new present in search of sleep. But the minute I lie down I sit right back up. I hear something cry out. Forgetting my boots, I unzip my tent and step out. I am instantly freezing.

It is darker than the darkness behind closed eyes.

Knife in hand, I feel my way forward with the bottoms of my feet. I instantly regret this. The ground is littered with sharp thistles and broken glass. Making an approach in these conditions will be difficult, if not impossible. Still, I listen for the sound of scraping in the grass. It takes me a moment, but then I hear it, there, in the empty dark. I estimate it is a few hundred meters ahead. I stop and steady my breath. I wait for the sound to move away before I begin again. After a couple of steps, I have left the safety of the base. I am alone with Chinko.

❀　❀　❀

Love is simple, he said. I had just turned twenty-one and sat across from this statement in a crowded bar. In the tequila blur, he insisted on this point, the proof: lips in my hair and two fingers along the top of my jeans. I decided I did not want to be evidence for his thesis.

No, I said.

What?

No.

After he punched me in the face I remember not screaming. I don't remember his face, but I remember everyone else around me and I remember that everyone else saw. The bartender continued to make some kind of pink and orange cocktail. Two men looked at us, then got lost in the laughter/argument that is typical of certain types of bars. I felt the blood run down my eye, then nose, and start to drip. I looked around and waited for someone to do something, but nothing happened. I got up and went to the one place I figured was a refuge, the women's restroom.

Because it was a Friday night, there was a long line and a crowd in front of the mirror. I looked above the girls pulling their faces into the right position for a photo and saw my eye starting to swell. There was blood across my mouth and cheeks and hands.

422

Oh gross!

A stall opened up. I went in and sat there and tried to think. I was in a city where I knew nobody. I tried to imagine something wonderful, something magical at my side, but my mind was blank. I thought of my car, parked miles away. I knew I could not possibly drive. I would find a taxi. Someone would come for me, they had to. Deep down, the Beast laughed.

Back at the bar, I saw the man was waiting for me. I pushed past him and went outside. He followed. I started to walk up the dark block, but he still followed. He ran up and caught my arm. He looked genuinely concerned.

You can't just wander off, it's dangerous in this neighborhood at night.

❖ ❖ ❖

When did I learn how to see in the dark? Maybe it's just the moonlight. I look up, but the forest cover is even, unbroken. If there were still tens of thousands of elephants, they would have cleared the area in a matter of months. The fact that the trees are all the same height is a testament to the mass slaughter, and how recently it must have happened.

I come across a clearing filled with fallen logs. This isn't right. There isn't any animal out here big enough to topple this many trees. I kneel down and feel the softness between my fingers. Ash. I stand and continue along the path of fallen trees. I see blood smears across some of the tall grass. The creature has been wounded, probably in a fight that didn't quite kill it. I quicken my pace. I know that an injured beast is a deadly thing. A creature can appear weak and vulnerable, but that is when it can rise up and strike with a terrible and wonderful lifesaving force. I know what a cornered animal is capable of.

I press onward.

Hours must have passed, because now I can definitely see the moon above. The blood on the ground is unmistakable. Large ink-black pools of it dot the path forward.

I follow a bend in the path and am greeted by an unmistakable growl. I hold my breath and turn my knife over in my hand. I am ready.

From the darkness it rises, ten feet, then fifteen, then fifty. Its great tail swishes out of the brush, and as it moves, its scales sparkle, black obsidian, sourced by a light I cannot see. Its huge yellow eyes blink slowly, taking in my form below. I step forward. I can see the wound, eight bullet holes in its left flank. Someone got here before me. I reach for my knife and it snorts and rears, but I hold up my other hand in surrender and it calms. I am able to draw closer. I place my palm on the wound and feel my hand grow wet. The knife is still at my side. A horrible helplessness fills me. What did I think I was doing, coming here? This is too easy.

It blinks again. I want to climb up and dive into those magnificent fiery eyes. It lowers its head and faces me and I consider.

* * *

I walked, broken and bruised, but I walked all the way home and nobody followed me.

Don't think about it.

Don't give them power to hurt you more.

They are sadder than you.

Bad things happen to everybody. You are not special.

Pain is not unique, nor is suffering.

This is the chorus of advice, both inside and outside myself.

Someone I used to call a friend told me I was a "victim," the word heavier with disdain than all the other words ever assigned to me. It used to bother me a lot until I heaped it onto the very top of the pile of names I'd been called before, and set it all on fire.

* * *

Night here is at once endless and momentary. There is nothing but blackness, but the sun is also rising, heavy, along the equatorial horizon. My knife is already discarded on the ground. I know I don't have much time and she knows that too. I place my foot onto her good shoulder and hoist myself onto her back. She doesn't wait for me to find something to grab onto. She is rising, her heavy wings more than three times her height, taking us higher and higher. I throw myself against her neck and hold on with all my strength. Moments later, we are one with the night, rising until my sweaty nightshirt freezes against my skin, and snow forms on my eyelashes.

Then we are swooping low. Our enemies lie hiding in the bush. I can see them, filled with fear at the sight of us. They raise their guns, but we are ready for them. At once, everything in sight is on fire. A spark in the dry grass catches so quickly and rises so fast that if they screamed, we couldn't hear them. We ride like this for miles and miles until the forest is alive with flames and she is empty of fire and satisfied that there is nothing left standing.

The sun begins to rival the burning land. We need to return. Some-
one will wake and see the smoke and sound the alarm. They will run
for the airplanes and use their computers and GPS to root out the cul-
prit. The smoke is very thick now, but I am not afraid. All they will be
able to make out is a massive beast, free at last, roaming the skies, and
a girl who from this angle looks just like a little kid, along for the ride.

✿ ✿ ✿

I was bullied well into adulthood. Every night I would fall asleep and
ask what I had done wrong. Each morning I would begin again, no wiser
than the day before. It was as if something elusive, something true, lay
out there, and all I needed to do was be strong or brave enough to find
it. I assumed it had to be something that could not be altered, no matter
how dutifully I dressed it up, or beat it into submission. This is how I
first became acquainted with the Invisible Beast. It was an answer and
I loved it because it was a relief. In this way I both hated and nurtured
the Beast inside me. I told myself that it was what the others despised
about me, why they shrank from me. But it was also a truth I desper-
ately wanted to know better and understand.

Now that I have met her, I know two things. The Invisible Beast in-
side all of us is real, but it is not the answer. It is the question.

What are you afraid of?

One day, your Beast will rise up and when it breaks free, nothing will
survive its path. It will destroy every wall you've dutifully built, and tear
down any and all defenses. It will seek revenge for being imprisoned
and will stop at nothing to get what it wants. If you are lucky, you will
survive its rampage, but you will never get it back. If you have spent
no time in its company, you will never know what it can teach you. The
Invisible Beast sees parts of yourself you cannot see on your own.

✿ ✿ ✿

It is time to leave Chinko. I am up in the plane. I am filled with a de-
sire to be dropped, to be lost in the trees and open plains with my eter-
nal companion. I am certain we could survive together. I know that
well-armed men and women lie waiting for me, waiting to destroy me
for their own gain. With my Beast at my side, they will not find me and
they will not hurt me. But I stay where I am and do not run.

I watch my Beast grow smaller beneath me. It stretches its obsidian
wings with ease and then takes off in the opposite direction of our plane.

425

It flies towards no roads or villages, only to the burned wasteland. I tell myself we are both plotting our own ending on our own terms. I do not know when I will see it again, but I know that when I am ready, I will not have to search far. It will always be out there, somewhere, full of fire, daring me to fly with her.

Once the plane lands and we disembark, I know what waits for me: my desk and my reports and my teetering understanding of how to do good in this world. Before I get home, I learn that something has happened in my absence.

Due to a huge electrical fire in my home in the capital of CAR, everything I own has been destroyed.

I return to what is left of my home, insisting on seeing what is left. Even the roof is gone. The sad cement structure is all that remains. I set my bag down in a pile of ash. I touch the ground. It is still hot. I run my hands through the ash, what is left of everything I own and the life I diligently packed up and brought here, and allow myself to be crushed under the weight of how utterly human I must now be as I figure out how to go on living, working, and surviving with nothing.

Suddenly, I feel so tired. I sit. I allow myself a moment to delight in the warmth of the smoldering ruins around me. I close my eyes and pull this blanket of the earth up over my head and fall asleep listening to the gathering whispers, the potential for growth there, somewhere within.

Nominated by New England Review

DRAFT / MOUTH

by PETER LABERGE

from WILLOW SPRINGS

If at our most dangerous / we blink. If winter reveals itself like a sol-
dier's gibbous mouth. If rows of silos give way to fire. If *Jonathan*, my
father's / ideal son. If evening, a painted face / I could peel off. If speak.
If with my own two hands, if stained / sky. If for three days I pull and
pull / the soft white thread of my name / from my father's throat / as he
registers me in the next room. If a house wraps itself in thread / until it
is no longer a house / but rather the drafted boy / I might one day be-
come. If no waning apology / in my father's mouth, if no lifted tracks. If
doused in petrol / my mouth's god like a field filled with silent / children.
If each twirls in the wind / until they lift apart. If match, if strike.

Nominated by Willow Springs

CITIZENSHIP

by JAVIER ZAMORA

from POEM-A-DAY AND UNACCOMPANIED (COPPER CANYON PRESS)

it was clear they were hungry
with their carts empty the clothes inside their empty hands

they were hungry because their hands
were empty their hands in trashcans

the trashcans on the street
the asphalt street on the red dirt the dirt taxpayers pay for

up to that invisible line visible thick white paint
visible booths visible with the fence starting from the booths

booth road booth road booth road office building then the fence
fence fence fence

it started from a corner with an iron pole
always an iron pole at the beginning

those men those women could walk between booths
say hi to white or brown officers no problem

the problem I think were carts belts jackets
we didn't have any

or maybe not *the* problem
our skin sunburned all of us spoke Spanish

we didn't know how they had ended up that way
on *that* side

we didn't know how we had ended up here
we didn't know but we understood why they walk

the opposite direction to buy food on this side
this side we all know is hunger

Nominated by Poem-A-Day,
Martha Collins,
Aimee Nezhukumatathil,
D. A. Powell

A DELIBERATE THING I SAID ONCE TO MY SKIN

by MEGAN BAXTER

from THE THREEPENNY REVIEW

To consider my tattoos we must first consider skin. Skin is our barrier against the world, enveloping our body so that we won't lose our precious water and evaporate like dew. The outer layer, the epidermis, lacks blood vessels and survives on oxygen alone, although it needs very little of it because many of its cells are already dead. A skin cell lives for a fortnight and is then pressed upward through the process of desquamation to flake off and float around your house as dust.

The strata of our skin resemble a slice of the earth, where twenty-five to thirty layers of skin cells separate us from the outside world. Scratch your epidermis and you might flake off a few dead cells, but cut into your dermis and you'll bleed and slap your hand to the cut in pain. It is in the dermis that tattoo ink is deposited and where, as the years of a life progress, the ink sinks like heavy water, fading away through layers of skin like a figure retreating into shadow.

There are marks that fate applies to our bodies, freckles, moles, and scars from falls, mean house cats, sharp kitchen knives, and slippery rocks in the water holes where we learned to swim, and then there are marks we etch into our skin deliberately, razor bites, piercings, tattoos.

The average adult lives within twenty square feet of skin, roughly the size of a large baby blanket, although shaped, of course, not like a blanket but like a human. A big canvas. Skin covered in ink doesn't much resemble our naked dead layers. It looks like snake and bird feather, scale and leather.

Tattoos are often the language of the dead because skin can speak for us when we are gone. Sailors hoped their ink would identify their bodies if they drowned at sea. Salt and water do horrible things to a body, erasing all personality, removing eyes, wiping faces clean, but even stretched and waterlogged, a tattoo remains locked in flesh. Anchors, pirate queens, bleeding hearts all offered something like an ID card. With the inked mummies of the Euro-Asian steppe, or the bodies of the Iceman and an Egyptian priestess, what did their dots and dashes and their swirling chimerical animals mean to their owners? Perhaps only that they had names, even in death.

I am certain that I began drawing on myself early. I drew on all things, so it seems likely that my skin was also my canvas. In school I doodled on my hands and arms, writing notes that blossomed into flowers and vines. But that ink scrubbed away or smeared off on my cheek in the night. Like most kids who grow up in the country, I was checked with scars on my arms and legs from bike accidents, barbed wire, the blade of the pocketknife I had stolen from my father, a fishhook, a mean pine bough, the barbs of blackberry and raspberry bushes.

My skin, if I consider it, is not particularly special. It is neither oily nor dry. It isn't a large hide, not quite twenty square feet, and beyond the scratches and scrapes of childhood it has escaped real damage, enduring only moderate acne during adolescence and again during a rough spot in my late twenties.

But I am inscribed with images, electric with ink. See me naked, or moving through the water swimming in clear lakes, see me in a sundress or walking the trash to the curb, see me stretching my muscles toward the sun, see me showering off the sweat of the day, and see my arms and legs illustrated, my back and foot patterned, my hipbone stamped with pigment, my shoulder opening wings of ink.

I am the poet of the body,
And I am the poet of the soul,
The pleasures of heaven are with me, and
  the pains of hell are with me,
The first I graft and increase upon myself—
  the latter I translate into a new tongue.

—Walt Whitman

Whitman might have seen tattoos in the hospital wards on the limbs of those dying boys that he tended with letters and words and ice cream. Martin Hildebrandt, a tattoo artist from New York City, enlisted in the Army of the Potomac and was known to ink men so that their bodies might be identified. There were no dog tags in the Civil War, and despite a six-year program undertaken in 1865 by the Quartermaster General to locate and inter the dead, only half of the war's fatalities were identified.

The first tattoo, a cross on my hipbone. My mother accompanied me because I was under eighteen, and she was trying, with her first and most willful child, to be cool. She talked the artist down to inking me with something no bigger than a quarter. It was over before I understood the pain. The waistline of my jeans wore it off over the course of a two-week hiking trip that I embarked on just after getting the tattoo. It was cloudy and mosaicked before I had it reworked four months later when I sat for my second tattoo. The man let me tattoo myself while he took a break to relax his hands. He guided me through the process as his feet pumped the machine.

You came into the world perfect, my mother muttered, after each tattoo, perhaps in protest.

Consider pain. Consider the skin under pain. That organ is the perfect vehicle for agony. It can be burned, cut, rubbed off, frozen, lashed, electrified, beaten, pierced, branded. There is pain in the skin; there has to be for us to walk through the world and know fire and ice and to pick up things like marbles and bowling balls and to tie shoelaces or zip up a dress. It is our barrier but it screams to us; those nerves woven through the dermis shoot electric warnings to our distant brains. Many tortures have been enacted upon skin. The saints at their martyrdom. The Death by a Thousand Cuts. The mind has dreamed up and then executed a thousand violations of that greatest of organs, that membrane that protects the individual from the universe.

Perhaps tired of traditional methods, or simply crueler than the rest, the Byzantine Emperor Theophilos had the brothers Theophanes and

432

Theodore tortured for their protest against Iconoclasm. Over the course of two days he had their faces tattooed with twelve lines of his metrically correct although artistically unsuccessful poetry. The brothers survived and continued their protests. Later, when they were venerated as saints, they became known as the *Grapti*, the "written upon" or "the inscribed."

There is a comma missing in the poem on my left leg. I didn't notice it was missing until a few months later. I have a very casual relationship with commas and am surprised I took note. Sometimes I draw it in with pen but to have it fixed permanently seems so fussy.

> *Stay together [missing comma] learn the flowers, go light.*
>
> —Gary Snyder

There is a line through the dark image on my left shoulder that a beloved cat tore as he escaped from my arms and into the yard at dusk. That too will remain while the image on my back simply fades away. That tattoo, a Celtic knot, sits on the sliver of skin that is exposed by my shirt hiking up my back as I lean to weed or plant. It has faded so that when I am deep summer tan it appears more like an elaborate birth mark than a tattoo; it is a memory of a deliberate thing I said once to my skin forever.

The pain of fading, the pain of mistake, is not as bad as the pain at its origin under the needle. Have you ever picked a scab and pulled its crust too deep? Have you felt the bite of a razor on your anklebone and a rush of sweet sharp something too? Can there be love without this exposure, or growth without that tingling ache in the bones? There are scales for pain but they aren't accurate. Each body has its own measure, and year-to-year, place-to-place on our hide, it changes. Consider the inside of your elbow or the smooth skin along your ribs, both dangerously sensitive to the needle, so that some artists won't touch you there for your first tattoo. Now run your hands over your deltoid and biceps, the rounded head of your shoulder and the meaty part of your upper arm, the skin on your calf. Thick and distant from bone. Here the needle sinks without getting too close to the tender parts. Here you'll not feel it shake your skeleton.

Sometimes a cat scratch. Sometime a burn. The needle will bite and then radiate out as the minutes become hours until the whole thing is a flooded field of red raw pain. A tattoo's pain can ache downward from the dermis to the muscle fiber to the bone. It'll start to move. Or maybe that's the pain from not moving, from sitting and becoming canvas. But even if you stretch, even if the artist offers you a Coca-Cola for the sugar rush, even if he leaves you for a while to smoke a cigarette or answer the phone, the skin will buzz. The needle vibrates like bees in the grass. Its hiss shocks you at first and you'll jump, but that's just the beginning. Then you'll know how it hurts. Then you'll know how a good artist will start light and then press deeper or start with the single needled out-liner and finish with the many needled shader, scratching in ink instead of drawing it like a fine-tipped pen across your bloody skin.

But the pain is essential. It releases endorphins that flood you with something like love and joy. A two-beer buzz. Sex. French fries and milkshakes. The good stuff. And after a while you won't be able to de-scribe the pain but you'll know that it is a key and the release is worth the scratch.

Unscrew the locks from the doors!
Unscrew the doors themselves from their jambs!

—Walt Whitman

I am an addict. I think I should say that. I fall hard for things, and I've had to cut them out, too. Booze and cigarettes are gone now. I have to watch that I don't get too involved with pastimes or specifics. Too in-terested. I'll pick at a scab until it becomes a scar. I'll keep looking for that sweet response. I know that.

Some people get addicted to tattoos. I have seven, the large one on my left arm being what I consider now my last. The pain was never that much of a high for me. Except during that last one, when, like a terri-ble night of drinking when you cheat on your beloved and crash your car and then swear never to touch the bottle again, I found the edge of my tolerance for the needle. That tattoo ink was cut with witch hazel to help me heal, but O! the sting! And the session lasted nine hours, instead of the normal two four-hour sessions, because the artist was leaving the next day. He began in the meaty part of my arm and finished in tender bits—my armpit, my elbow bone, until I rang with pain—inking in an image from an illustrated edition of *Leaves of Grass*, women holding babies, men pushing plows, birds breaking into the sky of my shoulder. Driving home delirious, I wondered if I might not be breaking the law.

Consider inspiration. Is it born in a dream or myth or pretty picture you saw once? I rolled my tattoos around in my mind for years before they spread out on my skin, except for one. The eagle on my shoulder landed on me.

There are seasons marked on my body like a castaway's notches to record the day. The Celtic cross and knots. The poets: Jeffers (his red-tailed hawk), Snyder, and Whitman.

In the season of the eagle tattoo, my heart was freshly broken and I was driving out west hoping hard to find adventure, or at least something other than the snow of another New England winter. Over the mountain passes of the Rockies I prayed for my car's engine. I wrote in cheap motel rooms and hoped someone would text or call me, but my phone was silent. To anyone who asked, I told lies about who I was and what I was doing, as if I were trying on different skins, but the one thing that stayed with me, state to state, dawn to dusk, were the eagles. I saw them or they saw me and followed me west, their white hooded heads sharp against the sky.

I joked that I would get an image of one of them inked on my arm. Joked to the tracks of Lynyrd Skynyrd and the Allman Brothers. Joked to the stale air in my car.

In Utah I settled in to a nest of a motel room a few minutes away from the gates of Zion. I could see the rim of some red rock formation from the window near my desk. The sun cast over its face like clock hands counting away hours. And the eagles hung above it, screaming silent in the desert sky. No, not screaming. Yipping. Hawks scream. Eagles yip like beagles.

When I couldn't write a word I drove. My car red with dust, I followed a brochure's map up a dirt road on the other side of Zion. It was the last day of the year. A man in a silver pickup truck looked down, worried, into my window as we passed on the tight road. As he drove down to the main highway I saw that his bed was full of hound dogs, their noses pressed to the grates of their cage.

The road ended or seemed to end at the gates of Grafton, a historic site, a ghost town whose fields were still farmed by a rancher down valley. Walking the main road, I felt like I'd been there before. Miles Romney, an architect sent by Brigham Young to oversee the construction of the St. George Temple, was housed in Grafton while final plans were drawn up. He wrote in his journal "when I studied Milton's *Paradise Lost* in school I never intended to spend the last part of my life in it."

435

The settlement spread out on the skirts of the Virgin River with the red cliffs behind and the clear sky above. Red, green, blue cut boldly into the earth. But it wasn't beauty that made me pause, for the West has plenty of that. I knew those old buildings worn by the desert sun. I knew the church and schoolhouse, the fences and barns.

An eagle circled. Hunting.

Then it came to me, but I didn't believe myself until I read it in the fine print at the bottom of the historical society's sign. Grafton had been in several movies, most notably *Butch Cassidy and the Sundance Kid*. The gentle schoolteacher Etta lived in this Paradise, and the outlaws came to her for food and love and shelter. Dusty, Redford, and Newman dragged themselves to the light of that house while the posse, nameless, faceless, bore down on them.

"There are no second acts in American lives," F. Scott Fitzgerald said, but Butch and Sundance got one by running away and living in Bolivia for over a decade before they were killed. Or not. Lula Parker, Butch's sister, claimed that he returned to Utah and died there of old age. In the movie they live forever in that long frozen shot as they blast out into the marketplace where the Bolivian Army's rifles can be heard. There's no pain in that ending.

I've always loved that movie, its evasion and veiled truth. Once I dreamt of Whitman and Galway Kinnell holed up together, bandaging their wounds, talking not of Australia and banks but of the body and the soul. I've read that hearing other people's dreams is boring, but I can't imagine why. I consider this dreamed scene often: on the count of three the poets ran out into the bullets and were frozen there on the screen.

> I believe in the flesh and the appetites,
> Seeing, hearing, feeling, are miracles, and each part and tag of me
>   is a miracle.
> Divine am I inside and out, and I make holy whatever I touch or am
>   touched from,
> The scent of these armpits aroma finer than prayer,
> This head more than churches, bibles, and all the creeds.
>
> —Walt Whitman

My body the only universe I'll really inhabit. And what have I inked upon it?

436

I have come to myself empty, the rope strung out behind me in the fall sun suddenly glorified with all my blood.

—Galway Kinnell

I wanted blood in Utah, and tattooing is a bloody art. As the needle tears into the dermis, blood wells up and things get messy. The artist smears your skin with A and D ointment, which helps keep the blood down but not enough; they'll wipe it away every few minutes with a paper towel so that briefly they can see the image they're carving.

Imagine having something to write but nothing to write on or with. You go tearing into your desk for a pen and paper. You rattle through all the stuff in your purse, the glove box, and you feel the words pounding on your skull demanding to be inscribed. Eagle. Eagle. Eagle, my skin said. Eagle my skin, I said.

Somewhere between magic and mysticism truth is suspended. Magic is just a trick that you haven't figured out yet. Mystics are something else entirely. They can talk to God and animals. Their dreams are worth paying attention to. When they die their skin becomes leather. Their bones are good luck. Their poems cause people to sway and see the Virgin Mary or taste spring water on their lips. There isn't any reason in them, though if there is, it is mythic reason, full-moon thought, and tidal. Theirs is the way of the spirit. They might begin as blank canvases but they become saints.

I don't believe in magic. I think it's a silly thing to even have to say. When I was three, my father told me Santa was fake to save me from having to believe a lie. But I believe in the body and the spirit and the skin living on air as it separates us from air, and in things that I don't understand pulling at me. I can't really tell you how the tides work but I know they are called by the moon's gravity and that the lunar cycle tugs at the blood in my belly, too. I don't speak Eagle but the Eagles told me to get back in my car and drive down Interstate 15 to St. George where I would find a man with ink in his needle on this, the last day of the Year of Our Lord 2009.

Tattoo shops, or parlors, or studios, are not welcoming places to walk into. Like all places that deal in blood, they are often tucked up in the armpits or off to the side of cities, especially nice cities like St. George, where you can see Miles Romney's beautiful white temple or walk over the tracks of Jurassic reptiles at the Dinosaur Museum. To find a tattoo shop you have to look for one. I followed a bumper sticker to a phone book to a strip mall where the only tattoo parlor open on New Year's Eve let me slip in as the last skin of the day. The place was tile and Fifties roadster revival, but empty, and the man who inked my shoulder was the owner of the store.

In the past, I had always walked in with artwork, something I had drawn that had been waiting for flesh, but in Utah I knew only the bird and where it would soar on my body. He drew me an eagle and placed it, in temporary ink, with its wings over my upper arm. It wrapped me up lovingly.

First the hair is shaved. Human skin, like that of most mammals, is hairy, even if those hairs are fine and light, and these tiny hairs will get caught in ink and needle. Then the rubbing of alcohol swabs, the cleansing. I settled forward in the chair, my arm out stretched. He assembled his kit. The ink quaked dark in its reservoirs. He banded the needle's necks to the machine and tapped it to life with his foot. Ointment slathered over the site. He pulled at my shoulder, testing its elasticity, its thickness, its bounce. Then ink into needle and needle into skin, the first touch a cut to form a wing, a test, then faster and longer with each line, until the bird is outlined. Blood wells so ruby, so shocking, dripping in orbs then running all wild with black ink shot through until purple and messy, just bruise.

A tattoo is a wound. Consider that you have just opened yourself to infection on the very surface that is meant to protect you from the world. You are now vulnerable in a way you weren't thirty minutes ago. The artist cleans the eagle up good and smears it with ointment, then he packs it away under a dressing and tapes the edges shut. The pain has made me excited. I shake as I drive away, back north to my motel. There are lights in the desert. The night is dark already when I arrive and peel the bandage off and gaze into the floor length mirror. The eagle is part blood, part ink.

If I worship one thing more than another it shall be the spread of my own body
—Walt Whitman

First the ink will rise up and the image will be branded on you. Then it'll scab, but don't scratch it. It'll peel, but don't pull it. One by one the

438

lines will fall away, and you will feel again your skin, smooth but full of ink now. The ink settles heavy in the dermis. Sitting above nerve and fat but below the dead layers that wear off. Deep enough to be forever in you.

Perhaps skin is the best place to be selfish. Under the dermis on our hands and feet there are papillae that extend outward toward the outside world. They press into the epidermis, forming the distinctive hurricanes of our fingerprints. These marks are created in the womb during the first trimester and they remain with us, unchanged, through all seasons. Unique. Pressed in ink, they are our identity. We are known through our skin.

Nominated by Threepenny Review,
Michael Bowden,
Joan Murray

IN THAT TIME

fiction by RICHARD BAUSCH

from NARRATIVE

Back in late June of 1949, when I was twelve years old, I spent a morning with Ernest Hemingway. This was shortly after I had been hauled down to Cuba, deeply against my will, by my parents, whom I had begun to think of as the Captain and his wife. The Captain had retired from the navy after twenty years' service, and was following a friend from his time on a destroyer in the Pacific during the war. They were planning to begin a charter fishing business. The friend, who left the navy as the war ended, was already living down there, and the charter fishing idea was his. My father had wired him funds toward getting things set up.

His half of the investment; it was a lot of money.

The friend's name, all I ever knew about him, was Coldrow, nickname Cookie. He was supposed to meet us at the harbor in Havana. The Captain and his wife sold and gave away things, and packed other things with a kind of unspoken urgency, and the three of us boarded the Holland America Line's MS *Veendam* on the seventeenth of June. When we arrived, the morning of the eighteenth, Cookie wasn't there. So the Captain rented us rooms a couple of blocks from the Floridita, in a place called Pepe's (I think the building is still there, under a different name), a big house with a double-decker porch and a café on the first level. There was no sign of Cookie, and no word from him, either. The address he had given my father turned out to be a burned-out cottage at the edge of the Canal de Entrada. Someone told my father that a man fitting Cookie's description had lived there, but no one knew what became of him after the fire. He was just gone. There was supposed to be a boat, but there was no boat—there was a little dock, but no boat.

So we stayed at Pepe's, and the long days went by. The Captain spoke Spanish, but his wife and I did not. They had been married only a little more than a year. They were either going to get used to each other, or they never would (they never did). By the fourth day, he was ready to give up trying to locate Coldrow—he had stopped using the nickname by then—and instead of looking for a place where we could set up house, he spent the next three days mostly in bed. The wife was restless and irritable, though she told me bravely that what he required now was rest, that we all must take time to acclimate. Money wasn't an immediate problem, even with the loss of what he had sent to Coldrow: he had sixty-eight days' retirement leave, a navy pension after twenty years' service, and income from an inheritance his first wife, my mother, left him.

Of course, I had nobody, and nothing to do. Nowhere to go. I was just *with* them: the Captain and his wife.

"Clark," she said to me somewhere around the tenth or eleventh morning, "go out and get us a newspaper and some bananas. Go busy yourself, be useful. You make me nervous."

Sitting on a sofa under the one tall window looking out on the city, with a book open on her lap and a cigarette between the index and middle fingers of her left hand, she put me in mind of a picture I'd seen on a paperback cover of a lady of shadows, though there was really nothing mysterious about her. She was a young woman who grew up in Virginia and had never been anywhere, and came from a family that catered to her whims in ways the Captain never did. No doubt she found this exciting about him at first; now she was too far from home, and fairly disenchanted. But she looked chic anyway—nails painted dark red, like her lips; natural blond hair in a perm. She was very pretty and had what I'd heard people call Betty Grable legs.

The cigarette sent its winding strand of blue smoke to the ceiling. I'd been trying again to get the radio tuned to something other than static. "They'll have newspapers at the Floridita. Go on, boy. Get."

My own mother died having me. I'd known this for as long as I could remember. And I'd spent most of my life with women my father hired to watch me. He was almost always gone in my growing-up years. Duty tours. The war, of course. But even when he was stationed where I could be with him, regularly I had governesses (his expression) attending to me. It was easy enough to think of him as the Captain.

"Give him some money," he said now from the other room.

"Really?" she called. "I'm stunned. You need money down here? We have to pay for things down here, even though we already *sent* money?" Then, low, to me: "There's some in my purse, over there on the table."

I brought the purse over to her and she rummaged through the mess inside. A lot of little tubes, a cigarette case, a billfold, some facial tissue, and a compact. "Here." She held out a ten-peso note, folded so tight it wasn't much bigger than a postage stamp. "And get yourself an egg or something."

The Captain coughed in the other room. "Bring some fruit. Any kind of fruit."

"Bananas," she called to him. "I *said* a newspaper and bananas."

"I hate bananas and you know it. Jesus Christ."

"You *said* any kind of fruit, Dwayne. And don't use that language. It's common."

"Screw you, how about that?"

"Your father," she said to me, "is a common, uncouth, low-life person."

"What're you telling him?" came from the other room. "It's not even nine in the morning. A lot of people are in bed at this hour on a Saturday. Christ. Any kind of fruit!"

That last was louder, meant for me.

I heard the strain he was under in his voice. He had more to worry about than losing money to a supposed friend, and though I was too young to understand it fully, I knew enough: he'd been duty officer when James Forrestal, former secretary of defense, jumped from a high window of the Naval Medical Center in Bethesda, Maryland. Two in the morning on May 22; he was found on the roof of the third-floor cafeteria, wearing only pajama bottoms. I'd heard my parents talking about it the day it happened. I was in my bed, supposed to be asleep, and the Captain's voice came low, down the hall: "The indignity of it. Pajama bottoms. He was a man of dignity. Something just doesn't add up."

And then her voice. "You're saying—?"

"There was broken glass in his bed, Abby. I was there. I saw it. Broken glass, and his room was across the hall from the window where he went out. Or was thrown."

"Thrown."

"They know he and I formed a bond."

"A what?"

"That's what *he* said. I even heard him say it over the phone. That's what he called it. He made a big deal about it. He said he felt a bond, that we'd formed a bond because we were navy men, and were against helping the Zionists. And the Zionists, and the government, they hated him. This goes all the way up to the president."

"Stop it."

"Forget I said that about the glass in his bed."

"You're kidding. Poor baby, you're imagining things."

"I was there in that room at six this morning. I came in and he wasn't there. Broken glass in the bed. Forget I said anything. I didn't say anything."

"Who would *I* talk to about it, honey?"

"No. Right."

"Dwayne. The man jumped. Come on. He was crazy."

"Explain the broken glass."

I heard the shrug in her voice. "He broke a glass."

According to the papers and the radio news, Forrestal was quite outspoken about his anti-Zionist sentiments. My father did not like the Zionists, either. I wasn't too sure, at the time, what Zionists were. I knew they had something to do with the Middle East and the new country carved out of the Partition. I had an idea, anyway. That stuff about Palestine and Israel was hard to miss, with the radio on every evening and the papers piled up on the coffee table in the living room of our apartment in Roselyn. The Captain believed the Zionists might have killed Forrestal, and that there was a chance they'd be coming after him too. He didn't speak of this, but it was in the air, in the disquiet you heard in his voice. He and Forrestal formed the bond (he kept using the phrase) while Forrestal was hospitalized. Now Forrestal was dead. The facts kept troubling him, and her. I was in the middle of it all.

Zionists, suicide, theft, murder. Cuba, where we knew no one. The uncertainty of everything. The sad Captain and the sad Captain's wife.

I had all this in my head as I went out to get a newspaper. I didn't want to be near them anymore. When I came down the stairs from the top deck, there was Hemingway sitting in the café, a newspaper open on the table, coffee at his elbow, with a squat brown bottle of something on the other side of it. Right away I knew who he was: I had been obsessed with lions and Africa, and the Captain had a magazine with pictures of the author-hunter that everyone called Papa. I knew the face, and now I heard the waiter say, "Algo más, Papa?"

"A couple more fried eggs, Alejandro. With chorizo this time, please."

"Enseguida."

Hemingway looked at me and smiled. "And what's yours this morning?"

It was really a wonderful smile. There was coffee in his beard, which still had some darkness in it close to the skin, and his mustache was ash-colored. He wiped the back of his hand across his mouth. He had on a black T-shirt, ragged, stained white shorts, and rope sandals. I saw the hair on his legs, his big knees. I stood there gaping.

"Why're you crying?" he said.

I hadn't known I was. "Nothing," I told him.

"Okay." He drank, and went back to reading the paper.

"Can I have that paper when you're finished?" I was being a brave unhappy boy.

He gave me a long, evaluative look, then poured into his coffee the last of whatever the clear liquid was in the bottle, and drank. His eyes were red, irritated looking. But friendly. "You had breakfast?"

I shook my head.

"Is that what you're crying about?"

"No."

"You want the paper that bad?"

"No."

He smiled again. "Tears from pain, or from pique."

I stared.

"Pique," he said. "You *mad* at somebody? Where are your people? Your parents."

"Upstairs."

"They mad at you?"

"You killed a lion," I said. I felt stupid. It was all I could think to say. I wiped my nose with my hand and then wiped my hands on my own dirty white shorts.

"You mad at *me*?" He put his fingers against his chest. "It was self-defense, I swear."

"I wish I could hunt lions," I got out.

He took the other chair at the table and turned it. "Sit down, partner."

I did so. He turned a page of the paper, and took a drink from his coffee cup. "Alejandro," he said to the waiter. "Tiempo para el vino, amigo. Un blanco frío."

444

"Sí, Papa."

"I'd like to go to Africa," I said.

He shook his head very slightly, remembering something. "Haven't been there in years. I did kill a lion, a big gazelle, and a charging buffalo—water buffalo. You know what that is, right? A great, big thing with horns. Black as outer space." He put the paper down and extended his arms into what looked like an embrace of something large. "Massive and ill tempered. Kill you out of meanness." Then he reached into the pocket of his shorts and brought out a clean white handkerchief. "Wipe your nose."

I did.

"What's your name?"

"Is a water buffalo fast?" I said.

He nodded. And there was the smile again. "Had to finish one with my bowie knife. Ever see a bowie knife?"

"No."

"Cut you in half. A man named James Black created it for Jim Bowie—you've heard of Jim Bowie."

I wasn't certain, but I nodded. It did sound familiar.

"Created the thing just for knife fighting, way back in 1827. Jim Bowie used it too, in a big duel called the Sandbar Fight, where he would've died if it wasn't for that knife. It saved him. Damn near as big as a broad-blade sword. And this bull, I got him in the neck as he was coming over me. Just missed getting trampled."

I was speechless for a few seconds, trying to imagine it all. "I saw a picture of you," I got out. "With a lion."

Alejandro brought a bottle of white wine in a bucket of ice, and one glass. He set the glass down, opened the wine, and poured a little. Hemingway just nodded, so Alejandro poured a little more, and then set the bottle into the ice. He picked up the squat brown bottle and the coffee cup. "Would you like something to eat?" he said to me in completely unaccented English. I think he was intentionally not noticing my sniffling.

Hemingway lifted one hand at me, palm up. It looked like it might weigh ten pounds, that hand. "Well? What do you say, kid? It's on me."

"Eggs?" I managed, wiping my nose with the handkerchief. "And bacon."

"You like the yolks soft?"

"Yes."

He said to Alejandro, "Three, sunny-side up, amigo. And five strips of bacon, and do the eggs in the bacon fat. And an English muffin." He looked at me. "You like orange juice?"

I nodded.

"Tell us your name."

I said it, looking down.

"Big glass of orange juice for Clark."

Alejandro wrote it down.

"That all sound good to you?" Hemingway asked me.

"And a waffle?" I said.

He gestured to Alejandro with that smile.

"Tenemos solamente panqueques."

"Only pancakes here, partner. That all right?"

I nodded.

"Coming right up." Alejandro walked off. I noticed that he had a crooked back, and a slight limp. He moved slowly.

"He speaks good English," I said.

"Better than we do. For some reason he doesn't like to speak it. But he's good."

"Sí," I said.

He nodded, that smile. "Feeling better, I see."

"I'd like to go to Africa."

"I was there way back in thirty-three. Alejandro a lot more recently. He fought against the Desert Fox, a brilliant German general. You ever hear of him?"

"No, sir," I said. The world was full of color now, and interest. Desert foxes and bowie knives and duels, lions and charging water buffalo.

He looked me over again. "How old are you?"

I told him.

"Your daddy never told you about the Desert Fox?"

"No."

"Great general. His name was Rommel. Irwin Rommel. He was forced to take cyanide by Herr Hitler toward the end. What were you, seven or eight when the war ended?"

"Yes, sir."

"You know about Hitler?"

"Yes, I do, sir."

"How come you don't like your name? A minute ago, you looked like you were ashamed of it."

"No," I told him.

"I think it's a good name."

"Yes, sir."

"You know it comes from the English word *clerk*. They still pronounce *clerk* there as Clark."

I simply nodded.

"I didn't like my name, either, when I was your age. Ernest. Ernie. That's what I *really* didn't like. Ernie. I thought it sounded puny."

"I think it sounds friendly," I said.

He nodded. "Are you gonna be a writer?"

I shrugged.

"Still not sure, myself." He made a little scoffing sound. "And you know about Hitler. What about Mussolini, and Stalin?"

"Yes," I said.

He lifted his newspaper and held it open, probably in some way intending to compliment me by being unsurprised that I knew the other names. On the other side of the page I saw Forrestal's picture. My heart jumped.

"My father *knew* him." I pointed.

He turned the edge down with his heavy fingers to look, then folded the section to the page with the article, holding it in one hand and sipping the wine. "That's right. The paralytic's navy boy. Your father knew him, huh?"

I repeated the phrase: "Paralytic's navy boy." I thought he might be referring to my father in some way.

"Franklin D.'s boy. Secretary of the navy. Franklin D. was *assistant* secretary of the navy before he got to be president. And Forrestal was our first secretary of defense. Did you know Franklin D. was a cripple?"

Nodding, I said, "You knew the president?"

"Sure."

"My father was in the navy," I said. "He was stationed at the hospital where Forrestal—" I didn't finish the sentence.

"Ah, right. Bethesda Naval Hospital."

"Yes, sir."

When Alejandro brought the orange juice, I said to him, "You were in Africa too."

He glanced at Hemingway, who returned the gaze, grinning now. It was like some kind of joke between them. Then it seemed suddenly serious from the expression on Alejandro's face.

"Just that you were there," Hemingway said quietly to him.

"Oh, sí, jovencito," Alejandro said to me. Then: "I was there, all right, young man. I was there." He went back to the kitchen.

Hemingway leaned close, and I saw the sun damage on both sides of his nose. "The war," he said, low. "Doesn't like to talk about it. He's a bloody hero, though. Served in a tank battalion. You know what that is, a tank battalion?"

I had enough of an idea of it to nod.

"Were you in the war too?" I asked him. I remembered seeing a picture of him standing with some soldiers behind some kind of truck or jeep. I wanted him to tell about it.

He looked serious for a moment, the index finger of his left hand tapping lightly on the table. "I've been in all of them," he said. "In this century, anyway." He straightened and stretched, arms up, fists at his ears. "With this latest one, I liberated the Ritz Bar, in Paris. You ever hear of the Ritz Bar?"

I nodded, and smiled at him for the first time.

"There," Hemingway said. "Good. You *are* feeling better. You never heard of the Ritz Bar."

"No, sir," I admitted.

He laughed. It was a surprisingly high-pitched laugh. When he took a sip of the wine, the sun from the far window sparkled in the straw color of it. "I have three sons, myself, you know. Grown men. You'd like them."

I nodded, but he was looking at the paper, reading the article about Forrestal. The silence lengthened. For a minute, it was like we were old friends, used to being in each other's company and not needing to talk. But the time went on, and I thought maybe he'd forgotten I was there. I still had his handkerchief, so I put it on the table. He looked over the paper at me, saw the handkerchief, and put it back in his pocket. "Says here that his family claims he was just exhausted. Not crazy."

"Does it say anything about broken glass?"

He looked back at the paper and then at me again. "Broken glass?"

"They found broken glass in his bed. It's a secret. My father said not to tell anyone."

"You just told *me*, kid."

"I know. I'm sorry." For a second I thought I might need the handkerchief again.

"Don't worry, partner. I won't tell anybody."

I nodded, and put on a smile.

"So your father and he were friends."

"They spent time. Every day, while Mr. Forrestal was in the hospital—yes, sir."

Hemingway combed one heavy hand through his thinning hair. "Did your father know him before the hospital?"

I hesitated, trying to decide exactly what the truth about it must be.

"Your father's navy. This guy was navy too."

"They formed a bond." I was just using the Captain's word.

"Well, what brings all of you down this way?"

"The Zionists may be after my father." I did not understand why I felt the need to lie just then. And I think this was when I realized that it might not exactly *be* a lie: certainly, the Captain was worried about the possibility.

"Do *you* know who Forrestal was?" Hemingway asked.

"Not really. The Captain's friend."

"The Captain."

"My father."

"You call him that?"

I shrugged.

"Does *he* know you call him that?"

I shrugged again, feeling caught out.

"Well, it's none of my business—no need to worry about it now, partner." Hemingway turned the newspaper over, and laid it flat, so the article about Forrestal was up. He smoothed it with both hands. "Forrestal was important in the government. But you knew that, right? So what about the feds? They after your father too?"

"Yes," I told him. "I believe the feds are too."

"So he's in hiding." Now Hemingway's smile was broad, stretching all the way across his wide jaw. "Down here. In the lion's den. Not a good place to hide from the feds. There's feds crawling all over the place down this way, kid. That's why I'm here instead of the Floridita."

I looked around the empty room.

"I'd like to talk to your father." His eyes narrowed. I felt that he was looking deep into me now. We just sat staring at each other for what seemed a long time.

Presently, two men came into the place and walked directly over to our table, as if they had an appointment with us. I shrank back at their approach, and Hemingway reached over to steady me. His rough hand was on my arm for a second. No one had touched me in a long time. It got me sniffling again. The taller of the two men was bald, with thin strands of black hair combed over from a part just above his left ear.

449

He had a camera on his chest, secured by a little strap hanging from his neck. "I'm Ed Volker," he said, and then tilted his head toward the shorter one with him. "This is Tye Blazedall. We're with the *Washington Star-Tribune*." Blazedall had a blue baseball cap on with a red W. He looked way younger. He was rubbing his hands together oddly, shifting his weight from side to side. It came to me that he was excited to meet the famous author and hunter.

The one named Blazedall saw the paper open on the table and read the name aloud in the headline: "Forrestal. What a thing."

Volker took a picture of Hemingway, who just sat there while he took two more.

"I know someone who covers politics in DC," Blazedall said, "and he swears you could see it coming a mile away. Guy was a suicide waiting to happen."

Hemingway took a sip of wine and simply gazed back at him.

"I can't imagine jumping, though, can you?"

"Evidently there's some question."

"Oh, that's thinking like a novelist," said Volker.

"No," Hemingway told him. "That's what this article's about. Family says he wouldn't do that to himself. Says he was terrified of heights." Then, looking at me: "What do you think, there, partner? That sound true?"

I gave him a look that I hoped communicated the need for secrecy. He nodded slightly and looked back at the man. "About jumping—not much of a way to go, I guess. I think drowning or freezing to death. I think you just go to sleep freezing to death."

Volker snapped another picture, then stood back and muttered, "Anyway, all that time falling. And from that height, a body would break open like a watermelon."

Hemingway reached over again and lightly patted my arm. And when I looked at him he winked. "I never liked watermelon."

"I guess if you've gone crazy, you don't really care how you do it."

"This young man's father knew him," Hemingway said, indicating me.

"That so," said Blazedall. But he seemed to brush this aside. "Well, actually, we do have a reason to be in Havana. Your wife said we'd find you here but that you'd probably be working."

"I'm being lazy this morning," Hemingway told him. "Miss Mary knows quite well I'm not working. I've just finished the best thing I've ever done. And I'm thinking of hunting big game with my partner here." He indicated me again, and winked. "What say we go to Africa, partner?"

450

Volker said, "What's it like spending time with Gary Cooper and In-grid Bergman?"

"I haven't seen those two fine people in a while. Supposed to see Coop soon enough, though. Do some hunting in Idaho. Fine fella."

"What're they really like?" Blazedall asked. "What's Marlene Diet-rich like?"

"She's as sexy as you think she is."

"And Coop?"

Hemingway smiled and nodded. "Coop's sexy too."

"No, really."

He stared. After a beat, he nodded, muttering, "They're fine people."

Blazedall took off his baseball cap and moved to stand next to Heming-way's chair. "Take another picture, Ed."

"Actually, we're about to eat," Hemingway said.

"Won't take a second," said Volker, focusing. He snapped it.

"Thank you so much," Blazedall said. "Listen, I know it's ridiculous, but the paper actually sent us to ask what your opinion might be about the Nobel Committee not awarding a prize in forty-eight."

Hemingway sipped the wine, and gazed at the shifting sunlight in it.

The two men glanced at each other. "Goddamn it, Tye, it's too soon," Volker muttered.

"What did Miss Mary tell you two? She tell you to get me talking? Have a drink with me?"

They were silent.

"She didn't say I'd be working. I know goddamn good and well she didn't say that."

"I can't drink at this hour of the morning," Volker said.

Hemingway's annoyance was obvious now. "No opinion."

"Seems odd, don't you think? No prize?"

"I just told you what I think."

"Can you say something more about your new book?" Blazedall asked.

This changed things a little. Hemingway took another drink of wine. "You should try this in the morning sometime. Very good for the spirit. Like fuel for an engine." He looked at me. "Isn't that right, partner?"

"Yes," I said.

"Alejandro," he called. "Isn't that right, amigo?"

Alejandro was standing in the entrance to the kitchen. "Sí, Papa," he said.

Hemingway looked at the two men; he was still holding his glass of wine. "Otro, amigo."

Alejandro retreated to the kitchen.

"Twenty-five years old and wounded at El Alamein. He took out a panzer single-handed with a sticky bomb laid into the tread."

The others said nothing.

"So. You boys want to talk about the new book."

"Man, yes we do," Blazedall broke forth in an enthusiastic tone that even an unhappy twelve-year-old boy could see was embarrassing.

"It's got everything I know in it," Hemingway said. "And it's built solid as the hull of a ship."

Alejandro brought the second bottle of wine, already opened. He filled Hemingway's glass and set the bottle in the bucket as he removed the empty one.

"You sure you don't want some of this?" Hemingway asked them.

"*Across the River and into the Trees*," Volker said. "Great title."

Hemingway smiled broadly. "You saw it in the magazine?"

"Do you want to tell us more about it?"

A woman came in then and walked over to the table. "Volker," she said. She was blond and wiry, with perfect skin. I thought of the Captain's wife, upstairs. The same long legs, the same dark lipstick. "Mr. Hemingway," she said. "Are you liberating this place?"

"You know that story."

"Doesn't everyone?"

"Well. Paris wasn't all fun and games. It was the end of the war, but it wasn't all fun and games. We saw plenty of fighting on the way in."

"I heard you had a sidearm. Against regulations."

Hemingway's jaw tightened. "I had a brigade, madam. At a place called Rambouillet. I was with a group of partisans. We had headquarters in a bombed-out hotel."

She said, "Can I quote you?"

"This is already out there," he said. "I'll tell you this, though—I saw action. I had a hundred-twenty-two sures before I got to Paris."

"Sures."

"Kills. Nazis. You remember the war?" His smile was brittle, and fleeting.

"Quite," she said.

"You with these two?" he asked her.

"We're in the same business," said the woman. "I'm Helen Talbot. I'm not averse to having a glass of wine."

"Did my wife send you?"

"I don't understand the question. *Vanity Fair* sent me."

"And you want to know what I think of the lack of a recipient of a certain award."

"That, and a couple other things. I didn't know about these kills."

"I don't talk about them. It's already been reported. Several times over."

"Will you write about them? About death?"

"I've been writing about nothing else. My whole life."

"How does it feel to be a legend?"

"How do *you* feel about it?"

She left a pause.

"I don't have an opinion about the forty-eight Nobel, all right? I never think of it. Nor of anything like it or near it."

"And about the new book? Can you talk about that?"

"Did you see it in the magazine?"

"Yes. But I wondered what you meant to say with it. The old soldier and the young girl."

"You remind me of somebody," he said. Then: "There's nothing else to say."

She stayed silent.

"What I have to say is *it*, itself. That. The book."

"I see."

"You'll excuse us." He gave her another brittle smile. "Quite probably you're nothing like who you remind me of. But let's call it a morning's work, all right?"

Alejandro brought our breakfasts out on a big tray. I felt an almost unreasonable sense of relief. I remember that I thought we could go back to talking about lions.

Volker was muttering at the woman, and Blazedall took hold of his elbow and was trying to move him toward the door. "We could stay and order breakfast," Helen Talbot said.

Blazedall said, "Can't you see he's having breakfast with his grandson."

They all went out and along the street, away. We were quiet, watching them go. Alejandro poured more wine.

"They were up early," Hemingway said. "Didn't she look like somebody to you?"

"No es la ex-esposa," Alejandro said.

"You sure? Not an ex-wife? You didn't think of her?"

453

Alejandro shook his head, walking away.

I had begun to eat the eggs. I said, "She reminded me of my step-mother."

Hemingway laughed.

"Upstairs," I said.

And he laughed again.

It made me very glad. I sat happily eating my eggs. I thought I had never tasted anything so good. He forked the chorizo into his mouth, chewing and looking off. "It seemed like they wanted the movie stars," I said, chewing.

He laughed again. It thrilled me. We were compadres.

"Tourists," he said. "And they're supposed to be journalists."

"Pah," said Alejandro, from the doorway. He waved one hand across his face and turned into the kitchen.

"Alejandro worked at the Floridita a while," Hemingway said to me. "Known him a couple years now." He drank more wine. Then: "Journalists. Christ."

I said, "Goddamn them." I had heard the Captain say that about journalists. I was merely repeating it, to please Hemingway.

"I started as a reporter," he said. "They disgrace it. I know some very good journalists." He watched me scrape the eggs from the plate. "You read the papers?"

I nodded. I had turned to the pancakes. "I wish I could see a lion."

"Yeah. Lions. You should hear the sound they make at night."

"And you killed one."

He nodded, grinning.

"And water buffalo," I said.

"Yep."

Because I wanted to keep talking about the lions, I offered what was the full extent of my knowledge about the buffalo. "They're even bigger." Then I added, "But lions kill them."

"Hunting in concert," he said. "Maybe some. But the water buffalo has no real enemies. The other animals don't bother them." He drained his wineglass, and poured still more. It had no effect on him, that I could see. "Want a taste?"

"No, thank you." I drank my orange juice and thought about how the Captain and his wife would be falling down drunk splitting one bottle.

"The water buffalo travel in herds," Hemingway said suddenly. "And they'll fight for each other. The lions stay away, mostly."

"You killed them."

454

"Killed one each."

I waited for him to go on. Then he was just watching me eat the remainder of my pancakes. Alejandro stood there watching me too. I began to feel self-conscious.

"Dawns on me I like to watch someone eat who's really hungry," Hemingway said, pouring the last of the wine. He held the glass up. "To us soldiers."

Alejandro said, "Soldiers." But he just nodded.

Hemingway drank, then belched soundlessly and put the glass down. I saw his eyes, the light in them and the way they moved, taking everything in. He kept watching the door; I hadn't noticed that earlier. "Those journalists, as they'd call themselves, thought you were my grandson."

I said, "Funny."

Suddenly I wanted to ask him if the things he had told me were true. I knew that I would not do so, but I also understood that there had been no stabbing of a charging water buffalo with a bowie knife, nor any killing of a hundred Krauts. So then I was sitting there with my full stomach wondering why a person of his size and fame and fortune would lie to a boy like me about such things. Also, I recall the sense that there was something to learn from him in the fact of it, to have an advantage as I went on with the Captain and his wife. I mean I thought it was part of being a grown-up.

But then too I remember hoping, with a guilty ache, that no one would ever catch him out in his lies. I said, "Thank you for the breakfast, Papa," and he clapped his hands together and leaned back, smiling that smile.

"My pleasure, Clark. My pleasure."

In the next minute, the Captain was there, in Bermuda shorts and a sleeveless undershirt. He scowled at me until it registered with him who was sitting across from me. Quickly, he offered his hand. "Very, *very* excited to meet you, sir."

Hemingway looked at me. "This your papa?"

I was ashamed, nodding.

"I'm his father," the Captain said quickly. "I hope he hasn't been bothering you."

"Not a bit of it."

"Get up, boy." He cuffed me lightly, painlessly, on the back of my head, though the fact of it hurt. "Don't overstay your welcome. Do you know who this is?"

"He's not bothering me, sir," said Hemingway. "We're talking about going on safari together, isn't that right, partner?"

I had stood out of my chair, fighting tears. Alejandro had come back into the room.

"Come on," Hemingway said gently to me. "Sit down. It's all right. Finish your breakfast. You've still got half a muffin left."

The Captain, uninvited, pulled another chair over, and then seemed to think about it. "Excuse me, would you mind if I just brought my wife down. I—I have to put a shirt on."

Hemingway turned to Alejandro, and indicated the bottle. "Uno más, amigo."

"Cierto."

"I'll be right back," the Captain said, backing toward the stairs. "Won't be a second."

"Good. We can talk about Forrestal."

He paused, straightened slightly—which was when I realized that he'd been hunched over, like somebody cringing in the cold—"Yes, of course." Then, looking at me: "Wait here." His voice was full of displeasure and suspicion. He turned and was gone.

I looked at Hemingway, who smiled that smile and then leaned toward me and, with his hand on the paper over the article about Forrestal, said, "Partner, really, it's all right."

I don't remember now how much time went by. It seemed long. Alejandro brought the wine, Hemingway downed a glass of it, then asked for a daiquiri, and Alejandro brought that. Another journalist, a slack-looking man, came in and also wanted to know what the lack of a prize for forty-eight meant. Hemingway waved his hand across his face and said, "Is that all you want to talk about?"

"My boss wants to know."

"You want a drink, some coffee? The price is we don't talk about that shit."

The journalist muttered that he had a job to do, and left.

"Did you notice," Hemingway asked me, "that none of his clothes fit him? They all looked a size too big."

At last the Captain came down, dressed, and alone. "I'm so sorry," he said. "She'll be right down. She just needs to freshen up a bit."

"Did you see this?" Hemingway asked him, indicating the paper lying open on the table.

The Captain stared at it for an awkward few seconds while Hemingway and Alejandro and I watched him. It occurred to me that he was reading it. He sat down slowly, still staring at it.

"Coffee, señor?" Alejandro said.

The Captain nodded absently. "I'm not supposed to say anything, but we found broken glass in his bed."

Hemingway glanced my way, while feigning surprise. "You don't say? You knew him well?"

The Captain looked at me.

"Clark here says you were his friend."

"Well."

Now Hemingway leaned back, clasped his hands under his chin, and smiled broadly. "Tough to be a real friend to that sort of character."

"You knew him?"

"Met him in France, during the war. To me he seemed like an unpleasant little son of a bitch. But very efficient, and very smart."

The Captain was quiet. Alejandro brought him his coffee.

"And you liked him," Hemingway said.

"Well."

"He seemed to me like a doubled-up fist," he went on. "The type who would depopulate a country to get his own way."

"He was very strict," my father said. "And, really—yes. Not very pleasant."

I couldn't believe it. The man who had formed a bond. I looked at him, at the folds of his white shirt, the collar, the one button that was undone halfway down the front. Suddenly I knew Hemingway was lying about knowing Forrestal, as he had lied about everything else, toying with the Captain, for my benefit, and that the Captain was suffering, and that this morning was all part of the badness of a suicide and fear and flight to a country none of us knew, and a friend who had lied and taken money and disappeared. In that moment, for the first time in my life, I saw my father as a person. I saw a man down on his luck. And I wanted Hemingway to stop. He had bought me breakfast and was supposed to be my friend. But I wanted him to leave my father alone.

I said, "We think the Zionists might've killed him. And they might be after us."

My father looked at me, and all the years of my little journey to twelve years old, when he was far from me and I was alone with one woman or another—all that time away shone in his eyes; I had the sense that he saw me suddenly as a stranger who was being kind. He leaned forward and took the last piece of my English muffin and put it to his lips. "Nothing to worry about, boy," he said, nodding at me. "Really. We'll be all right."

"But that's why you're in Cuba," Hemingway said to both of us.

My father explained about Coldrow and the charter fishing idea, the money, the burned-down cottage. It was as though he were a boy talking to a grown-up.

"So what'll you do?" Hemingway asked him, grinning.

"Oh, we'll probably head back north."

He leaned forward. "This place is crawling with feds, you know."

The Captain shook his head.

"Crime bosses own Havana. Everything goes through them. And the feds can only watch."

And then they were talking about that. For a while they were just two older men trading news accounts and rumors about Meyer Lansky and Lucky Luciano and the others.

I sat there.

Hemingway began to talk about his war, drinking the daiquiri, and the wine. My father had some wine, staring wide-eyed at the famous man going on about "sures," and his new book, the mistakes and incompetence of the military men he had known. It was all dull to me now, and I wanted to go back upstairs. I had found out that we were going to head back north. The blank future was ahead of us.

That future contained, of course, Hemingway's own suicide; the Captain's divorce from his wife, who returned to Virginia and raised a family; and his remarriage to a woman named Mavis—my now dear friend Mavis—who gave him years of unexpected happiness; my own time in the catastrophe of Vietnam; my years in a kind of careful friendship with the Captain; and his eventual adoption of that form of address too. I called him Captain through the last years, actually with great affection. Now and then we would talk about that time in Cuba, when we met Hemingway.

It was noon before my stepmother walked into the café, wearing a crisp, red, sleeveless dress with a steep V in front, and high heels. Hemingway was getting ready to leave. He glanced at her as she came in, then sat up a little and took her in. Alejandro had brought him another coffee. My stepmother said, "Good morning," to the room and sat down, arranging her dress over her thighs.

"This is Abby," the Captain said. "My wife."

"Hello, Abby," Hemingway said, smiling widely. "You're quite a bit younger than the Captain here, aren't you?"

"Fourteen years," she said.

It was clear, even to me, that he had only meant to compliment her youthful appearance. He hesitated only slightly, and went on: "Well,

Abby. I always liked that name. And you remind me of someone." His eyes were cloudy. He drained the coffee, building up to say something.

But she interrupted him. "We don't want to keep you." Reaching into her purse, she brought out a fountain pen and a piece of notepad paper, leaned forward, and offered it to Hemingway. "If you'd be so kind."

He smiled the wonderful smile, and gave a little sighing shrug, and I had a sudden sense of what the whole morning had cost him, the strain of being who he was in that place and at that time, the world as it was then, keeping up with his fabrications. And I'm convinced that I knew, somehow, sudden as a spark and a dozen years before it happened, how his life would end. Because I thought of Forrestal, and the newspaper man's political friends saying you could see his suicide from a mile away. At the time, it seemed only an importunate thought, random, having nothing to do with us. Hemingway took the pen, his hand trembling very slightly, and signed his name.

Nominated by Narrative

IN THE STUDIO AT END OF DAY

by CATHERINE BARNETT

from AMERICAN POETRY REVIEW

From my mother I've inherited dark eyes
and the desire to spend hours alone in a room
making things that might matter to no one.
She paints canvas after canvas, so many

she doesn't know what to do with them all.
Would you like one? Please,
come down to her studio,
she's giving them away now, as I write,

as I watch her and write and revise draft after draft
while not twenty feet from me she's spilling her paints
on the floor. She has more courage than I,
painting's not like writing, you can't get back

to earlier versions. Failure is hot right now,
said one of the children of her children,
and I think my mother was consoled.
I was, and then we were in it,

celebrating my mother and my father, both.
She made us laugh as she looked around the table
at the mutable world, her vast progeny—
so many of us she doesn't know what to do

with us all, and two already lost—
then raised a glass to my father
and their ninety years together.
Who's counting? Time passes

while my mother stands before the painting
as if it were a mirror
and paints the woman's face purple,
tilts the woman's head, blurs her outline.

She paints with whatever's at hand.
Chopsticks. Fingers. Elbow.
If she had a gun she'd use that.
My father built the storage racks

but there's no more room.
Try to hurry, try to get here fast,
before she leaves. Last night
she went home early,

and I was by myself in her studio,
which is like a womb. Everything
pulses. I turned the lights out
at the circuit breaker, as she taught me.

When they go off they make a kind of bang,
a shudder through the walls.
Tonight let's leave my mother
working here, she says she's not finished yet,

but take a painting on your way out
—tomorrow there will be another.
Read this draft, tomorrow there will be another.
Kiss her face.

Tomorrow there will be another.

Nominated by American Poetry Review,
Eleanor Wilner

EULOGY

by PATRICIA FOSTER

from PLOUGHSHARES

"I had to get away from her," my husband whispered as we lay together in bed. For thirty years, I'd heard only his sharp, flinted words, the stories about his mother no more than a few terse sentences—"She sacrificed me to my stepfather. She let him beat me. She beat me too"—his resentment flaring on this dark winter evening, the light fading, the wind up, tossing branches against the roof. Then, just as suddenly, the fuse fizzled. He shook his head. Old stuff. He didn't want to go there, dragging himself back into the past.

And yet, each time he mentioned his mother, I resented her. I disliked her. I felt embarrassed by her, this woman I'd never met who looked so working-class old and frumpy in the one picture I'd seen: shaggy hair, a beaky nose, dark circles shadowing brown melancholy eyes. A wicked witch! I thought: you dumped him in foster care as a child and didn't protect him once he was yours again.

Nobody deserved her.

But now, now that I've read the foster care files, the narrative has begun to shift, her story so much larger and more complicated than I could have imagined. True, I can't see her clearly, can barely scrape the surface of her life, but the difference is that I want—and need—to make her more than a monster. She died in 2000. She died and we didn't know it. Now I think that the only way to resurrect her properly is to write what I've come to know, to say goodbye before I've even said hello. And though I don't have the historical documents or personal anecdotes to

462

give her a proper eulogy, to chart even one hour of happiness, I like to imagine a night in spring as she sauntered down Millbury Street, the laundry done, the moon low and white over the trees, a new pack of cigarettes snug in her pocket.

I spread out the information I have: a 1940 US Census report (she was eleven); thirty-one pages of typed caseworker notes in a Health and Human Services file dating from 10/19/48 to 06/25/56 (the period that my husband—her son—was in foster care); a 1957 Worcester County Probate Court petition for adoption by her and her new husband, Orrin Campbell; a US Social Security Death Index (she was seventy-two); an online obituary; and a few random pictures, one in which she looks so young and lovely I can't quit staring at it. In this photo, she's a slender woman, auburn hair swept back from her face, a bright cranberry sleeveless shirt bloused over tan shorts, one sandaled foot lifted as she leans into her new husband. Her skin looks pale and creamy, her thin lips pressed close, her almond eyes dreamy, almost sleepy, as if she's been coaxed up from a nap for this quick photo in an ordinary 1950s kitchen with its bright white cabinets and blue-gray tile. A paper-towel rack is just visible behind her left shoulder.

Though she may indeed have been a monster, I know now that she was also a motherless daughter, an abandoned girl, a jilted lover, a young woman caught in the crosshairs of poverty with a deep, hungry love for a baby she couldn't afford to keep.

Her name was Ann.

She is listed as Anna C. Trigiano in the 1940 US Census, though I don't know what the C stands for or when the final *a* was dropped from her first name. *Ann.* I say the name out loud. My own middle name.

She was the last of five children born in May 1928 to an Italian Catholic family in Worcester, Massachusetts, immigrants from the province of Foggia, known as the "granary" of Italy and famous for its watermelons and tomatoes. The records show that her mother died when she was three years old and she was raised by an eleven-year-old aunt in a family whose social situation was listed as "poor" by social services, a 1950s code for economic and social dysfunction. When I read these words, I pause, alert to the genesis of trouble-*mother died; raised by an eleven-year-old aunt; already in the system.* In one paragraph, the seeds of despair, the constraints of a future. Adversity often repeats itself in traumatized families, as if the child who becomes the adult remains locked in the peril of her childhood, tangled in its black shadow, unable to detach.

For years, researchers have acknowledged, even insisted, that problems in mothering were "the most dramatic for those who'd lost a same-sex parent at an early age." Here, a trope of inevitability, a helplessness that cuts like glass. Unmothered. Untethered. Unprepared. Where's the gleam in that? Maybe her mother's early death explains why she felt "so unloved" in childhood, why she described herself to the caseworker as developing "a shy, inferiority complex with a defeatist attitude," why she became such an erratic mother, both detached and overly involved, trapped in her own twisted loyalties.

Maybe not being mothered left her empty. Maybe desire became demolition. Maybe it made her terribly hungry, reckless for any kind of love . . .

But I don't finish that sentence. I look out my window, but there's only inky darkness, the air blue with cold.

Ann.

She left school and her father's house after the ninth grade—she must have been fifteen or sixteen years of age—"because of my father," she confessed to the caseworker. After I read that sentence, I am indignant. I can't help but blame *him*: a shiftless worker, a gravedigger, a lay-about, the files note—his stubby fingers reaching for a cigarette, a beer—and who knows, maybe a domestic brute and an abuser of girls? Regardless, her home was known to social services as a place of "little security," where she felt "unloved" in an unsettled, shifting immigrant family dominated by men. At sixteen, she went to work in a factory, perhaps the Cudahy Packing Company, an Irish meatpacking plant on Franklin Street with its stench of offal and blood, sweat, and chemicals. Though I can't know exactly what hardships or abuse she attributed to her father, I sense her urgent need to escape, the desire to slip from the old life into a new world. Just as her son will do many years later.

And this is the way I see her: a halo of smoke circling her as she stands in sturdy brown shoes just outside the factory gates at 6:58 a.m., a last puff of her cig before the grind begins. It's the summer of 1944, the whole world at war, puckered and burning, refugees crowding the roads of Europe, dreaming of cabbage, of black bread slathered with butter, the cloying stench of carcasses wafting in the breeze. And yet here in America with its energy and bustle, its humming factories, there are jobs for women—even for girls like her—with so many of the men overseas, the Allies preparing to enter Rome just as she, an Italian American girl, steps through the factory door into hot, dusty air.

A year later, I lose her. She's vanished from social service records. I have no idea what happened to her right after the war. Did she stay in touch with her sister, with the aunt who raised her? Was she laid off from the factory once the veterans returned, men needing and deserving good jobs, their welfare a national priority? Is that why she began waitressing, surviving on tips, on her feet all day, carrying trays, chatting up the customers—old men with yellow teeth and bored smiles; married men who demanded their coffee *hot*—prepping for the next day, the steady, methodical folding of napkins, the clinking of silverware, the stacking of cups, a little more knowing now at seventeen or eighteen or nineteen? She's petite but voluptuous, a wary girl but quick with words—this last I sleuthed from my husband's comments—and an easy laugh. You can see I'm casting about; there's nothing concrete for me to know of her life—except that she was a waitress—until 1947 when she discovers her pregnancy, a fact she can't seem to reveal to the man she's fallen in love with and been dating for two years. The caseworker writes:

> Mother (A) talked freely about putative father and with a great deal of feeling. She said she had known him for over two years and he was a toolmaker, attending_____Institute during that time. A better job possibility had required him to leave the area shortly before she knew she was pregnant. She said she had heard from him in June (four months before the baby's birth), but at that time, she lost the purse containing the letter and she was not able to write to him.

When I read that last sentence, I blush. It has the feel of a nineteenth-century novel, the tragic heroine defeated by the most mundane of complications: a lost purse. Oh, dear! And yet this is the middle of the twentieth century and that lost purse, I suspect, is simply a face-saving excuse, an apt metaphor for so much more: the end of a relationship that once carried the potential for emotional and financial salvation. There's something so guileless about the comment, so vulnerable to easy critique that I imagine her glancing furtively away from the caseworker, embarrassed and uncertain if she's disguised the true state of things: she is alone and pregnant and abandoned by her boyfriend. The caseworker's notes continue:

She fully expects that he will soon be back in Worcester, and at that time, she will inform him about the baby. It was apparent to Worker that she is hopeful that marriage to [the baby's] father will ensue.

And what, I think cynically, could possibly go wrong with such a plan?

"I never knew who my father was," David said casually one evening on a road trip to Alabama to visit my mother. Driving on Interstate 55, through the piney woods of Mississippi, I pretended no surprise, squinting at the highway while he tried to find the next exit on the map.

"Your mother didn't tell you *anything* about him, not even his name?"

"Nope. She refused."

"She didn't say what she liked about him or why they didn't marry?"

"Nothing. Not one word."

"That seems odd. I wonder why."

He didn't answer. "Exit thirty-four," he said. "About four-and-a-half miles."

Now I believe she may have been one of those women who couldn't bear the loss, the betrayal, all hopes dashed, the man denying or simply rejecting the fact of a child. But perhaps she began to hate him too, to see that love can be duplicitous and slippery, can strangle the dignity of a woman while letting the man slip entirely free. I hope so. I hope anger singed her respect for him, but it's just as possible all the anguish turned inward, dulling and eroding the self, sneaking into her thoughts each morning to ambush her self-esteem. Perhaps she vowed never to mention his name, to keep him a private punishment and pleasure, a lifetime penance, the knowledge of his rejection like teeth sunk into her neck.

But she had the baby. Oh, yes! His baby. She had a part of him to love and delight in if not the man himself. He couldn't take that from her. Nobody could.

But of course that too turned out to be a lie.

"I never knew why I was put in foster care so early," David said to me one night, several months after he'd read the foster care files. We were sitting across the table from each other, having just finished dinner, our napkins crumpled, our plates not yet scraped.

"Honey, your mother didn't have anyone to keep you while she worked and she didn't make enough money as a waitress to hire someone to watch you." I tried to smooth out my napkin, my hands needing something to do. "The truth is," I said simply, "she couldn't keep you because she was poor." That's the real reason. Poor and alone. No family. No husband. No one to step in and help. Nobody to care. "After you were born, she stayed at the Girls' Welfare Society for six weeks, the file says, but I'm sure she could only stay for a certain amount of time."

He looked surprised. "But wasn't there welfare—"

"No, they didn't have welfare for unmarried mothers in 1948, you know. Only for widows. They didn't have daycare either, at least not what we think of as daycare, though I think there was some childcare in New York and Philadelphia after the war. But not in Massachusetts." Back then, it was all sharp corners and straight edges, no room for ambivalence or surprise.

David stared at me, uncertain. "I thought I was *taken* from her. I thought, you know, there must have been something *wrong* with her."

> It was apparent to Worker how very proud the Mother was of her child and how much feeling she had for him. Mother evidenced sheer delight in her intention of notifying all her friends and family about D [the baby].

I think of the articles I've read, how middle-class unwed mothers in the 1940s and 1950s were so degraded by illegitimacy and so shamed by their families that they were strongly advised to give up their children for adoption while lower-class mothers more often kept their babies. And yet, in postwar America, even for poor girls like Ann, marriage was still the prize, the only rescue. She might as well have been living in Jane Austen's England with Lady Catherine de Bourgh sniffing her body, pronouncing everything about her unworthy and inappropriate, while Mrs. Bennett fussed frantically to get her girls wed. And just as in Austen's time, the word *bastard* rang out a curse, "shame, shame, shame."

Bastard or no, when the Worker suggested her baby might be a hindrance "in terms of matrimonial possibilities," the "Mother was quick to voice her feeling that she would like to tell the whole world about the baby and that she would under no circumstances keep him a secret."

And in this moment, I like her very much. True, she must place her baby in foster care before he's three months of age, but during the first seven months of care, so the files note, she visited him four nights a week after work and took him to her brother's home for Christmas and his birthday. I imagine she thought she could manage, could make a go of it, sharing the baby with another woman.

But then suddenly the child's placement went to hell, the foster home was closed down for "unfavorable conditions," the baby moved, and Ann's visits in the new foster home were cut to once a week, her mind ragged with worry.

Because I'm writing this and because I can, I decide to give Ann a happy moment, an hour of delight playing with her one-and-a-half-year-old son. He's pushing a shiny red fire truck across the floor, a toy she's just bought him, though it will mean she'll have to scrimp on laundry soap and stockings. But as he bends down to a crawling position and runs the toy back and forth on her old wood floors, making *rrrrrhhhh-rrrrrhhh* sounds with his scrunched lips and saying, "Mommy, Mommy, look," she can't imagine why anyone would give a fig about new stockings. His hair sticks up in a ruff, his pants are a bit too long, but he's so gloriously occupied with the thick rubber wheels and the white plastic ladder that raises and lowers she forgets that very soon she'll have to take him back. Back to his foster home, back to sleeping in the hallway in a house where the older boy has taught him to sing out, "Bad boy! Bad boy!" with such glee he too thinks it's funny.

Each time my husband comes downstairs to get more coffee, I want to put this writing away. What the hell am I doing? I feel as though I'm being subversive, appropriating what's not mine, rewriting the story of his mother, making it neater, giving it boundaries, tampering with it instead of merely attending to the facts: she got pregnant, she gave birth, she put him in foster care, she reclaimed him seven and a half years later. I listen as he turns on the water in the sink. I hear the refrigerator door open, then the swish of it closing. I hear the hiss and rumble of his coffee brewing, my hands paused, waiting. And then, just like that, he's gone back to his study, but I remain uncertain, wavering, not sure how to continue. Ann is elusive. A quicksilver presence. I can't see her.

I can't know her. She was no saint. Of course, I'm making her up, embodying her, giving her purpose and consequence created out of the caseworkers' commentary and my own slender thoughts. But more than that, I'm shifting allegiance, allowing her to claim my sympathies. By giving her the benefit of the doubt, I've pushed past my husband's resentment, allowing the context of shadows and sociology, a feminist rebirth, a right to a voice. Sort of. But why does this need to be done? No one has asked me to consider her as anything but an impoverished, conflicted mother who never got her act together. No one is demanding a eulogy or a vindication. And yet, after reading the foster care files, I lay in bed one night, dizzy with all the information, all the uncertainty. I closed my eyes, letting my thoughts drift, my mind untethered, and what I saw was Ann sitting in the caseworker's office year after year in her sensible waitressing shoes, a woman unable to let her baby go, unable to rescue him. I sat up and reached for my notebook: *the girl in the woman, the woman in the girl.* She was the center of it all. And didn't she deserve a story, not just the tired old story of the "fallen woman" but a story with a little charity, a small pocket of hope to even out the class barbarism, the misogyny of the late 1940s and '50s?

I've no doubt that had she been born into the middle class instead of to the immigrant working class, she'd have had different opportunities— high school and maybe college, perhaps dancing and music, a room of her own and a closetful of clothes—and thus more choices, so many more ways to experience the world and perhaps so many more ways to fuck things up. "It's all about options," we say so casually today, the right to push against anonymity, to experience and value our difference, to thrust our thoughts into the air, saying *mine.*

And so every morning, I sit down to write about her. Every morning, I tell myself I should stick to the known, and yet the shadows beckon. What did she do with her private grief?

But perhaps I'm being romantic. Maybe she learned early to stifle the brooding, to get on with it, to avoid the mess of feelings, the push and heat of sorrow, enjoying instead her twenty-minute break from work with a piece of lemon meringue pie and a fresh cup of coffee. If I go this route, she's earnest and dutiful and repressed, a woman who accepts her lot, does her bit, and tries not to think too much beyond the present. After all, she grew up in an immigrant Catholic family in the 1930s and '40s, crowded with brothers and sisters and uncles and aunts, with little space for adventure or difference. "And don't forget the misogyny of the older Italian men," my husband reminded me the other day. "A father's perspective was to keep everything in line, and if that meant a little violence, some slapping about, well, who was to complain?" So maybe after the birth of the baby, she doesn't need a stern patriarch to keep her in line, someone whose fury boils and explodes. She's already transgressed. She's used. She's done. So why not enjoy the lemon meringue pie, her feet propped up on a chair, bare and plump in the warm afternoon sun.

Winter. Everything here in Iowa is either shrunken or dead—gone are the heart-shaped katsura leaves, the ivy, the geraniums, gone the red and pink impatiens, the lawn now khaki-brown or feathered white with frost, the trees mere sticks, branches rising upward and outward into skinnier and skinnier sticks. Only the fir trees blur silvery green in the late afternoon sun. When there is sun. But not today. Today the sky is empty, a gray swatch of color like lint or the inside of my purse, which is equally barren of money. "So much of possibility depends on economics," I told David last month in the midst of an argument about an IRA, and then more insistently, "Don't you know that to be financially independent is sometimes the defining moment in a woman's life? This isn't superstition or myth."

If I follow that lead, I see that David's mother *agreed to pay $6/week to Family Services for his board in foster care out of a salary of $32/week*. Mmmh. My shoulders tighten at that exasperating figure: a $128/month salary from a factory in Massachusetts in 1948 (the average monthly wage for a male worker in 1948 was $216.56). Simultaneously, I remember my mother's complaints about her monthly salary of $500 as a high-school biology teacher in Alabama in 1951. The comparison isn't merely the $372 difference in pay, but the fact that my mother's check was a secondary income added to my father's thriving medical practice. And yet, despite that reality, the whole of it stinks. Economic oppression *is* the dreary ballad of female history: for David's mother and my mother the world will not bend.

For three months, the files note that Ann dutifully pays $6 a week, but then *her salary is knocked back to $25 a week* and if she pays $6 for the baby's board, she has only $1 left to cover the cost of food and clothing and other essentials. And always something backfires: she hurts her back and must have osteopathic treatment for a chronic injury, losing four days of work; she leaves the meatpacking plant, goes to work at the Spanish Grille as a waitress, but quits this job to work at a girdle factory; when she's laid off, it takes two months before she finds a position at a hat company where she works as an inspector. The caseworker writes, *She looks very tired and admits that she does not eat properly, smokes usually too much.* Inevitably, she's asked again to think about adoption—it's been two years since her child entered foster care, meant only to be a temporary solution. After all, she can't make the payments and she's without a plan. Be practical, I imagine the caseworker saying, observing her, noting the pallor of her skin, the dark circles shadowing her eyes. She's thinner, her dresses beginning to sag, her hair needing a trim. The worker prods her, leans closer. "My dear, you need to think about the security of your child," but still, Ann shakes her head, telling the caseworker she just can't see her way to it, to letting him go. She promises she'll make a plan, but several weeks later she's hospitalized for neuritis in both legs.

She is twenty-three.

Let's say she finds a way to accept this life, to survive her frequent disruptions in employment and the child's transfer from home to home. Let's say she understands that if she can't live with her boy, she can at least visit him, hold and cuddle him, feed him and change him, make peek-a-boo eyes at him. I imagine she knows how to make friends with foster mothers, women not so different from her except that they're married and with husbands whose labor doesn't quite make ends meet. She understands this. She understands crowded bedrooms, three children to a room, one bathroom, thin towels, lines of diapers drying on the line, chipped bowls, dusty curtains, a pretty blue vase nudged high up on a shelf, out of reach. But after several years, she gets careless, forgetting that she's at the mercy of another woman, forgetting that her presence in the foster mother's house requires being attentive, pleasing, never lingering, always asking permission and showing gratitude for the favor of seeing her baby, now a toddler of two, and then three. It's not that she does something outrageous or stupid. It begins with her being late for the appointment to see him, not getting the ride she expected and having to rush, now two hours late and earning a frown of disapproval from

471

the foster mother who stands in the doorway. She knows she should spend five minutes apologizing and reprimanding herself before she crosses the threshold, insisting this is an aberration and then stay only an hour, leaving at the proposed time. But when she sees her son, his cheek a sweep of eczema, his right arm in a sling because he fell out of bed and broke his collarbone, his mouth crusted with old milk, she forgets all about the other woman. It's as if the foster mother vanishes as she sweeps him up, "How's my boy?" she whispers, and then hours later, it's past dark when she walks out the front door.

> Worker feels that foster mother is somewhat jealous of Mother's love for D and that Mother, in turn, is jealous of foster mother for having daily care of the baby.

How did it begin to go so wrong?

I wonder if this is the moment Ann realizes she's been naïve, walking through each day with her eyes half closed, seeing only what she's wanted to see: obliging women offering her son to her for a few hours every week. Then again, her life isn't the ordinary world of getting up and taking the bus to work, having a smoke break and chatting with girl-friends, flirting with the cook, paying rent and utilities, buying groceries and cigarettes, but a darker, restless world, an uncivilized place of men deserting and fathers berating and caseworkers always asking *when, when, when will you be able to make a plan for your son* as if she could simply sit outside in the evening and wish upon a star.

A plan is what you do if you've finished high school or maybe a year or two of college, had training in bookkeeping and dictation or plied some special talent: illustrating or drawing or hat design or sewing. To her, a plan means working extra hours at the Spanish Grille and trying to save a bit before the next layoff, the next bout of neuritis or bronchitis.

How is she supposed to make the unlikely probable?

And yet, somehow she does make a plan. It takes several years, but by scrimping and flirting—everything seems to require a bit of badness—she's able to rent seven rooms in a rundown three-decker, fix them up with repairs, a coat of paint, and some cheap leased furniture and rent out rooms to boarders. It's the first thing she's ever managed and to her surprise, it works. She talks easily to carpenters, fixes them

472

coffee, takes out icy lemonade on a sweltering day, handing a glass up to a man on a ladder who's resetting the window, where she's aware that, for a moment, he's turned his attention to her, barefoot in blue shorts and a knit top, her eyes moist from cutting onions for the potato salad, her thick auburn hair pulled up, exposing her pale, smooth neck. Sometimes they stay later, do a bit of extra work, unclogging a drain, repairing a soffit, replacing a rotting step, chatting with her, and not charging her a penny.

At night, she feels the warmth of a man, the rustle of bedding, and in the dark, she smiles. She'll get her boy back. She will.

But even with this entrepreneurial success, she can't get her son back. Most of her boarders are old men on pensions, their payment enough to cover the rent and utilities and furniture payment, but she still has to work. It turns out that getting him back also requires a husband. She isn't opposed to the idea. For a little while, during that spring when the elm trees are dressed out in green, when lilacs and daffodils bloom, there is a softness that surprises her, like a little cushion of air surrounding her, protecting her. Her son is safe and growing, a sweet but highstrung, mischievous boy who lives a 45-minute bus ride away in a small town, almost a village, where he tramps down the hill to first grade, kicking rocks and jumping puddles and printing his name in big round letters. *[He] identifies Mother to the foster mother as his "best girl,"* which makes her grin. Sometimes he playfully calls her Ma when she picks him up for the one overnight visit a month and refers to his foster mother as Aunt Adeline, and yet now he seems quite happy to return to his foster family after spending a night with her, throwing her a kiss even as he runs to eat Aunt Adeline's chicken and dumplings. Though at first the ease of his leaving stuns her, this new cloud of possibility steadies her.

A house and a husband. It isn't exactly that she makes a plan, only that there is someone already there, one of the carpenters, a big, strapping Scotsman who's lingered more than the others, taking a little longer than necessary to sand a door. This, she was to understand, had been an odd job for him, something to tide him over while he waited for a construction job opening up in the summer. And yet, when she came home from her waitressing job, hot and sweaty, her hair pulled up, a few auburn strands loosed and tangled, tucked inside her collar, he didn't seem to mind being there, would often stay for a beer. Then more.

Now the construction job's come through and he's drinking, blowing money on Friday and Saturday nights, but always back to work on

473

Monday. It's a way of life. Familiar. Familial. Favorable perhaps to having no one. When her son comes to visit, the man plays with the boy, laughs, and lets him sit on his big, wide lap. And hasn't she seen this man, Soup, catch a green fly in his bare hands and drop it casually out the window, then glance up at her and sheepishly smile?

How can she know—can any woman know?—that the very thing that is her salvation will also be her undoing? How can she know that though the husband will adopt the boy, he'll come to resent him and resent her for having him, will punish the boy for being such a pain in the ass without even a drop of his blood? How can she know he'll beat him, step on his hands with his construction boots, mock him, berate him, make him stand naked in a chalked circle for punishment? "I gave the kid a name, for shit's sake," he'll yell at her years later, as if he's the one who's been played for a sucker.

This man, who once seemed so easygoing, so playful, eating a huge forkful of birthday cake, thick with frosting, while holding her boy in his lap, will, in three years, become an alcoholic, crashing again and again into Bridgewater State Hospital's detox unit, while she'll be passive and hopeful, then devious and resentful, and finally depressed.

And yet, in the summer of 1956, she's in the three-decker with its ruffled curtains, its rented sofa, its secondhand TV. She's attained the impossible: a husband, a reclaimed son, another on the way, even as the air of possibility now gusts past her, skittering down the block while she hovers in the doorway, exhausted, blinking, uncertain just how it is that she failed. For years, when her son looks at her, he seems hopeful and loving, but by age twelve, he's wary, then angry, and finally, at sixteen, he refuses to look at her at all.

"My best girl," she murmurs one night, staring into his empty room.

He's gone, his closet stripped of clothes and books and guitar strings and dirty socks. She stares at the bare mattress, the stripped sheets, aware of how time folds in on itself, and yet she doesn't cry as she pulls closed the door.

Full circle.

Today, the sun's come out after days of rain. I leave the computer and step out onto my deck in Iowa City, the air fresh and clean, the sun warming my face. OK, OK, I breathe with relief, glad to feel nothing but this. Pleasure. The leaves just budding on the trees, the daffodils and tulips in bloom. When I go back to writing, I wonder if I've shifted the balance, made the intolerable tolerable, brushed a bit of color onto the cheeks of a sordid story. The truth is, I think I've only made myself feel better.

"I believe I should be able to forgive my mother," David said one evening while we were making a snack in the kitchen, "because now I know from the files that she loved me. And she really tried." He looked both sad and relieved at the thought.

"She did," I agreed. And though I've been trying to re-see her, I wasn't sure that I forgave her either. After working so hard to reclaim him, she seemed unable to protect him, to make him feel wanted and worthy and necessary to the world. Once she'd pulled it all together, everything just went to hell.

"Anyway, it's good that I got the foster care files. After reading them I didn't feel so much like a victim." He washed the French press to make his evening coffee and began measuring out the dark roast. "And I didn't hate her anymore, because they let me see a different part of her." He glanced at me. "So, I'm just saying I'm glad you helped, glad—" but he didn't finish. Maybe he couldn't.

"Me too." I got out rice crackers and almond butter and handed him a plate.

After he poured the hot water into the press, he waited, staring at the brewing coffee as if meditating. When he looked up, he gave me a rueful smile. "Family." He shook his head. "It's all Bosch and Brueghel."

Delighted, I laughed. At the moment it seemed true.

But I also think of his mother on the Greyhound bus riding out of Worcester on a Saturday or Sunday to see her seven-year-old son at his foster home in Sturbridge, watching the city's shoe factories with their rising plumes of smoke give way to the countryside, goldenrod and blue-bells blooming on the side of the road, grazing cows in the distance, fat trees crowding the far end of a pasture. What must she be thinking, sitting alone on that bus for thirty-five minutes, going to see a child she hasn't put to bed or fed or talked to in three weeks? She's never seen him catch grasshoppers, do his arithmetic homework, or read his first series of books at a desk, never taken him to the dentist or to buy shoes. And yet, when she's there with him, for two hours or four hours or sometimes an overnight visit, I like to imagine that the uncertainty of her choices lifts and for that little bit of time, she's someone else, someone better. I like to think that she holds onto this thought, slippery as it is, her face softened, her shoulders eased, the possibility of connection there only because she's kept it alive.

"I'm glad," I imagine her whispering to him, summing up her plight. "I'm glad and I'm sorry." Five honest words.

Nominated by Rosellen Brown

DANTE ON BROADWAY

by HAL CROWTHER

from NARRATIVE

One of New York City's most neglected historical landmarks is a tiny park almost directly across Columbus Avenue from Lincoln Center, the cultural mecca where multitudes of New Yorkers satisfy their passions for opera, dance, theater, jazz, and classical music. Situated at Sixty-Third Street where Broadway crosses Columbus and bends to the east, the park is a perfect triangle that measures one-seventh of an acre of Manhattan's precious real estate. Though I lived in the city for more than a decade, attended many Lincoln Center performances, and once rented an apartment just thirty blocks up Broadway—though I've visited Manhattan hundreds of times since I moved to the provinces— I never noticed the park or the statue that graces it until last spring. How many times had I passed it in a taxicab, passed deep beneath it in a subway car, or even walked within sight of it, never registering that tall figure on the pedestal, standing there among the trees?

New York City guidebooks describe the park as an overlooked, all-but-forgotten curiosity, and mention the trees that obscure the statue with their branches, even when you're almost in its shadow. Even if you were staying at the Empire Hotel, with its front entrance a few yards across Sixty-Third Street from the park, you might miss it if you were in a hurry. I had never stayed at the Empire before this visit in May; since I was in no hurry one morning, I sat down at a little iron table at the edge of the park with my Starbucks coffee and the *New York Times*— and looked up.

Which heroes of the past do we expect to see honored by urban statues? In the South, mostly generals. Everywhere, politicians, saints, philanthropists, famous athletes. I couldn't see the statue's head, up there among the spring leaves, but the larger-than-life-size (nine and a half feet, actually) male figure was dressed in an outfit that looked nothing like a military uniform, more like an academic gown or a priest's cassock that covered the big fellow down to his shoes. A medieval aristocrat's everyday street wear, as it turned out, specifically Italian, Florentine, thirteenth century. If I had been sitting on the other side of the little park, I would have seen its name on a large iron sign: Dante Park.

Dante Alighieri. I wouldn't have been more surprised if I'd found a statue of Joan Rivers. Dante, prince of poets, author of *The Divine Comedy*, first bright beacon of the Italian Renaissance that ended Europe's Dark Ages. How did his graven image come to its perch above Broadway, and how long has it been staring north past Lincoln Center?

Since 1921, I discovered, since decades before Lincoln Center was developed, since a time when many of New York's cabs were still drawn by horses. For nearly a century Dante's statue has struck its attitude of lonely contemplation above one of the city's busiest thoroughfares. Dante Park was part of the generous vision of one remarkable immigrant, Carlo Barsotti (1850–1927), banker and publisher of the Italian-language newspaper *Il Progreso Italo-Americano*. Barsotti's fund-raising talent and passion for his native Italy were largely responsible for Dante and for statues of at least three other Italian heroes—Columbus, Garibaldi, and the composer Giuseppe Verdi—that still stand watch in Manhattan today. A much larger statue of the poet—one account says it was fifty-nine feet tall—was commissioned by Barsotti from the same sculptor, Ettore Ximenes, and delivered in 1915. But the city fathers rejected it as too grandiose, and it was last seen gathering cobwebs in a warehouse in Hoboken, New Jersey.

I had barely made Dante's acquaintance and noted that his head, way up there in the branches, wore a crown of laurels, when my attention was deflected to a white panel truck that had stopped for a red light at Sixty-Third Street. In very large letters on its side panel, legible from a block away, was the name and nature of the owner's business:

PRO SHRED
Information Destruction at Your Door
Onsite Paper and Hard Drive Destruction

I'm serious. Look up Pro Shred online. Call me a slave to irony, a pushover for symbolism—I'm a relic of college English departments and

478

graduate schools before Big Theory reared its ugly head. But with peripheral vision I could actually see Dante and the truck in the same visual frame, poet on the left, Pro Shred on the right, an ironic juxta-position so jarring I could have spit up my coffee. Representing the thirteenth century, Dante, father of the modern Italian language, pro-genitor of the Renaissance, disciple of Aristotle, a great poet whose sa-cred mission was to preserve the wisdom and literature of the ancient Greeks and Romans and protect their precious, fragile links to his own time and culture. Representing the twenty-first century, *Information Destruction at Your Door.*

Irony doesn't hit us much harder than that. I like to think that a lot of people, if they had shared my vision at that moment, would have been as blindsided as I was. Realistically I know that 95 percent of the people who pass through Dante Park have never heard of the poet ("Dante? A wide receiver for the Browns?") and would have no negative response to a Pro Shred truck. And that, of course, is a huge part of the problem.

Dante and the great Italian writers who immediately followed him—Boccaccio, Petrarch—were devoted above all to continuity, the spinal cord of civilization. They were committed to saving and illuminating everything they judged profound, essential, and eloquent among the contributions of previous generations and previous civilizations. *Illumi-nation* is the key word, the password of the Renaissance—shedding light. Setting aside the actual physical destruction of printed and digi-tal information, the Pro Shred Final Solution, isn't it clear that the twenty-first century, awash and adrift in technology, is veering in the opposite direction? Whose hand is on the dimmer switch, who benefits when we obscure, neglect, and trivialize the accumulated knowledge of the past and its printed artifacts?

In America's social-media century, with an illiterate Twitter-addicted liar steering the ship of state, even yesterday—the past twenty-four hours and their printed, taped, and digitalized record—is routinely erased, distorted, denied. There are idiots afoot who must start every day like the first day of creation, as empty of memory as Adam waking up in the Garden of Eden. In *The Divine Comedy*, Dante locates the shade of Aristotle, his philosophical idol, in hell—he was a pagan, sorry—but honors him with the august title "Master of those who know." What can we make of a country where the flow of information is domi-nated by the "Master of those who know nothing"?

"As a society, we have somehow fallen into a collective amnesia in thinking that it doesn't matter when the highest officeholder in the land

479

doesn't tell the truth," wrote Mark Sanford, the Republican congressman from South Carolina who lost his reelection primary because he refused to kiss the stumpy ring finger of Donald Trump. The philosopher Hannah Arendt, a Jew who fled Nazi Germany after she was jailed by the Gestapo, wrote about the degradation of language and information in a fascist society: "In an everchanging, incomprehensible world the masses had reached the point where they would, at the same time, believe everything and nothing, think that everything was possible and that nothing was true."

The political implications of cultural amnesia are frightening enough. We elected a president who dismisses every unwelcome fact as "fake news" and tells his supporters, "What you're seeing and what you're reading is not what's happening." He's not merely implying, he's declaring unequivocally that any information he hasn't supplied or sanctioned is worthless. And if you buy that, you might enjoy making Russia, Turkey, Syria, or the Philippines your homeland. You have no business in the United States, where a free and obstreperous press is a priceless legacy and our only real insurance against tyranny.

But the political crisis may not be the most depressing aspect of America's decline. Electoral politics can turn on a dime, as we learned in 2016. There may yet be someone sane and competent at the wheel before chaos engulfs us. Maybe even someone honest. What disturbs me even more is my sense of a culture turning away from language, from clarity, from complexity, from the liberal arts and our best educational traditions. From illumination in every form. The false populism that has empowered the Republican Party is anchored unashamedly in anti-intellectual prejudice, in rejecting an "elite" identified with erudition and expertise. The same spirit dominates social media, with their legions of furious, flesh-eating "trolls" and volcanoes of uninformed and misinformed opinion. The novelist Jonathan Franzen expressed his frustration in a recent interview:

"The internet is all about destroying the elite, destroying the gatekeepers. The people know best. You take that to its conclusion, and you get Donald Trump: 'What do these Washington insiders know? What does the elite know? What do papers like the *New York Times* know? Listen, the people know what's right.'"

It's no rhetorical flourish to assert that this all-American brand of "populism" privileges, sanctifies, and enthrones Ignorance. It disrespects education, creativity, originality, and taste; it's a poisonous influence on the arts and on all our cultural artifacts. Dante's living descendants, serious American writers like Franzen whose books can no longer compete with James Patterson's, are beginning to articulate their distress. Richard Russo has written that a novel like his *Empire Falls* (2001) published today "would have to be set in a tribal America that has stopped listening, that may have little interest in a novelist's musings." And consider America's once-illustrious film industry, now devoting most of its energies and financial resources to grindingly stupid superhero sequels—squads of embarrassed actors in tights and belted underpants, playing airborne mutants who vanquish various avatars of Doctor Evil. I've been told that several important "intellectuals" are addicted to Marvel Comics superheroes, and I'll regard that as the intellectual equivalent of the bubonic plague until someone can explain it for me.

In the annals of irony, my epiphany in Dante Park is a gift that keeps on giving.

Dante and his contemporaries had ample darkness to deal with—endless local wars and factional bloodshed, an entrenched Catholic Church with its inquisitors burning heretics and its religious orders that had monopolized and censored intellectual activity for centuries. Not to mention a real bubonic plague, the Black Death that killed half the people in Europe a few years after Dante's death. But there's no question that they believed, from the thirteenth century forward, that they were emerging from the Dark Ages and generating light for a brighter day to come. For artists and scholars who laboriously copied ancient manuscripts and wrote millions of words with quill and ink in longhand, the concept of "information destruction" would have seemed as bizarre as gender reassignment or animal rights. At the time Dante died, the Republic of Florence was supporting six elementary schools and four high schools with more than ten thousand students. The high schools taught literature and philosophy, and it's even recorded that a few of their students were girls.

Seven centuries later in America, a republic with infinitely more wealth and a much higher technical rate of literacy, only the most stubborn optimist could overlook the intellectual stagnation and cultural dry rot that make another Dark Age seem possible, if not imminent. Notable journalists, experiencing scorn and bewilderment, are writing books with titles like *The Death of Truth*.

In a benighted age, Dante was one of the first to understand that language is the essential battleground of civilization. A fluent Latinist, he wrote his greatest poetry in the Tuscan vernacular to expand the reach and influence of "those who know." His scholarly Latin treatise *De vulgari eloquentia* is a masterwork of modern philology, defending the vernacular and probing the nature, origins, and purpose of language. An Italian American, the novelist Don DeLillo, was our first prominent writer to sound an alarm about the rapid degradation of public language and its dire consequences. In *White Noise* (1985), he bemoans an American landscape of "abandoned meanings." The central conflict in another DeLillo novel, *The Names* (1982), is between characters who represent the holy and the profane uses of language—as a means of opening up this bright world we've been gifted, or as a means to control it. A character in *The Names* says, "Language is the River of God."

That's a sweet theology few subscribe to in the consumer society where American English is beaten mercilessly from dawn to dusk, where cell phone texts and things called "tweets" are the new lingua franca, where "information destruction" is a respectable vocation. If language is civilization's critical battleground, the philistines and cynics, the inarticulate and proud of it like the president, have been winning many skirmishes—and perhaps some major battles—against the forces of light. Who can say whether the tide of battle is reversible? When Dante and Boccaccio struggled against an uncooperative Church to expand the community of "those who know," could they have comprehended a community, numbered in the tens of millions, who don't know, don't wish to know, and don't wish to hear from those who do? What sort of people will be walking by the poet's statue, if it's still standing there on Broadway, fifty years from today?

Nominated by Narrative

INFIDELS

fiction by JOANNA SCOTT

from CONJUNCTIONS

It was a damp November afternoon in Paris in 1887 when the man who would be identified in the book only as "C" suffered the first symptoms of the affliction that would make him noteworthy. He had risen from his nap and settled comfortably into his armchair by the window overlooking the Place des Vosges. Droplets from the thick fog ran like tears down the exterior of the glass. A wood fire crackled and filled the room with its soothing fragrance.[1]

Long married but with no heirs, recently retired from a position as director of a champagne export business, C did not lack for friends. He and his wife dined out most evenings, and he was an active member of the Société de Géographie. But C also guarded his solitude and spent most of his afternoons alone in his library. He was well educated and fluent in several languages. He longed to author something of his own but didn't know how to begin. He was secretly critical of contemporary men of letters and blamed novelists, especially, for pandering to the public and emptying their work of useful information. The worst of them, in his opinion, was Victor Hugo, who used to live in an apartment across the square. C had read a couple of novels and a book of verse by his former neighbor. He wasn't inclined to read more. He wasn't at all curious. What was there to be curious about if there was nothing to learn?

---

1. I came across the story of C when I was browsing at a used bookstore in Ithaca. I read the case history while standing in the aisle. Stupidly, I left without purchasing the book. When I returned for it later, the book was gone. I don't recall the title. C's story, however, left an indelible impression in my mind.

He had read enough to reach the verdict that the whole of Hugo's oeuvre was overrated.

In general, he preferred reading biographies and military histories. On this particular day in 1887, we find him reading a volume he'd purchased for a few francs from a bookseller near the Pont Marie. It was an English edition about the Crusades, and C was reading with interest about the disorder in the ranks of the early Christian pilgrims.[2]

". . . The vulgar, both the great and small, were taught to believe every wonder, of lands flowing with milk and honey," he read.

". . . Their ignorance of the country, or war, and discipline, exposed them to every snare," he read.

". . . A pyramid of bones informed their companions of the place of their defeat," he read, and he continued to read the sentence stating that "three hundred thousand perished before a single city was rescued from the"—

And then he stopped, or was stopped, as if he had run with his eyes closed into a brick wall. His eyes were wide-open, but he couldn't read the word that followed in the sentence. The word was *infidels*. It should have been a familiar word to C even if he hadn't been entirely fluent in English, since it was nearly identical in French: *infidèles*. He knew the word in English just as he knew it in French. He knew it in Latin and Spanish. Really, it should have been easy enough for C to comprehend. Yet, to his dismay, the word was utterly unintelligible. His eyes processed the letters in their correct order. His brain received the information in the usual fashion. He inhaled, and his oxygenated blood flowed briskly. All organs were seemingly in working order, and C was very much awake, utterly sober and self-aware, but the eight letters of that English word were as devoid of meaning as if he had never learned to read.

It's true that many of us have experienced the odd momentary sensation when a simple word is suddenly unrecognizable. Scientists call this phenomenon "semantic satiation" and explain it as a result of overuse of a specific neural pattern. They hypothesize that intense repetition of a specific word creates a reactive inhibition, slowing the neural activity associated with the meaning of that word. We can read the word

---

2. The book C was reading consisted of late chapters extracted from Edward Gibbon's classic work and republished in a pocket edition titled simply *The Crusades*. I have checked the quotes for accuracy.

want, for instance, without difficulty. But reading it over and over interferes with comprehension: *want want want want want want want want want want want want want want want.*[3]

This, however, was not what C experienced that day in 1887. He didn't perceive the word as a familiar one that he'd once known. The letters were so unrecognizable that *infidel* wasn't even a word to him. It was a solid blankness, a splotch of spilled ink, an absolute nothing.

He removed his spectacles, rubbed them with his handkerchief, and returned them to his face. The one printed word he didn't recognize became two, and two seeped into a sentence. He squinted and shifted in his chair. He opened the window shade. He tried to reread the preceding paragraph. With relief, he experienced some recognition: he knew what *pyramid* signified, and *bones*, and *defeat*. Yes, he knew what each of those words meant, thank God. *Pyramid, bones, defeat.*

Awareness was painfully brief. *Py . . . ra . . . , bo . . . n . . . , defe . . . a . . .* It was as if the light within each letter went out one by one, until each word was dark.

With rising concern, he turned to words in his native language. He tried and failed to read the front page of the newspaper that lay open on his desk. The titles of the books on his shelves were unintelligible. He couldn't even read the name printed on his own stationery.

Naturally, he would go on to consult his doctor. His doctor would refer him to a specialist, who would study him with interest and publish his case history. That C retained his speaking fluency gave the scientific community much to ponder. If you had conversed with him, you wouldn't have seen signs of his impairment, which affected only his perception of printed words. In other ways, he lived a normal life.

For our purposes, however, it is enough to know that once C fully lost his ability to read, he never recovered it. I won't even bother telling you about his first appointment with his doctor. What concerns us here is

---

3. One study has gone so far as to suggest that the recent dramatic uptick in this phenomenon is due to the simplification of writing necessitated by mobile devices. Smaller screens demand a smaller vocabulary, increasing both our exposure to a smaller number of words and the concurrent increase in semantic satiation. See Leonardo, T.; Pissoralüpa, S.; Merendeskewski, J. M. 2018. Neurosemantic Frequency Patterning in ERP DHA Measured Outcomes. *The Journal of Neuromorphological Studies.* 1752(2-3):132-145.

C's adventure that day after he decided that all he needed was a good, brisk walk around the square to clear his confused mind.

Back in 1981, when I was a student studying in Paris, I used to make my way to the Place des Vosges to get away from the bustle of the city. I remember how the streams of clear water gushed from the mouths of stone lions in the central fountain, and the groomed lawns bordered by metal wickets looked as perfect as if they'd been painted green. Linden trees grew in stately rows. An artificial hush seemed to mute the noise of traffic on the adjacent streets, as if a volume dial had been adjusted.

It was a warm spring that year, and I would sit on a bench and enjoy the sunlight on my face. One day, I fell into conversation with an old woman who was feeding crumbs to the pigeons. She saw my backpack and identified me as an American. She asked if I liked Paris. I said I liked it very much. She asked if I liked the Place des Vosges. I said I thought it was beautiful. Though the sky was clear, the woman wore a tan raincoat that was oversized on her small frame. Her cheeks had the deep creases of boots that had gone unworn for decades. She was eager to talk, and I was glad to have the chance to practice my French. When she asked, out of the blue, if I believed in ghosts, I said, "Oui, madame," just to play along.

And so it was from this old woman that I learned something about the bloody history of the Place des Vosges. Long ago, she explained to me as she tore off pinches of bread to toss to the birds, the large square was occupied by the Palais des Tournelles, named for numerous turrets that decorated its rim. It was here, in the courtyard of the palace, that Henri II was wounded in a tilting match with the Duke of Montgomery, whose spear splintered against the king's visor, sending shards through his eyes and into his brain. The king suffered for eleven days in painful agony before finally dying. In mourning, his wife, Catherine de' Medici, ordered the palace to be destroyed.

This is where a ghost enters the story: the old woman claimed the Place des Vosges was haunted by Henri II. I asked her whether she had ever seen the king herself. *"Bien sûr!"* she said. It was impossible to predict when he would make an appearance. Some said he came on the nights when Venus was closest to earth while others maintained that he could be seen during a lunar eclipse, or on the anni-

486

versary of his death, or birth, or marriage. He would appear in his armor suit walking slowly across the grass to the fountain. He would remove his helmet with his broken visor and dip his hands into the water being spit out by one of the stone lions. He would wash the blood from his face, then he would put his helmet back on and walk away.

The old woman was fourteen years old when she had first seen the king on her way home from a tavern where she worked sweeping the floors. She had seen him three times since then. With a theatrical grimace, she tried to convey how frightening he was to behold. When her lips peeled back, I saw that she was missing several upper molars.

I didn't bother to wait around to see if the ghost of Henri II would make his entrance that evening. It had become increasingly obvious to me that the woman was suffering from senility. I could only hope that she was receiving adequate care. As for me, though I appreciate a good ghost story, I thought I could tell the difference between fiction and fact—until I stumbled across the story of C.

My sense of C is that he was even more of a skeptic than yours truly. He must certainly have been aware of the square's history, but superstition made him impatient. And though he was a dutiful Catholic and went to confession once a week, he much preferred forms of knowledge that could be verified. When in doubt, he would always side with duplicable proof. As for human attempts to expose the secrets of mortality, he believed that the truth was visible in every corpse: you could see just by looking at a man without a heartbeat that death was the end of life. There was no world elsewhere. C was convinced that heaven and hell existed only as imagined places. His pragmatic mind had no room for phantoms.

The fog that had settled over the city of Paris the day C lost his ability to read was so dense, and the winter dusk had come so early, that he could barely make out the outlines of the tall buildings across the square. He felt the unnerving sensation of being lost, though he knew exactly where he was. He resisted the urge to grab the arm of a woman who was walking ahead of him along the gravel path. Feathers sticking up from the bulb of her hat shook in the swirling mist. C gasped, mistaking the feathers for a live bird. He took a few steps backward and would have stumbled, but luckily his hand found the iron handle of a bench. He lowered himself onto the seat. With a few deep breaths, he was able to calm his agitation.

The quiet of the square had a restorative effect, and he began to appreciate the effect of the fog on the scenery. It would have been fine weather for spectral illusions. C smiled at the thought. Of course he'd heard the silly stories about Henri II. He enjoyed the feeling of superiority that overcame him when he considered how susceptible other people were to superstition, how easily they would mistake a tree trunk, blurred by the heavy cloud, for the ghost of a dead king.

He tipped his head back and closed his eyes. Voices of passersby seemed to come from far away. He could almost fancy that he was at the seashore. He found himself remembering the sensation he'd loved so much when he was a young boy and let the gentle waves wash the sand over his toes.

A nearby cough had the startling effect of shattering glass. C blinked. That's when he noticed the man at the opposite end of the bench. He didn't know how long the man had been there—probably he had just arrived. He wore an old-fashioned sack suit with a tailcoat that was unbuttoned, revealing a plaid vest and the froth of a white ruffled shirt. His black cravat was tied in a bow and brushed against the rough curls of his white beard. He had a pencil out and was writing on a piece of paper. His expression had the fixed aspect of a statue and gave little indication of his thoughts. From C's perspective, there was an air of loneliness about the man, a perfuse, sad loneliness that kept him helplessly sealed off from the rest of humanity.

C tried not to stare. There was something familiar about the stranger; a moment of reflection brought clear identification as C recognized his former neighbor, Victor Hugo. Victor Hugo!

But that was impossible—Victor Hugo was dead. He had been dead for two years. C had been inconvenienced by the author's huge funeral procession in front of the Panthéon.

Oh, but it was him, there was no denying. Victor Hugo, buried in a tomb he shared with Zola and Dumas, was sitting beside C on an iron bench in the Place des Vosges. C was overtaken by a clarity of mind that came in stark contrast to the confusion he'd experienced earlier. He could no longer find meaning in printed words, but he could see reality for what it was.

Hugo brought the back of his hand to his mouth and coughed again. He was old and haggard, but his poor health couldn't stop him from scribbling on the paper. C felt a wave of pity for Hugo and wanted to reach out to him and tell him . . . what? What could he possibly say? He searched his memory for a passage from one of Hugo's verses. Instead, a scene from the famous early novel about the hunchback came to mind. He remembered the passage almost word for word. He remembered how Djali, the little pet goat of La Esmeralda, gets his horns tangled in the folds of a noblewoman's dress. C's heart ached as he thought of all the ugly, contemptuous aristocrats mocking La Esmeralda, calling her a witch and ordering her to make the goat perform a feat of magic.

C wasn't prone to sentimentality, but who could resist when the actors on the page were so vividly rendered? It occurred to him that he had judged Hugo's work too harshly through the years. His inclination to find faults had dominated his reading experience. He realized that in his urge to be critical, he had missed the sheer, absorbing pleasure of Hugo's books. Why, he had only to gaze at the sad, decrepit ghost beside him and realize that the stories he'd left behind would survive the eroding effects of time. Centuries would pass, and the books would continue to be read . . . though not by C, since C could no longer read.[4]

Awareness filled him with horror. He would never again be able to read about La Esmeralda disentangling Djali's horns from Madame Aloïse's dress! He didn't need a doctor to examine him to conclude with absolute certainty that his impairment was permanent. Printed words forever on would be impenetrable. If he wanted to read, he would have to be read to. It wasn't the same when the words were spoken aloud. No, it wasn't at all the same as digesting words visually and letting them transport him far from his armchair into a world illuminated by the light of his solitary consciousness. He had failed to fully savor the distinct satisfaction that comes with reading selflessly, propelled by selfless interest. All through his adult life, when his intellect was at its sharpest, he had positioned himself in competition with the

---

4. C was probably wrong about the survival of Victor Hugo's books. Predictive patterns based on data by Leonardo et al. (ibid.) indicate that by the year 2150, the majority of the human species will be illiterate.

books in his library. Now it was too late to start over. He had missed his chance.

Casting a sorrowful glance at C, Victor Hugo stood, fluffed out the tails of his coat, and walked away. C resisted calling out to him. He watched silently as the ghost dissolved in the mist. After Victor Hugo had disappeared entirely, C bravely fought against despair and invited a return of cold common sense. He told himself that he had imagined the whole encounter. There had been no ghost. He said it over and over to himself: There had been no ghost!

He would have been persuaded if he hadn't seen, beside him on the bench, the piece of paper Victor Hugo had left behind. C was reluctant to pick it up. It would cause him too much distress, since he wouldn't be able to read what Hugo had written. It would only be painful to peruse the scrawl of ink and fail to make sense of it. Hugo had probably written something brilliant; C would never know. He would leave the paper there. He would not allow himself to be tormented. But an unusual curiosity overtook him, and he gingerly lifted a corner of the paper.

It took extra scrutiny in the dim light to realize he was looking not at words but at a drawing. At first it seemed a busy patterned design, flowers tumbling behind a web, but with further consideration he came to see the circles, one dark, one hollow, that represented eyes, and a grim, skewed oval of a mouth lined with monstrous teeth, and wisps of a beard trailing like Medusa's snakes. C finally recognized in the image the shape of a ghostly face, dissolving into a net of lines, as if printed on lace.

Victor Hugo had left behind a drawing. This was his gift to C, who from that day on could no longer read but could still see with perfect clarity. In the picture Victor Hugo had made in C's presence, C saw the self-portrait of the very ghost with whom he had shared the bench. It did not take much effort to see that the illustration succeeded in capturing all the mysterious brilliance of the artist on a single sheet of paper. He was filled with admiration and at the same time he perceived in the image the full imaginative depths he'd missed in the previous years. It felt as if he were looking through ice at a spectacular underwater garden.

The effect of the drawing was so disorienting that in the days to come C would put it in a drawer, out of sight. Anyway, medical examinations and experimental treatments would keep him so busy he wouldn't have time for anything else. He decided that rather than leave the drawing to languish in his desk, he would donate it to the city of Paris. When the Victor Hugo Museum was established on the Place des Vosges in 1902, it would be displayed among the author's papers in a second-floor gallery. It remains there to this day. I know, for I have seen it myself.

Nominated by Conjunctions

IF YOU FIND A MOUSE ON A GLUE TRAP

by SUZANNE FARRELL SMITH

from BREVITY

If you find a mouse on a glue trap, he'll eyeball you with one black shiny eye while breathing in and out faster than you have ever seen anything breathe. You will panic, though you know the mouse is panicking harder. When your husband points out that the mouse is not alone in the furnace room, you will notice a second glue trap, stuck with the coiled carcass of a garter snake. When the mouse starts to struggle, you will tell your husband to kill it, no save it, and you will run to your phone and search "how to remove a mouse from a glue trap." Articles will tell you to use oil, so while your husband brings the glued mouse out to the back walkway so that your three young sons, in jammies and waiting with popcorn bowls for a Saturday-night Christmas movie, don't see it, you will hunt for the carafe. Outside, the mouse will sniff and stretch from the trap. Wearing snow boots over your own jammies, you will, for a moment, think he can free himself. But he won't. You will cover his body with an old tri-fold cloth diaper and douse his legs with olive oil. Your husband will say, "He's going to smell too good to predators," and you will tell the mouse, in all honesty, "I'm sorry, I'm sorry you smell delicious." You will dig under his legs with a plastic paint scraper. When his front feet clear the glue and hit the cold slate, the mouse will yank his back legs so hard you'll think he's pulling them clear off. The rear left foot will pop free. When the mouse stops reaching for a moment to rest, you and your husband will peer at his rear right leg, which is now bent like a wishbone. You will dig under it with gusto. The leg will stretch again, like nylon. You will sob and apologize to the mouse, because you knew the glue trap was left in the furnace room by your home's previous owner, but by the time you remembered to remove it, it will have served its purpose, *her* purpose. You will tell your husband, the mouse, and yourself, that you are the kind of person who rescues stinkbugs, who found a hopping frog in the kitchen and talked it into a cup, who feeds the chipmunks and squirrels and made friends with the garter snake before finding it perished. Resolved, you will say to your husband, we have to kill the mouse, it's only humane, and he will say, "I'm not a person who kills things!" And yet here you are, two people who don't believe in glue traps and who don't kill things, kneeling on their new walkway and killing something, killing it slowly. You will free the mouse's back right leg. He will try to scurry on the mangled stick, land in a hump of snow, and spin round and round, toiling to get somewhere but too broken to go. You will collect yourself. The mouse will stop circling and lie still. You will dig a hole around him and say, "The furnace room is so warm, isn't it? That's why you found your way in there." You will hope for hypothermia. Your husband will throw out the paint scraper, the diaper, and the entire bottle of olive oil. You will retrieve from the kitchen pretzels, granola, chia seeds, and a piece of cheese and sprinkle a snack circle around the mouse. You will say goodbye, then tell him to surrender. You will return to your family and watch a holiday movie as the boys munch on popcorn and ask for more. When they are in bed, you will not take any more chances and will search the furnace room, garage, and crawlspace for more glue traps. In the morning, you will find the mouse's frozen body, graying and covered in frost, still in the snow grave, all the snacks gone except for the seeds.

Nominated by Brevity,
Jennifer Lunden,
Ron Tanner,
Jessica Wilbanks

YOUNG HARE

by DIANE SEUSS

from AMERICAN POETRY REVIEW

Oh my love, Albrecht Dürer, your hare
is not a spectacle, it is not an exploding hare,
it is not a projection of the young hare
within you, the gentleness in you, or a disassembled hare,
nor a subliminal or concealed hare,
nor is it the imagination as hare

nor the soul as a long-eared, soft-eared hare,
Dürer, you painted this hare,
some say you killed a field hare
and brought it into your studio, or bagged a live hare
and caged it so you could look hard at a wild hare
without it running off into thorn bushes as hares

will do, and you sketched the hare
and laid down a watercolor wash over the hare
and then meticulously painted-in all the browns of hare,
toast brown, tawny, dim, pipe-tobacco brown of hare,
olive, fawn, topaz, bone brown until the hare
became dimensional under your hand, the thick hare

fur, the mottled shag, the nobility of the nose, the hare
toenails, black and sharp and curved, and the dense hare
ears, pod-shaped, articulated, substantial, erect, hare
whiskers and eyebrows, their wiry grace, the ruff of hare

neck fur, the multi-directional fur over the thick hare
haunches, and did I say the dark inside the hare

ears, how I want to follow the darkness of the hare
and stroke the dark within its ears, to feel the hare
ears with my fingers, and the white tuft, the hare
anomaly you painted on its side, and the fleshy hare
cheeks, how I want to squeeze them, and the hare
reticence, how I want to explore it, and the downturned hare

eye, it will not acknowledge or appease, the black-brown hare
eye in which you painted the reflection of a window in the hare
pupil, maybe your studio window, in the hare's
eye, why does that window feel so intimate in the hare's
unreadable eye, why do I press my face to the window to see the
    hare
as you see it, raising your chin to look and then back to the hare

on the page, the thin hair of your brush and your own hair
waving gold down your back, hair I see as you see the hare.
In the hare's eye you see me there, my swaying black hair.

Nominated by American Poetry Review,
John Allman,
Laura Kasischke,
Maxine Scates,
Lee Upton,
Allison Benis White

PETRONIA PETRONIA JYEKUNDENSIS
Rock Sparrow/Steinsperling
[collected September 4, 1935]

by JAN VERBERKMOES

from ECOTONE

if it was a hunt i wouldn't have known he blocked light from my body
with a new name stoneshot to the skull there was wind in the cypress
smell of pepper and pine rigged in my hammerthroat *ein grüner wind*
in the cypress my feather-mess falling *ein grüner wind in den bäumen*
he preened my skin from the bones now black crown now body-less
night what did you say night cliffs were there pepper and pine cliff-face
black black black crown of my head *pfeffer und kiefer* my cliffs were
there crownless wet rock-face what blood faced my *schwarze felsen*
felsen waren da green wind in the cypress *pfeffer und kiefer fer ein*
grüner wind stößt die felsen black rock burst my body from the green-
knit cypress when cliffs were if black cliff if if if *felsen waren da* if cliff
if *felsen da da kalt läuft das wasser den stein hinunter* washed my cliff
my cliff-face cold *er riss meinen dunklen körper nieder*

In the 1930s, German zoologist Ernst Schafer and American naturalist Brooke Dolan II made two natural
history expeditions to Tibet and China. They collected roughly 3,000 birds over the course of these trips,
including newly discovered species and subspecies. The birds were then transported back to the Academy of
Natural Sciences in Philadelphia and the Museum für Naturkunde Berlin, where they remain today.

Nominated by Ecotone

OASIS

fiction by DEBORAH FORBES

from THE HUDSON REVIEW

In the dry season dust sifts down over all things inside and outside, living and inanimate. Every day Corinne's maid sweeps and mops the floors; every third day she goes down on her knees to work lavender scented wax into the colonial-era parquet; but at the end of every day Corinne's feet are still brown-black with the earth that has come in through the windows. It grits between her teeth and coats the lining of her throat. It reddens the sun as it sets and the moon as it rises.

There are many things she hasn't known how to tell her husband since she followed him to this posting in Lusaka, Zambia, and one is how she loves the dust. Not "loves"—she wants a word less willed and compromised, more elemental. The dust seems to her not dirty but clean, fine enough to filter out impurities. When it collects in her hair and under her fingernails, it's proof she's here, alive—a fact she finds wildly improbable, most days.

During the long hours when Grant is at the office, she takes her laptop to the bar at the InterContinental Hotel, where the internet connection is halfway decent. She copyedits articles for an anthropology journal, a sort-of job her college mentor got her. The first time, her waiter is a young man built like a teenager, his head slightly out of proportion, large and square. His nametag says "Joseph."

He meets her look and smiles. "Good morning, madam."

He takes her order for a cappuccino, but instead of opening her laptop she watches him walk back toward the bar. No Zambian has met her look with as much warmth and familiarity as Joseph just did. Corinne's maid keeps her face averted, and Corinne understands this is the custom,

497

understands the American habit of looking people dead in the eye is considered rude in many places—but understanding doesn't stop her from feeling invisible. That first day she leaves Joseph a thirty-percent tip, because she took up the table for two hours but also because of his smile. From then on he always takes her order, shooting warning looks at the other staff.

"How is your family, madam?" he asks the next time.

"It's only me and my husband."

"Yes?" he says, his face going blank, and she realizes the question was a courtesy, not a request for information.

"How is your family?" She tries to right the exchange.

"Fine, we are all fine, madam."

The correct formula, the answer she should've given. But instead of stopping here, she asks more questions and confirms that he's not a teenager; he has a three-year-old son and six-month-old daughter.

"My sister has a baby the same age," she says. "What's her name?"

"Oh-ah-sees."

"I'm sorry?"

"Oh-ah-sees. Like this." He points to the header of her menu: Oasis Bar and Lounge.

"Oh, Oasis!" Corinne says. Joseph's brow furrows at the hard "ay."

"It's a lovely name," she adds quickly. "A green place in the desert."

Her remark doesn't seem to register. "It is to give thanks to God," he says. "This is the place from which our blessings come."

Later that morning, the suck of the hotel door opening against the air conditioning causes her to lift her head, and the gasping, hollow sound lodges in her chest when she sees it's Pieter Graff who's striding into the hotel lobby. She knows him from the expat barbeques and Sunday lunches that now make up her social world. He's in Lusaka to do a consultancy for the humanitarian organization that employs Grant, a white-blond Afrikaner with a radiant Indian wife. When Corinne first met them she couldn't keep her eyes off Radha, velvet-skinned in saffron yellow and orange and lime green. She barely noticed Pieter. He has a prominent nose and lips that look as if they've been carved out of some unyielding substance, leaving an impression of unfriendliness.

After a few encounters, Corinne noticed that while she was watching his wife, Pieter was watching her. She supposed he disliked her. She met his gaze with a bland smile, which he refused to return. Then she thought she must be mistaken—she wasn't the kind of woman men generally looked at—but it kept happening. At parties he managed to be in the same room as she was, in the same clump of people talking. He got up to close a window the moment goosebumps rose on her flesh. Looking forward to these attentions has become a harmless game—something to give shape to an otherwise shapeless time.

They've been alone together only once, a few nights ago. Pieter and Radha came to a dinner party she and Grant were hosting for Tim, a marketing guy visiting from the D.C. office.

Midway through dinner, Tim had asked her, "What do you do while Grant's off in the trenches?"

She could've said, I sit in the empty house and listen to the wind creak the bamboo until I'm alive and dead as the wind is. It would've been true, but even on her third glass of wine she wasn't that drunk. Neither did she attempt to smile charmingly and shrug, which likely would've been enough to satisfy him. She tried for something in-between: "I've sort've reverted to a 1950s housewife. But we have a maid, because everybody does, so I don't even do housework. Maybe I'm a colonial Madam, but without the racism—" She could feel Pieter's eyes on her.

"Her degree's in anthropology," Grant broke in. "She was working in D.C., but she quit her job to come out with me, so now—"

"I get to decide what to do with my life. I'm a 1950s housewife in a 21st-century marriage."

"That doesn't sound half bad," Radha said, and then everyone knew they could laugh.

The talk turned to fundraising appeals. Grant was explaining: "You want to make the hardship of people's lives real without making them sound so desperate that they're beyond help. You want to show their suffering without shortchanging their dignity and resourcefulness."

"Is that possible?" Corinne asked and saw the new line in her husband's forehead deepen. "Can you give the real truth of another person's suffering without showing how helpless it makes them? Without feeling helpless yourself?" These questions weren't rhetorical, but the conversation tilted and shifted away as though they were. Grant's job is to help the country cope with the deepening poverty wreaked by the AIDS crisis; Corinne loves him for defying his family's expectations that he become an engineer and choosing this work instead. But when he talks about it, he talks about documents and meetings. She hasn't met the people whose needs have brought them halfway around the world. Four months in, the mystery of their obligations to this place has only deepened.

"The problem is poverty isn't sexy enough. There's no hook," Tim was saying. "Since 9/11, people—"

"—Americans," Pieter corrected.

"Okay, Americans think about other countries in terms of terrorism. Good guys versus bad guys."

"That's why we're working the defense angle," Grant said. "Hundreds of thousands of kids orphaned by AIDS, growing up without adult supervision—if that's not a security threat, what is?"

There was pleasure in her husband's voice, a quickening on the trail of a solution, but she was listening to something else. Hundreds of thousands of orphans. She tried to steady the fact in her mind. This is why we are here.

"I've got something even better," Tim said. "Plane crashes. Think of all that attention to the planes going down. Child mortality in sub-Saharan Africa is like plane crashes. Seventy-seven plane crashes every day. That's one every eighteen minutes. And every plane filled with children."

Corinne scraped her chair hard against the floor but kept her steps as even as she could as she walked to the kitchen. She pressed her palms into the counter. She knew people in Grant's line of work got used to terrible statistics. She knew they had to get hardened to pain and death, like surgeons had to harden themselves to the open wound. Everybody else was okay; what was wrong with her?

She made herself open the plastic container and distribute raspberries onto the dessert plates. They were imported, shamefully expensive, but she couldn't resist the contrast they'd make against the whipped cream and dark cake. Every eighteen minutes, a planeload of children was falling from the sky—children weakened by hunger as well as disease. Either this was not real or the raspberries and cake weren't real. They couldn't be real at the same time.

She looked up to find Pieter standing a couple of feet away, watching her without embarrassment. There was a burst of laughter from the other room.

"We must seem loathsome to you," he said.

"No . . . I'm sorry . . . what?"

"Pain parceled out in acronyms. Passed around. As if we're immune."

She closed her mouth on an impulse to say, you don't really mean that, I don't understand. Instead, for once, she held his look. His eyes were expressionless, bleached-out gray like pebbles in a shallow river.

"It's all right," he said after a moment. "Sometimes I'm loathsome to myself."

"It's good work," she said a beat too late. It helped that she believed it. "You and Grant do good work." But he'd already turned without saying what he'd wanted.

Later that night, she was reading in bed when Grant came to join her. He stretched out on his back, and she put down her book to look at him. The maid had ironed the fresh T-shirt he was wearing so that he looked seamless. No hollows or handholds for her. He asked the ceiling, "Why did you tell everyone you're a 1950s housewife?"

"You didn't like it."

He rolled onto his side to face her. "I didn't get it. We made the decision to come here together. You made it sound like I forced you to give up something—"

"You didn't like how it sounded," she said stonily. She wasn't sure why she was angry.

"I don't care how it sounded. Who cares what those people think? I care about what you think."

This softened her. "I was trying to say how—strange it feels. Not to be working. Waiting for you to come home every day."

"Don't then," he said. "Look for opportunities—volunteering, or researching grad schools, or something online—"

Her husband the problem solver. He'd left engineering because he wanted his skills to mean something. His "skills"—that's how he put it, a man impassively carrying around a toolkit. He wanted to solve the problems that were most intractable, and that meant socioeconomic problems, and that meant Africa.

She nodded. "Okay."

He was sitting up to turn off the light but paused to check her face. "Anything else?"

This was the moment she could've asked whether he felt anything when Tim was talking about plane crashes, but she didn't. She was afraid she wouldn't be able to explain why it mattered. She was afraid of his versions of no. Instead she ducked her face away and stood up to slip out of her yoga pants. He switched off the lamp before she finished undressing, as if he were trying to avoid seeing her naked, though more likely it hadn't even occurred to him to want to.

There was one way she resembled a 1950s housewife, she thought as she pulled the covers up over her shoulder. She'd thought—she had hoped—that her and Grant's love would be enough. There was a time before they were married when all she thought about was how soon he could be inside her. All she wanted was to stop pretending their separate lives were real, because the only part that was real was the part they lived in each other's skin.

There came a time, after they were married, when he no longer reached for her with the same urgency, and she began to worry that his urgency had been the whole point. That his desire for her was all she understood about him. That she hadn't even tried to understand herself. She tried back in D.C. to explain this to him, but he always answered with some version of: don't make this about us. This is about you. The problem must be her boring-but-stressful administrative job. The problem must be her lack of direction. She learned to tuck her uncertainties and longings out of sight, because when she released them into the space between her and Grant, they became charged with hurt, seduction, blame—difficult to defend.

The red wine tingled up and down her nerves as she lay next to him in the dark. She curled onto her side, facing the wide featureless expanse of his back. She could tell from his breathing that he was still awake. We're here because you care about people you don't even know, she told him in her head. It didn't feel true.

Pieter told the truth. The shock of it had been physical, and it was still thrumming through her body like the wine. *We must seem loathsome to you. I'm loathsome to myself.* She possessed all the luxuries of a colonial Madam and all the freedom of a modern marriage—even her free-floating sadness was a luxury in this country of griefs. She wondered if Pieter could see the black ribbon of self-hatred she too carried under her skin.

❋   ❋   ❋

Pieter doesn't notice her on the raised platform of the hotel bar, so for once she's free to watch him. His body is small for a man's, compact. He pushes up on the balls of his feet when the line at Reservations moves forward. She listens to him speak to the mixed-race girl behind the counter in what must be Afrikaans, a fluency and variation in tone she's never heard in his English. When the girl laughs, Corinne looks away.

She gathers that he's running meetings in the hotel. He must see her by the second day, the third, but he doesn't speak to her. Her nerves become tuned to his quick, firm step as he passes the bar. Why doesn't he greet his colleague's wife? She argues with herself: he's as unfriendly as she first suspected; he hasn't seen her; he doesn't want to interrupt; he's busy; it's all in her head. Why does she care?

"How is Oasis?" she asks Joseph, taking care to keep the "a" soft, the "i" an "ee" that makes a little hiss at the end.

"She is just okay, madam. This morning my wife is worrying, because Oasis, she don't eat."

"It's hard at that age, I think. My sister's trying to get her baby to eat solid foods, and sometimes she wants them and sometimes she doesn't."

Pieter stands before her. Joseph discreetly vanishes.

"There's something I need to discuss with you," he says without preamble. "Could you come to room 428 in ten minutes or so?"

She knows. Of course she knows. It's only afterward that she tries to convince herself that she thought he wanted to talk about work, maybe wanted her to pass some message to Grant. When she comes to the room, he gestures her in, and she takes the only chair. He sits on the bed and looks at her the way he always looks at her.

"You said you wanted to discuss something," she says finally, a note of pleading in her voice.

"No," he says, and she knows he isn't going to make this easy for her, and she knows there's no question of getting up and walking out.

"I'd like to discuss everything with you," he continues, leaning forward and resting his elbows on his knees. "But we haven't much time."

She rises and he seizes her. That's how she remembers it. She'd like to tell herself that's all she remembers, that the breach happened in total blackness.

She remembers that the force of the first kiss pushed her backward, until she was pressed up against the curtained window. She remembers the glass creaking in its frame, thinking it would break; something must break, but nothing broke. She remembers that she was holding his bottom lip between her teeth when he first entered her—not biting him, just holding him still, wait, is this happening—and then the metallic tang of his blood filling her mouth. They stripped each other blindly but never lay down.

She remembers that some moments it was like drowning and some moments like being saved.

Afterward he holds her, still standing, while their bodies stop shuddering. It's a new feeling to be waist to waist, shoulder to shoulder—not her husband bending to meet her. "What does this mean?" she asks, softly enough that he can pretend not to hear.

"I don't know."

This doesn't sound like a statement of uncertainty to Corinne. It sounds like: we don't have to know. Or: it doesn't mean; it just is. As if they've entered a sealed-off world that doesn't have to have any relation to anything else.

Wishful thinking.

The last thing she remembers is the bed pulled tight and smooth, innocent of them.

*　*　*

Every morning she returns to her usual table, going through the ritual of questions with Joseph. Oasis is eating again, but she has diarrhea.

"The mother is worrying," Joseph repeats every time she asks. Corinne doesn't know enough yet to know about the taboo against complaint in Zambia. His refrain should sound like a siren screaming down the street.

"I'm sure she'll be fine," she says, putting on the voice she uses when her sister frets over her kids.

The second time Pieter greets her casually, the wife of his colleague. A little while later she asks Joseph for the bill. By the fourth time she doesn't have to ask—Pieter comes and Joseph brings the bill. She tips extra those days. Then she goes to Pieter, always in the same room.

Once they're alone, what Corinne wants becomes very specific. Not to explore. No long detours of touch. She wants to be obliterated, circuits lit up so fast they black out. Afterward they take turns washing up and leaving. She hears the click of the door shutting behind him as she stands with her foot balanced on the sink, wiping herself down. She doesn't mind the mirror. She could be anyone, this woman who looks back at her—a little flushed, unhurriedly buttoning her shirt.

"Africa is starting to agree with you," Grant tells her one evening after she and Pieter have met.

She looks up from her magazine and smiles at him, but not for so long that he might take it from her hands. There's an emptiness in her chest where guilt might've been. She felt guiltier before she took up with Pieter—more miserable over her failure to give an accounting of herself. She knows this is wrong and knows she should be scared that she can't feel the wrongness of it.

The fifth time, she and Pieter get lazy. They linger in the anonymous bed—not sleeping; she can never sleep afterward—feeling their bodies go quiet, letting their minds wander. She curls away from him, facing the window. He puts his hand over her breast.

"I've been thinking about this since Tuesday," he says.

504

"Mmmm."

"Do you think about it? When we're not together?"

"I try not to."

"Don't lie to me."

"I said 'try.'"

He rolls her back toward him and pins her to the bed. He slips the condom on with one hand, so neatly that a plain fact breaks through: it's not just me. This is what he does.

"Pieter," she says. She doesn't want him inside her, but it's too late.

"Corinne. So contained. So clean."

She doesn't know if he's talking about her name or herself, but she can feel him trying to hurt her, scribbling heavy and dark over whatever line she meant to draw. If she were a different kind of woman, she'd fight back, tear his flesh, commit fully to the violence they're doing to each other.

She's not that kind of woman. The realization comes as he finishes and heaves himself off of her. It comes as he says, "I'm tired of containment, life in little pieces. That's why we understand each other, yes?"

No.

She turns away from him again. She's okay. Isn't she? She presses her face into the bedspread, elaborately patterned to hide stains.

"I don't like this room," she says once she trusts her voice. "It's always the same. Think of how many bodies have been here. Each time we come, it's like we were never here."

"We were never here."

"What?" She cranes her neck back to look at him, but he's studying the ceiling the way Grant does when he's considering whether to say something. This reflected image makes her think of reflections on dark water, something that could pull her under—

"That's how this is possible. You try not to think about it, in your other life."

She feels cold and wants someone to hold her, but not him.

*　*　*

When she returns to the Oasis Bar and Lounge the following day, a woman she's never seen—breasts and belly straining against the maroon vest of the hotel uniform—asks if she wants to see a menu.

Corinne scans the room. "Where's Joseph?"

"Funeral, madam. We are expecting him tomorrow."

She follows the woman toward a different table than her usual one near the edge of the riser. She takes a quick extra step to catch up. "I hope it's no one close to him?"

"You are wanting a different table, madam?"

Corinne stops, puzzled. The woman looks at her expectantly. "No. I meant—the funeral. Who it's for."

"The baby, madam."

"I'm sorry?"

"It's for the baby girl."

"Not Oasis?"

The woman stares at Corinne.

"Not Oasis," Corinne repeats stubbornly. "The daughter."

"Eh, yes, madam. The baby."

"No. What happened?"

The woman backs away from her, clearly sorry she's said anything.

"What happened?" Corinne's voice is blunt and hard, like the butter knife lying on the table. The patrons at the next table look up. Blunt and hard and useless.

"I don't know, madam. The baby, she was growing weaker. She had diarrhea."

Babies don't just die of diarrhea, Corinne wants to shout at her. But they do. They do here. The woman retreats behind the bar, eyeing Corinne as she dries a glass.

She won't sit down and let someone else take her order. She won't wait, queasy and ambivalent, for Pieter to walk by. Her decision takes hold as she sees him approach the hotel entrance and open the heavy glass door. She reaches him before it swings shut.

"I can't do this anymore," she says.

"What's the matter with you?" he hisses, looking over her shoulder.

"Pretend we're talking about work," she says more quietly. "Pretend you're just talking to your colleague's wife."

They move away from the door to the small alcove next to the reservations desk. When he looks at her again, his face is composed. "That will not be difficult."

She stares at him, searching for bravado, pain, confirmation that his indifference is sincere, anything. Nothing. She doesn't know this man. She never knew him. This is a relief, because it makes it easier to leave. And this is a horror.

"Is it ever difficult for you?" she asks. The first time she's curious about him—not just about what he does to her—and too late.

"You have no idea."

Tell me, she could've said. I'll meet you upstairs and you can tell me. Months and then years later she'll wonder if her first feeling was right: that he understood something about her no one else had guessed. That he could tell her something she needed to know. But today she pushes out onto the hot, cracked concrete and drives blindly home.

That night she tells Grant about Joseph.

"That's why you're crying? Because the waiter's baby died?" There may be relief in his voice.

"I know it happens all the time," she says, so he won't say it. As if it happening all the time is a consolation. "I know infant mortality is really high here—"

"But still." He lifts a hand to touch her hair.

"I feel responsible."

"How could you be responsible?"

"He told me she was sick. I didn't pay attention."

"It's not your fault." He strokes her hair mechanically, a little too hard. She moves her head away.

"How do you do it?" she asks, looking into his face. When is the last time she really tried to see him? He looks tired. His eyes move back and forth, settling on one of her eyes and then the other, not finding a point of focus.

"Do what?"

"This work. It can't be good for you. Going where the suffering is. Having to absorb it."

"I don't have to absorb it. I just have to help where I can."

"But . . . you can't help but feel something? At least a little bit?"

The muscle in his jaw tenses. "Would it help you if I got upset?"

"No," she says, defeated. "No, it wouldn't."

She wraps her arms around him so that they don't have to look at each other anymore. Beneath the waxy layer of his soap she catches his real smell, like something burning up quickly. His words make a wall she can't scale, but his body is saying something else. Numbness is the other side of feeling too much. We're in danger of both.

She should be frightened as she holds him—by what she's done, by the secret she'll now have to protect—but instead she feels a pulse of strength. She'll be able to live in this new country. She won't dissolve into the wind and dust. She'll move, miraculously intact, between the reality where children are starving and the reality where she pays two weeks of her maid's salary for a pint of raspberries, the reality where

507

she reaches for Grant and the reality where she intersected with Pieter. She'll give up the indulgence of self-loathing—old habit of a woman who expected to be whole.

She returns one last time to the hotel, early morning, to see Joseph. It's reassuring to find him in his uniform, same as ever, only his movements a degree more deliberate, the volume of his voice a notch lower. She tells him she's sorry for his loss. She tells him, with perfect honesty, that she cannot imagine it. She gives him some money toward the funeral expenses—an incommensurate, helpless gesture, but he thanks her.

While they are speaking, a plane full of children crashes into the earth. How much do you have not to think about, not remember, in order to live?

Nominated by The Hudson Review,
Maura Stanton

SPECIAL MENTION

(The editors also wish to mention the following important works published by small presses last year. Listings are in no particular order.)

FICTION

Benjamin Soileau — Boosh Bourgeois (Colorado Review)
D.R. MacDonald — In The Blackhouse (Epoch)
Whitney Collins — The Pupil (Grist)
Justin Hocking — Gallery (Signal Fire)
Karen E. Bender — Where To Hide In A Synagogue (Epiphany)
Jacob M. Appel — Iceberg Potential (Reservoir Journal)
Amy Neswald — Late Bloomer (Bat City)
Kevin Wilson — The Lost Baby (American Short Fiction)
Abby Lipscomb — Mill Pond (Quiddity)
Lindsay Starck — Hibernation (Cincinnati Review)
Amy Stuber — People's Parties (Copper Nickel)
Amber Dermont — So What If I Love You That's None of Your
    Business (Iowa Review)
Roxane Gay — Boy In A Coma (Wigleaf)
Lara Markstein — Our Hendrina (Chicago Quarterly Review)
Lee Conell — Posthumous Portrait (Oxford American)
Joe Cary — Disembodied (One Story)
Michaela Hansen — The Devil in The Barn (American Short Fiction)
Jim Shepard — Our Day of Grace (Zoetrope)
Emily Nemens — Prospects (Iowa Review)
John Jodzio — The Narrows (The Sun)
Uche Okonkwo — Our Belgian Wife (One Story)
Gershon Ben-Avraham — Yoineh Bodek (Image)

Patrick Nathan — Host (Ninth Letter)

Alexandra Chang — Tomb Sweeping Day (Glimmer Train)

Catherine Lacey — Family Physics (Sewanee Review)

Brendan Missett — Labor (Bellevue Literary Review)

Kathryn Scanlan — The Candidate (Noon)

Matthew Vollmer — How To Write A Love Story (Epoch)

Steven Schwartz — The Bad Guest (Ploughshares)

Jane McCafferty — The Strong, Silent Type (Iowa Review)

Christine Sneed — The Monkey's Uncle Louis (New England Review)

Amanda S. Torres — Fortuna (Glimmer Train)

Caitlin Fitzpatrick — The Laws of Motion (Colorado Review)

Louis B. Jones — Everybody's Long-Term Welfsre (ZYZZYVA)

Therese Eiben — Pass The Baby (December)

Marti Boone Mattia — No Moon Night (New Ohio Review)

Stephen Dixon — Things Fall (Idaho Review)

Carlos Fonseca — Art Brut (Brooklyn Rail)

Aaron Hamburger — Refugees (Bennington Review)

Tommy Orange — Freyr (Zoetrope)

Katie Coyle — The Little Guy (Tin House)

George Singleton — Apology Letter From Starkburg County Jail
(Prairie Schooner)

Anthony Wallace — The Overcoat (Southern Review)

Joyce Carol Oates — The Bloody Head (Idaho Review)

Steve Almond — Play This Right Kid And You're The Hero (Cincin-
nati Review)

Nell Freudenberger — Rabbits (Paris Review)

Karen Russell — Black Corfu (Zoetrope)

Peter Gordon — Elizabeth (Missouri Review)

Deborah Eisenberg — The Third Tower (Ploughshares)

Benjamin Nugent — Safe Spaces (Paris Review)

Hannah H. Kim — Listen (Kenyon Review)

Kate McIntyre — Prairie Vision (Cincinnati Review)

Sidik Fofana — Mr. Battles (Sewanee Review)

Ann Beattie — Cass and Charlene (Sewanee Review)

Dina Nayeri — The Woman In Bed Fifteen (Alaska Quarterly Re-
view)

Elizabeth Tallent — The Lights (Threepenny Review)

Benjamin Guerette — Goal: Full or Success ! Yes ! (Notre Dame
Review)

S.P Tenhoff — The Book of Explorers (Southern Review)

Maddy Raskulinecz — Barbara From Florida (ZYZZYVA)
Michael Martone — Versed (StoryQuarterly)
Anne Sanow — The Racers (The Collagist)

NONFICTION

Molly Gallentine — American Gothic (Gulf Coast)
Hudson Jungck — Resurrection (Baltimore Review)
Aaron Hamburger — Sweetness Mattered (Tin House)
Krista Christensen — Theories of Negativity (Potomac Review)
Alice Mattison — The Writing Daughter (Speak)
Justin Taylor — Safe In Heaven Dead (Sewanee Review)
Brendan O'Byrne — Irish Mist Adrift In the Fog Of War (War Horse)
Scott Russell Sanders — At The Gates of Deep Darkness (Orion)
Sonja Livingston — Miracle of the Eyes (Cincinnati Review)
Bernard Cooper — Greedy Sleep (Granta)
Michael Deagler — Ivan Among The Two Street String Bands — Michael Deagler (StoryQuarterly)
Sonya Huber — Women & Pain "Between One and Ten Thousand" (Another Chicago Magazine)
Sara A. Lewis — Safe Houses (Oxford American)
Madison Davis — Land Not Theirs (The Common)
Andrew Kay — Wrestling In Paris (The Point)
Eliza Smith — All These Apocalypses (Pinch)
Phil Klay — Tales of War and Redemption (American Scholar)
Serene Taleb-Agha — A Hiker's Guide to Damascus (Ploughshares)
Kapka Kassabova — Border Ghosts (World Literature Today)
Erica X. Eisen — Have You No Home to Go To (Harvard Review)
Leslie Jamison — I Met Fear On The Hill (Paris Review)
Xujun Eberlein — The Cremation (Brevity)
Julie Marie Wade—503A (Iowa Review)
Gary Fincke — Faith (Pleiades)
Robert Boyers — The Ways Of The Will (Raritan)
Georgi Markov — Wastewaters (Ploughshares)
Christopher Collins — The Dark Month (Creative Nonfiction)
John Blanton Edgar — The Auction (Chattahoochee Review)
Bonnie Friedman — Minding the Store (Agni)
Daniel Blue Tyx — Riding The Tornado (Oxford American)
Jonathan Malesic — When Work and Meaning Part Ways (Hedgehog Review)

J. Drew Lanham — Forever Gone (Orion)

Alice Hatcher — General Grant Wore A Pink Dress (Fourth Genre)

Elizabeth Becker — Report (Crazyhorse)

Sydney Lea — Earthquakers and Angels (River Teeth)

DeWitt Henry — On Cursing (Massachusetts Review)

Grace Schulman — Twisted Branches (*Strange Paradise*, Turtle Point)

Tom Montgomery Fate — Fishing For My Father (Fourth Genre)

Kiese Laymon — Quick Feet (Virginia Quarterly)

Tyrese L. Coleman — Speculum (Black Warrior Review)

Rachel Wiseman — Switching Off (The Point)

J. Malcolm Garcia — The Garden Center (The Sun)

JoAnna Novak — Frosting (Bennington Review)

Merrill Joan Gerber — True Believer: My Friendship With Cynthia
    Ozick (Salmagundi)

Lee Huttner — Once We Were Snow (Pinch)

Navtej Singh Dhillon — Homecomings (n+1)

Suzanne Rivecca — Ugly and Bitter and Strong (ZYZZYVA)

Tammy Lynne Stoner — Butterflies & Bullfrogs (*Sugar Land*, Red
    Hen Press)

David Gessner — Montaigne In the Age of Trump (Ecotone)

EJ Levy — Sweeties (High Desert Journal)

Nyssa Chow — How To Become A Monster (Ploughshares)

POETRY

Jill Osier — Blood (Southern Review)

Triin Paja — Forest Brothers (Portland Review)

Deborah Bacharach — Women's Work (Pembroke Magazine)

Mara Pastor — Despues De La Tormenta (The Common)

John Gallaher — Brand New Spacesuit (New England Review)

Torrin a. Greathouse — Hapnophobia or the Fear of Being Touched
    (Palette Poetry)

Dean Rader — Elegy Pantoum (Palette Poetry)

Oliver de la Paz — from *Labyrinth* (Poetry Northwest)

Corey Marks — Lark (New England Review)

Kathy Fagan — Fountain (Plume Poetry)

Anna Rose Welch — This is How You Beg, *We, the Almighty Fires*
    (Alice James Books)

Carl Dennis — War and Peace (New Letters)

Kristin Chang — Ode to Intestines (foglifter)

Maggie Smith — How to Preserve a Fistful of the Neighbor's Tulips, (Palette Poetry)

Ralph Burns — The Valium Song (*Field*)

James Allen Hall — On Dark Days, I Imagine My Parents' Wedding Video (The Iowa Review)

Kimberly Johnson — Fire-work (New England Review)

Taylor Johnson — This is a Review for *Blue in Green* by Miles Davis (Indiana Review)

Cate Lycurgus — Avowal (Colorado Review)

Fred Marchant — On a Collage by Peter Sacks (Salamander)

Sonia Sanchez — Belly, Buttocks and Straight Spines, (Valley Voices)

Lisa Russ Spaar — Last Rose Madrigal (Literary Imagination)

PRESSES FEATURED IN THE PUSHCART PRIZE EDITIONS SINCE 1976

A-Minor
About Place Journal
Abstract Magazine TV
The Account
Adroit Journal
Agni
Ahsahta Press
Ailanthus Press
Alaska Quarterly Review
Alcheringa/Ethnopoetics
Alice James Books
Ambergris
Amelia
American Circus
American Journal of Poetry
American Letters and Commentary
American Literature
American PEN
American Poetry Review
American Scholar
American Short Fiction
The American Voice
Amicus Journal
Amnesty International
Anaesthesia Review
Anhinga Press
Another Chicago Magazine

Antaeus
Antietam Review
Antioch Review
Apalachee Quarterly
Aphra
Aralia Press
The Ark
Arroyo
Art and Understanding
Arts and Letters
Artword Quarterly
Ascensius Press
Ascent
Aspen Leaves
Aspen Poetry Anthology
Assaracus
Assembling
Atlanta Review
Autonomedia
Avocet Press
The Awl
The Baffler
Bakunin
Bare Life
Bat City Review
Bamboo Ridge
Barlenmir House

Barnwood Press

Barrow Street

Bellevue Literary Review

The Bellingham Review

Bellowing Ark

Beloit Poetry Journal

Bennington Review

Bettering America Poetry

Bilingual Review

Birmingham Poetry Review

Black American Literature Forum

Blackbird

Black Renaissance Noire

Black Rooster

Black Scholar

Black Sparrow

Black Warrior Review

Blackwells Press

The Believer

Bloom

Bloomsbury Review

Blue Cloud Quarterly

Blueline

Blue Unicorn

Blue Wind Press

Bluefish

BOA Editions

Bomb

Bookslinger Editions

Boston Review

Boulevard

Boxspring

Brevity

Briar Cliff Review

Brick

Bridge

Bridges

Brown Journal of Arts

Burning Deck Press

Butcher's Dog

Cafe Review

Caliban

California Quarterly

Callaloo

Calliope

Calliopea Press

Calyx

The Canary

Canto

Capra Press

Carcanet Editions

Caribbean Writer

Carolina Quarterly

Catapult

Cave Wall

Cedar Rock

Center

Chariton Review

Charnel House

Chattahoochee Review

Chautauqua Literary Journal

Chelsea

Chicago Quarterly Review

Chouteau Review

Chowder Review

Cimarron Review

Cincinnati Review

Cincinnati Poetry Review

City Lights Books

Cleveland State Univ. Poetry Ctr.

Clover

Clown War

Codex Journal

CoEvolution Quarterly

Cold Mountain Press

The Collagist

Colorado Review

Columbia: A Magazine of Poetry and Prose

The Common

Conduit

Confluence Press

Confrontation

Conjunctions

Connecticut Review

Constellations

Copper Canyon Press

Copper Nickel

Cosmic Information Agency

Countermeasures

Counterpoint

Court Green

Crab Orchard Review

Crawl Out Your Window

Crazyhorse

Creative Nonfiction

Crescent Review

Cross Cultural Communications

Cross Currents

Crosstown Books

Crowd

Cue

Cumberland Poetry Review

Curbstone Press

Cutbank

Cypher Books

Dacotah Territory

Daedalus

Dalkey Archive Press

Decatur House

December

Denver Quarterly

Desperation Press

Dogwood

Domestic Crude

Doubletake

Dragon Gate Inc.

Dreamworks

Dryad Press

Duck Down Press

Dunes Review

Durak

East River Anthology

Eastern Washington University Press

Ecotone

Egress

El Malpensante

Electric Literature

Eleven Eleven

Ellis Press

Empty Bowl

Ep;phany

Epoch

Ergol

Evansville Review

Exquisite Corpse

Faultline

Fence

Fiction

Fiction Collective

Fiction International

Field

Fifth Wednesday Journal

Fine Madness

Firebrand Books

Firelands Art Review

First Intensity

5 A.M.

Five Fingers Review

Five Points Press

Florida Review

Foglifter

Forklift

The Formalist

Foundry

Four Way Books

Fourth Genre

Fourth River

Frontiers: A Journal of Women Studies

Fugue

Gallimaufry

Genre

The Georgia Review

Gettysburg Review

Ghost Dance

Gibbs-Smith

Glimmer Train

Goddard Journal

David Godine, Publisher

Graham House Press

Grand Street

Granta

Graywolf Press

Great River Review

Green Mountains Review

Greenfield Review

Greensboro Review

Guardian Press
Gulf Coast
Hanging Loose
Harbour Publishing
Hard Pressed
Harvard Review
Hawaii Pacific Review
Hayden's Ferry Review
Hermitage Press
Heyday
Hills
Hollyridge Press
Holmgangers Press
Holy Cow!
Home Planet News
Hopkins Review
Hudson Review
Hunger Mountain
Hungry Mind Review
Ibbetson Street Press
Icarus
Icon
Idaho Review
Iguana Press
Image
In Character
Indiana Review
Indiana Writes
Intermedia
Intro
Invisible City
Inwood Press
Iowa Review
Ironwood
I-70 Review
Jam To-day
J Journal
The Journal
Jubilat
The Kanchenjunga Press
Kansas Quarterly
Kayak
Kelsey Street Press
Kenyon Review

Kestrel
Kweli Journal
Lake Effect
Lana Turner
Latitudes Press
Laughing Waters Press
Laurel Poetry Collective
Laurel Review
L'Epervier Press
Liberation
Linquis
Literal Latté
Literary Imagination
The Literary Review
The Little Magazine
Little Patuxent Review
Little Star
Living Hand Press
Living Poets Press
Logbridge-Rhodes
Louisville Review
Love's Executive Order
Lowlands Review
LSU Press
Lucille
Lynx House Press
Lyric
The MacGuffin
Magic Circle Press
Malahat Review
Manoa
Manroot
Many Mountains Moving
Marlboro Review
Massachusetts Review
McSweeney's
Meridian
Mho & Mho Works
Micah Publications
Michigan Quarterly
Mid-American Review
Milkweed Editions
Milkweed Quarterly
The Minnesota Review

Mississippi Review
Mississippi Valley Review
Missouri Review
Montana Gothic
Montana Review
Montemora
Moon Pie Press
Moon Pony Press
Mount Voices
Mr. Cogito Press
MSS
Mudfish
Mulch Press
Muzzle Magazine
n+1
Nada Press
Narrative
National Poetry Review
Nebraska Poets Calendar
Nebraska Review
Nepantla
Nerve Cowboy
New America
New American Review
New American Writing
The New Criterion
New Delta Review
New Directions
New England Review
New England Review and Bread Loaf
   Quarterly
New Issues
New Letters
New Madrid
New Ohio Review
New Orleans Review
New South Books
New Verse News
New Virginia Review
New York Quarterly
New York University Press
Nimrod
9×9 Industries
Ninth Letter

Noon
North American Review
North Atlantic Books
North Dakota Quarterly
North Point Press
Northeastern University Press
Northern Lights
Northwest Review
Notre Dame Review
O. ARS
O. Bl k
Obsidian
Obsidian II
Ocho
Oconee Review
October
Ohio Review
Old Crow Review
Ontario Review
Open City
Open Places
Orca Press
Orchises Press
Oregon Humanities
Orion
Other Voices
Oxford American
Oxford Press
Oyez Press
Oyster Boy Review
Painted Bride Quarterly
Painted Hills Review
Palo Alto Review
Paper Dart
Paris Press
Paris Review
Parkett
Parnassus: Poetry in Review
Partisan Review
Passages North
Paterson Literary Review
Pebble Lake Review
Penca Books
Pentagram

Penumbra Press

Pequod

Persea: An International Review

Perugia Press

Per Contra

Pilot Light

The Pinch

Pipedream Press

Pitcairn Press

Pitt Magazine

Pleasure Boat Studio

Pleiades

Ploughshares

Plume

Poem-A-Day

Poems & Plays

Poet and Critic

Poet Lore

Poetry

Poetry Atlanta Press

Poetry East

Poetry International

Poetry Ireland Review

Poetry Northwest

Poetry Now

The Point

Post Road

Prairie Schooner

Prelude

Prescott Street Press

Press

Prime Number

Prism

Promise of Learnings

Provincetown Arts

A Public Space

Puerto Del Sol

Purple Passion Press

Quaderni Di Yip

Quarry West

The Quarterly

Quarterly West

Quiddity

Radio Silence

Rainbow Press

Raritan: A Quarterly Review

Rattle

Red Cedar Review

Red Clay Books

Red Dust Press

Red Earth Press

Red Hen Press

Release Press

Republic of Letters

Review of Contemporary Fiction

Revista Chicano-Riqueña

Rhetoric Review

Rhino

Rivendell

River Styx

River Teeth

Rowan Tree Press

Ruminate

Runes

Russian *Samizdat*

Salamander

Salmagundi

San Marcos Press

Santa Monica Review

Sarabande Books

Saturnalia

Sea Pen Press and Paper Mill

Seal Press

Seamark Press

Seattle Review

Second Coming Press

Semiotext(e)

Seneca Review

Seven Days

The Seventies Press

Sewanee Review

The Shade Journal

Shankpainter

Shantih

Shearsman

Sheep Meadow Press

Shenandoah

A Shout In the Street

Sibyl-Child Press
Side Show
Sixth Finch
Small Moon
Smartish Pace
The Smith
Snake Nation Review
Solo
Solo 2
Some
The Sonora Review
Southeast Review
Southern Indiana Review
Southern Poetry Review
Southern Review
Southampton Review
Southwest Review
Speakeasy
Spectrum
Spillway
Spork
The Spirit That Moves Us
St. Andrews Press
Stillhouse Press
Storm Cellar
Story
Story Quarterly
Streetfare Journal
Stuart Wright, Publisher
Subtropics
Sugar House Review
Sulfur
Summerset Review
The Sun
Sun & Moon Press
Sun Press
Sunstone
Sweet
Sycamore Review
Tab
Tamagawa
Tar River Poetry
Teal Press
Telephone Books

Telescope
Temblor
The Temple
Tendril
Terrapin Books
Texas Slough
Think
Third Coast
13th Moon
THIS
Thorp Springs Press
Three Rivers Press
Threepenny Review
Thrush
Thunder City Press
Thunder's Mouth Press
Tia Chucha Press
Tiger Bark Press
Tikkun
Tin House
Tipton Review
Tombouctou Books
Toothpaste Press
Transatlantic Review
Treelight
Triplopia
TriQuarterly
Truck Press
Tule Review
Tupelo Review
Turnrow
Tusculum Review
Twyckenham Notes
Undine
Unicorn Press
University of Chicago Press
University of Georgia Press
University of Illinois Press
University of Iowa Press
University of Massachusetts Press
University of North Texas Press
University of Pittsburgh Press
University of Wisconsin Press
University Press of New England

Unmuzzled Ox
Unspeakable Visions of the Individual
Vagabond
Vallum
Verse
Verse Wisconsin
Vignette
Virginia Quarterly Review
Volt
The Volta
Wampeter Press
War, Literature & The Arts
Washington Square Review
Washington Writer's Workshop
Water-Stone
Water Table
Wave Books
Waxwing
West Branch
Western Humanities Review
Westigan Review
White Pine Press

Wickwire Press
Wigleaf
Willow Springs
Wilmore City
Witness
Word Beat Press
Wordsmith
World Literature Today
WordTemple Press
Wormwood Review
Writers' Forum
Xanadu
Yale Review
Yardbird Reader
Yarrow
Y-Bird
Yes Yes Books
Zeitgeist Press
Zoetrope: All-Story
Zone 3
ZYZZYVA

THE PUSHCART PRIZE

FELLOWSHIPS

The Pushcart Prize Fellowships Inc., a 501 (c) (3) nonprofit corporation, is the endowment for The Pushcart Prize. "Members" donated up to $249 each. "Sponsors" gave between $250 and $999. "Benefactors" donated from $1000 to $4,999. "Patrons" donated $5,000 and more. We are very grateful for these donations. Gifts of any amount are welcome. For information write to the Fellowships at PO Box 380, Wainscott, NY 11975.

FOUNDING PATRONS

The Katherine Anne Porter Literary Trust
Michael and Elizabeth R. Rea

PATRONS

Anonymous
Margaret Ajemian Ahnert
Daniel L. Dolgin & Loraine F. Gardner
James Patterson Foundation
Neltje
Charline Spektor
Ellen M. Violett

BENEFACTORS

Anonymous
Russell Allen
Hilaria & Alec Baldwin
David Caldwell
Ted Conklin
Bernard F. Conners
Catherine and C. Bryan Daniels
Maureen Mahon Egen
Dallas Ernst
Cedering Fox
H.E. Francis
Mary Ann Goodman & Bruno Quinson Foundation

Bill & Genie Henderson
Bob Henderson
Marina & Stephen E. Kaufman
Wally & Christine Lamb
Dorothy Lichtenstein
Joyce Carol Oates
Warren & Barbara Phillips
Stacey Richter
Glyn Vincent
Kirby E. Williams
Margaret V. B. Wurtele

Gwen Head
The Healing Muse
Robin Hemley
Bob Hicok
Jane Hirshfield
Helen & Frank Houghton
Joseph Hurka
Christian Jara
Diane Johnson
Janklow & Nesbit Asso.
Edmund Keeley
Thomas E. Kennedy
Sydney Lea
Stephen Lesser
Gerald Locklin
Thomas Lux
Markowitz, Fenelon and Bank
Elizabeth McKenzie

McSweeney's
John Mullen
Joan Murray
Barbara and Warren Phillips
Hilda Raz
Stacey Richter
Schaffner Family Foundation
Sharasheff—Johnson Fund
Cindy Sherman
Joyce Carol Smith
May Carlton Swope
Glyn Vincent
Julia Wendell
Philip White
Kirby E. Williams
Eleanor Wilner
David Wittman
Richard Wyatt & Irene Eilers

MEMBERS

Anonymous (3)
Stephen Adams
Betty Adcock
Agni
Carolyn Alessio
Dick Allen
Henry H. Allen
John Allman
Lisa Alvarez
Jan Lee Ande
Dr. Russell Anderson
Ralph Angel
Antietam Review
Susan Antolin
Ruth Appelhof
Philip and Marjorie Appleman
Linda Aschbrenner
Renee Ashley
Ausable Press
David Baker
Catherine Barnett
Dorothy Barresi
Barlow Street Press
Jill Bart
Ellen Bass
Judith Baumel
Ann Beattie
Madison Smartt Bell
Beloit Poetry Journal
Pinckney Benedict
Karen Bender
Andre Bernard
Christopher Bernard
Wendell Berry

Linda Bierds
Stacy Bierlein
Big Fiction
Bitter Oleander Press
Mark Blaeuer
John Blondel
Blue Light Press
Carol Bly
BOA Editions
Deborah Bogen
Bomb
Susan Bono
Brain Child
Anthony Brandt
James Breeden
Rosellen Brown
Jane Brox
Andrea Hollander Budy
E. S. Bumas
Richard Burgin
Skylar H. Burris
David Caligiuri
Kathy Callaway
Bonnie Jo Campbell
Janine Canan
Henry Carlile
Carrick Publishing
Fran Castan
Mary Casey
Chelsea Associates
Marianne Cherry
Phillis M. Choyke
Lucinda Clark
Suzanne Cleary

Linda Coleman
Martha Collins
Ted Conklin
Joan Connor
J. Cooper
John Copenhaver
Dan Corrie
Pam Cothey
Lisa Couturier
Tricia Currans-Sheehan
Jim Daniels
Daniel & Daniel
Jerry Danielson
Ed David
Josephine David
Thadious Davis
Michael Denison
Maija Devine
Sharon Dilworth
Edward DiMaio
Kent Dixon
A.C. Dorset
Jack Driscoll
Wendy Druce
Penny Dunning
John Duncklee
Nancy Ebert
Elaine Edelman
Renee Edison & Don Kaplan
Nancy Edwards
Ekphrasis Press
M.D. Elevitch
Elizabeth Ellen
Entrekin Foundation
Failbetter.com
Irvin Faust
Elliot Figman
Tom Filer
Carol and Lauerne Firth
Finishing Line Press
Susan Firer
Nick Flynn
Starkey Flythe Jr.
Peter Fogo
Linda Foster
Fourth Genre
John Fulton
Fugue
Alice Fulton
Alan Furst
Eugene Garber
Frank X. Gaspar
A Gathering of the Tribes
Reginald Gibbons
Emily Fox Gordon

Philip Graham
Eamon Grennan
Myrna Goodman
Ginko Tree Press
Jessica Graustain
Lee Meitzen Grue
Habit of Rainy Nights
Rachel Hadas
Susan Hahn
Meredith Hall
Harp Strings
Jeffrey Harrison
Clarinda Harriss
Lois Marie Harrod
Healing Muse
Tim Hedges
Michele Helm
Alex Henderson
Lily Henderson
Daniel Henry
Neva Herington
Lou Hertz
Stephen Herz
William Heyen
Bob Hicok
R. C. Hildebrandt
Kathleen Hill
Lee Hinton
Jane Hirshfield
Edward Hoagland
Daniel Hoffman
Doug Holder
Richard Holinger
Rochelle L. Holt
Richard M. Huber
Brigid Hughes
Lynne Hugo
Karla Huston
Illya's Honey
Susan Indigo
Mark Irwin
Beverly A. Jackson
Richard Jackson
Christian Jara
David Jauss
Marilyn Johnston
Alice Jones
Journal of New Jersey Poets
Robert Kalich
Sophia Kartsonis
Julia Kasdorf
Miriam Polli Katsikis
Meg Kearney
Celine Keating
Brigit Kelly

John Kistner
Judith Kitchen
Stephen Kopel
Peter Krass
David Kresh
Maxine Kumin
Valerie Laken
Babs Lakey
Linda Lancione
Maxine Landis
Lane Larson
Dorianne Laux & Joseph Millar
Sydney Lea
Stephen Lesser
Donald Lev
Dana Levin
Gerald Locklin
Rachel Loden
Radomir Luza, Jr.
William Lychack
Annette Lynch
Elzabeth MacKieman
Elizabeth Macklin
Leah Maines
Mark Manalang
Norma Marder
Jack Marshall
Michael Martone
Tara L. Masih
Dan Masterson
Peter Matthiessen
Maria Matthiessen
Alice Mattison
Tracy Mayor
Robert McBrearty
Jane McCafferty
Rebecca McClanahan
Bob McCrane
Jo McDougall
Sandy McIntosh
James McKean
Roberta Mendel
Didi Menendez
Barbara Milton
Alexander Mindt
Mississippi Review
Martin Mitchell
Roger Mitchell
Jewell Mogan
Patricia Monaghan
Jim Moore
James Morse
William Mulvihill
Nami Mun
Joan Murray

Carol Muske-Dukes
Edward Mycue
Deirdre Neilen
W. Dale Nelson
New Michigan Press
Jean Nordhaus
Celeste Ng
Christiana Norcross
Ontario Review Foundation
Daniel Orozco
Other Voices
Paris Review
Alan Michael Parker
Ellen Parker
Veronica Patterson
David Pearce, M.D.
Robert Phillips
Donald Platt
Plain View Press
Valerie Polichar
Pool
Horatio Potter
Jeffrey & Priscilla Potter
C.E. Poverman
Marcia Preston
Eric Puchner
Osiris
Tony Quagliano
Quill & Parchment
Barbara Quinn
Randy Rader
Juliana Rew
Belle Randall
Martha Rhodes
Nancy Richard
Stacey Richter
James Reiss
Katrina Roberts
Judith R. Robinson
Jessica Roeder
Martin Rosner
Kay Ryan
Sy Safransky
Brian Salchert
James Salter
Sherod Santos
Ellen Sargent
R.A. Sasaki
Valerie Sayers
Maxine Scates
Alice Schell
Dennis & Loretta Schmitz
Helen Schulman
Philip Schultz
Shenandoah

Daniel Halpern

Edward Hoagland

John Irving

Ha Jin

Mary Karr

Joan Murray

Wally Lamb

Rick Moody

Joyce Carol Oates

Sherod Santos

Grace Schulman

Charles Simic

Gerald Stem

Charles Wright

CONTRIBUTING SMALL PRESSES FOR PUSHCART PRIZE XLIV

(These presses made or received nominations for this edition.)

The A 3 Review, Calle Peñuelas 25, 4-4, Madrid 28005, Spain
AbstractMagazineTV.com, 1305 E. Boyd St., Norman, OK 73071
Abyss & Apex, 116 Tennyson Dr., Lexington, SC 29073
Academy of American Poets, 75 Maiden Ln, #901, New York, NY 10038
The Account, 2501 W. Zia Rd., #8204, Santa Fe, NM 87505
Adirondack Review, 11 Smith Terrace, Highland, NY 12528
The Adroit Journal, LaBerge, 1223 Westover Rd., Stamford, CT 06902
Aeolus House, PO Box 53031, 10 Royal Orchard Blvd., Thornhill, ON L3T
    3C0, Canada
Adelaide Books, 244 Fifth Ave., Ste. D27, New York, NY 10001
After Happy Hour Review, 136 Conneaut Dr., Pittsburgh, PA 15239
Agape Editions, 865 Brookside Dr., Ann Arbor, MI 48105
Agni Magazine, Boston Univ., 236 Bay State Rd., Boston, MA 02215
Alaska Quarterly Review, ESH 208, 3211 Providence Dr., Anchorage, AK
    99508-4614
Alice James Books, 114 Prescott St., Farmington, ME 04938
Alien Buddha Press, 3107 N. 53rd Dr., Phoenix, AZ 85031
Altadena Poetry Review, 468 E. Marigold St., Altadena, CA 91001
Altered Reality, UNI, 1001 Bartlett Hall, Cedar Falls, IA 50614-0502
Always Crashing, 1401 N. St. Clair, #3A, Pittsburgh, PA 15206
American Chordata, 589 Flatbush Ave., #2, Brooklyn, NY 11225
Alternating Current Press, PO Box 270921, Louisville, CO 80027
American Journal of Poetry, 14969 Chateau Village Dr., Chesterfield, MO
    63017
American Literary Review, 1155 Union Cir, #311307, Denton, TX 76203
American Poetry Journal, 24 Cushing Green So., Pawling, NY 12564

The American Scholar, 1606 New Hampshire Ave. NW, Washington, DC
  20009
American Short Fiction, P.O. Box 4152, Austin, TX 78765
Anaphora Literary Press, 1108 W 3rd St., Quanah, TX 79252
Anchala Studios, 106 Suffolk Pl., Chapel Hill, NC 27516
Ancient Paths, 3316 Arbor Creek Lane, Flower Mound, TX 75022
Anomaly, 2031 Arch St., #105, Philadelphia, PA 19103
Anti-Heroin Chic, 6784 Route 113, Thetford Center, VT 05075
Anvil Press, 278 East First Ave., Vancouver, BC V5T 1A6, Canada
Appalachian Heritage, Howard, CPO 2166, Berea, KY 40404-0001
Apparition, 3718 McMillan St., Charlotte, NC 28205
Apple Valley Review, 88 South 3rd St., #336, San José, CA 95113
Apt, Aforementioned Productions, 8 Dana Ave., Albany, NY 12208
Arc Poetry Magazine, Box 81060, Ottawa, ON K1P 1B1, Canada
The Ardent Writer Press, 1014 Stone Dr., Brownsboro, AL 35741
Ariel Chart, Rossi, 227 Laurel Landing Blvd. Kingsland, GA 31548
Arkana, Thompson Hall, 2019 Bruce St., Rm 324, Conway, AR 72034
Arkansas International, UAR, Kimpel Hall 333, Fayetteville, AR 72701
ArLiJo, PO Box 3812, Arlington, VA 22203
Arts & Letters Journal, Box 89, Georgia Coll., Milledgeville, GA 31061
Arundel Books, 212 First Ave S., Seattle, WA 98104-2558
Ascent, Concordia College, 901 8th St. S, Moorhead, MN 56562
Ashland Poetry Press, 401 College Ave., Ashland, OH 44805
Atticus Review, 623 Eagle Rock Ave., #154, West Orange, NJ 07052
Auburn Avenue, PO Box 824, Ellenwood, GA 30294
Aurora Poetry, 1918 S. Harvard Blvd., #10, Los Angeles, CA 90018
The Aurorean, PO Box 187, Farmington, ME 04938
Authreo Media, PO Box 141, Red Wing, MN 55066
Autumn House Press, 5530 Penn Ave., Pittsburgh, PA 15206
Awst, P.O. Box 49163, Austin, TX 78765-9163
Azure, 104 Adelphi Sr., #422, Brooklyn, NY 11205

The Baltimore Review, 6514 Maplewood Rd., Baltimore, MD 21212
Bamboo Ridge Press, PO Box 61781, Honolulu, HI 96839-1781
Banshee, 18 Pacelli Rd., Naas. Co. Kildare, Ireland
Barcelona Review, Correo Viejo 12-2, 08002 Barcelona, Spain
Bards and Sages, 201 Leed Ave., Bellmawr, NJ 08031
Bare Life Review, 1442-A Walnut St., PMB 317, Berkeley, CA 94709
Barrelhouse, 793 Westerly Parkway, State College, PA 16801
Bat City Review, English, 1 University Sta, B 5000, Austin, TX 78712
Bayou Magazine, UNO, 2000 Lake Shore Dr., New Orleans, LA 70148
Bear Review, 4211 Holmes St., Kansas City, MO 64110
Bear Star Press, 185 Hollow Oak Dr., Cohasset, CA 95973

Belletrist Magazine, 3000 Landerholm Circle SE, Bellevue, WA 98007

Bellevue Literary Review, NYU Medicine, 550 First Ave, OBV-A612, New York, NY 10016

Bellingham Review, MS-9053, WWU, Bellingham, WA 98225

Beloit Poetry Journal, PO Box 1450, Windham, ME 04062

Belt Magazine, 1667 E. 40th St., Ste. 1G1, Cleveland, OH 44103

Beltway Poetry Quarterly, 626 Quebec Pl., NW, Washington, DC 20010

Bennington Review, 1 College Dr., Bennington, VT 05201

Better Than Starbucks, 7711 Ashwood Lane, Lake Worth, FL 33467

Big Muddy, SMSU, 1 University Plaza, Cape Girardeau, MO 63701

Big Pond Rumours, 116 Stuart St., Sarnia, ON N7T 3B1, Canada

Big Windows, 4800 East Huron River Dr., Ann Arbor, MI 48105-4800

bioStories, 175 Mission View Dr., Lakeside, MT 59922

bird's thumb, 701 S. Wells St., #2903, Chicago, IL 60607

Birmingham Poetry Review, English, UAB, Birmingham, AL 35294

BkMk Press, UMKC, 5101 Rockhill Rd., Kansas City, MO 64110-2446

Black Dandy Press, 1/15 Sunward Risc, Auckland, 0629 New Zealand

Black Earth Institute, P.O. Box 424, Black Earth, WI 53515

Black Fire Stories, 1993 Hayden, Corinth, TX 76210

Black Fox, 336 Grove Ave., Ste. B, Winter Park, FL 32789

Black Lawrence Press, 279 Claremont Ave., Mount Vernon, NY 10552

Black Warrior, Univ. of Alabama, Box 870170, Tuscaloosa, AL 35487

Blank Spaces, 282906 Normanby/Bentinck Townline, Durham ON N0G 1R0, Canada

Blink Ink, P.O. Box 5, North Branford, CT 06471

Bloodroot Literary Review, 71 Baker Hill Rd., Lyme, NH 03768

Bloomsday Literary, 1039 Orchard Hill S., Houston, TX 77077

Blue Fifth Review, 267 Lark Meadow Circle, Bluff City, TN 37618

Blue Heron, N66W38350 Deer Creek Ct., Oconomowoc, WI 53066

Blue Light Press, PO Box 150300, San Rafael, CA 94915

Blue Mesa Review, UNM, MSC 04 2700, Albuquerque, NM 87131

Blue Unicorn, 13 Jefferson Ave., San Rafael, CA 94903

BOA Editions, 250 North Goodman St., Ste. 306, Rochester, NY 14607

Bodega Magazine, 451 Court St., #3R, Brooklyn, NY 11231

Body, D35 a.s., Antala Staska 5H/40, 140 00 Praha 4, Czech Republic

Body Without Organs, PO Box 1332, Gambier, OH 43022

The Boiler, 311 Jagoe St., #7, Denton, TX 76201

Bold + Italic, 1234 Bloomfield St., Hoboken, NJ 07030

Boned, 1341 Washington, #8, Denver, CO 80203

Booth, 4600 Sunset Ave., Indianapolis, IN 46208

Border Crossing, 650 W. Easterday Ave., Sault Ste. Marie, MI 49783

Bosque Press, 508 Chamiso Lane, NW, Los Ranchos, NM 87107

Bottom Dog Press, PO Box 425, Huron, OH 44839

Boulevard, 4125 Juniata St., B, St. Louis, MO 63116

Box Turtle Press, 184 Franklin St., New York, NY 10013

Boxcar Poetry Review, 14706 NE 28th St., Vancouver, WA 98682

Brain Mill Press, 2351 Sunrise Crt., Green Bay, WI 54303

Brevity, c/o Moore, 265 E State St., Athens, OH 45701

Briar Cliff Review, 3303 Rebecca St., Sioux City, IA 51104-2100

Brick Road Poetry Press, 513 Broadway, Columbus, GA 31901

Brilliant Flash Fiction, 149 Bonner Spgs Ranch Rd., Laporte, CO 80535

Brink Literacy Project, 1050 S. Monaco Pkwy #8, Denver, CO 80224

Broad Street, 4214 Southampton Rd., Richmond, VA 23235

Broadkill Review, PO Box 63, Milton, DE 19968

Broadsided Press, P.O. Box 24, Provincetown, MA 02657

Broadstone Books, 418 Ann St., Frankfort, KY 40601-1929

Broken Sleep Books, Tegfam, Cwm-Cou, SA38 9PD, Wales, UK

Brooklyn Poets, 135 Jackson St., #2A, Brooklyn, NY 11211

Brooklyn Rail, 253 36th St., Ste. C304, Unit 20, Brooklyn, NY 11232

Brooklyn Review, 35 Eastern Parkway, #3F, Brooklyn, NY 11238

Brown Orient, 788 Harrison St. #411, San Francisco, CA 94107

BTS Books, 22 Bramwith Rd., Sheffield, S11 7EZ, UK

Bull & Cross, Julian, C/Mestre Racional, 12, 4, Pta 9, 46005 Valencia, Valencia, Espanā

Burningword Literary Journal, PO Box 6215, Kokomo, IN 46904-6215

Burrow Press, P.O. Box 533709, Orlando, FL 32853

Button Poetry, 1219 Marquette Ave., Ste. 390, Minneapolis, MN 55403

Cagibi, 801 Avenue C, #4C, Brooklyn, NY 11218

cahoodaloodaling, 2100 College Dr., #65, Baton Rouge, LA 70808

California Quarterly, PO Box 2672, Del Mar, CA 92014

Calliope, 2506 SE Bitterbrush Dr., Madras, OR 97741-9452

Calypso Editions, Davidson, 2540 Goldsmith, Houston, TX 77030

CapsuleCrit, Lacina, 2031 Arch St., #105, Philadelphia, PA 19103

Capturing Fire Press, 1240 4th St NE, #239, Washington, DC 20002

Carbon Culture Review, 845 Fenimore St., Winston Salem, NC 27103

Catamaran, 1050 River St., #118, Santa Cruz, CA 95060

Catapult, 1140 Broadway, Ste. 704, New York, NY 10001

Cave Wall Press, PO Box 29546, Greensboro, NC 27429-9546

Cease, Cows, 133 Chaucer Manor Cir, #C, Kernersville, NC 27284

Central Avenue Publishing, 396-5148 Ladner Trunk Rd., Delta BC V4K 5B6, Canada

Chaffin Journal, Mattox 101, 521 Lancaster Ave., Richmond, KY 40475

Chaleur Magazine, PO Box 1205, Madison, NJ 07940

Chattahoochee Review, 555 N. Indian Creek Dr., Clarkston, GA 30021

Chatter House, 7915 S. Emerson Ave., Ste. B303, Indianapolis, IN 46237

Chatwin Books, 80 S. Washington St, Ste 202, Seattle, WA 98104

Chautauqua, Cr. Writing, 601 S. College Rd., Wilmington, NC 28403

Cheap Pop, 6021 Mission Trail, #3, Granger, IN 46530

Chicago Quarterly Review, 517 Sherman Ave., Evanston, IL 60202

Chinese and Foreign Pen, Rm 706, 2, 398 Ln, Dapu Road, Shanghai, 200023, China

Chiron Review, 522 E. South Ave., St. John, KS 67576-2212

Cholla Needles, 6732 Conejo Ave., Joshua Tree, CA 92252

Chrome Baby, 602 Graham Ave., #219, Fredericton, NB E3B 4C3 Canada

Cimarron Review, English, Oklahoma State Univ., Stillwater, OK 74078

Cincinnati Review, English, PO Box 210069, Cincinnati, OH 45221

Circling Rivers, PO Box 8291, Richmond, VA 23225

Cirque Press, 3978 Defiance St., Anchorage, AK 99504

Citron Review, 291 Walnut Village Lane, Henderson, NV 89012

Cleaver Magazine, 8250 Shawnee St., Philadelphia, PA 19118

Cleveland State University Poetry Center, 2121 Euclid Ave., Cleveland, OH 44115-2214

Clockhouse, PO Box 784, Middleburg, VA 20118

Cloudbank, PO Box 610, Corvallis, OR 97339-0610

Coal City, English Dept., University of Kansas, Lawrence, KS 66045

Codhill Press, 1 Arden Lane, New Paltz, NY 12561

Cold Mountain Review, ASU Box 32052, Boone, NC 28608

Coffin Bell Journal, 1109 Orchard Park Rd., West Seneca, NY 14224

Collective Unrest, 4960 Coronado Ave., San Diego, CA 92107

Colorado Review, CSU, English, Fort Collins, CO 80523-9105

Columbia Poetry Review, 600 So. Michigan Ave., Chicago, IL 60605

The Common, Frost Library, Amherst College, Amherst, MA 01002

The Common Reader, Box 1098. 1 Brookings Dr., St. Louis, MO 63130

Concho River Review, Angelo State Univ., San Angelo, TX 76909-0894

Conjunctions, 21 East 10th St., New York, NY 10003

Connecticut River Review, 9 Edmund Pl, West Hartford, CT 06119

Constellations, 127 Lake View Ave., Cambridge, MA 02138

Contrary, S. Beers, 615 NW 6th St., Pendleton, OR 97801

Copper Nickel, Campus Box 175, Denver, CO 80217-3364

The Courtship of Winds, 55 Cortland Lane, Boxborough, MA 01719

Cowboy Jamboree, 605 Wright's Crossing, Cobden, IL 62920

Crab Creek, P.O. Box 1682, Kingston, WA 98346

Crab Fat Magazine, 1128 Hermitage Rd., #303, Richmond, VA 23220

Crab Orchard Review, English, So. Illinois Univ., Carbondale, IL 62901

Crack the Spine, 6449 Sea Isle, Galveston, TX 77554

Craft, 70 SW Century Dr., Ste. 100442, Bend, OR 97702

Crave Press, 256 Abbey Lane, Leesport, PA 19533

Crazyhorse, College of Charleston, 66 George St., Charleston, SC 29424

Cream City Review, UW-M, PO Box 413, Milwaukee, WI 53201
Creative Nonfiction, 5119 Coral St., Pittsburgh, PA 15224
Creative Talents Unleashed, PO Box 605, Helendale, CA 92342
Crisis Chronicles, 3431 George Ave., Parma, OH 44134
Critical Read, 276 Fifth Ave., Ste. 704, New York, NY 10001
Cultural Weekly, 3330 S. Peck Ave., #14, San Pedro, CA 90731
Cumberland River Review, English, TNU, Nashville, TN 37210-2877
Cutthroat, A Journal of the Arts, PO Box 2414, Durango, CO 81302

D. M. Kreg Publishing, 3985 Wonderland Hill Ave., #201, Boulder, CO 80304
Darkhouse Books, 160 J St., #2223, Niles, CA 94536
Dash, Cal State Fullerton, English, PO Box 6848, Fullerton, CA 92834
David Robert Books, PO Box 541106, Cincinnati, OH 45254
december, P.O. Box 16130, St. Louis, MO 63105
decomP, 3002 Grey Wolf Cove, New Albany, IN 47150
Deep Magic, PO Box 1564, Cottage Grove, OR 97424
Deerbrook Editions, PO Box 542, Cumberland, ME 04021-0542
Delmarva Review, PO Box 544, St. Michaels, MD 21663
Diagram, New Michigan Press, 8058 E. 7th St., Tucson, AZ 85710
Digging Through the Fat, 130 W. Pleasant Ave., #307, Maywood, NJ 07607
Diode Editions, PO Box 5585, Richmond, VA 23220
The DMQ Review, 16393 Bonnie Lane, Los Gatos, CA 95032
Dream Pop Press, 6 Balsamo Ln., Ranchos de Taos, NM 87557
Dreamers, 585 Bruce St., Hepworth, ON N0H 1P0, Canada
Dreams and Nightmares, 1300 Kicker Rd., Tuscaloosa, AL 35404
Driftwood Press, 14737 Montoro Dr., Austin, TX 78728
Drunk Monkeys, 252 N Cordova St., Burbank, CA 91505
Dying Dahlia Review, 95 York St., Lambertville, NJ 08530

EAP: The Magazine, 1892 Colestin Rd., Ashland, OR 97520
Eastern Iowa Review, 6332 33rd Avenue Dr., Shellsburg, IA 52332
Eastern Shore Writers Association, Sauder, 615 N. Pinehurst Ave., Salisbury, MD 21801
Eckleburg Review, 205 North Pointe Terr, Middletown, MD 21769
Eclectia, 6030 N. Sheridan Rd., #805, Chicago, IL 60660
Ecotheo Review, 352 Kelley Rd., Unit A, Bastrop, TXJ 78602
ecotone, UNCW, 601 S. College Rd., Wilmington, NC 28403-5938
805 Lit + Art, 1301 Barcarrota Blvd W, Brandenton, FL 34205
Ekphrasis, PO Box 161236, Sacramento, CA 95816-1236
Electric Literature, Ste. 26, 147 Prince St., Brooklyn, NY 11201
Elm Leaves, English, Ketchum 301A, 1300 Elmwood Ave., Buffalo, NY 14222
The Emrys Journal, PO Box 8813, Greenville, SC 29604
Encircle Publications, P.O. Box 187, Farmington, ME 04938

Entre Rios Books, 733 25th Ave. So., Seattle, WA 98144
Epoch, 251 Goldwin Smith Hall, Cornell University, Ithaca NY 14853
The Esthetic Apostle, 1418 N. Maple Ave., La Grange Park, IL 60526
Etched Press, Dublin, 3 Bayside Village Pl., San Francisco, CA 94107
Ethel, 1001 Willow Pl., Lafayette, CO 80026
Evansville Review, UE, 1800 Lincoln Ave., Evansville, IN 47722
Event, PO Box 2503, New Westminster, BC, V3L 5B2, Canada
Exit 13, PO Box 423, Fanwood, NJ 07023
Exposition Review, 23619 Via Clasico, Valencia, CA 91355
Eye to the Telescope, UNI, Gotera, 1001 Bartlett Hall, Cedar Falls, IA 50614-0502

failbetter, 2022 Grove Ave., Richmond, VA 23220
Fairy Tale Review, English Dept., Univ. of Arizona, Tucson, AZ 85721
Fiction, College of NY, English, Convent Ave & 138th St, NY, NY 10031
Fiction Week Literary Review, 887 South Rice Rd., Ojai, CA 93023
Fictive Dream, 79 Court Lane, Dulwich, London SE21 7EF, UK
Fiddlehead, Box 4400, Univ. New Brunswick, Fredericton NB E3B 5A3, Canada
Field, 50 North Professor St., Oberlin, OH 44074-1091
fields magazine, 3502 E. 12th St., Unit A, Austin, TX 78721
Fifth Wednesday, P.O. Box 4033, Lisle, IL 60532-9033
Figure 1, 286 Union Ave., #4A, Brooklyn, NY 11211
Finishing Line Press, P.O. Box 1626, Georgetown, KY 40324
Five Oaks Press, 6 Five Oaks Dr., Newburgh, NY 12550
Five Points, Georgia State University, Box 3999, Atlanta, GA 30302
Flash Frontier, 45 Glendale Rd., Whangarei 0110, New Zealand
Fledging Rag, 1716 Swarr Run Rd., J-108, Lancaster, PA 17601
Floating Bridge, 909 NE 43rd St., #205, Seattle, WA 98105
Flock, PO Box 7944, Roanoke, VA 24019
Florida Review, PO Box 161346, Orlando, FL 32816—1346
Flowersong Books, 1218 N. 15th St., McAllen, TX 78501
Flying Island, 1125 Brookside Ave., #B25, Indianapolis, IN 46202
Flyway, English Dept., 206 Ross Hall, Iowa State Univ., Ames, IA 50010
Foglifter, 214 Grand Ave., #40, Oakland, CA 94610
Folded Word, 79 Tracy Way, Meredith, NH 03253-5409
Fomite, 58 Peru St., Burlington, VT 05401-8606
The Font, A. Shishin, 306-801 Okubo Machi, Okubo-Cho, Akashi-shi, Hyogo-ken, 674-0067, Japan
Foothill Poetry Journal, 165 E. 10th St., Claremont, CA 91711-6186
Forge, 4018 Bayview Ave., San Mateo, CA 94403-4310
Foundlings Press, 14 Fairfield Sr., #2, Buffalo, NY 14214
Foundry, 10 Halley St., Yonkers, NY 10704

4 X 4 Magazine, 70 Morningside Dr., New York, NY 10027

Four Way Review, c/o White, 1217 Odyssey Dr., Durham, NC 27713

Fourth Genre, 434 Farm Lane, Rm 235, MSU, East Lansing, MI 48824

Fowlpox Press, 28915 Hwy 7, PO Box 47, Moser River, NS B0J 2K0, Canada

Free State Review, 3222 Rocking Horse Lane, Aiken, SC 29801

Freedom Voices, PO Box 423115, San Francisco, CA 94142

Freeze Frame, 8419 Somerset Dr., Prairie Village, KS 66207

Freshwater Literary Journal, ACC, 170 Elm St., Enfield, CT 06082

Frontier Poetry, 818 SW 3rd Ave., #21-5911, Portland, OR 97204

Galleywinter Poetry, Simmons, 2778 Elizabeth Pl., Lebanon, OR 97355

Garden Oak Press, 1953 Huffstatler St., Ste. A, Rainbow, CA 92028

Gargoyle Magazine, 3819 13th St. N., Arlington, VA 22201-4922

Gemini Magazine, PO Box 1485, Onset, MA 02558

genre2, 303 Wyoming Ave., Billings, MT 59101

The Georgia Review, University of Georgia, Athens, GA 30602-9009

The Gettysburg Review, Gettysburg College, Box 2446, Gettysburg, PA 17325

Gigantic Sequins, 209 Avon St., Breaux Bridge, LA 70517

Gimmick Press, 598 Ann St., Plymouth, MI 48170

Gingerbread House, 378 Howell Ave., Cincinnati, OH 45220

Gival Press, PO Box 3812, Arlington, VA 22203

Glass Lyre Press, PO Box 2693, Glenview, IL 60025

Glass Poetry Press, 1667 Crestwood, Toledo, OH 43612

Glassworks, 260 Victoria St., Glassboro, NJ 08028

Glimmer Train Press, P.O. Box 80430, Portland, OR 97280-1430

Glint, FSU, English Dept., 1200 Murchison Rd., Fayetteville, NC 28301

Gobshite Quarterly, 338 NE Roth St., Portland, OR 97211

Gordon Square Review, 7405 Detroit Ave., Cleveland, OH 44102

Grain Magazine, PO Box 3986, Regina, SK S4P 3R9, Canada

Granta, 12 Addison Ave., Holland Park, London W11 4QR, UK

The Gravity of the Thing, 17028 Rhone St., Portland, OR 97236

great weather for MEDIA, 515 Broadway, #2B, New York, NY 10012

Green Hills Literary Lantern, TSU, English, Kirksville, MO 63501-4221

Green Linden Press, 208 Broad St South, Grinnell, IA 50112

The Greensilk Journal, 228 N. Main St., Woodstock, VA 22664

Grief Diaries, DiLallo, 657 24th Ave., #38, Santa Cruz, CA 95062

Grist, 301 McClung Tower, Univ. of Tennessee, Knoxville, TN 37996

Groundhog, 6915 Ardmore Dr., Roanoke, VA 24019-4403

Guernica, 157 Columbus Ave., c/o The Yard, New York, NY 10023

Gulf Coast, English, University of Houston, Houston, TX 77204-3013

Gyroscope Review, 1891 Merrill St., Roseville, MN 55113

Habitat, 150 West 30th St., Ste 902, New York, NY 10001

Half Mystic Press, 67 Rosewood Dr., #05-33, 737876 Singapore, SG

Halophyte, 450 E. 100 S, #17, Salt Lake City, UT 84111

Hand Type Press, P.O. Box 3941, Minneapolis, MN 55403-0941

Harpur Palate, Binghamton Univ., PO Box 6000, Binghamton, NY 13902

Harvard Review, Lamont Library, Harvard Univ., Cambridge, MA 02138

Harvard Square Editions, 2152 Beachwood Terr, Hollywood, CA 90068

Haus Publishing, 4 Cinnamon Row, London SW11 3TW, UK

Hayden's Ferry Review, P.O. Box 871401, Tempe, AZ 85287-1401

Healing Muse, SUNY Med. Univ., 618 Irving Ave., Syracuse, NY 13210

Hedge Apple, BSH 127, 11400 Robinwood Dr., Hagerstown, MD 21742

Hedgehog Review, UV, P.O. Box 400816, Charlottesville, VA 22904

Heyday, P.O. Box 9145, Berkeley, CA 94709

High Desert Journal, PO Box 23012, Federal Way, WA 90893

Highland Park Poetry, 376 Park Ave., Highland Park, IL 60035

Hip Pocket Press, 5 Del Mar Court, Orinda, CA 94563

Hippocampus Magazine, 222 E. Walnut St., #2, Lancaster, PA 17602

Hobart, PO Box 1658, Ann Arbor, MI 48106

The Hollins Critic, P.O. Box 9538, Roanoke, VA 24020-1538

The Hopper, 1511 Grove St., #B, Boulder, CO 80302

Hot Metal Bridge, English, Univ. of Pittsburgh, Pittsburgh, PA 15260

Hub City, 186 West Main St, Spartanburg, SC 29306

The Hudson Review, 33 West 67th St., New York, NY 10023

Huizache, UHV University Center, #130, 3007 N. Ben Wilson St., Victoria, TX 77901

Hunger Mountain, Vermont Coll., 36 College St., Montpelier, VT 05602

Hypertrophic Press, P.O. Box 423, New Market, AL 35761

Hysterical Literary, 1116 Manhattan Ave., #2R, Brooklyn, NY 11222

I-70 Review, 5021 S. Tierney Dr., Independence, MO 64055

Ibbetson Street Press, 25 School Street, Somerville, MA 02143

The Idaho Review, Boise State, 1910 University Dr., Boise, ID 83725

Ilanot Review, English Dept., Bar-Ilan Univ., 52 900 Ramat-Gan, Israel

Image, 3307 Third Avenue West, Seattle, WA 98119

In Translation, c/o Brooklyn Rail, 253 36th St., Ste. C304, Unit 20, Brooklyn, NY 11232

Indiana Review, 1020 E. Kirkwood Ave., Bloomington, IN 47405-7103

Indianapolis Review, 1712 Provincial Dr., South Bend, IN 46614

Ink in Thirds, 707 Halstead Ct. SE, Huntsville, AL 35803

Intima, 36 N Moore St., #4W, New York, NY 10013

Into the Void, 112 Claremont St., Toronto, ON M6J 2M5, Canada

Inverted Syntax, PO Box 2044, Longmont CO 80502

The Iowa Review, 308 EPB, University of Iowa, Iowa City, IA 52242

Isthmus, PO Box 9573, Seattle, WA 98109

J Journal, 524 West 59th St., 7th Fl, New York, NY 10019

Jabberwock Review, MSU., P.O. Box E, Mississippi State, MS 39762

Jacar Press, 6617 Deerview Trail, Durham, NC 27712

Jelly Bucket, 521 Lancaster Ave., Mattox 101, Richmond, KY 40475

Jellyfish Review, Medit. 1, D15KC, TJD, 11470 Jakarta Barat, Indonesia

Jerry Jazz Musician, 2207 NE Broadway, Portland, OR 97232

Jersey Devil Press, Sweeney, 813 Waverly Ave., Neptune, NJ 07753

Jet Fuel Review, English, Lewis University, 1 University Pkwy, Romeoville, IL
    60446-2200

JMF Chapbooks, 92 Parkview Loop, Staten Island, NY 10314

jmww, 2105 E. Lamley St., Baltimore, MD 21231

Joao Rogue Literary Journal, 3 Burlington, UB7 9FE W. Drayton, UK

The Journal, Ohio State Univ., 164 Annie & John Glenn Ave., Columbus, OH
    43210

Juked, 108 New Mark Esplanade, Rockville, MD 20850

Juniper, 47 Robina Ave., Toronto, ON M6C 3Y5, Canada

JuxtaProse, 4430 Aster St., Springfield, OR 97478

Kairos Literary Magazine, 640 Santander Ave., #7, Coral Gables, FL 38134

Kallisto Gaia Press, 1801 E. 51st St., Ste. 365-246, Austin, TX 78723

Kelsay Books, 502 S. 1040 E, #A119, American Fork, UT 84003

Kelsey Review, MCCC, 1200 Old Trenton Rd., West Windsor, NJ 08550

Kenyon Review, Finn House, 102 W. Wiggin St., Gambier, OH 43022

Kerf, COR, 883 W. Washington Blvd., Crescent City, CA 95531-8361

Kestrel, Fairmont State Univ., 1201 Locust Ave., Fairmont, WV 26554

Kore Press, PO Box 42315, Tucson AZ 85733-2315

Kweli Journal, P.O. Box 693, New York, NY 10021

KYSO Flash, 3348 Videra Dr., Eugene, OR 97405

L'Éphémère, 253 College St., #1312, Toronto, ON M5T 1R5, Canada

La Presa, 6505 Carlinda Ave., Columbia, MD 21046

Lady/Liberty/Lit, 667 Country Club Dr., Incline Village, NV 89451

Lake Effect, Humanities, 4951 College Drive, Erie, PA 16563-1501

Lake Mesa, PO Box 57060, Calgary, AB T1Y 5T4, Canada

Lantern, 128 2nd Place, Garden Suite, Brooklyn, NY 11231-4102

Lascaux Review, 275 Conner St., Clinton, AR 72031

Latah Books, 31 W. Maine Ave., Spokane, WA 99021

Latterly, 3583 Randolph Rd., Mogadore, OH 44260

Laurel Review, NWMSU, 800 University Dr., Marysville, MO 64468

Lavender Review, P.O. Box 275, Eagle Rock, MO 65641-0275

Levee Magazine, 3928 Henderson Way, Sacramento, CA 95608

Light, 500 Joseph C. Wilson Blvd., CPU Box 271051, Rochester, NY 14627

Light 2000, 14 Gleann Ruairi, Rostrevor BT34 3GE, Co. Down, N. Ireland

Likely Red Press, 735 S. 2nd St., #303, Louisville, KY 40202

Lillicat Publishers, 402 N Cuyamaca St., El Cajon, CA 92020

Lindenwood Review, 400 N. Kingshighway, St. Charles, MO 63301

Lips, P.O. Box 616, Florham Park, NJ 07932

Liquid Imagination, 7800 Loma Del Norte Rd. NE, Albuquerque, NM 87109

The Literal Latté, 41 5th Ave., #4B, New York, NY 10003

The Literary Hatchet, 328 French St., Fl. 2, Fall River, MA 02720

Literary House Press, Washington College, 300 Washington Ave., Chesterton, MD 21620

Literary Yard, 5810 W. Jefferson Commons Cir., Unit 314, Kalamazoo, MI 49009

LitMag, Greeley Square Station, PO Box 20091, New York, NY 10001

Little Fiction/Big Truths, 1608-1910 Lake Shore Blvd. W., Toronto, ON M6S 1A2, Canada

Live Mag!, P.O, Box 1215, Cooper Station, New York, NY 10276

Livingston Press, Stn 22, Univ. West Alabama, Livingston, AL 35470

Loch Raven Review, 1306 Providence Rd., Towson, MD 21286

Locarno Press, 475 Main St., #217, Vancouver, BC V6A 2T7, Canada

Longreads, 189 Smith Ave., Kingston, NY 12401

Longridge Review, 325 W. Colonial Hwy, Hamilton, VA 20158

Loose Moose Publishing, 303 E. Gurley St., #449, Prescott, AZ 86301

Loosey Goosey Press, 1111 Shive Ln, #200, Bowling Green, KY 42103

Los Angeles Review, 11122 Kling St., Toluca Lake, CA 91602

Los Angeles Review of Books, 6671 Sunset Blvd., Ste. 1521, Los Angeles, CA 90028

Lost iN, Brunnenstr 191, 10119, Berlin, Germany

Lost Balloon, 1402 Highland Ave., Berwyn, IL 60402

Lost Horse Press, 105 Lost Horse Lane, Sandpoint, ID 83864

Louisville Review, Spalding U., 851 South 4th St., Louisville, KY 40203

Love's Executive Order, Lippman, 781 Hammond St., Chestnut Hill, MA 02467

Loving Healing Press, 5145 Pontiac Trail, Ann Arbor, MI 48105-9238

Lowestoft Chronicle Press, 1925 Massachusetts Ave., #8, Cambridge, MA 02140

Lumina, Sarah Lawrence College, 1 Mead Way, Bronxville, NY 10708

Luminare Press, 438 Charnelton, Ste. 101, Eugene, OR 97401

Lummox Press, 3129 E. 6th St., Long Beach, CA 90814

Lunch Ticket, 400 Corporate Pointe, Culver City, CA 90230

The MacGuffin, 18600 Haggerty Rd., Livonia, MI 48152

Mad Swirl, Olson, 3600 Commerce, #105, Dallas, TX 75226

Madcap Review, 245 Wallace Rd., Goffstown, NH 03045

Madville Publishing, PO Box 358, Lake Dallas, TX 75065

The Magnolia Review, PO Box 1332, Reynoldsburg, OH 43068

MAKE Literary Productions, 2712 W. Medill Ave., Chicago, IL 60647

Mambo Academy of Kitty Wang, PO Box 5, North Branford, CT 06471

Manhattan Review, 440 Riverside Dr., #38, New York, NY 10027

The Mantle, 4422 Milgate St., Pittsburgh, PA 15224

Manzano Mountain Review, English Dept., 280 La Entrada Rd., Los Lunas, NM 87031

Map Literary, 300 Pompton Rd., Wayne, NJ 07470

The Margins, Asian American Writers' Workshop, 110-112 W. 27th St., #600, New York, NY 10001

Marsh Hawk Press, PO Box 206, East Rockaway, NY 11518

Mason Jar Press, 1439 Medfield Ave., Baltimore, MD 21211

Massachusetts Review, Photo Lab 309, 211 Hicks Way, Amherst, MA 01003

Matador Review, 4608 N. Beacon St., #B-1, Chicago, IL 60640

Matchbook, 333 Harvard St., #5, Cambridge, MA 02139

Matter, 212-30 23rd Ave., #1K, Bayside, NY 11360

McSweeney's, 849 Valencia Sr., San Francisco, CA 94110

The Meadow, VISTA B300, 7000 Dandini Blvd., Reno, NV 89512

Medusa's Laugh, 340 Quinnipiac St., Bldg. 40, Wallingford, CT 06492

Memoir Magazine, 2025 Sprunt Ave., Durham, NC 27705

Menacing Hedge, 424 SW Kenyon St., Seattle, WA 98106

Meniscus Literary Journal, Webb, Canberra Univ., ACT2601, Australia

Mercer University Press, 1501 Mercer University Dr., Macon, GA 31207

Mercurial Stories, 5-2-16 #204 Rakurakuen, Saeki-ku, 731-5136, Hiroshima Japan

Mica Press, Bell, 47 Belle Vue Rd., Wivenhoe, Colchester, Essex CO7 9LD, UK

Michigan Quarterly Review, 0576 Rackham Bldg., 915 E. Washington St., Ann Arbor, MI 48109

Mid-American Review, BGSU, English, Bowling Green, OH 43403

Midnight & Indigo, 300 Prospect Ave., Ste. 5H, Hackensack, NJ 07601

Midway Journal, 216 Banks St., #2, Cambridge, MA 02138

Midwest Review, UW-M, 21 N. Park St., #7101, Madison, WI 53715

Minerva Rising, 9501 Bessie Coleman Blvd, #21082, Tampa, FL 33622

Miracle Monocle, UL, 2211 South Brook, Louisville, KY 40292

Misfit Magazine, 143 Furman St., Schenectady, NY 12304-1113

Mississippi Review, USM, 118 College Dr., #5037, Hattiesburg, MS 39406

Missouri Review, 357 McReynolds Hall, UMO, Columbia, MO 65211

Mizna, 2446 University Ave. West, #115, Saint Paul, MN 55114

Mobius, Journal of Social Change, 149 Talmadge, Madison, WI 53704

MockingHeart Press, PO Box 116, Youngsville, LA 70592

Modern Haiku, PO Box 930, Portsmouth, RI 02871-0930

Modern Language Studies, Susquehanna Univ., English, 514 University Ave., Selinsgrove, PA 17870

mojo, WSU, Lindquist Hall 620, 1845 Fairmount St., Wichita, KS 67260

Molotov Cocktail, 1218 NE 24th Ave., Portland, OR 97232

Monkeybicycle, 611-B Courtland St., Greensboro, NC 27401

Montana Mouthful, 736 N. Ewing St., Helena, MT 59601

Moon City, English, MSU, 901 So National Ave., Springfield, MO 65897

Moon Park Review, 12312 Mt. Pleasant Dr., Laurel, MD 20708

Moonpath Press, PO Box 445, Tillamook, OR 97141-0445

Moon Pie Press, 16 Walton St., Westbrook, ME 04092

Moonrise Press, PO Box 4288, Sunland, CA 91341-4288

Moria, Woodbury U., 7500 N. Glenoaks Blvd., Burbank, CA 91504

Moss, 30 Columbia Pl., #AF, Brooklyn, NY 11201

Mount Hope, RGU, 1 Old Ferry Rd., GHH Bldg., Bristol, RI 02809

Mud Season Review, Post, 80 Austin Dr., #94, Burlington, VT 05401

Muddy River Poetry Review, 15 Eliot St., Chestnut Hill, MA 02467

mudfish, 184 Franklin St., New York, NY 10013

Muse-Pie Press, 73 Pennington Ave., Passaic, NJ 07055

Muzzle, S. Edwards, 2307 Longmeadow St., Denton, TX 76204

Narrative, 2443 Fillmore St., #214, San Francisco, CA 94115

Narrative Northeast, 32 Valley View Rd., Verona, NJ 07044

Nasiona Magazine, 807 Lyon St., San Francisco, CA 94115

Nat. Brut, 17820 Wildflower Way, #1404, Dallas, TX 75252

Natural Bridge, English, UMSL, 1 University Blvd., St. Louis, MO 63121

Naugatuck River Review, PO Box 368, Westfield, MA 01086

Nazim Hikmet Poetry, ATA-NC, 303 E. Durham Rd., #F, Cary, NC 27513

NELLE, UAB, English, HB 217, 1530 3rd Ave. So., Birmingham, AL 35294

Negative Capability Press, 64 Ridgelawn Dr. E., Mobile, AL 36608

Neologism Poetry Press, 34 Glenbrook Dr., #2C, Greenfield, MA 01301

Never Mind the Press, PO Box 8106, Berkeley, CA 94707

New Delta Review, LSU, Allen Hall 9, Baton Rouge, LA 70803

New England Review, Middlebury College, Middlebury, VT 05753

New Feral Press, P.O. Box 358, Oyster Bay, NY 11771

New Flash Fiction, 210 W. Lincoln Ave., Indianola, IA 50125

The New Guard, Writer's Hotel, PO Box 472, Brunswick, ME 04011

New Letters, 5101 Rockhill Rd., Univ. MO, Kansas City MO 64110

New Limestone Review, Univ. of KY, 1249 Patterson Office Tower, Lexington, KY 40506

New Madrid, FH - 7C, Murray State University, Murray, KY 42071

New Millennium Writings, 4021 Garden Dr., Knoxville, TN 37918

New Ohio Review, OU, English, 360 Ellis Hall, Athens, OH 45701

New Orleans Review, Loyola Univ., 6363 St. Charles Ave., New Orleans, LA 70118

New Poetry in Translation, 365 Fairfield Way, U-Box 1057, Storrs, CT 06269

New Pop Lit, 2074 17th St., Wyandotte, MI 48192

New Rivers Press, 1104 7th Ave. S., Moorhead, MN 56563

The New Southern Fugitives, 29 Jackson St., Newnan, GA 30263

New Verse News, Les Belles Maisons H-11, Jl. Serpong Raya, Serpong Utara, Tangerang-Baten 15310, Indonesia

New World Writing, 85 Hardwood Rd., Glenwood, NY 14069

Newfound Journal, 4505 Duval St., #156, Austin, TX 78751

Newtown Literary, 61-15 97th St., #11C, Rego Park, NY 11374

Night Ballet Press, Borsenik, 123 Glendale Ct., Elyria, OH 44035

Nightboat Books, 310 Nassau Ave., Unit 202, Brooklyn, NY 11222-3813

Nimrod, Univ. of Tulsa, 800 South Tucker Dr., Tulsa, OK 74104

Nine Muses Poetry, 'Y Dderwen' 17 Snowdon St., Y Felinheli, Gwynedd LL56 4HQ, Wales

Ninth Letter, 608 S. Wright St., Urbana, IL 61801

Nixes Mate Review, PO Box 1179, Allston, MA 02134-0014

No, Dear, 133 Conselyea St., #1F, Brooklyn, NY 11211

No Tokens, 1736 Bay Blvd., Atlantic Beach, NY 11509

Nomadic Press, 2301 Telegraph Ave., Oakland, CA 94612

Noon, 1324 Lexington Ave., PMB 298, New York, NY 10128

The Normal School, 5245 N. Backer Ave., M/S PB 98, CSU, Fresno, CA 93740-8001

North American Review, UNI, Cedar Falls, IA 50614-0516

North Carolina Literary Review, ECU Mailstop 555 English, Greenville, NC 27858-4353

Notre Dame Review, B009C McKenna, UND, Notre Dame, IN 46556

NUNUM, Miller, 4-4-3-101, Kitashinagawa, Shinagawa, Tokyo, 140-0001, Japan

O-Dark-Thirty, 5812 Morland Drive No., Adamstown, MD 21710

Oakwood Magazine, SDSU, Pugsley Center 302, Box 2218, Brookings, SD, 57001

Obsidian, Illinois State U., Campus Box 4241, Normal, IL 61790-4241

Ocean State Review, Swan 114, 60 Upper College Rd., Kingston, RI 02881

The Offbeat, MSU, 434 Farm Lane, East Lansing, MI 48824

Okay Donkey, 3650 Watseka Ave., #15, Los Angeles, CA 90034

Olive Press, UMO, Lang/Lit, 634 Henderson Dr., Mt. Olive, NC 28365

One Sentence Poem, 1220 Daybreak Dr., Merced, CA 95348

One Story, 232 3rd St., #A108, Brooklyn, NY 11215

Ooligan Press, Portland State Univ., PO Box 751, Portland, OR 97207

Orange Quarterly, Peters, 20 E. Pine St., Cadillac, MI 49601

Orchards Poetry, 4441 Greenview Dr., El Dorado Hills, CA 95762

Origami Poems Project, 1948 Shore View Dr., Indialantic, FL 32903

Osiris, 106 Meadow Lane, Greenfield, MA 01301

Out/cast, 5008 Oaklyn Dr., Des Moines, IA 50310

Outlook Springs, 193 Leighton St., Bangor, ME 04401

Outrider Press, Inc., 2036 North Winds Drive, Dyer, IN 46311

Ovunque Siamo, 17 Douglas St., Ambler, PA 19002

Oxford American, P.O. Box 3235, Little Rock, AR 72203-3235

Oyster River Pages, 1 Greenwood Ave., Glen Burnie, MO 21061

P. R. A. Publishing, PO Box 211701, Martinez, GA 30917

Pacific Standard, 801 Garden St., #101, Santa Barbara, CA 93101

Paddock Review, 452 Gen. John Wayne Blvd., Georgetown, KY 40324

Palette Poetry, 818 SW 3rd Ave., #221-5911, Portland, OR 97204

Paloma Press, 110 28th Ave., San Mateo, CA 94403

Panel Magazine, Eromu utca 6, 2em 7, 1117 Budapest, Hungary

Pangolin Review, 16, Louvet Avenue, Quatre Bornes, Mauritius

Paper Darts, 1310 West 28th St., #3, Minneapolis, MN 55408

Paper Nautilus, 424 Waupeloni Dr., #G13, State College, PA 16801

Parchment Press, 10254 Oxbow Dr., Komoka, ON N0L 1R0, Canada

The Paris Review, 544 West 27th St., New York, NY 10001

Parallel Magazine, 2754 Broadway, New York, NY 10025

Passages North, English Dept., NMU, Marquette, MI 49855-5363

Paul Dry Books, 1700 Sansom St., Ste. 700, Philadelphia, PA 19103

Peach Mag, 174 Crestwood Ave., Buffalo, NY 14216

Peacock Journal, 12702 Eldrid Pl., Silver Spring, MD 20904

Pelekinesis, 112 Harvard Ave., #65, Claremont, CA 91711

Pembroke Magazine, P.O. Box 1510, Pembroke, NC 28372-1510

Pen + Brush, 29 East 22nd St., New York, NY 10010

Penn Review, 3805 Locust Walk, Philadelphia, PA 19104

Permafrost, Univ. of Alaska, P.O. Box 755720, Fairbanks, AK 99775

Pershing Park Press, PO Box 4945, Albuquerque, NM 87196

Perugia Press, PO Box 60364, Florence, MA 01062

Petigru Review, SCWA, Mathues, 510 Darlington Ave., Greenville, SC 29609

Philadelphia Stories, Sommers, 107 West Main St., Ephrata, PA 17522

Phoebe, George Mason Univ., MSN 2C5, 4400 University Place, Fairfax, VA 22030

Phoenicia Publishing, 207-5425 de Bordeaux, Montreal QC H2H 2P9, Canada

The Pickled Body, 54 Manor St., Dublin 7, Ireland

Pigeon Pages, 443 Park Ave. S., #1004, New York, NY 10016

The Pinch, English Dept., 467 Patterson Hall, Memphis, TN 38111

Pinesong, Griffin, 131 Bon Aire Rd., Elkin, NC 28621

Pink Umbrella, 13323 W. Rancho Dr., Litchfield Park, AZ 85340

Pithead Chapel, 918 North Hill Dr., West Chester, PA 19380

Plain View Press, 1101 W. 34th St., Ste. 404, Austin, TX 78705

Platypus Press, 67 Cordwell Park, Shropshire, SY4 5BE, UK

Pleiades, UCM, English, Warrensburg, MO 64093-5214

Ploughshares, Emerson College, 120 Boylston St., Boston, MA 02116

Poet Lore, 4508 Walsh St., Bethesda, MD 20815

poeticdiversity, 6028 Comey Ave., Los Angeles, CA 90034

Poetry Box, 3300 NW 185th Ave., #382, Portland, OR 97229

Poetry, 61 West Superior St., Chicago, IL 60654

Poetry Nook, 6600 JFK Blvd. E—6C, West New York, NJ 07093

Poetry Northwest, 2000 Tower St., Everett, WA 98201-1390

Poetry Society of Texas, 6717 Talmadge Lane, Dallas, TX 75230

Poetry South, 1100 College St., MUW-1634, Columbus, MS 39701

The Poet's Billow, 6135 Avon St., Portage, MI 49008

Poet's Haven, PO Box 1501, Massillon, OH 44648

Poets Reading the News, PO Box 264, Big Sur, CA 93920

The Poets' Touchstone, PO Box 118, Amherst, NH 03031

Poiema Poetry, 117 Ecclestone Dr., Brampton, ON, L6X 3P4, Canada

The Point, 2 N. LaSalle St., Ste. 2300, Chicago, IL 60602

Ponder Review, 1100 College St., MUW-1634, Columbus, MS 39701

Porkbelly Press, 5046 Relleum Ave., Cincinnati, OH 45238

Port Yonder Press, 6332 33rd Avenue Dr., Shellsburg, IA 52332

Portland Review, 1609 SW 10th Ave., Rm 104, Portland, OR 97201

Posit, 245 Sullivan St., #8A, New York, NY 10012

Post Road, Boston College, 140 Commonwealth Ave., Chestnut Hill, MA 02467

Potomac Review, 51 Mannakee St., MT/212, Rockville, MD 20850

Prairie Journal, 28 Crowfoot Terr. NW, PO Box 68073, Calgary, AB, T3G 3N8, Canada

Prelude, 589 Flushing Ave., #3E, Brooklyn, NY 11206

Presence, Caldwell U., English, 120 Bloomfield Ave., Caldwell, NJ 07006

Press 53, PO Box 30314, Winston-Salem, NC 27130

Pretty Owl, Andrews, 7712 Brashear St., #1 Pittsburgh, PA 15221

Priestess & Hierophant Press, 4432 Myrtlewood Dr., #D, Huntsville, AL 35816

Prism International, UBC, Buch E462, 1866 Main Mall, Vancouver BC V6T 1Z1, Canada

Prism Review, Univ. of La Verne, 1950 Third St., La Verne, CA 91750

Prismatica Magazine, 9384 E. Indigo Mountain Way, Vail, AZ 85641

Progenitor, ACC, Box 9002, 5900 S. Santa Fe Dr., Littleton, CO 80160

Promethean, English, CCNY, 160 Convent Ave., New York, NY 10031

Provincetown Arts, 650 Commercial St., Provincetown, MA 02657

Psaltery & Lyre, 4917 E. Oregon St., Bellingham, WA 98226

Psychopomp, 17574 Gillette Way, Lakeville, MN 55044

Puerto del Sol, NMSU, PO Box 30001, Las Cruces, NM 88003-8001
Pulp Literature Press, 8336 Manson Crt., Burnaby, BC V5A 2C4, Canada
Puna Press, PO Box 7790, Ocean Beach, CA 92107

Qu Magazine, 306 Estes Dr. Exit, Apt. B-18, Carrboro NC 27510
Quiddity, PO Box 1046, Murphysboro, IL 62966
Quiet Lightning, 734 Balboa St., San Francisco, CA 94118
Quill and Parchment, 2357 Merrywood Dr., Los Angeles, CA 90046

Rabid Oak, 8916 Duncanson Dr., Bakersfield, CA 93311
Radius, 65 Paine St., #2, Worcester, MA 01605
Radix Media, 522 Bergen St., Brooklyn, NY 11217
Raleigh Review, Box 6725, Raleigh, NC 27628
Raritan, Rutgers, 31 Mine St., New Brunswick, NJ 08901
Rattle, 12411 Ventura Blvd., Studio City, CA 91604
Raven Chronicles, 15528 12th Ave. NE, Shoreline, WA 98155
The Raw Art Review, 8320 Main St., Ellicott City, MD 21043
Read Furiously, PO 284, East Brunswick, NJ 08816
Red Fez, Lambert, 1115 Kinney Ave., Unit 23, Austin, TX 78704
Red Hen Press, 1540 Lincoln Ave., Pasadena, CA 91103
Red Mountain Press, PO Box 32205, Santa Fe, NM 87594
Redactions, 604 N. 31st Ave., Apt. D-2, Hattiesburg, MS 39401
Redivider, 120 Boylston St., Boston, MA 02116
Remembered Arts, POB 40072, 1210 S. Glebe Rd., Arlington, VA 22204
Rescue Press, 526 Reno St., Iowa City, IA 52245
Reservoir Journal, 511 1st St. North, #302, Charlottesville, VA 22902
RhetAskew Publishing, 15701 S. 257 E. Ave., Coweta, OK 74429
Rhythm & Bones Press, 568 Fire Tower Rd., Birdsboro, PA 19508
Riddled with Arrows, 117 McCann Rd., Newark, DE 19711
Riggwelter Press, 58 John St., Heyrod, Stalybridge, Cheshire, SK15 3BS, UK
Ristau: A Journal of Being, 1935 Gardiner Ln, #A-8, Louisville, KY 40205
River Styx, 3139A South Grand, Ste. 203, St. Louis, MO 63118-1021
Roanoke Review, Miller Hall, Roanoke College, Salem, VA 24153
Rogue Agent, 5441 Covode Place, Pittsburgh, PA 15217
Rosebud, c/o Clark, N3310 Asje Rd., Cambridge, WI 53523
Rumble Fish Quarterly, Sions, 2020 Park Ave., Richmond, VA 23220
Ruminate, 1041 N. Taft Hill Rd., Ft. Collins, CO 80521
The Rumpus, 742 Halstead Ave., Mamaroneck, NY 10543
Running Wild Press, 2101 Oak St., Los Angeles, CA 90007
Rust + Moth, 2409 Eastridge Court, Fort Collins, CO 80524

Salamander, Suffolk U., English, 8 Ashburton Pl., Boston, MA 02108
Salmagundi, Skidmore College, 815 N. Broadway, Saratoga Springs, NY 12866

Salmon Creek Journal, Washington State University Vancouver, 14204 NE Salmon Creek Blvd., Vancouver, WA 98686
the Same, 12911 Peach View Dr., Knoxville, TN 37922
San Julian Press, 2053 Cortlandt, Ste. 200, Houston, TX 77008
San Pedro River Review, P.O. Box 7000-760, Redondo Beach, CA 90277
Sand Journal, c/o Schneider, Willibald-Alexis-Str. 16, 10965, Berlin, Germany
Santa Fe Literary Review, 6401 Richards Ave., Santa Fe, NM 87508
Santa Monica Review, 1900 Pico Blvd., Santa Monica, CA 90405
Saranac Review, SUNY, English, 101 Broad St., Plattsburgh, NY 12901
Saturnalia Books, 105 Woodside Rd., Ardmore, PA 19003
Saw Palm, 4202 East Fowler Ave., CPR 107, Tampa, FL 33620
Scarlet Tanager Books, PO Box 20906, Oakland, CA 94620
Scattering Skies Press, 3950 Kalai Waa St., D-103, Kihei, HI 96753
Schuylkill Valley Journal, 334 Crawford Ave., #5, Morgantown, WV 26505
Scoundrel Time, 5425 Wisconsin Ave., 6th flr., Chevy Chase, MD 20815
Screen Door Review, 1932 6th St. So., Birmingham, AL 35202
Scribble, 7137 Cedar Hollow Circle, Bradenton, FL 34203
Scribendi, MSC06-3890, 1 University of New Mexico, Albuquerque, NM 87131-0001
Seems, Lakeland Univ., W3718 South Drive, Plymouth, WI 53073-4878
Salt Hill Journal, Syracuse Univ., 100 University Pl., Syracuse, NY 13244
Serving House Journal, PO Box 28386, Bellingham, WA 98228
Settlement House Books, PO Box 12004, Silver Spring, MD 20908
Seven Kitchens Press, PO Box 492, Loveland, OH 45140
SFK Press, 29 Jackson St., Newnan, GA 30263
Shadelandhouse Modern Press, PO Box 910913, Lexington, KY 40591
Shanghai Review, 365 Clinton Ave., #2E, Brooklyn, NY 11238
Sheila-Na-Gig, 203 Meadowlark Rd., Russell, KY 41169
Shenandoah, Washington & Lee Univ., English, 204 W. Washington St., Lexington, KY 24450-2116
Sibling Rivalry Press, P.O. Box 26147, Little Rock, AR 72221
Sidereal Magazine, 11719 Clifton Blvd, Apt. 2, Lakewood, OH 44107
Signal Fire, P.O. Box 361, Tucson, AZ 85702
Signature Editions, PO Box 206, RPO Corydon, Winnipeg, MB R3M 3S7, Canada
Silver Needle, 236 Glenda Ct, Pleasant View, TX 37146-7970
Sinister Wisdom, 233 McIntosh Rd., Dover, FL 33527
Sixteen Rivers Press, PO Box 640663, San Francisco, CA 94164-0663
Sixth Finch, 95 Carolina Ave., #2, Jamaica Plain, MA 02130
Sky Island Journal, 1434 Sherwin Ave., Eau Claire, WI 54701
Slag Glass City, English, 2315 No. Kenmore Ave., Chicago, IL 60614
Slag Review, 457 Zaicek Rd., Ashford, CT 06278
Sleet Magazine, 1846 Bohland Ave., St. Paul, MN 55116

Slice Literary, PO Box 659, New York, NY 10014

Slipstream, Box 2071, Niagara Falls, NY 14301

Small Beer Press, 150 Pleasant St., #306, Easthampton, MA 01027-1264

SmokeLong Quarterly, 5229 Sideburn Rd., Fairfax, VA 22032-2641

So It Goes, Kurt Vonnegut Museum, 340 N. Senate Ave., Indianapolis, IN 46204

The Sonnetarium, PO Box 1491, Pensacola, FL 32591

The Southampton Review, 239 Montauk Hwy., Southampton, NY 11968

Southeast Review, English, Florida State U., Tallahassee, FL 32306

Southern Humanities Review, 9088 Haley Center, Auburn Univ., Auburn, AL 36849

Southern Indiana Review, USI, 8600 Univ. Blvd., Evansville, IN 47712

The Southern Review, LSU, 338 Johnston Hall, Baton Rouge, LA 70803

Spadina Literary Review, 101-639 Dupont St., Toronto, ON M6G 1Z4, Canada

Speak The Magazine, 2212 Queen Anne Ave. N., Seattle, WA 98109

Spelk, 20 Bell Rd., Belford Northumberland, NE70 7NY, UK

Spillway, Marsha de la O, 1296 Placid Ave., Ventura, CA 93004

Spineless Wonder, Unit 13/66-72 Shepherd St., Chippendale, New South Wales, 2012, Australia

Spinifex Press, PO Box 105, Mission Beach, Qld 4852, Australia

Split Lip Magazine, PO Box 49, Manchester, MA 01944

Split Rock Review, 30330 Engoe Rd., Washburn, WI 54891

Split This Rock, 1301 Connecticut Ave. NW, Washington, DC 20036

Spoon River, ISU, 103 Williams Hall Annex, Normal, IL 61790-4241

Star*Line, UNI, Gotera, 1001 Bartlett Hall, Cedar Falls, IA 50614-0502

StepAway, 2, Bowburn Close, Wardley, Gateshead, Tyne & Wear NE10 8UG, UK

Still, 89 W. Chestnut St., Williamsburg, KY 40769

Still Point Arts, 193 Hillside Rd., Brunswick, ME 04011

Stillwater Review, Poetry Center, Sussex County College, Newton, NJ 07860

Stone Canoe, YMCA, 340 Montgomery St., Syracuse, NY 13202

Stoneboat Literary Journal, P.O. Box 1254, Sheboygan, WI 53082

Storm Cellar, 1901 St. Anthony Ave., St. Paul, MN 55104

Story Quarterly, English, Rutgers, 311 N. Fifth St., Camden, NJ 08102

Streetlight Magazine, 56 Pine Hill Ln., Norwood, VA 24581

Strix, 1 Sunset Rise, Meanwood, Leeds, LS6 4LN, England

subTerrain, P.O. Box 3008 MPO, Vancouver, BC V6B 3X5, Canada

Sugar House Review, PO Box 13, Cedar City, UT 84721

Sum Journal, 18204 Lexington Farms Dr., Alpharetta, GA 30004

The Summerset Review, 25 Summerset Dr., Smithtown, NY 11787

The Sun, 107 North Roberson St., Chapel Hill, NC 27516

Sundog Lit, 10 rue Mélingue, 75019, France

Sunlight Press, 221 Valley Rd., Merion Station, PA 19066

Sunshot Press, 4021 Gordon Dr., Knoxville, TN 37918

Swamp Ape Review, 777 Glades Rd., CU, #306, Boca Raton, FL 33431

Sweet, 10144 Arbor Run Dr., Unit 157, Tampa, FL 33647

Sycamore Review, English, Purdue University, 500 Oval Dr., West Lafayette, IN 47907

Synaeresis: arts + poetry, 443 Three Valleys Crescent, London, ON, N5Z 3E6, Canada

Syndic Literary Journal, 5131 Pleasant Dr., Sacramento, CA 95822

Syntax & Salt Magazine, 1106 Platt St., Lansing, MI 48910

TAB, Chapman Univ., English, 1 University Dr., Orange, CA 92866

Tahoma Literary Review, PO Box 924, Mercer Island, WA 98040

Tar River Poetry, ECU, MS 159, Greenville, NC 27858-4353

Taurolog Books, 12608 SW 267th Pl., Vashon, WA 98070

Technoculture, English Dept., PO Box 43719, Lafayette, LA 70504

Temz Review, 845 Dufferin Ave., London, ON, N5W 3J9, Canada

Terrain.org, P.O. Box 19161, Tucson, AZ 85731-9161

Terrapin Books, 4 Midvale Ave., West Caldwell, NJ 07006

Territory, 2606 Hampshire Rd., Cleveland Heights, OH 44106

Texas Review Press, SHSU, Box 2146, Huntsville, TX 77341-2146

Thin Air, English Dept., PO Box 6032, Flagstaff, AZ 86011

Third Coast, Western Michigan Univ., Kalamazoo, MI 49008-5331

Third Flatiron, 4101 S. Hampton Cir., Boulder, CO 80301

32 Poems, English Dept., 60 South Lincoln St., Washington, PA 15301

Thirty West Publishing, 2622 Swede Rd., #C8, Norristown, PA 19401

This Broken Shore, 15 Sandspring Dr., Eatontown, NJ 07724

Thomas-Jacob Publishing, P.O. Box 390524, Deltona, FL 32739

3: A Taos Press, P.O. Box 370627, Denver, CO 80237

3 Elements Review, 198 Valley View Rd., Manchester, CT 06040

3 Mile Harbor Press, PO Box 1, Stuyvesant, NY 12173

Three Rooms Press, 561 Hudson St., #33, New York, NY 10014

Threepenny Review, PO Box 9131, Berkeley, CA 94709

Thrush Poetry Journal, 889 Lower Mountain Dr., Effort, PA 18330

Tiger Bark Press, 202 Mildorf St., Rochester, NY 14609

Timeless Tales, 12445 Alameda Trace Cir. #724, Austin, TX 78727

Tin House, 2601 NW Thurman St., Portland, OR 97210

Tinderbox, 6932 Kayser Mill Rd. NW, Albuquerque, NM 87114

Tiny House, 61306 Huckleberry Pl., Bend, OR 97702

Tipton Poetry Journal, 642 Jackson St., Brownsburg, IN 46112

The Tishman Review, PO Box 605, Perry, MI 48872

TranceMission Press, 301 S. Clark Blvd., Clarksville, IN 47129

TRACK//FOUR Journal, 338 Quincy Mall Center, 58 Plimpton St., Cambridge, MA 02138

Trestle Creek Review, North Idaho College, 1000 W. Garden Ave., Coeur d'Alene, ID 83814

TriQuarterly, Northwestern Univ., 339 East Chicago Ave., 6th Floor, Chicago, IL 60611

True Story, 5119 Coral St., Pittsburgh, PA 15224

Tupelo Press, 60 Roberts Dr., #308, North Adams, MA 01247

Turtle Point Press, 208 Java St., 5th Floor, Brooklyn, NY 11222

Two Cities Review, 138 Gatwick Dr., Oakville ON L6H 6N3, Canada

Two Sylvias Press, PO Box 1524, Kingston, WA 98346

Twyckenham Notes, 2420 Erskine Blvd, South Bend, IN 46614

Typehouse Magazine, PO Box 68721, Portland, OR 97268

U.S. 1 Poets' Cooperative, PO Box 127, Kingston, NJ 08528-0127

Umbrella Factory, ILacqua, 838 Lincoln St., Longmont, CA 80501

Under the Gum Tree, PO Box 5394, Sacramento, CA 95817

Under the Sun, 2121 Hidden Cove Rd., Cookeville, TN 38506

University of Arizona Press, PO Box 210055, Tucson, AZ 85721-0055

University of Louisiana at Lafayette Press, P.O. Box 43558, Lafayette, LA 70504

University of North Texas Press, 1155 Union Circle #311336, Denton, TX 76203

University of Wisconsin Press, 1930 Monroe St., 3rd Flr, Madison, WI 53711

Untethered Magazine, 17 Plaxon Dr., Toronto, ON M4B 2P6, Canada

Up North Lit, 8230 Rhoy St., Victoria, MN 55386

Up the Staircase Quarterly, 716 4th St., SW, Apt. A, Minot, ND 58701

Upset Press, PO Box 301025, Brooklyn, NY 11230

Utterance Journal, 902 NW Carlon Ave., #3, Bend, OR 97703

Valley Voices, MVSU 7242, 14000 Hwy 82 W., Itta Bena, MS 38941

Vallum, 5038 Sherbrooke St. W., PO Box 20377 CP Vendome, Montreal, QC H4A 1T0, Canada

Vastarien, 1238 Fern St., New Orleans, LA 70118

Vegetarian Alcoholic Press, 643 S. 2nd St., Milwaukee, WI 53212

Veliz Books, PO Box 920243, El Paso, TX 79902

Vessel Press, 188 Lincoln Pl., Irvington, NJ 07111

Vestal Review, 5 Dogwood Dr., Upton, MA 01568

Vinyl, 1 College Dr., Bennington, VT 05201

Voice of Eve, 15615 Avenida Alcachofa, #G, Rancho Bernardo, CA 92128

Waccamaw Journal, 133 Chanticleer Drive West, Conway, SC 29526

The Wall, 136 Muriel St., Ithaca, NY 14850

The War Horse, PO Box 399, Richlands, NC 28574-0399

War, Literature & the Arts, 2354 Fairchild Dr., Ste. 6D-149, USAF Academy, CO 80840-6242

Washington Square Review, 58 W. 10th St., New York, NY 10011

Water~Stone Review, MS A1730, 1536 Hewitt Ave., St. Paul, MN 55104

Wave Books, 1938 Fairview Avenue East, #204, Seattle, WA 98102

Waxwing, Kaneko, 761 Hawthorne St. NE, Grand Rapids, MI 49503

Wesleyan University Press, 215 Long Lane, Middletown, CT 06459

West Marin Review, P.O. Box 1302, Point Reyes Station, CA 94956

West Texas Literary Review, 5239 94th St., Lubbock, TX 79424

Western Humanities Review, Univ. of Utah, English Dept., Salt Lake City, UT 84112-0494

Whale Road Review, 3900 Lomaland Dr., San Diego, CA 92106

What Are Birds, 13630 Via Varra, #303, Broomfield, CO 80020

White Stag, 3682 W. McCauley Ct., Anthem, AZ 85086

Wigleaf, Univ. of Missouri, 114 Tate Hall, Columbia, MO 65211

The Wild Word, Zimmermannstrasse 6, 12163 Berlin, Germany

Willow Springs, 668 N. Riverpoint Blvd., #259, Spokane, WA 99202

The Wire's Dream, 180 N. 1st St., #115, El Cajon, CA 92021

Wisconsin People & Ideas, 1922 University Ave., Madison, WI 53726

Wising Up Press, PO Box 2122, Decatur, GA 30031-2122

WMG Publishing, PO Box 269, Lincoln City, OR 97367

The Worcester Review, PO Box 804, Worcester, MA 01613

Words On The Street, 6 San Antonio Park, Salthill, Galway, Ireland

Wordsmithery, 5 Curzon Rd., Chatham, Kent, ME4 5ST, UK

Wordworksbooks, PO Box 42164, Washington, DC 20015

World Literature Today, 630 Parrington Oval, Ste. 110, Norman, OK 73019-4033

World Poetry Books, 156 River Rd., #2101, Willington, CT 06279

World Weaver Press, PO Box 21924, Albuquerque, NM 87154

Woven Tale Press, PO Box 2533, Setauket, NY 11733

Write Bloody, 5617 Hollywood Blvd., Ste. 117, Los Angeles, CA 90028

Writing Disorder, P.O. Box 93613, Los Angeles, CA 90093-0613

Wyrd & Wyse, 205 Lincoln St., S, Northfield, MN 55057

Wyvern Lit, 47 Railroad S., #306, Great Barrington, MA 01230

Yellow Medicine Review, SMSU, 1501 State St., Marshall, MN 56258

Your Impossible Voice, 1081 E. Dunedin Rd., Columbus, OH 43224

Zephyr Press, 400 Bason Dr., Las Cruces, NM 88005

Zoetic Press, PO Box 1354, Santa Cruz, CA 95061

Zoetrope: All Story, Sentinel Bldg., 916 Kearny St., San Francisco, CA 94133

Zone 3 Press, APSU, P.O. Box 4565, Clarksville, TN 37044

ZYZZYVA, 57 Post St., Ste. 604, San Francisco, CA 94104

CONTRIBUTORS' NOTES

FARAH ALI is from Karachi, Pakistan. Her work has been published in *Copper Nickel*, *Kenyon Review*, *Ecotone*, and elsewhere.

KAVEH AKBAR is founding editor of *Divedapper*. Born in Iran, he teaches at Purdue, Randolph College and Warren Wilson.

CATHERINE BARNETT previously appeared in PP XXIX with her poem "untitled."

GRAHAM BARNHART is a US Army veteran. He received a Wallace Stegner Fellowship from Stanford University and other awards.

RICHARD BAUSCH is a winner of The Rea Award for The Short Story and other accolades. He teaches at Chapman University.

MEGAN BAXTER is the author of the essay collection *The Coolest Monsters*. She has three dogs and seven tattoos.

LISA BELLAMY teaches at The Writers Studio and is author of *The Northway* and *Nectar* poetry collections

JASON BROWN's latest story collection is forthcoming from Missouri Review Books. He lives in Eugene, OR.

CHEN CHEN teaches at Brandeis University. He has been long listed for The National Book Award and has received several honors including a Thom Gunn Award.

YE CHUN lives in Providence, RI, and previously appeared in PP XLI.

BRUCE COHEN has published five volumes of poetry. His most recent is out from New Issues Press

WHITNEY COLLINS lives in Lexington, KY. This is her first Pushcart selection.

HAL CROWTHER was a finalist for The National Book Critics Circle Award. This is his third PP appearance.

CLAIRE DAVIS is the author of two novels and a short story collection. She teaches at Lewis-Clark State University, Lewiston, ID.

TOI DERRICOTTE'S *I: New and Selected Poems* is recently published by University of Pittsburgh Press. She has received two Pushcart Prize selections, and many other awards. She co-founded the Cave Canem Foundation.

NATALIE DIAZ is a member of the Gila River Indian Tribe. She is a 2018 MacArthur Fellow and a Lannan Literary Fellow.

RYAN ERIC DULL lives in Irvine, CA. This is his first Pushcart Prize.

CAMILLE T. DUNGY lives in Ft. Collins, Co. She also appeared in PPXLII with her poem "Natural History." She is the author of four poetry collections.

EMMA COPLEY EISENBERG's first book, *The Third Rainbow Girl*, is due soon from Hachette.

JULIA ELLIOTT won a Rona Jaffe Writer's Award and two Pushcart Prizes. Her story collection is *The Wilds*.

NAUSHEEN EUSUF's first poetry collection, *Not Elegy, But Eros* was published by NYQ Books. She is a PhD Candidate at Boston University.

CALLY FIEDOREK graduated from Yale and Oxford. This is her first PP selection.

DEBORAH FORBES lived in Lusaka, Zambia in the early 2000s.

PATRICIA FOSTER won the 2017 Clarence Casan Award and teachers at the University of Iowa.

ALLEN GEE is the author of *My Chinese America* and teaches at Columbus State University.

LOUISE GLÜCK has appeared in thirteen Pushcart Prize volumes. She teaches at Yale and Stanford.

ALLAN GURGANUS is the author of *Oldest Living Confederate Widow Tells All* and other fictions.

BECKY HAGENSTON lives in Starkville, MS. She is the author of three story collections.

FRANCINE J. HARRIS teaches at the University of Houston. Her third poetry collection is due from FSG.

JEFFREY HARRISON's sixth book of poetry will soon be published. He lives in Dover, MA.

JUAN FELIPE HERRERA is a former poet Laureate of The United States and the son of migrant farm workers.

EDWARD HIRSCH's tenth book of poems, *Stranger By Night*, will soon be published by Knopf. He lives in Brooklyn, NY.

TONY HOAGLAND died in 2018. He was a finalist for The National Book Critics Circle Award and the author of several poetry collections. He was featured in eight previous Pushcart Prize editions.

FADY JOUDAH has published four award winning poetry collections. He lives in Houston with his wife and kids and practices internal medicine.

MAIA JENKINS lives in Ocean Springs, MS. Her work has appeared in *Litro*, *Grazia*, and *Smokelong Quarterly*.

PETER LABERGE is founder of *Adroit Journal*. His work has appeared in *Crazyhorse*, *Iowa Review*, *Pleiades* and elsewhere.

SHARA LESSLEY is Poet-In-Residence at Randolph College and is Assistant Poetry Editor for Acre Books. She is the author of two poetry collections.

SAMANTHA LIBBY is a human rights advocate who has lived and worked around the world. She recently completed her first novel.

CLAIRE LUCHETTE's work has been featured in *Iowa Review*, *Glimmer Train*, *Kenyon Review* and elsewhere. She lives in Chicago. Her first novel is out soon from FSG.

REBECCA McCLANAHAN lives in Charlotte, NC. She previously appeared in PPXVI with her story "Somebody."

TIFFANY MIDGE is a citizen of standing Rock Sioux Nation. Her work has appeared in *Lit. Hub*, *The Offing*, *Belladonna* and elsewhere.

MARY MILLER is the author of two novels, *Biloxi* and *The Last Days of California*. She lives in Oxford, MS.

OTTESSA MOSHFEGH's new novel, *My Year of Rest and Relaxation*, was published in 2018. She lives in Whitewater, CA.

HOA NGUYEN was born in the Mekong Delta and now lives in Toronto. She is the author of three poetry collections.

MEGHAN O'GIEBLYN has appeared in PP XL and PP XLII. She lives in Madison, WI.

LUCIA PERILLO published seven poetry collections as well as short stories and a book of essays. She died in 2016.

KIKI PETROSINO is the author of *Witch Wife* (2017). She teaches at The University of Virginia.

LESLIE PIETRZYK's story collection, *This Angel on My Chest*, won the 2015 Drue Heinz Prize. She teaches at Converse College.

DAN POPE is a graduate of the Iowa Writers Workshop and the author of two novels and many short stories.

ROGER REEVES is the author of *King Me*. He has received a Whiting Award and Fellowships from the NEA and Ruth Lilly / Poetry Foundation.

ALISON C. ROLLINS is the author of a debut poetry collection, *Library of Small Catastrophes* (2019), from Copper Canyon. She is a cave Canem and Callaloo fellow.

JOANNA SCOTT's most recent novel is *Careers For Women*.

DIANE SEUSS lives in Kalamazoo, MI and previously appeared in PP XXXVII.

ERIN SINGER grew up in Yukon and Saskatchewan. She now lives in Las Vegas.

BEN SHATTUCK received the 2017 PEN America Best Debut Short Story Award. He lives in South Dartmouth, MA.

SEAN SHEARER is founder of BOAAT Press. His poems have been published in *Boulevard*, *Jubilat* and *Copper Nickel*.

CHARLES SIMIC lives in Strafford, NH. He has appeared in seven previous Pushcart Prize editions.

TOM SLEIGH's many books of essays and poetry have received numerous awards. He teaches at Hunter College and was a past poetry editor for The Pushcart Prize.

DANEZ SMITH is the author of recent, poetry collections from Graywolf Press, and was a finalist for The National Book Award.

SUZANNE FARRELL SMITH is the author of *The Memory Sessions* and *The Writing Shop*.

MAUREEN STANTON teaches at the University of Massachusetts, Lowell. Her *Body Leaping Backward : Memoir of a Delinquent Girlhood* is just published from Harcourt.

RON STOTTLEMYER lives in Helena, MT. His work has appeared in *Streelight*, *Temenos*, and elsewhere.

ARTHUR SZE's latest poetry collection is *Sight Lines* (Copper Canyon). He is a past poetry editor for The Pushcart Prize.

MARY SZYBIST's most recent poetry collection is *Incarnadine*, winner of the 2013 National Book Award.

NANCY TAKACS is a graduate of the Iowa Writers Workshop and winner of The Juniper Prize and other awards

MARGARET WARDLAW is a pediatrician. She lives in Seattle, WA.

MALERIE WILLENS is at work on a novel. Her work has appeared in *Agni*, *Tin House* and *Granta*.

DIANE WILLIAMS is founder and editor of *Noon*. She is the author of nine books of fiction.

JOY WILLIAMS's most recent book is *Ninety-Nine Stories of God*. She lives in Tucson, AZ.

C PAM ZHANG's debut novel, *How Much Of These Hills is Gold*, will soon be published by Riverhead Books. She currently lives in San Francisco.

JAVIER ZAMORA was a 2018–2019 Radcliffe Fellow at Harvard. He migrated to the US from El Salvador when he was nine years old.

INDEX

The following is a listing in alphabetical order by author's last name of works reprinted in the *Pushcart Prize* editions since 1976.

560

563

565

573

574

581

584

585

597

AFTERWORD

"I don't think the value of the small presses can be over-estimated in any degree. In truth, I feel they are the backbone of the national literature.

"Speaking for myself, I don't believe I would have had a literary life, or not much of one anyway, had it not been for small press publishers and the little magazines. My first three books were poems and they were published by Kayak Press and Capra Press. And my first fiction that was ever published in book form was a chapbook from Capra . . . Small presses and little magazines sustained me for more than a decade, when none of the larger magazines would publish my work . . . the mere fact that someone was publishing my work in whatever form was an indication to me that somebody cared. . . . The best of the small presses are doing work that is every bit the equal, if not superior to, the literature being issued by the larger better know and certainly more financially sound presses."

Ray Carver
(From a letter to Pushcart Press)